ARAMINTA STATION

MONOMANTIC SEMINARY
Warning! Keep out!

Glawen ignored the sign and started up the road. Back and forth he trudged: a hundred yards to the left, a hundred yards to the right, with each traverse broadening the vista across the steppes of Lutwiler Country.

The seminary loomed across the sky. The road made a final turn and swung back to pass before the front of the structure. Glawen halted to catch his breath where three stone steps led up to a small porch and a heavy timber door.

Glawen squared his shoulders, settled his jacket and looked up the face of the building. The tall narrow windows seemed blind and vacant, as if no one troubled to look out at the view. A most cheerless place in which to study, thought Glawen, with the single advantage: there would be no frivolities or entertainments to distract the students. He stepped forward, raised and let fall the brass door-knocker.

A moment passed. The door opened; a burly round-faced man, somewhat taller than Glawen, with round close-set eyes, looked forth. He wore a gown of gray-brown fust and a cowl leaving only his face exposed. He gave Glawen a scowling inspection.

About the Author

Born in 1916 and educated at the University of
California, Jack Vance wrote his first story
while serving in the US Merchant Navy during
the Second World War. His first book, THE
DYING EARTH, was published in 1950 and he
went on to become one of the acknowledged
masters of fantasy and science fiction.

He has enjoyed success both as a screenwriter
and author of mystery and suspense novels –
THE MAN IN THE CAGE won the coveted
Edgar award – and he has won both of the
major awards for science fiction, THE
DRAGON MASTERS winning the Hugo and
THE LAST CASTLE taking both the Hugo and
the Nebula. Jack Vance's hobbies include
blue-water sailing and early jazz. He lives near
Oakland, California.

Araminta Station

The Cadwal Chronicles
Book One

Jack Vance

NEW ENGLISH LIBRARY
Hodder and Stoughton

To David Alexander, Kim Kokkonen, Norma Vance

Copyright © 1988 by Jack Vance

First published in the United States of America in 1988 by Tor Books

First published in Great Britain in 1988 by New English Library hardbacks

First New English Library paperback edition 1989

British Library C.I.P.

Vance, Jack, *1916–*
Araminta station.
I. Title II. Series
813'.54 [F]

ISBN 0-450-49733-X

Printed and bound in Great Britain for Hodder and Stoughton paperbacks, a division of Hodder and Stoughton Ltd., Mill Road, Dunton Green, Sevenoaks, Kent TN13 2YA (Editorial Office: 47 Bedford Square, London WC18 3DP) by Richard Clay Ltd., Bungay, Suffolk.

Araminta
Station

Oddments and Notes, to be Read if
One is so Inclined

These are excerpts from the Introduction to *The Worlds of Man*, by Fellows of the Fidelius Institute, and will assist in bridging the gap between now and then, here and there:

. . . In this work, now thirty years in preparation, we attempt neither exhaustive detail nor analytical profundity, but, rather, a pastiche of a million parts, which, so it is hoped, will coalesce into a focused picture.

. . . Order, logic, symmetry: these are fine words but any pretense that we have crammed our material into molds so strict would be obvious sham. Each settled world is *sui generis*, presenting to the inquiring cosmologist a unique quantum of information. All these quanta are mutually immiscible, so that efforts to generalize become a muddle. We are yielded a single certainty: no event has occurred twice; every case is unique.

. . . In our journeys from one end of the Gaean Reach to the other and, on occasion, Beyond, we discover nothing to indicate that the human race is everywhere and inevitably becoming more generous, tolerant, kindly and enlightened. Nothing whatever.

On the other hand, and this is the good news, it doesn't seem to be getting any worse.

. . . Parochialism derives, apparently, from an innocent egotism, which, if verbalized, would express itself thus: "Since I choose to live in this place, it therefore and perforce must be excellent in all its aspects."

Still and yet, the preferred destination of first-time travelers is almost always Old Earth. Latent in all exiles, so it would seem, is the yearning to breathe the native air, to taste the water, to work the mother soil through the fingers.

Further, spaceships arriving at the ports of Earth each day discharge two or three hundred coffins of those who, with their last breaths, chose to return their substance to the dank brown mold of Earth.

. . . When men arrive on a new world the process of interaction begins. The men attempt to alter the world to suit their needs; at the same time the world, far more subtly, works to alter the men.

Thus the battle is joined, of man versus environment. Sometimes the men overcome the resistance of the planet. Terrestrial or otherwise alien flora is introduced and adapted to the chemical and ecological environment; noxious indigenes are repelled, destroyed or circumvented, and the world slowly takes on the semblance of Old Earth.

But sometimes the planet is strong, and forces adaptation upon the intruders. At first from expedience, then from custom and finally from innate tendency, the colonists obey the dictates of the environment and in the end become almost indistinguishable from true indigenes.

CHAPTER I

PRELIMINARY

1   The Purple Rose System of Mircea's Wisp
(Excerpted from *The Worlds of Man*, by Fellows of the Fidelius Institute.)

Halfway along the Perseid Arm a capricious swirl of galactic gravitation has caught up ten thousand stars and sent them streaming away at an angle, with a curl and a flourish at the end. This is Mircea's Wisp.

To the side of the curl, at seeming risk of wandering away into the void, is the Purple Rose System, comprising three stars: Lorca, Sing and Syrene. Lorca, a white dwarf, and Sing, a red giant, swing close together around their mutual center of gravity: a portly pink-faced old gentleman waltzing with a dainty little maiden dressed in white. Syrene, a yellow-white star of ordinary size and luminosity, orbits the gallivanting pair at a discreet distance.

Syrene controls three planets, including Cadwal, the single inhabited world of the system.

Cadwal is an Earth-like planet seven thousand miles in diameter, with close to Earth-normal gravity.

(A list and analysis of physical indices is here omitted.)

2   The World Cadwal

Cadwal was first explored by the locator Rudel Neirmann, a member of the Naturalist Society of Earth. His report prompted the dispatch of an expedition which, upon its return to Earth, recommended that Cadwal be protected forever as a natural preserve, secure from human exploitation.

To this end, the Society asserted formal possession of Cadwal, and issued a decree of Conservancy: the Charter.

The three continents of Cadwal were named Ecce, Deucas and

Throy,[1] each differing markedly from the other two. Ecce, straddling the equator, palpitated with heat, stench, color and ravenous vitality. Even the vegetation of Ecce used techniques of combat in the effort to survive. Three volcanoes, two active, the third dormant, were the only protrusions above a flat terrain of jungle, swamp and morass. Sluggish rivers coiled across the landscape, eventually emptying into the sea. The air reeked with a thousand odd fetors; ferocious creatures hunted each other, bellowing in triumph or screaming in mortal fright, as dictated by their roles in the event. The early explorers gave Ecce only cursory attention, and across the years others generally followed their example.

Deucas, on the opposite side of the world and four times as large as Ecce, sprawled across the north temperate zone. The fauna, at times both savage and formidable, included several semi-intelligent species; the flora in many cases resembled that of Earth—so closely that the early agronomists were able to introduce useful terrestrial species, such as bamboo, coconut palms, wine grapes and fruit trees, without fear of an ecological disaster.[2]

Throy, to the south of Deucas, extended from under the polar ice well into the south temperate zone. Throy was a land of dramatic topography. Crags leaned over chasms; the sea dashed against cliffs; forests roared in the wind.

Elsewhere were oceans; great empty expanses of deep water barren of islands save for a few trifling exceptions: Lutwen Atoll, Thurben Island and Ocean Island off the east coast of Deucas, a few rocky islets off Cape Journal in the far south.

3   Araminta Station

At Araminta Station, an enclave of a hundred square miles on the east coast of Deucas, the Society established an administrative agency to enforce the terms of the Charter. Six bureaus were organized to perform the necessary work:

Bureau   A: Records and statistics
         B: Patrols and surveys: police and security services
         C: Taxonomy, cartography, natural sciences
         D: Domestic services
         E: Fiscal affairs: exports and imports
         F: Visitors' accommodations

[1] The first three cardinal numbers in the language of Ancient Etruria.
[2] The biological techniques for introducing new species into alien surroundings without danger to the host environment had long been perfected.

The original superintendents were Deamus Wook, Shirry Clattuc, Saul Diffin, Claude Offaw, Marvell Veder and Condit Laverty. Each was allowed a staff of forty persons. A tendency to recruit this staff from family and guild kinships brought to the early administration a cohesion which otherwise might have been lacking.

Six temporary dormitories, each associated with one of the bureaus, housed the agency personnel. As soon as funds became available, six fine residences were constructed, each outdoing the others in grandeur and richness of appointment; these became known as Wook House, Clattuc House, Veder House, Diffin House, Laverty House and Offaw House.

Centuries passed; work never ended at any of the six houses. Each was continually enlarged, remodeled and refined in its details with carved and polished wood, tiles and panels of local semiprecious stone, and furnishings imported from Earth or Alphanor or Mossambey. The grandes dames of each house were determined that their own house excel all the others in style and palatial luxury.

Each house developed its own distinctive personality, which its residents shared, so that the wise Wooks differed from the flippant Diffins, as did the cautious Offaws from the reckless Clattucs. Likewise, the imperturbable Veders disdained the emotional excesses of the Lavertys.

At Riverview House on the Leur River, a mile south of the agency, lived the Conservator, the Head Superintendent of Araminta Station. By order of the Charter he was an active member of the Naturalist Society, a native of Stroma, the small Naturalist settlement on Throy.

Araminta Station early acquired a hotel to house its visitors, an airport, a hospital, schools and a theater: the Orpheum. In order to earn foreign exchange, vineyards began to produce fine wines for export, and tourists were encouraged to visit any or all of a dozen wilderness lodges, established at special sites and carefully managed to avoid interference with the environment.

With the new amenities came problems of principle. How could so many enterprises be staffed by a complement of only two hundred and forty persons? Elasticity of some sort was necessary, and "collaterals," in the guise of "temporary labor," began to serve in many managerial capacities.

The collaterals were a class which almost imperceptibly had come into being. A person born into one of the houses, but denied full "Agency status" by reason of the numerical limit, became a collateral, with diminished status. Many collaterals emigrated; others found more or less congenial employment at the station.

13

The Charter exempted children, retired persons, domestic servants and "temporary labor not in permanent residence" from the count. The term "temporary labor" was extended to include farm labor, hotel staff, airport mechanics—indeed, labor of every description—and the Conservator looked the other way so long as this work force was allowed no permanent residence.

A source of cheap, plentiful and docile labor, conveniently close at hand, was needed. What could be more convenient than the population of Lutwen Atoll, three hundred miles northeast of Araminta Station? These were the Yips, descendants of runaway servants, illegal immigrants and others.

In such a manner the Yips became part of the scene at Araminta Station. They lived in dormitories near the airport and were allowed work permits of only six months' duration. Thus far strict Conservationists were willing to bend, but no farther; any new concessions, they argued, would formalize the Yip presence, and gradually lead to Yip settlements on Deucas continent, which could not be tolerated.

As time passed, the population of Lutwen Atoll increased to an unreasonable figure. The Conservator notified the headquarters of the Naturalist Society on Earth, and urged that drastic steps be taken, but the Society had fallen on hard times and offered no help.

Yipton became a tourist attraction in its own right. Ferries from Araminta Station conveyed tourists to the Arkady Inn at Yipton: a structure built entirely of bamboo poles and palm fronds. On the terrace beautiful Yip girls served rum punches, gin slings, sundowners, Trelawny sloshes, malt beer and coconut toddy, all mixed liquors brewed or distilled at Yipton. Other more intimate services were readily available at Pussycat Palace, famous up and down Mircea's Wisp and beyond for the affable versatility of the attendants—though nothing was free. At Yipton, if one requested an after-lunch toothpick, he found the reckoning on his bill.

The tourist traffic increased even further when the Oomphaw (the title of the Yip ruler) introduced a startling new set of entertainments.

4 Stroma

Another problem involving the Charter had been settled to a more definite effect. During the first few years, Society members, when they visited Cadwal, were lodged at Riverview House. The Conservator finally rebelled and refused to cope any further with the constant comings and goings. He proposed that a second small enclave be established thirty miles to the south, with guesthouses reserved for the use of visiting Naturalists. The plan, when presented at the Society's

14

annual conclave (held on Earth), found a mixed reception. Strict Conservationists complained that the Charter was being gnawed to shreds by first one trick, then another. Others replied: "Well and good, but when we go to Cadwal, either to undertake research or to take pleasure in the surroundings, are we to live in a tent?"

The conclave adopted a compromise plan, which pleased no one. A new settlement was authorized, but only on the condition that it be built at a specific location overlooking Stroma Fjord on Throy. This was a site almost comically unsuitable, and obviously intended as a ploy to discourage proponents of the plan from taking action.

The challenge, however, was accepted. Stroma came into being: a town of tall narrow houses, crabbed and quaint, black or dark umber, with doors and window trim painted white, blue and red. The houses were built on eight levels with majestic views down Stroma Fjord.

On Earth the Naturalist Society fell prey to weak leadership and a general lack of purpose. At a final conclave, the records and documents were assigned to the Library of Archives, and the presiding officer struck the gong of adjournment for the last time.

On Cadwal the folk of Stroma took no official notice of the event, though now the sole income of Stroma was the yield from their private off-world investment, which had more or less been the case for many years. Young folk ever more frequently departed to seek their fortunes. Some were seen no more; others succeeded and returned with influxes of new income. By one means or another Stroma survived and even enjoyed a modest prosperity.

5   Glawen Clattuc

Something over nine hundred years had passed since Rudel Neirmann's first landing on Cadwal. At Araminta Station summer was verging into autumn, and Glawen Clattuc's sixteenth birthday, formalizing his transition from "childhood" to "provisional staff," was upon him. On this occasion he learned his official "Status Index," or SI: a number calculated by a computer, after it digested masses of genealogical data.

The number seldom surprised anyone, least of all the person most directly concerned; he would long have been counting on his fingers and casting projections.

Since the habitancy of each house was established at forty persons, half male, half female, any SI of 20 or under was excellent, from 21 to 22 good, 23 or 24 fair; anything over was ambiguous, depending upon conditions within the House. A number beyond 26 was discouraging and prompted mournful speculations in regard to the future.

Glawen's place on the genealogical chart was not exalted. His mother, now dead, had been born off-world; his father, Scharde, an official at Bureau B, was the third son of a second son. Glawen, a sober and realistic youth, hoped for a 24, which would still allow him a chance at Agency status.

6 Days of the Week

A final note concerning days of the week. On Cadwal, and generally around the Gaean Reach, the traditional seven-day week remained the norm. Using a nomenclature based on the so-called Metallic Schedule avoids the ear-grinding incongruity of contemporary equivalents (i.e., "Monday," "Tuesday," et cetera).

Linguistic notes: Originally, each term was preceded by the denominator *Ain* (literally: "This day of"), so that the first workday of the week was "Ain-Ort," or "this day of iron." As the root language became archaic and was superseded, the *Ain* was lost and the days were designated simply by the metal names alone.

The days of the week:

(Ain)-	Ort	iron
	Tzein	zinc
	Ing	lead
	Glimmet	tin
	Verd	copper
	Milden	silver
	Smollen	gold

1

Glawen Clattuc's sixteenth birthday was the occasion for a modest celebration which would culminate in Housemaster Fratano's formal salute and his announcement of Glawen's SI, or Status Index—a number which in large measure would determine the direction of Glawen's future.

For the sake of both convenience and economy, the celebration would be superimposed upon the weekly "House Supper," which all in-House Clattucs must attend, with neither age nor indisposition serving as an excuse for truancy.

The morning of the celebration went quietly. Glawen's father,

Scharde, gave him a pair of silver and turquoise epaulettes, as worn by gentlemen at the most exclusive resorts of the Gaean Reach, if the fashion journals were to be believed.

Scharde and Glawen took breakfast in their chambers, as usual. They lived alone; Glawen's mother, Marya, had died in an accident three years after his birth. Glawen dimly remembered a loving presence, and sensed latent mystery, though Scharde would never discuss the subject.

The bare facts were simple. Scharde had met Marya when she visited Araminta Station with her parents. Scharde escorted the group around the circuit of wilderness lodges and later visited Marya at Sarsenopolis on Alphecca Nine. Here the two had married, and shortly after returned to Araminta Station.

The off-world marriage took Clattuc House by surprise, and provoked an unexpected furor, instigated by a certain Spanchetta, grandniece to Housemaster Fratano. Spanchetta was already married to the mild and uncomplaining Millis and had produced a son, Arles; nevertheless, she had long, shamelessly and vainly, marked Scharde for her own.

Spanchetta at this time was a flashing-eyed young woman, buxom and large, with a tempestuous spirit and a great roiling mass of dark curls which usually lay in a cylindrical heap on top of her head. To justify her fury, Spanchetta seized upon the problems of her sister Simonetta: "Smonny."

Like Spanchetta, Smonny was large and burly, with a round face, rounded shoulders and large moist features. Where Spanchetta was dark-haired and dark-eyed, Smonny showed taffy-colored hair and golden-hazel eyes. Often she was jocularly assured that with yellow skin she might have passed for a Yip, which never failed to annoy her.[1]

To gain her ends Smonny was purposeful but lazy. Where Spanchetta preferred to bluster and domineer, Smonny used a wheedling or peevish persistence which rasped away at her adversary's patience, and eventually reduced it to shreds. Through indolence she failed her courses at the lyceum, and was denied Agency status. Spanchetta at once placed the blame upon Scharde, for introducing Marya into the house, thereby "rolling" Smonny out.

---

[1] Couplings between Yips and ordinary Gaeans yielded no progeny; Yips apparently were a subspecies of man in the process of differentiation: at least such was the speculation.

Yips, both men and women, were physically attractive; indeed, the beauty of Yip girls was proverbial.

"That is absurd and illogical," she was told, by no less than Fratano the Housemaster.

"Not at all!" declared Spanchetta, eyes glittering and bosom heaving. She took a step forward and Fratano drew back a step. "The worry absolutely destroyed Smonny's concentration! She made herself sick!"

"Still, that's not Scharde's fault. You did the same thing when you married Millis. He's out-House too, a Laverty collateral, as I recall."

Spanchetta could only grumble. "That's different. Millis is our own sort, not just some little interloper from God-help-us!"

Fratano turned away. "I can't waste any more of my time with such nonsense."

Spanchetta gave an acrid chuckle. "It's not your sister who is being victimized; it's mine! Why should you care? Your position is secure! As for wasting your time, you are anxious only to get to your afternoon nap. But there will be no nap for you today. Smonny is coming to talk with you."

Fratano, not the most obdurate of men, heaved a deep sigh. "I can't talk to Smonny right now. I'll make a special exception. She can have a month for study and another examination; I can't do any better. If she fails, she is out!"

The concession pleased Smonny not at all. She set up a howl of complaint: "How can I cover five years of material in a month?"

"You must do your best," snapped Spanchetta. "I suspect that the examination will only be a formality; Fratano hinted as much. Still, you can't get by with nothing! So, you must start studying immediately."

Smonny made only a perfunctory attempt to encompass the material she had so long ignored. To her consternation, the examination was of the usual sort, and not just a pretext for granting her a passing grade. Her score was even worse than before, and now there was no help for it: Smonny was out.

Her eviction from Clattuc House was a long and contentious process, which climaxed at the House Supper, when Smonny delivered her farewell remarks, which escalated from sarcastic jibes, through a revelation of disgraceful secrets, into a shrieking hysterical fit.

Fratano at last ordered the footmen to remove her by force; Smonny jumped up on the table and ran back and forth, followed by four bemused footmen, who finally seized her and dragged her away.

Smonny took herself off-world to Soum, where she worked briefly in a pilchard cannery; then, according to Spanchetta, joined an ascetic religious group, and subsequently vanished no one knows where.

In due course Marya gave birth to Glawen. Three years later, Marya drowned in the lagoon, while two Yips stood on the shore at no great distance. When asked why they had not gone to her rescue one said: "We were not watching." The other said: "It was none of our affair." Both, puzzled and uncomprehending, were immediately sent back to Yipton.

Scharde never spoke of the event and Glawen never asked questions. Scharde showed no inclination to remarry, even though the ladies considered him eminently personable. He was quiet and soft-spoken, of medium stature, spare and strong, with coarse short prematurely gray hair and narrow sky-blue eyes gleaming from a bony weathered face.

On the morning of Glawen's birthday, the two had barely finished breakfast before Scharde was called away to Bureau B on special business. Glawen, with nothing better to do, lingered at the table, while the two Yip footmen who had served the breakfast now cleared away the dishes and set the room to rights. Glawen watched them, wondering what went on behind the half-smiling faces. The quick sidelong glances: what did they signify? Mockery and contempt? Simple placid curiosity? Or nothing whatever? Glawen could not decide, and Yip behaviour gave no clue. It would be interesting, thought Glawen, to understand the quick sibilant Yip idiom.

Glawen finally rose from the table. He departed Clattuc House and wandered down to the lagoon: a series of brimming ponds fed by the River Wan, with trees along the shore both native and imported: black bamboo, weeping willow, poplar, purple-green verges.[1] The morning was fresh and sunny; autumn was in the air; in a few weeks Glawen would be entering the lyceum.

Glawen came to the Clattuc boathouse: a rectangular structure with an arched roof of green and blue glass supported on pillars of black iron, built to outdo in elegance the other five boathouses.

The Clattucs of this particular time, save perhaps for Scharde and Glawen, were not keen yachtsmen. The boathouse sheltered only a pair of punts, a beamy little sloop twenty-five feet long and a fifty-foot ketch for more extended blue-water cruising.[2]

---

[1] A large number of Earth-native plants and trees had been introduced to enhance the already rich flora of Cadwal. In every instance the biologists had adapted the plant to the environment, imposing ingenious genetic safeguards to prevent ecological disaster.

[2] Since islands were almost absent from the oceans of Cadwal, the principal discouragement to cruising lay in the lack of pleasant destinations. Dedicated yachtsmen might sail south to Stroma on Throy, or circumnavigate Deucas or even Cadwal itself: in the latter case making no landfall other than the dangerous coast of Ecce.

The boathouse was one of Glawen's favorite resorts, where he could almost always find solitude, which today he wanted above all else so that he might compose himself for the ordeal of the House Supper and his birthday celebration.

Such affairs were little more than formalities, so Scharde had assured him. Glawen would not be required to deliver a speech or embarrass himself in any other manner. "You are merely going to dine with your kin. For the most part they are a tiresome group, as you are well aware. After a moment or two they will ignore you, and become busy with their gossip and little intrigues. At the end Fratano will declare you a provisional, and announce your SI, which I should guess to be a fairly safe 24, or at worst a 25, which is still not too bad, considering the creaking joints and gray hairs around the table."

"And that is all?"

"More or less. If someone troubles to talk to you, answer politely, but otherwise you can dine in silence and no one will be the wiser."

Glawen sat on a bench where he could look across the lagoon and watch the play of sunlight and shadow on the water. He told himself: "Perhaps it will not go so badly, after all. Still, I'd be relieved if my SI turned out to be a point or two lower than what I fear it will be."

The scrape of footsteps broke into his thoughts. A bulky shape appeared at the end of the dock. Glawen sighed. Here was the person he least wanted to see: Arles, two years older than himself, taller by a head and heavier by fifty pounds. His face was large and flat, with a snub nose and a ripe heavy mouth. A smart cap with a stylish slantwise visor today confined his black curls.

At the age of eighteen and an SI of 16, by reason of his direct lineage, through Spanchetta and Valart, her father, to Past Master Damian, who was father to the current Master, Fratano,[1] only serious malfeasance or failure at the lyceum could cause Arles difficulties.

Coming into the cool dimness from the sunlight, Arles stood blinking. Glawen quickly picked up an abrasive block and, jumping aboard the sloop, busied himself at the taffrail. He crouched low; perhaps Arles would not see him.

Arles strolled slowly along the dock, hands in pockets, peering right and left. At last he took note of Glawen. He stopped and stared, puzzled by Glawen's activity. He sauntered close. "What are you up to?"

---

[1] Genealogical details and SIs need not be remembered. They will be cited as sparingly as possible.

Glawen said evenly: "I am sanding the boat, to prepare it for varnish."

"That's what I thought you were doing," said Arles coldly. "After all, my eyes are in very good condition."

"Don't just stand there; get busy. You'll find another sanding block in the locker."

Arles gave a snort of derisive laughter. "Are you serious? That's work for the Yips!"

"Why haven't they done it, then?"

Arles shrugged. "Complain to Namour; he'll put them right. But don't involve me; I have better things to do."

Glawen continued to work, with a sober concentration that at last caused Arles exasperation.

"Sometimes, Glawen, I find you absolutely unpredictable. Haven't you forgotten something?"

Glawen paused and gazed dreamily out over the water. "I can't think of anything. Of course, if I'd forgotten it, that's what one would expect."

"Bah! More of your larky talk! Today is your birthday! You should be up in your chambers, making preparations—that is, if you want to cut any kind of a figure. Do you have white shoes? If not, you should get some in double-quick time! I tell you this out of kindness; no more."

Glawen darted a side glance at Arles, then continued his work. "If I came to supper barefoot, no one would notice."

"Hah! That's where you're wrong! Never underestimate fine shoes! It's the first thing the girls look for!"

"Hm . . . That's something I didn't know."

"You'll find that I'm right. Girls are clever little creatures; they can size up a fellow in no time at all! If your nose is dripping or your fly is open or if your shoes aren't truly sporting, they'll tell each other: 'Don't give that turnip-head the time of day!'"

"Those are valuable tips," said Glawen. "I'll keep them in mind!"

Arles frowned. One could never be sure how to take Glawen's remarks; often they verged upon the caustic. At the moment Glawen seemed sober and respectful, which was as it should be. Reassured, Arles continued, even more grandly than before. "Perhaps I shouldn't mention this, but I have taken the trouble to work out a manual of foolproof methods for getting along with the girls, if you know what I mean." Arles gave Glawen a lewd wink. "It's based on female psychology and it operates like magic, every time!"

"Amazing! How does it work?"

"The details are secret. In practice, one needs only to identify signals which instinct enforces on the little darlings, and then make the response recommended in my manual, and so forth."

"Is this manual generally available?"

"Emphatically not! It's top-secret, for the use of Bold Lions only." The Bold Lions included six of the most raffish young scapegraces of Araminta Station. "If the girls got hold of a copy, they'd know exactly what was going on."

"They already know what's going on; they don't need your book."

Arles blew out his cheeks. "That is often true, in which case the manual recommends strategies of surprise."

Glawen rose to his feet. "I guess I'll have to work out my own methods—although I doubt if I'll need them at the House Supper. In the first place, there won't be any girls on hand."

"You're joking! What of Fram and Pally?"

"They are too old for me."

"But not for me! I take them as I find them, young or old! You should get involved with the Mummers! There are some real sizzlers in the troupe this year: Sessily Veder, for one."

"I don't have any talents along those lines."

"There's nothing to it! Master Floreste uses you to your best advantage; Kirdy Wook has no trace of talent; in fact, he's a bit of a lummox. Goody-goody, so to speak. In *Evolution of the Gods* he and I are primordial beasts. In *First-Fire* I am a being of clay and water, and I get struck by lightning. I change costumes and once again Kirdy and I are hairy beasts groaning for enlightenment. But the flame is stolen by Ling Diffin, who plays Prometheus. Sessily Veder is 'Bird of Inspiration,' and she inspired me to write my manual. Even that stick Kirdy drools to see her."

Glawen turned his back on the taffrail. Sessily Veder, whom he knew only from a distance, was a girl of charm and vitality. "Have you tried the manual on Sessily?"

"She hasn't given me the opportunity. That's the one flaw of my system."

"A pity . . . Well, I must get on with the sanding."

Arles settled himself upon a bench to watch. After a moment he said: "I suppose that you find this a good way to relax your nerves."

"Why should I be nervous? I've got to eat somewhere."

Arles grinned. "You don't improve matters lurking and glooming down here at the boathouse. Your SI is already calculated and there is nothing you can do about it."

Glawen only laughed. "If there were, I'd be doing it."

Arles' grin faded. Was there nothing sharp enough to puncture Glawen's self-possession? Even his mother, Spanchetta, had termed Glawen the most detestable child of her experience.

Arles spoke in an important voice: "Perhaps you're wise! Enjoy your peace of mind while you can, because after today, you'll be a provisional, with the five-year worries on your neck."

Glawen gave Arles one of the sardonic side glances which Arles found so annoying. "And these worries trouble you?"

"Not me! I'm a 16. I can afford to relax."

"So did your Aunt Smonny. How are your grades at the lyceum?"

Arles scowled. "Let's just leave me out of the conversation, shall we? Anytime my grades need attention, I can easily take care of them."

"If you say so."

"I say very much so. As for the matter under discussion—and I don't mean my grades—I know a great deal more than you might expect." Arles gazed up toward the blue and green glass dome. "In fact—I shouldn't tell you this—I've been privately notified of your SI. I'm sorry to say that it is not encouraging. I tell you only so that you won't be taken by surprise at the supper."

Glawen turned Arles another quick side glance. "No one knows my SI but Fratano, and he would not tell you."

Arles gave a knowing laugh. "Mark my words! Your number is close to the 30s. I won't tell you exactly, but shall we hint at somewhere between 29 and 31?"

At last Glawen's composure was breached. "I don't believe it!" He jumped to the dock. "Where did you hear such nonsense? From your mother?"

Arles suddenly sensed that he had spoken far too loosely. He tried to bluster. "Are you suggesting that my mother talks nonsense?"

"Neither you nor your mother are supposed to know anything about my SI."

"Why should we not? We can count and the lineage is a matter of record—or, more accurately, is not a matter of record."

An odd remark, thought Glawen. "What do you mean by that?"

Arles saw that once again he had spoken indiscreetly. "Nothing much. Nothing, really, at all."

"You seem oddly full of information."

"The Bold Lions know everything that's worth knowing. I'm familiar with scandals you can't even imagine! For instance, what old lady tried to pull Vogel Laverty into bed last week, almost by sheer force?"

"I have no idea. How far did he let himself get pulled?"

"Not at all! He's not even my age! Another situation: I could point out right now someone who will shortly have a baby and the father is very much in doubt."

Glawen turned away. "I had nothing to do with it, if that is what you came to find out."

Arles gave a hoot of laughter. "That is a fine joke! Quite the wittiest remark you have made today." He rose to his feet. "Time is getting on. Instead of varnishing the boat, you should be up in your chambers, cleaning your fingernails and rehearsing your deportment."

Glawen looked at Arles' plump white hands. "My fingernails are cleaner than yours are right now."

Arles scowled and thrust his hands in his pocket. "Conditions are different; keep that in mind! If I should speak to you, answer: 'Yes, sir' or 'No, sir.' That's proper conduct. If you have doubts about your table manners, just watch me."

"Thank you, but I will probably be able to muddle through the meal."

"As you wish." Arles turned on his heel and stalked from the dock.

Glawen stood looking after him, seething with irritation. Arles passed between the pair of heroic statues which flanked the entrance to the Clattuc formal garden, and was lost to view. Glawen pondered. Between 29 and 31? After five years as a provisional, his SI might have declined to 25. That meant collateral status and out of Clattuc House: away from his father, away from all the niceties of life, away from the prestige and perquisites of full Agency!

Glawen looked off across the water. Just such a grim event had altered the lives of thousands before him, but the full tragedy of the situation had never touched him before.

And what of the girls, whose good opinion he valued? There was Erlin Offaw, already embarked on what promised to be a long career of breaking hearts, and Ticia Wook, blond, fragile, fragrant and graceful as a gillyflower, but, like all Wooks, remote and proud.[1] Then there was Sessily Veder, who had been conspicuously amiable the last few times he had encountered her. If he were ranked with an SI of 30, his future was blasted and none of them would look twice at him again.

---

[1] Had each house rated the other five in order of perceived prestige, and had the six estimates been combined, the consensus would have placed the Wooks and the Offaws at the top of the list, with the Veders and the Clattucs just below, then the Diffins and the Lavertys, though even in the most unkind estimation, the difference between top and bottom was not great.

Glawen left the boathouse and followed Arles back up the slope to Clattuc House: a thin, somber dark-haired figure inconsequential in the scope of the landscape, though highly important to himself and to his father, Scharde.

Entering the house, Glawen went up to his chambers at the eastern end of the second-floor gallery. To his great relief, he found Scharde at home.

Scharde instantly sensed Glawen's perturbation. "You're getting the shakes early."

Glawen said: "Arles told me that he knew my SI, that it was between 29 and 31."

Scharde raised his eyebrows. "31? Even 29? How is that possible? You'd be out with the collaterals before you even started!"

"I know."

"I'd pay no heed to Arles. He just hoped to put you in a turmoil, and he seems to have succeeded."

"He says he heard it from Spanchetta! And he said something about my not having any lineage!"

"Oh?" Scharde considered. "Did he, now? What did he mean by that?"

"I don't know. I told him that he could not possibly know my SI, and he said: why not; that my lineage was a matter of record, or— more accurately—my lack of lineage."

"Ha," muttered Scharde. "Now I begin to see. I just wonder . . ." His voice dwindled away. He went to stare out the window. "There is indeed the flavor of Spanchetta in this business."

"Could she change my number?"

"That's an interesting question. She works at Bureau A and has access to the computer. Still, she'd never dare fiddle with the machinery; that's a capital crime. Whatever she has done, if anything, is bound to be legal."

Glawen shook his head in puzzlement. "Why should she want to do such a thing? What difference does my number make to her?"

"We don't know yet whether or not anything has been done. If so, Spanchetta may or may not be responsible. If so again, the answer is simple. She forgets and forgives nothing. I'll tell you a story you've probably never heard before.

"Long ago she made up her mind to marry me, and she actually schemed with the House Mistress and Dame Lilian the Chatelaine so that they all began to take the match seriously, even without so much as consulting me. One evening, we were playing epaing. Spanchetta was on the court, shouting and cursing and making flamboyant signals, and calling fouls where none existed and gray balls when they were pink, and yelling in outrage when someone dropped in a lob. Wilmor Veder called over to me: 'Well, then, Scharde, looks like your marriage will be quite an adventure.'

"I said: 'I'm not getting married; where did you hear that?'

"'It's all over! Everybody is talking about it.'

"'I wish someone would let me in on the secret. Who is the lucky woman?'

"'Spanchetta, of course! I heard it from Carlotte.'

"'Carlotte is talking doodle. I'm not marrying Spanchetta! Not today, not tomorrow, not last year, not at the second coming of Pulius Feistersnap. In short, never, and not even then! Does that set matters straight?'

"'It sounds definite to me. Now you need only convince Spanchetta, who is standing right behind you.'

"I looked around and there stood Spanchetta breathing flame. Everybody laughed and Spanchetta tried to murder me with her epaing bat, which made everyone laugh even more.

"So then, just for spite, she married poor Millis, and also took up with Namour. But she never forgave me.

"About a year later, I married your mother at Sarsenopolis on Alphecca Nine. When we returned to Araminta Station, there were unpleasant incidents, many of them. Marya ignored them; so did I. Then you were born, and Spanchetta dislikes you in triplicate: because of me and your mother and because you are everything Arles is not. And now it just might be that she has found an opportunity to express herself."

"It's hard to believe."

"Spanchetta is a strange woman. You wait here; I want to make some inquiries."

2

Scharde went directly to the Bureau A offices in the New Agency, where, in his capacity as Commander of Police, he was able to make his investigation without hindrance.

Time was short; in two hours the House Supper, as inexorable in its regularity as the motion of Lorca around Sing, would begin. Scharde returned to Clattuc House and took himself to the pleasant high-ceilinged apartments occupied by Housemaster Fratano.

As Scharde entered the reception hall, he met Spanchetta coming from the inner parlor. Both stopped short, each thinking that here was the person he least wanted to see. Spanchetta spoke sharply: "What are you doing here?"

"I could ask the same of you," said Scharde. "But, as a matter of fact, I have Agency business to take up with Fratano."

"The time is late. Fratano is dressing." Spanchetta looked Scharde up and down. "Are you coming to the Supper in that outfit? But why should I ask? You are notoriously lax where propriety is concerned."

Scharde gave a rueful laugh. "I neither admit nor deny, but never fear! I'll be on hand when the soup is served! Now I have business with Fratano; please excuse me."

Spanchetta grudgingly moved aside. "Fratano is occupied with his own dressing and won't wish to be bothered. I'll take in your message, if you like."

"I must see to this matter myself." Scharde stepped in front of Spanchetta, holding his breath against the warm and heavy scent, half perfume, half female fecundity, which she exuded. He entered Fratano's private parlor and carefully closed the door, almost in Spanchetta's face.

Fratano, wearing a loose lounge-robe, sat in an easy chair with one long pallid foot propped on a cushioned stool, while a Yip maidservant massaged his lower leg. He looked up with a questioning frown. "Well, then, Scharde, what is it now? Can't you come at a more convenient time?"

"The time will never be more convenient, as you will learn. Send the girl away; our conversation must be private."

Fratano made a peevish clicking sound with his tongue. "Is it so vital as all that? Paz is not interested in our talk."

"Possibly not, but I have noticed that Namour knows everything about everybody. Need I say more? Girl, take yourself from the room, and close the door as you leave."

After a glance at Fratano, the maid rose. She took up her pot of ointment and with a cool half-smile for Scharde, left the room.

"So, now!" growled Fratano. "What is of such importance that it interferes with my massage?"

"Today is Glawen's sixteenth birthday, and he becomes a provisional."

Fratano blinked, suddenly thoughtful. "What of it?"

"Have you been notified of his official SI?"

"Yes, so I have." Fratano coughed and cleared his throat. "Again —what of that?"

"Spanchetta brought it to you?"

"That is inconsequential, one way or the other. It has to arrive from

Bureau A by some means. Usually Dame Leûta brings it over. Today it was Spanchetta. The SI is the same."

"Has Spanchetta ever handed it in before?"

"No. Now tell me, once and for all, what are you up to?"

"I think you know. You've looked at the number?"

"Of course! Why not?"

"And what is the number?"

Fratano tried to draw himself up. "I can't tell you that! The SIs are confidential!"

"Not if Bureau B decides to concern itself."

Fratano pulled himself up in his chair. "Why should Bureau B interfere in House business? I insist on knowing what you are getting at!"

"I am investigating what may be a criminal conspiracy."

"I don't know what you are talking about."

"When Spanchetta claims to know Glawen's SI, and tells Arles, who crows about his knowledge to Glawen, that is already wrongdoing. If the Housemaster is involved, the question of criminal conspiracy arises."

Fratano gave a poignant cry. "What are you saying! I am guilty of nothing!"

"Where is the SI?"

Fratano pointed to a square of yellow paper on the side table. "The number is there. It is the official computer printout."

Scharde looked at the paper. "30? You saw this number?"

"Yes, naturally."

"And you were going to read it off at the House Supper?"

Fratano's loose-jowled face sagged even lower. "As a matter of fact, I thought the number rather high."

Scharde gave a scornful laugh. "High, you say? What, at a guess, should be Glawen's SI?"

"Well, I would have guessed 24 or thereabouts. Still—" Fratano pointed to the yellow paper. "It is not my place to argue with the computer."

Scharde grinned: a crooked sinister grimace which for an instant showed the tips of his teeth. "Fratano, I have just come up from Bureau A. The computer is functioning with its usual accuracy. But it must depend upon the information fed into it. Do you agree?"

"That is so; yes."

"This morning, as is my right, I examined the input to the computer —the information upon which it had based its judgment—and do you know, someone had altered the records? To such an effect that Glawen was declared illegitimate—a bastard."

Once more Fratano cleared his throat. "If the truth be known, rumors have been circulating to this effect for some time."

"I have heard none of them."

"It is said that your marriage to Marya was illegal and void, with the result that all issue was illegitimate."

"How could my marriage be illegal? I can show you the marriage certificate at any time. Now if you like."

"The marriage was void because Marya was already married, and had neglected to certify a legal divorce. Naturally, I paid no heed to such meretricious chatter. Still, if unfortunately it were true—"

"Spanchetta told you all this? She is the source of the so-called rumor?"

"The subject indeed came up in our conversation."

"And you accepted her statement, without so much as referring it to me?"

"The facts speak for themselves!" bleated Fratano. "On her tourist entry she signs herself as 'Madame' Marya Chiasalvo."

Scharde nodded. "Bureau B can construct against you a clear case of either 'criminal conspiracy' or 'felonious default of duty.'"

Fratano's jowl quivered and his eyes became large and moist. "My dear Scharde! You know me better than that!"

"Then why did you accept, without protest, such an outrageous printout from Spanchetta? I admit to a sense of sheer outrage! You know Spanchetta and her spite! You have let yourself become her tool! So you must bear the consequences!"

Fratano said miserably: "Spanchetta can be very convincing at times."

"Here are the facts, which you could have learned from me over the telephone. Marya's family subscribed to a popular religion of Alphecca Nine known as the Quadriplar Revelation. Children enter the religion at the age of ten by dedicating themselves in a mock-marriage with their patron saint. Marya's patron saint was Chiasalvo, the Jewel of Kind Being. The marriage is a religious formality, which the patron saint renounces as part of the marriage ceremony. It is so certified on the marriage certificate, which you could have seen at any time the question arose. The marriage, despite Spanchetta's vicious assertions, is as legal as your own. How she could dare introduce this distortion into the genealogical record is beyond my understanding."

"Bah!" muttered Fratano in a subdued voice. "Spanchetta and her intrigues will someday drive me crazy! Luckily, you were in time to catch out the mistake."

"Don't use the word 'mistake.' There is malice at work here!"

"Ah well, Spanchetta is a sensitive woman. At one time she had reason to believe . . . But no matter. This is a sorry mess. What shall we do?"

"You can count and I can count. Here is the Clattuc roster. Glawen clearly should rank after Dexter and before Trine. That gives him an SI of 24. I suggest that you formalize this number by executive fiat, as is your privilege, and, in this case, your duty."

Fratano studied the roster. He counted with his long white finger. "Just possibly Trine might pick up a point or two by virtue of his mother's aunt's altitude among the Veders."

"The same applies to Glawen. Elsabetta, his grandmother's older sister, is a high Wook, and he can also show Dame Waltrop of Diffin as input. And don't forget, Trine is eight years younger than Glawen! He doesn't need a 24 at his age."

"True enough." Fratano turned a cautious side glance toward Scharde. "And there will be no more talk of criminal conspiracy—which of course is only a bad joke in the first place?"

Scharde gave a grim nod. "So be it."

"Very well. Common sense says 24 and we will assume that the computer meant to give us a 24." Fratano took the yellow sheet and with a stylus marked through the '30' and wrote '24' in its place. "Now all is well and I must dress."

At the door Scharde turned to speak over his shoulder. "I suggest that you lock the outer door after me. Otherwise you might have Spanchetta on your hands again."

Fratano gave a sour nod. "I can manage the affairs of my own department. Gunter? Gunter! Where the devil are you?"

A footman entered the room. "Sir?"

"Lock the door with double bolts after Sir Scharde departs. Admit no one, and bring me no messages; is this clear?"

"Yes indeed, sir."

3

As they stood ready to leave their chambers, Scharde subjected Glawen to a last inspection. His curt nod concealed far more pride than he cared to put into words. "For certain, no one will find fault with your appearance; you may rest easy on that account."

"Hmmf. Arles will disapprove of my shoes, at the very least."

Scharde chuckled. "Only Arles. No one else will look twice in your direction—unless you commit some awful vulgarity."

Glawen said with dignity: "I am not planning any vulgarity whatever. That is not my idea of a birthday celebration."

"Sound thinking! I suggest also that you say nothing unless you are directly addressed, and then reply with a platitude. Before long everyone will think you a brilliant conversationalist."

"More likely, they'll think me a surly brute," growled Glawen. "Still, I will guard my tongue."

Once again Scharde showed his crooked half-smile. "Come; it is time we started down."

The two descended the staircase to the first floor and passed through the reception hall into the main gallery: a pair of erect figures, with similar austere features and mannerisms which suggested innate grace and strength under careful control. Scharde stood a head taller; his hair had become a coarse nondescript gray; wind and weather had darkened his skin to the color of old oak. Glawen was somewhat more fair, and more compact at chest and shoulder. Scharde's mouth was taut and ironic; Glawen's mouth, when he was relaxed or moody, took on a pensive droop at the corners, as if his mind were off among the clouds. Girls, when they looked at Glawen, as often they did, found that this droop, with its suggestion of sweet flights of fancy, tended to play strange tricks upon their hearts.

The two proceeded to the dining room. At the portal they halted, and took stock of those already at their places. Most of the in-House Clattucs had arrived, and now lounged at their ease in the stiff-backed chairs, gossiping, laughing and sipping lively Bagnold from the Laverty winery, or, as often, the heavier and sweeter Pink Indescense, as formulated by the Wook oenologists. At stations around the walls stood Yip footmen, resplendent in the gray and orange Clattuc livery, their faces powdered white and their hair concealed by wigs of combed silver floss.

Scharde pointed across the table. "You will sit there, next to your Great-aunt Clotilde. I will be at your other side. Lead the way."

Glawen set his coat, squared his shoulders and advanced into the dining room. The company on hand stilled its talk; flippant remarks hung in the air; chuckles and titters dwindled into silence; all heads turned to stare at the new arrivals.

Looking neither right nor left, Glawen marched around the table, with Scharde coming behind. There were mutters and whispers; clearly rumors regarding Glawen's SI and his imminent shock had already seeped around the table. Such an item of news, with its implications and scope for tragic drama, was too choice to be contained. All now awaited the moment when Fratano's announcement would blast Glawen's life and everyone covertly studied the victim-to-be. Scharde smiled his faint smile.

Glawen arrived at his place, with Scharde close behind. A pair of footmen pulled back their chairs and slid them forward after Glawen and Scharde had seated themselves. The company resumed its previous occupation; all was as before, and Glawen was ignored: an almost insulting indifference, in Glawen's view. The dinner, after all, was in celebration of his personal birthday. He turned a haughty glance around the table, but no one noticed. Perhaps some grotesque and splendid vulgarity might be in order, after all.

Glawen put the idea aside; it had no real temptation for him, and his father would be embarrassed. He studied the company: his uncles, aunts and cousins of high and low degree, together with a single great-grandparent. All were arrayed in fine garments and stylish ornaments, and seemed to take pleasure in the act. The ladies wore gowns of rich fabric and feather-weave, and many displayed their jewels: alexandrites, emeralds, rubies, and carbuncles, topaz and purple tourmaline from sites about Deucas;[1] sphanctonites from dead stars, and Maidhouse crystals, found at a single site in all the expanse of the Gaean Reach.

The gentlemen wore coats and tight trousers of soft twill in contrasting colors: often dark buff and blue, or maroon and cedar green, or black and deep mustard ocher. Among the young gallants, white shoes were all the rage, and the more dashing clasped the left side of their scalps with silver mesh from which lifted clusters of silver prongs, to striking effect. Among this latter group was Arles, who sat six places around the table from Glawen, with Spanchetta beside him.

There could be no question as to Spanchetta's intense and pungent vitality. Not the least of her attributes was the remarkable mass of raven-black curls, barely disciplined, which surmounted her head and swayed perilously as she looked this way and that. The placement of her glittering black eyes, close by the bridge of her nose, accentuated the expanse of her marmoreal cheeks. Today she wore a magenta gown, cut low to display the white pillar of her neck and a good deal of what depended below. Spanchetta had darted a single glance toward

---

[1] The Conservator ignored the almost universal passion for gem collecting, so long as no significant mining operations were attempted.

32

Glawen which assimilated every detail of his appearance; then, with a faint sniff, she looked away and paid him no further heed.

Next beside Spanchetta sat Millis, her mild and diffident husband, distinguished principally by his drooping ash-blond mustache. He was now concerned with the problem of drinking wine without wetting his mustache.

Fratano stood at the side table reserved to retired Clattucs, making polite conversation with his father, Damian, a long-retired Past Master, now well over ninety years old. Resemblance between the two was striking; both were gaunt, pallid, high of forehead, long of nose, upper lip and chin.

The table was almost full. Only Garsten and Jalulia, Glawen's grandparents, were not yet present. The footmen poured wine for Glawen and Scharde, Green Zoquel and Rimbaudia, both Clattuc wines, and prizewinners at last year's Parilia. Glawen essayed a goodly gulp of the Zoquel, which caused Scharde surprise and mild alarm. "The wine is strong! Much more and you'll be snoring on the table with your hair in the soup!"

"I'll be careful." Glawen shifted his position and tugged at his new coat, which felt stiff and tight, while the new trousers not only constricted his shanks, but rode high in the crotch, causing him acute discomfort. Such, he told himself, was the price one paid for the enjoyment of high style, and little could be done about it. He forced himself to sit quietly, hands in his lap. Arles bent down his head and turned him a pursy grin. No matter if Housemaster Fratano fixed his SI at 50. Glawen swore that he would betray emotion by not so much as a twitch.

Minutes went by at a slow march. Fratano continued to chat with Damian. Garsten and Jalulia still had not arrived. Glawen sighed. Would dinner never be served? He looked around the table. Never had his senses seemed so alert, nor his perceptions so keen! He studied the faces of his kin. All were strangers. Remarkable! It was as if a curtain had slipped, revealing, if only for an instant, truth not intended for his knowing . . . Glawen sighed and raised his eyes to the ceiling. An odd but useless notion. Foolishness, of course. He essayed another sip of wine. Scharde made no comment.

Voices rose and fell, or lapsed momentarily into silence, as if everyone had decided to use the same instant to formulate his next words. The time was middle afternoon; light from Syrene slanted through tall windows, reflecting from high ceilings and white walls, playing across the tablecloth, glinting on the glass and silver.

At last Garsten and Jalulia entered the room. They paused behind

33

Glawen, and Garsten touched his shoulder. "Today: the great occasion, eh? I remember my own sixteenth; how long ago it seems now! But I still remember the tension! Even though I was born A-bc, I was still in dread of being sent off across the Reach, into some dark cold hinterland. But the Mad Dog[1] coughed up a 19, and I was in, and lucky for you, eh? Otherwise you'd be hunkered down over a plate of beans on some cold far world while the leeches hopped around the mud and the natives howled, and gargoyle hawks ravaged your flocks."

Jalulia chided him: "What nonsense you talk! If you had actually failed and had been turned out, we would never have met and Glawen would not be here now."

"All to the same effect! Well, we can only hope that the Mad Dog plays you fair."

"I hope so too," said Glawen.

Garsten and Jalulia went to their places; Fratano stepped down to his own chair. He looked at a slip of paper beside his service plate, read, then turned to inspect the faces around the table. "Ah, Glawen, there you are. Today you come into the proud estate of provisional! The opportunities of life are now open to you! I am sure that through diligence and duty you will, at the very least, arrive at the condition of noble and self-reliant manhood, no matter whether your life is to be lived here, as an agent of the Conservancy, or elsewhere, in what might prove an equally rewarding career!"

Glawen listened, feeling the attention of all eyes.

Fratano proceeded. "I will today utter no lengthy peroration; should you feel the need of instruction or wise counsel, you need only apply to me, and it shall be forthcoming. Such is my obligation to every Clattuc of the House, from low to high.

"Now, then: to definite matters. I see no reason to prolong the suspense. I have here the official statement of your SI." Fratano lifted the paper, threw back his head and looked down his nose at the inscription. "Here, as yielded by impersonal and accurate processes of calculation, is your SI. I announce the number to be—" he raised his head and gazed around the attentive faces— "24."

Eyes blinked, then swung to fix upon Glawen. From Spanchetta came a startled cry, which she quickly stifled. Arles stared first at Glawen, then turned to gaze numbly at his mother, who sat hunched forward, scowling down into her wine.

Glawen was now expected to utter a few remarks. He rose to his

[1] Mad Dog: colloquial term for the Bureau A computer.

34

feet and bowed politely toward Fratano. His voice quavered so slightly that no one noticed but Scharde. "Thank you, sir, for your good wishes. I will truly do my best to become both a good agent of the Conservator and a credit to Clattuc House."

Fratano asked: "And where will you work, or have you chosen?"

"I have already been accepted into Bureau B."

"A sound choice! We need careful and vigilant patrols if we are to keep Marmion Land[1] clear of the Yips."

The Yip footmen smiled somewhat self-consciously at Fratano's remarks, but otherwise showed no reaction.

Glawen sat down to a spatter of applause, and footmen began to serve the supper. Conversation once more became general, and all declared that never for an instant had they believed the wild rumor in regard to Glawen, which was on the face of it absurd. Furtive glances were turned toward Spanchetta, who sat like a stone, until suddenly, as if at a signal, she became animated, even ebullient, and conducted four conversations at once.

Now that Glawen was no longer to be considered a pariah, his Great-aunt Clotilde, a tall breezy woman of middle age, condescended to speak with him. She keenly enjoyed the game of epaing, and considered herself knowledgeable in regard to the game's tactical intricacies; she now conveyed to Glawen a number of her opinions.

With Scharde's advice in mind, Glawen carefully suppressed all evidence of independent thought, and later Clotilde remarked upon Glawen's intelligence to her cronies.

The Supper culminated with a festive pudding of iced custard and fruit. The company drank a ritual, if rather perfunctory, toast to Glawen, then Fratano rose to his feet, and the Supper was at an end.

A number of folk, as they left the room, paused to wish Glawen good luck. Arles sauntered across the room. "A good number!" he stated. "A very fair number, considering everything. I'd placed it a bit higher, as you know, but I'm glad to see that all turned out favorably. Although you don't want to be overconfident! 24 is by no means a free pass."

"I know."

Scharde took Glawen's arm and the two returned to their chambers,

---

[1] Deucas was divided into sixty districts, or "lands." Marmion Land was that strip of pleasant savanna along the northeast coast directly opposite Lutwen Atoll. Already Yips were crossing over to set up camps and remain until apprehended and ejected by Bureau B patrols.

where Glawen instantly rushed into his bedroom and changed into ordinary clothes.

He returned to the parlor to find Scharde at the window, brooding across the landscape. Scharde turned and pointed to a chair. "Sit. We have important matters to discuss."

Glawen slowly seated himself, wondering what was afoot. Scharde brought out a bottle of the light fresh wine known as Quiritavo and poured a pair of goblets half full. He noticed Glawen's expression and grinned. "Relax! There are no dreadful secrets to be shared with you on your sixteenth birthday—just some precautions: practical planning, so to speak."

"In regard to Spanchetta?"

"Quite right. She has been humiliated and everyone is laughing at her. She is seething with fury and padding back and forth like some awful beast in a cage."

Glawen said thoughtfully: "If Arles is wise, he will slip down to the Lions' Lair and hide under the table."

"And if he is very wise indeed, he will never mention that due to his loose tongue we were able to catch her out in her tricks."

"Isn't what she did illegal?"

"In principle: yes. But if we brought charges, she would simply assert that she had made a mistake, and it would be hard to prove otherwise. To Spanchetta, it's already water under the bridge, and unless I miss my guess, she'll be scheming and plotting in new directions."

"That is insanity!"

"Insanity or not, be warned and be careful, but don't let her become an obsession. The world can't stop because of Spanchetta. You've now got lyceum to think about, which will be more than enough to keep you busy, especially with Bureau B's supplementary work."

"When will I start going out on patrols?"

"That's a long way off. First there's the matter of your flying permit, then your special training. Of course, if some emergency comes up anything can happen."

"By emergency, you mean the Yips."

"I don't see how to avoid it. Every day there are more Yips with no place to go but Yipton."

"Then you really think there will be trouble."

Scharde considered before responding. "It's not inevitable, if proper decisions are made and made soon. Already the Yip Oomphaw is starting to act oddly, as if he knows something we don't."

"Is that possible? What could he know?"

"Probably nothing, unless he's been talking with the Fairness and Peace people at Stroma."

"I've never heard of them."

"They are a political faction among the Naturalists. We have, essentially, two options: to capitulate and abandon the Conserve, or to maintain order by whatever means is necessary."

"That doesn't seem a hard choice to make."

"Not at Bureau B. We believe that sooner or later the Yips must be vacated from Lutwen Atoll and be resettled off-world. In terms of the Charter, no other solution is possible." Scharde gave his head a gloomy shake. "The hard facts are that our opinions have little force. We are agents of the Society at Stroma. It's the Society's problem and they must make the decisions."

"Then they should do so, or so it seems to me."

"Ah, but it's not so simple. Nothing ever is. At Stroma the Society is split down the middle. One faction supports the Charter, while the opposition rejects any actions which might lead to bloodshed. The present Conservator identifies with the second group: the Party of Fairness and Peace, they call themselves. But he is retiring and a new Conservator is moving into Riverview House."

"And what party is he?"

"I don't know," said Scharde. "He'll be here for Parilia, and then we'll know more about him."

Parilia, a three-day festival in praise of the wines of Araminta, was celebrated each autumn and considered the high point of the year.

Glawen said: "It would seem that the Yips would want to be resettled, rather than living in what amounts to a warren at Yipton."

"Naturally! But they want to settle Marmion Province."

Glawen made a disconsolate sound. "Everyone at Stroma must know that if the Yips were allowed into the Marmion littoral, they'd swarm over all of Deucas."

"Tell that to the Fairness and Peace people at Stroma, not me. I already believe you."

4

The long summer came to an end. Master Floreste's troupe of Mummers returned from a successful off-world tour, the profits of which would help fulfill Floreste's great dream: a magnificent new Orpheum for the glorification of the performing arts. Glawen celebrated his sixteenth birthday and immediately started flight training under the supervision of the airport manager: one Eustace Chilke, a native of Old Earth.

The lessons, the flyers and Eustace Chilke himself, with his tales of odd folk in remote places, for a time dominated Glawen's life. Chilke, while barely past the first flush of youth, was already the veteran of a hundred picaresque adventures. He had traveled the Gaean Reach far and wide, at every level of the economic ladder: all of which had yielded him a working philosophy which he often shared with Glawen. "Poverty is acceptable because then there is no way but up. Rich people worry about losing their wealth, but I like this worry far more than the worry of scratching the wealth together in the first place. Also, people are nicer to you when they think you are rich—although they'll often hit you over the head to find out where you hide your money."

Chilke's appearance, while not at all remarkable, combined an unobtrusive flamboyance with a droll corded face. His features were weather-beaten and somewhat irregular, under a coarse and tattered crop of short dust-colored hair. He stood at average stature, with a short neck and heavy shoulders which caused him to hunch slightly forward.

Chilke described himself as a farm boy from the Big Prairie. He spoke so feelingly of his old home, the neat little prairie towns and the wide windy landscapes that Glawen inquired if he ever planned to return.

"Indeed I do," said Chilke. "But only after I've amassed a fortune. When I left they called me a vagabond and threw rocks after the car. I want to return in style, with a band playing and girls dancing ahead of me throwing rose petals in the street." Chilke thought back over the years. "All taken with all, I suspect that the consensus was correct. Not that I was mean and vicious; I just took after Grandpa Swaner, on my mother's side. The Chilkes never thought highly of the Swaners, who were felt to be society folk from the city and hence worthless. Grandpa Swaner was also considered a vagabond. He liked to deal in junk: purple bric-a-brac, stuffed animals, old books and documents, petrified dinosaur droppings. He had a collection of glass eyes of which he was very proud. The Chilkes laughed and jeered, sometimes behind his back, sometimes not. He wasn't troubled in the least, especially after he sold the glass eyes to a fervent collector for a princely sum. The Chilkes stopped laughing and began looking around for glass eyes of their own.

"Grandpa Swaner was a canny old bird, no question about it, and always turned a handsome profit on his deals. The Chilkes finally had to stop calling him names out of embarrassment. I was his favorite. He gave me a beautiful *Atlas of the Gaean Worlds* for my birthday. It was an enormous book, two feet high by three feet wide and six inches thick, with Mercator maps of all the settled worlds. Whenever Grandpa Swaner came upon an item of interesting information regarding one of these worlds he'd paste it to the back of the map. When I was sixteen he took me to Tamar, Capella Nine, aboard a Gateway Line packet. It was the first time I'd been off-world and I was never the same again.

"Grandpa Swaner belonged to a dozen professional societies, including the Naturalist Society. I vaguely remember him telling me of a world at the end of Mircea's Wisp which the Naturalists kept as a preserve for wild animals. I wondered if the animals appreciated what was being done for them, so that they would abstain from eating people like Grandpa Swaner. I was just an innocent kindly child. Strange to say, here I am now, still innocent and kindly, at Araminta Station."

"How did you happen to come here?"

"That's a peculiar story, and I haven't sorted it out yet. There are two or three puzzling coincidences which are very hard to explain."

"How so? I'm something of a vagabond myself, and I'm interested."

Chilke was amused by the remark. "The story starts off sedately enough. I was working as a tour-bus operator out of Seven Cities, on John Preston's World." Chilke told how he became aware of "a big white-skinned lady wearing a tall black hat" who joined Chilke's morning tour four days in succession. At last she engaged him in conversation, commenting favorably upon his amiable manner and sympathetic conduct. "It's nothing special: just my stock-in-trade," said Chilke modestly.

The lady introduced herself as Madame Zigonie, a widow from Rosalia, a world to the back of the Pegasus Rectangle. After a few minutes of conversation she suggested that Chilke join her for lunch: an invitation which Chilke saw no reason to refuse.

Madame Zigonie selected a fine restaurant where they were served an excellent lunch. During the meal she encouraged Chilke to talk of his early years on the Big Prairie and the general facts of his family background. Presently the focus of the conversation shifted and touched upon a number of various subjects. As if on sudden impulse, Madame Zigonie revealed to Chilke that she was conscious within herself of strong clairvoyant powers which she ignored only at grave risk to herself and her fortunes. "Perhaps you have wondered at my manifest interest in you," she told Chilke. "The fact is that I must hire an overseer for my ranch, and this mysterious inner voice insisted that you were the right and proper person for the position."

"Interesting!" said Chilke. "I'm an old farm boy, no question as to that. I hope that your inner voice recommends a high salary."

"Adequately high," said Madame Zigonie. "Shadow Valley Ranch comprises twenty-two thousand square miles with a hundred or more employees. It is a responsible post. I can offer a salary of ten thousand sols per year, along with travel and living expenses."

"Hm," said Chilke. "It sounds like an important job. The proper salary would seem to be twenty thousand sols: less than a sol per square mile, which I consider a bargain."

Madame Zigonie said decisively: "The salary is not reckoned on that basis, since not every square mile needs careful supervision. Ten thousand sols is quite adequate. You will reside in a private bungalow, with ample room for all your belongings. It is important to be surrounded by one's little treasures; don't you think?"

"Absolutely."

"You will find conditions quite congenial," said Madame Zigonie. "I shall see to it personally."

Chilke spoke with great earnestness: "I want to reassure you in regard to a rather delicate matter. Never fear that I might become overfamiliar! Never, never, never!"

"You are remarkably emphatic!" said Madame Zigonie coldly. "The possibility had never occurred to me."

"It is wise to be clear on these things, if only for your peace of mind. You need expect nothing from me except dignified and formal conduct. The fact is, I am sworn to celibacy, and I am already married, to boot. Also, if the truth be known, I am somewhat underpowered, shall we say, which makes me nervous and flighty when ladies get too friendly. Hence, you may rest easy in this regard."

Madame Zigonie gave her head a toss which almost dislodged her tall black hat. She noticed Chilke staring at her forehead, and quickly rearranged the russet curls which fringed her face. "That is only a birthmark you see; pay it no heed."

"Just so. It is rather like a tattoo."

"No matter." Madame Zigonie carefully adjusted her hat. "I take it that you will accept the post?"

"Regarding the salary, fifteen thousand sols would seem a nice compromise."

"It would also seem an inordinate sum for a person of your inexperience."

"Oh?" Chilke raised his eyebrows. "What does your clairvoyant power tell you in this regard?"

"It inclines to the same opinion."

"In that case, let us abandon the entire idea." Chilke rose to his feet. "I thank you for the lunch and for an interesting conversation. Now, if you will excuse me—"

"Not so fast," snapped Madame Zigonie. "Perhaps something can be arranged. Where are your belongings?"

"They're more or less the clothes on my back and a change of underwear," said Chilke. "I tend to travel light, in case I want to make a hasty move somewhere."

"Still, you must have the goods you inherited from your grandfather. We shall ship everything to Rosalia and you will feel comfortably at home."

"Not necessarily," said Chilke. "There's a stuffed moose in the barn, but I don't want it in the front room of my bungalow."

"I'm interested in such things," said Madame Zigonie. "Perhaps we should go to Big Prairie and make an inventory, or I could go by myself."

"The family wouldn't like it," said Chilke.

"Still, we must do our best to bring you your things."

"It's not all that necessary."

"We shall see."

In due course Chilke arrived at Rosalia, a rough-and-ready little world at the back of the Pegasus Rectangle. Lipwillow on the banks of the Big Muddy River was the principal town and spaceport. Chilke spent a night at the Big Muddy Hotel and in the morning was conveyed to Shadow Valley Ranch. Madame Zigonie housed him in a small bungalow under a pair of blue-pepper trees, and put him in charge of a hundred indentured workers of an unfamiliar race: handsome golden-skinned young men known as Yips.

"The Yips were a source of total frustration; I could never entice them to work. I tried to be nice and I tried to be cruel. I begged, I threatened, I reasoned, I intimidated. They just smiled at me. They were quite willing to talk about work, but they always had some more or less sane reason why a certain job could not or should not be done.

"Madame Zigonie watched for a while, laughing to herself. Finally she explained how to handle the Yips. 'They are sociable creatures, and detest solitude. Take one of them to a job, tell him that's where he stays, alone, until the job is done. He'll howl and cry, and explain that he needs help, but the more he complains, the faster he'll work,

41

and if it isn't done right, he must stay and do it all over. You'll find that they'll work briskly enough once they get the idea.'

"I don't know why she waited so long to tell me. She was an odd one, no question as to that. She was not often in residence at the ranch. Every time she showed up I asked for my salary, and she said: 'Yes, of course; it slipped my mind. I'll see to it directly.' But the next thing I knew she was gone again and I was still penniless. Finally I was reduced to gambling with the Yips and taking what little money they had. When I think back and remember their sad faces I feel just a bit ashamed.

"On one occasion Madame Zigonie was gone several months. She came back in a tense mood. I had lunch with her at the big house and out of a blue sky she said that after careful thought she had decided to marry me. We were to join our lives, mingle our hopes and dreams, share our possessions and live in connubial bliss. I sat stunned, with my mouth hanging open. I have mentioned my first impression of Madame Zigonie at Seven Cities. She had not become more appealing in the meantime. She was still tall and portly; her face was round with round cheeks, and her skin was still the color of lard.

"I said in a polite way that the idea did not fit in with my plans, but, just out of curiosity, what was the sum total of her wealth, and would it be signed over to me at once, or only upon her demise?

"At this she became a bit haughty and asked what I proposed to contribute to the union. I frankly admitted that I had nothing but a barnful of purple bric-a-brac and a hundred stuffed animals. She didn't like it, but said it would have to do. I said no, not really. It wasn't fair to her, what with all my peculiar hang-ups in regard to ladies; also we mustn't forget that I was already married to a lady in Winnipeg, which made another marriage not only redundant but also unthinkable to a man of honor. Madame Zigonie became angry and discharged me on the instant, without paying my salary.

"I made my way into town and went to Poolie's Place, at the end of a pier reaching fifty yards out into Big Muddy. I sat down with a cold lager and tried to decide what to do. Who should I meet there but Namour, fresh from delivering a gang of indentured Yips to one of the outback ranches. This was a private side enterprise to his regular work, so he told me. I asked how he was able to recruit the Yips; he said it was no problem and actually a fine opportunity for any who showed diligence, since, after working out their indenture, the Yips could take up land and become ranchers themselves. I told him that in my opinion the Yips were next to worthless as workers. He just laughed and told me I didn't know how to handle them. He used the telephone, then notified me that he had spoken to Madame Zigonie, who said I could have my old job back if I wanted it. Namour thought it was a good idea, and that I'd been far too hasty in leaving for town. I told him: 'You marry the lady, so she's comfortably taken care of, then come talk to me.' He said: 'Not bloody likely,' but there was another possibility: how would I like managing the airport at Araminta Station? I said: 'Yes indeed, I surely would.' He said he could guarantee nothing, but the position was open and he thought he could push the job my way. 'But don't forget,' he said, 'first and foremost I'm a businessman and I'll take something in return.' I told him he could have his choice of a purple vase with two handles or a stuffed mink eating a stuffed mouse. Namour finally said he'd help me with the job anyway, and if he ever got to Earth he might go pick out something he liked. I said that could be arranged, if a few loose ends were tied up, such as my getting the job. He said not to worry; the details would sort themselves out."

Upon Chilke's arrival at Araminta Station, Namour introduced him to the Bureau D authorities, who put Chilke through an intensive grilling. Chilke declared himself supremely qualified for the position, and in the end no one could prove otherwise and he was hired on a probationary basis.

It soon became evident that, if anything, Chilke had understated his capabilities and the appointment was made permanent.

Chilke at once instituted a general shake-up which in due course ran him afoul of Namour. At issue were the Yips assigned to the airport staff, where they performed such tasks as keeping the field in order, washing and cleaning the aircraft, checking spare parts in and out of the warehouse, and a few simple tasks of routine maintenance, or even mechanical work, under Chilke's supervision.

Up to this time Chilke had not yet been assigned an assistant manager. To lighten his own work load, he trained his four Yips with care, and finally brought them to a level where they actually seemed interested in what they were doing. Nevertheless, at the end of their six-month stint, Namour sent them back to Yipton and assigned Chilke four fresh Yips.

Chilke protested with fervor: "What the bloody hell is going on? Do you think I'm running a ruddy educational institution here? Not on your life!"

Namour said coldly: "These people are here on six-month permits. That is the rule. I did not make this rule, but I am required to enforce it."

"And sometimes you do," said Chilke. "Sometimes you are busy elsewhere. At the hospital Yip orderlies get new cards every six months and nothing is said; also in the tailor shop and much of the domestic help. I'm not complaining; it only makes sense. Why train these geezers if you intend to send them back to Yipton? There's no flyers at Yipton, so far as I know. If you want trained Yips for Yipton, you train them yourself."

"You're talking nonsense, Chilke!"

With amiable pertinacity Chilke continued. "If I can't keep the ones I have now, don't send any at all. I'll bring in my own help."

Namour drew himself up to his full height. Slowly turning his head, he brought a glacial stare to bear on Chilke. He said: "Listen well, Chilke, so that there will be no misunderstanding. Your orders come from me and you will do exactly as you are told. Otherwise, two roads lead into the future. The first is uneventful: you resign with your health and leave Araminta Station by the first ship."

Chilke's ropy grin grew even broader. He put his hand upon Namour's face and pushed with great force, to send Namour reeling back against the wall. Chilke said: "That kind of talk makes me nervous. If we're going to stay friends, you'll beg my pardon with full sincerity and leave, smiling and closing the door quietly on your way out. Otherwise I'm going to tousle you around a bit."

Namour, a Clattuc and no coward, was nonetheless a trifle daunted. At last he said: "Come on, then; we'll see who gets tousled."

The two men were much of a weight. Namour, with a good physique, stood taller by two inches. Chilke was more compact, burly at the chest and shoulders, with long arms and heavy fists. As the Yips and some boys from the lyceum watched, the two fought an epic battle, and in the end Chilke stood grinning his twisted grin down at Namour, half propped against the wall.

"Now, then," said Chilke. "Let's face the facts. Why you brought me here I don't know. You weren't concerned for my welfare, and I don't think you're avid for the stuffed owl I owe you."

Namour started to speak, then checked himself and painfully rubbed the side of his face.

Chilke went on. "Whatever the reason, I'm here. So long as I stay and keep your scheme going, I'm paying you all I owe you. Otherwise, and except for the owl, we're even. You keep to your line of work and I'll keep to mine. Now back to the help. I'll take your six-month Yips, if you insist! But I'll use them for dog work only and fill out with my own staff, which is the way I want it anyway."

Namour pulled himself to his feet. "For your information, the Conservator won't allow any more Yip extensions. If you don't like it,

44

go down to Riverview House and tousle him around like you did me."

Chilke laughed. "I may be wild but I'm not reckless. I'll have to puzzle this one out."

Namour departed without further words. Relations thereafter between the two were polite but not overly cordial. Namour gave no more orders to Chilke, while Chilke made no further complaints in regard to the six-month Yips. Bureau D allowed him the services of Porric co-Diffin, to be trained as an assistant manager, while the Yips were employed only at "dog work."

5

With the onset of autumn anticipation of the wine festival, Parilia, with its banquets, masques and revels began to color the thoughts of everyone. At Parilia almost any kind of eccentric behavior was not only condoned but encouraged, so long as a costume purported to conceal identities. Araminta Hotel had long been booked and overbooked, so that, during the week of Parilia, all manner of desperate expedients would become necessary. In the end, no one would suffer disappointment; if necessary, the six great houses would throw open their guest chambers and feed the visitors in the formal dining halls, and no one so lodged had ever been known to complain.

Glawen had undertaken no special role at Parilia. He lacked proficiency with musical instruments, and the antics of Floreste's Mummers interested him not at all. His studies at the lyceum had given him no difficulty, even though he had continued flight training, and at the end of the first quarter-term he was awarded a Certificate of Excellence. Arles received an Urgent Notice of Unsatisfactory Achievement.

Glawen's methods were disarmingly simple: he did his work methodically, promptly and thoroughly. Arles used a different philosophy. From the beginning his work was meager, late and incomplete. He was nevertheless confident that through clever manipulation, bluff and sheer élan he could avoid tedious drudgery and drill and yet promote good grades for himself.

Upon receiving the Urgent Notice, Arles was both impatient and exasperated. In a single decisive gesture he crumpled the message and flung it aside; such was his opinion of all pedagogues! Why did they bother him with such priggish little messages? What did they hope to achieve? The notice told him nothing he wanted to hear; the pedants lacked all largeness of perception! Surely it was obvious that he could not cram his large and sweeping talents into the petty little pigeonholes which they had designated, and which were all they knew! Ah well, he must ignore, or by some means slide around, all this pettifoggery. One way or another things would sort themselves out and he would be graduated into full Agency. Any other possibility was unthinkable! If worse came to worst, he might even be forced to study! Or his mother, Spanchetta, would set matters right with a few well-chosen words, although involving Spanchetta was a risky business. Far better, if at all possible, to let sleeping dogs lie.

At the end of Arles' second term—this would be at the beginning of summer, before Glawen's sixteenth birthday—Arles had failed promotion into the third-year class. It was a serious situation which Arles could remedy only by attending summer school and passing an examination. Unfortunately, Arles had made other plans involving Master Floreste and the Mummers, which he did not wish to alter.

The Honorable Sonorius Offaw, superintendent of the lyceum, called Arles to his office and made the situation clear: if Arles failed to meet the lyceum's minimum requirements before his twenty-first birthday, his Agency status would be canceled and he would become a collateral without option, which meant that under no circumstances could he regain Agency status, unlike collaterals who had met the educational qualifications.

Once or twice Arles tried to interrupt, in order to express his own views, but the superintendent made Arles listen to the very end, so that Arles became more annoyed and edgy than ever.

At last Arles said: "Sir, I understand that my grades should be better, but, as I tried to explain, I was ill during both of the midterm examinations, and did poorly. The instructors in each class refused to make allowances."

"Rightly so. The examinations measure your scholastic achievements, not the state of your health." He looked at Arles' card. "I see you have opted into Bureau D."

"I intend to be an oenologist," said Arles sullenly.

"In that case, I advise that you attend summer school and make up your failed work; otherwise you will be cultivating your grapes in very far vineyards."

Arles scowled. "I'm already committed to Master Floreste for the summer. I am a member of the Mummers Troupe, as you probably know."

"That is irrelevant. I can hardly express myself more succinctly but I will try. Either do your schoolwork or fail to graduate."

Arles cried out in pain: "But we will be making an off-world tour to Soum and Dauncy's World, which I don't want to miss!"

Sonorius Offaw rubbed his forehead with the tips of his fingers. "You may go. I will communicate with your parents and inform them of your problem."

Arles departed the office, and a day later intercepted the official note before it reached Spanchetta: an act of subtle ingenuity, Arles told himself with a grin. If his mother had read the note, she might well have kept him home all summer, with his nose pressed to the scholastic grindstone. What a bore! He desperately wanted to make this particular tour, if only to prevent Kirdy Wook from having a free hand with the girls. Not that Kirdy, a large earnest fresh-faced youth, was all that much of a threat.

So Arles avoided summer school, and toured off-world with the Mummers, returning to Araminta Station a few days before Glawen's birthday, much too late for summer session. When lyceum started, Arles found himself enrolled at the second-year level.

How should he best explain the matter to his mother?

By not explaining at all: that was the answer. The matter would probably evade her notice; then, by one means or another, he would repair the difficulty.

The final day of the quarter-term was a half day, and the students were allowed a free afternoon. Glawen, Arles and four others took themselves to the dock beside the airport, to oversee the arrival of the ferry from Yipton with a contingent of workers for the grape harvest.

The group consisted of Glawen, Arles, Kirdy Wook, Uther Offaw, Kiper Laverty and Cloyd Diffin. Kirdy, the oldest and, like Arles, a Mummer, was a large careful young man, somber of manner, with round blue eyes, large features, and a fair, almost pinkish complexion. He used a terse mode of speaking, perhaps to disguise his shyness. In general the girls thought Kirdy dull and a trifle self-righteous. Sessily Veder, whose pretty face and irrepressible personality charmed all who saw her, referred to Kirdy as a "fussy old pussycat." If he heard her, he gave no sign, but a week later, to the surprise of everyone, he joined the Bold Lions, as if to demonstrate that he wasn't such a dullard after all.

Kiper Laverty, who was Glawen's age, contrasted in every way with Kirdy, in that he was brash, noisy, active, not at all shy, and ready for any and all mischief.

Uther Offaw, a complicated individual almost as old as Kirdy, performed meticulous work at the lyceum, but in private demonstrated a wry mentality which spun off ideas wild, quaint and sometimes reckless. His hair, a straw-colored ruff, grew back from a high forehead which seemed to funnel directly into a long nose. Uther was also a Bold Lion.

Cloyd Diffin, another Bold Lion, presented a staid imperturbable face to the world. He was strong and stocky, with dark hair, a heavy hooked nose and massive chin. Cloyd formulated few ideas of his own but could be counted upon to follow the lead of others.

The six youths strolled up Beach Road to the dock, where the ferry from Lutwen Atoll was about to discharge its cargo of Yips. At the debarkation gate stood Namour, the labor coordinator: a man tall and handsome with a head of glistening white hair. Namour, a Clattuc collateral, had fared far and wide across the Reach; he had known good times and bad; he had engaged in a hundred exploits and adventures, most of which he refused to discuss. He claimed to have seen everything worth seeing and to have done everything worth doing: a cool flat statement which no one had ever challenged. His experiences had left him with a patina of urbane good manners and an understated elegance, which Arles thought to use as a model for his own conduct.

The six youths joined Namour, who acknowledged their presence with an austere nod. Arles asked: "How many in today's load?"

"According to the roster, one hundred and forty."

"Hmmf! That's quite a parcel. Are they all grape workers?"

"I expect we'll use some of them at Parilia."

Arles inspected the Yips lined up along the ship's rail: young men and women dressed alike in knee-length white kirtles. They waited quietly, with mild expressions: by and large a well-favored folk. The young men were of uniformly good physique, if somewhat slender, with bronze skins, ringlets of dusty-blond hair, golden-hazel eyes set faunlike, widely apart. The faces of the girls were softer and rounder, and their hair showed generally a darker copper-gold color. Their arms and legs were slim and graceful: no question but that the Yip girls were beautiful. Some folk were especially intrigued by what they considered a hint of an alien, or nonhuman, quality, which just as many others failed to perceive.

The gates opened; the Yips filed past a desk, announced their names in soft slurred voices and received their work permits. Namour and the six youths stood to the side, watching the process.

"Alike as peas in a pod," Kiper reported to Glawen. "That's how they look to me."

"It might be that we look exactly alike to them."

"I hope not," said Kiper. "I wouldn't want even a Yip to think that I looked like Uther or Arles."

Uther laughed, but Arles turned a haughty glance over his shoulder. "I heard that, Kiper. Such remarks are not well advised."

"Kiper is very ugly," said Uther. "I endorse his remark."

"Well, yes," said Arles. "On those grounds I do too."

Uther asked: "Have you noticed the odor, when the breeze blows this way? It's the typical Yip reek, that you notice when you go out on the Concourse at Yipton." He referred to a faint soft scent, like waterweeds, with a hint of spice and indefinable human exudation.

"Some say it's a result of their diet," Namour told the group. "Personally, I suspect that a Yip smells like a Yip, and that is that."

"I'm not bothered," said Arles. "Oh, my sacred Clattuc elbow! Look yonder at those three lovely creatures! I'll smell them from morning till night, and ask for more! Namour, you may assign them to me, here and now!"

Namour turned him a cool glance. "Certainly, if you're willing to pay."

"How much?"

"They come high, especially those with the black earrings. That means they're associated with a man. In loose terms: married."

"What of the others? Are they virgins?"

"How should I know? They still come high."

"What a pity!" moaned Arles. "Can't I have just one of them free?"

"You'd have a knife in the ribs just as quickly. The men are not meek; don't let those placid faces fool you. They don't like us in the first place, and even less when we start fooling with their girls—unless we pay. They'll do anything for money, but never try to cheat them. A few years ago a tourist forced himself on a Yip girl while she picked grapes. Like a fool he refused to pay. Two Yips held him while a third pushed a grape stake down his throat—all the way. A nasty business."

"What happened to the Yips?"

"Nothing. If you play, pay. Better yet, leave the Yip girls alone."

Uther Offaw glanced skeptically toward Namour. "Does that apply to you? There always seems to be a pretty Yip girl fluffing out your pillows and another running your bath."

Namour allowed a faint smile to appear on his handsome face. "Never mind about me. Over a lifetime I've learned a hundred little tricks which I call lubrications. Most of them I keep to myself, but I'll share one of them with you, free of charge: 'Never push too hard at anything; it might start pushing back.'"

Uther frowned. "Very profound, and I'm grateful, especially since it's free. But what's it got to do with Yip girls?"

"Nothing. Or perhaps everything. You puzzle it out." Namour went off to deal with the new contingent of workers.

The six youths returned along the Beach Road to the lyceum. In the open-air refectory they discovered a group of girls regaling themselves with fruit ices. Two, Ticia Wook and Lexy Laverty, were legitimate beauties; the other two, Jerdys Diffin and Clöe Offaw, were definitely attractive. All were a year or two older than Glawen and outside his field of interest.

Uther Offaw, though a freethinker, could be most courtly and polite when the need arose. He now called out in his best voice: "Girls! Why do you bloom here unseen in the shade of the gadroon tree?"

"They're not really blooming," said Kiper. "They are eating right and left like little gluttons."

Ticia in a single glance had gauged the quality of the boys. All were either too young or too callow and good for nothing but practice. She looked down at her dish. "A mango smash? That's far from gluttony."

"In that case, why bother?"

Jerdys said: "If you must know, this is a meeting of the 'Medusa Cult', and we are planning our program for next year."

Clöe said: "We intend to conquer Araminta Station and enslave all the men."

"Hush, Clöe!" exclaimed Jerdys. "You're giving away cult secrets!"

"We can make up some more. Secrets are easy. I use up dozens every day."

"Ahem!" said Arles. "Have you noticed our presence? Must we stand here like storks, or are we invited to sit at your table?"

Ticia shrugged. "Do as you like. But please pay for your own ices."

"No fear. Aside from Glawen and Kiper, you are in the company of cultivated gentlemen."

The four older boys found chairs and managed to squeeze up to the table. Glawen and Kiper were pushed aside and forced to sit somewhat apart at another table: a situation which they accepted philosophically.

Lexy Laverty asked: "Well then, what have you 'cultivated gentlemen' been up to?"

"Just wandering about, discussing our investments," said Uther.

Kiper called across the gap: "Arles is behind in his classwork, so we studied anthropology at the ferry slip."

Arles said with dignity: "More to the point, we looked over some space yachts. There's a new Purple Prince which I swear I will buy before ten years is out!"

Kiper, who knew no inhibition, called out: "I thought you were saving up for one of the Yip girls."

"Aha!" said Ticia. "So that's where you've been! Drooling over the Yip girls like the precocious little lechers you are!"

"Not Arles!" said Uther. "All he wanted to do was smell them."

Kiper said: "That may or may not be lechery—although it's definitely odd."

"I'm inclined to agree," said Uther. "Ticia, what do you think? Has anyone ever wanted to smell you?"

"I think that you are both lunatics! That's what I think."

Arles said primly: "I know better than to fool with Yip girls. Do you think I want to be strangled and killed and burned alive and then stabbed just for a bit of naughty conduct?"

Kiper said: "If your mother caught you at it, you'd fare even worse."

Arles' face became a thundercloud. "Let's leave my mother out of it, shall we? She has nothing to do with the case at hand!"

"What was the case at hand?" asked Kirdy, speaking for the first time. "I've forgotten what we were talking about."

Jerdys said plaintively: "Let's discuss something really wonderful and interesting, like the Medusa Cult."

"I'm willing," said Cloyd. "Do you have a gentlemen's auxiliary?"

"Not now," said Jerdys. "We used them all for sacrifices."

"Ha-hah!" Lexy cried out. "Who is divulging secrets now?"

"Those secrets are well used and no good to anyone."

Arles said: "Speaking of secrets, I have a splendid idea! Have you noticed that there are four Medusa-type girls here, and also four Bold Lions? Glawen and Kiper don't count; in fact, they were on the point of going home. I suggest that we join forces and go off to somewhere quiet where we can drink wine and sort out all our old secrets, and maybe work up some new ones."

"That's one of Arles' rare good ideas," said Cloyd. "I'll vote yes."

"And I," said Kirdy, smiling self-consciously. "There's two yes votes. Arles will probably vote yes also, which makes three. Uther?"

Uther pursed his lips. "I think that I will reserve my vote until the ladies are heard from. I assume that they will all vote in the affirmative."

"Silence means assent," said Arles. "So then—"

"To the contrary," said Lexy crisply. "Silence in this case means shock and astonishment."

Jerdys asked: "What do you take us for? This is the Medusa Cult: a very select group!"

Clöe suggested: "Go try the Nixies or the Girls' Philosophy Club."

Ticia rose to her feet. "It's quite time that I was getting home."

"I wonder why we waited this long," said Jerdys with a sniff.

The girls departed. The Bold Lions looked after them nonplussed. Kiper broke the silence. "How very odd! One mention of the Bold Lions and the girls dash away as if they were running a race."

Glawen stated: "Arles has written a book for the use of Bold Lions only. It is called *Manual of the Erotic Arts*. On the first page he should print a warning: 'Never admit to being a Bold Lion! If you do, the warranty on this book becomes void.'"

Kiper said smugly: "I'm glad that I'm not a Bold Lion. What of you, Glawen?"

"I'm quite happy the way I am."

Arles declared grimly: "Neither of you will ever be invited into the group; you can be sure of that!"

Kiper jumped to his feet. "Come, Glawen! Let's leave before Arles changes his mind!"

Glawen and Kiper departed. Uther made a wry comment: "For a fact, our public image seems to be, shall we say, not superb."

"Most odd!" said Cloyd. "After all, we're not deep-dyed ruffians."

"Not all of us, at any rate," growled Kirdy Wook.

Arles demanded sharply: "What do you mean by that?"

"Your suggestion to the girls that we go somewhere and cuddle was preposterous, if not vulgar."

"You voted for it!"

"I did not want to hurt anyone's feelings," said Kirdy virtuously.

"Hmmf! Well, it was an idea. They could have said yes or they could have said no. Who knows? Next time it might be yes. That's the theory behind a whole section in my book, entitled: 'Go for it; what can you lose?'"

Kirdy rose to his feet. "I've got schoolwork to do. I'm going home." He departed.

Arles said thoughtfully: "Kirdy can be just a bit pompous at times. He's not what I would call a typical Bold Lion."

Cloyd said: "If just for this reason, he improves our image."

Uther sighed. "You may well be right. Except for Kirdy, we're a fairly erratic group, at the fringe of civilization . . . I'm going home too. I'm a bit behind in mathematics."

"I guess I'll do the same," said Arles dubiously. "Old Sonorius hit me with an Urgent Notice that I'm supposed to show my mother."

Uther asked in interest: "Are you going to do so?"

"Small chance of that!"

But when Arles returned to his chambers he found that the lyceum had sent his mother a separate notification.

As soon as Arles appeared at Clattuc House, Spanchetta demanded an explanation of the Urgent Notice. "Apparently you are repeating last year's work, a fact which I am now learning for the first time! Why was I not notified at the start of the term?"

"Of course you were notified!" declared Arles. "I told you myself, and you said, 'You must do better this year,' or something like that, and I said I would."

"I recall no such occasion."

"You might have been thinking about something else."

"How is it that you are doing so poorly even on the repeat course? Don't you ever study?"

Throwing himself down in a chair, Arles cast about for some plausible excuse. "I'm certainly capable of better work, but it's not all my fault! I blame it mostly on those dreary little bookworms who call themselves instructors. You can't imagine the stupefying boredom to which they put you nowadays! I'm not the only one who complains. But I get singled out for criticism and bad grades!"

Spanchetta surveyed him with eyes half closed. "Odd. Why should that be?"

"I suppose it's because I have an inquiring mind and I can't take everything for granted, just to get a good grade. I consider them a snobbish little clique of pettifoggers, and they know it."

Spanchetta nodded with ominous deliberation. "Hmm. Why do other students manage so well? Glawen has won a certificate."

"Don't talk to me of Glawen! He uses every smarmy little trick imaginable to ingratiate himself! Everyone knows it and everyone but Glawen feels as I do! We all want reasonable teachers, who play no favorites!"

"I'll have to look into this," said Spanchetta.

In sudden alarm Arles asked: "What are you going to do?"

"I am going to get to the bottom of the situation, and one way or another straighten things out."

"Wait!" cried Arles in poignant tones. "I'd prefer that you just give me a letter, stating that I have many responsibilities and don't need such a heavy concentration of mathematics and science! It won't look well if you go down there yourself."

Spanchetta gave her head an impatient shake, which caused her great pile of ringlets to sway and lurch, but by some miracle maintain their shape. "When I want something, I get it, no matter how it looks. You must learn to be thick-skinned if you want to get on in life."

"Bah," muttered Arles. "I'm doing quite well enough already."

"If you lose Agency because of bad grades you will sing a different song."

The next morning Spanchetta took herself to the lyceum and approached Instructor Arnold Fleck in the hall outside the mathematics classroom.

Spanchetta halted. Looking Fleck up and down, she took note of his slight physique, thin pale face and mild blue eyes. Could this be the malevolent ogre of the many revenges so feelingly described by Arles?

Fleck recognized Spanchetta and instantly divined the nature of her mission. "Good morning, madame. Can I assist you in any way?"

"That remains to be seen. You are Instructor Fleck?"

"I am indeed."

"I am Spanchetta Clattuc of Clattuc House. My son, Arles, so I believe, is under your supervision?"

Fleck considered. "Nominally so, and for a fact I see him from time to time."

Spanchetta frowned. She wanted a brisk businesslike understanding, without evasions or glib little ambiguities. This Instructor Fleck had made a bad beginning. "Please, sir, if you will! You are Arles' instructor in mathematics?"

"Yes, madame."

"Hm. He seems to be having problems and he insists that he is not to blame. He feels that the material is presented incorrectly."

Instructor Fleck smiled a cool sad smile. "I will teach him any way he likes, so long as he does the work. He cannot absorb the subject by osmosis; he must do the drills and work out the problems, all of which is admittedly tedious."

Spanchetta glanced around at the circle of students who had paused to watch and listen, but was in no wise deterred. She lowered her voice an ominous half octave. "Arles seems to feel that he has been singled out for harassment and criticism."

Fleck nodded. "In this case, Arles has reported the facts correctly. He is the only member of the class who takes a surly attitude toward his work. Inevitably, he is the only one criticized."

Spanchetta sniffed. "I am thoroughly disconcerted. Clearly, something is amiss."

"It is a sad case!" said Fleck. "Would you care to sit down and rest until you feel better?"

"I am not ill, but outraged! It is your duty to teach the subject fairly and fully to each member of the class, making every allowance for individual temperament!"

"Your remarks are well-taken! I would feel gloom and guilt, but for a single consideration: each of Arles' other instructors finds the same problem: a kind of obstinate laziness which defeats the best of intentions." Fleck looked around the circle of onlookers. "Have you people nothing better to do? This matter is no concern of yours." Then, to Spanchetta: "Step into the classroom, if you will. It is unoccupied at this time and I have something to show you."

Spanchetta followed Fleck to his desk, where he handed her several sheets of paper. "Here is a sample of Arles' work. Instead of finishing the problems, he draws grotesque faces and what appear to be dead fish."

Spanchetta took a deep breath. "Bring Arles here! We shall hear what he has to say."

Fleck spoke into the telephone and presently Arles sidled into the room. Spanchetta shook the papers in his face. "Why do you draw corpuscles and dead fish instead of solving your problems?"

Arles cried out indignantly. "Those are· art studies: drawings of nude human figures!"

"Whatever you call them, why are they here instead of the proper work?"

"I was thinking about something else."

Fleck looked at Spanchetta. "Is there any other way I can help you, Madame Spanchetta? If not . . ."

Spanchetta jerked her hand at Arles. "Go back to your class!"

Arles gratefully departed.

Spanchetta turned to Fleck. "I need not emphasize that Arles must receive a passing grade. Otherwise he will lose his Agency status."

Fleck shrugged. "He has much work to make up. The sooner he starts and the harder he works, the better his chances of passing."

"I will put this to him. Strangely, I dreamt of this entire episode last night. The dream began in just this fashion; I remember every word!"

"Amazing!" said Fleck. "Madame, I wish you good day."

Spanchetta paid no heed. "In the dream poor Arles was given a failing grade, which seemed to set in motion a whole string of misfortunes which even involved the instructor. It was a most realistic and rather terrible dream."

"I hope it is not precognition," said Fleck.

"Probably not. Still—who knows? Odd things happen."

Fleck considered a moment. "Your dream is the oddest of them all. As of this moment Arles is dropped from the class. Superintendent Sonorius Offaw will henceforth deal with his case. Good day, madame. There is nothing more to be said."

On the following day, Superintendent Sonorius called Arles and Spanchetta to his office. Spanchetta emerged shaking with rage; Arles, morose and glum, marched along behind her. Spanchetta had learned that she must hire a special tutor in mathematics, at her own expense, and that at the end of each quarter-term Superintendent Sonorius himself would supervise the examinations.

Arles at last saw that, like it or not, the halcyon times of indolence and languor had come to an end. Grumbling and cursing, he set himself to his toil, under the bleak tutelage of an instructor appointed by Superintendent Sonorius.

For hours on end, during all his spare time, Arles drilled on fundamentals and all the material that he had scamped before, and presently, somewhat to his own surprise, he discovered that the subject was not as difficult as he had assumed.

To make the situation even more irksome, Sessily Veder now returned to Araminta Station. Sessily, one of Floreste's Mummers, had met her mother and her younger sister, Miranda (better known as Squeaker) at Soumjiana on the world Soum. The three had then gone on to visit a wealthy Veder connection at his villa on the romantic Calliope Coast, between Guyol and Sorrentine on the world Cassiopeia 993:9.

Sessily, a year or so younger than Glawen, was totally charming; everyone conceded as much. A joyful providence had graced her with every natural asset: a cheerful intelligence, a fine sense of humor, a friendly affectionate disposition; and in addition—almost unfairly—glowing good health, a beautiful slim body and an impish snub-nosed face under a cap of loose brown curls.

Sessily's only detractors were one or two of the older girls, namely Ticia and Lexy, who seemed pallid and severe when Sessily joined the company. "Vain little exhibitionist!" they muttered to each other, but Sessily only laughed when the comments were reported to her.

For Sessily schoolwork came easily. She entered lyceum a year earlier than ordinary, which placed her in Glawen's class. When she traveled, she took her lesson books with her and on her return to Araminta Station merged effortlessly into the work of her class.

Sessily seemed to bring a vital new dimension to the lyceum. She was perhaps not consciously a flirt; still she took an innocent delight in exercising the wonderful new knack she had so recently discovered.

Sessily was the main reason why Arles had so reluctantly given up the Mummers, thus abandoning Sessily to the attentions of Kirdy Wook, Banceck Diffin and others, even though Sessily had shown no one conspicuous favor.

This year Floreste's spectacles at Parilia would be curtailed. Sessily would take part, along with the orchestra and some others, but to Arles' relief, neither *Evolution of the Gods* nor *First-Fire* would be presented, thus depriving Arles' rivals of opportunities denied to Arles himself.

For her part Sessily felt no partiality for anyone connected with the Mummers. At Soumjiana one or two incidents had taught her something of the almost frightening forces she could generate but not control. She had decided that after Parilia she would retire from the troupe. "I guess things will never be the same," Sessily told herself. "Isn't it odd? The only boy I like hardly looks at me, while the others become familiar if I'm so much as polite!"

In this latter category Arles was pre-eminent. He had developed a tactic for intercepting her when she came to the refectory for lunch and taking her willy-nilly to a side table and there devoting the entire hour to a discussion of himself and his plans for the future. "The truth is, Sessily, that I'm one of those fellows who are not satisfied with just the ordinary! I know what is absolutely top quality in this world, and I propose to get it. That means going after it, with no ifs, ands, or buts! I'm not one of this world's losers! That's for sure! I'm telling you this so you'll know the kind of fellow I am! And I'll tell you something else, quite frankly." Arles reached across the table and took her hand. "I'm interested in you. Very much so! Don't you think that's nice?"

Sessily pulled away her hand. "No, not really. You should broaden your interests in case I'm not available."

"Not available? Why not? You're alive and I'm alive."

"True. But I'm going away on a solitary tour of the universe, or I might become a Trappist monk."

"Ha, ha! What a joke! Girls can't be Trappist monks!"

"Still, if I did, I'd be very unavailable."

Arles said crossly: "Can't you be serious?"

"I am very serious . . . Excuse me, please. I see Zanny Diffin over yonder and there's something I must tell her."

On the following day, despite Sessily's attempt to hide by holding a folder in front of her face, Arles found her sitting alone in the shade of the gadroon tree, and sat down at her table. With one plump white finger he pushed down the folder and smiled a wide toothy smile at her over the top. "Peekaboo! It's Arles. And how is the young Trappist monk today?"

"I plan to cut off all my hair and paint my face blue, and wear a mustache, so people won't recognize me," said Sessily.

"Ha, ha! That's marvellous! Can I do the cutting and the painting? I wonder what Master Floreste would say, especially if I painted myself red, and we showed up hand in hand!"

"That act would be called 'Nightmare of a Maniac.' Floreste will never see it. I'm quitting the Mummers."

"Really? That's good news! I'm out of the Mummers too, until my grades get better. We'll be together all next summer."

"I think not. I'm working at Opal Springs Lodge."

Arles leaned forward. Today he had primed himself with a strategy from his *Manual of the Erotic Arts*. "There's something I want to talk to you about. Would you like to own a space yacht?"

"What a foolish question. Is there anyone who wouldn't?"

Arles said earnestly: "You and I should make plans together, about the kind of yacht we want. For instance, how do you like those new Spang Vandals? Or the Model Fourteen Nasebys with the after-saloon? They're not so common and maybe not quite so dashing, but the appointments are truly superb! What's your opinion!"

"Anything would be nice," said Sessily. "However, there's the matter of ownership. I'm too much of a coward to steal and too poor to buy."

"Don't worry there! Just trust me in that department! I'll find the money, and we'll buy one together, and go roaming! Think of the fun we could have!"

Sessily gave her hand a flippant wave. "My mother has much more money than I do. Why don't you talk it over with her? You could take your mother along too, and you'd all have a wonderful time."

Arles stared at her with black eyebrows lofted in displeasure. According to the *Manual*, girls never responded in this fashion. Was Sessily some kind of a little freak? He asked peevishly: "Wouldn't you like to visit the Glass Towns of Clanctus? And the canals of Old Kharay? And don't forget Xanarre, with the alien ruins and the floating cloud-cities."

"Right now I've simply got to visit the girls' room. You sit here and dream away to your heart's content."

"Wait one moment! I've decided to escort you to Parilia! What do you say to that?"

"I say, make another decision, since I have different plans."

"Oh? With whom are you going?"

"Tra-la-la! That's my secret! I may even stay home and read a book."

"What! During Parilia? Sessily, I insist that you be serious!"

"Arles, please excuse me! If I stand here and wet myself I will be very serious indeed!"

Sessily departed, leaving Arles glowering after her. Sessily, so he noticed, did not go directly to the girls' room, but stopped to talk to Glawen, where he sat alone. He looked up smiling and pointed to something in the book which lay open on the table. She put a hand on his shoulder and bent over to look; then she said something and went off to the girls' room. When she emerged a few moments later she went directly to join Glawen, without so much as a glance elsewhere.

With ostentatious displeasure Arles rose to his feet and left the refectory.

Glawen, like many others, had also become captivated by Sessily. He liked her saucy mannerisms, her jaunty style of walking, her trick of glancing sideways with a half-smile hinting of delicious mischief. But whenever Glawen thought to talk with her, it seemed that someone else came bustling up to monopolize her attention. He was therefore pleasantly surprised when she joined him at his table. "Well, Glawen, I'm back, and I've got to ask you a question."

"Very well. Ask away."

"Someone told me that you said, in your opinion, I was a hateful little frump."

"Did they, now!" said Glawen, startled.

"Do you admit to that, Glawen?"

Glawen shook his head. "Somebody else must have said it. Arles, possibly."

"And you don't even think that I am?"

"Definitely not. I'd like to tell you sometime what I really think, but you're always with half a dozen others, and I can't get a word in."

Sessily said thoughtfully: "Arles just asked if he could escort me to Parilia. I said no, because I was going with someone else."

"Oh? Who?"

"I don't know yet. I suppose someone nice will ask me before too long."

Glawen started to speak but the bell rang for classes. Sessily jumped to her feet and was gone. Glawen sat looking after her. Could she possibly have been suggesting something so unexpected and so wonderful as to be almost incredible?

Arles tried to walk Sessily home as often as possible, but on this particular afternoon he was delayed in class and Sessily gratefully set off by herself. Glawen, who had been waiting, almost missed her, but ran to catch up.

Sessily looked over her shoulder. "For a dreadful moment I thought it was Arles."

"No, it's me, and I've been thinking over your problem."

"Really, Glawen? How very kind! Has anything occurred to you?"

"Yes! I thought that I might ask to be your escort."

Sessily stopped short and turned to face him. She smiled up into his face. "Glawen! What a surprise! Are you sure you're not just being kind?"

"Quite sure. Very sure indeed!"

"And you don't think me a hateful little frump?"

"I never did."

"In that case—yes!"

Glawen turned and looked at her in sheer joy and took her hands. "For some reason I feel very strange inside, as if I were full of bubbles."

"I do too. Could it be for the same reason?"

"I don't know."

"Probably not exactly the same. Don't forget, I'm a girl and you're a boy."

"I haven't forgotten for an instant."

"We're supposed to have different reasons for doing the same things. At least that's what Floreste says. It's what makes the world go round, according to Floreste."

"Sessily, what a wise person you are!"

"It's nothing, really." Sessily moved a step forward and kissed him. Then she jerked back as if aghast at her own daring. "I shouldn't have done that! You'll think me very bold."

"Well—not too bold."

"I've been wanting to kiss you for weeks, and I just couldn't wait any longer."

Glawen reached to put his arm around her, but Sessily became perversely coy. "Only I may do the kissing; not you."

"That's not fair!"

"Perhaps not . . . Don't delay, then; we don't want to be late getting home from school!"

Arles, sauntering along Wansey Way, turned his head and saw

Glawen and Sessily where they stood in the shade of a weeping willow. He halted to stare, then gave a hoot of mocking laughter. "Haw, haw! I have interrupted a tender moment! Isn't this a somewhat public place for intimacies? Glawen, I never expected such conduct from you!"

Sessily laughed. "Glawen has been kind and that is why I am kissing him. I may well do it again. Are you leaving?"

"What's the hurry? I might learn something interesting."

"In that case, we'll go." Sessily took Glawen's arm. "Come; the neighborhood has gone to pieces."

The two departed with full dignity, and Arles was left standing in the road. Sessily looked anxiously up at Glawen. "I hope you haven't let him annoy you."

Glawen gave his head a dour shake. "I feel foolish." Sessily's arm stiffened and Glawen added hastily: "Because I couldn't make up my mind what to do! Should I have punched his face? I stood there like a dummy! And, truly, I'm not afraid of him!"

"You did exactly right," said Sessily. "Arles is a lummox! Why trouble yourself and get all sweaty? Especially since you have no real chance of beating him."

Glawen blew out his breath. "I suppose you're right. But if it happens again . . ."

Sessily squeezed his arm. "I don't want you involved in foolish rows on account of me. Are you going to walk me home?"

"Of course!"

At the portal giving on the avenue to Veder House, Sessily looked up and down the way. "I must be careful; my mother already thinks I'm a hoyden." She tilted her face and kissed Glawen, who tried to catch her in his arms. Sessily laughed and drew back. "I must go."

Glawen said huskily: "Will you meet me this evening, after supper?"

Sessily shook her head. "There's a chart I must draw for school and I must practice the tunes I'm supposed to play at Parilia. After that I am supposed to be in bed . . . Still, now that I think of it, tomorrow night Mother will be at her committee meeting, and I won't be under such strict control—which evidently would seem to be necessary."

"Tomorrow night, then. Where?"

"Do you know our rose garden, on the east side of the house?"

"Where all the statues stand on guard?"

Sessily nodded. "I'll come out, if I can, about two hours into the evening. I'll meet you where the steps come down from the upper terrace."

"I'll be there."

The next day was Milden;[1] there was no school. For Glawen the day seemed to drag on interminably: minute after minute after minute.

An hour after sunset he changed into dark blue trousers and a soft gray shirt. Scharde noticed the preparations. "What's all this afoot? Or is it a secret?"

Glawen made a casual gesture. "Nothing of any consequence. Just a social engagement."

"Who is the lucky girl?"

"Sessily Veder."

Scharde chuckled. "Don't let her mother catch you. She's Felice Veder, who was born a Wook, and has never relinquished her virtue."

"I'll have to take my chances."

"I don't blame you. Sessily is a charmer; no doubt of it! Be off with you, and need I say—"

"I already know, or at least I think I do."

"Just as you like."

Glawen paused by the door. "Whatever else, don't tell anyone, especially Arles!"

"Naturally not. Do you take me for a fool?"

"No. But you've taught me yourself never to take anything for granted."

Scharde, laughing, squeezed Glawen's shoulders. "Absolutely right! Just don't get caught!"

Glawen laughed nervously and departed the chambers. He descended the staircase and stepped out into the night. On feet charged with energy he half walked, half ran to Veder House; then, making a wide circuit through the meadow, he approached the rose garden. He passed between a pair of great marble urns, pale in the starlight and trailing fronds of dark ivy, and so entered the rose garden. To right and left heroic statues stood in a pair of opposing rows, with beds of white roses between. Beyond loomed the towers and tiers, bays and balconies of Veder House, black except for a few random rectangles of soft yellow glow across the streaming stars of Mircea's Wisp.

Glawen walked up the central way to the far steps. He paused to listen, but the garden was silent. The scent of the white roses hung in the air; and forever after, the scent of roses would remind Glawen of this night.

---

[1] Originally "Ain-Milden" (literally "this day of silver"), equivalent to contemporary "Saturday." The word *Ain* gradually dropped from usage and only the metal name remained. The days of the week, beginning with Monday: Ort, Tzein, Ing, Glimmet, Verd, Milden and Smollen. Translated: iron, zinc, lead, tin, copper, silver and gold.

He was alone in the garden except for the statues. He went quietly to the place of rendezvous. Sessily had not yet arrived. He went to sit on a bench in the shadows and composed himself to wait.

Time passed. Glawen looked up at the stars, many of which he could name. He found the constellation known as Endymion's Lute. At the very center, a telescope of sufficient power would discover Old Sol . . . He heard a faint sound. A soft voice called: "Glawen? Are you here?"

Glawen stepped from the shadows. "I'm here, by the bench."

Sessily made a small wordless sound and ran to meet him; they embraced. Intoxication! Overhead: the flow of Mircea's Wisp streaming across the void; in the garden the pale roses and the marble statues silent in the starlight.

"Come," said Sessily. "Let's go over to the arbor, where we can sit." She led him to a round open-sided pergola with vines growing up the pillars. The two seated themselves on an upholstered bench which went halfway around the inner circumference. Minutes passed. Sessily stirred and looked up. "You're very quiet."

"I was thinking some rather strange thoughts."

"What kind of thoughts? Tell me!"

"They are hard to describe: more a matter of mood than thoughts."

"Try anyway."

Glawen spoke haltingly. "I looked up at the sky and the stars, and I felt a sudden openness—as if my mind were aware of the whole galaxy. At the same time I felt all the millions and billions of people who had spread through the stars. Their lives, or the people, seemed to give off a whir or a hum, really a soft slow music. For just an instant I could hear the music and I felt its meaning and then it was gone, and I was looking at the stars and you asked me why I was quiet."

After a moment Sessily said: "Thoughts like that make me gloomy. I like to pretend that the world started when I was born and will go on forever, and never change."

"That's a very mysterious universe."

"Who cares? It works nicely enough, and suits me very well, so I don't worry about the machinery." She sat up and twisted around so as to face Glawen. "I don't want you thinking peculiar thoughts or humming weird music to yourself. It distracts your attention from me. I'm much more fun than the stars—I think."

"I'm convinced of it."

In the eastern sky a flush of pale vermilion announced the coming of Sing and Lorca, the other two stars of the system. As they watched, first Sing, then Lorca bumped up over the horizon: Sing like a wan

63

orange moon; Lorca, a very bright star flashing prismatic colors.

Sessily said: "I can't stay out late. The committee is meeting at our house, and your Great-aunt Spanchetta is on hand. She and Mother always quarrel, and the meeting breaks up early."

"What committee is this?"

"They're planning the Parilia program. There's to be less entertainment at the Orpheum, and they are dealing with Master Floreste right now, which will be a trial for everyone since Master Floreste can be remarkably single-minded. The dream of his life is a new Orpheum directly across from the lyceum, and every sol from the Mummers' off-world tours goes into his fund."

"Have you told him that you are resigning?"

"Not yet. He won't care. It's something he expects. He just adapts his material to the talent, which is why he is so successful. At Parilia he'll have three short presentations and I'll be involved in all of them: musical novelties, Verd and Milden evenings and a spectacle Smollen night, when I'm to be a butterfly with four wings. I'd like to make my own costume, out of real butterfly wings."

"That sounds complicated."

"Not if you help me. Are you allowed to fly?"

Glawen nodded. "Chilke signed off my advanced novice rating as of last week. I'm checked out on any of the Mitrix trainers."

"Then we can fly down to Maroli Meadow and gather butterfly wings."

"I don't see why not—if your mother will approve of the idea, which somehow I doubt."

"I doubt it too—if I asked in advance. So I'll tell her after we get back, if she asks. It's time that I was developing independence, don't you think? But not too much; I'm happy to stay a little girl for a while yet . . . I must go in, before Mother comes looking for me. She has her own ideas about independence."

"When do you want to go to Maroli Meadow? I should know a day or two in advance."

"A week from next Ing is a school holiday. The Calliope Club is planning a swimming party and picnic up at Blue Mountain Lake. Perhaps you and I can go to Maroli Meadow on our own picnic."

"Very well. I'll have Chilke reserve a Mitrix for me."

Sessily stirred. "I hate to leave—but I must! Now, do be careful walking home! Don't fall down and hurt yourself, and don't get carried away by a big night bird or an owl!"

"I'll be careful."

Chilke had given Glawen his flight training and made no difficulty about providing a Mitrix flyer for what would go on the log as a "cadet day patrol."[1]

On the appointed bright sunny Ing morning, Glawen and Sessily arrived at the airport, Glawen with a pair of mesh baskets and a long-handled net while Sessily carried a picnic hamper.

Chilke pointed to a nearby flyer. "There's your Mitrix. But why the baskets and the net?"

Sessily said: "We're putting down on Maroli Meadow for butterfly wings. I need them for my Parilia costume. I'm to be a beautiful four-winged butterfly in the spectacle."

"You'll be that without a doubt," said Chilke gallantly.

Sessily warned him: "Don't tell anyone! It's supposed to be a surprise."

"Never fear! I'll hold my tongue."

Glawen asked: "What of your own costume?"

"Me? Costume? I'm just one of the help."

"Come now, Chilke! All of us know better than that! Surely you'll be at the festival!"

"Well—maybe so. It's the one affair where I'm allowed, but only because the mask hides my face. I'll be Chitterjay the Clown, which you'll probably consider not much of a disguise. What of you?"

"I'm a Black Imp, in a tight black velvet skin, with even my face painted black."

"You're not one of the Bold Lions, then."

"Not a chance! They'll all be in Lion costume." Glawen pointed to the Mitrix. "Is it ready to go?"

"Approximately, considering it's an Araminta flyer. Let's see if you remember the checkout."

Chilke watched as Glawen performed the routine inspections. "Fuel: charged," said Glawen. "Emergency power: charged. Navigator: nulls all proper. Time: correct. Circuits: blue light. Radio: blue light. Backup box: blue light. Emergency flares: in case. Pistol: on rack, at ready. Emergency water: full. Emergency gear: in cabinet. Engines: alarms quiet. All systems alert: blue light."

Glawen went on to complete the checkout, to Chilke's satisfaction.

---

[1] Flights of inspection across the Conservancy, to monitor the movement of animal herds; to search for evidence of plague or blight; to take note of natural cataclysms such as floods, fires, storms and volcanic eruptions, and, most urgently, to discover and check any Yip encroachment into the mainland. Qualified cadets were therefore not discouraged from flying short patrols.

"Two things to remember," said Chilke. "At Maroli Meadow, make sure to land on the pad. If you break open a hummock you'll have bugs everywhere, and curse the day you were born. Second: don't stray off into the forest; tangle-tops have been sighted in the neighborhood. So keep your eyes open, and stay close to the flyer."

"Very well, sir. We'll take care."

Glawen and Sessily stowed their gear, climbed into the flyer, waved to Chilke, then, to Glawen's touch, were taken aloft. With the autopilot engaged, they flew south at a conservative altitude of a thousand feet.

The Mitrix drifted at no great speed over plantations and vineyards, across the River Wan and the Big Lagoon, then away from the enclave and out over the wilderness: here a placid savanna of low hills grown over with a carpet of low blue-gray plants and pale green bushes, marked by dark green dendrons, alone or in copses, and occasional smoke trees, holding puffs of fragile blue foliage three hundred feet into the air. To the west the hills rolled higher, one rank behind another, and at last swelled enormously to become the Muldoon Mountains, with plain-to-be-seen Flutterby Pass: that notch through the mountains which funneled the migrating butterflies down Maroli Valley to their rendezvous with the sea.

Ten miles, twenty miles, thirty miles: below was Maroli Meadow, a garish sight splotched with a hundred colors. The flyer settled slowly through a myriad butterflies. Glawen sighted through the optic finder, fixed the pale green disk on a pad of concrete established for the convenience of tourists in omnibus flyers. Glawen pushed the landing toggle, and the Mitrix lowered itself to the pad.

For a minute the two sat quietly, looking around the meadow. They were alone. Except for the butterflies, nothing moved. A hundred yards to the right rose a rim of forest, ominously dense and dark, with similar forest to the left, even closer. Ahead, at a somewhat greater distance, the meadow opened upon the ocean beach, with blue ocean beyond.

The two opened the door and stepped down to the pad. The sky flickered with the wings of a million butterflies arriving from all parts of Deucas. The throb of their wings created a low near-inaudible hum; the air reeked with a rich sweet stench. In shoals and schools each of distinctive color: scarlet and blue; lambent green; lemon yellow and black; purple, lavender, white and blue; purple and red, they slanted down into the meadow, to swirl and circle, often flying through a swarm of a different sort, producing what seemed previously unknown colors of amazing pointillist brilliance.

The swarms, after milling and wheeling, at last settled into that tree dedicated to their own sort. At once they nipped off their wings, to create a rain of colored snow under the tree, and give the meadow a curiously garish aspect.

The butterflies, now two-inch grubs, identically pale gray, with six strong legs and horny mandibles, ran down the tree trunk to the ground, and scurried at full speed toward the ocean.[1]

Glawen and Sessily took long-handled nets and trays from the flyer and Glawen, mindful of Chilke's remarks, thrust the pistol into his belt.

Sessily asked quizzically: "Why the gun? There are plenty of loose wings; you needn't shoot the butterflies."

Glawen said: "It's one of the first things my father taught me: never go even three feet into the wilderness without a gun."

"The principal danger around here is stepping into something wet and sticky," said Sessily. "Come; let's get our wings and leave; I can barely breathe because of the fearful chife."

"Do you know what colors you want?"

"Let's get some blues and greens from that tree yonder, and some reds and yellows, from over there, a few blacks and purples and that should do nicely."

---

[1] The life cycle of the butterfly is of considerable interest. After abandoning its wings, it makes for the sea, but not without adventure along the way. First the grubs must pass hummocks of cemented soil four feet high from which issue parties of warrior insects, who seek to capture or kill the grubs and carry them back into the hummocks. The grubs are neither helpless nor overmatched; with jets of ink they first blind their adversaries, then nip off their heads, and proceed. Across Maroli Meadow ferocious battles rage, while the ex-butterfly hordes march past unheeding.

Arriving upon the beach the grubs, having toiled so far, and now but ten yards from their goal, find a new hazard: darting, swooping birds. The survivors of this depredation face one last danger: the yoot, a bulky animal, hybrid of mandoril and rat (mandoril hybrids are widespread across all of Cadwal), lethargic of habit, wandering the beach, sucking up grubs through a long proboscis. A repellent creature, semiaquatic, with hide mottled pink and black, the yoot exudes a noxious odor, as do many other creatures of Cadwal.

The grubs which have escaped warrior insects, birds and animals still number in the millions. These plunge into the surf, to begin a new phase in their remarkable life cycles.

Among the rocks and reefs close to shore the ex-butterflies consume plankton, lose their legs, form a flexible carapace, a fishlike tail, and, indeed, presently become fish six inches long. Reacting to some mysterious signal, they swim to the east and away from Deucas, to begin a migration which will take them halfway around the world. Finally they arrive at a place south of Ecce, where an enormous bank of seaweed is trapped in a curl of the ocean current. Here the ex-butterflies, now foot-long fish, breed and lay eggs in the seaweed. With their destiny fulfilled, they die and float to the surface. The eggs hatch into kril, feed on the carcasses of their parents. Growing and undergoing ten molts to the condition of nymphs, the creatures crawl out on the seaweed and dry their wings. In due course they flutter into the air, and without ceremony depart for the west coast of Deucas.

They picked their way carefully across the meadow to the specified trees. With the net Glawen caught the wings as they drifted down from above and turned them over into the baskets: first, emerald green and blue, then pomegranate red and rich yellow, and finally purple, black and white.

Sessily stood, hesitant. Glawen asked: "Is this enough?"

"I'm sure it is," said Sessily. "I'd like some of those yellow-reds and greens, but it's too far to walk, and this smell is making me sick."

"I see another reason," said Glawen in a suddenly flat voice. "Let's get back to the flyer, and fast."

Following his gaze, Sessily saw across the meadow a long massive beast, black except for its white oddly human face. It trotted on six taloned legs and clasped a pair of hooked pincers to its chest in the attitude of prayer. This was the semi-intelligent Muldoon tangle-top, so named for the squirming black tendrils at the top of its head.

Glawen and Sessily started back toward the flyer, as inconspicuously as possible, but the tangle-top instantly noted the movement. It turned and trotted forward, denying them the refuge of the flyer.

The creature halted a hundred feet away to appraise the situation, then uttered a querulous whine, a rumbling rasping groan, and with dire deliberation began to stalk them.

Glawen said between clenched teeth: "My father was right, as always." He pulled the heavy pistol from his belt and aimed it toward the tangle-top, which stopped short; from somewhere it had learned that men pointing weapons were even more dangerous than itself. It gave another querulous whine, then turned and ran on long loping lunges to the beach, where it pounced on one of the yoots. A horrid squealing protest became a mournful sobbing sound, then silence.

Glawen and Sessily had long since run to the flyer, where they packed baskets and net and without delay took the flyer aloft.

Glawen spoke in heartfelt emotion: "Safety! I've never appreciated it so much!"

"It was nice of the beast to go away," said Sessily.

"Very nice. It decided to give me another chance. My hands were shaking so badly I could never have hit it. I wonder if I could have pulled the trigger . . . I'm not pleased with myself."

Sessily said soothingly, "Of course you would have hit it, no doubt in some very painful place. The beast realized this. Also, I told it to go away."

"You did what?"

Sessily laughed airily. "I used telepathy and told it to run off. It recognized a stronger will than its own and obeyed me."

"Hmf," muttered Glawen. "Shall we go back and try again?"

"Glawen! It's wicked to tease me so. I was only trying to help."

Glawen brooded: "I wonder if we should tell anyone what happened. It may sound too alarming, like a dangerous emergency—which it was."

"We'll say nothing about it. Do you feel hungry?"

"I still feel nothing but fright."

Sessily pointed. "There's a nice hilltop where we can have our lunch."

8

Early in the afternoon Glawen and Sessily returned to Araminta Station. Glawen landed the flyer in the park at the back of Veder House, where Sessily alighted with her wings, net and picnic hamper. Glawen then flew the Mitrix to the airfield and landed beside the hangar.

Chilke came out to greet him. "How went the butterfly hunt?"

"Quite well," said Glawen. "Sessily is pleased with her wings."

Chilke looked over the Mitrix. "The flyer seems to be in one piece. Why are you so pale?"

"I'm not pale," said Glawen. "At least I don't think I am."

"I'd call you just a bit spooky."

"For a fact, there was something, but I don't particularly want to talk about it."

"Come, now! It can't be that bad. Speak!"

Glawen's story came out in a rush. "Here is what happened. We had finished netting the wings. Then just as we started back to the flyer, a big black tangle-top came out of the forest. It spotted us right away and began to stalk us, approaching really close. I had the gun ready but I didn't need to shoot, because it turned away and ran down to the shore, where it ate a yoot. Sessily says she chased it away by telepathy; for all I know, she did; I was too scared for anything even that sensible." Glawen took a deep breath. "I had buck fever so bad I could hardly hold the gun."

"A very moving tale," said Chilke. "Is there more?"

"Just a bit. We left Maroli Meadow at full speed, and glad to get away. About ten miles north we got some of our nerve back and put down on a hilltop for our lunch. I was still annoyed with myself. I thought I'd practice shooting the gun, and getting a feel for it. I aimed at a rock, and pulled the trigger. The gun went *click!* I examined the chamber and found that there was no ammo in the gun."

Chilke's jaw dropped. "Isn't that a situation! You wasted your buck fever on an empty gun!"

"I didn't think of it quite that way."

For a moment Chilke whistled tunelessly through his teeth. At last he said: "If there's a need for blaming people, we can start with you. Checking ammo in the gun is the operator's responsibility; that's the rule."

Glawen hung his head. "I know. I missed it."

"Second on the list is me. I stood here and watched you go past the gun. My only excuse is that I charged that gun myself three days ago. We've both learned a lesson, so I hope. And now we'll get down to brass tacks. Why was there no charge of ammo in the gun? Here we must look to that scoundrel Sisco. Ah! It's a great aggravation! I'll beat that Sisco well. First, we've got to find him. It's pure pleasure listening to the Yips lie, especially when they suspect that they're caught dead to rights."

Chilke looked into the hangar. "Sisco? Where are you? Asleep? Oh, I see. Not asleep. Just lying down resting. Why are you tired? You haven't done any work. But never mind that. Come out here; I want to talk to you."

Sisco emerged from the hangar: a young man with tawny golden skin, hair of almost the same color, a fine physique and features of classic beauty. If his appearance were to be faulted in any wise, it might be said that his eyes were spaced a trifle too widely apart. He looked back and forth between Glawen and Chilke, then, smiling the vague Yip smile, came gingerly forward.

Chilke spoke gently. "Sisco, do you know the difference between a Class A beating, a Class B beating and the beating of a lifetime?"

Sisco smilingly shook his head. "You talk in riddles. I know nothing of these bad things, which are never nice in the polite conversation."

"Do you know the difference between what is yours and what is mine?"

Sisco's face clouded over with puzzlement. "For my answer to be right you must say what thing of yours and what thing of mine. Or is it another vulgarity, that you are talking, and even in front of this boy?"

Chilke gave his head a sad shake. "Sometimes, Sisco, you make me blush for your odd notions."

"That is not what I started to do."

"No matter. What I want is for you to come with me now, to where you put the ammo from the gun."

Sisco said blankly: "Gun? Ammo?"

"I want to get it now, before I start beating on you."

"Ha, ha, ha."

"What's funny?"

"All your jokes, about things like ammo. They are funny."

"They're not jokes. Glawen isn't laughing. You watch him. When he laughs, you laugh."

"Certainly, sir. Shall I watch him now, at this time, or shall I go to my work?"

"First: the ammo from the gun in the Mitrix. Where is it?"

"Oh! That ammo! Why didn't you say so? You caused me worries! It wasn't any good and I took it out to put in much better stuff for protection, and then I was asked to do a thousand duties. When I came back the ammo was gone. Someone had seen it was bad and thrown it away."

"Glawen, have you ever heard such lies? Fetch me that rope, so that I can tie Sisco up."

"Now, then," said Sisco uneasily. "I know that you like to make jokes between friends, but sometimes it is nicer to use what I call happy words. Otherwise, what will this boy think? I am a fine person."

"For the last time: where is the ammo?"

"Oh, that stuff! I think I saw something like it at the back of the shop. Some unruly person, or maybe a thief, must have put it there."

"That's just about right. Today Glawen tried to shoot a tangle-top which was charging him. He pointed the gun and pulled the trigger, but there was no ammo, because you had stolen it. Luckily, the tangle-top was frightened and ran away."

"That was a brave adventure!" said Sisco. "You, young sir, have a deep power! I can feel it! Can you feel it, my friend Chilke? It is a noble force! What a blessing for you! And now I am rested and I have my duties."

Chilke said: "Let's get the ammo before the beating. At the back of the shop, you say?"

Sisco held up a tremulous finger. "It has just come to my mind! Without thinking I believe that I took the useless old stuff to my room! You may sit still and rest! I will run to fetch it!"

"I will come too, but not on the run. Glawen, what about you?"

"I've had enough excitement for the day. I'm going home."

"Very well. When you have some free time, I'll show you how to use that gun. There's the right way and the wrong way. It never hurts to be ready; the folk who turn their backs on trouble only get their arses kicked."

"I'd appreciate that very much." Glawen departed.

Scharde was not on hand when Glawen returned to their chambers in Clattuc House. Glawen flung himself wearily down on the couch and immediately fell asleep.

He awoke to find that Syrene had set and dusk had come to Araminta Station. Scharde still had not returned: an unusual circumstance.

Glawen washed his face and hands, brushed his hair and went down to the refectory for his dinner. A few minutes later Arles appeared. He took note of Glawen, who looked away, but in vain. Arles marched across the room and settled into the seat beside Glawen. He asked: "What's behind all this uproar? Why did you cause such a dustup?"

"I don't know what you are talking about."

Arles uttered a bark of laughter. "Do you expect me to believe that? You took Sessily out in the flyer and landed where you could go hard at it, in peace and quiet. Then, as I hear it, you lost the gun, and when you got back blamed the Yip, so that he got in trouble for nothing."

Glawen stared at Arles in indignation. "Where did you hear such absolute nonsense?"

"No matter where I heard it! And that's not all!"

"You mean there's more?"

"Of course! Chilke, who passed you on the flyer but wouldn't pass me on a technicality, believed you again and started to abuse the poor Yip. Namour wouldn't allow it and told Chilke where he stood! There were words, and in the end Namour discharged Chilke from his position. And that's the outcome of your little expedition."

Glawen spoke in a contemptuous voice: "You are wrong in every detail. Sessily and I went to Maroli Meadow for butterfly wings, not to go hard at it, as you elegantly put it."

Arles uttered another unctuous laugh. "More fool you, then! I've seen the way she acts whenever there's a fellow around: don't tell me she's all so innocent!"

"I'm telling you only the truth. I lost no gun; I merely discovered that Sisco had stolen the ammo, and so informed Chilke."

"Hmf! Namour doesn't believe it, because he fired Chilke. That's that, and that's what counts."

Scharde came into the refectory. He settled into the chair across from Glawen and asked: "Where have you been during the excitement?"

"I've been asleep. Arles says that Namour has fired Chilke from his job. Is that the excitement?"

Scharde looked at Arles in surprise. "Namour has no such authority. He's in charge of the Yips, no more. Where did you pick up that choice bit of nonsense?"

"From my mother," growled Arles. "She said that Namour was supervisor of all outside labor."

"She is quite incorrect. Both Namour and Chilke work out of Bureau D, at about the same level. Secondly, there never was any question of discharging Chilke. If anyone, Namour has the explaining to do. Bureau B has been looking into the matter all afternoon, and I'll be going back as soon as I get something to eat."

Arles said in a surly tone: "That's not the way I heard it. But I suppose you know what you are talking about."

"I can tell you this," said Scharde. "There is more to the matter than meets the eye. I'll say no more now, but you'll hear about it tomorrow."

9

The following afternoon Glawen went to Veder House, to help Sessily construct her butterfly wings. As they worked, he reported the events subsequent to his return of the Mitrix. "I saw Chilke this morning," said Glawen. "According to him, I missed all the fun. He says it was like a trained-animal extravaganza, with one dramatic deed following hard on the one before. Namour started out automatically defending Sisco, without any concern for the facts. He said to Chilke: 'Of course they purloin an oddment now and again! We all know it! What do you expect of them? It's an unspoken perquisite of the job!'

"'No longer!' said Chilke. 'That perquisite stopped the moment I took over as manager.'

"This is when Namour fired Chilke. He said: 'In that case, you're relieved of the job here and now! Get your gear together and get off the planet, because you're definitely not going to change the way we do things at Araminta Station.'

"Chilke just laughed at him. He said: 'Stealing charges of ammo isn't just a prank. If you think it is, maybe you better leave instead of me. It's a very serious matter. Let's go right now and look in Sisco's room. Anything from the airport I want back, right now. That's my responsibility.'

"Namour refused to make a move. Chilke said in that case he was going to look into Sisco's room, regardless. Namour seemed to lose his head. He told Chilke that if he made a move the Yips at Namour's orders would pitch him out of the compound.

"Chilke got bored with wrangling and telephoned Bureau B from the dispensary. Namour suddenly cooled off and began to make reasonable noises. While they were waiting, Sisco sneaked off to his room, evidently intending to hide the loot. Chilke had been watching for just that and followed Sisco into the room. He found an amazing hoard: a gun, many charges of ammo, tools, flyer parts: all stuff that Sisco had stolen from the airport.

"Spanchetta had appeared on the scene. She became very excited, and asked Chilke: 'How dare you threaten poor Sisco on such paltry grounds?' And: 'Don't you think that this is an intolerably arrogant act, to be taking the law into your own hands, especially after you have been discharged from your post?'"

Sessily asked in fascination: "What did Chilke say to that?"

"He said: 'Madame, I was not discharged, and I was not taking the law into my own hands. I was taking airport property into my own hands. It represents a considerable sum of money.'

"Spanchetta said that principles were more important than money, but now Bureau B arrived: my father, Wals Diffin and old Bodwyn Wook himself. No one agreed with Spanchetta, not even Namour."

"And what will happen to Sisco?"

"He'll be sent back to Yipton without wages; that's about all that can reasonably be done to him. But the case isn't closed yet. Everyone is down at the compound now, making a tour of inspection, and even the new Conservator has been notified. I should be there too, but I won't be missed and I'd rather be here with you."

"Thank you, Glawen. I'd hate to miss Parilia because of Sisco's crimes, as I might if these wings don't get done."

"I think we're coming along quite nicely."

"I do too." Already they had built four frames of bamboo withe, over which they had stretched transparent film; now they glued wings to the film, in accordance with a pattern. They worked in a combination studio-storage room under the west wing of Veder House, with sunlight entering through a line of high windows. Sessily wore soft pink trousers and a gray pullover shirt: garments which failed to disguise the contours of her body, of which Glawen became ever more conscious. At last, he came to stand beside her, where she bent over the table. She felt his nearness and looked up, half smiling. Glawen caught her in his arms and kissed her with an intensity she could not fail to understand, and to which she responded. At last they pulled apart and stood facing one another.

Glawen said huskily: "I don't know whether it's because of ideas Arles put into my head or because I've begun thinking them of my own accord. Either way I find it hard to stop."

Sessily, smiling ruefully, said: "To blame Arles because you want to love me—that's not very flattering."

Glawen said hastily: "I didn't mean it that way. It's just that—"

"Hush," said Sessily. "Don't explain. Talk is always a distraction. Think, instead."

"Think? Of what?"

"Well . . . Perhaps of Arles."

Glawen was puzzled. "If you like. For how long?"

"Only an instant. Just long enough to realize that I have feelings too, and Arles said nothing to me." She took a step back. "Glawen, no. I shouldn't have said that. My mother might be looking in at any moment . . . In fact, listen! I hear her coming now. Get busy."

Footsteps approached, certain and brisk. The door opened and it was indeed Felice Veder who came into the room: a pretty woman of early maturity, not much larger than Sessily, characterized by an innate decisiveness, as if her conduct were controlled by patterns of absolute validity which needed no attention.

Felice paused a moment to appraise Glawen and Sessily. Her gaze took in Glawen's uneasy posture and Sessily's flush and somewhat tumbled brown curls. She came to the table and inspected the wings. "Oh, how beautiful! Those will be truly spectacular, especially when they glow in the light! Am I wrong, or is it a trifle warm down here? Why don't you open the windows?"

"Yes, it's a bit warm," Sessily agreed. "Glawen, would you please —but no! If the wind blows in, it will shift all the patterns."

"True," said Felice. "Well, I have much to do. Keep up the good work!"

She departed. A few minutes later another set of footsteps sounded in the hall. Sessily listened. "It's Squeaker. Mother decided that we need supervision." She glanced sidelong at Glawen. "With good reason, perhaps?"

Glawen grimaced. "Now she'll make sure that we're never alone."

Sessily laughed. "Small chance of that . . . Although sometimes I want things to go on forever, just as they are."

Into the room came a girl: a slight little creature about ten years old, with Sessily's snub nose and brown curls. Sessily looked up. "Hello, Squeaker. What are you doing down here among the rats and vermin and jumpy bugs?"

"Mother says that I am to help you, and that Glawen must work very hard so that his mind does not wander off among the flowers. Isn't that a strange thing for Mother to say?"

"Very strange. She is unpredictable. She means, of course, that Glawen is something of a poet, and unless you and I direct his every move, he'll just stand and daydream."

"Hm. Do you really think that's what she meant?"

"I'm sure of it."

"When can I have a turn directing Glawen?"

Sessily said: "Sometimes, Squeaker, I suspect that you are far wiser than you let on. You definitely may not have a turn with Glawen. Not until I have put him through all his paces, and proved that he is tame. Now, then, come over here and make yourself useful."

"Are there really rats and vermin down here?"

"I don't know. Go look in that dark corner, behind those boxes. If something jumps out at you—well, we'll all know not to do it again."

"It's not all that important, thank you."

Sessily told Glawen: "Squeaker is very brave in such matters, remarkably so."

"Not exactly," said Squeaker. "In fact, not at all, though it's nice of you to say so. Also, I've been thinking lately that I'd rather not be called Squeaker anymore. Glawen, did you hear that?"

"I certainly did. What should we call you?"

"My real name is Miranda. It sounds more like a girl than 'Squeaker.'"

"Perhaps so," said Glawen. "What does 'Squeaker' sound like, in your opinion?"

"I know what it sounds like! When anyone says 'Squeaker' they think of me."

"Exactly right!" said Sessily. "Well, we must change our ways. Especially since 'Miranda' is a pretty name just right for a nice girl who is not a brat, like so many other little sisters I know."

"Thank you, Sessily."

10

Just after sundown Glawen returned to Clattuc House, and once again Scharde was gone from their chambers. Glawen stood indecisively, disturbed by a feeling of guilt for some deed or misdeed which he could not define, but for which Scharde's absence seemed to reproach him. What could his father be doing at this quiet hour of the evening? The matter of Sisco's larceny must long since have been settled . . . Glawen telephoned Namour's office but made no contact. He called Bureau B headquarters at the New Agency and was told that in all likelihood Scharde was still occupied at the compound.

Glawen waited no longer. He left the chambers, departed Clattuc House and started for the compound, only to be met by Scharde. Glawen said hurriedly: "I was just starting out to look for you. What has kept you so long?"

"Quite a good bit," said Scharde. "Wait for me in the refectory. I'll be down as soon as I wash up."

Ten minutes later Scharde joined Glawen at the table where he sat nibbling on cheese and salt biscuits. Scharde asked: "And where have you been hiding yourself all afternoon? You were needed."

"I'm sorry," said Glawen. "I was helping Sessily with her costume. I wasn't aware that anything was going on."

"I might have guessed," said Scharde. "Parilia must proceed, or so I suppose. We managed without you, and probably saved your young lives in the process. Although, now that I think of it, you had a hand in the matter yourself."

"But what happened?"

Scharde was silent while the Yip waiter served them soup. Then he said: "It is truly a wonderful chain of circumstances. Parilia seems to have a charmed life of its own."

"How so?"

"If it were not for Parilia, Sessily would never have wanted butterfly wings. You would not have heroically tried to shoot tangle-tops with an empty gun. Chilke's honor would not have been outraged and he would not have forced his way into Sisco's room, to make his awesome discovery. Bureau B would not have been called down to the compound, where we searched room after room, and found not only mounds and heaps of stolen goods and aircraft parts, but also a small arsenal. Every Yip at the compound owned a weapon: knives, dart shooters, spantics, and twenty-eight guns. The place was an armed camp. Namour declares himself dumbfounded. He is very subdued at the moment, and he admits Chilke was right, although for the wrong reasons."

Glawen asked: "But what is the meaning of all this?"

"Nobody knows for sure. The Yips just simper and smirk, and look off into space with their eyes crossed. The guns were presents from tourists, for being nice. So they say. That means that tourists visiting Yipton were provided Yip girls during their stay and paid off in guns. It's quite possible. We'll squeeze down on that right away; there'll be no more guns taken out to Yipton.

"The Yips won't tell us anything of their plans. But next week is Parilia. On Ort the ferry was to bring in a new gang of Yips, perhaps with more weapons. Everyone wonders if, say, Tzein or Ing night, when folk are standing around in their costumes, drunk and careless, if there might not have been a sudden screaming attack and a fine massacre, with the Yips pouring into Araminta by the thousands. Then they fly south to Throy and blow Stroma into the fjord, and it's all over; the hay is in the barn, and Deucas is thereafter known as Yipland, with Titus Pompo the Oomphaw of Cadwal. But"—and here Scharde held up his finger—"Sessily decided she wanted butterfly wings and Chilke is a man who won't be denied and so Parilia will proceed as usual, and very few folk will know how near they were to something else."

"What will happen next?"

"That will be decided after Parilia. Right now all Yips except domestics are confined to the compound. Chilke wants to send them out to Rosalia with indenture to pay their fares. It seems that Namour is already keeping a business like that in operation."

"It sounds like a sensible idea."

"Decisions like that come from Stroma, where nothing is ever simple. It seems now that there's a faction, the Freedom, Peace and Mother-Love Society, or some such title, that won't allow anything done which might hurt the Oomphaw's feelings. Well, we'll see. Incidentally, good news for you!"

Glawen looked up in apprehension. "Oh? What?"

"You've been assigned some important official duties over Parilia."

Glawen's heart sank. "I'm to guard Yips at the compound."

"Quite right! That's good thinking! Additionally, you'll have a most prestigious post. The new Conservator is named Egon Tamm. He will be residing at Clattuc House over Parilia, until the old Conservator moves out of Riverview House. He will bring his family, which includes two children: Milo, a boy about your age, and Wayness, a girl somewhat younger. They are pleasant intelligent young people, very well-mannered. You have been selected to take them in charge and do your best to keep them amused during Parilia. Why were you chosen? Be ready for a compliment. Because you too are considered pleasant, intelligent and well-mannered."

Glawen sat limply back in his chair. "I'd rather have fewer compliments and more free time."

"Put all such thoughts aside."

"My social life is ruined."

"A Clattuc is not only reckless and brave; he is resourceful and bides his time. At least, that's how the tradition goes."

"If I must, I must," growled Glawen. "When does this activity start?"

"As soon as they arrive from Stroma. They are probably modest and conventional; do not get them drunk so that they make themselves public spectacles; the Conservator would not like it and he would form a poor opinion of you."

"All very well," muttered Glawen. "But suppose they are the unruly ones: who will protect me?"

Scharde laughed. "A Clattuc is a gentleman under all circumstances."

CHAPTER 2

1

On Verd morning the satyr Latuun jumped upon an abutment near the lyceum, jerked his knotted brown arms, stamped goatish legs, then blew a skirling flourish on his pipes, to signify the beginning of Parilia. Jumping down into Wansey Way, then, blowing a melody of reedy phrases and rasping ground tones, he led a parade up Wansey Way, kicking out his hairy legs, leaping, stamping, strutting like a young animal. Costumed celebrants followed close behind, jigging and cavorting to the urgent music of Latuun's pipes, along with a score of decorated wagons, mechanical monsters, gorgeous ladies and stately gentlemen in sumptuous carriages. Musicians accompanied the procession, marching or riding on wagons; a phalanx of eight Bold Lions in costumes of tawny fur reared, charged and pounced on pretty girls along the way. Lines of gleeful children: small Pierrots and Punchinellos ran back and forth throwing handfuls of flower petals, darting sometimes under the rearing legs of Latuun himself. And who might be this satyr under his leering mask? Latuun's identity was supposed to be a profound secret, but clearly Latuun and the man who represented him were quite comfortable with each other's personalities, and it was generally suspected that Latuun was none other than that gallant scapegrace Namour.

So began the final three days and nights of revelry, pomp, feasting, along with amorous titillation and giddy dalliance. On Verd and Milden evenings Floreste's Mummers would present one of their little interludes, which Floreste called Quirks, and on Smollen night a more extended Phantasmagoria. Then: the climactic Grand Masque, until midnight when the bittersweet music of the pavane brought an end to Parilia, amid unmasking and tears of emotion, sometimes for the sheer tragic glory of life, and the wonder attendant upon its coming and going.

Such was Parilia, in the form now conventionalized after a thousand years of celebration.

Glawen's plans for Parilia were disrupted by a pair of unrelated circumstances, both surprises, both irksome: the discovery of the Yip arsenal and the arrival of the new Conservator and his family at Clattuc House.

As a result of the first case, Glawen found himself, in his capacity as a Bureau B cadet, assigned to a three-hour nightly patrol of the fence surrounding the Yip compound. The patrol was intended to counter the possibility that the Yips, drawing upon other caches of weapons, might still attempt a violent episode: in Glawen's opinion, an extremely farfetched hypothesis.

Scharde emphatically endorsed Glawen's thesis. "You are exactly right! The chances of a sudden Yip attack are remote indeed: probably, on any given day, not more than one in ten thousand. This means that twenty or twenty-five years might pass before we are surprised and murdered by raging grinning Yips!"

Glawen grumbled: "Now you're making fun of me. I'll be patrolling with Kirdy Wook, which makes it worse."

"Oh? I thought that you liked Kirdy."

"I have nothing against him except that he's a bore."

The Yips reacted to the surveillance with what seemed no more than bemused bewilderment—but seasoned Yip-watchers thought to sense bitter disappointment beneath the usual affability.

Not everyone admitted even the slight possibility of a bloody Yip rampage. Namour, cool and sardonic, commented: "I'm glad I'm not in charge around here. If I laid down decisions like this, I'd be laughed out of my job."

Chilke chanced to hear the remark. "You're not surprised by that pile of loot out yonder?"

"Of course I'm surprised."

"Who do you think they expected to shoot with those guns? Tourists?"

Namour shrugged. "I stopped trying to understand the Yips long ago. But I know this: not one of them could organize so much as a frog fight without falling out of a tree."

"Maybe someone is helping them plan."

"Maybe. But I'd surely like to see some pieces of hard evidence before I turned the station topsy-turvy."

Kirdy Wook, senior to Glawen, had been put in charge of the patrol. Kirdy, a large fair young man with rather heavy features and round china-blue eyes, begrudged every instant of the three-hour patrol.

"The emergency is over, if it existed in the first place," he declared in curt, positive tones. "So why are we trundling back and forth in the dark?"

"I know why I'm here," said Glawen. "Because Bodwyn Wook gave the orders."

Kirdy grunted. "I'm certainly not here of my own accord. It's carrying caution too far! Just possibly the Yips might have run riot and cut a throat or two, but anything more I find unreasonable."

"More? What more do you want?"

Kirdy uttered a peevish curse. "Must I explain everything in words of one syllable or less? The Yips have never done it before, have they?"

"That's why we're here talking about it."

"I don't quite pick that up," said Kirdy.

"If the Yips had killed our grandmothers we would never have been born."

"Bah," grunted Kirdy. "There's no talking with you when you're in this kind of silly mood."

Glawen was reminded of one of Uther Offaw's remarks in connection with Kirdy: "No mystery: Kirdy is simply old before his time." Arles had replied somewhat dubiously: "I'm not so sure! He's a most ardent Mummer, and a roaring Bold Lion!" Uther Offaw shrugged. "He's probably just a bit shy."

Kirdy now grumbled: "I wonder how long they'll keep this patrol going."

"Until after Parilia, at least, so my father says."

Kirdy made a mental calculation. "So then on Smollen we'll have the late evening duty! Do you know what that means? We'll miss the Phantasmagoria and the Masque!"

In dismay Glawen realized that Kirdy was exactly right, and that he would not see Sessily in her butterfly costume. Despondently he said: "There's nothing we can do about it. So we might as well like it."

Kirdy grunted. "I notice that the bigwigs aren't out here in the dark walking patrol—just the cadets and junior officers."

"That's in the elemental nature of things. I'm not clever, but I know at least that much."

"I know it too, but I don't like it . . . Well, just another twenty minutes; then we can go home and sleep."

The next morning was the start of Parilia week. Over breakfast Scharde notified Glawen that today the new Conservator would be arriving at Clattuc House. "So wash well behind your ears and practice saying: 'Yes, Lady Wayness,' and 'Quite right, Sir Milo.'"

Glawen looked up in shock, then realized that Scharde was joking. "Just the same, I wish I knew what to expect. Are they odd, or peculiar? Should I talk about the ecology of Cadwal? Or avoid the subject? Will I be required to dance with the girl?"

Scharde grinned. "Of course! Where is your gallantry? Would you rather dance with the boy?"

"Hmmf. I won't know for sure until after I see the girl."

Scharde threw his arms into the air. "Upon this note I retire from the field!"

After breakfast Glawen telephoned Veder House and told Sessily of his various misfortunes.

Sessily was properly sympathetic. "You must patrol with Kirdy? What a bore!"

"I'm afraid so! Even though the fellow means well. But he's only the tip of the iceberg. According to the schedule, we'll be patrolling Smollen evening during the Mummers spectacle, and I won't see you in your wings!"

"Ha! Maybe that's just as well, since I'm not sure that the joints will last out the performance."

"That's not all. Today my unknown guests arrive from Stroma, and I must keep them well-fed and jolly all during Parilia."

"That sounds rather exciting!"

"'Exciting' is not the word I would use. I expect a pair of hearty red-cheeked Naturalists, very tall, with booming voices, smelling of fish and oiled leather and turpentine."

"Oh, come, now! The Naturalists I've seen were never like that."

"It's just my luck to get such a pair."

"Feed them well on lots of plain wholesome food and take them for long runs up and down the beach. But I'm sure it won't be as bad as you fear. What are their names?"

"Milo and Wayness Tamm."

"They might be entertaining and clever, so that you enjoy their company. I wouldn't give up hope just yet."

"Hmmf," said Glawen. "You show great courage in the face of my forthcoming agonies."

"I have problems of my own. Floreste has been absolutely vexing. He makes all kinds of demands on me and every ten minutes changes the program. Now I'm to play two nights in the trio and I don't know the tunes, and out of sheer caprice he's just rearranged all the routines for Milden night. In this case, I'm thankful. Floreste plans a short comic pastiche of six nymphs teasing Latuun the satyr, who of course will be Namour."

"I didn't know that Namour had any interest in Mummery!"

"He doesn't really. He just likes to handle the nymphs, and his costume gives him scope for naughtiness. He's been more familiar with me than I like and he's even made some quiet suggestions. I told Floreste that I couldn't play in the trio and be a nymph at the same time, so he excused me, and put Drusilla in my place."

"Who is Drusilla?"

"Drusilla co-Laverty. She's somewhat older than we are, and works in the hotel."

"Now I know who you mean. Isn't she a trifle overblown for the part?"

"I care not at all. I'm having enough trouble learning to use four butterfly wings in the proper rhythm. I've learned a great new respect for the insects who do it all so easily."

3

During the evening Glawen telephoned Sessily. "Glawen here."

"Oh! I've been wondering about you all day. What's been going on?"

Glawen thought that Sessily sounded tired and a trifle dispirited. He said: "Nothing much. Just my official duties."

"You sound suspiciously jaunty."

"That's due to some marvelous good luck. I've been relieved from the patrol, so that I can give full attention to our visitors. Guess who has been assigned to fill the vacancy."

"Namour? Chilke? Floreste?"

"Good guesses, but all wrong. The fortunate fellow is Arles. There was quite an uproar when Arles heard the news. He was in top form. Spanchetta also had some remarks to make."

"It sounds like a lively affair."

"But all for naught. Tonight Kirdy and Arles trudge through the dark, entertaining each other with Bold Lion stories."

"In Bold Lion costume, I suppose?"

"No chance! What would the Yips think to see a pair of Bold Lions slinking around their fence?"

"I suspect that they'd run to guard their womenfolk."

"Ha! In any event, Arles and Kirdy must turn out in regulation Bureau B gear."

"Well, that's good news for you. By this time you're on easy terms with your guests?"

Glawen said cautiously: "We're still a bit formal, although I've lost my fear of them."

"Wayness is not seven feet tall and does not smell of fish after all?"

"That was just a joke. She is quite normal, and has no perceptible odor."

"And she's amazingly pretty? So that I seem just a tired old bundle of junk?"

"What foolishness! You're the prettiest bundle of junk I've ever seen!"

"Glawen! Should I take that as a compliment? I can't quite figure it out."

"I intended a compliment. What are you doing?"

"Better to ask what should I be doing, which is practicing my parts. But tell me more about your guests. Are they lofty or difficult?"

"Not at all! They're quite agreeable, and very well-mannered."

"Hmmm. The Naturalists I've seen out at the lodges were all slightly peculiar, as if they thought differently from the way I did."

Glawen glanced over his shoulder toward the library table where Milo and Wayness stood turning the pages of off-world periodicals. "They don't seem extra-peculiar, although I know what you mean."

"What do they look like?"

Again Glawen chose his words carefully. "They are not what I would call bad-looking."

"Fascinating! Tell me more."

"They have black hair which makes a remarkable contrast with their pale olive skin. Milo has quite a good physique."

"And Wayness: has she a good physique too?"

"In a certain sense. She is slim, rather boyish, in fact. Milo is an inch taller than I am and is quite handsome, I should say, in an aristocratic way."

"Wayness is not aristocratic, then?"

"They're much the same in that respect. Both are very much in charge of themselves."

"What are they wearing?"

"I haven't noticed. One minute while I look."

"Hurry, because Mother is calling me for my fitting."

"Wayness is wearing a short gray skirt, black stockings which show her knees, a black jacket and a gray ribbon around her hair with two tassels, dark red and dark blue, hanging to the middle of her neck. Milo—"

"Never mind about Milo. I'm sure he's decently clad."

84

"Oh, quite. They're still looking at fashion books . . . Now they're laughing, why I don't know."

"Here comes Squeaker, I mean Miranda, with urgent news from Mother. I must go."

Glawen turned away from the telephone. For a moment he studied his guests, then slowly approached the table. "I see that I'm not indispensable after all. You're getting along nicely without me."

"Yes, with the help of these silly fashions," said Milo. "Look at this funny creature."

"Sad to say, it's a lady and she's in deadly earnest."

"Hm. Which reminds me: I was much impressed by the coiffure of your Aunt Spanchetta."

"We're all quite proud of it. Unfortunately, after Spanchetta's hair and the fashion books, there's not much else of interest around here." Glawen went to the sideboard, and poured wine into goblets. "This is our own Green Zoquel, which we Clattucs claim to be the wine which gave Parilia its start."

The three went to sit on the sofa. Aside from themselves the library was empty. Glawen said: "It's quiet downstairs tonight. Everyone is busy with their costumes. What of yourselves? We'll have to find costumes for you."

Wayness asked: "Does everyone go about in costume?"

"Almost everyone, from tomorrow until Smollen night. We can always find something in the Mummery wardrobe. We'll go to look first thing in the morning."

"Costumes encourage conduct which otherwise might be repressed," said Milo. "Don't ask me how I know; the idea just came to me."

Wayness said: "I've always assumed that people picked out costumes representing parts they wanted to play."

"In many cases, that's the same thing," said Glawen. "There are always more demons and half-naked maenads strolling around the Quadrangle than nice little birds or baskets of fruit."

Wayness asked mischievously: "What is your costume to be? A nice bird?"

"No," said Glawen. "I shall be a black demon, sometimes invisible —which is to say, when the lights go out."

"I'll be just a thing in a sack," said Milo. "In that way I escape, or at least confuse, all attempts at psychoanalysis."

"You'd be more comfortable as a Pierrot," said Wayness. "Also less conspicuous." She told Glawen: "Milo feels that ostentation indicates an insipid personality."

"I'll have to give the matter some thought," said Milo. "Now, if you'll excuse me, I think I will be off to bed."

"And I as well," said Wayness. "Goodnight, Glawen."

"Goodnight."

Glawen went to his own chambers. Scharde looked him over and said: "You seem none the worse for your ordeal."

Glawen spoke with nonchalance: "It wasn't as bad as I expected—especially when I thought of Arles marching on patrol around the compound fence."

"That compensates for a great deal," said Scharde. "What do you think of your seven-foot Naturalists?"

"They're not an embarrassment."

"That's a relief."

"At first it wasn't all that easy. I thought they would want to talk about ecology and the most nutritious kinds of fish oil, but when I brought these subjects up, they showed very little interest. Eventually I opened a bottle of Green Zoquel, and the talk went more easily. I still find them a bit stiff."

"Away from home and in new surroundings they probably feel uncomfortable and shy."

Glawen gave his head a dubious shake. "Why should they be shy? They're well-mannered and nicely dressed, and even handsome, in a quiet sort of way. Though the girl is a trifle plain."

Scharde raised his eyebrows. "Plain? I had a different impression. Agreed, she's not buxom, but her face glows with intelligence; she's a pleasure to look at . . . What did you finally find to talk about?"

"I told them about Sisco and the stolen gear. They were very much interested—much more than I had expected. It seems that at Stroma the Yips are a major political issue."

"So I am told," said Scharde. "One faction is ready for changes; at least, it renounces force and violence as instruments of policy. The second faction is made up of old-fashioned Naturalists, who aren't all that squeamish. They want the Yips either to stop breeding or to leave Cadwal, or both. The Conservator must be neutral, but privately he seems to lean toward the Chartists."

"Milo put it even more strongly, especially after he heard Chilke's theory."

"You're ahead of me there," said Scharde. "What is Chilke's theory?"

"He thinks that the Yips have been stealing flyers from us a piece at a time. He says that the inventory records, even though they are a mess, indicate something of the sort."

"That's an interesting notion."

"Milo put it this way: 'If the Yips steal flyers, it means that they want to fly somewhere. If they steal guns, it means that they want to shoot someone.'"

Scharde rubbed his chin. "And all because you pulled the trigger on an empty gun."

4

In the morning, Glawen took Milo and Wayness down Wansey Way, past the lyceum to the Mummers' warehouse, where stage properties and costumes were stored. The building was empty; the three walked along the wardrobe racks, inspecting costumes and holding them up to themselves. Milo finally selected a harlequin costume of black and yellow diaper with a black tricorn hat. Wayness wavered between half a dozen costumes but finally chose an overall pink garment, fitting snugly to arms, legs and torso, with black pompons down the front. A tight hood with slanting eyeholes left only nose, mouth and chin exposed, with a crown of delicate silver spirals clasping her hair.

Without perceptible self-consciousness, Milo and Wayness slipped from their outer garments and tried on the costumes.

Milo said sorrowfully: "Glawen's finally got us disguised and bedizened, and now we'll probably commit all sorts of disgraceful acts. Glawen will have a great load on his conscience."

"Not unless you get caught," said Glawen. "Be careful, and if you can't be careful, at least be furtive."

"This is a nice costume, and I intend to be very nice," said Wayness. She studied her reflection in a tall mirror. "I look like a scrawny pink animal."

"You look more like a pink cloud-fairy, which is how you are supposed to look."

"Shall we stay as we are or get back into our own clothes?"

"Stay as you are. I'll change into my costume, then we'll go out in search of adventure."

At Clattuc House Glawen became a black demon, then telephoned Sessily. "We're all in costume and about ready to go out. Shall we stop by for you?"

"Hopeless. My relatives are here from Cassiopeia and I've been dragooned into walking them around town until noon."

"We'll meet you for lunch in the Old Arbor."

"I'll try to be there. If not, we'll share a table tonight under the lanterns. What are your friends wearing?"

"Milo is a harlequin, in yellow and black. Wayness is a pink cloud-fairy. What about you?"

"I'm not sure. Miranda has decided to astound everyone as a Pierrot, and I'll probably be the same, at least for today."

The morning went by pleasantly, or so it seemed to Glawen. At noon the three found a table in the Old Arbor: a place half restaurant, half open-air tavern under an arbor overgrown with lilac and native jelosaria. An open arcade overlooked the Quadrangle and a number of folk already costumed for Parilia.

Sessily presently appeared, costumed not as a Pierrot but as a whimsical entity she had patched together from bits of this and that. She identified herself as a Kalaki temple dancer from ancient Earth.

"So that's what they looked like," said Milo.

"Don't count on it," said Sessily. "I make no guarantee . . . What shall we have for lunch?"

Milo asked: "What do you suggest?"

"Everything is good here. I especially like the skewers of meat, with hot sauce and bread."

Glawen said: "Cold ale goes along very nicely."

"Not for me," said Sessily. "Floreste changed his mind again and I've got to learn two new programs before Milden afternoon. It's not difficult, but it takes all my time . . . Look! There he goes now!" Sessily pointed to a tall sharp-featured man with a great soft bush of gray hair, striding on long lean legs across the Quadrangle.

"Everyone admits he's a genius, including Floreste himself," said Sessily. "He wants to build a grand new Orpheum, and bring artists and audiences to Araminta from all over the Reach. He'd sell his grandmother to get funding."

Wayness asked Sessily: "What kind of music will you be playing?"

"Different kinds. On Verd evening I'll play flute and tzingal with the trio. On Milden evening I'll just have a few runs on the mellochord. On Smollen night, for the Phantasmagoria, I'll play flute in the orchestra until my butterfly part, and then it's over!"

"I wish I had your competence," said Wayness. "I'm inept. My fingers won't work together."

Sessily gave a grim laugh. "Your fingers would work well enough if your mother's name was Felice."

"Really? Is that all there is to it?"

"Well—not quite all. Musical instruments are like languages; the more you know, the easier it is to learn a new one—if you have the knack in the first place. Having a mother named Felice teaches you scales and exercises. I'm grateful she never admired lion tamers or people who walk on red-hot coals; these would be new skills for my repertory."

"We'll leave those for Squeaker to learn," said Glawen. "And speaking of lion taming: look what just prowled in."

"What is it?" asked Wayness.

"It's called a Bold Lion. Eight of them have formed an exclusive society."

"Evidently not a temperance group," suggested Milo.

"Definitely not. You can tell this one is drunk by the way it drags its tail along the floor. I think I recognize my distant cousin Arles Clattuc."

"Ho, ho!" exclaimed Sessily. "See that Ruby Empress out on the Quadrangle? That is his mother, Spanchetta. Poor Arles! She has seen him."

"Worse than that," said Glawen. "She intends to have a word with him."

Spanchetta entered the arbor and went to confront Arles. The tawny shoulders hunched; the massive Bold Lion head sagged forward.

Spanchetta made a crisp remark, to which Arles gave back a surly grumble, whose tenor Glawen deduced and reported. "Arles asks: 'Is this not Parilia? Let the flowers bloom freely!'"

Spanchetta spoke again, then turned on her heel and departed the Old Arbor. Arles went to a table and was served a bowl of fish chowder.

Spanchetta, returning to the Quadrangle, went to sit on a bench, where she was joined by a masked satyr with horns and hairy goat legs.

"There's Latuun," said Sessily. "It's actually Namour, who is said to maintain a discreet relationship with Spanchetta."

"It's incomprehensible," said Glawen. "Still—there they sit!"

A small girl wearing loose white pantaloons, a white blouse and a tall conical white hat approached the table. Her face was disguised by white paint and a large lumpy nose.

Glawen said: "I notice the arrival of a certain Miranda, long ago known as Squeaker but no longer. She carries important news, as usual."

"How do you know?" asked Miranda.

"I can tell by the way your nose twitches."

"You can't see my nose! It's hidden behind this false nose."

"Oh. My mistake."

"Glawen! My nose isn't a big lumpy thing! You know better than that!"

"I remember now. Well, what's the news?"

"Mother wants Sessily to come."

Sessily sighed. "It would be so easy to get drunk like Arles and wallow around in front of Mother and make inarticulate noises when she spoke."

Miranda cried out: "Go ahead, Sessily! I'll get drunk with you! We'll do it together. Mother wouldn't dare to kill us both."

"Don't be too sure," said Sessily. "I suppose I must go. Come, Miranda."

"Maybe Glawen will get drunk with me."

"You keep your greedy little hands off Glawen! He's mine!" Sessily rose to her feet. "Come along, you naughty creature! Let's go find Mother."

The afternoon passed, and the evening. Before retiring Glawen telephoned Sessily. "Has Floreste made any more changes?"

"Just one small change, but I'm delighted. I don't have to play flute Smollen night in the Bugtown orchestra. But I still can't make the wings behave properly. It's a matter of exact coordination. I must practice and practice."

"Butterflies manage without any practice."

"Butterflies aren't standing on a pedestal with colored lights shining on them and everyone watching."

"True."

"I've told Floreste to turn off the lights if I start making mistakes. Incidentally, why did you assure me that Wayness Tamm was plain and built like a boy?"

"Isn't she?"

"I noticed the difference instantly."

"I guess it's just something I missed."

"Anyway, I'm tired and I'm going to bed. I won't see you tomorrow, but on Glimmet perhaps we can have lunch at the Arbor."

"I hope so. We'll still be together at the Masque?"

"Yes! After I change from the wings, I'll meet you to the side of the orchestra, near the bass viol."

Ing passed and Glimmet; and on Verd morning Latuun led the parade along Wansey Way to open the official three days of Parilia.

Everywhere was color and gaiety; along Wansey Way the wine-tasting booths sold the great vintages of Araminta Station in quantities ranging from bottles to casks and dozens of casks, to buyers from worlds near and far. Each night the revelers dined at tables arranged along the side of the Quadrangle, just under the outdoor proscenium of the Old Orpheum. On Verd and Milden evenings, Sessily performed in truncated Mummer presentations: the first night playing in a trio, on the second playing mellochord accompaniment to a set of pastiches by the Mummer mimes.

On Smollen night Parilia reached its climax, with the banquet and Floreste's Phantasmagoria, to be followed by the Grand Masque, which would end at midnight to the stately music of the Farewell Pavane. Then, as the gong struck the hour, Latuun would jump down from the proscenium and run through the crowd, to be pelted with grapes and sent fleeing into the dark; and with the departure of Latuun, Parilia would come to its end. General unmasking would follow, and sad-sweet singing of traditional songs while folk wandered away to their beds, leaving only a few maudlin celebrants in the Quadrangle to await the dawn.

Glawen's plans for himself and Sessily had been thoroughly disrupted, partly by Felice Veder, who wanted Sessily to make a good impression upon her off-world relatives, and partly by reason of Glawen's duties in connection with Milo and Wayness Tamm.

Glawen had made a fatalistic adjustment to the situation. At the banquet he sat beside Wayness, with Milo at her other side. Arles, looking somewhat untidy in spite of his Bureau B cadet uniform, sat at a nearby table beside Spanchetta. He would miss most of the banquet, Phantasmagoria and the Grand Masque by reason of the patrol, and his posture suggested disgust and resentment. From time to time he reached to replenish his goblet with wine, only to be halted by Spanchetta's peremptory signal and a reminder that sobriety was an essential component of a proper and vigilant patrol.

Glawen had been watching. He told Wayness: "Arles keeps trying to pour wine for himself, but Spanchetta won't allow it. Arles is becoming more rebellious every minute. He and Kirdy may just hide in the bushes with a bottle, and let the patrol go hang. We'll know, if the Yips come screaming across the Quadrangle and cut our throats."

Wayness gave her head a dubious shake. "The Yips wouldn't dare such an outrage during Parilia! They'd incur enormous disapproval, even from the LPF."

"Who are the LPF?"

"The Life, Peace and Freedom people. That's what they call themselves. They call us Alligators. But I don't want to talk about such things now."

Glawen studied her profile. "Are you having a good time?"

"Of course!" She turned him a quick side glance. "Were you afraid I might not?"

"To some extent. I wasn't sure that you'd like Araminta Station. Or me, for that matter."

Wayness laughed. "Oh, you're inoffensive enough. As for the Station, when I first arrived I was afraid that everyone would be so sophisticated that I'd feel naive and foolish."

"And do you?"

"No. Thank you for asking."

"Not at all."

"I have been wondering what attending school at the lyceum is like. Is it very difficult?"

"Not if you keep up with the work. Arles is a good case in point. He wants to be an oenologist and for two years he tried to get good grades by drinking gallons and gallons of wine. Naturally he failed miserably."

"Interesting, but how does this apply to me?"

"I think it's fair to say that drunkenness and wine drinking won't make learning any easier."

"Hm. Did Arles mend his ways?"

"To some extent . . . There he goes now, the fine young cadet marching off to patrol the back fence."

"Poor Arles! He'll miss the Phantasmagoria."

"He's seen it all before. He's an ardent Mummer, if you can believe it. So is Kirdy, for that matter."

"What about you?"

"I've never had the urge. And you?"

"There aren't any pageants or performances at Stroma."

"Why is that?"

Wayness shrugged. "I suppose that the folk at Stroma don't care to sit like clams and watch other people perform."

"Hm. I must think this over a bit."

The banquet proceeded, while on the Orpheum stage Floreste presented his Phantasmagoria: a potpourri of pantomime, frivolity, ballet and sheer spectacle, controlled by a loose weft of ideas.

The production was entitled *The Charming Antics of the Bugtown Folk*, and dealt with the affairs of assorted insects, all dressed as peasants. Foliage and painted scenery indicated a village of small cottages and shops in a dark nook of the forest, with a broken pedestal of gray-green marble to the rear. Insects scurried here and there, transacting bits of business, usually with droll consequences. A company of small beetles danced to the chirping, scratching, honking music of an insect orchestra. A white chrysalis hung on a tree to the side; from time to time the sides bulged and jerked as if from activity within. The bugs gathered to watch, in awe and reverence.

The activity inside the pale shell became more urgent, and the orchestra began to accent the thrusts and bumps with plangent guttural tones.

The chrysalis began to break open; light focused on the activity and left the rest of the stage in darkness.

The chrysalis broke open; instantly the orchestra became still. Out of the aperture hopped a horrid little white imp, with distorted features defined in black. It made gleeful chittering sounds, then went fleeting from the stage in bounds and jumps, while insects and orchestra produced sounds of consternation.

The light shifted from the broken shell and for a moment the stage was passive. Then: a sudden splash of new light to the top of the pedestal, and there stood Sessily the butterfly, body encased in a soft gray stuff, antennae sprouting from her forehead. The wonderful wings waved as if of their own accord, in exact gentle rhythm.

Sessily turned slowly upon the pedestal, wings beating continually, her face a study in entranced concentration. She sank to a cross-legged sitting pose, the wings quivering and vibrating, to show off their startling color: purples and greens, deep reds, burning dark yellows, velvet black, as rich as any of the colors.

Sessily slowly rose to her feet, as if lifted by the wings. She stood smiling a rapt half-smile, delighted with the easy movement of the wings. Every eye watched her in fascination; she made an image of irresistible appeal and Glawen's heart seemed to contract in his chest.

Other parts of the stage had gone dark. From the side came a grinding roar. The lights fled from the pedestal; white glare picked out a band of imps armed with grotesquely tall halberds. The insects recoiled in confusion, then rallied and attacked with all ferocity. The imps were stung, rasped, pinched by mandibles, constricted by centipedes, gnawed by beetles. The stage spotlight, wan and diffuse, swam here and there about the stage. It touched the pedestal; the butterfly was gone.

From the orchestra came an outburst of frenzied polyphony which almost at once went quiet; except for a white spotlight wandering here and there the stage was dark.

The insects, glimpsed in the moving light, had become busy. With huge mallets, presses and rollers they flattened the imps to thin stiff sheets, distorting the features into near-abstract patterns.

From the direction of the pedestal came the sound of pounding.

The light, straying upon the pedestal, discovered insects nailing flattened imps into a crude representation of a white and black butterfly.

A curtain of opaque air swept down to conceal the stage. Floreste came briskly out upon the proscenium. "The Mummers and I hope that you have enjoyed our efforts. As you probably know, all our talent is recruited here at Araminta Station; they work with great dedication to produce our effects.

"Now I will make my pitch, but it will be short. This Orpheum has given us many hours of pleasure, but it is small and sadly obsolete, so that every production played here becomes an adventure in itself.

"Many of you know that we are planning a new Orpheum. When the Mummers play off-world all proceeds go into a fund to build a new Orpheum, the finest such complex in the Gaean Reach.

"Shamelessly I request your contributions, that we may bring the reality of the New Orpheum closer. Thank you."

Floreste jumped down from the stage and was gone.

Glawen turned to Wayness and Milo. "And there you have it: one of Floreste's inventions. Some like them; others don't."

"At the very least, he holds your attention," said Wayness.

Milo grumbled: "I'd like it better if I knew what was going on."

"Most likely Floreste doesn't know himself. He improvises left and right and devil take the hindmost."

"There is certainly something to be learned here," mused Milo. "Floreste shows a few perplexing incidents, then comes out on the stage to demand money, and no one even laughs at him."

The orchestra had begun to gather in preparation for the Grand Masque. Glawen said: "The first dance is always the 'Courtesy Pavane'; they're almost ready to start and I must step it off with Sessily, even though I don't like leaving you alone. Perhaps you'll join the dance?"

Wayness looked at Milo, but found no encouragement. "I think we'll just sit here and watch."

"Sessily has probably finished changing from her wings," said Glawen. "We've arranged a place to meet, and if you'll excuse me, I'll go wait for her."

Glawen went to the designated rendezvous and stationed himself where he could look along the passageway which led both backstage and to the kitchens.

At the moment the results of the wine competitions were being announced from the stage. As usual, the Wook winery took the grand award for overall excellence and the single best wine, with other houses winning awards for special products, such as Clattuc House's Green Zoquel.

The announcements were completed. The orchestra began to tune and along the Quadrangle couples took their places for the "Courtesy Pavane." Since Wook House had won the award, the place of honor went to Wook Housemaster Ouskar Wook and Ignatzia, his spouse.

Glawen became restive. Where was Sessily? If she did not hurry, they would miss the start of the pavane . . . Could there have been a mistake in the rendezvous? He thought back over the conversation. Directly behind him stood the bass violist, with his imposing instrument.

Glawen caught sight of Miranda and called to her. She ran up bubbling with excitement. "Did you see me, Glawen? I was the number three imp—the one who was killed by the wisselrode bug."

"Certainly I saw you. You died with great pathos. Where is Sessily?"

Miranda peered down the passageway. "I haven't seen her. Our dressing rooms are different. We've got just a little closet backstage; Sessily has what is called the Ladies' Dressing Room, out along the dock past the kitchen."

"Would you go see if you can find her? Tell her to hurry or we'll miss the pavane."

Miranda paused only an instant, to ask: "If she's sick do you still want her to dance?"

"No, of course not! Just find her. I'll wait here in case she shows up."

Miranda ran off. Five minutes later she returned. "Sessily is not in the dressing room, and the maid says she hasn't been there. She's nowhere along the way."

"Could she have gone home? Where is your mother?"

"She's stepping the pavane with my father. Glawen, I'm frightened. Where can she be?"

"We'll find out. How are your parents dressed?"

"Mother's the Sea Queen: see her there in green? Father is the Dombrasian Knight."

Glawen went out on the dance area, and accosted Carlus and Felice Veder where they performed the ritual measures of the pavane. Addressing Carlus Veder, Glawen said: "Sir, I'm sorry to bother you, but we can't find Sessily. She was to step the pavane with me, but she never came out from backstage, and she's not there now."

"Come, let's go look!"

A search revealed no trace of Sessily, nor was she discovered later, even though the grounds were carefully examined. Sessily was gone, without a trace of her going.

An aura of tragic glamour surrounded the disappearance of Sessily Veder. Standing high on the pedestal, face exalted, body taut, wings and arms raised in farewell salute, the girl-butterfly became an image of primordial glory, and never would anyone present recall the occasion without feeling an eerie thrill along the nerves of his or her back.

A frantic search revealed no trace of Sessily; it was as if she had been whisked away into another dimension. Araminta Station was then examined again, more thoroughly, with no better result.

Everyone immediately supposed that she had been carried away in a flyer, but records at the spaceport revealed that neither flyer nor space vehicle had used the sky above Araminta Station during the critical period.

Perhaps, then, a boat or a surface vehicle had been used to carry her away? A similarly explicit assurance could not be made; still, when cars, trucks, vans and power wagons were checked, all were found to be in their accustomed places, and no one reported suspicious movements. As for boats, such employment downstream of the Orpheum—which was to say, parallel to Wansey Way—would have been instantly conspicuous, and could be ruled out upstream by reason of the reeds which fringed the riverbank. Forcing a boat to shore through the reeds or the transport of a body out to a boat would have left obvious and unmistakable traces. The same could be said for the possibility of carrying a body into the river, so that it might drift downstream and out to sea.

Mysteries of this sort were rare at Araminta Station though not unknown. The typical victim might be a Yip girl who had resisted a conventional seduction, with unhappy consequences.[1] The perpetrator, upon definite identification, was forthwith hanged, or, at his own option, dropped into the ocean a hundred miles offshore.

Crimes at Araminta Station, or anywhere about Deucas, were investigated by agents of Bureau B, an IPCC affiliate.[2] Director of Bureau

---

[1] Almost any Yip girl would willingly perform sexual services if the remuneration were adequate. (Knowledgeable consensus held the money to be wasted, by reason of apathy.) In Yipton, a place called Pussycat Palace had been set aside for the amusement of tourists; here the girls (and boys) were trained to simulate at least the rudiments of enthusiasm, in order to encourage return trade.

[2] IPCC: the Interworld Police Coordination Company, ages before a private concern, now a semiofficial police organization operating across the length and breadth of the Gaean Reach.

B was the septuagenarian Bodwyn Wook, who was small, thin, mercurial and something of a martinet. He was bald as a stone, with darting blue eyes, a bony chin and a long inquisitive nose. His captains were Ysel Laverty, Rune Offaw and Scharde Clattuc. These four senior officers were discreetly known by the junior staff as the Zoo, through a fancied resemblance to illustrations in a famous old Earthly bestiary. Scharde: a gray wolf; Ysel Laverty: a boar; Rune Offaw: a stoat; and Bodwyn Wook: a small bald orangutan.

The entire Zoo applied itself to the Sessily Veder case, along with as many sergeants, ordinaries and cadets as could be spared from routine duties.

The search of Araminta Station and its environs was conducted with meticulous care. Every structure was inspected, as well as the ground surface within a reasonable perimeter. Each day a chemist tested river water for traces of decomposing flesh, again without result. Sessily Veder had dissolved into nothingness, leaving behind no clues and very few theories.

One such theory, to the effect that Sessily, becoming deranged, had run wildly away to hide in the wilderness, was scoffed at as nonsense, but if insane flight, submersion in the river and kidnap by aircraft were all ruled out—what, then? At Bureau B it was recognized that the general bafflement must be a source of comfort to the criminal.

Every person who had been present during the Phantasmagoria— tourist, wine buyer, resident, collateral, guest, worker, Mummer, musician—all were questioned and asked to describe the movements both of themselves and of anyone else of whom they had knowledge. Such information was collated in the Bureau A computer, and the readout allowed a large number of visitors to depart Araminta Station.

Another set of investigators tried to trace Sessily's movements immediately after her descent from the pedestal. Her route should have taken her across the backstage area to a door leading out into a passageway. Here she would have turned to the left, walked some twenty feet and out upon a loading dock, then to the left and to the dressing room annex, past the corner of the Orpheum proper: an inconvenient arrangement frequently cited by Floreste during his pleas for a new Orpheum.

Sessily had been assisted down from the pedestal by Drusilla co-Laverty, a Mummer girl two or three years older than Sessily. Drusilla and several other Mummers had seen Sessily depart the backstage and go out into the passageway. Thereafter no one admitted to knowledge regarding her movements. The two wardrobe maids asserted that she had never arrived in the dressing room. Somewhere between backstage and dressing room Sessily had disappeared—which meant from the loading dock.

At this hour the dock was deserted and poorly illuminated, while the service area beyond was not illuminated at all. Kitchen workers had access to the dock through a storage pantry, but all, when questioned, declared that they had been busy serving the banquet and had not gone out on the dock, including Zamian, a Yip scullion.

Because of their proximity to the dock, the kitchen workers were questioned in careful detail. The statements, when digested by the computer, revealed discords in the testimony of Zamian. He was immediately brought to the Bureau B offices for questioning. Scharde Clattuc ushered him into the presence of Bodwyn Wook, then went to sit quietly in the shadows.

Bodwyn Wook leaned back in his massive high-backed chair and fixed Zamian with a minatory gaze.

Zamian, slender and erect, with regular features and close-cropped tawny golden curls, responded to the scrutiny with a nod of grave courtesy. "Sir, how may I oblige you in your desires?"

Bodwyn Wook waved a paper in the air. "You made a statement regarding your movements on the last night of Parilia. Do you remember this?"

Zamian smilingly nodded his head. "Yes, quite so! Your informant was utterly truthful, and you may trust his word. I am happy to have been of help to you. May I go now?"

"I am not quite done yet," said Bodwyn Wook. "A few trifles remain. First, do you know the meaning of the word 'truth'?"

Zamian raised his eyebrows in surprise. "Of course, sir, and I will willingly explain the word to you as best I can; but would you not prefer to learn the precise and official definition from the dictionary?"

Bodwyn Wook coughed. "I suppose you are right. I'll take care of the matter a bit later . . . No, don't go yet; I am not quite done with you. In this statement, you claim that during the time which was specified to you, roughly from the end of the Phantasmagoria to the start of the Grand Masque, you did not leave the kitchen."

"Naturally not, sir! I had my important duties which were entrusted to me. How could I do them, and do them well, if I were somewhere else, such as down near the beach, or walking by the river? I am surprised that you ask this question, since you know that the duties were done expertly."

Bodwyn Wook raised a handful of other papers. "These are statements which assert that you left the kitchen on several occasions in order to hide bags of stolen food. What of that?"

Zamian gave his head a rueful sidewise shake. "As you well know, sir, there is always scandal in the kitchen. One hears constantly a dozen or more stories. This one sweats too freely; that one breaks wind every time he bends over to peep into the oven. I pay no heed to such talk. Usually it is not true."

"But in this particular case, the reports are accurate?"

Zamian glanced up toward the ceiling. "Sir, I barely remember."

Bodwyn Wook spoke to Scharde. "Take Zamian to a very quiet dark room where he will be able to think without distraction. I want him to remember everything in complete detail."

Zamian raised his hand, his smile now somewhat tremulous. "Why make such trouble for yourselves? Now that I gather my thoughts, I find that I remember quite well!"

"That is good news! The mind is a wonderful organ! What happened that evening?"

"Now I remember! I went out into the pantry a time or two, to stretch my legs. And then—but I can't be sure."

"Tell us anyway."

Zamian spoke with great earnestness. "Truly, sir, it is wrong to make reports when one is not sure. An injustice might be done, and I would not want the weight upon my soul unless for at least a large sum of money."

Scharde told Bodwyn Wook: "He wants to know how much we'll pay."

Bodwyn Wook threw himself back into his chair. "I think we should take Zamian to where he can think quietly in the dark until he is sure of his facts. He will be saved worry; we will be saved expense, and it will be best for all of us."

"Quite right, sir: sound thinking."

Bodwyn Wook added: "Before you leave him explain how accessories after the fact are punished, just as the criminal is punished."

Zamian spoke with dignity: "Such talk is not in good taste when people are eagerly trying to help. I would never withhold knowledge of crime. Still I think we agree that a little gift is always nice and shows good faith and happy feelings on all sides."

"If we were faithful and happy we would never catch criminals," said Bodwyn Wook. "That is why we are cruel and merciless. Tell us what you know and be quick about it."

Zamian gave a forlorn shrug. "As I mentioned, I stepped into the pantry to rest and think. While there, I thought I heard a voice cry out. It stopped quickly. I listened and heard talking, and I thought: 'Ah, then, all is well.' Then the voice cried again. This time it said: 'You're breaking my wings!'"

"And then?"

"I went to the door and looked out. I saw no one. The truck from the winery had come in earlier with wine for the banquet; it was backed up to the dock with the curtain down. I decided that someone was in the back of the truck. But of course such things are not my affair."

"Then what?"

"That is all. At midnight, after the unmasking, old Nion came for his truck, but it was unoccupied then."

"How do you know?"

"He put an empty cask into the back."

"And you cannot identify the persons who were in the truck?"

"I know nothing."

Scharde approached Zamian and spoke quietly, almost into his ear: "If, by chance, money were offered, would you remember more?"

Zamian spoke in anguish: "As always, I am the sport of a malicious fate! When my great chance finally arrived, instead of looking through the curtain and writing down names, I sat daydreaming in the pantry. I could have gathered gold by the handful; instead I have none."

"Yes, very sad," said Bodwyn Wook. "Still, you overestimate the money you could have earned from us. As for blackmail, of course we can only speculate."

Zamian departed. Bodwyn Wook and Scharde immediately located and studied the statement made by Nion co-Offaw, master vintner at the Joint Winery. Nion stated that he had brought three casks of wine down from the winery, unloaded them to the dock; then, arrayed in a makeshift clown costume, he had gone to the Quadrangle to dine with friends, watch the Phantasmagoria and enjoy a modest carouse until half an hour after the midnight unmasking, when he had returned to the winery in his truck. He had noticed nothing particularly unusual and had remained ignorant of the horrid circumstances until the next morning.

Bodwyn Wook threw the statement aside. "Well, we have advanced a trifle or two. The attacker apparently took the girl into the truck and assaulted her there. What is your thinking on this?"

"Not much more. Apparently he knew of the route she would take, and planned to waylay her—though those plans were probably made on short notice."

"That's the way it feels to me. So then, our attention turns to the truck."

"It certainly should be carefully examined."

"That is a good job for you."

6

The week after Parilia was somber and quiet. The wine buyers were gone, their purchases choking the holds of every departing ship. Tourists had also moved on, including the Clattuc houseguests: some home to far worlds, others to the wilderness lodges, still others by ferry across three hundred miles of ocean to Yipton: a destination as exotic as any. Here they would test the semibarbaric appointments of Arkady Inn, or explore the labyrinthine bazaars, or ride by gondola along the surprising canals, or look from a balcony across the Stewery. And others still might test the options available at the Pussycat Palace.

At Bureau B inquiries into the disappearance of Sessily Veder continued without cessation, taking precedence over all but the sea patrols along the Marmion littoral.

Surveillance of the Yip compound was delegated to special squads of the militia. Kirdy Wook was reassigned to Bureau B; Arles, however, was still required to trudge a nightly stint, to his intense dissatisfaction.

Glawen had become obsessed with the investigation, and could think of nothing else. Even his interest in food was lost and only Scharde's concerned insistence prompted him to eat.

Glawen had clung to the hope that Sessily might still be alive, that for some inscrutable reason she had changed from butterfly wings into a new costume; then, so disguised, had taken herself off to a secret place from which, sooner or later, she would either return or send news of herself—until Scharde reported Zamian's testimony.

Zamian's account shattered all such hope; there could be little doubt but that Sessily had come to a violent end, and Glawen's viscera crawled with hatred for the person responsible.

What had happened to the body?

The question had not lacked answers, including immersion in river, lagoon, ocean; destruction by chemical, fire; maceration, implosion, ionic disassociation; levitation by balloon, tornado or the clutch of a giant night-flying gambril down from the Maughrim Mountains. In each hypothesis one or more flaws had been discovered and the problem still hung in the air.

Upon hearing of Zamian's disclosures, Glawen immediately asked: "What of the truck? Has anyone gone to look at it?"

"I'm on my way now," said Scharde. "I thought you might like to join me."

"Yes. I would indeed."

"Come along, then."

The time was middle afternoon of a blustery cool day; from the northeast came a keen wind to chase shreds and tatters of a broken overcast out to sea. Scharde and Glawen drove to the end of Wansey Way, around the Orpheum and inland along a dirt road leading eastward, first across garden plots, paddies, orchards and fields, then into a region of gentle slopes and swales planted to vineyards. Something less than a mile from the Station, the Joint Winery occupied the top of a low rise: a group of gray-brown concrete structures, inconspicuous in the context of the landscape, and of little distinction otherwise.

At the Joint Winery, secondary yields from the six wineries were blended by Master Oenologist Nion co-Offaw, to produce wines of good character, suitable both for home consumption and for export.

Where the garden plots gave way to the vineyards Scharde stopped the car. "This ground has been examined foot by foot, not once but twice, out to a quarter mile from the road. That's considered double the maximum distance a man could carry a body, perform a burial and return to the road within the time strictures. In my opinion it exceeds the maximum by a factor of four, rather than two."

"That's only a bit more than a hundred yards."

"A hundred yards in the dark, carrying a body and tools, leaving no tracks or marks? I'd call that incredible in itself."

"The whole affair is incredible," muttered Glawen. "How could anyone destroy poor little Sessily?"

"Aha! But when she was destroyed she was glorious wonderful Sessily, too beautiful for her own good, and someone felt impelled to pluck the highest fruit from the Tree of Life. I suspect that he regrets nothing."

"Not until we catch him, at any rate."

"He'll regret getting caught," said Scharde. "No doubt as to that."

"The winery has been searched, of course?"

"I searched it myself. She's not there: not in any closet, bin, vat, cubbyhole, on the roof or under the foundations. Nion is a crusty old devil, so don't expect cordiality. Also, just to be difficult, he pretends to be deaf."

Scharde put the car into motion; the two continued along the road, which presently veered, climbed a gentle slope and ended in front of the winery.

Scharde halted the car; the two alighted and took stock of the surroundings. The front façade of the winery rose in front of them. A tall door stood open, allowing a glimpse of the shadowed interior: a row of tall vats, oddments of machinery, the gleam of piping. About fifty feet to the side, Nion's truck was parked under a tree.

Scharde and Glawen went to the open door and looked into the winery, to discover Nion in the seat of a mobile lift, loading wine casks into a modular shipping case. The two came forward and stood politely waiting until Nion should choose to take note of them.

Nion flicked a sidewise glance toward them, but worked until he came to an optimally convenient opportunity to stop. Then he swung around in the seat, appraised his visitors, and at last grudgingly stepped down to the floor: a man well into middle age, stocky of frame, ruddy of face, with coarse russet-gray hair, narrow red-brown eyes under bristling eyebrows. He asked in a barely courteous voice: "What is it this time? I have nothing to do with your mysteries."

"We have had some new information," said Scharde. "It now appears that the criminal used the winery truck during your absence, probably to transport the girl's body."

Nion started to utter an automatic snort of derision, stopped short, scowled and reflected a moment, then gave a heavy shrug, jerked his head back. "As to that, I can tell you nothing. If it's true, they have a great audacity, using my truck for their dirty business."

Glawen started to speak, then, at a glance from Scharde, held his tongue. Scharde asked: "Earlier that evening you brought three casks of wine down from the winery?"

"That I did, at the specific request of the wine steward. He is the man to question on that score, and if that's all you're wanting to know, I'll get back to my work."

Scharde paid no heed. "You backed the truck against the dock to unload the casks?"

Nion stared at Scharde in astonishment. "Surely, man, you can't be so dense as all that! Would there be any other way?"

Scharde smiled grimly. "Very well. I take it, then, that you backed the truck against the dock. When you returned, which according to your statement was after midnight, did you find the truck as you left it?"

Nion blinked. "Now as I think on it, some sky-larking fool had jockeyed it about, and finished off his prank by nosing it in against the dock. I would have taught him tricks if I had caught him at it."

Scharde smiled once again. "Did you find any indication as to who might have played the trick? Any oddment or piece of property in the truck?"

"Nothing."

"Have you used the truck since that night?"

"Indeed I have! Every day I deliver a module—that's four casks in a shipping case, mind you—down to the spaceport. Sometimes more when there's a ship to be laden. Now, then, is there more you want to know?"

"We'll have a look at the truck."

"As you like."

Scharde and Glawen returned outside and went to the truck. Scharde glanced briefly into the control compartment, which was discouragingly stark and clean. "We'll find nothing here."

Glawen had pulled aside the canvas curtain at the back, allowing light to play into the empty cargo space. An inch-thick carpet of elastic sponge covered the bed, with a pair of planks four feet apart running the length of the bed, apparently to accommodate the wheels of a loading dolly.

Scharde jumped up into the cargo space and looked about. Almost immediately he noticed stains at the center of the bed, halfway between the two lengthwise planks. Scharde bent his head and examined the stains. They were dark red in color and might be blood. Without comment he went to the forward end of the bed; dropping to his hands and knees, he examined the floor area inch by inch. Glawen also noticed the stains, but held his tongue. With nothing better to do, he looked about the control cab but found nothing of interest, and returned around to the rear, just in time to see Scharde pluck some sort of object from where it had caught on the splintered inner edge of the left-hand plank. He asked: "What have you found?"

"Hair," said Scharde laconically, and continued his search.

Glawen could no longer tolerate inactivity. He climbed up into the cargo space, and began his own search in an area Scharde so far had neglected: the crack, or seam, where the elastic sponge met the side panel. Before long he made a discovery of his own and gave a sad exclamation.

Scharde looked around. "What did you find?"

Glawen held up a black and orange fragment. "A bit of butterfly wing."

Scharde took the bright wisp and placed it into an envelope. "There's no longer much doubt about the time and place."

"Just the 'who.'"

The two searched half an hour or so longer and Scharde found another tuft of matted fiber but nothing else of obvious significance. Descending to the ground, they examined their findings: the wing fragment and the tufts of coarse brown hair. "Not much," said Scharde. "But still better than nothing. Perhaps we'd better have another word with Nion."

Glawen looked dubiously toward the winery. "He doesn't seem too interested in helping us."

"We'll still give him a try. The trail must lead somewhere."

The two returned to the winery. Nion, standing in the doorway, observed their approach without display of emotion. He asked as they drew near: "What have you found, if anything?"

Scharde displayed the articles taken from the truck bed. "Do these mean anything to you?"

"The colored bit would seem to be part of the girl's costume. The other stuff: I don't recognize it, offhand."

"You don't use a rug, or sacking, or any such material?"

"I do not."

"Very well. We'll just take another look into the winery."

Nion shrugged and stood aside. "What do you hope to find? You've been through the place like a bad smell, into vats and all."

"True. But somewhere, somehow, we're missing something."

"How so?"

"This is the end of the trail. She was murdered in the truck. When you came for the truck, it had been moved and the body was gone. Time is limited; the body apparently was not buried; we would have markings in the soil, and the road shows the truck went no farther than the winery. What happened to the body?"

"I can't help you. Search if you like."

Scharde and Glawen stepped through the doorway and into the winery, with Nion coming behind. Ten vats loomed above them, five to either side, each vat painted a different color, and a console at each vat to control operations and supply information. During Scharde's previous visit, Nion had pumped dry each vat in turn, revealing no trace of Sessily.

Nion noticed Scharde's obvious interest in the vats. He asked gruffly: "What now? Must I pump my vats again? I waste a gallon of good wine every time I pump over a vat."

"Are your gauges so accurate?"

"Certainly. The meters read to the tenth part of a gallon, which is important for careful blending, when even a half gallon of Diffin's No. 4 Bitter Malvas too much or too little can affect a blend."

"So what is your procedure?"

"In simplest terms, I pump from the vats to the blending tank in proper proportions, to the amount of six hundred and sixty gallons, which is twelve casks, or three cases. This is a convenient batch size. Then I slide the casks along the easeway to the filling machine. I inspect the interior of each cask, the pump loads exactly fifty-five gallons of wine; I set the lid in place and the machine seals and clamps the lid to the cask. I slide away the full cask, and fill another to the number of twelve. These are held in stock over against the wall until I receive an order, when I load a shipping case appropriately and deliver it to the cargo bay at the spaceport."

Scharde looked along the wall. "Your stock on hand is very low."

"There is no stock to speak of. Everything was sold during Parilia."

"And delivered to the spaceport?"

"True."

"And shipped?"

"I would suppose so."

"And one of those casks might well have contained a body?"

Nion started to speak, then stopped short. He looked toward the blending tank and seemed to stammer under his breath. When he looked back at Scharde, his ruddy color had gone ashen. "I can assert almost definitely that this is what happened."

"Hm. How so?"

"On Ort morning I filled casks from what remained in the vat, and when I was finished I discovered an overage of almost thirteen gallons."

Glawen turned and departed the winery. Nion and Scharde looked after him. Nion heaved a deep sigh and turned back to the blending tank. "At the time, I wondered at the error; how could it be, when my meters are accurate to a small fraction of this amount? How much did the girl weigh?"

"Glawen could tell us, but he is not present. I would guess about a hundred pounds, or a hundred and five."

"She would thereby displace something less than thirteen gallons of wine, and I would find the overage, and puzzle as to its source. Now all is clear."

"Who would know how to fill and seal a cask?"

Nion made a harsh wild gesture. "It could be anyone: the oenology students, those who work the six House wineries, anyone who has ever watched me at work. I will go on to say this! With these two hands I would strangle the man who so despoiled the wine! It is a sickly perversion beyond all ordinary calculation!"

Scharde inclined his head in profound agreement. "It is a crime doubly vicious; that is true. I join you in your disgust."

"Will we ever capture this person?"

"I can say only that we are making progress in our investigation. One other matter, in regard to the cask itself: can we trace it? What would be the label on the cask?"

"It would be the Graciosa, and I have shipped fifty or sixty such casks since Parilia to a large number of destinations. It would be virtually impossible to locate the spoiled cask."

"The casks carry no serial number? No coding of any kind?"

"None. Such a task would swamp me in paperwork, and serves no purpose."

"Not until now."

"It shall not happen again, not while I am alive." Nion struck his chest with his fist. "I have been mild and guileless! I have trusted persons with suppuration and gangrene for brains. They have looked at me and breathed this air; I have displayed my secrets and given my best; still they do this to me! Never again."

"It is a bad situation," said Scharde. "Still, we must not throw the good out with the bad. The innocent should not suffer for the crimes of the guilty."

"We shall see."

"A final word, and here your advice will be most important. I personally see no reason to cause a great public outcry over this matter. I will recommend absolute discretion in our announcements; otherwise we will sell little of your good Graciosa for long years to come, if your winery is to become the subject of vulgar jokes."

Nion's ruddy face had gone gray. "Still—sooner or later someone will make a terrible discovery."

"We can only hope that it will be later rather than sooner. When the time comes, we can adjust the matter in the field, and hope that no one takes any great notice. If they do, we will blame it on warehouse bandits."

"Yes; that is correct," said Nion. "Ah, me! What an affair!"

7

By order of Supervisor Bodwyn Wook, the full Bureau B roster, including captains, sergeants, junior sergeants, collateral ordinaries, and cadets gathered in the New Agency auditorium. Promptly upon the stipulated moment Bodwyn Wook marched into the room, seated himself on the rostrum and addressed his subordinates.

"Tonight I will report a late development in the Sessily Veder case, which puts to rest a certain amount of speculation. Because of the continuing inquiry I will take no questions; the information contained in my statement must and will suffice for the moment.

"As everyone knows, Sessily Veder's disappearance has puzzled us all. Now new information from certain sources has clarified the mystery. In brief outline, Sessily, after changing costume, was lured by a false message to a rendezvous, where she met a Pierrot, who escorted her to the beach, using guiles and pretexts we cannot imagine.

"The two set off along the beach to the south. Two hours later the Pierrot returned alone. His manner, according to information, was bewildered and distrait.

"We must accept the conclusion that someone probably known to Sessily had taken her down the beach, murdered her, and set her body adrift in the longshore currents.

"This completes my statement. I now instruct everyone to avoid discussing the case with persons not employed by the Bureau, inasmuch as speculation, gossip and scandal will interfere with the continuing investigation. You may succinctly report what I have told you but no more. Am I clear? Persons found in violation of this order will be quite sorry.

"Tomorrow certain reassignments will be made. That is all."

As Scharde and Glawen were leaving, Kirdy Wook came after them. "You're wanted in the supervisor's office; don't ask me why; I just carry messages."

Scharde and Glawen climbed the stairs to Bodwyn Wook's office on the second floor. He greeted them with a wave of the hand. "Be seated, wherever you like. This is an informal meeting. Kirdy, make us a nice pot of tea, if you will; then you may go."

With a single gelid glance toward Glawen, whom he outranked, Kirdy went to the sideboard and busied himself with pot and hot water, then turned and started to leave. Bodwyn Wook, noticing Kirdy's stiff demeanor, called out: "On second thought, you might as well stay and add your wisdom, such as it is, to ours. We have some deep thinking to do, and we'll need all the convolutions available."

Kirdy gave a curt nod. "Just as you say, sir."

Bodwyn Wook turned to Scharde. "How did my statement go over?"

"Well enough, I would say. No one can contradict you."

"That's the way it shall be, then. Now, as to our investigation. I see it moving down two roads: first, the material you took from the truck. We'll want to analyze that and trace it to its source. Second, I received a most singular message today from Zamian the Yip. I will read it to you." He waited while Kirdy served tea and then seated himself.

Bodwyn Wook cleared his throat and looked down at a sheet of paper. "This is the message:

"Respectable Supervisor of the Investigation Forces
"Dear Sir:
"I hope that your work goes well so that crimes are halted here and everywhere. Be confident of my help.
"I am writing to let you know how I am doing, which is well. As I told you, with true honesty, I am sorry that I did not investigate all suspicious things as they occurred, and did not ask for the true explanation. But remember, please! I told you that I would not stop my thinking and now I see that my efforts have been good ones, and I have reached success, unless I am quite wrong, or if we cannot find some small funds to make a certain person feel that he does not take great risks for just 'Thank you! You are a truly fine man!' After all, remember this! Success costs money! But it is cheap, at any price.
"One more thing. I should not say this, but I feel that I must state: there is cause for hurry, since this gentleman may ask for money from another place. Such an act is wrong sometimes, but money is right all times. This is a little joke, but how true! Anyway, it would be wise tomorrow morning to let me know, with perhaps some kind generosity for me, too. I am, as always
    "Your good friend and helper,
        "Zamian Lemew Gabriskies."

Bodwyn Wook looked up from the message. "Zamian's attitudes are refreshingly artless; it is a pleasure following the flow of his thoughts. He is at all times lucid; one is never in doubt as to his desires, but he is as gentle as a bottlesnake stealing milk. No doubt he finds us equally quaint." Here Bodwyn Wook looked from face to face, then gave the letter a flick of the fingers. "Still, we are not poets nor are we sociologists, and we must not abandon ourselves to the delectations of either. Glawen, you have been brooding with obvious intensity. What are your opinions?"

"They are nothing so settled as opinions: speculations, rather."

"That is appropriate, under the circumstances. Proceed."

"First of all, Zamian's tone seems different, as if now he has something definite and new to sell. Probably this 'certain person' also worked in the kitchen or pantry near the loading dock—the source of information, so to speak. For some reason, Zamian and the 'certain person' seem to have been working at least half-independently, and

109

the 'person' seems to have discovered information which at the time Zamian neglected or was unable to get."

"That seems to hang together. Zamian now is the front man, and conducts negotiations from this end while the 'person' tries some blackmail. Presumably they have agreed to share proceeds. Kirdy, what is your analysis?"

"Sorry! I haven't thought all that deeply about the case, what with the other duties to which I was assigned—rather foolishly, so I feel."

Bodwyn Wook returned a bland grin to the remark. "You refer to that odious patrol of the compound? Who knows? You might have saved us the indignities of a screaming Yip riot or worse—if there is anything worse. They'd be nasty customers once they forgot the 'yes-sirs' and 'no-sirs.' Or they might remain polite, and it would be: 'Excuse me, sir; please hold still while I cut your nose off.' Ah well, Kirdy! Your gallant sacrifice brought us all peace of mind. It was by no means in vain!"

Glawen said: "Certainly I slept better, knowing that Kirdy and Arles were out there on guard."

"It was a noble episode," said Bodwyn Wook. "But back once more to Zamian and his intrigues. Scharde, what are your ideas?"

"Taking up where Glawen left off: we have Zamian and a 'certain person' in the kitchen, or pantry. What could the 'person' have seen that Zamian missed? He might have seen the murderer as he waited for Sessily. Or Zamian might have notified him that something was going on in the truck. They noticed its departure and resolved to watch for its return. Apparently Zamian was otherwise occupied and so the 'person' took care to watch and see who alighted from the truck on its return."

"Exactly so!" declared Bodwyn Wook. "That is my own reconstruction of events. Zamian at this time has committed himself to the pose of helping us and so lacks leverage. Or the 'person' decides to go it alone and freeze Zamian out. By means of this letter, Zamian ensures that he will get his share of any proceeds, either from us or by way of blackmail. He does not reckon that we too can go it alone and pay nothing to anyone." Bodwyn Wook reached in a drawer and brought out a folder. "These are statements from the kitchen help. Four Yips were on duty: Zamian and three others. Two of these were at all times occupied in food service and can be dismissed. Zamian and Xalanave had more general duties which took them into the pantry. I therefore nominate Xalanave as the 'certain person' and propose to put him through the wringer as soon as possible: let us say, tomorrow morning. Kirdy, you and Glawen pick him up and bring him here."

"At what time?"

"An hour or two into the morning."

"What of Zamian?"

"We'll take them separately. With any luck Xalanave will crack open the case for us."

For a moment the four sat thinking their separate thoughts, then Scharde said: "You may be overoptimistic. Remember the truck on its return was parked down at the other end of the dock. Xalanave would not have had a good view from the pantry."

"In that case, why would he not stroll down the dock until he could see as much as he liked? It is what I would do."

"Also, don't forget that the driver almost certainly wore costume."

"True again, and we know something about this costume. That shall be the second string to our bow. In any event we'll have the truth out of Xalanave tomorrow. Now, what about the fuzz or hair or whatever it is?"

"It seems to come from a shaggy brown fabric: a coarse rug, or imitation fur."

Bodwyn Wook gazed up toward the ceiling. "As I recall, Latuun's goat legs were covered with the stuff. Six Bold Lions, the bravos of Araminta Station, wore fur as they swaggered, staggered, pounced, lurched, romped, rambled and swilled wine."

Kirdy made an instant declaration: "Please exclude me; I drank very little!"

Bodwyn Wook paid no heed. "I saw a Kazakh robber with fur pants, a mang, and also a Tantic giant with a fur vest."

"The giant was a frame on Dalremy Diffin's shoulders. In that costume he could not conveniently have used the truck," said Scharde.

Again Bodwyn Wook ignored the remark. "No doubt there were others, but no need to explore these avenues until we make our inquiries of Xalanave. Junior Sergeant Kirdy and Cadet Glawen: here are your orders. Tomorrow morning go to the compound, make a proper and official approach to Xalanave and bring him here, at, let us say, two hours before noon; that should be convenient for all." Bodwyn Wook rose to his feet. "This has been a tiring day and I am off to bed."

8

Glawen was only just finishing his breakfast when Kirdy arrived. "I'll be right with you," said Glawen. "I did not expect you quite so early. Will you take a cup of tea?"

111

"No, thank you," said Kirdy, and added in a voice of bored disapproval: "I knew you would not be ready; that's why I came ten minutes early."

Glawen raised his eyebrows in wonder. "But I'll be ready in less than ten minutes. In fact, I'm ready now, as soon as I slip on my jacket."

Kirdy looked him up and down. "You're not going like that? Where is your uniform?"

"To go down to the compound? Do we need uniforms for that?"

"It's official business. We represent the Bureau." Kirdy himself was meticulously turned out in correct Bureau B sergeant's uniform. Glawen glanced at Scharde, who looked out the window.

"Oh, very well," said Glawen. "I suppose you are right. Just a moment. I'll still be ready on time."

Correctly attired, the two marched to the compound. Kirdy inquired at the entry office for Xalanave, and the attendant telephoned Xalanave's chambers.

No one responded. Investigation revealed that Xalanave was neither in his chambers nor anywhere in the compound.

The attendant suggested: "He may be working double-shift at the hotel; he'll do that once or twice a week."

A call to the Hotel Araminta kitchen revealed that Xalanave was not on the premises. "He worked the evening shift last night until midnight," stated the kitchen manager. "I don't expect him back until this afternoon."

"Thank you, sir," said Kirdy. "You have been very helpful."

"Wait!" said Glawen. "Ask if Xalanave received any calls during the evening, or if anything unusual happened."

Kirdy glanced at Glawen with a frown, then turned and spoke into the telephone; response came in the uncertain negative. Kirdy thereupon telephoned Bodwyn Wook, and explained the situation.

"Find Namour," said Bodwyn Wook. "Explain the circumstances to him, and ask him to find Xalanave. If he has any questions he can call me."

Namour's inquiries yielded no more information of significance. Xalanave had departed the Hotel Araminta kitchen at midnight and had not been seen since, by anyone who cared to admit to the meeting.

When Kirdy and Glawen, upon instructions from Bodwyn Wook, went to seek out Zamian, they were thwarted once again. Zamian, like Xalanave, was nowhere to be found within the precincts of Araminta Station, but for a different reason. Zamian had departed aboard the morning ferry to Yipton. A scrutiny of the passenger manifest indicated that the same was not true in the case of Xalanave, and there was a consensus at Bureau B that Xalanave had been attacked in the shadows at the back of the hotel, carried down to the hotel dock and dropped into the sea.

9

The day passed and the night which came after. Early in the morning, before dawn had lightened the sky, Scharde slipped from Clattuc House and set off down Wansey Way in the direction of the ocean.

The air was cool and still. No sound could be heard but the soft crisp scrape of Scharde's footsteps on the crushed-stone way. A high haze frosted the sky; Lorca and Sing, halfway down the west, swam in a pool of rose-pink luminosity; as Scharde passed under the riverbank poplars, he traversed spatters of wan rose light and black shade.

At the shore road, Scharde turned left and a few moments later came to the airfield. A drooping-eyed Chilke awaited him in the office.

Chilke's greeting was subdued. "This is not my time of day. All this wet dew and early birdcalls just irritate me. As I see it, the only good thing about morning is breakfast."

"At least you're happy and cheerful."

"Am I? I guess it's because the worst is over. I'll be back in bed before you're twenty feet off the ground."

The two went out to the flyer, which stood ready beside the hangar. Chilke watched as Scharde performed the routine preflight check.

"All in order," said Scharde. "Even the gun is loaded."

Chilke gave a sour chuckle. "You might find a sick fuel cell, or broken landing gear, or fused radio crystals, but there'll be a charge in the gun. That I guarantee. May I ask where you are going, as I am required to ask by regulation? And why so much stealth—which I am not required to ask?"

"Certainly you may ask. I'll even answer. I'm off for a day's fun at Yipton. If anyone else asks, I'm out on patrol."

"And why should anyone ask?"

"If I knew, I might not need to go. But I'm bound for the Lutwen Islands, and I'll be back before tonight if all goes well, as naturally it won't since nothing goes well at Yipton."

"Good luck to you, and my best to the Oomphaw."

Scharde took the flyer aloft and flew out over the ocean and away into the northeast, where dawn colors were now beginning to show.

113

Behind him Lorca and Sing cast a pink trail along the water, which presently became indistinct in the reflections of dawn.

Syrene appeared: a blue-white spark on the horizon, then a sliver, then a segment; in the west Lorca and Sing faded from view in the morning light.

Ahead a great float of dun-colored stuff lay flat upon the water: the Lutwen Atoll, a rim of narrow islands surrounding a shallow lagoon, now totally crusted over by the structures of Yipton. Details began to emerge from the haze: a veining of gunmetal waterways suddenly flashing silver when the sunlight struck at the proper angle.

Below, fishing boats had appeared on the face of the ocean: frail craft of tied bamboo bundles, propelled by sails of felted fiber.

The details of Yipton came into focus. Rickety structures two, three or four stories high supported a set of vast roofs, each of a thousand segments, each segment and slant a different shade of pallid brown—ash brown, dun, grayed umber, mud color. In nooks, crannies, corners grew clumps and tufts of bamboo, with coconut palms leaning seaward from laboriously formed little plots around the periphery of the islands.

Canals webbed Yipton without perceptible pattern, sometimes flowing in the open, sometimes disappearing into tunnels under the structure. Boats moved sluggishly along the canals, like corpuscles in an artery. Other boats lay at permanent mooring alongside the banks of the canals; from their minuscule braziers rose wisps of smoke, finally curling and folding, to disappear into the still morning air.

At the southern verge of Yipton stood the bizarre, fascinating and erratic shape of the famous Arkady Inn: a structure of five levels, a hundred swaying balconies, and a roof garden where the tourists dined to the light of colored lanterns, while Yip boys and girls performed acrobatic entertainments sometimes naive, always incomprehensible, to a thin music of flutes and soft bells, which, if beyond the appreciation of the tourists, at least created a soft and pleasant sound.

Beside the hotel a pier projected into the ocean, where the ferry to Araminta Station docked; beyond lay a minimal airstrip, with a surface of marl compounded from shells, fresh coral pulverized with mussel-like bivalves which yielded a tough adhesive. Scharde approached the landing strip from the sea, taking care not to fly above Yipton proper, so to avoid as long as possible the "Big Chife": next to Pussycat Palace the most notorious of all the strange and wonderful aspects of Yipton. Everywhere across the Gaean Reach, when knowledgeable talk turned to the subject of bad smells and intolerable stinks, someone would insist that the Big Chife of Yipton must be numbered high among the contenders.

114

A recipe for the Big Chife had been proposed in a semifacetious paper written on the subject by a savant in residence at Vagabond House:

The Big Chife
a tentative recipe

Ingredient	Parts per 100
Human exudations	25
Smoke and charred bones	8
Fish, fresh	1
Fish, rotting	8
Decaying coral (very bad)	20
Canal stink	15
Dry fronds, mats, bamboo	8
Complex cacodyls	13
Unguessable (bad)	2

Tourists were never notified in advance of the Big Chife, since their shock and confusion afforded a never-failing source of pleasure for the initiated. In any event, noses quickly became desensitized and the Big Chife lost its authority.

Scharde landed the flyer and stepped out upon the marl. With only a momentary wince for the Big Chife, he locked and sealed the flyer, though at Yipton pilferage was a relatively mild annoyance, through the orders of the Oomphaw, Titus Pompo.

Scharde climbed a flight of broad steps to the hotel verandah. A pair of houseboys, wearing short white aprons slit at the sides, embroidered vests, white gloves and small cylindrical white caps, came to take his luggage; discovering that he carried none, they stopped short in puzzlement, then quickly performed bows of welcome and retreated, twittering in amusement for the ridiculous outlander without luggage and their own mistake.

Scharde crossed the terrace and entered the broad airy lobby, which had been renovated since his last visit ten years previously. The bamboo walls were painted white; new rugs patterned in green and blue covered the floor; the furniture, of soft white wicker, was upholstered in pale sea green. Scharde was favorably impressed; he remembered dark varnished bamboo and spartan furniture, neither clean nor comfortable.

At this early hour only a few of the hotel guests had come down from their chambers. A dozen sat at breakfast on the terrace; another group stood in the center of the lobby discussing their plans for the day, which included a trip by gondola through the canals.

Scharde went to the registration counter. Behind sat four functionaries in crisp white uniforms. From the left ear of each dangled a black pearl on a silver chain, signifying a member of the Oomphaw's personal staff: an Oomp. One of these came to serve him: a person of early middle age, grave and handsome. He asked: "Sir, how long will you be staying with us?"

"Not long at all. I am Captain Scharde Clattuc of Bureau B at Araminta Station. Please inform Titus Pompo that I want a few words with him on an official matter, at his earliest convenience; in fact now, if possible."

The clerk glanced at his colleagues; the three, after quick curious glances to gauge Scharde's seriousness, or, perhaps, sanity, returned to their work, disassociating themselves from so bizarre a problem. The clerk who had come forward spoke carefully: "Sir, I will see that your message is immediately disposed for the Oomphaw's attention."

A nuance in the clerk's phrasing caught Scharde's attention. "What does that mean?"

The clerk smilingly explained: "The message will be expedited to the Oomphaw's offices. No doubt an appropriate member of the staff will deliver to you, probably today, an application form upon which you may freely explain your needs."

"You don't quite understand," said Scharde. "I don't care for an application form; I want a few words with Titus Pompo, as soon as possible. Now would not be too soon."

The clerk's smile became strained. "Sir, let me use an open vocabulary. You do not seem an impractical visionary, with eyes raised to the glory of the ineffable. Still you apparently expect me to run to the Oomphaw's bedchamber, shake him awake and say: 'Up, sir, and out of bed quickly! A gentleman wants to talk with you.' I must inform you that this is not feasible."

Scharde nodded. "You express yourself well. May I have a sheet of hotel stationery?"

"Of course. Here you are, sir."

"What is your name?"

The clerk raised his eyebrows in wary perplexity. "I am Euphorbius Leliantho Jantifer."

Scharde wrote on the paper for a moment, then said: "Please date and sign this document and ask your associates to sign as witnesses and participants."

The clerk, now concerned, read the document aloud in muttering

116

tones: "I, Euphorbius Leliantho Jantifer, affirm that on the morning of this date, I refused to notify Titus Pompo that Captain Scharde Clattuc of Bureau B, Araminta Station, had arrived to speak with him on urgent and official business. I admit that Captain Clattuc notified me that he could not wait upon formalities and must immediately return to Araminta Station, and that the penalties ensuing upon my act would include cessation of ferry service for an indefinite period, or until a fine of one thousand sols was paid over." He looked up with a sagging jaw.

"Just so," said Scharde. "Sign the paper, then I will go. There will be a final ferry to pick up persons now at the hotel, then no more. Sign, if you please—though of course it is not necessary, since there are witnesses to your conduct."

The clerk pushed the document away and managed an ironic grin. "Come, come, sir. This document is ridiculous, as you well know."

"I am going out upon the terrace for breakfast," said Scharde. "When I am finished I will return to Araminta Station, unless you bring me a definite response from Titus Pompo."

Euphorbius the clerk, now somewhat crestfallen, said: "Sir, you are truly most importunate. But I will see what can be done."

"Thank you." Scharde went out on the terrace, selected a wicker table under a pale green parasol and made a breakfast upon the piquant foods of Yipton.

Toward the end of his meal three members of Titus Pompo's elite Oomps marched out upon the terrace and approached his table. The officer in charge of the detail halted in front of Scharde, performed a crisp bow. "Sir, you are summoned by Titus Pompo the Oomphaw to an audience, at this moment."

Scharde rose to his feet. "Lead the way."

The Oomps marched from the terrace, with Scharde coming a few paces behind: across the lobby and into a fastness of corridors, dogleg halls, creaking bamboo stairs; past ranked doors and apertures giving into unlit spaces, up creaking bamboo stairs and down, high under the roof, where chinks in the palm fronds showed glints of light, low to where he could hear the plash of lagoon water around bamboo posts, finally through a bamboo door into a room furnished with a pink rug patterned in dark red and blue, a couch upholstered in deep rose-pink, with a pair of small side tables, each supporting a shaded lamp casting a subdued glow about the room.

Scharde advanced slowly into the room, looking right and left and not liking what he saw. He studied the couch a moment, then turned to examine the opposite wall, which was constructed of bamboo rods woven into a mesh, with interstices two inches square opening into dark space, or so it seemed.

The Oomp captain indicated the couch. "Be seated; make no disturbance."

The Oomps departed; Scharde was left alone. He stood listening. No sound could be heard, save a far faint all-pervading noise.

Scharde again examined the couch and the wall behind. He turned away and went to stand by the side wall. He was obviously under surveillance: possibly through the mesh. There seemed no reason, however, except for the joy of deceit for its own sake.

Scharde leaned back against the wall and settled himself for the wait which his ruffling of sensibilities almost guaranteed, and which a show of impatience could only extend. He closed his eyes and pretended to doze.

Minutes passed: ten, then fifteen, the irreducible minimum to be expected under the circumstances.

At half an hour, Scharde yawned and stretched, and began to consider his options, which at the moment were confined to waiting with all the dignity he could muster.

At about forty minutes, when "absentminded indifference, colored with contempt" began to verge into "purposeful insult,"[1] there came a scrape of movement in the space at the other side of the mesh.

A voice spoke: "Scharde Clattuc, what is your business with Titus Pompo?"

Scharde's diaphragm jerked and twitched, for reasons unclear, since the voice was unfamiliar. He asked: "Who is talking?"

"You may accept these as the words of Titus Pompo. Why are you

---

[1] Cultural psychologists have defined the symbology of "wait times" and its variation from culture to culture. The significance of the intervals is determined by a large number of factors, and the student can easily list for himself, out of his own experience, those which are relevant to his own culture.

"Wait times," in terms of social perception, range from no wait whatever to weeks and months. In one context a wait of five minutes will be interpreted as "unpardonable insolence"; at another time and place a wait of only three days is considered a signal of benign favor.

The use of an exactly calculated wait time, as every person familiar with the conventions of his own culture understands, can be used as an assertion of dominance, or "putting one in one's place," by legal and nonviolent methods.

The subject has many fascinating ramifications. For instance, Person A wishes to assert his superior status over Person B, and keeps him waiting an hour. At the thirty-minute mark, which B already feels to be unacceptable and humiliating, A sends B a small tray of tea and sweetcakes, a gesture which B cannot rebuff without loss of dignity. A thereby forces B to wait a full hour and B must also thank A for his graciousness and bounty in the matter of the inexpensive refreshments. When well-executed, this is a beautiful tactic.

not using the couch which was provided for your convenience?"

"That was a kind thought, but I don't like the color."

"Really? It is my favorite."

"The couch also looks as if it might fold suddenly backward when one least expected it. I prefer not to risk pranks of this sort."

"You have an uneasy temperament!"

"Still, I am visible . . . No doubt you have good reasons for not showing yourself."

There was silence for a moody few seconds, then: "In response to your demands, an audience has been conceded to you; do not waste the occasion by belaboring the obvious." The voice, of neutral timbre and measured intonation, seemed almost mechanical, and rasped, as if it had been modified by overloaded filters.

"I will try to keep to the business at hand," said Scharde. "This is a recent murder at Araminta Station. There was a witness, or a near-witness, named Zamian Lemew Gabriskies. He is now here at Yipton. I therefore request that you find this person and give him into my custody."

"Certainly, and without hesitation! But I must charge you a service fee of one thousand sols."

"You will be paid nothing for conduct required of you by the law, which you know as well as I do, perhaps better."

"I know your law, certainly, but on the Lutwen Islands we use my law."

"Not so. I agree that you exercise a personal rule here, but only by default, in the absence of established authority, which may be re-asserted at any time. The situation is tolerated only as a temporary stopgap, and because, in general, proper social order seems to be maintained—give or take a few distasteful circumstances. In other words you are allowed to rule because it is expedient, not because you have the acknowledged right to do so. The moment you step out of line and start flouting established law, this temporary accommodation comes to an end."

"Use whatever words you like," said the voice. "The Lutwen Islands are in fact independent, like it or not. Let us all recognize reality, starting with the Conservator. His penalties are insufferably impertinent."

"I know nothing of penalties."

"You haven't heard the news? The Conservator now allows us payment only in scrip. Tourists are no longer allowed to bring sols to Lutwen City: only scrip, which then must be spent at the Araminta commissary for approved goods."

Scharde chuckled. "Evidently weapons are not on the list."

"I assume as much. The tactic is inept. We acquire as much hard currency as we need."

"How is that accomplished?"

"I see no need to advertise our resources."

Scharde shrugged. "As you like. I am not here to discuss politics with you. I only want Zamian."

"And you shall have him. My inquiries are complete, and I too regard him as a miscreant. He worked for private gain at detriment to my personal interests."

Scharde chuckled again. "In other words, he failed to cut you in for a share of the loot."

"Just so. He intended blackmail for his personal profit alone. He gave you to believe that one Xalanave was the blackmailer. In fact, Xalanave knew nothing, but nevertheless was killed."

"By whom?"

"That is irrelevant, from my point of view. I pressed no inquiries in that direction."

The statement, so Scharde noted, was not altogether responsive. He said: "I still do not grasp your meaning. Do you or do you not presume to know?"

"I see no reason to speculate—other than to cite the possibility that Zamian himself might be, in this case, guilty."

"That's not a reasonable theory," said Scharde. "If Xalanave in fact knew nothing of the original crime, Zamian had not the slightest reason either to harm him or to leave Araminta Station. It seems clear that he fled out of fear. If we extend this idea further . . ." Scharde fell silent.

"Continue," said Titus Pompo softly, and even the electronic transvocalization failed to eliminate an overtone of mockery, or savage glee.

"Like you, I don't care to speculate," said Scharde. "I am anxious only to hear what Zamian can tell me."

"Now it's Zamian you want? Go out into the corridor, descend the stairs; in the chamber immediately to the right you will find Zamian and members of the Oomps, who will conduct you to your flyer."

"I will intrude upon your time no longer. Thank you for your courtesy."

From behind the mesh came only silence; Scharde could not determine whether or not someone still stood there, watching him from the dark.

Beset by an emotion akin to claustrophobia, Scharde turned and marched on long strides from the room. He strode heavily down the corridor, descended the stairs. On his right hand he found a bamboo door, painted dull red, which he pushed open. An Oomp sitting on a bench by the wall rose to his feet. "You are here for Zamian?"

Scharde looked around the room. "Where is he?"

"Over here in the hole, for safekeeping. He was a kitchen helper? Don't expect him to do his work like before; he's been used a bit." The Oomp went to where a rope hung from a windlass into a hole in the floor, and turned the windlass crank. Scharde looked into the hole. Ten feet below, the dim light revealed mounds and flats of black slime laced by rivulets of lagoon water. The rope stretched to the head of a naked man floundering in the slime. His arms had been taped behind his back; a strip of tape covered his mouth. He heaved and squirmed against the attack of what seemed to be a hybrid of rats and children, with mottled dark skin, pointed nonhuman faces. They gnawed at what remained of his legs and burrowed into his abdomen with furious avidity, and only reluctantly dropped away when the Oomp worked the windlass to lift Zamian from the slime, by the rope which had been glued into the hair of his scalp.

Zamian's head appeared above floor level, then his torso. "The yoots have been getting to him," said the Oomp. "I don't know what good he'll be to you now."

"Probably none," said Scharde.

Zamian still lived. He saw Scharde with recognition, and made noises behind the tape.

Scharde jumped forward, cut away the tape. "Zamian! Do you hear me?"

The Oomp said: "He can't talk, much less think; he's been dosed with nene so that he spilled all he knew to the Oomphaw. Now there's nothing left. That's the good and bad of the stuff. Still, he's yours; take him away."

"Just a minute," said Scharde. "Zamian! It's Scharde! Speak to me!"

Zamian made incomprehensible wet noises.

"Zamian, answer! Who drove the truck? Who killed the girl?"

Zamian's face contorted. His mouth opened; his voice came clear. "When he came back I saw his fur. But no head."

"Who was it? Do you know his name?"

The Oomp said: "Take him if you want him; I'll hold him no longer."

"One moment," said Scharde, and to Zamian: "Tell me his name!"

The Oomp walked away from the windlass. The drum sang; the rope ran free; Zamian disappeared into the hole. Scharde uttered a sick groan, squeezed his eyes shut and held back from an attack on the Oomp.

Scharde looked down into the hole. The yoots had rushed back;

Zamian sat staring at them in confusion as they tore at his body. His world had become constricted; it seemed certain that he would have no more to say.

Scharde turned away. In a flat voice he said: "I'll go now to my flyer. I'm done here."

10

Glawen, meanwhile, had risen at his usual hour, taken a solitary breakfast and spent the morning dealing with neglected tasks, and preparations for the resumption of classes after the Parilia recess.

An hour before noon he received a telephone call. "Glawen Clattuc here."

A small clear voice responded. "Glawen, this is Miranda. I've discovered something very odd and I want to talk to you about it."

"Certainly; talk away. What's it all about?"

"Glawen! Not over the telephone!" Miranda's voice faded momentarily.

Glawen called out: "Are you still there?"

"I was looking over my shoulder; I'm starting to be nervous about noises. Properly so, in this case, since the noise was Mother."

"Very well; we'll talk. Shall I come to Veder House?"

"No. I'll meet you down in the Way, in about ten minutes."

"I'll be there."

Glawen arrived at the rendezvous a minute early, and watched as Miranda came running down the avenue from Veder House: a slim big-eyed little creature with a mop of brown curls, keenly aware of her own importance, at least within the realms of her private universe. Glawen, waiting in the shadow of the gateposts, thought that she seemed subdued and uneasy.

Miranda arrived breathless at the bottom of the avenue. Glawen stepped forward. "I'm over here."

Miranda jerked around. "Oh—I didn't see you at first. I was startled."

"Sorry," said Glawen. "What's the problem?"

"Come along," said Miranda. "I don't want to talk here."

"Whatever you say. But at least tell me where we're going."

"To Archives."

The two went up Wansey Way in the tree shadows, past the Arbor and along the riverside path to the venerable Old Agency.

As they walked, Miranda began to talk, at first in disconnected ideas: "—all the time, as if she's sitting just out of sight . . . Sometimes I think I've gone just a bit crazy, or become old ten or twenty years too soon."

"That's an original thought, certainly," said Glawen. "As far as that goes, I suddenly feel old as the hills."

Preoccupied with her own thoughts, Miranda hardly heard him. "I don't like the way I feel, so full of hate that I get sick in my throat . . . One night while I lay in bed I tried to imagine how it happened. Whoever did it must have watched Sessily during the Phantasmagoria, but before the end he went around to the back and hid in the truck."

Glawen asked in surprise: "How do you know about the truck? That's supposed to be a secret."

"I heard Mother and Father talking when they thought I couldn't hear. Anyway, I thought of the Archive cameras; they must have photographed him going around to the loading dock."

"That's very sensible. Even the Bureau B staff thought of it. Captain Rune Offaw has been studying the photographs every day."

"I know. He's taken spools away from me several times."

"Ah, I see! You've been down in the Archives, helping Bureau B study the photographs!"

Miranda gave him a reproachful look. "Glawen, are you laughing at me? Before even seeing what I have to show you?"

"Not really. And I admit that I'm curious."

Miranda acknowledged the response with a dignified nod as they entered the Old Agency.

The two went down the wide hall, footsteps echoing from the marble floors and odd intricate walls of cast iron and greenstone medallions. Miranda said thoughtfully: "Perhaps I had better tell you what I was looking for."

"I think I know. Someone going around to the back of the Orpheum."

"Someone wearing fur. Like Latuun, or a Bold Lion, or one or two others."

"So you know about the fur too."

"Why shouldn't I know?"

"No reason, I suppose. Especially if you found something."

"I'll show you!"

Miranda tugged open the heavy door; the two entered the stately precincts of Bureau A. Miranda led the way to a counter, filled out a slip and dropped it into a slot; a moment later she was tendered a small black box.

The two went into a viewing chamber. Miranda dimmed the light and started the projection. "The first time I did this I could hardly bear to look at Sessily. Now I just don't think about it anymore. I guess I've become hard-hearted, or something of the sort." There was a break in her voice. "I guess not altogether. Still, don't worry. I won't start crying or fling myself on the floor."

Glawen patted her head and ruffled her hair. "In my opinion, Squeaker, you're uncommonly wise for your age."

"You are too, for that matter. Also, if you don't mind—"

"It was a mistake. I'll be more careful."

Miranda gave a curt nod. "I've looked at all the spools a dozen times. Often they show the same area from different angles, so that you see everyone present. The archivists haven't completely finished yet, but almost everyone has been identified. For instance—" Miranda worked buttons to bring a tracer-spark down the screen. She stopped it on one of the faces and touched another button. A name appeared at the bottom of the screen: GLAWEN CLATTUC. "Of course, I wasn't looking for you. I wanted to find someone skulking around to the back of the Orpheum. But whoever did it was careful to keep away from the cameras and I found nothing. After a bit, I started using the zoom, looking here and there, with nothing particular in mind. And I happened, by sheer chance, to notice this."

11

Bodwyn Wook and his captains met in the high-ceilinged office on the second floor of the New Agency. After the customary small talk Bodwyn Wook leaned back into the depths of his massive black chair. "I'll now hear reports. Captain Laverty?"

Ysel Laverty said: "I've been working with fibers taken from the floor of the truck. They turn out to be synthetic stuff, produced off-world, probably on Soum. I have secured samples from what I shall call 'hairy' costumes, including Latuun's legs, the Bold Lion pelts, and a number of others. I have had ambiguous results. The fiber exactly matches only the fur from Latuun's legs, although I discovered a number of close similarities among the Bold Lion costumes. How did these folk account for their time? Two of the Bold Lions, Arles Clattuc and Kirdy Wook, were occupied patrolling the Yip compound; the other six Bold Lions were here and there, but often enough in the purview of reputable witnesses during the critical time as to eliminate them from suspicion. Latuun, or, I should say, Namour, states that for a time he stepped the pavane with Spanchetta Clattuc, then strolled around, but never left the environs of the Quadrangle. Spanchetta corroborates the statement, as do other witnesses; despite the evidence of the fur, we must also dismiss Namour. So then—" Ysel Laverty flung out his hands in a gesture of frustration. "What remains? In connection with the fur, very little, if anything. According to Namour, his costume came from the Mummers' wardrobe. Floreste got the material off-world specially for 'primordial' costumes; and a swatch or two was left over. I won't say the mystery is deeper than before, but it certainly hasn't been clarified."

"This bears thinking about," said Bodwyn Wook. "Who's next? Scharde?"

"I learned a great deal at Yipton," said Scharde. "In fact, considerably more than I wanted to know. But not much seems to bear on our case. I did not see Titus Pompo; he takes obsessive precautions to hide himself; he is a mystery in himself that we should take steps to solve. I talked with him, and after a fashion heard his voice."

Bodwyn Wook looked at him with eyebrows raised high. "After a fashion? Either you heard him or you did not hear him. Please elucidate."

"I heard what I think to be a re-creation of his voice. Analogues of his words, if you like. I suspect that when he spoke, his words were piped into a transvocalizing machine, broken into digits, then re-formed into new sounds, with dials set to eliminate lilt, adjust the pacing, then alter timbre, pitch and overtones. In the end the voice had no more character than a video-cell reading a printed page. And still it made a connection in my head. I'm convinced that I've heard that voice before."

"Very well," said Bodwyn Wook. "So much for the voice. Now, then: tell us what happened."

Scharde described his experiences. "Somebody made a mistake and Zamian managed to transmit a few words of information. He said, quite clearly: 'When he came back I saw his fur. But no head.'"

"Ha!" Bodwyn Wook struck the table with his hand. "So we can't simply disregard Ysel Laverty's work, after all!"

"True. We can also deduce that the man was not Namour, whom Zamian naturally knew well and had no reason to protect, so far as I know. Zamian was dying and in shock. Nothing he said can be trusted completely. As for the phrase 'but no head'—I would guess that the murderer took off the head to his costume, if only to drive the truck more easily. There's room for speculation here, but personally, I don't feel it's worth the effort."

Bodwyn Wook looked around the table. "Captain Rune Offaw,

125

what is your news? You are suspiciously serene, and I detect in you that rather tiresome suggestion of omniscience which over the years has vitiated the popularity of the Offaws."

"It is comparison with the Wooks which makes the Offaws seem so effortlessly able. Still, in the case at hand, I believe that I can at least provide an iota of progress, and at best nip up our criminal by the heels."

"That is cheerful stuff indeed! Well, then: what do the cameras tell us? Did Namour 'tread measure after measure of dreamy delight' with Dame Spanchetta as he claims, or did he pursue 'pleasures more ghastsome and dire'? In short: is he guilty of this one crime? Or, as is more likely, half guilty of twenty others?"

"In this case, at least, Namour seems safely in the clear," said Rune Offaw. "Without shame he treads the measures and twirls Spanchetta this way and that with reckless aplomb. Not for the whole three hours, of course, but well past the critical time. Strike Namour from the list, fibers or no fibers. The same tiresome pattern applies across the board. Everyone even remotely under suspicion is shown doing what he claims he was doing.

"Except in one case. Yesterday, a mixture of diligence and luck yielded a significant fact." (The "luck" was Glawen's insistence that Miranda report her findings to Rune Offaw. "Let him take care of the news! He'll be a useful friend and you won't make enemies elsewhere.") "I found, as might be expected, that the movements of the Bold Lions during the critical time were much less structured and static than those of other folk. Still, I managed well enough, and accounted for all eight: Arles Clattuc and Kirdy Wook marching patrol, and I have here a copy of their sign-in sheet, one signature and a countersignature each half hour, signifying a patrol out and back. The other six Bold Lions were not so easy to account for, but I had no real problem. So: eight Bold Lions; like Namour, off the list. At this point, when I was about ready to put the job aside, my attention was called to a furtive shape in the shadows behind the Arbor, just barely within the camera's field. I applied both zoom and enhancement and came up with this." Rune Offaw, working the controls of Bodwyn Wook's video equipment, brought an image to the wall screen. "It is a Bold Lion and a great mystery, since all are accounted for! As the figure moves, it becomes recognizable as Arles Clattuc, purportedly on patrol at the Yip compound. The time is right; Sessily is still on the pedestal. He could be our man."

"Ha-ha!" said Bodwyn Wook. "The good dutiful Arles! Has he been approached, or questioned?"

"No. I thought that we should jointly consider how best to handle the matter. Sergeant Kirdy Wook, also on duty, would seem to have serious questions to answer, such as why he failed to report Arles' dereliction when the fact would obviously have bearing upon our investigation."

"Hm," said Bodwyn Wook. "That question at least is easily asked— if perhaps not so easily answered. First, let me see that patrol record."

Rune Offaw passed over the sheet. "You will notice that on the three nights previous the sign-ins were occasionally done by Arles: two or three each night, although Kirdy, being the superior officer, signed in most of the patrols. On the night of the murder Kirdy signs them all."

Bodwyn Wook looked around the table. "Well, gentlemen? Are there any comments?"

Ysel Laverty said: "There are still the fibers to be explained. The murderer wore fur; fibers were found in the truck. But the fibers from Arles' costume don't match the fibers in the truck. Hence, Arles cannot be proved guilty."

Bodwyn Wook said: "He might have had two costumes, old and new. Well, there's no help for it; we must ask Arles some questions, before the day is any older. I'll take care of Kirdy later."

"Now is as good a time as any," said Scharde. "It's still early; Arles will be in his chambers. So will Spanchetta."

Rune Offaw said thoughtfully: "I have some urgent affairs, and there would seem no need for the four of us."

Ysel Laverty said quickly: "A mound of paper is swallowing my desk; I must take care of it this morning, or both desk and I may disappear forever."

"Hmmf," said Bodwyn Wook. "I'm not afraid of Spanchetta." He spoke into the mesh. "Who's in the office? I need an experienced man, large, tough, quick on his feet and lacking all fear. Who is available?"

"Sorry, sir. There's no one in the office now except Cadet Glawen Clattuc."

Bodwyn Wook looked sidewise at Scharde. "Glawen, eh? He'll do admirably. Have him report to my office in uniform, at once."

12

Bodwyn Wook, Scharde and Glawen presented themselves at the door to the apartment in Clattuc House occupied by Millis, Spanchetta and Arles. Bodwyn Wook touched the call button, and a footman admitted them to the foyer: an octagonal chamber furnished with a central octagonal settee upholstered in green silk. Four alcoves dis-

127

played four fine cinnabar urns in which bouquets of glass flowers had been carefully arranged. At the end of the room, a pedestal carved of black chert supported a silver censer from which smoldering incense sent a wavering ribbon of smoke into the air.

Bodwyn Wook looked critically around the room. "I find this neo-classic romanticism a bit overwhelming. No doubt it is the preference of Millis. I am told that Spanchetta's tastes are simple and modest."

"That would be my guess," said Scharde.

"A pity we won't have the pleasure of seeing Spanchetta today," said Bodwyn Wook. "But there may be another occasion soon, should Arles be executed."

Spanchetta swept into the room, still wearing her morning gown of ruffled and pleated lilac satin, with slippers of pink fluff. Her tumultuous masses of dark curls were constrained in a lace cylinder which let a number of vagrant ringlets overflow the top. She looked from face to face. "What is all this hurly-burly? Bodwyn Wook. Scharde. And who is that? Glawen? In a uniform? An imposing group of dignitaries."

Bodwyn Wook performed a curt bow. "I fear that there has been a mistake; we asked for Arles."

"Arles is resting. What is the problem?"

"Principally, it seems to be that when we ask to see Arles, you appear."

"What of that? I am his mother."

"Just so. Still, as our uniforms indicate, we are here in an official capacity and in fact are investigating the murder of Sessily Veder."

Spanchetta threw back her head and half lowered her heavy eyelids. "Murder? Must you use that dreadful word when the case has not yet been proved? I have had it on excellent authority that she simply skipped away with an off-world lover, in a most irresponsible fashion. In any event, the case cannot conceivably concern Arles."

"This is what we hope to establish. Please bring him here, instantly, or I will ask Sergeant Glawen Clattuc to bring him out by force, if necessary."

Spanchetta gave Glawen a glacial glare, then said: "That will not be necessary. I will see if he wants to talk to you." She swung about and departed the room.

Ten minutes passed, during which Spanchetta's passionate contralto and Arles' grumbling tones could faintly be heard through the walls.

At last Arles shuffled into the room, wearing a brown daygown and red leather slippers of extravagant cut. For a moment he hesitated in the doorway, looking from face to face, then was impelled forward by Spanchetta.

Bodwyn Wook said: "I suggest that we remove into the parlor, where we can ask our questions in greater comfort."

"Come," said Spanchetta curtly, and led the way into the adjoining parlor.

"This will do nicely," said Bodwyn Wook. "Arles, sit yonder if you will. Spanchetta, we will need you no longer: you may go."

"Just a moment!" snapped Spanchetta. "Of what is Arles accused?"

"At the moment there are no charges. Arles, if you wish, you may have Fratano present, or another adviser, or even your mother; or you may choose to speak to us alone or, finally, simply refuse to talk. In the latter case, you will be taken into custody, charged and prosecuted."

"On what grounds?" cried Spanchetta. "I demand to know!"

"Oh—no doubt we can scratch up something. Arles, have you any ideas?"

Arles licked his heavy lips and looked sidewise toward his mother. In a peevish voice he said: "I don't need anyone's advice. I prefer to talk to you alone."

Spanchetta finally departed and Scharde closed the door behind her.

"Now, then," said Bodwyn Wook, "answer our questions simply, directly and without evasion. You are not required to inculpate yourself, but you must report the guilt of any other person. To begin with: do you know who killed Sessily Veder?"

"Of course not!"

"Describe in careful detail your actions the night she was killed."

Arles cleared his throat. "Whatever I did, it had nothing to do with Sessily."

"So you say. We know that you abandoned your post at the compound, dressed in Bold Lion costume and were seen returning the winery truck to its place at the loading dock."

"That's not possible," said Arles. "I wasn't there. Your information is wrong."

"Where were you?"

Arles looked toward the door and spoke in a low voice. "I had an appointment with a young lady. I had made it before I knew about the patrol and I didn't want to break it."

"Who was the young lady?"

Arles darted another glance toward the door and spoke in a voice so low as almost to be inaudible. "It's someone my mother does not like. She would fall into a rage if she knew."

"Who is the girl?"

"Will my mother find out?"

"Quite possibly. Your misconduct cannot be concealed, and no doubt you will be duly punished."

"Punished for what? It was sheer foolishness, parading along that fence in the dark. One person on patrol was just as good as two."

"That may well be. Why did not Kirdy report your absence?"

"He knew where I was going; he knew I had been there and nowhere else. He realized that under the circumstances, such a report would cause a great hullabaloo over nothing. So he agreed to say nothing. We're both Bold Lions, don't forget!"

"I'll keep that in mind. You'll be able to practice roars while you are being flogged."

"Flogged?" Arles' voice rose in pitch.

"I can't predict the penalty. You probably won't get what you deserve. Who was the young lady?"

"A girl I knew from the Mummers. Her name is Drusilla co-Laverty."

"And where did you spend time?"

"In a dark corner of the Arbor, where we could watch the Phantasmagoria. Afterward we just sat there talking."

"Did anyone see you?"

"Of course. Lots of people. I don't know if anyone took any particular notice."

There was a pause. Glawen asked a question. "What of your costume? Did you bring that with you on patrol?"

Arles merely shrugged, apparently regarding questions from Glawen as below his dignity. Bodwyn Wook said gently: "Answer the question."

"I left my costume at Clattuc House. I didn't want to waste time so I went into the Mummers' warehouse and used a primordial costume, with a kind of gargoyle head. No one noticed the difference. Not even the Bold Lions."

"I see. Then what?"

"Before midnight I dropped off the costume and went back on duty and discovered all the patrols had been signed off. Nothing had gone wrong and I felt that I had done no great harm."

Bodwyn Wook shook his head in deep disparagement. "It is not a pretty story," he said in his reediest, most nasal voice. "You have scamped your duty. You have falsified official documents and trespassed on the trust of your superior officer . . . What are you saying?"

Arles, who had been trying to interject a remark, apparently in his own defense, thought better of it. "Nothing," he said in surly tones. "Nothing whatever."

Bodwyn Wook threw the papers down on the desk. "Whatever else you have done we will discover in due course. You may go now."

CHAPTER 3

1

Days went past, then weeks. Autumn settled into winter and the rhythm of the seasons, broken by tinkling spangling many-colored Parilia, resumed. The disappearance of Sessily Veder receded into the past; public outrage lost its edge, even though everyone knew that somewhere among them walked a man with a dreadful secret behind his face.

The urgency of Glawen's emotions likewise dwindled, although often at night he lay staring into the dark, trying to look into the face of the murderer. At times he felt himself standing on the loading dock with the event occurring before his eyes. There! The truck and there in the cargo space! a silent dark shape. And here came Sessily: running as fast as butterfly wings allowed: out upon the dock, stopping short and innocently approaching the truck at a call from someone she knew, while Glawen strained to drive his vision into the face which Sessily saw as she approached the truck. At times Glawen glimpsed the features of Arles, but often the face remained no more than a pallid blur.

By all tenets of logic—so Glawen told himself—the guilty person was Arles. Drusilla had proved an extremely weak reed when asked to verify Arles' account of the evening. Her manner was careless and flippant; the alibi she provided Arles was almost worse than none at all.

The interview with Drusilla had been conducted on the seaside terrace of the Hotel Araminta, where Drusilla had just finished her breakfast. Now she sat sidewise on a bench, arms clasping her knees, a breeze rippling her pale pinkish-blond hair, her lavish buttocks stretching taut the fabric of her white knee-length trousers. As she thought back to the fateful night of the Grand Masque, a coy smile brought dimples to her cheeks.

"Do you want the plain truth? You do? Then here it is! I was drunk, far beyond the call of duty." She shook her head in rueful pride for the magnitude of her achievement. "No question about it, and I feel no remorse whatever. I had just decided that everyone I knew was either a sour fish, a yahoo or a stinken scoundrel. I was furious with Florrie"— here she referred to Floreste— "and my fiancé just laughed when I told him about it. That's Namour, as you probably know: charming and debonair, but something of a cad. I really don't know how I put up with him! Spanchetta, strange to say, can twist him around her finger. My word, how she hates me! Foof!" The sound was intended to convey the intensity of Spanchetta's dislike. "Anyway I thought I'd just show them all; I went tinkety-tanko and had a famous time all to myself, and I still don't care!"

"What of Arles?"

"Yes, true. Arles was there, for a while—I remember watching part of the Phantasmagoria with him; we couldn't miss that since we're both Mummers. But I haven't a clue as to what happened next—at least after he tried to take me off down the riverbank—I remember that well enough—but I wouldn't go, down there among all those frogs and brambles and pinchbugs, and he marched off in a huff. After that it's all a great glorious whirl. I think I went to sleep on the bench; at least that's where I woke up, and it was already long after midnight, with the dismasking already done. Arles came back and I made him take me home, as I wasn't feeling my best."

Drusilla's testimony brought only gloom to Bureau B. Arles was considered probably guilty, but no one could formulate a decisive case against him, since another person, using the second primordial costume, could easily have done the deed.

The uncertainty was reinforced by a peculiar circumstance, which cost Sergeant Kirdy Wook dear. He was ordered to go to the Mummers' wardrobe and take the two primordial costumes into custody. The time was late in the day; Kirdy's schoolwork urgently needed attention; he postponed the task until the next day. At that time, when he went to take up the costumes, they were gone, and the wardrobe attendant could only say that they had been there the day previously.

Kirdy's negligence on this occasion, compounded by his failure to report Arles' absence from patrol, earned him a demotion and a reprimand from Bodwyn Wook.

Kirdy listened to the admonitions with a wooden half-smiling composure which only irritated Bodwyn Wook the more. He snapped: "Well, then, sir, what do you have to say for yourself?"

Kirdy said: "I was prepared for the reprimand and I accepted it, as I'm sure you noticed, with good grace. The demotion however is excessive, and truly not fair!"

"Indeed!" said Bodwyn Wook. "How so?"

Kirdy frowningly considered the matter and expressed himself as delicately as he could. "Sometimes, sir, a person must be guided by his principles."

The statement jerked Bodwyn Wook bolt upright in his chair. He responded in a voice ominously gentle: "You feel then that the orders of your superiors must run in concert with your personal convictions before you feel obliged to obey them?"

Kirdy hesitated, then said: "I suppose that, to be honest, I would have to answer yes."

"Amazing. Where and how did you develop this inconvenient idea?"

Kirdy shrugged. "Last summer with the Mummers I did a great deal of thinking, and also exchanged views with Floreste."

Bodwyn Wook eased back into the depths of his chair. He placed the tips of his fingers together and studied the ceiling. At last he said: "Ha-hah! Let us review your case."

"That was what I hoped you'd say, sir."

Bodwyn Wook paid him no heed. "First, you are a Wook. Few Wooks indeed have become prancing, dancing, gallivanting performers. We do not consider histrionics to be a dignified profession. Therefore I make the following analysis with extreme reluctance."

Kirdy's large earnest features sagged. "And how is that, sir?"

Bodwyn Wook slowly brought his gaze down from the ceiling. "On the basis of what you have told me, you apparently have two options for a career: the Mummers or Bureau B. Much can be said for the Mummers. You can indulge your fantasies to the utmost, and your temperament is allowed full sway. If you are chanting a popular ditty and Floreste requires that you make an ogling grimace to the right while thrusting your pelvis to the left, you can claim that your 'principles' stand in the way. Floreste will perhaps blink at you nonplussed, but because of his insights, he will concede your right to thrust your pelvis in whatever direction you choose. So much for the Mummers. At Bureau B conditions are different. Oh my word but they are different! Here 'principles' mean the same as orders from high-ranking officers. The philosophy which guides your professional life is not your own, not Floreste's, but mine. Is all this absolutely clear?"

"Certainly, but surely there are—"

"None whatever."

"What if I am ordered to perform tasks contrary to my conscience?"

"If you have even a twinge of apprehension, as of this instant I will accept your resignation from Bureau B."

Kirdy said mulishly: "I could with as much justice ask you to resign."

Bodwyn Wook could not restrain a chuckle. "So you could. In five seconds, which of us do you think would be ejected from the office?"

Kirdy stood silent, his large pink features disconsolate.

Bodwyn Wook asked briskly: "Well, then: which is it to be?"

"It is obviously in my best interests to make a career with Bureau B."

"That is not the point, and you have not answered my question."

"I choose Bureau B. I have no choice."

"And what of the 'principles'?"

Kirdy's round blue eyes were limpid with hurt and resentment. "I suppose that I must compromise them."

"Very well." Bodwyn Wook jerked his thumb toward the door. "That is all."

Kirdy made a final bitter complaint: "I still do not consider the demotion justified!"

"That sort of reaction is not unusual," said Bodwyn Wook. "Out with you, before I stop laughing and start thinking."

Kirdy swung about and departed.

2

Winter ran its course and spring came to Araminta Station. Grudgingly the obsessions which gripped Glawen's mind yielded to the vernal influences. He had done his utmost; he could do no more—at least, not for the moment. Sessily Veder receded to a melancholy ache in his memory.

Glawen turned his pent energies into schoolwork and gained his usual high levels of achievement. Arles, compelled by the most urgent pressures, performed well enough to avert the imminence of expulsion.

The year went its course, and another year followed. Glawen arrived at his nineteenth birthday with an SI, or Status Index, of 23: somewhat too high for comfort, and Glawen began to feel cold fingers of apprehension, although Scharde assured him that there was definitely no cause for panic. "At least not yet," said Scharde.

In the three years since his sixteenth birthday Glawen had changed little. He had grown as tall as Scharde, and from some source had gained an indefinable air of competence and decision, which was almost precocious. Like Scharde he was now spare and slender, with square shoulders and narrow hips. Again like Scharde, he carried himself with an understated economy of motion, almost elegant in its simplicity. His face, while less gaunt, bony and predacious than that of Scharde, was further softened by luminous dark hazel eyes, a cap of short thick black hair and a long generous mouth with a pensive droop at the corners: a face somewhat irregular and by no means classically handsome but one which romantic maidens found fascinating to consider. Glawen nowadays seldom thought of Sessily Veder except sometimes when he walked alone in the country or stood on the shore looking out to sea, when he might whisper: "Sessily, Sessily, where have you gone? Is it lonesome out there?"

Across the years the facts of the case, as known to Bureau B, had seeped into the public awareness, and Arles' guilt had become accepted as fact, provable or not. The situation titillated some and repelled others, while Spanchetta could hardly speak for mortification. Only the Bold Lions provided refuge for Arles—not so much from either loyalty or tolerance, but because it was felt that Arles' membership lent a special rakehelly devil-take-all panache to the group.

As the months and years passed, folk of the station became inured to his presence. Arles gradually regained something of his former standing, and in due course swaggered about affairs with near his old aplomb, although now his wit had a truculent overtone which seemed to imply: "So you take me for a deviate and a murderer? Very well, if that's what you think, don't be surprised by what you get, and be damned to all of you!"

With the coming of summer Arles went off-world with the Mummers, where he functioned as Floreste's aide, and the atmosphere at Araminta Station seemed easier and lighter for his absence.

Glawen's SI dramatically improved, by reason of a death and a retirement, which brought his number down to an encouraging 21, an almost sure guarantee of Agency status, and a great weight was lifted from his soul.

Another noteworthy event marked the end of summer: the return of Milo and Wayness Tamm from a long sojourn on Earth. They took up residence at Riverview House, and enrolled for the fall term at the lyceum.

Their presence gave rise to a flutter of discussion. According to the stereotypes of Araminta Station, Naturalists tended to be odd, crotchety and unconventional, with puritanical tendencies. Milo and Wayness, however, confounded the popular expectation. Both were conspicuously clean, intelligent and well-favored; both wore their simple Earth-style clothes with flair; both conducted themselves with a total lack of either self-consciousness or affectation: all of which aroused not a few pangs of envy and sniffs of deprecation among those who regarded themselves as the arbiters of taste.

Glawen found the two much as before. Milo, tall and austerely handsome, still seemed wry, clever and saturnine: an intellectual aristocrat. Despite his careful good manners, Milo made few friends. Uther Offaw, the most intelligent of the Bold Lions, discovered in Milo a kindred soul, but Uther Offaw himself was considered bizarre and rather untidy, if not actually unstable; why else would he remain among the vulgar Bold Lions?

Seixander Laverty, arbiter of another group known as the Intolerable Ineffables, felt Milo to be "an elitist: caustic and insufferably vain": an opinion which Milo found gratifying. Ottillie Veder, of the Mystic Fragrances, wondered if Milo hoped "merely to show his face to bring girls cringing up to clasp his knees."

Milo, in response to the report, said no, this was not what he hoped.

Another Fragrance, Quhannis Diffin, found Milo "—shall we say, a bit hoity-toity. Of course the same would apply to Wayness, though unquestionably she's stunning to look at."

In Glawen's opinion, three years had worked few changes on Wayness. She had grown taller by an inch, but her figure remained as before: the next thing to boyish, and her glossy dark hair, dark luminous eyes and dark eyebrows still made a striking contrast with her beautiful pale olive skin. How, Glawen marveled, could he ever have thought her plain?

Wayness was discussed no less carefully than Milo. The statuesque Hillegance Wook, also a Mystic Fragrance, discerned in Wayness no figure whatever. "I've seen wet weasels with more shape," said Hillegance. This opinion was definitely not endorsed by Seixander Laverty of the Ineffables ("She's round where it counts, with nothing left over for slop and that's how it should be"), nor by any of the Bold Lions, who studied her with fascinated interest. Wayness showed little tendency to flirt, which experts among the Bold Lions diagnosed as a case of sexual frigidity, but they could not agree as to the best method for curing the unfortunate girl of her affliction.

The term began. Milo and Wayness entered classes and adapted themselves to the new routines. Glawen undertook to be of assistance and explained the traditions and special customs of the school as best he could. Milo and Wayness accepted their generally cool reception by the other students with equanimity. Milo told Glawen: "You would find it even more difficult at Stroma, where the cliques are, in effect, little secret societies."

"Still—"

Milo held up his hand. "Truly, it's quite inconsequential. I definitely don't care to join any groups, nor, I'm certain, does Wayness. Your concern is wasted."

"Just as you say."

Milo laughed and clapped Glawen about the shoulders. "Come, now, don't be annoyed! I'm happy that you like me well enough to worry."

Glawen managed a laugh of his own. "The situation would still annoy me, even if I didn't like you."

Toward Wayness Glawen felt something more complicated than simple liking, and he was not sure how to deal with the emotion. She entered his thoughts ever more regularly and almost against his will, since he wanted no more heartaches. It would be dreadful, he thought, to fall in love with Wayness and then discover that she reciprocated not at all. And then what would he do?

Wayness' impersonal amiability gave no clue as to her feelings. Glawen even suspected sometimes that she went out of her way to avoid him, which caused him new pangs of doubt and puzzlement.

In sheer frustration Glawen threw himself down in a chair, gazed out the window and tried to come to some sort of decision. If he attempted a closer relationship with the girl, and she politely but definitely discouraged him, as seemed probable, then he would be miserable. On the other hand, if he failed to make the effort and simply went brooding about his affairs, then he lost even more definitely by default and would also be miserable—in fact, more miserable than ever because now he would feel shame for his cowardice . . . Glawen took a deep breath. What was he, then? A Clattuc or a milksop? Girding himself with all his courage, Glawen called Wayness on the telephone: "It's Glawen here."

"Indeed! And to what do I owe this honor?"

"This is a personal call. I'd like to do something special with you tomorrow, but I have to ask you first."

"It's certainly polite of you to give me a choice, and I'm favorably impressed. In fact, I'm even a bit excited. What do you have in mind? I hope it's something I like—although I'd probably agree anyway."

"Tomorrow should be a fine day for sailing. I thought we could take the sloop down to Ocean Island for a picnic."

"That sounds quite nice."

"Then you'll go?"

"Yes."

The day could not have been finer had Glawen made all the arrangements himself. Syrene shone bright in the blue morning sky; a cool breeze from the northeast left an invigorating tingle on the skin as it passed by, and also blew from exactly the right quarter.

Glawen and Wayness, arriving early at the Clattuc boathouse, boarded the sloop, hoisted sail and cast off lines. The boat drifted out upon the river, caught the breeze, danced and plunged, then swung about and moved downstream: across the lagoon, through the river mouth and out upon the ocean. Glawen set the wind vane to hold a course south by east; the sloop sailed away from the shore and into a region of endless slow swells of transparent blue water, just barely ruffled with cat's-paws.

They made themselves comfortable on the cockpit cushions.

"I like this kind of sailing," said Wayness. "The world is serene, and it induces me to be serene. There is nothing to be heard but the soft sound of my voice. Guilt and remorse are wisps of the imagination. Responsibilities are of even less account. Schoolwork: less than bubbles in the wake!"

"If only it were so," said Glawen. "I'm sorry you reminded me."

"Reminded you of what? Surely it can't be that bad!"

"You're just lucky that you're a girl and it can't happen to you."

"Glawen, please don't be cryptic. I don't like mysteries. What has disturbed you so? Is it me? Do I talk too much? I like it out here on the ocean!"

"I probably shouldn't discuss the matter," said Glawen. "But—why not? Last night Bodwyn Wook ordered me to do something awful."

Wayness uttered a nervous laugh. "I hope it doesn't have anything to do with me. Like marooning or throwing overboard."

"Worse," said Glawen gloomily.

"Worse? Is there anything worse?"

"Judge for yourself. I am commanded to join the Bold Lions."

"Bad, I agree. But not worse . . . What did you say?"

"First I'll tell you what I should have said: 'If you are so keen on the Bold Lions, join them yourself!' But I was tongue-tied for shock. Finally I asked: 'Why me? Kirdy is already in the group!' He said: 'I am quite aware of the fact. Kirdy, however, is a bit moony, and not always predictable. We need you!' I asked again: 'But why? Why me?' All he would say was: 'You'll find out in due course.' I said: 'Evidently I am to be a spy.' He said: 'Naturally! What else?' I mentioned that at last I could cherish Arles' enmity, since he would never allow me in the group. He just laughed and said never fear; I would be a Bold Lion before the week was out. And that is why I am surly and glum."

"Poor Glawen! But we need not worry today. How far is Ocean Island?"

"Not far. We'll sight it almost anytime . . . In fact, see that gray smudge on the horizon? That's Ocean Island."

The sloop sailed on: up the blue slopes, down the wide wet swales. Ocean Island, the tip of a sea mountain, took on definite form: a low cone with a shattered irregular tip a mile in circumference, with coconut palms fringing the shore and a forest of native trees ranging up the slopes of the central crag.

Glawen anchored in a sheltered cove, a hundred feet off a beach of white sand. He jumped overboard into four feet of water. "Come," he told Wayness. "I'll carry you ashore."

Wayness hesitated, then put her arms around his neck. He caught her under the knees, carried her to the beach, then returned to the boat for the lunch basket.

In the shade of a massive clarensia tree Glawen built a fire over which they grilled skewers of meat, which were then dipped into pepper sauce, caught in a slice of bread and devoured, along with a bottle of mild white Clattuc wine.

The two leaned back against the tree and looked along the curving beach, where coconut fronds moved in the breeze, and water eased up and down the sand. Glawen sighed. "Here there are no Bold Lions. There they are waiting for me. It seems foolish to go back. So why go back when we could live in utter tranquillity here, at peace with the elements? There is much to be said for the idea."

"I'm not so sure," said Wayness demurely. "There isn't any more lunch. What would we eat?"

"The bounty of nature. Fish, edible roots, seaweed, coconuts, rats and land crab. It is the ultimate dream of a million romantic poets."

"True, except for the cuisine, which might become tiresome, night after night either rat or fish for supper. By the same reasoning, you might well become bored with me after ten or twenty years—especially if we ran out of soap."

"Soap is no problem. We can make it out of coconut oil and ashes," said Glawen.

"In that case there is only a single obstacle: my mother. She is quite conventional. A romantic sojourn on Ocean Island—or any other island, for that matter—would interfere with her plans for my marriage."

"Your marriage!" Glawen looked at her in astonishment. "You're too young to be married!"

"Don't get excited, Glawen. Nothing is definite. My mother simply is thinking ahead. This person thinks he might like to marry me, at least so he's told my mother. He has a private fortune and is already influential at Stroma. My mother thinks it would be an excellent match, even though he is totally LPF in all his views."

"Hmmf. And what do you think of all this?"

"I haven't given it much thought."

Glawen spoke casually. "And this LPFer—what's his name?"

"Julian Bohost. He was on Earth while we were there, and I saw quite a bit of him. He's rather strong-minded and earnest, and Mother is probably quite right: Julian would surely prefer that his bride had not lived ten or twenty years during her youth on Ocean Island with another gentleman."

"Do you like him?"

Again Wayness laughed. "Aren't I allowed any secrets whatever?"

"I'm sorry. I shouldn't ask such things." Glawen rose to his feet and looked up at the sun. "Anyway it's time the romantic idyll was ending for today. The breeze has backed around into the east which is good news, but it has a tendency to slack off in the late afternoon, and it's probably a good time to be leaving."

Glawen carried the lunch basket to the boat. He turned to find Wayness at the water's edge preparing to wade to the boat. He called: "I'll carry you, if you will wait."

Wayness made an airy gesture. "I don't mind getting my legs wet." Nevertheless she waited until Glawen returned and made no protest when he lifted her.

Halfway to the boat Glawen halted. Their faces were close together. Wayness asked in a husky whisper: "Am I too heavy? Are you going to drop me into the water?"

Glawen sighed. "No . . . I see no real reason to do so."

He carried her to the boat and climbed aboard himself. While Glawen stowed the lunch basket and made ready for departure, Wayness sat on the coach roof combing her hair through her fingers and watching him with an enigmatic expression. She jumped up to help him hoist the sails and raise the anchor; the sloop departed Ocean Island and drove off across the blue afternoon sea on an easy starboard tack.

Neither Glawen nor Wayness had much to say on the voyage home; each seemed absorbed in thought, though they sat close together on the port cockpit seat.

With the breeze starting to fail and the sun declining into the west,

Glawen drove into the mouth of the River Wan and upstream to Clattuc boathouse. Securing the sloop, Glawen conducted Wayness to Riverview House on the Clattuc power wagon. She hesitated a moment, as if thinking; then, turning to Glawen, said: "In regard to Julian Bohost, Father is dubious. He considers Julian something of a demagogue."

"I'm more interested in your opinions," said Glawen.

Wayness tilted her head and pursed her lips as if holding back a smile. "He's noble; he's high-minded; he's strong! What more could a girl want? Something more like Glawen Clattuc? Who knows?" Bending, she kissed Glawen's cheek. "Thank you for a lovely day."

"Wait!" cried Glawen. "Come back!"

"I think not," said Wayness, and ran off up the path to Riverview House.

4

Bodwyn Wook summoned Glawen to his office and waved him to a seat. Glawen settled himself and waited patiently while Bodwyn Wook straightened papers on his desk, rubbed his bald pate, and finally, leaning back into his massive leather-upholstered chair, fixed a sharp gaze upon Glawen. "So! Here's our bully new Bold Lion!"

"Not yet," said Glawen. "If ever."

"If ever, eh? And what am I supposed to understand by that?"

"It's not likely that I'll be allowed into the group," said Glawen.

"Indeed. You will find that I am right and you are wrong. You will be elected a Bold Lion with facility."

"Just as you say, sir, although I don't understand the reason for any of this."

Bodwyn Wook laced his fingers together, tucked them under his bony chin and gazed toward the ceiling. "In a month or so the group will visit Yipton, so I am told, for several days of social studies. You will be included in this junket. That should be a pleasant prospect."

"Not really, sir. I'm not good at conviviality, or group frolics."

"Hm. Very much the loner, aren't you, Glawen?"

"I suppose that's the way of it."

"Well, you shall go to Yipton and frolic and make merry and be as convivial as the others. Dissimulation is the necessary camouflage of the spy."

"But what am I spying for?"

"All this will be made clear in due course. Until then: become a good Bold Lion! Learn to carouse and frolic, since at Yipton you must participate in all the fun if you are not to compromise your cover."

Glawen gave a somber nod. "If I must, I must. The expenses will certainly be considerable—"

Bodwyn Wook jerked upright in his chair, became suddenly wary. "Quite so. Money spent on pleasure is money well-spent; look at it that way."

"—but no doubt you will supply me with Agency funds."

Bodwyn Wook sighed. "Glawen, I have misjudged you. You are truly a rascal after all, despite that look of pensive innocence which no doubt drives the girls wild. Please do not hoodwink me again."

"Sir—"

Bodwyn Wook rose to his feet. "I have heard enough. I no longer have doubts as to your role as a Bold Lion. It may well be that you are the most feckless of the lot. That is all for now."

Glawen, with a hundred questions pressing at his lips, departed the office for his morning classes at the lyceum.

At noon Glawen sat at a table to the side of the terrace, pretending to read a book but in fact waiting for Wayness to appear. The minutes passed by, but no Wayness. He became edgy. Either his imagination was playing him tricks or she was purposely avoiding him. It was illogical; why should it be? Caprice? Second thoughts in regard to Julian Bohost? Impossible to guess what might be going on in her mind . . . Here she came now, with two of her friends. Glawen rose to his feet but she appeared not to see him and went to a table across the terrace. As she sat down, she turned a quick side glance in his direction and gave him a quick little flicker of the fingers. She had seen him after all!

In a dark mood Glawen crouched over his book, while watching her through his eyelashes. Something was different; something was changed. What could it be? Her hair? The same loose dark curls. Her face? Fascination, the stuff of magic: as before. Her clothes—ah! Instead of the knee-length dark skirts and jackets which she had brought from Earth, she wore pale blue Araminta-style trousers, tight at the hips, loose under the knees and gathered at the ankles, with a short-sleeved gray-tan shirt open at the neck: a costume which admirably showed off her slim figure.

Glawen became resolute. If she would not join him at his table, he would go sit with her . . . On the other hand, that might be exactly the wrong procedure. What would his father do in like circumstances? Glawen pictured Scharde's face, grim and whimsical all at once.

Scharde, he decided, would simply laugh and read his book and let Wayness straighten things out for herself.

Kirdy Wook dropped into the chair opposite him. "I'm told that you want to become a Bold Lion."

Glawen gave his head a slow shake. "Quite wrong."

"Eh? What's this? I had it straight from Old Birdcage."

"It's his idea, not mine."

Kirdy's ruddy features twisted in puzzlement. "What does he have in mind?"

"Ask him yourself."

Kirdy grimaced. "There's no talking to the old codger. Things go his way or not at all. Someday I expect I'll go in and find him sitting in the chandelier, scratching his arse with one hand and eating a banana with the other."

Glawen grinned, but made no comment.

Kirdy looked gloomily off across the terrace. "There's only one way to deal with him. It's simple and practical: I obey orders to the exact iota and keep my ideas to myself. He'll find out what he's been losing one of these days but then it will be too late, and it will serve him right."

"Yes, no doubt. What's involved in joining the Bold Lions?"

"Nothing much." Kirdy tossed a packet of papers down on the table. "Memorize the Roars and Growls; that's important. Then study the bylaws well, in case someone gets officious and tries to put you through the Tail March."

"And what's that?"

"Just an exercise where you demonstrate your extreme leoninity."

Glawen glanced through the papers. "What's this mean: 'Agrolio, agrolio, agrolio'?"

"That's just one of the formal roars."

Glawen threw down the paper. "This is foolishness."

Kirdy grinned widely. "Of course it is! But out on the beach, with a keg of beer, it becomes quite the thing! Be sure to memorize everything correctly."

"Why bother? I'll never get by Arles."

"Don't worry about Arles; tomorrow night he goes to his makeup class at the lyceum. The Grand Pouncer—that's Uther—will call an emergency meeting, and we'll run you through. It's as simple as that."

"Arles will be upset."

Kirdy said ponderously: "I know this. I don't like it but we've had our orders. Arles must learn how to cope with small adversities." Rising to his feet, Kirdy said: "Tomorrow evening, then, in the Den."

143

Kirdy went off about his affairs. Glawen looked to where Wayness had been sitting but discovered that she had departed the terrace.

During the evening Glawen tried to concentrate on serious matters but at last he jumped to his feet and telephoned Wayness at Riverview House. "It's Glawen."

Wayness' voice seemed cautiously friendly. "The instant I heard the chime I knew it was you! A clear case of telepathy!"

"Or anxiety?"

"Oh, perhaps a bit of anxiety," said Wayness carelessly. "But please don't be stern with me."

"Are you busy?"

"No more than usual. Why do you ask?"

"May I come to see you?"

"Here? At Riverview House?"

"Certainly; where else?"

There was a pause of three seconds, then a somewhat dubious response: "That would be nice. However . . ."

Glawen waited, but the silence persisted. Finally, in a flat voice, he said: "Very well. I won't come."

Wayness said: "I don't quite know how to explain . . . Except simply state the facts. You can come if you like. But after you leave, I'll have to participate in another earnest discussion with my mother."

"Another?"

"After we came home from sailing I made the mistake of telling her that it was a beautiful day and that I liked you."

"She disapproves of me?"

"No, but that's not the point. She's convinced that it's impractical for me to see you, except on a very polite and impersonal basis. She says that anything else can't possibly lead anywhere, and she wonders why I am not sufficiently clearheaded to see this for myself. I can only say that I, too, am perplexed. Then she becomes analytical. She asks a rhetorical question: suppose the relationship proceeded and we were even foolish enough to marry? To save me the exertion of thinking, she answers the question herself. It would turn out to be a tragedy, says Mother. Where would we live? On Stroma? Not feasible. You would be a fish out of water. At Clattuc House? The same applies to me." Wayness gave a soft laugh. "Of course she's right; I can't argue with her. Then she asks the question I keep asking myself: What am I going to do with my life? Unlike me, she has an answer."

"And his first name is Julian."

"I learn that it's an opportunity which comes only once in a lifetime. I tell her that I don't want to worry about such things just yet. She explains that time has a way of sliding past, and before you know it, you're stringy and gaunt and your back hurts, and where are the opportunities now? Gone. This leaves me depressed and tired. Tonight I'm not up to it, and I think that you'd better not come."

"Does that mean tomorrow night too, and all the other nights?"

Wayness laughed again: a rather desperate sound. "It does sound like that, doesn't it? I'll have to ponder on this. I'm not meek, but I want no more dreary discussions with Mother, especially when she may be right."

"Just as you like."

"Glawen! Now you're angry with me!"

"I don't know what to think. On top of all else, I now must become a Bold Lion, and I sorely wish that Bodwyn Wook were learning the roars and growls instead of me."

Wayness tried to maintain a tone of sober sympathy, without total success. "You're probably being prepared for an important mission; when you learn the details you'll no doubt think better of the program, despite the yelps and howls."

"Roars and growls, to be exact."

"In either case it's a recondite skill, totally unknown to Julian Bohost—who, incidentally, is coming to visit Riverview House before too long. Perhaps you'll want to meet him."

"It will be a pleasure."

"Goodnight, Glawen."

"Goodnight."

5

At the appointed hour, Glawen arrived at the Old Arbor. He made his way to that corner preempted by the Bold Lions for their Den, and took a seat, somewhat apart, in the shadows.

Three of the members, Kirdy Wook, Cloyd Diffin and Jardine Laverty, were already on hand, and a moment later Shugart Veder and the two Offaws, Uther and Kiper, appeared.

Grand Pouncer Uther Offaw addressed the group. "This meeting was called tonight by reason of an alarming development requiring our instant attention. As we know, there has been chronic trouble with the Yips and it seems to be getting worse—so bad in fact that the authorities were canceling all excursions, including the Rip-roar! However, I am happy to report that Kirdy today made forceful representations in high places. He pointed out that we had already made our preparations, and in short exerted full lion power. As a result he managed to get the order rescinded. For this we owe Kirdy three rousing growls: let's hear them loud and clear! Hurrah, Kirdy!"

Dutifully the Lions voiced three growls of approval.

"Very good! Happily the disaster is averted! Kirdy, do you have anything to say?"

"Well, yes. Tardy Diffin's resignation leaves an opening in the group, for which place I'd like to nominate a fine long-tailed creature with a resplendent mane: Glawen Clattuc! He will bring agility and clever new tactics to our pride!"

Uther Offaw cried out: "A great choice! I'll second that nomination myself! Is there any discussion? Any objection? In that case, I declare Glawen Clattuc unanimously elected a full-fledged Bold Lion. Three growls of acclamation for Glawen Clattuc, and let them ring loud!"

The growls were rendered with gusto and Glawen thereby became a Bold Lion.

On the following day Arles waited by the portal which opened between Wansey Way and the lyceum terrace. Presently Uther Offaw came past. Arles stepped forward. "Uther, just a minute, if you please!"

Uther paused. "Make it quick, like a good fellow; I can spare just a minute."

"What I have to say is important," declared Arles. "It may take more than a minute."

"Well, one way or another, get on with it! What do you want: the assignment sheet? Here it is; you'll have to work the problems yourself; I haven't got to them yet."

Arles pushed the sheet aside. "I've just heard about last night's meeting. To my utter shock, I find that Glawen has been taken into the Bold Lions."

"True, by unanimous acclamation. An excellent choice; don't you agree?"

"In no way, shape, form, color or smell! And I'll tell you why: Glawen simply does not have the right stuff! He's the bashful sort, always peeking around corners. As I see it, the Bold Lions are a driving hell-for-breakfast bunch who always come out on top, and devil take the hindmost! Glawen? A sorry little milksop, if truth must be told."

Uther pursed his lips. "I am surprised to hear this! The rest of the membership feels that we've made quite a good catch."

"Doesn't anyone have common sense? Why go out of our way to enroll a Bureau B spy to report every little peccadillo to the authorities?"

Uther gave a wry laugh. "Come now! Kirdy is Bureau B and you don't raise a howl."

Arles blinked and considered. "Well, Kirdy is a Mummer and that makes a difference, believe me. He's not a prig and knows when it's best to ignore the red tape."

Uther said reasonably: "It really makes no difference. I for one intend to break no laws."

"Nor do I! But now we'll have to gauge every innocent little indiscretion, just to make sure Glawen is not offended."

Kirdy Wook had come up to listen. He said in disgust: "Arles, you are hysterical!"

"Call it what you like! I just don't want Glawen keeping score every time I blow my nose."

Uther appeared to ponder. "It's a difficult situation. What should we do?"

Arles pounded his fist into the palm of his meaty hand. "Obviously: reconsider this flawed election!"

Kirdy chuckled. "It's clear that Arles must have his way. Uther, what is proper procedure, as defined in the bylaws?"

"Proper procedure be blowed!" declared Arles. "We need only tell the blighter that a mistake was made and that he is not a Bold Lion after all."

"Impossible," said Kirdy. "He was voted in unanimously."

"Well, we can't have dissension," said Uther. "Tonight we'll call a special meeting and Arles can bring an action to expel if he's willing to take the risk."

Arles stuttered: "I did not say expel! I said 'not admit'!"

"We must work within the bylaws," said Uther. "You need six votes out of eight to expel, and if you fail, you're out yourself. You won't get Glawen's vote; that's certain. Kirdy?"

"I nominated Glawen; I'd look pretty silly voting to turf him out."

"I seconded the nomination, and the same applies to me. Arles, it looks as if the vote has gone against you. Do you propose to resign?"

"No," said Arles. "Forget the special meeting. I'll work this out some other way."

6

A remarkable set of events, each controlling the shape of the next in sequence, received its first impulse at a class in social anthropology at the lyceum.

The class, a prerequisite for graduation, was taught by Professor Yvon Dace, one of the least predictable of a notably unconventional faculty. Dace looked his part, with a high forehead, a few lank wisps of dust-colored hair, mournful dark eyes, a button nose, a long upper lip and an odd little crabapple of a chin.

Professor Dace's somewhat diffident appearance was belied by his conduct, which was often surprising. At the beginning of the term he made his position clear. "Whatever you have heard about me, dismiss it. I do not regard my class as a confrontation between the clear light of my intellect and twenty-two examples of sloth and wilful stupidity. The exact number may be only half that, if we are lucky, and of course varies from term to term. Despite all, I am a kindly man, patient and thorough, but if I must elucidate the obvious more than twice, I often become gloomy.

"As for the subject matter, we can hope only to acquaint ourselves with the large outline, though we will often pause to focus upon interesting details. I recommend subsidiary reading, which, incidentally, will improve your grade. Anyone who negotiates the ten volumes of Baron Bodissey's *Life* in addition to the assigned texts will automatically receive at minimum a passing grade. Needless to say, I will satisfy myself that this reading has actually taken place.

"Some of you may consider my teaching techniques rather casual. Others will wonder how I arrive at your proper grade. There is no mystery here. I grade partly from examination results, partly from a subjective, or even subconscious, evaluation. I lack sympathy with both mysticism and stupidity; I hope that you will control any such tendencies during our discussions. I must admit that beautiful girls face a special handicap; I must constantly guard against giving these delicious creatures all that they want and more. I might add that ugly girls fare no better, since then I must take into account my kindly pangs of guilt and pity.

"Enough of the side issues; to the work itself, which you will find to be fascinating, rich in drama, humor and pathos. Your first assignment is Parts One and Two of *The World of the Goddess Gaea*, by Michael Yeaton. Are there questions? Yes?"

Ottillie Veder said: "I am a girl. How will I know whether my bad grade is because you admire me or because you find me disgusting and repulsive?"

"Nothing could be simpler. Arrange to meet me out on the beach with a blanket and a bottle of good wine. If I do not appear, your most pessimistic fears will be confirmed. Now, then, as for today . . ."

The girls of the class, along with Ottillie Veder, included Cynissa

148

and Zanny Diffin; Tara and Zaraide Laverty; Mornifer and Jerdys Wook; Adare and Clare Clattuc; Vervice Offaw; Wayness Tamm from Riverview House, and others. The Bold Lions were represented by Glawen and Arles Clattuc, Kiper Laverty, Kirdy Wook, Ling Diffin and Shugart Veder.

Two weeks of the term went by, then one day Professor Dace leaned back into his chair. "Today we deviate from our usual procedure, and undertake some anthropological fieldwork here in the class. Everyone has doubtless taken note of the individuals normally present during this period. Two of these persons derive from cultures somewhat alien to that of Araminta Station. One of them is myself, but I could not, without flagrant loss of dignity, allow the class to use me as a case study. Therefore we will focus our attention upon that intriguing individual who calls herself Wayness, and hope that her dignity is proof to the trial. Observe her now as she sits at her desk, evaluating this startling turn of events. Her composure is worthy of note; she neither titters, rolls her eyes nor crouches in a nervous huddle. Aha! At last she laughs! She is mortal after all! To a keen and educated eye a variety of subtle signals indicates her alien background: for instance, the odd manner in which she holds her pencil."

Kiper Laverty, sitting next to Wayness, called out: "That is not a pencil; she has borrowed my new fidget rod."

"Thank you, Kiper," said Professor Dace. "As always, you bring a fresh perspective to our ruminations. Returning to Wayness, I suspect that the events of her life have been almost incommensurable with those of the rest of us. Furthermore, she interprets these events differently than we might. Am I right, Wayness?"

"I would expect so, sir, since you are the professor."

"Hm, yes; quite so. Well, then: how would you describe the differences between life here and life at Stroma?"

Wayness reflected a moment. "There are differences, certainly, although they are hard to explain. Our customs are much the same; we use the same table manners and wash when we are dirty. At Araminta Station class distinctions are important and carefully defined, but you have no perceptible politics. At Stroma, politics and political skills are the source of prestige, even more than wealth. But we have no class distinctions."

"That is an interesting observation," said Professor Dace. "And which do you consider the better system?"

Wayness pursed her lips in mild perplexity. "I've never troubled to think about it. I've always taken it for granted that ours is the best way."

Professor Dace shook his head. "That is not necessarily so, although today we will not explore the topic in depth. Continue, if you will."

"Whatever the case," said Wayness, "politics at Stroma is very important; in fact it's a continuous wrangle which involves everyone."

"And what, in brief, are the issues?"

"There are two main factions: the Life, Peace and Freedom group, who are anxious to make what they call 'progressive changes,' and the Old Naturalists, whom the LPFers call the Old Naturals or Bird-watchers, who want to maintain Cadwal as a wilderness preserve."

Professor Dace asked: "And what are your own views?"

Wayness, smiling, shook her head. "The Conservator is officially neutral. I'm part of his household."

Adare Clattuc asked: "Where do you prefer to live? Here or at Stroma?"

"I often ask myself the same question. There really is no basis for comparison."

"But isn't Araminta far nicer? How can you even hesitate?"

"Well—since Throy isn't nice at all, the word simply doesn't apply. Throy is a land of force and grandeur: not necessarily harsh or cruel but certainly not kindly. When I think of Throy I feel two emotions: a lifting of the spirits in response to the natural beauty, and awe. These emotions are always with us, and often challenge our courage. In our winter cabins out on the seaward crags, we can feel the force of the storm and watch the great waves smashing against the rocks. Part of the joy comes from the thrill of fear, even though we know we are safe and comfortable. Certain bold persons claim to enjoy what is known as storm-sailing; they go out on the sea to challenge the worst of the storms. Sometimes I think that mostly they enjoy the sensation of returning alive to the dock. Naturally, the storm boats are very strong and very heavy; they make a wonderful sight as they ride over the waves. Once when I was small I watched from our cabin as a storm boat struck a submerged rock and sank; even now when I think of it I feel a strange emotion which I can't describe.

"Sometimes we go out to one of the famous old inns instead of our cabin. The Iron Barnacle, which is built out on an offshore crag, is my favorite place to be when the storm is wildest. The green waves come in from the sea to crash against the rocks, and white foam spatters a hundred feet into the air. Wind roars; clouds tumble across the sky, while rain and hail fall on the roof and firelight stirs the soul like beautiful music. There is a special hot soup prepared for such occasions, and rum punch. When finally we go to bed, all the wild black night we hear the roar of the sea and the wind wailing through the rocks. When we travel from Throy and go far away, memories of the Iron Barnacle always make us homesick."

Professor Dace said: "Visitors often wonder why the Society built Stroma on Throy, when easier sites were at hand. Can you explain?"

"I think that they wanted to keep the population low, without imposing a numerical limit."

"And the population now?"

"Six hundred or so. When the Society was still sending subsidies, it reached fifteen hundred."

"And what of the Society now? Does it still concern itself with Conservancy policy?"

"Not at all, as far as I know."

"Tell us something of your daily routine at Stroma."

Wayness hesitated. "I don't think anyone would be interested."

"Include a saucy anecdote or two; you'll instantly have everyone's attention, especially when they realize that your remarks will form the basis of an examination."

"Let me think. Where shall I start? Everyone knows that Stroma overlooks the Stroma Fjord. We live in the best of the old houses; others have been pulled down, and only the gardens remain. At the end of the sound are the greenhouses; almost a hundred acres are under glass.

"Almost every family has a cabin: along the sea cliffs, at a mountain lake or out on the moors, where friends are entertained. This is great fun, especially for the children. During the day and sometimes at night we walk out, often alone, to enjoy the solitude. The andorils[1] have learned not to bother us. The toctacs[2] sometimes set up elaborate ambushes, which we take pains to avoid. One day out on the moor I came upon an enormous master andoril, sitting on a rock. He must have been twelve feet tall, with curving black shoulder horns and a crest of five bones. He watched very closely as I walked past, with about a hundred feet between us. I knew he would like nothing better than to eat me, and he knew that I knew. He also knew that I would not kill him unless he attacked me, and therefore sat quietly, wondering whether I'd make a better roast than a stew. I could see every detail of his face, which was disconcerting, since I felt that I could read his thoughts."

Zaraide Laverty gasped: "Weren't you frightened?"

---

[1] Andorils: large vicious andromorphs. Because of the difficulties of research, their habits remain obscure.

[2] Toctacs are two-legged wolves.

"In a way. But I had my handgun ready, and there was no real danger. If I were out walking by night, I'd be wearing a sensor harness against ambushes. Here at Araminta, of course, I don't bother with such things."

"You go out to walk at night? Alone?"

Wayness laughed. "Sometimes I swim, when the sea is calm—especially when Lorca and Sing are up."

Glawen, looking sidewise, saw Arles jerk up his head and fix a hooded stare upon Wayness. After a while Arles lowered his head and for a period pretended to take notes. Then, after a moment, he surreptitiously glanced up again, to study Wayness more carefully.

Vervice Offaw, one of the Fortunate Five, in her relations with Wayness, tended to use a cool condescension. She said now: "You must find Riverview House dull and overcivilized after all your exciting battles with the elements, not to mention andorils. Are you bored living here?"

Professor Dace said lazily: "Allow me to offer a judgment which Wayness herself might be too charitable to make. She has spent considerable time on Earth where true overcivilization is not unknown, and I seriously doubt if she thinks of Riverview House in those terms. Dull? The Conservator frequently entertains guests from both Stroma and off-world. I suspect that Wayness finds Riverview House both stimulating and pleasantly placid, though never dull. Araminta Station may well seem a languid little backwater, where all the styles and fads are ten years out of date."

Vervice decided that she hated Professor Dace more thoroughly than any man she had ever met.

Wayness smiled at the remark. "Riverview House is certainly peaceful. I have more time to myself than ever before, which I find that I like."

Ottillie Veder asked: "What of love affairs at Stroma? Who arranges your marriages?"

"Arranged marriages are unusual at Stroma.[1] Love affairs? They are very common."

Professor Dace straightened up in his chair. "And on this note we shall excuse Wayness, before the questions become overpersonal."

---

[1] As often as not, at Araminta Station young men and women marry to their own inclinations, even, despite family pressure, with collaterals. Nonetheless, when Agency status is at stake, the Housemaster will do his best to arrange an advantageous marriage.

Early in the evening the Bold Lions gathered at the Old Arbor, to drink a goblet or two of wine, gossip, formulate plans and discuss space yachts. Almost all brought books, as if they intended to study, but little was ever accomplished in this direction.

The conversation veered to a topic of general interest: how to judge a girl's erotic proclivities from a study of her mannerisms, signs, signals and physical characteristics. Each of the Bold Lions had given thought to the subject and each contributed his own insights. Several of the group, almost as an article of faith, asserted that breast dimension infallibly corresponded with erotic enthusiasm. Ling Diffin tried to justify the theory on the basis of psychological compulsion: "It's only sensible. A girl looks down and can't see her feet by reason of an extraordinary bust, so she tells herself: 'Oh my word! Everywhere I go I brandish these truly notable sex symbols! Whether I realize it or not, I must be a real five-star high-output performer! No other explanation is valid! So why fight it?' The obverse situation, when the girl can see not only her feet, but her ankles and heels as well, exerts the negative influence."

"Scholarly but absurd," said Uther Offaw.

Kiper Laverty said: "Girls are curious creatures, but their motives yield to close observation. I learn all I need to know by watching how a girl twitches her fingers, especially her little fingers."

"Total nonsense!" said Kirdy Wook. "Why would a girl attempt such subtle refinements? She's got better things to wave than her little finger."

Shugart Veder said, somewhat ponderously: "In my opinion, there are no valid shortcuts; one must study the whole picture."

"Possibly yes, possibly no," said Arles. "Still, I can pick out a sizzler at a distance of fifty yards, simply by watching the way she walks."

Uther Offaw shook his head. "In this case I must side with Shugart. Personally, I keep a schematic image in my notebook, and I synthesize information from several key parameters. I have never known the system to be at fault."

Arles put on a patronizing grin. "Specifically, then: how do you and your index rate, let's say, Ottillie, zero being a dead fish and ten a real go-for-broke steamer?"

"As I recall, my figures indicate that Ottillie can be had, by the right man in the right place at the right time."

"Very informative," said Arles. "What is the line on Wayness?"

Uther frowned. "In this case, I am not satisfied with my figures. She puts out too many contradictory signals. At first I thought she was prim; now I find her strangely attractive."

"It's not strange at all," said Kiper. "In those tight pants she's practically edible."

"Quiet, Kiper," said Shugart. "You curdle the moral atmosphere."

Kirdy Wook addressed Kiper: "I thought that you were a proponent of the 'twitching finger' theory."

"I looked at her fingers first," said Kiper. "Then I changed."

"I wish you chaps would talk of something else," grumbled Kirdy Wook. "I came down here to study."

"So did I," said Arles. He looked down at his books with disfavor. "This stuff is dry as dog bone. Uther, you're a mathematical genius; work out these problems for me! They're due tomorrow, and I've only just started."

Uther smilingly shook his head. "I refuse to start down a long, futile road. Face the facts, Arles. To pass the course, you must be able to solve such problems."

Arles spoke in a voice of reproach: "Is this the brave Grand Pouncer, Sage of the Pride, who dispenses such bleak mercy to a pack member with a sore paw?"

"I am the Grand Pouncer and a roaring true Bold Lion! If I solved your problems tonight, tomorrow you would stare even more blankly at the next set. In the end I would drudge through all your work until the examination, which you would fail, with gratitude for no one, least of all me."

Shugart Veder said: "I thought you were working with a tutor."

Arles grunted. "He was inept in every respect! First, he tried to put me through a lot of meaningless drills: elementary stuff! What I needed was a clear and easy way to solve the problems, and all he would say was: 'In due course!' and 'First things first!' Finally I told him either to teach me properly or to stand aside for someone who could."

"Those were strong words! What did he say?"

"Nothing much. He knew I'd caught him out fair and square, so he just gave a hollow laugh and walked away. Curious chap."

"So who worked your last problem-set, when the tutor refused to do so?"

Kirdy Wook murmured: "Could it have been Spanchetta, noblest of lion mothers?"

Arles scowled blackly and slammed the book shut. "She might have given me a hint or two. What of it?"

"Face facts, Arles! Spanchetta can't take the examination for you."

"Bah!" muttered Arles. "You sound like my tutor." He pushed back his chair and rose to his feet. "I'm not worried. I know how to deal with these so-called facts, if the need arises!"

All around the table faces looked blankly at Arles. Uther Offaw said coldly: "I don't understand what you are saying. Do you care to explain?"

"Certainly I'll explain, if you're too dense to catch on for yourself! Changes are coming around here! Some will be pushed forward; others will get left behind. I wanted the Bold Lions to be in the lead. Now I don't know. The group is getting worse instead of better. Now do you understand?"

"I do not, but I must say that I don't like the tone of your words."

Arles grinned. "Don't be such a tame little lap-pussy! Maybe we'll have to vote in a new Grand Pouncer after all! Someone who'll get things properly done." Arles gathered his books together. "I'm leaving; there are things I'd rather be doing elsewhere."

Arles departed the Old Arbor, leaving behind an uncomfortable silence. Shugart finally said: "Not a nice scene, at all. I can't imagine what he's talking about."

"Whatever it is, I don't like it," said Uther in a troubled voice. "It's downright sinister."

Cloyd Veder said: "When he gets into this kind of mood he's unpredictable . . . I wonder what he had in mind when he said he wanted the Bold Lions in the lead."

Kirdy Wook drained his goblet and collected his books. "Arles is just full of big talk."

"And what does he mean 'the group is getting worse'? That's not a proper thing to say."

Kirdy rose to his feet. "He can't get used to seeing Glawen in the group . . . Where is Glawen? He was here the last time I looked."

Kiper said: "He left a minute ago—slipped away like a shadow, just after Arles went. He's another odd one."

Kirdy said: "That applies more or less to all of us . . . I'll be getting along too."

"And I," said Uther. "The meeting, such as it was, is adjourned."

8

Glawen unobtrusively departed the Old Arbor and went out into Wansey Way, where he paused to look and listen . . . He heard only a muffled murmur of voices from the Old Arbor. The Quadrangle lay quiet and empty in the starlight. Wansey Way went off toward the beach between patches of dappled starlight and heavy shade. But nowhere could be seen the dark moving shape which might indicate the present location of Arles: a fact which suddenly had become a matter of grave importance.

Where, then, was Arles? At the meeting he had seemed edgy and preoccupied, as if something were gnawing at his mind.

Glawen thought that he might be able to guess what was troubling Arles.

Where was he now?

The first and obvious place to look was Clattuc House. Glawen turned and ran up the avenue. He pushed open the main portal and looked into the foyer. The footman on duty gave him a polite salute. "Good evening, sir."

"Has Arles come in just recently?"

"Yes, sir: about five minutes ago."

The response took Glawen by surprise. "And he hasn't come down again?"

"No, sir. Dame Spanchetta met him here on her way out and gave firm instructions in regard to schoolwork. Master Arles went up to his chambers but without enthusiasm."

"Hmmf," muttered Glawen. "Most peculiar . . ." Upstairs, his own rooms were dark and silent; Scharde was gone. Feeling puzzled and dissatisfied, Glawen flung himself into a chair and sat staring into space.

A new concept entered his mind. He went to his bedroom, opened the window and clambered out upon the roof. Nearby a great oak tree grew close to the roof, affording a secret route to the ground when, in years previous, the mood had so inclined him. Now he went quietly around the roof until he could see the windows giving upon Arles' bedroom. The window was open, but the room behind was dark.

Glawen returned across the dank old tiles to his bedroom. Verification was necessary. He called Arles on the telephone. There was no answer.

Cursing under his breath, Glawen now struggled to resolve a new predicament. If he telephoned Riverview House, while precautions might be taken, he inevitably would be made to seem the source of an overexcitable clamor and probable false alarm, to his helpless embarrassment.

Furious with himself for worrying over such paltry considerations, Glawen turned away from the telephone. Now: every minute was important; Arles had a goodly head start. Glawen left his rooms, descended the stairs and departed Clattuc House at best speed. He ran down the avenue to Wansey Way, out to the Beach Road, then south toward Riverview House: at all times peering ahead lest he overtake Arles—assuming that Arles were, for a fact, hunching along the road ahead.

Glawen stopped to listen. The ocean was still. A pink flush at the horizon signaled the imminent appearance of Lorca and Sing. He heard the soft sound of the surf and occasionally the hushed call of a night bird in the palms and tanjee trees beside the road.

Glawen proceeded, but more slowly and cautiously. If Arles were also traversing the road on his secret business, he could not be far ahead, and it would not be comfortable to come hard up on Arles out here in the dark. Glawen gave a grimace; he should have brought a weapon.

Glawen trotted soundlessly ahead . . . Aha! He stopped short. At the edge of his vision: a lurching shadow which could only be Arles, and Glawen felt a grim satisfaction that his intuition had been confirmed.

Reality also brought a thrill of fear. Glawen had no illusions regarding his ability to cope with Arles, and again he wished he had brought a weapon.

With even greater caution, Glawen started forward once again, keeping to the shadows whenever possible, proceeding just fast enough to keep pace with the dark shape ahead. There was something odd about its contours; was it definitely Arles? Glawen could not be sure, but dared draw no closer, though the figure, moving at a lumbering half trot, seemed oblivious to the possibility of anyone coming behind.

The road approached the grove of trees surrounding Riverview House, with starlight glinting on the river lagoon beyond . . . Another hundred yards and the dark figure stopped short and seemed to appraise the landscape. Glawen dropped into a patch of deep shadow. Riverview House, on a knob of land extending into the lagoon, could now be placed by a glimmer of lights from its windows.

Glawen, skulking through the shade, moved closer to the dark figure. Suddenly, as if perturbed by a psychic impulse, it turned and looked back the way it had come. The movement caused its outlines to billow; with a flush of something like horror, Glawen saw that it wore a long loose cloak and some sort of loose mask to conceal its features. Glawen was now close enough to identify the shape; it was a secret and horrid version of Arles, hitherto unknown—at least to Glawen. Again he regretted the lack of a weapon. Groping along the ground, Glawen found the dead frond of a parasol tree. Carefully he stripped away the fiber spokes, to produce a flexible pole with a bulb of heavy dank sponge at one end. He backed into the shadows, and with great caution broke off the tip, to produce a serviceable cudgel three feet long.

Glawen crept foward again. Out over the sea Lorca and Sing had appeared, to cast a pallid pink light over the scene. But now, where was Arles? He was nowhere to be seen.

Glawen jumped to his feet and stared south down the beach. Arles could not have gone far. The beach stretched away blank and empty. Where, then, was Arles?

Glawen moved slowly forward. Arles might have ventured down the path toward Riverview House. Or he might have gone down to the shore of the lagoon, where he could watch and wait unseen in the deep shade under the weeping willows.

Glawen listened. From the direction of the lagoon came the plash of nocturnal water animals: otterlings—or water cats—timorous creatures who would dive deep and hide at any alarm. If Arles had come this way, he had used great stealth indeed.

The sounds halted—which might mean much or nothing.

Glawen ran crouching up the path to the shore of the lagoon. To his left he saw a boathouse, a dock and ripples glinting pink and white where someone was swimming and disturbing the surface of the water. All was now explained: here was the source of the splashing sounds, and unquestionably Arles was near at hand.

Step by slow step Glawen moved around the shore, wincing at every shift of position for fear of snapping a twig or otherwise alerting Arles to his presence.

His caution was perhaps exaggerated. Absorbed in the view, Arles lacked interest in extraneous details, and in any event what could concern him? He felt majestic in his power. All contingencies had been dealt with; there was nothing to fear. If anyone should ask, the footman would attest that he had never left Clattuc House, and who would or could contradict him? Disguised in mask and cloak, Arles had marched through the night like a god incognito: a creature of force and mystery, the stuff of legends. He also carried clever devices to be used as needed, even though tonight he had come out with no fixed plan—"on the prowl," so he told himself. And tonight he had prowled to good effect. He leaned forward, avid and keen, absorbed in what could be seen of the nude body where it glimmered pale in the dark water.

The swimmer was Wayness. She floated now with only her face and the top of her head exposed, arms outstretched, holding position by deft twitches of her hands. Moving her legs, she brought them to the surface and lay floating lazily on her back, gazing up at the stars. Arles began to breathe hard through clenched teeth.

Wayness kicked her feet, churning the water and propelling herself toward the dock, where she had left a robe, sandals and a towel. Along the shore moved Arles, watching her every movement. She was about to come from the water and most convenient to hand. Ha! Could there be any choice? A man exposed to this kind of stimulation could not be expected to restrain himself!

Wayness climbed a ladder to the dock and for a moment stood looking over the water and letting herself drip, while the light of Lorca and Sing invested her skin with a wonderful ruddy glow.

Wayness picked up the towel, rubbed her hair, dried her face, arms and torso, gave her back, haunches and legs a few desultory wipes, then threw the robe over her shoulders, thrust her feet in the sandals and stepped down from the dock.

A shape came up behind her and attempted to drop a loose bag over her head. Wayness gave a startled cry, threw up her arms and pulled away the bag, which fell to the ground. Jerking around, Wayness saw a looming dark shape, anonymous behind dark cloak and black mask. Her knees loosened and gave way; she sagged back against the dock.

The dark shape came forward and spoke in a hoarse whisper. "I'm sorry I startled you, but there was no other way."

Wayness tried to hold her voice firm. "No other way for what?"

"Don't you know? Of course you do. It's what girls are made for."

Wayness' voice trembled despite her best efforts. "Don't be absurd. It's Arles, isn't it? You're absolutely grotesque in that outfit."

"No matter who it is, or how I look!" The heavy whisper had become annoyed. "That's got nothing to do with it."

"Well, whatever you've got in mind, I'm not at all in the mood for it. In fact, you're acting very badly. So goodnight and please don't come scaring me anymore." She started to move away, but Arles caught her arm.

"Not so fast. We haven't even started yet. Let's go over yonder, in that grass, where it will be easier on your pretty little backside."

Wayness pulled back. "Arles, are you crazy? You can't do this and not be punished!"

"It's all in knowing how," said Arles. "You might like it so much that you'll come out every night looking for more."

Wayness said nothing. Arles reached out and twitched away the robe. "I was right. You have a beautiful figure." He chuckled. "What there is of it." He touched her breasts. "I like them somewhat bigger, but these do you very nicely. Come along, over here, and don't think

159

to yell, because I know how to stop that kind of foolishness. Shall I show you?"

"No."

Arles nevertheless gave a great flourish of the hands, then thrust his thumbs into a pair of sensitive places under the turn of her jaw. Wayness jerked back and for a moment broke loose. She turned to run, but Arles was on her, and bore her to the ground. "Now lie there! And don't move!" He spread out the robe and rolled her over upon the fabric. "Now: isn't that nice? What do you think of all this?"

"Please let me go home!"

"That's the wrong thing to say!" Arles' voice was half jesting, half ugly. "Girls like you need attention; that's why you go running around naked looking for it." He reached down and began fondling her body. Wayness stared up at the sky, wondering how Arles dared do this to her. Unless . . . Her mind refused to put the idea into words.

Arles threw aside his cloak, dropped his trousers and lowered himself. From the shadows a dark figure stepped forward. There was motion, a swishing sound, a sodden thud, and Arles fell forward senseless.

Glawen reached down and pulled Wayness to her feet. "You're safe now. It's Glawen."

"Oh Glawen . . ." She pressed against him and started to cry, while he tried to comfort her. "Wayness, poor Wayness! You're safe, safe, safe. Don't cry."

"I can't help it. I think he intended to kill me."

"That's certainly how it might have ended up." Glawen reached for her robe.

"Put this on, then go for your father. Can you do that?"

"I'd rather that you came with me."

Glawen looked down at the twitching hulk. A knife hung at Arles' belt, with which Glawen cut strips from Arles' cloak and tied his ankles and wrists. "There! That will keep him quiet for a few minutes, at least." He looked at Wayness. "Are you feeling well?"

"Well enough."

"Come along, then." Glawen took her hand and they went up the path to Riverview House.

Five minutes later Egon Tamm and Milo returned down the path with a hand lamp to find Arles struggling against the bonds.

At the approach of the two men Arles desisted in his efforts and lay blinking up into the light. "I say, who are you?" he growled. "Turn that damned light out of my eyes and cut these cords. It's an absolute outrage! I've been attacked and injured."

"What a shame," said Milo.

"Turn him loose," said Egon Tamm grimly, and held the light while Milo cut the cords.

Arles rose shakily to his feet. "This is a very bad situation; when I came to help Wayness, someone attacked me. I suggest that we run out to look along the beach."

"I want to look in your pouch. Hand it over."

Arles began to expostulate. "Now, just a moment! By what right—"

Egon Tamm twitched the light toward Milo. "Take his pouch."

"Oh, very well," grumbled Arles. "Here! I carry just a few things, of a personal nature—" His voice trailed away.

Egon Tamm said: "You can go home. Do not try to leave Araminta Station. I will deal with you when my mind is settled."

Arles turned and lurched away through the night. Egon Tamm and Milo returned to Riverview House. Wayness and Glawen were sitting on the couch, sipping the tea served by Cora Tamm.

Egon accepted a cup of tea, then turned a somber gaze upon Glawen. "I am grateful for your timely help. But I am puzzled that you could be so ready at hand when the need arose."

"In other words," said Glawen, "why was I skulking around the neighborhood while your daughter was swimming in the nude?"

Egon Tamm smiled a wintry smile. "You have a nice turn of phrase."

"You have a right to ask. If you recall, Sessily Veder was murdered."

"I remember very well."

"Arles became a prime suspect in the case, although nothing was definitely proved. When Wayness mentioned during class that she often walked alone by night, Arles showed extreme interest. Tonight I kept watch on him. He went up to his bedroom and departed by a secret way across the roof. I followed him up the beach, and along the path to the lake. I would have interfered sooner, except that I had to wait until I could safely come up behind him and bash him decisively. I am sorry if the delay brought extra travail to Wayness. That is your explanation."

Wayness took Glawen's arm and hugged it. "I at least am grateful to Glawen."

"My dear, I am grateful too. But let me ask this: when Arles began to act in a suspicious manner, why not simply use the telephone and let me deal with the matter."

Glawen gave a rueful laugh. "Sir, if I were to answer your question, you might think me rude. You must try to divine the answer for yourself."

"It seems to me that you are being unnecessarily cryptic," said Egon Tamm. "Cora, do you understand his allusions?"

"Not in the slightest. Your suggestion seemed most sound."

Wayness laughed. "But not from Glawen's point of view. Do you want to know why?"

"Of course!" said Cora Tamm. "Why else should the question be asked?"

"Then I'll tell you. Glawen foresaw a conversation like this. Suppose Mother had answered the telephone. Glawen tries to find words to tell you that he thinks someone might be inclined to attack me. You say: 'What's all this nonsense again? Aren't you being just a bit excitable?'

"And Glawen says: 'I don't think so, madame. This is my belief.'

"So, after much cool skepticism and putting Glawen properly in his place, I am warned not to swim, and Father goes out to look up and down the beach. He carries his light, flashes it back and forth; Arles sees him and goes home. Father finds nothing, and comes in disgruntled. He blames Glawen for his preposterous false alarms, and thereafter whenever Glawen's name is mentioned, someone says: 'Oh, yes, that hysterical young man from Clattuc House.' There is the answer to your question, and no doubt better that I should tell you than Glawen."

Egon Tamm looked sternly at Glawen. "Is she correct in all this?"

"I'm afraid so, sir."

Egon Tamm laughed, and his face became suddenly warm. "In that case, it seems that we must mend our ways. I see now that you have handled yourself quite properly, and I truly am grateful to you."

"Say no more, sir. And now I will be going home. One last matter: I hope that my name won't figure in the case, if only to make matters easier for me at Clattuc House."

"Your name will not be mentioned."

Wayness took Glawen to the door. She put her arms around him and hugged him. "I won't even try to thank you."

"Of course not! Think how badly I would feel if something happened to you!"

"I'd feel even worse." On an impulse she turned up her face and kissed Glawen's mouth.

Glawen asked: "Is that just from gratitude?"

"Not entirely."

"Let's do it again, and you tell me which part is which."

"Mother is coming. She wants to know too. Goodnight, Glawen."

9

The time was an hour short of midnight. Arles arrived home to find Spanchetta waiting up for him. Arles, his attention fragmented, had not yet decided upon what should be his version of the night's events and so was forced to improvise a tale with Spanchetta's unwinking stare fixed upon his face.

Spanchetta made no secret of her skepticism. "Please, Arles, it is insulting to be lied to; it is even more insulting to be taken for a half-wit. I find your story bewildering. As I understand it, you had an appointment to meet a girl along the beach, where you intended to help her with her schoolwork. Who was the girl, incidentally? Not that awful Drusilla?"

"She's not awful and she doesn't go to school," muttered Arles. "She's out doing promotional work for the Mummers."

"Well, then: who was it?"

Arles had been told that the most proficient liars used as much truth as possible. "If you must know, it was Wayness Tamm, from Riverview House. She's just a bit of trollop, if the truth be known—very selectively, of course."

"Hmf," said Spanchetta. "So selectively that she beat you and gave you that awful black eye when you made advances?"

"Of course not! When I went out on the beach, I found that a couple of drunken tourists had accosted her and were giving her trouble. I piled into them and set them right, but in the process I took a blow or two myself. I think I'll stay home from school until the black eye is better and my face is less swollen."

"Absolutely not!" declared Spanchetta. "You can't afford to miss any more school."

"I look a fright! What shall I say when people ask questions?"

Spanchetta shrugged. "Apparently you intend to tell no one the truth. Just say that you fell out of bed. Or that you were playing whack-doodle with your grandmother."

So in the morning Arles willy-nilly went slouching off to the lyceum, where, as he had feared, his appearance aroused attention. When asked questions, he followed Spanchetta's advice and said: "I fell out of bed."

Wayness and Milo came to school as usual, but paid no attention to Arles. After the social anthropology class, Arles waited for Wayness in the hall. She walked wordlessly past, but he called out to her. "Wayness, I want to say something to you."

"As you like, but make it short."

"You didn't take me seriously last night, did you?"

Wayness clamped her lips and turned her face away. She said softly: "If I were you I'd be ashamed even to bring the matter up."

"I am, in a way. It seems that I became overexcited, so to speak." Arles attempted a lame grin. "You know how it is."

"I think that you intended to kill me."

"Nonsense!" scoffed Arles. "What a fantastic idea!"

"So it is," said Wayness with a shudder. "I don't want to talk anymore."

"One question! Last night somebody hit me. Who was it?"

"Why do you ask?"

"Hah! Need you ask? It was a cowardly thing to do! Look at me, with this ridiculous black eye!"

"You can express your indignation to my father. You'll be seeing him shortly."

"I don't want to see your father," growled Arles. "So far as I'm concerned, the matter is closed."

Wayness merely shrugged and turned away.

Two days later, during the noon recess, Arles emerged from the cafeteria to be met by four Naturalists in military uniform. Arles, turning pale, looked from one to the other. "What do you want?"

"You are Arles Clattuc?"

"What of it?"

"Come with us."

Arles hung back. "Just a moment. Where? And why?"

"You are going to Riverview House, where you will be dealt with according to law."

Arles took a step back and tried to bluster. "This is Araminta Station! Your law is no good around here."

"Society law controls all of Cadwal. Come."

Protesting and struggling, Arles was placed into a power wagon and conveyed to Riverview House. Spanchetta, when apprised of the event, first called Housemaster Fratano, then Bodwyn Wook, only to learn that both had been called to Riverview House.

The two Araminta dignitaries returned during the middle afternoon. Both spoke with Spanchetta and assured her that Arles could consider himself lucky; he had been stopped short of a capital crime.

During the late afternoon Arles was returned to Araminta Station and released into the Quadrangle. He looked pale and crestfallen, and smelled of antiseptic ointments. As chance would have it, a group of Bold Lions came past as Arles was thrust from the power wagon.

164

Cloyd Diffin called out: "So where have you been, and what did they do to you?"

Kiper said critically: "My word, what a state of bedragglement!"

Shugart bleated: "And all for waxing a pair of drunken tourists? Hard lines, I call it."

"It's a bit more complicated than that," muttered Arles. "I don't want to talk about it now . . . It was all bluff, anyway, I'm sure of it. They'd never dare do such a thing to me."

Uther Offaw asked: "You're rambling dreadfully, you know. Try to be lucid and tell us what happened."

"Nothing: just a misunderstanding. It's bound to be a bluff."

"You smell of hospital," said Kirdy Wook. "Were doctors there? These drunken tourists that you chastised: were they doctors, by any chance?"

"I've got to go home now," said Arles. "We'll talk about it later."

CHAPTER 4

1

In response to a summons from Bodwyn Wook, Glawen presented himself to the Bureau B outer office and was directed to a door at the end of a short corridor. An elderly clerk admitted him to an anteroom and after a question or two allowed him entry into Bodwyn Wook's private office: a tall chamber of irregular dimension, with chest-high wainscoting of green baize rectangles surrounded by dark moldings, and dark paneling to the ceiling. High on the wall at the end of the room a group of stuffed animal heads glared down from the shadows; another wall was decorated with dozens of old photographs.

Bodwyn Wook turned away from the window and went to his chair. He indicated another chair for Glawen, then, leaning back, clasped his hands over his bald pate and inspected Glawen through half-closed yellow eyes. "Well, then, Sergeant Clattuc! What are you prepared to tell me?"

An odd question, thought Glawen, and one perhaps calling for a meticulously careful reply. He said: "I have prepared no statement whatever, sir."

"Really? I thought that you had been consorting with the Bold Lions."

"True. I have observed them carefully and listened to their conversations. There is always wild talk which no one takes seriously; in fact, I have learned nothing of any consequence."

"No scurrilous gossip? No defamatory anecdotes? My tastes are catholic."

"Nothing which would justify a report, sir."

"I inquire not just from frivolity," said Bodwyn Wook. "I am hoping always to intercept one unguarded sentence, or a phrase, or even a word which might unlock some startling mystery. I don't know this word or sentence, but I will recognize it when I hear it, and it is this word or sentence for which you must be on the alert."

"I will keep my ears open, sir."

"Good. In connection with Arles: exactly what took place the other night?"

Glawen looked up in surprise. "Did not the Conservator discuss the matter with you?"

Bodwyn Wook darted a yellow stare across the desk, but Glawen had already perceived his transgression and had pulled his head down between his shoulders: enough, apparently, to amuse Bodwyn Wook, who gave a civil answer to the question. "He provided a perfunctory account of what took place. Since his daughter was involved, I did not press for details. What, then, are the full circumstances?"

"It started in a class at the lyceum," said Glawen. "Arles heard Wayness say that sometimes she went out alone at night, to walk along the beach, or even swim. The idea interested Arles. That same night he donned a cloak and mask, and skulked along Beach Road to Riverview House. He came upon Wayness swimming in the lagoon and attacked her. It seems to be something he likes to do. In any event, someone who wants to remain nameless followed him to Riverview House, and stopped him before he did anything worse than scare Wayness out of her wits."

"And how did this nameless person accomplish such a feat?"

"He hit Arles over the head with a club."

"Ha-ha! So Arles still wonders who interfered with his gallantry?"

"He probably suspects Milo, which suits me very well."

Bodwyn Wook nodded. "Apparently—and this is the opinion of the Conservator—he did not go out intending to kill the girl. He disguised himself; he carried a bag to put over her head, and even a bag of knockout gas. These items saved his life, according to the Conservator."

"Perhaps so. But once she recognized him, I suspect that, after apologizing with great courtesy, he would have killed her. If you recall, Sessily Veder is dead."

"Not so fast! In this case Arles is demonstrably guilty. In the case of Sessily Veder, he is only a prime suspect."

"More so than ever, it seems to me."

"I would not argue with you there."

Glawen asked: "And what now with Arles? Is there an official Bureau position?"

"The case is closed," said Bodwyn Wook. "He has been definitively punished, according to the Conservator, and anything more would be in the nature of double jeopardy."

"Can't we even expel him from Clattuc House?"

167

"On what charge? And who will bring it? And, most cogently, who will deal with Spanchetta?"

"In the meantime, he swaggers around as if nothing had happened," said Glawen in disgust. "I can't bear to look at him."

"You must control your emotions. It is good training for you. When will the Bold Lions make their excursion to Yipton?"

"During the half-term holidays. But I'm not going."

Bodwyn Wook waved his finger. "There you are wrong! That is the main reason you have become a Bold Lion." He reached into a drawer and withdrew a folded sheet of paper, which he opened out and placed on his desk. "This is a chart of Yipton, in as much detail as we are able to achieve. Here is the dock, and here is the Arkady Inn. These blue marks are canals. They open into the ocean, as you will notice, at the passes between the rim islands. The pink-shaded area is the Caglioro, or the Pot. All these passages and canals have names, but each Yip, for whatever reason, tells us something different.

"Now then"— Bodwyn Wook tapped another section of the chart — "here is Pussycat Palace. Notice this gray area beside the dock. It's also just behind the hotel, which must be sheer chance. The Yips are evasive about this area, and we want to know what goes on here. As a Bold Lion you're expected to be undisciplined and erratic, and you'll have more latitude than the ordinary visitors: possibly just enough for you to learn something. It won't be easy; in fact, it may well be dangerous, but it's a job which needs to be done. What about it?"

"I'll do my best."

"I expect no more. Naturally you will say nothing to anyone in regard to this mission, except your father, Scharde."

"Very well, sir."

2

The school term proceeded. Arles attended classes in surly silence and once again managed to jerk himself back from the brink of dismissal.

Wayness and Milo followed their own routines, indifferent to the presence of Arles. For a time Wayness was attended by whispers and covert glances, stimulated by Arles' wild explanations of his black eye, but the scandal collapsed of its own improbability.

Toward Glawen Wayness continued to use elusive tactics, or so it seemed. Try as he might, he could arrive at no explanation for her distant behavior. One day, when Milo had not come to school, Glawen walked Wayness home. For a space she held him at arm's length with flippant remarks and comments on schoolwork, but at last Glawen became impatient. Taking her hand, he swung her smartly round, so that she stood facing him. She cried out, half laughing: "Glawen! I had to jump and skip to keep from turning a somersault! Is that what you had in mind?"

"I want to know why you are acting so oddly."

Wayness put on an airy attitude. "Please, Glawen, don't be cross. It's not easy being me nowadays."

"One would never guess. You make it seem so effortless."

Wayness smiled. "I don't lack for help. Mother is training me for a life of dignity and decorum. You want me to be a full-fledged Clattuc, ready for anything, fearless of scandal or disgrace."

"Yes; it gives one a fine feeling of freedom!"

"But there is someone else with even more influence over me. This person urges me in quite a different direction, with advice that I can't ignore."

"Oh? Who is this wise individual?"

"Me."

Glawen presently asked: "And what advice do you hear from yourself?"

Wayness turned away; the two walked south along the Beach Road. "It concerns something which I've never mentioned before, and I'd prefer not to talk about it now."

"Why not? Is it a secret, or a mystery?"

"It's something I learned when Milo and I were last on Earth, and it's become an obsession with me. I intend to go back to Earth as soon as I've finished school. With Milo, if he'll come."

The light from Syrene suddenly seemed less bright and cheerful. Glawen asked: "Do you intend to enlighten me, ever?"

"I hadn't thought about it, one way or the other."

"And this is why you want to break off our relationship."

Wayness burst out laughing. "That's very poor logic! I said nothing of the sort! Anyway it's not the reason. In fact, there isn't any reason except that I know myself and I'm afraid."

"Afraid of what?"

Wayness gave an oblique answer. "At Stroma our love affairs are very demure. Just to sit in a corner with someone, drinking tea and eating cookies, is considered high adventure."

Glawen made a glum sound. "We haven't even reached that stage yet."

"Don't be in such a hurry; it drags on forever and it's tiresome, especially if Mother hangs around."

"What's the next stage?"

"That's the one of which I'm afraid. I don't want to start something which takes my mind off—more important things."

"I take it you mean your trip to Earth?"

Wayness nodded. "Perhaps I shouldn't have brought the subject up, except that I'd have to tell you sooner or later and it's only fair to tell you sooner, so that you can avoid me, if you're of a mind to do so."

"And this is why you've been hiding from me?"

Wayness again gave an oblique answer. "I've decided not to hide from you anymore."

"That's good news."

They arrived at the path which led through the trees to Riverview House. Wayness hesitated, moved first in one direction then another, until Glawen caught her and kissed her: once, then twice. "The answer then is yes?"

"Yes? To what?"

"To our so-called relationship."

Wayness gave her shoulders a jerk, squinted, squirmed, tilted her head, twitched her nose, made a fluttering gesture with her fingers.

Glawen asked in wonder, "What's that all mean?"

"It's a complicated way of not saying no." Wayness started off down the path.

"Wait!" cried Glawen. "I'm still not clear on a number of things!"

"Clarity is not what I had in mind." Wayness stepped close and kissed him. "Thanks for walking me home. You're a nice kindly young gentleman, even handsome in a grim sort of way, and I like you."

Glawen tried to catch her but she ran off along the path. Just before passing from sight she turned, waved, then disappeared among the trees.

3

On Verd evening of each week the Bold Lions met in a corner of the Old Arbor, to conduct business, drink wine and discuss the trends and fashions. A peculiar mood characterized these occasions, based on the premise that each Bold Lion was inherently noble and superior in all his phases to the general ruck of man. Golden haze hung over the table; large schemes were proposed and analyzed; each of the eternal verities in turn came under examination and from time to time were amended.

Each Bold Lion sat at his dedicated place around the table.[1] At the far end, with his back to the arcade, sat Arles, with Kirdy Wook to his right and Uther Offaw to his left. Jardine Laverty faced Arles from the far end of the table, while the others sat to either side in their wonted places. Glawen, arriving late, took his seat between Cloyd Diffin and Jardine Laverty. Several jugs of wine had already been consumed, and the conversation was going well. Jardine Laverty, suave, handsome and carefully dressed, was making a point: "—musty old laws quite irrelevant to our needs. Still they exist and every day we are thwarted and demeaned by some long-dead prejudice."

Jardine in this case referred to the laws which banned the mining of precious gems: a sore point among the Bold Lions, since a month or two of prospecting the Magic Mountain mineral beds might well make millionaires of them all.

Kiper Offaw, who already had tippled at least adequately, called out in a rather wild voice: "Put it to the vote! All in favor? All opposed?"

Kiper was considered somewhat brash and no one paid him any heed. He contented himself singing the refrain of an old song:

"Oh sell no more drink to my father!
"It makes him so strange and so wild!"

Shugart Veder, who represented the conservative point of view, stated: "Certainly these old rules should be brought in line with new concepts, but this would mean rewriting the Charter, which could only be effected at a Grand Conclave of the Naturalist Society."

"Bah!" growled Arles. "Fat chance of that. Over the years they've ossified and become an odd type of subrace, like the Yips. They don't want change! Give them a fish and a pound of seaweed, they'll make soup and never ask for anything better."

Kirdy frowned. "Let's be reasonable. We're petty functionaries in the service of the Naturalists, and like it or not we've got to mind our manners."

[1] The Bold Lions at Their Table

Arles Clattuc

Kirdy Wook	Uther Oftaw
Cloyd Diffin	Shugart Veder
Glawen Clattuc	Kiper Offaw

Jardine Laverty

Arles drank down the contents of his mug at a gulp. "I don't like it."

"Well, you must put up with it, or leave. Those are the cold facts."

Arles gave a throaty chuckle. "You're a Wook and that's Wook thinking. I'm a Clattuc and I have other notions."

Shugart Veder put a petulant inquiry: "Can someone tell me where the Charter actually resides? It's not at Riverview House, nor at Stroma. If someone wanted to verify the text, where would he look?"

"Ha, ha!" cried Kiper. "It's all a great joke! There isn't now and never has been a Charter! We've been dancing jigs to the music of ghosts!"

Jardine raised his elegant eyebrows. "Kiper, if you please! Either talk sense or pay for the wine!"

"Or both," said Uther.

"Exactly so," said Kirdy. "But let's clear up this foolish talk once and for all. The Charter is obviously in the Society Archives on Earth, and if any benighted soul is ignorant of the text, copies abound."

"That's not the point!" argued Jardine. "Was the Charter designed to enforce poverty upon the folk of Araminta Station? It's hard to believe anyone would be quite so niggardly!"

"Wrong, as usual," said Uther Offaw. "The Charter was drafted by Naturalists, with conservancy in mind."

"And nothing but conservancy," added Kirdy Wook.

Arles grumbled: "They're all peaceably dead, and we're still suffering for their mistakes."

Kirdy gave a caw of scornful laughter. "Mistakes? Nonsense! They wanted workers at Araminta Station, not millionaires."

"Strange folk indeed," sighed Jardine. "Then and now."

"High-stepping old pettifoggers in tight black pants!" declared Kiper. "Who cares what they wanted? I know what I want, and that's what counts!"

Cloyd called out: "For once Kiper is on the mark! Bravo, Kiper!"

Shugart put on a lewd smirk. "He'll have to wait for Pussycat Palace; then he can have as much as he likes."

"All he can pay for, at any rate," said Uther. "Credit forms are not accepted."

Cloyd Diffin made a sly suggestion: "Since Arles is coming we should try for the wholesale rate."

Arles lowered his heavy eyebrows and scowled down the table. "I've heard about enough of this talk! It's far off the mark, and everyone knows it!"

Shugart Veder said brightly: "Come, now, fellow Growlers! Let's concentrate on our goals! Yesterday I saw an advertisement for the new Black Andromeda that actually made me salivate with longing!"

"Bah! Too small!" said Kiper. "I'll take a Pentar Conquestor, maybe with recessed pods, for that sleek look!"

Jardine gave a contemptuous snort. "Have you no taste? What of the Dancred Mark Twenty? There's true style for you! A bit pricy, of course, but what's money?"

"Nothing very important," said Cloyd. "Just the elixir of life."

"A delightful word," sighed Uther. "It tinkles with sweet overtones: poetry and luscious fruits and the pit-a-pat of beautiful girls!"

"Pit-a-pat?" asked Kiper. "What is 'pit-a-pat'? I'm old enough now to know."

"Take it and pay for it and don't ask questions," said Uther. "That's my best advice."

Shugart said: "Money has always been our great problem, even though the basic philosophy is simple."

"I wish I found it so," said Kiper wistfully.

"Nothing to it," said Shugart. "First, locate someone with money. Second, learn what he wants more than the money. Third, make this available to him. It works every time."

Kiper asked: "In that case, how is it that you are not rich?"

"You've heard enough for now," said Shugart with dignity. "I suggest that you lean back in your chair, drink wine and dream of pit-a-pat while your betters discuss serious matters."

Jardine said: "There's Namour! He knows all about such things . . . Hoy, Namour! Over here! Join the Bold Lions for a change!"

Namour turned his head and appraised the table. Tonight, fixed into his silver hair on the right side of his head, he wore a small but elegant confection of black iron, polished jet cabochons, with a single carbuncle glowing with the sultry fury of a red star: presumably the present of an admirer. With a languid step he approached the table. "Hard at your lucubrations, so I see."

Cloyd blinked. "Quite right, or so I suppose. We're also doing some deep thinking. Draw up a chair! Jardine, pour Namour a mug of that good Sancery! Namour, drink up!"

"Thank you." Namour seated himself. A black twill jacket with a high-collared black shirt set off his aquiline features to perfection. He tasted the wine, and his eyebrows vaulted high. He looked askance into the mug. "Sancery, did you say? Good Sancery? What are they serving you? Waiter, if you please! What is this dark-colored liquid? I've been told it's Sancery, but that is hard to believe."

"It's from the keg we call Bold Lion Reserve, sir."

"I see. Bring me something from a keg less confused as to its antecedents: some of that Laverty Delasso will do nicely."

Uther Offaw looked ruefully into his own mug. "Well, at least it's cheap."

"Never mind the wine," said Shugart. "Our problem is that we want to buy a space yacht."

"That's a fairly common ambition," said Namour. "I'm in the market myself."

"Really? What do you have in mind?"

"Oh—I don't know. Maybe a Merlin or an Interstar Majestic."

Kiper asked innocently: "How do you plan to pay for it?"

Namour laughed and shook his head. "Now you are probing too deeply!"

Shugart turned to the other Bold Lions. "Perhaps we should take Namour into our syndicate! It might expedite things for all of us!"

Arles looked toward Namour. "What do you say to that?"

Namour pursed his lips thoughtfully. "My favorite philosopher declares: 'Not only does he travel fastest who travels alone, he travels twice as fast as two people, three times as fast as three people and four times as fast as four.'"

"Ha-hah!" cried Uther Offaw. "And what is the name of this misanthropic philosopher?"

"He is Ronsel de Roust, of The Galcidine. Still, I'm willing to listen to anything, if it's to my advantage, and if it's definite! I can't waste time on a lot of wild talk."

"Naturally not," said Shugart. "We're all in earnest, and we don't propose to be thwarted!"

"What exactly do you have in mind?"

"Well—we have several ideas, such as a big new tourist resort on Sunrise Strand. We're short of capital, but if you guaranteed cheap labor to the project, we might get a bank loan for the balance. We envision everything first-class, with a gambling casino, a cosmopolitan restaurant, and naturally a corps of Yip girls to jolly up the patrons."

Cloyd asked anxiously: "What do you think? Could it be arranged?"

"You'd never get past the Conservator."

Jardine pounded the table. "We're suffering financial problems and this is a great solution! He's got to see it our way!"

Namour sipped his wine. "What if he won't? Do you plan to bring pressure to bear? If so: how?"

"Well, persuasion of some sort. After all, what does it matter to the Naturalists?"

Cloyd demanded: "How could they stop us if we were resolute? I hardly think they'd use force."

"Hmm." Namour mused a moment. "They're not particularly numerous, and half of them are social idealists called LPFers."

Uther Offaw, somewhat the worse for wine, said: "Still, they claim to own the planet, and they've got the Charter to prove it."

"That's what we're told, at any rate," said Namour.

Once again Shugart pounded the table. "Devil take them, LPFers, black pants and all! The Bold Lions insist on justice!"

Kiper, flushed in the face, cried out: "Three great growls for Shugart and his manifesto of justice!"

Kirdy said: "Quiet, Kiper! You are far too obstreperous. Namour, you were about to speak?"

Kiper refused to restrain his advocacy. "I'm a Bold Lion, brave and free! I want money so bad I can taste it!"

"Please, Kiper! Namour is experienced in these matters! Let him speak!"

"With pleasure! Speak, Namour, to your heart's content!"

"Only this," said Namour. "Perhaps you are making the wrong sort of plans. Cadwal is due for change: everyone knows this. Those who will profit are those who ride the changes and control them, not the folk who lament for the old days."

Kirdy's big features twisted into ropes of perplexity. "I don't quite follow you. Surely—"

Namour made an easy gesture. "I offer no program! I merely point out that it's better to win through decisive action, even force, than lose everything through hand-wringing and confusion."

Arles became excited. "How else has the Reach been expanded across the galaxy? By games of pattycake and cat's cradle? Not on your life!"

Namour said: "One thing is sure. Changes are on their way. We can't keep the Yips away from the Marmion Low Plain forever, and it may go farther than that when the time comes. And in the end, some will survive and others will not. I hope to survive."

"The Bold Lions as well!" cried Cloyd.

"That seems a sensible choice," said Namour mildly.

Jardine slapped the table. "Namour, you may well be the wisest man at Araminta Station, in spite of being a Clattuc."

"Kind of you to say so." Namour rose to his feet. "Well, I'll amble on and leave you Lions to roar in peace. Goodnight, all."

On the following morning, during breakfast, Scharde took note of Glawen's preoccupation. He said: "You're very quiet. How went the meeting?"

Glawen gathered in his thoughts from far places. "Much as usual, or so I suppose. I heard wild talk by the bucketful, if that's any clue."

Scharde chuckled. "A lively affair, in short."

"A bit too lively, I should say. No one seems to notice where sanity stops and hysteria begins. At times I couldn't believe what I was hearing."

Scharde leaned back in his chair. "Kirdy reports to Bodwyn Wook from a somewhat different perspective."

"No doubt. Kirdy may be the worst of the lot. He enjoys every minute of it."

"Kirdy is experiencing a late and rather ponderous adolescence," said Scharde. "What strikes you as lunacy, he considers just high spirits and playacting."

Glawen gave a disparaging grunt. "That theory is all very well for Kirdy, and maybe Arles, who are Mummers, but how do you explain Namour, who wisely considers even Kiper's crazy notions? Is Namour just being polite? Is he, too, playacting? Or does he have something else in mind? I find him hard to understand."

"There you're not alone. Namour plays whatever role he thinks immediately useful, and sometimes just for practice. I could talk all day about Namour and still not finish."

Glawen went to look out the window. He grumbled: "I can't say that I like this undercover work. It's absolutely embarrassing to sit as a full high-tailed Bold Lion, roaring and growling at the signal."

"The job won't last forever. I might mention that you have already gained Bodwyn Wook's approval, and if you do well as a Bold Lion, you'll be established in your career—no matter what your Status Index."

"Another depressing thought," said Glawen. "It's only two years to cutoff."

"You worry too much! Somehow we'll work it out, even if I must take an early retirement. If worse comes to worst you can marry into the House."

"I don't know about that. Namour never seemed to like that solution."

"Namour could have married back a dozen times. Although

Spanchetta wouldn't let him marry her sister Smonny, or so the rumor goes."

"What a thought! If ever I marry, which is doubtful, I have someone else in mind."

"In any case, it's too early to think about such dismal matters."

"I'm certainly in no hurry."

Scharde presently departed the chambers on business of his own. Glawen stood by the window looking out over the countryside.

The morning was fine. Syrene shone bright in a cloudless sky. The Clattuc gardens were at their best, and Glawen's gloom began to dissipate.

A pleasant thought entered his mind. He went to the telephone and called Riverview House.

To his relief, Wayness answered the chime. At the sight of Glawen's face, she allowed her own image to appear on the screen. Her voice was cordial, if a trifle prim. "Good morning, Glawen."

"That is an understatement. The day is superb!"

Wayness clapped her hands. "How nice that you have notified me so early in the day!"

Glawen said modestly: "I would have called even earlier, but I wanted to make certain of the facts."

"Thank you, Glawen! I approve of such caution. If you called at dawn with your glad news, and we dragged ourselves from bed to find a torrent of rain, everyone would be somewhat nonplussed."

"Exactly so." Glawen took note of Wayness' dark green blouse with white cuffs and a white lace collar. "Why are you dressed in such finery? Are you going somewhere?"

Wayness smilingly shook her head. "It's our Naturalist vanity. We can't allow anyone to think that he can catch us in dishabille simply by calling at dawn."

"Come, now! It's later than that. You're off on some sort of outing."

"As a matter of fact, guests are visiting from Stroma and today I'm on my best behavior. I must also dress the part, so that I am not considered a bedraggled little tomboy."

"If you continued to wear nice clothes and guaranteed to behave yourself, would you be allowed to come sailing for an hour or two?"

"Today? When the guests include that important young philosopher Julian Bohost?"

"The answer seems to be no."

"Emphatically! If you and I went frolicking off in a boat leaving Julian standing on the shore, we could expect a cool reception on our return, and only haughty glances from Julian."

"And still he is considered a philosopher?"

"As a matter of fact, we are demeaning poor Julian. He is actually rather a pleasant fellow, although prone to impromptu political speeches."

"Hm. Someday I would like to meet this splendid young prodigy!"

"That is easy enough. Julian is quite approachable, even amiable, if you don't annoy him." Wayness seemed to reflect. "There is nothing to stop you from calling today, if you were of a mind to do so."

"Why not?" said Glawen.

"Spoken like a true Clattuc! Why not indeed? But you must come as if paying a formal visit, or Mother would politely ask you to call another day, in order to give Julian a free hand with me."

"A formal visit?"

"It's a common custom in Stroma, and considered a compliment to the hostess."

"I need no invitation?"

"Not for a formal call. Best of all, she is obliged to be agreeable." Wayness turned a quick look over her shoulder. "But you must conduct yourself by the proper etiquette."

"That goes without saying. I may be a Clattuc but I do not dip my chin in the soup."

Wayness made an impatient gesture. "Listen carefully! You must wear a hat, if only your sailing cap."

"I understand. Proceed."

"Pick a nice bouquet of flowers, then come to the front door at Riverview House."

"And then?"

"Listen carefully! Every detail is important! Sound the chime, and stand close by the door. If Mother appears, you must step forward into the doorway, proffer the flowers and say: 'Dame Cora, from my house to yours comes this blessing of flowers.' Say no more, no less. Etiquette requires that Mother take the flowers and make a formal acknowledgment. No matter what she says, pay no heed, even if it is something like 'Thank you, Glawen; today we are all sick.' Just pretend you did not hear. Step forward and hand her your cap. She must now say: 'What a great pleasure! How long will we enjoy your company?' You will say: 'Today only!' And that is the whole of it. You have used the proper ritual and you are now a welcome guest, on a level with Julian."

"What if someone else answers the door?"

"Then you must step forward into the doorway, but not into the house—just so that the door cannot be closed—and say: 'I bring a token for Dame Cora Tamm.' Then wait until Mother appears, and proceed as before. Can you remember all this?"

"I'm afraid I'll feel embarrassed."

"Julian Bohost would perform the ritual with total aplomb and excite Mother's admiration."

"I'm not embarrassed after all," said Glawen. "I'll be there as soon as possible."

"Today should be interesting," said Wayness.

Glawen changed into garments he thought suitable for the occasion, pulled a soft cap slantwise over his forehead and left the chambers. From the House gardener he obtained a bouquet of beautiful pink jonquils, then took himself at best speed south, down the Beach Road, to Riverview House.

He halted before the massive front door, where he discovered that his heart seemed to be beating faster than usual. He muttered under his breath: "Am I really such a coward after all? Dame Cora is a gracious lady! I have no real cause for fear."

He settled his jacket, arranged the bouquet, marched forward and sounded the chime.

Moments passed, one after the other. The door opened, to reveal Dame Cora herself, stately in a gown of soft dark blue weave, enlivened by stripes of rose red. She looked at Glawen in mild surprise, which became startlement as he stepped forward into the doorway and thrust the bouquet into her hands. "Dame Cora, from my house to yours comes this blessing of flowers!"

Dame Cora at last found her tongue. "The flowers are beautiful, Glawen, and I am pleased to find that you are familiar with the old courtesies, even if you don't quite understand all their implications." She went on, rather lamely: "I fear that both Milo and Wayness are occupied today. But you'll see them soon at school. I will tell them that you called."

Glawen grimly stepped forward, so that Dame Cora was forced to sway back. He took off his cap and pushed it into her limp fingers. "Indeed, Glawen, this is a great surprise and a great pleasure. How long may we expect to enjoy your company?"

"Today only, sad to say."

Dame Cora closed the door with a hint of unnecessary emphasis.

Glawen took occasion to look about the room, which was pleasantly dim. Age-darkened wainscoting covered the walls; on the floor a heavy rug displayed patterns worked in odd combinations of black, black-red, sour green and blue-green, with accents of dark orange, white and red. Across the room a line of glass-fronted cabinets displayed oddments and curios collected across eras of time and light-years of space.

Dame Cora, turning from the door, stood irresolute a moment, chewing on an invisible bit of thread. Then she said crisply: "Naturally, Glawen, we are always happy to see you, but—"

Glawen bowed. "No more need be said, Dame Cora. I am happy to be here."

Wayness entered the room. "Who is it, Mother?" She had changed from her dark green blouse and now wore a dusky-pale frock almost the same color as her skin; in the dimness her eyes seemed large and luminous. "Glawen? How nice to see you!"

Dame Cora said: "Glawen has presented himself as a guest, despite the inconveniences which our other guests may impose upon him."

Wayness came forward. "You need not worry about Glawen; he is flexible and not at all diffident. In any case, either Milo or I will see to his comfort."

"That is the point," said Dame Cora. "Both you and Milo will be needed with Julian. I am afraid that Glawen may feel quite out of things."

"Nonsense, Mother! Glawen will fit very nicely. If not, Milo can take Julian for a long walk, while Glawen and I entertain each other."

Glawen said graciously: "That will suit me very well, if worse comes to worst! Please do not worry on my account."

Dame Cora bowed. "I will leave you with Wayness. Remember, my dear, you must not chatter so incessantly with your school chum that you neglect poor Julian." She turned to Glawen: "Julian is one of our most respected young thinkers. He is highly artistic and very progressive! I am sure that you will like him immensely; in fact, he and Wayness are making serious plans for the future."

"That is exciting news!" said Glawen. "I must congratulate the gentleman."

Wayness laughed. "It would be extremely premature. Julian would think I had set my cap for him, which is far from the case; in fact, our 'serious plans' are only for an excursion to Mad Mountain Lodge later this year."

Dame Cora said coldly: "Truly, Wayness, you are far too frivolous; Glawen will make embarrassing assumptions about your character." She nodded to Glawen and departed the room, leaving behind a heavy silence.

Glawen turned to Wayness. He bent forward to kiss her, but she drew back. "Glawen! Have you lost your mind? Mother might come back at any instant! And then you'd hear some talk about frivolity!

180

Let's go to the parlor! It's far more cheerful." She led the way along a passage and into a wide airy parlor. Windows overlooked a placid expanse of lagoon. Three green rugs lay upon the bleached wooden floor; couches and chairs were upholstered in green and blue fabrics.

Wayness took Glawen to a couch; he seated himself at one end, and Wayness settled herself at the other. Glawen watched her sidelong, wondering if he would ever understand the workings of her mind. He asked: "Where are your guests?"

Wayness tilted her head to listen. "Julian and Milo are in the library studying charts of the Mad Mountain district. Sunje lounges with one hip on the table hoping that someone will notice her intellect. The two Wardens are raking Father over the coals. It's an annual ritual which the Conservator must tolerate with good grace. Warden Algin Ballinder is Sunje's father; Warden Clytie Vergence is Julian's aunt. Dame Etrune Ballinder, who is Sunje's mother, is gossiping with Mother in the upstairs sitting room. They take turns, each telling grim little tales of her daughter's vice and folly, while the other makes horrified noises. It is good catharsis and I approve; Mother will be quite nice to me for three or four days. Finally, in the parlor, sitting with full punctilio at one end of the couch, and for the moment behaving himself well, is the mettlesome Glawen Clattuc of Clattuc House."

"Who is happy to be here, even though he can't quite understand the reason for his presence."

Wayness showed a trace of vexation. "Must everything have a reason attached to it, like a label?"

"In this case, the possibilities are so tantalizing that I can't help but speculate."

Wayness looked off across the room. In a soft voice she recited lines from an antique poem: "'Never put questions to the wet dark sea; you might learn the drowning of your most darling argosies.' So sang the mad poet Navarth."

The words hung in the air. At last Glawen said: "Tell me something of your guests."

"They come in all sizes and shapes. Julian and Warden Vergence are flagrant LPFers. Warden Ballinder is no less definitely a Chartist. Dame Ballinder doesn't care, so long as everyone is polite. Sunje, with Julian nearby, calls herself a New Humanist, which means whatever she says it means. And that is the lot."

"I look forward to meeting them, especially Julian. Your mother is sure that we will like each other immensely."

Wayness grinned. "Mother's dream worlds are inhabited by charming people who always behave nicely. I am to marry, breed two dear quiet children and glow with pride whenever Julian issues a manifesto. Milo is destined to become a force for the good. He will be clean, honest, forthright and virtuous: he will never be rude to the Yips, much less fight them. Conservationism is a noble ideal, even though Mother is afraid of ugly beasts who growl and make bad smells. Perhaps they should be kept behind a fence."

"And how does your father respond to these opinions?"

"Oh, Father has mastered the art of amiable vagueness. Perhaps he'll say: 'That is an interesting opinion, my dear. We must look to see how it accords with the Charter.' And that's all there is to the matter." She lifted her head to listen. "Here come our guests from the library."

A tall young woman came swinging jauntily into the room. She wore tight plum-colored trousers and a black jacket; her face was small and pale in a cap of straight black hair. Sparkling black eyes, arched eyebrows and a wide quizzical mouth caused her to seem knowing, mischievous and privy to all manner of exotic secrets. A tall spare young man, evidently Julian Bohost, sauntered behind her, talking over his shoulder to Milo. He was somewhat lanky and loose-jointed, with round blue eyes and a fine straight nose. An aureole of light brown curls surrounded his fresh fair face; his voice, tenor and resonant, carried easily across the room: "—when one considers the lay of the land, the mysteries multiply . . . Hullo! Who's this?"

Milo, bringing up the rear, also stopped short at the sight of Glawen. "Well, well! Today the house overflows with celebrities! Shall I perform the introductions?"

"Please do," said Wayness. "But try to be brisk; your introductions are often like eulogies at a funeral."

"I shall do my best," said Milo. "Here we have a female in purple pants, named Sunje Ballinder. Beside her, somewhat less eye-catching but equally influential, is Julian Bohost. Neither has a criminal record and both are ornaments of fashionable Stroma society. Over here we discover the distinguished Glawen Clattuc of Clattuc House, already a high-ranking official of Bureau B."

"I am honored to meet you both," said Glawen.

"And I no less," said Julian.

Sunje inspected Glawen sidelong. "Bureau B? What a fascinating line of work! As I understand it, you patrol the shores and guard the Conservancy from attack?"

"That is a fair statement," said Glawen. "Although for a fact we have other duties as well."

"Would you think me impertinent if I asked to see your gun?"

Glawen smiled politely. "You are under a misapprehension. We handle guns only when out on patrol."

"Oh, what a shame! I have long wondered whether the patrollers truly filed notches for every Yip they had killed."

Again Glawen smiled. "I'd be filing every minute of my spare time! My business is killing Yips, not keeping a head count, which never could be wholly exact. When I set fire to a crowded boatload, I can only estimate the casualties. In any event, it's a useless statistic, since for every Yip I kill, two or three step forward. The sport has lost its zest."

Milo asked: "Could you possibly take Sunje out on a patrol and let her shoot a few Yips of her own?"

"I don't see why not." Glawen turned to Sunje. "Mind you, I can't guarantee any sport. Sometimes days or even weeks go by without a single honest shot."

Julian looked at Sunje. "What do you say? Here's your chance, if you're ready for it."

Sunje stalked across the room and flung herself into a chair. "I think you're all rather vapid."

Milo told Glawen: "Perhaps I should mention that Sunje endorses the program of the New Humanists, who are in turn the cutting edge of the Peefers."

"LPFers, if you don't mind."

"These are terms and phrases from the nomenclature of Naturalist politics," Milo explained to Glawen. "L, P and F stand for 'Life,' 'Peace' and 'Freedom.' Julian is an ardent member of the group."

Glawen said: "With such a slogan, how dare anyone raise his voice in opposition?"

"It's generally agreed that the slogan is the best part of the program," said Milo.

Julian ignored Milo's remark. "Against all sanity, opponents to the great LPF movement not only exist but flourish like noxious weeds."

"These are evidently the 'DWSers': the advocates of 'Death,' 'War' and 'Slavery.' Am I right?" said Glawen.

"They are clever and devious!" said Julian. "Never would they flaunt their true colors so brazenly. Instead they call themselves Chartists and think to hold the high ground by waving funny old documents at us."

Milo said: "These documents are known as the Articles of the Naturalist Society and are otherwise known as the Charter. Julian, why do you not read them someday?"

Julian made a debonair gesture. "Far easier to argue from ignorance."

"All this comes as a shock to me," said Glawen. "At the Station we consider the Charter to be the First Law of the Universe. Anyone who thinks otherwise must be a Yip, a madman or the Devil himself."

Wayness said: "Julian, which is it with you?"

Julian considered. "I have been called a bumptious young pest, a shrike and a doodle-wit, and today already the epithet 'vapid' has been used, but I am neither Yip, madman nor Devil! When all is taken with all, I am no more than an earnest young fellow not greatly different from Milo."

"Hold hard there!" exclaimed Milo. "I'm not entirely sure that Julian intends a compliment!"

"It must be a compliment!" said Wayness. "Julian would never identify himself with anything other than the finest and best, or at least the most stylish."

Milo said reluctantly: "I agree to points of similarity. We both wear our shoes with the toes pointing forward. We both use proper table utensils, if only to keep from biting our fingers. But we do have differences. I am staid and methodical, while Julian spatters clever ideas in all directions like a dog scratching off fleas. Where he gets them I'm sure I don't know."

"I can offer a rather pitiful explanation," said Julian. "When I was little, I read a great deal, night and day, and thereby absorbed the ideas of five hundred savants. Upon trying to assimilate this massive lump of squirming postulations, I suffered spasm after spasm of intellectual indigestion which—"

Wayness held up her hand. "I should mention that lunch will soon be served and if you are about to extend your metaphor into details of the consequent diarrhea, you might put some of us out of appetite. Poor Sunje already looks a bit clammy and ill."

Julian bowed. "Your point is well-taken. I will moderate my language. Briefly, when an idea, clever or otherwise, enters my head, I wonder as to its source. Is this idea truly mine or am I simply regurgitating the notions of someone else? Therefore I often hesitate to put a wonderful concept forward as my own for fear that someone wiser and more erudite than myself will recognize it and jeer at me for my plagiarism."

"An interesting idea!" said Milo.

Glawen nodded. "I thought so too when first I came upon it a few days ago."

"Eh?" said Julian. "What's all this?"

184

"By chance I am able to verify your thesis, although I emphatically disclaim erudition superior to your own."

Milo asked: "Exactly what are you telling us?"

"A day or so ago I had reason to check into the works of the philosopher Ronsel de Roust, which are part of Bjärnstra's *Pocket Guide to Five Hundred Notable Thinkers with Annotations of Their Thoughts*. In the foreword Bjärnstra described difficulties similar to your own, using very similar if not identical terms. A coincidence, of course, but still illuminating."

Milo said: "I believe we have a copy of Bjärnstra over yonder on the shelf."

Sunje, sprawled in the chair like a great rag doll, uttered a raucous hoot of laughter. "I must find a copy of this useful book!"

"No problem," said Wayness. "It seems to be everywhere."

Milo asked: "One puzzle remains. Why, Glawen, were you interested in Ronsel de Roust?"

"Simple enough. Namour announced his favorite philosopher to be de Roust, so from idle curiosity I looked him up in Bjärnstra. There's no more mystery than that, except perhaps for Namour's own interest in de Roust."

Julian asked: "And who might be this scholarly Namour?"

"He's labor coordinator for the Station, and in fact a Clattuc collateral."

Wayness said: "Whenever anything extraordinary happens, you can be sure that there's a Clattuc involved."

A set of soft musical tones sounded through the house. Wayness jumped to her feet. "Lunch is ready. Please be orderly and use your best manners."

Lunch was served on a verandah in the shade of four fine marquisade trees, with the lagoon spreading away beyond. Dame Cora seated the group. "Egon, you will take your usual place, of course. Then—how shall we do this?—Sunje, there, then Milo, then Clytie, if you please, and Glawen. On this side, Wayness, to the right of your father. Next Julian—I'm sure you two will find much to discuss—then Etrune, please. Algin, you shall sit here, beside me. Now, then, in the interest of sweet peace and harmony, shall we invoke a rule against politics?"

"On humanitarian grounds I vote no," said Milo. "The effect would be to stifle Julian."

Dame Cora said: "Now, then, Milo, please moderate your banter. Julian might not understand that you meant no offense."

"Quite right! Julian, no matter what I say, please take no offense."

"I would not dream of doing so," said Julian lazily. "In fact, I intend simply to sit here and enjoy the occasion as meekly as possible."

"Well spoken, Julian!" said his aunt, Clytie Vergence, a handsome if rather stern woman of early middle age, with a ruff of chestnut curls, sharp gray eyes, strong features and impressive physical proportions. "This is indeed a delightful occasion. The forest air is most refreshing."

So went the lunch: from a pale soup of sea fruits gathered along the beach to a salad of greens, a brace of small roast fowl at each platter; then, bubbling in brown earthenware pots, a cassoulet of beans, sausages, herbs and black morels; and, finally, a dessert of chilled melon.

After the first flask of wine the company relaxed; conversation twittered and tinkled back and forth about the table, along with murmurs of decorous laughter and, from time to time, one of Julian's resonant perorations—these sometimes droll, sometimes wise, but always of exquisite refinement. Glawen, on the other hand, with Dame Cora to one side and Warden Clytie Vergence to the other, was able to find few topics of mutual interest and for the most part sat quietly.

The group finished dessert and sipped green tea. Dame Cora mentioned Julian's proposed visit to Mad Mountain Lodge. "Have the maps helped you in any way?"

"Oh, decidedly! But I won't form any opinions until I make a personal inspection."

Warden Ballinder turned his head sharply. "Am I supposed to know anything about this?"

"Not necessarily," said Warden Vergence. "I have long felt that the Mad Mountain situation should somehow be modified. I want Julian to study the conditions before I make my recommendations."

"As to what?" Warden Ballinder, massive as a bull, with burning black eyes, thick black hair, a great prognathous jaw under a skim of black beard, stared suspiciously at his colleague. She responded in a cold voice, as if instructing an obstinate child: "Tourists flock to Mad Mountain Lodge and there are plans to add an annex. I question the desirability of this expansion. The tourists come to watch the slaughter on the plain. Since we make facilities available, we put ourselves in the position of pandering to the most disgusting of human traits."

"That is unfortunately true," said Warden Ballinder. "Still, the spectacles will continue willy-nilly whether we turn a profit or not, and if we refuse to take the tourists' money they will only spend it elsewhere."

"Quite so," said Warden Vergence. "But perhaps we can stop these dreadful engagements altogether, which would be a most constructive and benign achievement."

Warden Ballinder's face became stony. "I seem to detect the rich ripe odor of Peefer ideology."

Dame Clytie gave him a contemptuous grin. "What of it? Someone must bring a moral authority to bear upon this medieval society. It has been sadly lacking heretofore!"

Warden Ballinder rolled up his eyes, blew out his cheeks, then declared: "Enjoy your morals, by all means! Fondle them! Adore them! Hang them around your neck! But do not inflict them upon the Conservancy!"

"Come, come, Algin! Please don't be so pompous, and for once in your life use some amplitude in your thinking, instead of simply throwing back your head and braying. Morals are useless unless they are put to work. Across all Cadwal there is a crying need for a new moral perception, and Mad Mountain is a case in point."

"You are one hundred and eighty degrees wrong. The activity has persisted across millions of years; it obviously fulfills a fundamental ecological purpose which I for one would not care to fiddle with. These are the basic prohibitions imposed by the Charter."

Warden Clytie Vergence snorted. "I have arrived at a stage of life when I cannot be cowed every time you flap an old document in my face."

Julian declared: "And there you hear the voice of progressive realism, ringing loud, bold and clear! The time is now! I too have felt the clammy dead hand of 'then' on my arm and I have spurned it aside! Forward, the LPF!"

Milo clapped his hands. "Splendid, Julian! You have great style! Have you considered a career in politics?"

Sunje spoke with languid amusement: "Milo, what an idiot you are! He is already in politics!"

"And a very gallant advocate of his cause!" called out Dame Cora. "Wayness, don't you agree?"

"Of course! Julian is quite articulate! Glawen, I noticed you wincing and squirming while the Warden Vergence was speaking. Were you trying to endorse her views?"

Everyone turned to look at Glawen, who, after a thoughtful side glance at the Warden Vergence, said: "Our hostess prefers that we avoid the topic of politics, so I will keep my opinions to myself."

Dame Cora smiled and patted Glawen's shoulder. "How considerate of you! If only Milo could follow your example!"

Milo said: "That is why I am anxious to hear Glawen's point of view! His meekness and abnegation suggest that he supports the Peefers. Glawen, is this true? Tell us at least this much!"

"Some other time," said Glawen.

The Warden Vergence asked him: "I believe that you are employed by Bureau B?"

"That is true."

"What might be the nature of your duties?"

"I still undergo training, first of all. Then I do odd jobs for the Supervisor: small tasks below the dignity of the upper officers. And of course, I fly patrols out over all the sections of Deucas."

Julian said blandly: "The best sport, of course, is to be found over the Marmion Foreshore."

Glawen shook his head. "Contrary to Julian's obsessive belief, our patrols serve very serious purposes. In a word, we guard the territory of the Conservancy, and we overfly every province several times a year."

Dame Clytie said: "Off the top of my head I can't imagine what you'd be looking for."

"We provide information to the scientists; we support and sometimes rescue their expeditions. We observe and report upon any number of events: natural disasters, abnormal movement of herds, out-of-season tribal migrations. Sometimes we find human intruders, from off-world or otherwise, and we take them into custody, usually without event. For a fact, when we go out on patrol we never know what to expect. We might find a krabenklotter bogged down in the swamp, which represents a good deal of dirty work and a challenge to our professional skills."

Wayness asked: "What do you do in such a case?"

"We land, rig the proper tackle, drag the beast to safety, then run like blazes to escape the ungrateful creature."

"You do this alone?"

"We lack manpower for anything better. Still, we do our best and usually the job gets done, if only out of vanity. The intent of Bureau B training is to make us competent under any circumstances."

Sunje demanded: "And that's how you regard yourself?"

Glawen grinned. "I'm just learning. I'd like to be as resourceful as my father."

Julian asked blandly: "What happens when you find human intruders?"

"Most of these are petty bandits, hoping to loot the jewel beds."

"I should think that they'd be dangerous folk and quick with their weapons."

"Sometimes they are, but we have techniques to deal with them. Sensors warn us that intruders are present. Our first step is to locate

188

and disable their vehicles, to prevent their escape. Then with our loud-hailer we warn them against violence, and instruct them to surrender. Usually that's all there is to the matter."

"What happens next?"

"If they surrender at once, they'll serve three years or so on the Cape Journal Roadway. If they use weapons and resist, they are killed on the spot."

Sunje gave an exaggerated shudder. "The Bureau B personnel seem very brisk. You allow your prisoners no representation, no legal process, no rights of appeal?"

"Our rules are widely known. The legal processes you mention are automatically raised, argued and denied, in a single brief sentence. It is something like an all-inclusive hotel bill. To bring these points again would be redundant. If the bandits find our rules unacceptable, they can go elsewhere."

Sunje asked in a metallic voice: "Have you killed any of these bandits yourself—knowing that they might be ignorant of your rules?"

Glawen smiled a small wry smile. "When bandits try to kill us, our compassion is quickly lost. We don't even wonder whether they might be ignorant."

Dame Clytie said coldly: "Let me ask you this, since the subject has been broached: what of the Yips whom you capture along the Foreshore? Do you kill them with the same careless ease?"

Glawen showed a faint smile. "I cannot answer your question directly, since the Yips almost always surrender without offering violence."

"So then: what is their fate?"

"It has changed over the years. At first, they were merely tattooed for identification and sent back to the Lutwens. This policy dissuaded no one, so for a period trespassers were sent to Cape Journal to work on the road, until we could absorb no more. We now use a new technique, which seems to work very well!"

"And how do you operate this new technique?"

"The Yips no longer serve time at Cape Journal; instead they are sent off-world, to Soumjiana or Moulton's World, where they are indentured into suitable employment for a term of one or two years. The proceeds pay all our expenses; after the indenture is satisfied, the Yip finds himself employed and free to do as he likes, except return to Cadwal. He has in effect become an emigrant from Yipton off-world, which is our goal. Everyone is happy except, conceivably, the Oomphaw, who prefers to work out his own indentures."

Egon Tamm looked up and down the table. "Are there any more

questions? Or have we studied the work of Bureau B in sufficient detail?"

Dame Clytie said grimly: "I have learned even more than I wanted to know."

Dame Cora glanced at the sky. "I believe that the breeze has come up, and it's a trifle boisterous. Shall we go indoors?"

The company made its way to the parlor. Dame Cora called out for attention. "All are now free to relax as they please. Etrune and I are going to look at some of my leaf block-prints. They are truly exquisite, and as the textbook asserts they 'seem to vibrate with the essence of vegetation.' Clytie, would you care to join us? And Sunje?"

Sunje smilingly shook her head. Dame Clytie said: "Thank you, Cora, but I am not at all in a vegetative mood."

"As you wish. Milo, you might show Sunje and Glawen the secret rock pool you found the other day."

"Then it wouldn't be secret any longer," said Milo. "They can go seek it out themselves, if they want to. Meanwhile I'll show Julian our new encyclopedia of combat devices."

"In the name of precious Gaea herself," gasped Dame Clytie, "whatever for?"

Milo shrugged. "Sometimes it's more convenient to kill opponents than to argue with them, especially if you happen to be late for an appointment."

Dame Cora compressed her lips. "Milo, your humor approaches the bizarre and might even be considered tasteless."

Milo bowed. "I accept your judgment and retract everything! Come, Julian, I'll show you the rock pool."

"Not quite so soon after lunch," said Julian. "I am a trifle enervated."

"You must do as you like," said Dame Cora graciously. "Etrune, shall we look over the blocks?"

The two ladies departed. Others of the group disposed themselves around the room. Glawen reflected that now might be as good a time as any to take leave of the party. Wayness sensed his half-formed intent; with a mere twitch of the fingers and a meaningful glance she indicated that she did not want him to go.

Glawen seated himself at the end of the couch as before. Dame Clytie paced the length of the room, then seated herself opposite Julian.

Milo and Wayness busied themselves at the sideboard, and served cups of sweetened brandy along with sticks of dense dark pastry. Wayness told Glawen: "This is how we while away the long winter evenings at Stroma. You must dip the end of the hard-cake into the brandy, then gnaw away the part that has become soft. The process will seem pointless at first, but you'll find that you don't want to stop."

Dame Clytie waved away the proffered plate. "I lack patience for so much gnawing."

Milo suggested: "Simply drink the brandy, if you're of a mind."

"Thank you, no. I am somewhat disturbed and brandy would only make me dizzy."

Milo asked solicitously: "Would you like to lie down and rest for a while?"

"Certainly not!" snapped Dame Clytie. "My disturbance is purely mental. Not to put too fine a point on it, I am shocked and surprised at what I have heard over lunch."

Warden Ballinder smiled coldly. "Unless I misread the signs, it appears that we are about to share Dame Clytie's surprise and perhaps participate in her distress."

"I can't understand why you are not already affected," declared Dame Clytie. "You heard this gentleman, a Bureau B patrol officer, describe his work. Surely you noted his lack of self-consciousness—or could it be a moral vacuum? I find it unnerving in a person so young."

Glawen tried to utter a word of remonstrance but his voice was overborne by that of Dame Clytie, who would not be diverted from her thesis: "And what do we learn of Bureau B? We discover indifference for human dignity and disregard for basic human rights. We learn of dire deeds done with a chilling finality. We find a swaggering arrogant autonomy, which the Conservator apparently does not dare to challenge. Clearly he has abdicated his responsibility, while agents of Bureau B range the continent capturing, killing, deporting and who knows what else? In short, I am appalled!"

Warden Ballinder turned to Egon Tamm. "There you have it, Conservator! How do you answer these extremely blunt charges?"

Egon Tamm gave his head a dour shake. "The Warden Vergence speaks with gusto! If her charges were accurate, they would be a serious indictment of me and my work. Luckily they are balderdash. The Warden Vergence is an estimable person, but she has a selective comprehension which notices only what fits her preconceptions.

"Contrary to her fears, I monitor the work of Bureau B with care. I find that the personnel faithfully administers Conservancy law, as defined by the Charter. It is as simple as that."

Julian Bohost stirred himself. "But in the end it is not so simple, after all. The law you mention is clearly obsolete and very far from infallible."

Warden Ballinder demanded: "You are referring to the Charter?"

Julian smiled. "Please! Let's none of us be truculent, or irrational, or even hysterical! The Charter is not divine revelation, after all. It was designed to control a certain set of conditions, which have changed; the Charter remains: a stark moldering megalith, glooming over the past."

Dame Clytie chuckled. "Julian's metaphors are perhaps a bit exaggerated, but he speaks to the right effect. The Charter, as of now, is moribund, and at the very least must be revised and brought into phase with contemporary thought."

Again Glawen tried to speak, but Dame Clytie's ideas seemed to have a momentum of their own. "We must come to an accommodation with the Yips; this is our great problem. We cannot continue our abuse of these submissive folk: killing them and sending them away from their homes. I see no harm in allowing them the Marmion Foreshore; there is still ample space for the wild animals."

Milo spoke in wonder: "My dear Dame Clytie! Have you forgotten? The original franchise to the Naturalist Society established Cadwal as a Conservancy forever, and specifically prohibited human residency, except as specified by the Charter. You can't contravene this state of affairs."

"Not so! As a warden and a member of the LPF party I can and I will; the alternate course means war and bloodshed."

She would have spoken on, but Wayness interrupted. "Glawen, have you something to say? What is your opinion of all this?"

Glawen looked at her sidewise; she was smiling quite openly. Something cold clamped at his brain. Had she brought him here only so that he might put on an amusing performance? He said stiffly: "I am, in a sense, an outsider; it would be presumptuous for me to enter your discussion."

Egon Tamm looked from Glawen to Wayness and back to Glawen. "I for one do not consider you an outsider and I would like to hear your opinions."

"Speak, Glawen!" called Warden Ballinder. "Everyone else has brayed his best; let's hear your performance!"

Sunje said silkily: "If you fear that you might be chased from the house by an angry mob, why not make your farewells now, before you begin your speech?"

Glawen paid her no heed. "I am puzzled by a conspicuous ambiguity which the rest of you seem to ignore. Or perhaps I am ignorant of an accommodation, or a special convention, which everyone else takes for granted."

Milo called out: "Speak, Glawen! Your misgivings are of no interest; you have us hanging in midair! Break the suspense!"

Glawen said with dignity: "I was trying to introduce a ticklish subject with a certain degree of tact."

"Never mind the tact; get to the point! Do you want a gilded invitation?"

"We are ready for the worst," declared Egon Tamm. "I ask only that you do not question the chastity of my wife, who is not here to defend herself."

"I could go call her," said Wayness, "if that is what Glawen has in mind."

"Don't bother," said Glawen. "My remarks concern Dame Clytie. I notice that she has been elected to an office which derives directly from the Charter, with duties and responsibilities defined by the Charter, including unqualified defense of the Conservancy against all enemies and interlopers. If Dame Clytie demeans or diminishes or in any way seeks to invalidate the Charter, or despoil the Conservancy, she has instantly removed herself from office. She cannot have it both ways. Either she defends the Charter in whole and in part or she is instantly expelled from office. Unless I misunderstand her, she has already made her choice, and is now no more Warden than I am."

The room was silent. Julian's mouth had sagged open to show a pink gap. Wayness' grin had faded to a shadow. Egon Tamm pensively stirred a bit of hard-cake into his brandy. Warden Ballinder stared at Glawen under lowering eyebrows. Sunje said in a husky whisper: "If you are going to make a run for it, the coast is clear."

Glawen spoke: "Have I gone too far? It seemed to me that this question needed clarification. If I have been rude, I apologize."

Warden Ballinder said dryly: "Your remarks have been sufficiently polite. Still, you have said to Dame Clytie's face something which no one has cared previously to point out, even from an appreciable distance. You have gained my respect."

Julian said carefully: "As you yourself surmised, there are complications and subtleties here which you, as an outsider, could not be expected to perceive. The paradox you cite is only apparent; Dame Clytie was duly elected Warden and is as secure in office as any other, despite her progressive philosophy."

Dame Clytie drew a deep breath and addressed Glawen: "You question my right to office. But I claim my franchise, not from the

Charter, but from the votes of my constituency. What do you say to that?"

Egon Tamm said: "Allow me to answer that question. Cadwal is a Conservancy, administered by the Conservator through Araminta Station. It is not in any sense a democracy. Governing power is drawn from the original grant to the Naturalist Society. That power flows to the Conservator through legitimate Wardens and may only be used in the interests of the Conservancy. This is my reading of the situation. In short, the Charter may not be invalidated by the votes of a few disgruntled residents."

"Do you call a hundred thousand Yips a few?" snapped Dame Clytie.

"I call the Yips a very grave problem which we surely cannot solve at this moment."

Glawen rose to his feet. "I think that I must take my departure. It has been a pleasure to make the acquaintance of you all." And to Egon Tamm: "Please convey my thanks to Dame Cora." And to Wayness: "Don't get up; I'll find my own way out."

Wayness nevertheless accompanied him to the door. Glawen said: "Thank you for the invitation. I enjoyed meeting your friends, and I'm sorry if I caused a disturbance."

Glawen bowed, turned, started up the path. He felt the pressure of Wayness' eyes on his back, but she did not call after him and he did not look back.

5

Syrene had dropped behind the hills; night had come to Araminta Station; stars blazed across the sky. Sitting by the open window Glawen could see, almost overhead, that strangely regular constellation known as the Pentagram, and off to the south the twisting progress of the Great Eel.

The day's events had receded in perspective; Glawen felt drained and quietly depressed. All was finished; nothing could make any difference now. Conceivably events had turned out for the best—still how vastly preferable if he had never gone to Riverview House that day! Or perhaps ever.

Brooding was futile. The episodes of today, or something equivalent, had been inevitable from the beginning. Wayness had known as much. More or less tactfully she had tried to tell him, but, stubborn and proud as any other Clattuc, he had refused to listen.

In regard to the events of the day, a mystery lingered. Why had Wayness brought him out to Riverview House, where, one way or another, he was sure to make a spectacle of himself? He might never know the answer, and, in the course of time, he might not even care.

A chime summoned him to the telephone. The last person he had expected to see looked at him from the screen. "Glawen? What are you doing?"

"Nothing much. What about you?"

"I decided that I'd had enough society and I'm now supposed to be in bed with a headache."

"I'm sorry to hear that."

"I don't really have a headache; I just wanted to be alone."

"In that case, you need not heed my condolences."

"I'll pack them away in fine linen and use them another time. Why did you run from me as if I had a loathsome disease?"

The question took Glawen by surprise. He stammered: "It seemed like a good time to be leaving."

Wayness shook her head. "Not quite. You left because you were furious with me. Why? I've been staring into the dark it seems forever, and I'm tired of being mystified."

Glawen groped for an answer which would leave him a few shreds of dignity. He muttered: "I was more furious with myself than anyone else."

"I'm still baffled," said Wayness. "Why should you be angry with either one of us?"

"Because I did what I did not want to do! I had planned to be suave and polished, to charm everyone with my tact, and to avoid all controversy. Instead I blurted out all my opinions, caused a grand uproar and confirmed your mother's worst apprehensions."

"Come, now," said Wayness. "It wasn't all that bad; in fact, not bad at all. You could have done far worse."

"No doubt, if I'd really put my mind to it. I could have become drunk and punched Julian in the nose, and called Dame Etrune a silly old blatherskite, and on my way out stopped to urinate in one of the potted plants."

"Everyone would have thought it simple Clattuc high spirits. The main question remains, and you've made no attempt to answer it: why were you, or are you, furious with me? Tell me, so I won't do it again."

"I don't want to talk about it. As we both know, it doesn't make a particle of difference anymore."

"Oh? Why not?"

"You've made it clear to me how impossible it is to have any close

195

relationship between us. I tried not to believe it but now I know that you are right."

"And that's how you want it?"

"What an odd thing to say! My inclinations have never been considered at any time. Why are they under investigation now?"

Wayness laughed. "Through an oversight I neglected to notify you that I've been reassessing the situation."

A sardonic chuckle rose in Glawen's throat, which he wisely held back. "When will we know the results?"

"A few of them are in now."

"Would you like to meet me down on the beach and tell me about them?"

"I don't dare." Wayness looked over her shoulder. "About the time I was climbing out the window, Mother and Sunje and Dame Clytie would come peeping in to see if I was resting nicely."

"My best ideas turn out to be impractical."

"Now, then: tell me what I did to infuriate you."

Glawen said: "I'm just a bit puzzled why you invited me to Riverview House in the first place."

"Poof!"—a flippant feckless sound. "Could it be that I wanted to show you off to Sunje and Julian?"

"Really?"

"Really. Is that all?"

"Well—no. I can't understand why you're so mysterious about your trip to Earth."

"It's simple. I can't trust you not to tell someone else."

"Hmmf," said Glawen. "That's not a nice thing to say."

"You asked, and I told you."

"I didn't expect to hear anything quite so honest."

"It's more a matter of realism. Think, now. Suppose you swore silence by everything you held sacred, which induced me to tell you what I know and what I want to do. After thinking it over, you might decide that your higher duty lay in breaking faith with me and notifying your father. For the same high motives, your father might then inform Bodwyn Wook, and then who knows how far the information might travel? If it reached the wrong ears, very serious consequences might be the result. I avoid this worry by telling no one. Now I hope you understand and are no longer angry with me, at least on that account."

Glawen thought for a moment, then said: "If I understand you correctly, you are involved, or plan to involve yourself, in a matter of importance."

"That's true."

"Are you sure that you can take care of the business alone?"

"I'm not sure of anything except that I must do what needs to be done without attracting attention. It's a real dilemma for me; I want and I may need help, but only on my own terms. Milo is the best compromise and he is coming with me, for which I'm grateful. Now, then: have I made everything clear?"

"I understand what you've told me, yes. But suppose you and Milo are killed: what happens to your information?"

"I've already made arrangements."

"I think you should consult your father."

Wayness shook her head. "He'd declare that I was too young and inexperienced for such a venture, and I wouldn't be allowed to leave Riverview House."

"Is it possible that he might be right?"

"I don't think so. I believe that I am doing exactly the right thing . . . Anyway, that's the situation and I hope that you feel better."

"I don't feel anything, which is better."

"Goodnight, Glawen."

The following morning Wayness called Glawen again. "Just to bring you up to date: Warden Ballinder and Dame Clytie quarreled this morning. As a result Dame Clytie, with Julian in tow, is returning early to Stroma."

"Indeed! What of Julian's investigation of Mad Mountain?"

"The subject never arose. It's either been postponed or forgotten."

6

In response to a question from Bodwyn Wook, Glawen stated: "I'm not at all comfortable with the Bold Lion assignment. I feel a spy and a sneak."

"Why should you not?" snapped Bodwyn Wook. "That is your function. A Bureau B agent never fools himself with words. Forget the terminology; just do the work."

"Meanwhile I must consort with the Bold Lions. They grow more tiresome by the hour."

"Including Kirdy?"

"Kirdy is inconsistent. He can even be amusing, in a sarcastic way. But give him an extra mug of Bold Lion Reserve and he is as callow as Cloyd or Kiper. Sometimes worse!"

"Odd! Few Wooks are callow. Let me advise you: never underestimate Kirdy, or take him casually! At times he shows a Machiavellian clarity of vision. For example, like yourself, he felt awkward bringing me weekly reports of seditions and criminal conspiracies. He therefore recommended that I assign this work to you. Chicanery may be expected anywhere and at any time."

Glawen smiled ruefully. "I will certainly keep what you say in mind."

Bodwyn Wook leaned back in his chair. "Kirdy does not understand this, but the Bold Lions are in the nature of a camouflage. There is a certain person in whom I am interested. He seems to have a fairly close association with Titus Pompo, though he does not advertise the fact. I refer to Namour."

Glawen made no comment. Bodwyn Wook continued: "Namour is deft and gracious: so much so that we suspect him without knowing exactly why. Give careful attention to Namour and every word he says, without being obvious. When do the Bold Lions meet next?"

"Milden afternoon they're driving up to Sarmenter Cove for a clam roast. Namour will not be on hand. I also hope to avoid the event."

"How so? It might be a jolly affair!"

Glawen shook his head. "Everyone will be drunk but me. There will be a lot of secret Bold Lion ritual: pounces, growls and roars, with penalties for making mistakes. New songs composed by Kiper and Arles will be introduced, which everyone must memorize and sing with gusto. Kiper and Jardine will vomit. Arles will be Arles. Kirdy will pontificate; Uther will vex him by laughing and sneering. There is little to attract me."

"No girls?"

"What girls would go anywhere with the Bold Lions?"

"Still, you must be on hand. Be watchful and formulate theories."

"As you say, sir."

"One final word. Today I spoke with the Conservator. He mentioned that you had been a recent visitor to Riverview House."

"Yes. I'm afraid I talked too much."

"Not according to Egon Tamm. He tells me that when you were asked for your opinions, you stated them clearly and vigorously, but with perfect gentility. Your remarks, so he tells me, were exactly appropriate, and what he wanted to say himself. In short, you have gained his good opinion." He waved his hand. "That is all for now."

Glawen rose to his feet, bowed stiffly and departed the office.

On Milden afternoon, three wagons driven by Kirdy, Uther and Glawen conveyed all the Bold Lions save Jardine Laverty north along the beach road to Sarmenter Cove. Jardine would arrive shortly with a cask of wine, which he hoped to obtain by illicit means from the Laverty warehouse.

Jardine, however, was late. The others gathered fuel for a fire, then went off to dig in the sand for the clamlike molluscs indigenous to Sarmenter Beach.

The clams were dug; the fire was ready, and at last Jardine arrived, in a most disconsolate state of mind.

The story he had to tell was not a cheerful one. Instead of a cask of the fine Yermolino he had hoped to purvey, he had brought only a few jugs of ordinary white Tissop. "I walked into a trap," said Jardine bitterly. "Old Volmer was lying in wait and caught me dead to rights. I'm sure that he was tipped off; there's no other explanation! Anyway, I've had no end of trouble; I'm in hot water with the Housemaster, and no telling what they'll do to me. When I finally got away, I picked up some Tissop at the Arbor, but it's on our account and we'll have to pay."

"What a sordid situation!" said Shugart. "Did Volmer hint as to the source of his information?"

"Not Volmer! He's a tight old goat."

"It sounds suspiciously as if there's an informer somewhere," said Arles. His gaze rested a thoughtful moment on Glawen.

Uther Offaw said: "We'll work something out tomorrow, but for now we've got clams on the fire and wine in the jug! Let's rejoice as best we may."

"Easy for you to say," grumbled Jardine. "I don't know what the charges will be against me. They're not taking the matter lightly. I'm lucky not to be in the Carcery."

Cloyd Diffin said: "It's a wicked situation, and no two ways about it."

Jardine gave a dour nod. "I'd like to lay hands on the sneak who shopped me. I'd make him sing some high notes, I assure you!"

Arles said in a pompous voice: "I don't like to make accusations, but logic is logic and facts are facts. Need I point out that Glawen is a real bark-scratcher in Bureau B?"

"Nonsense," said Kirdy. "I'm in Bureau B too. I keep business out of my social life, and no doubt Glawen does the same."

"That's just a pious hope," said Arles. "If you recall, I advised against his membership in the first place, and now our troubles have started."

Jardine said in a troubled voice: "Glawen wouldn't nail me over a cask of wine! At least, I don't think he would!"

"Ask him," said Arles.

Jardine turned to Glawen. "Well: would you? More to the point: did you?"

Glawen said: "It's beneath my dignity to answer you. Think what you like."

"Come, now!" cried Arles. "That's not good enough! We want an answer, and we want it straight and for the record! Because I know very well you tell old Bodwyn Wook everything that goes on."

Glawen gave a stony shrug and turned away. Arles took his shoulder and whirled him around. "Answer, if you don't mind! We want to know whether you are a spy or not!"

"I am an officer in Bureau B," said Glawen. "What, if anything, I report to my superiors is official business, which I am not free to discuss."

Arles gave Glawen's shoulder a shake. "That is not what I asked you!"

Glawen pushed away Arles' hand. "You are becoming very tiresome, Arles."

Kirdy came forward. "Come, now! Let's not quarrel and spoil the whole day!"

"Bah!" cried Jardine. "The day is already spoiled!"

"And I say Glawen is responsible," cried Arles in a passion. "Answer me, Glawen! Do you inform on us or don't you? Give us a straight answer! Or consider yourself expelled from the Bold Lions!"

"Expelled? Bah! I resign from your drunken group!"

"That's good to hear, but it's still not an answer." Arles reached again to seize Glawen's shoulder; Glawen thrust the arm away. Arles struck out with his other fist, buffeting Glawen glancingly on the neck. Glawen drove one fist into Arles' belly and struck up at Arles' heavy chin, hurting his own knuckles. Arles snorted in fury and lurched forward, windmilling blows. Glawen backed away. Kiper, squatting on the sand, cleverly thrust out his foot; Glawen tripped and fell. Arles rushed forward and kicked Glawen in the ribs, and tried to do so again, but Kirdy intervened and pushed him aside.

"Come, now!" said Kirdy sternly. "Let's have fair play! Kiper, that was a rotten act."

"Not if he's a spy!"

"Quite right!" panted Arles. "This smirking little sneak deserves nothing better! Allow me just one more good kick, where it will do the most good!"

"Absolutely not," said Kirdy. "Now, stand back, or you'll be dealing with me as well. As far as the wine is concerned, Glawen obviously had nothing to do with it. No one knew what was up but Jardine and myself."

"He probably heard you talking."

Glawen picked himself up, conscious of a sharp pain in his side. He contemplated Arles, standing ten feet away and watching him with a grin. Glawen turned and limped away: up the beach to the Clattuc power wagon. He climbed into the seat and drove back to Araminta Station.

From Clattuc House he called Bodwyn Wook by telephone. "I am no longer a Bold Lion."

"Oh? How so?"

"Jardine Laverty tried to steal a cask of wine and was caught in the act. Arles accused me of informing. We had some words, and I was expelled from the Bold Lions, which is easily worth a kick in the ribs."

"Confound and blast," said Bodwyn Wook. "There go my plans."

Glawen thought it wise to hold his tongue. Bodwyn Wook made thoughtful hissing sounds through his teeth. "I take it you do not care to rejoin?"

"That is correct."

Bodwyn Wook slapped his hand gently down on the desk. "You shall still go to Yipton, and in the company of the Bold Lions. Kirdy will invite you. It may work out just as well."

"Whatever you say."

7

Two ferries plied the route between Araminta Station and Yipton: the old *Spharagma*, now dedicated to the transport of cargo and a few Yip laborers; and the new *Faraz*: a catamaran with comfortable accommodation for a hundred and fifty passengers. At speeds of forty to sixty miles an hour the *Faraz* skated across the blue ocean, making the passage to Yipton in six to eight hours, laying over for the night and returning the next day, thus making three round trips each week.

A few days before the half-term holiday Jardine Laverty sheepishly sought out Glawen. "In the matter of that ridiculous wine cask, I stand embarrassed. I find that Volmer simply happened to be working when he should have been off duty. You were most unfairly blamed and so, herewith, I tender my apologies. Words, I realize, are insufficient, but at the moment I can offer nothing else."

Glawen said stiffly: "I can't pretend to have happy memories of the event."

"Naturally not! It's a pity that you felt compelled to resign from the Bold Lions." Jardine hesitated, then went on somewhat lamely: "I suppose that you could be reinstated if you so chose—though Arles might be a bit difficult."

"No, thank you," said Glawen. "My term as a Bold Lion is done. However, I'll still be going to Yipton next week, and for company I may mingle with the group, unless there is any objection."

"You'll be most welcome, I'm sure!" Jardine thought a moment. "There's a meeting tonight; I'll explain about Volmer, and I'll mention that you'll be among the party."

The half-term ended; the recess began. On Milden morning early the Bold Lions, Glawen and about eighty tourists arrived at the ferry terminal, changed sols for scrip at the Currency Control desk, then boarded the *Faraz*.

The Bold Lions numbered eight: Uther and Kiper Offaw, Jardine Laverty, Shugart Veder, Arles Clattuc, Cloyd Diffin, Kirdy Wook and a new member, Dauncy Diffin. All save Arles gave Glawen a courteous welcome, and explained how they had never believed the allegations against him. "The idea is foolish on the face of it," said Uther Offaw.

Arles merely grunted. For the occasion he wore a fine new black cloak, with an embroidered silver cincture at the beltline. Casting a morose side glance toward Glawen, Arles said: "He's still a Bureau B snoop, and, mark my words, he's coming along to Yipton on some kind of funny business."

Kirdy came forward, his big pink face screwed up in irritation. "Let's all relax and have a good time!" Today Kirdy wore the costume of a backcountry Soum rancher: a light brown twill shirt, blue-and-white-striped knee-length trousers, with a broad-brimmed tan bush ranger's hat.

"Just so long as he realizes he's here on sufferance," muttered Arles. Glawen only laughed and turned away.

Upon boarding the *Faraz*, each of the passengers received a pamphlet entitled "Information for Visitors to the Lutwen Islands." As Glawen waited for departure, he went to stand by the rail and read the pamphlet:

The visitor to the Lutwen Islands—Yipton, as the place is familiarly known—will surely enjoy his visit and find a truly amazing diversity of entertainments, so long as he exercises common courtesy and strictly obeys Yip regulations.

REMEMBER: Yipton is not just a picturesque suburb of Araminta Station, but more like an independent settlement on a far world. Yip society is unique in the Gaean Reach.

DO NOT try to understand the Yip society or deal with it in ordinary terms; you will only make difficulties for yourself. Learn the following rules and abide by them.

BE WARNED! The Yips lack reverence for what you might call "human rights." The Yips live a harsh and practical existence, and often cannot spare the luxury of tedious legal exercises. It is easier to eliminate a problem than to solve it; the Yips are not averse to cutting the Gordian knot. Protect yourself by prudent behavior, keeping out of PRINCIPAL SOURCES OF TROUBLE.

NOTHING IS FREE except the air you breathe. You will be charged when you use the hotel toilet. Should you ask directions, pay your informant five dinkets. The Yip is neither grasping nor avaricious; he is merely exact, practical and meticulous. Everything costs; when you avail yourself of an item, or a service, you must pay.

NEVER ATTEMPT TO CHEAT OR SHORT-CHANGE, even as a joke. You might suffer a harsh penalty. PAY. This one word has eased a multitude of people through difficulties. If you think a Yip is overcharging, or mulcting you, take revenge in this fashion: wait till he visits you in your community, then overcharge him. This is a classical expedient, known across the ages.

SEXUAL MORALITY DIFFERS FROM YOUR OWN. This is safe to say, no matter how particular, or idiosyncratic, are your own preferences. Fornication is a casual act, with no emotional envelope. What you may consider apathy is usually simple disinterest or even boredom. Like any other service, it is priced according to an exact schedule. These schedules, incidentally, make amusing souvenirs; they are for sale at three sols[1] per copy. This may seem exorbitant, but shrewd old Titus Pompo charges what the market will bear.

Question: Is Yipton dangerous for the tourist?
Answer: Not at all, if he obeys the rules.
Question: What are some rules, other than those outlined above?
Answer:

RULE: Do not wander at random. Almost certainly you will get lost. At worst you will never be seen again—though this is the extreme case. Keep to those ways and canals marked on the attached chart. Even better: hire a guide.

RULE: Accept nothing, neither goods nor services, without first inquiring and settling upon a price. To reiterate, nothing is free. Find out the price first!

---

[1] The value of the sol is fixed at the worth of one hour of unskilled labor, under standard conditions.

RULE: Do not try to become friendly with any Yip, male or female. Your efforts will be in vain. Yips tolerate outsiders only because they bring in money. Their natural feelings toward you are a mild but definite detestation. Do not be deceived by politeness; it is a social lubricant. You might as well respond in kind, though the Yips will not particularly mind if you are cross. Complaints are not worth the breath it takes to utter them. If you are really annoyed about something, write the Oomphaw a letter.

RULE: Never, never, never go down upon the floor of the Caglioro (the Pot). You will lose all your possessions, including your clothes to the last stitch. If you resist you will be injured.

RULE: Confine your drinking of wines, punches, beer and so forth to the hotel. It is advisable to eat only what is served at the hotel, for a variety of reasons.

RULE: Never interfere in any Yip activity. The Yips live by their own rules which seem to serve them fairly well.

RULE: Never touch, caress, stroke, pat or hug a Yip in an idle or casual manner. He or she strongly objects to such contact. Above all, do not strike a Yip; no one will protect you from his response. This applies to man or woman alike; the Yip knows no gallantry nor special concern for the female. To the contrary.

RULE: Should you visit that section known as Pussycat Palace, it is wise to go with a guide from the hotel, who is paid to ensure that you do not come to grief, though the experienced person may go alone in perfect safety.

IN BRIEF: Be cautious! Attempt no reckless acts of individualistic enterprise.

Question: Do the Yips have a sense of humor?

Answer: No. Not in a sense you would understand.

Question: Are the Yips human?

Answer: This is a subject of ongoing controversy. The answer would seem to be: he is not a true Gaean. It is probable that the Yips form a new and superior species of *Homo sapiens terrestrialis.*

THE CHIFE: no mention of Yipton is complete without reference to the Big Chife. At first contact, you will be amazed and appalled. Gradually the impact diminishes. The influence permeates your clothes and lingers, finally attenuating to an almost pleasant musky intimation. This can be considered another souvenir of Yipton. Unlike almost everything else, it is free.

We hope these brief remarks will help you enjoy yourself to the fullest!

Glawen looked up from the pamphlet, to find the *Faraz* drifting away from the dock. The Bold Lions, so he noted, sat at a table in the main saloon with flasks of wine in front of them; Kiper already showed signs of jocundity. Kirdy, who hated the ocean and felt an almost obsessive dread of deep water, sat in a corner where he would not be forced to look out over the sea.

Glawen remained at the rail, watching the familiar contours of Araminta Station receding across the water. On knife-edge keels the *Faraz* sliced into the northeast, cutting narrow furrows into the face of the transparent dark blue sea.

Glawen went to the forward observation lounge, where he sat considering his mission. The Bold Lions had put no definite term on the excursion; most talked in terms of three days, though wondered if the resources of Pussycat Palace could be exploited in anything less than five days. If all went well, three days might be adequate to learn what they wished to know. Still, soft and easy were the guiding words, and he must make sure that Kirdy fully subscribed to this doctrine.

Almost as if awaiting his cue, Kirdy dropped into the seat beside him, with his back to the observation windows, so that he was not obliged to look at the sea. "So here you are! I wondered if you had fallen overboard." He grimaced and risked a glance over his shoulder. "Horrible thought!"

"No, I'm still aboard."

"You should be in the saloon with the others," said Kirdy, using the chiding tone he tended to take with Glawen. "It's no mystery why you're not popular. You act as if you consider yourself a superior being."

From time to time Glawen suspected that Kirdy did not like him much. He gave a noncommittal shrug. "Better to say, I act as if I prefer to avoid Arles' insults."

"Still, it's only decent to be diplomatic."

"It makes no great difference, one way or the other."

"Wrong!" declared Kirdy. "The Bold Lions are supposed to be your cover."

"It's far more placid here. Kiper has been drinking, which means growls and roars."

Kirdy gave his head a dour shake. "He wanted three great roars for Pussycat Palace, but the lounge steward told him to quiet down, and he's been out of sorts ever since."

"Oh, very well," said Glawen. "I suppose it's proper tactics to join them."

"One moment," said Kirdy. "There's something we must discuss." He frowned and turned his round blue eyes toward the ceiling. "In regard to this mission, I conferred with the Supervisor yesterday. He emphasized that we must work together as a team."

Glawen heaved a sigh. At times Kirdy could be most tiresome. He wondered how best to detach himself from a close association. He said: "I've had rather definite instructions myself, and—"

"These instructions have been superseded." Kirdy turned his bright blue gaze on Glawen. "It's been decided that, since I have an edge on you in both seniority and experience, I should be in command of the mission."

Glawen sat stock-still for a long ten seconds. "I have not been notified of this."

"I'm notifying you now," snapped Kirdy. "That should be sufficient. Do you believe me or not? We'd better have an understanding here and now."

"Oh, I believe you well enough," said Glawen. "Only—"

"Only what?"

"I should think that Bodwyn Wook would have notified me in person."

"Well, he told me and that should be quite enough. If you don't like it, complain when we get back. If the truth be known, Glawen, this is exactly what is wrong with you in a professional sense. You think too much. For instance, let's say that there's a pile of something nasty in the walk and you've been ordered to remove it. Well, you'd dither and sniff and wonder whether to use a shovel or a shingle, and meanwhile an old lady comes along and steps in it. I don't wish to be unkind but that's the sort of thing we've got to avoid, in favor of decisive leadership. I pointed this out to Bodwyn Wook and he agreed in every respect. So that's how it is. Perhaps I'm coming on a bit stronger than might be tactful, but in an operation like this, there can't be any slipups."

"I see. What were your precise instructions?"

Kirdy said in a measured voice: "I was told that you had what information we would need. You might as well brief me now."

"You've memorized the map of Yipton?"

"What map?"

"This."

Kirdy took the map and examined it. His mouth drooped in distaste. "What a mess. I'll look it over after a bit."

"It's to be destroyed before we go ashore. Notice this gray outline?"

"What of it?"

"That's the area we're supposed to investigate."

"And what are these other markings?"

"This is the dock and this is the hotel."

Kirdy studied the map. "The gray area seems to be down the dock from the hotel."

"Correct."

"And what exactly are we looking for?"

"I guess we'll know when we see it."

"Hmf. It's rather a disorganized way of handling an operation of this sort."

"As I understand it, we're supposed to do the best we can without taking chances."

"That's my own appraisal of the situation. I don't see any great tactical challenge. This road runs right past the structure, and we're sure to find clues everywhere."

"If you say so."

"Of course I say so. Let's go join the others."

"And the map?"

"I'll take care of it for now. Have you any other papers I should have?"

"No."

Early in the afternoon fishing boats appeared: light craft little more than rafts formed of bundled bamboo poles, lashed into the shape of a boat; and larger vessels with hulls of laminated bamboo strips. At the same time a smudge appeared on the northeast horizon, which in due course became, first, a floating crust, then a line of rickety structures among tufts of bamboo and coconut palms. At this time the first intimation of the Big Chife reached the *Faraz*, and passengers looked from one to the other with bemused expressions.

The *Faraz* approached the atoll: once the crater and surrounding rim of a volcano, now a circlet of a dozen sickle-shaped islands around a shallow lagoon.

The seaward aspect of Yipton focused into detail. The structures, of two, three, four and five spindly stories, standing on frail-seeming poles, leaned against each other for support, with porches and balconies cantilevered out in unlikely directions. Colors were muted: black, rust, the gray-green of old bamboo, a hundred tones of brown. On the breeze came a new waft of the Big Chife, causing another stir among the passengers.

The ferry slowed, settled lunging and surging into the water, veered behind a breakwater of lashed bamboo poles, drifted across the harbor and up to the dock. The Big Chife, no longer thinned by the breeze, attained full force.

On a choice area at the back of the dock, the Arkady Inn rose five rambling irregular stories to overlook harbor, breakwater and the sea beyond. The ground floor opened upon a terrace with tables shaded under pink and pale green parasols. Patrons of the hotel sat at their lunch while watching the activities of the harbor, apparently oblivious to the Chife, as indeed they were, and the incoming tourists felt somewhat more hopeful. The folk on the terrace seemed jovial and quite relaxed. Unless appearances deceived, the admonitions of the blue pamphlet could not be enforced so severely as to cause terror and apprehension. Or perhaps, as a gaunt gentleman in a Byronish pillow hat nervously suggested, these happy patrons were those who had paid, and paid, and paid, and as a consequence felt no fear.

Boats plied the harbor, moving in and out of canals; putting out to sea, or returning; or simply floating while the crew cleaned fish, shelled molluscs or repaired their gear. Along the shore bamboo grew like jets of greenery, sixty feet tall, while coconut palms, rooted in minute plots of soil, leaned out over the canals. In boxes on the balconies grew potherbs and greens; jardinières trailed blue fronds and rose-pink tockberries.

The passengers from the *Faraz* filed across a gangplank of squeaking bamboo poles to the dock, through a gate and past a wicket manned by a pair of Oomps.[1] One Oomp stood watching faces with grave attention; the other collected a landing fee of three sols from each arrival. With bland expressions they both ignored the grumbling and complaints.

The Bold Lions paid over their fees with disdainful flourishes, in a manner of *noblesse oblige*, which Glawen preferred not to emulate. Then all walked up the flight of broad stairs to the hotel.

At the registration desk Arles stepped forward: "We are the Bold Lions! There will be eight rooms reserved for us."

---

[1] Oomps (contraction of Oomphaw's Police Sergeantry): members of an elite militia, responsible only to the Oomphaw. They were men of extraordinary physique, with heads shaved bald, ears cropped to points and lips tattooed black. They wore crisp tan tunics, white knee-length kirtles, and ankle boots of a tough black metalloid substance exuded by a sea snail. A band of this same glossy black substance encircled their foreheads; to this band were attached spikes symbolic of rank. Most intriguing of all was the emblem, or ideogram, embroidered on the back of each tunic, in black and red; a symbol of unknown meaning.

"Just so, sir. A fine block of rooms on the fourth floor. How long will you be staying?"

"So far, this is indefinite. We will see how it goes."

Glawen came forward: "I am with the group, though without reservation, and will need a room."

"Of course, sir. You may have a nice chamber in the same block as the others, if you like."

"That will serve very well."

Upon climbing to the fourth floor, Glawen found his room at the end of the corridor: a pleasant cubicle with a small canal directly below, and, beyond, a wilderness of roofs. Mats covered the floor; the walls were formed of split bamboo, in several layers; from the ceiling hung a globular lume in a basket of black withe. Furnishings consisted of a bed cushion, now rolled against the wall, a table, a chair and a wardrobe. The bathroom and latrine were across the corridor, with an old woman in attendance to collect fees as specified on the schedule.

Glawen read the placard affixed to the wall which listed services and entertainments available to the tourist, with the associated charges. The day was warm and humid; Glawen changed into light clothing and went down to the lobby. This was an expansive area with walls and ceiling of the ubiquitous bamboo, varnished honey brown. Along the back wall hung dozens of grotesque masks, carved from blocks of black johowood—irresistible souvenirs for the tourist. On the floor lay dramatic rugs woven in startling colors and odd patterns, which added an attractive vivacity to the atmosphere of the room. A line of doorways opened on the terrace, where hotel guests loitered over their lunch.

Glawen seated himself on a wicker couch to the side of the lobby, despite himself fascinated by the ambience of Arkady Inn. Groups of tourists sat about the lobby, regaling newly arrived contingents with descriptions of their remarkable experiences along the byways and canals of Yipton. A dozen barefoot barboys wearing only white kirtles moved quietly back and forth serving rum punch, ling-lang toddy, smiler juice (mixed from secret ingredients) and green elixir ("salubrious, clarifying of the mental waylocks, conducive to merry diversities").

A group of Bold Lions descended the stairs: Arles, Cloyd, Dauncy and Kiper. Arles took note of Glawen from the corner of his eye, but ostentatiously turned away and led the group to a table across the room.

Glawen brought out the chart supplied in the information pamphlet.

The area of Bodwyn Wook's interest, north and east of the hotel, was labeled: "Industrial and Warehousing: nontourist area."

Glawen sat back wondering how best to deal with Kirdy, who almost certainly had misrepresented the degree of authority extended him by Bodwyn Wook.

Glawen considered what he felt to be his range of options and in the end decided that the least attractive of these, simple submission to Kirdy's dictates, was by all odds the most practical. He must swallow dignity, exasperation and half a dozen other emotions and adapt himself to his new role as Kirdy's assistant.

Even as Glawen swallowed this bitter pill, Kirdy came down the stairs. He looked around the lobby, then came to sit beside Glawen. "Aren't you going on the tour?"

Glawen looked at him blankly. "What tour?"

"It's what the Yips call their Orientation Tour. The charge is four sols, which pays for a guide and canal transportation. We'll be back for supper; then it's off and away to Pussycat Palace."

"I haven't been invited on the tour," said Glawen. "As for Pussycat Palace, I'll pass that up as well."

Kirdy stared at Glawen in wonder. "How so?"

Glawen sighed; Kirdy already was about to become tiresome. "It's no great matter. The girls are apathetic, which makes me feel foolish. Also, I'd be wondering who had just preceded me on the premises."

"That's sheer tommyrot!" scoffed Kirdy. "I'm an old hand at it and I never feel foolish. It's a treat for them; otherwise they'd be out tending sea lettuce. They'll give you all kinds of action if you just hint that you're displeased; in fact, sometimes they'll do it all over again, rather than be reported, which means a whipping for them."

"This is valuable information and I'll keep it in mind," said Glawen. "It's clear that you know how to handle women. But for me the process still lacks appeal."

Kirdy's face became set. "People in our line of work can't afford such qualms and quirks; you're too finicky by far. I want you to mingle with the Bold Lions in all situations; otherwise you call attention to yourself and arouse suspicion, which we don't need."

Glawen scowled across the lobby. Uther and Shugart had just come downstairs to join the others. Arles stood poised with one foot raised to a low table; his black cloak hung to striking effect. He noticed Glawen's attention and turned away. Glawen said: "Certain of the group clearly prefer not to associate with me."

Kirdy chuckled. "A pity that your feelings are so vulnerable. Don't go grieving to Bodwyn Wook; he'll only laugh at you."

Glawen said mildly: "You quite misunderstand my remarks."

"Be that as it may. I am as of now inviting you on the tour, and no more need be said. As for Pussycat Palace, it would be better for tomorrow, but I was outvoted. Cloyd, Dauncy, Kiper, Jardine—they're in a state of ferment."

A thought arose from the back of Glawen's mind. "No doubt Arles is also pawing the ground?"

"For a fact Arles has been almost subdued," said Kirdy. "We had a party last night and he's probably still under the weather." He arose. "We'd better join the others. Give me four sols; that's the fee for the tour."

Glawen paid over the money; the two crossed the lobby. The full complement of Bold Lions was now on hand: a group brash and bumptious, exchanging banter in overloud voices. Kirdy asked: "Who is handling the tour money?"

"I am," said Shugart. "Surely you can't be afraid I'll abscond?"

"Not while you're in plain sight. Here's another four sols. Glawen is going with us."

Shugart took the money, and turned a dubious glance toward Arles, who had stepped over to the wall to examine the array of grotesque masks. "I suppose there's no reason why not," said Shugart.

"None whatever," said Kirdy.

Arles, returning to the group, noted the presence of Glawen and stopped short. He turned to Shugart: "This is a club affair, for members only! I thought that had been made clear!"

Shugart spoke in a placatory voice: "Glawen's an ex-Bold Lion, which is close. He's paid his four sols; there's no reason why he shouldn't come."

"I should think that he could take a hint. He knows how everyone feels about him!"

Glawen ignored the remarks. Kirdy spoke sharply to Arles: "I invited him! He is my guest and I'll thank you to show him ordinary courtesy, if nothing else."

Arles could think of nothing to say and turned away. Meanwhile their guide had entered the lobby: a young man three or four years older than Kirdy or Shugart, with the clever vivacious features of a faun, a superb physique, a cap of bronzed curls. He wore a short white kirtle and a pale blue vest which barely covered his shoulders. His manner was polite and he spoke carefully, as if he were addressing a class of young children. "I am your guide. My name is Fader Campasarus Uiskil. We shall have a good time, but remember! you must stay with the group! Do not straggle; do not stray. If you wander off by yourself, you might encounter inconvenience. Is this clear to all? Stay with the group, where you will be safe." He paused to eye Arles up and down, then said: "Sir, you will not be comfortable in that cloak, and it may well become soiled. Give it to the floor boy; he will take it to your room."

With poor grace Arles followed the suggestion.

Fader continued his remarks: "This is an introductory tour. It includes passage along the canals in a boat, a visit to the Caglioro, the bazaar and other destinations as listed in the brochure. Options will be explained along the way, or they may be the theme of a new excursion tomorrow. Which of you is captain of the group?"

Arles cleared his throat, but Kirdy said: "That would seem to be Shugart, who controls all our money. Step forward there, Shugart! Exert your lionship!"

"Very well," said the portly Shugart. "If I must lead this unruly pride, so be it. You spoke of options; should we discuss them now?"

"They will be explained along the way, since we are a minute or two behind schedule. Come along; follow me, if you please. We will start out by boat, up the Hybel Canal."

The group descended a ramp to the hotel basement, where a landing ran parallel to a narrow canal. Here they found a canoelike craft, high at bow and stern, with a crew of four paddlers. The Bold Lions clambered aboard and seated themselves on cushioned thwarts. Fader went to stand aft by the steering wheel.

As soon as all were seated, the boat slid away from the landing, through an opening and out into sunlight and the canal proper.

The Bold Lions found themselves crossing the harbor, with the hotel terrace above them. Almost immediately the boat turned off into the Hybel Canal.

For half an hour the boat followed the swings and swerves of the canal, with dark and oily water below. To right and left rickety structures rose four and five stories, each supporting its sagging neighbor. The visual effect was a microscopic intricacy of windows, balconies hung with bits of cloth, green foliage trailing from brick-red pots, peering faces, braziers exuding small wisps of smoke. At odd intervals tufts of bamboo found a few square feet of soil to anchor their roots. The Big Chife pressed down as always.

The canoe proceeded at no great speed and the paddlers seemed to exert themselves very little, as if they too were enjoying the cruise. Glawen spoke to Kirdy: "See that boat with the red rag dangling from the stern? I've noticed that at least twice before. These rascals are taking us in a circle and laughing at us."

"By Balthasar's goat! I think you're right!" Kirdy indignantly called back to Fader: "What kind of games are you playing? You've circled us so many times we're getting dizzy! Can't you do better than that?"

Jardine echoed the complaint. "You must take us for ninnies! We've just been drifting back and forth through heat and stink!"

Fader replied with smiling candor: "The canal scenery is much the same everywhere; we were just making it easy on ourselves."

Shugart cried out: "That's not how the tour is described! The brochure speaks of 'picturesque environs' and 'glimpses of secret Yipton' and 'naked girls bathing.'"

"Quite right!" called Cloyd. "Where are the girls? I've seen nothing but old women chewing on fish heads."

Fader responded in a flat voice, evidently reciting a statement he had made many times before. "There is a reason for everything. Ours is a very practical society, of many tiers and levels which we understand, but which I will not even try to explain. We waste nothing; everything is planned. The tour you have selected, Number 111, provides a thought-provoking study of mature living. It documents the victory of patience and abnegation: qualities so important in the modern world. The message of the tour is truly inspiring! If you are interested in other phases of Yipton, Tour 109 provides a visit to the crèches where you may examine the infants of Yipton at your leisure. Tour 154 demonstrates the techniques of fish cleaning and fish scaling and the efficient use of fish by-products. Tour 105 takes you first through the sick-house, then out for an inspection of the death raft, where at sunset you may listen to traditional songs, which are said to be of high quality; and you may request your favorite upon payment of a small fee. You also may visit the girls' area now, if you choose to do so, at an extra charge of five sols for the group."

Shugart stared in astonishment. He spoke in a severe voice: "This sounds suspiciously as if we are starting upon the death of a thousand cuts. Please understand, Fader, that your gratuity will help defray the cost of all extras, and now, as I think of it, the specifications for this tour stipulated a visit to the girls' quarters."

"That is Basic Tour 112. This is Basic Tour 111."

"So what? The prices are the same. Tour 111, according to the brochure, caters to folk whose religion—and now I read from the brochure—'forbids them the sight of naked women or members of the female sex.' We are not all that easily offended. You have jumped to conclusions."

"Not so. The booking clerk at the hotel apparently misunderstood you. Tours cannot be pieced together, a bit of this with some of that. You must apply to the booking clerk for your refund."

Shugart gave a snort of derision. "Do you really take us for fools? This was Tour 112 from the start, and please don't try any more tricks on us."

Fader tendered a sheet of paper. "How is that possible, sir? Tour 112, you will notice, is limited to eight persons. There are nine aboard the boat."

"What's all this?" demanded Arles.

Kirdy made an irritated gesture. "Arles, be good enough to control yourself! You are like a mad dog!"

Shugart demanded of Fader: "Let me see the brochure."

"I cannot do that, sir. This is my only copy."

"Then hold it where I can read it."

Reluctantly Fader complied with the request. Shugart read aloud: "'Tours 111, 112 and 113 are similar: 111 is for folk who may be offended by nudity; 112 passes through the female residences; 113, which is slightly longer, avoids the female residences and visits the sanitary rotundas. The charge for all tours will be thirty-two sols, for up to a total of eight persons. Extra persons may be accommodated at the discretion of the tour captain, but each must pay a charge of four sols. A ten percent gratuity will be expected.' Just so. We have paid thirty-six sols, and here is the receipt to prove it!"

Fader said without accent: "You should have shown this in the first place; it would have saved trouble. Nevertheless, in my opinion, the boat is overloaded for Tour 112."

Shugart spoke crisply: "Enough of your pettifogging! Take us either on Tour 112, or back to the hotel at once, where we will make a furious complaint!"

Fader shrugged wearily. "Everyone wants something for nothing, and we must comply to maintain goodwill. So let it be. Give us our gratuities now and we shall once again bend our backs to the task."

"In no mode, manner, way, shape, intimation, hint or form! You will pine for your lost gratuities forever, unless you instantly mend your ways!"

"Ah, you rich Araminta workers are hard to deal with. Tour 112 it is, by your insistence." He called to the paddlers. "We are in luck! They want to take the shortcut past the dormitories rather than through the bathing rotundas."

Jardine called out: "Bathing rotundas! The brochure said something about sanitation!"

"It is all one," said Fader. "The die is cast."

The Bold Lions fell glumly silent. The boat threaded a set of canals, under built-over areas, beside a strip of land densely planted with bamboo and salpiceta, and tended, so it seemed, by almost as many workers as there were plants. Beyond, the canal turned sharply seaward, and passed between a pair of tall structures. Seven levels of balconies overlooked the canal, with plaited frond doors opening into cubicles. As the Bold Lions scrutinized the balconies, they occasionally glimpsed a Yip girl as she came out to hang a bit of cloth to dry or tend a potted plant, but these were few; the residences seemed almost comatose.

Kiper's disappointment was extreme. He spoke to Fader in bewilderment. "This is truly rather dull. Where are all the girls?"

"Many are bathing in the rotundas," said Fader. "Others are out on the water tending mussel racks and beds of sea lettuce. Here, however, are the residences. The morning girls are sleeping. At midnight they will be off about their duties and the afternoon girls will sleep. Each habitancy by this means serves two people. Eventually we will move to the land and there will be space for all; this is our destiny, and it cannot come too soon. In any case, you have now seen the residences. Some folk find it more amusing to watch the girls as they bathe; I prefer it myself."

"Yes, Fader," muttered Shugart. "You are the clever one, no doubt about it, and you can bid your gratuity a tearful goodbye."

"I beg your pardon?" inquired Fader. "Were you addressing me?"

"No matter. Let us get on with the tour."

"Just so. We will go ashore at yonder dock."

The boat eased up to the dock and the Bold Lions alighted, with Fader assisting them so that they would not fall. As Shugart climbed ashore, Fader's attention was distracted; he looked away just as the boat gave a sudden lurch and Shugart fell with a great splash into the canal.

Fader and others helped Shugart to the dock. "You should have been more careful," said Fader.

"I realize this," said Shugart. "I spoke a trifle too loudly."

"One learns by his mistakes. Well, no doubt you will dry off soon. We cannot waste time in commiseration. This way, then. Stay together and do not get lost, as a substantial fee is charged if we must find a missing person."

The Bold Lions walked along a trestle, climbed steps, passed through a narrow doorway into a corridor which after ten yards gave upon a balcony overlooking a murmurous murk so large that the far wall could only be sensed. A dozen dingy skylights provided illumination; as their eyes adapted to the gloom, the Bold Lions saw below a multitude of Yips. They stood in small groups, or squatted around tiny fire pots where they toasted morsels of skewered fish. Some sat spraddle-legged in circles playing at cards, or dice, or other games; some cut hair or clipped toenails; others played soft breathy music on bamboo pipes, evidently for their private amusement, since no one troubled to listen. Others stood alone, lost in their thoughts, or lay supine staring at nothing. The sound of so many folk came to the balcony as a great soft whisper with no definable source.

Glawen unobtrusively studied the faces of the Bold Lions. Each, predictably, wore a different expression. The brash Kiper would have given voice to facetious jokes, had he dared. Arles maintained a supercilious impassivity, while Kirdy seemed awed and thoughtful. Shugart, still damp from his immersion, clearly found the conditions deplorable. Later he described the Caglioro to his friends: "—ten billion pale eels! The nightmare of a diseased mind! A human miasma!"

Similarly, Uther Offaw would later describe the circumstances, a trifle less trenchantly, as "psychic soup."

Fader addressed the group, speaking without inflection: "This is where men come to rest, to think their thoughts and think the thoughts of others. Women, of course, have similar facilities."

Dauncy asked Fader: "How many folk are out there?"

"It is hard to guess. Persons come; persons go. Notice yonder around the balcony: a party of tourists is amused to throw coins out on the floor! As you see, it causes something of a scramble. Sometimes the tourists throw large sums, and persons become seriously hurt in the tumult."

Jardine asked suspiciously: "Is coin throwing permitted without payment of fees?"

"Yes; we stretch a point in this case. You may indulge yourself as you wish. If you have no small coins you may change sols at the wicket yonder."

Kiper said excitedly: "I'm out of coins! Who'll lend me a few dinkets?"

Kirdy said sternly: "Learn some dignity, Kiper! It's a stupid and pointless waste, throwing money away!" He looked at Fader: "We are not all of us lummoxes, despite your conviction."

Fader smiled, and shook his head. "I deal with many kinds of people, but I make no judgments."

Cloyd Diffin spoke: "You said that the women had separate facilities. Can these be visited?"

"You may select from Tours 128, 129 or 130, as listed in the brochure. They are similar save for optional features."

"Where do men and women meet? How do they marry and form families?"

Fader said: "Our social system is complex. I cannot even provide a generality within the limits of Tour 112. Payment of tutorial fees will provide instruction to any desired level of expertise. If you care to undertake this course of study, please make arrangements with the tour secretary tonight."

The irrepressible Kiper called out: "Tonight Cloyd performs his own research! He intends to gain wisdom at the very source of such lore!"

Cloyd was not amused. "That will be about enough from you, Kiper."

Arles pointed across the Caglioro, to where the other group of tourists stood staring up toward the ceiling. "What is going on over there?"

Fader turned to look. "They are paying for a spectacle. You must not look; that is the rule. If you participate in the viewing, you must pay what we call a subsidiary fee."

"Pure and total bosh!" declared Arles. "I have paid to look out over the Caglioro. If your 'spectacle' interferes with my enjoyment of the view, I will feel free to claim a partial refund!"

Fader emphatically shook his head. "If you are inconvenienced, simply turn your back and do not look."

Kirdy said: "Fader, be sensible. We have paid to inspect the Caglioro, together with—and here I quote the brochure to the best of my memory—'all the picturesque episodes and quaint incidents for which this surprising chamber is notorious.' Any spectacles occurring during our visit are implicitly included."

"Just so," said Fader. "Consider very carefully the thrust of that sentence. The Caglioro is not notorious for this particular spectacle, nor any other single and specific spectacle. Hence, if you watch one of these events, a subsidiary fee must be applied."

"In that case, we will look across the Caglioro as is our right, but we will ignore any and all spectacles. Fellow Bold Lions, do you hear this? Look out over the Caglioro to your heart's content, but if a spectacle interferes with your view, pay no heed. Neither enjoy it nor acknowledge its existence; otherwise we must listen to Fader's ratchety legalisms. Is that clear? Look, then, at will! But give no notice to any spectacle, should one chance to occur!"

Fader had nothing to say. Meanwhile, on a walkway high up under the roof, a pair of old men shuffled out upon a circular platform ten feet in diameter. They wore only loose trunks: one white, the other black. The old man in white showed disinclination, and peered with raised eyebrows and a slack jaw down at the floor far below. He turned and would have scuttled back to the walkway had not a gate barred his exit. The old man in black hobbled forward and seized him; the two wrestled, lurching this way and that, until the man in white tripped and tumbled headlong, whereupon his opponent fell upon him, dragged him clawing and scratching to the edge of the platform, and pushed him over the side. Sprawling, toppling, the old man in white fell, to land upon a target studded with sharp staves, which pierced and broke his body. The Yips ranged around the floor of the Caglioro gave no more than a glance to the proceedings. Up on the high platform the old man in black trunks shuffled wearily away and was lost to view in the high shadows.

Kirdy turned and addressed the Bold Lions: "I saw nothing unusual, in the nature of a spectacle. Did anyone?"

"Not I." "Not I." "Not I." "Nothing but ten thousand Yips engrossed in their machinations."

Uther Offaw turned to Fader: "I have just noticed a high platform up yonder. What is the reason for that, and I do not wish to pay an educational fee."

Fader allowed the shadow of an ironic smile to form on his face. "That is used for certain spectacles which we present to tourists willing to pay. Indigent old persons approaching death, if they so choose, are allowed a luxury supplement to their rations. In return they must wrestle upon the platform, until one of them falls to his death. It is a procedure beneficial in every respect. Old persons enjoy a good diet in their nonproductive years and generate income by their passing, which otherwise would be wasted."

"Interesting! Men and women both enjoy the advantages of the scheme?"

"Naturally!"

"It seems a rather cynical exploitation of these old people," said Uther Offaw.

"By no means!" declared Fader. "I am not encouraged to argue with you, but I will point out that because of strictures imposed upon us from without, we must use any and every means to survive."

"Hm. Might a spectacle be arranged with children as participants, rather than old men?"

"Quite possibly so. The tour clerk will be able to quote you the exact charges."

"It seems that almost anything can be arranged for a fee."

Fader held out his hands. "Is this not true anywhere? I must announce that time is on the move. Have you seen enough of the Caglioro?"

Shugart looked around the group. "We are ready to move on. Where next?"

"We pass through the Gallery of Ancient Gladiators. Had you been attentive a few moments ago, you might have glimpsed a pair of these doughty warriors wrestling on the high platform. Since you failed to notice, I cannot charge a fee."

"Do we incur charges by traversing the gallery?"

Fader made a reassuring sign. "It is on the way to the bazaar. Come."

Fader led the group into a long passage giving on a series of cubicles. In each an old man sat cross-legged on a dingy cushion. Some occupied themselves at a trifle of handicraft. One embroidered; another tatted; another wove strands of fiber into small toy animals. Others sat staring listlessly into space.

As the Bold Lions moved along the gallery they caught up with the party of tourists which had arranged the spectacle in the Caglioro. These numbered about twenty: Glawen adjudged them to be Laddakees from the world Gaude Phodelius IV, by reason of their squat physiques, fresh complexions, round faces and distinctive wide-brimmed hats with trailing black ribbons. The group leader seemed to be arranging another spectacle, the so-called Double Bubble, with the tour guide, but was deterred by what he considered excessive charges. Others of the party clustered around a cubicle, conversing with the old man inside. The Bold Lions stopped to listen.

A question had been put to the old man; he responded: "What choices are open to me? I can no longer work; should I sit in the dark and starve?"

"But you seem reconciled to this sort of death!"

"I care little, one way or another. It is a proper end to my life. I have achieved nothing, discovered nothing; I have brought not a twitch of change to the cosmos. I will soon be gone and no one will know the difference."

"It seems a negative philosophy," stated the Laddakee. "Is there nothing you have done of which you are proud?"

"I have been a grass-scraper all my life. One stalk is much like the others. Still, long ago, an odd mood came on me and I carved a bit of wood into the similitude of a fish, with every scale in correct detail. Folk who saw it thought it very fine."

"And where is this fish now?"

"It fell into the canal and drifted away on the tide. Not long ago I started another such fish—you see it here—but I lost heart and never finished it."

"So now you are ready to die."

"No one is ever quite ready."

One of the Laddakees pushed forward from the rear of the group. "If the truth be told, I am ashamed of this sort of thing. Instead of buying this gentleman's death, let us take up a collection and ensure his survival. Is not that more worthy of humanity and our religion?"

A mutter went around the group. Some seemed to agree; others were doubtful. A very stout man said plaintively: "That's all well and good, but we have already paid for the spectacle; the money would be wasted!"

Another said: "More to the point, there are thousands in the same case! If we rescue this old gaffer and his fish, then another will come to take his place; must we then rescue another, who perhaps has carved a bird? The process is endless!"

The leader said: "As you all know, I am a merciful man, and an Elder in the Church, but I must come down on the side of practicality. As I understand it, this spectacle conduces not to morbidity or perverse spasms, but to a healthy catharsis. Brother Jankoop's scheme does him credit, but I would suggest that on our return home, he show an equal solicitude for his neighbors and put his goats out to pasture."

Grateful laughter greeted the sally. The leader turned to Fader. "Perhaps your party would care to join us at the Double Bubble spectacle. The fee, thus prorated among the two groups, would make the cost less daunting."

Arles inquired: "What, in fact, is the fee?"

Fader calculated. "The charges would be five sols per individual. That is a flat rate." He held up his hand to the instant chorus of protests. "There will be no prorating; prices are fixed."

Arles said with a shaky laugh: "After a financial shock like that, I truly need some catharsis. I will take part, despite the expense."

"Include me," said Cloyd. "What about you, Dauncy?"

"I don't want to miss anything. I'll come."

"Include me as well," declared Kiper.

"It's disgusting," said Uther Offaw. "I won't have any part of it."

"Nor I," said Glawen.

Shugart also excluded himself from the event; Jardine at last decided to participate, "from sheer curiosity," as he put it. Kirdy hesitated, his big rubicund face showing first one expression, then another. At last, feeling Glawen's eyes upon him, he said, rather sulkily, "It's not for me."

While Fader collected the five-sol charges, Glawen chanced to notice the half-finished fish. He pointed. "May I see it?"

The old man handed him the object: a bit of wood eight inches long, with head and about half of the scales carved in exact and minute detail. On an impulse Glawen asked: "Would you sell this to me?"

"It is nothing: not even complete. When I am dead it will be thrown away. You may have it without charge."

"Thank you," said Glawen. From the corner of his eye he felt Fader's observation fixed upon him. He told the old man: "At Yipton nothing is free. I will pay you this coin for the carving. Is that agreeable?"

"Yes, just as you like."

Glawen paid over the coin and took the wooden half-fish. He noticed that Fader had turned away.

The Laddakees' tour guide called out: "Time for the spectacle! On your feet, old man! You must pump and blow hard if you wish to enjoy the evening supper."

Fader, with Kirdy, Uther, Shugart and Glawen, waited in the gallery. The others entered a room where a peculiar contrivance had been arranged: a pair of glass cylinders three feet in diameter and seven feet tall stood side by side, joined to each other by pipes. Into each of the cylinders an ancient gladiator was lowered, until he stood on the bottom; then lids were clamped over the top.

Into the bottom of each cylinder water began to gush, rising ever higher. By working a lever arm, each old man could pump water from his own cylinder into that of his adversary. At first both men seemed apathetic, but as the water rose up around their waists, each essayed a few strokes of the pump and at last both began to pump in earnest. The old gladiator in one tube displayed more desperation and more stamina; at last he succeeded in pumping water over the head of the old man who had carved the fish, who thereupon ceased his exertions, clawed and kicked at the glass for a moment or two, then drowned, and the spectacle came to an end.

The Bold Lions who had been on hand returned to the gallery. Kirdy said: "Well?"

Jardine spoke in a hollow voice: "If that is catharsis, I have had enough."

Fader said briskly: "Come, now; time is short. To the bazaar. Prices, incidentally, are fixed; do not haggle. Please stay together; it is easy to become lost."

221

By way of trestles, galleries, passages and bridges, past many a glimpse of men at work: scraping sea grass, shelling and pounding molluscs, processing bamboo, weaving mats and panels of fronds, the Bold Lions arrived at the bazaar: a low-ceilinged area of innumerable small booths, where Yips of both genders and all ages produced and sold articles of wood, metal, shell, glass, earthenware and knotted cord. Other booths displayed rugs, fabrics, dolls, grotesques of a hundred variants.

The Bold Lions lacked interest in making purchases. Sensing their mood, Fader said: "We will now visit the Hall of Music, where you are at liberty to bestow gifts as you so wish, at no extra charge."

In the Hall of Music elderly men and women sitting in booths played instruments and sang melancholy songs, each with a small bamboo pot in front of him, containing coins presumably contributed by persons who had been affected by their music. Shugart Veder changed a sol into small coins, which he distributed into each pot without regard for the excellence of the music. Kirdy asked one of the musicians: "How do you spend all the money you collect?"

"There's not much to spend. Tax takes more than half; the rest goes for gruel. I haven't known the taste of fish in five years."

"Pity."

"Yes. They'll have me in the Gladiators' Gallery before long. That's when the music stops."

"Come along," said Fader. "Time is up, unless you care for overtime charges."

"Not at all likely."

Once back at the hotel, Fader said: "Now, in the matter of my gratuity, ten percent is considered paltry and mean."

Shugart said: "What is nothing at all considered, after you refused to take us to the rotunda and threw me in the canal?"

"Nothing at all is considered careless, and it involves wondering what you are eating when you take your meals."

"You make a persuasive point. Very well. You shall have ten percent and think of us however you like. To be candid, I am as unconcerned with your good opinion as you are with mine."

Fader could not be bothered with a comment. The gratuity was paid over; Fader accepted it with a cool nod. "You are going to Pussycat Palace?"

"Yes; later this evening."

"You will need a guide."

"Why? The way is clearly marked."

"Let me warn you; footpads are rife! They spring at you from side corridors; you are hurled to the ground, and an instant later your money is gone. You are given a kick or two in the face for good measure, and they are gone, all inside half a minute. But they dare not attack if you are protected by a guide. My charges are nominal, and you will go to Pussycat Palace in dignity and assurance."

"What, then, are the charges?"

"Nine persons: nine sols."

"I will consult with my fellows at dinner."

As Syrene sank low, the Bold Lions, who had gathered on the terrace, settled at a table overlooking the harbor, directly above the *Faraz*, where it lay alongside the dock.

For a period the Bold Lions refreshed themselves with rum punches and ling-lang toddies, and congratulated themselves upon the romantic ambience of the situation.

"Naturally, we exclude the Big Chife when we discuss the local delectations," said Dauncy Diffin whimsically.

Kiper spoke bravely: "The Big Chife, bah! I've almost forgotten it. What's a bit of stink, after all?"

"Speak for yourself," said Uther. "I am not so tolerant."

Kiper told him: "It's all in your head! A person must have a brain well-stocked with all manner of vileness before he can identify a bad smell. My mind is noble and pure; hence I am unaffected."

"We can learn much from Kiper," said Shugart. "When I fell in that filthy canal, he advised me to take a dispassionate view of the situation, and enjoy it along with everyone else."

Jardine grinned. "As I recall, this was also Fader's opinion."

"I'm lucky he did not charge me for a bath," growled Shugart. "He thought of everything else, and now he wants another nine sols for taking us to Pussycat Palace. He claims it's the only way to avoid attack by footpads, presumably led by himself."

Uther, ordinarily casual, now became incensed. "That is extortion, plain and simple! I'm of a mind to report him to the Oomps!"

Kiper, grinning like a fox, pointed. "If you're serious, there they stand: two of the elite."

Uther jumped to his feet and strode off to confront the Oomps. They listened politely as he explained his grievance, and made what appeared to be a sympathetic response. Uther turned on his heel and came back to the table.

"Well?" asked Kiper.

"They wanted to know how much Fader charged. I told them and they agreed that it wasn't too much. I asked why they did not apprehend the footpads; they said that as soon as they started to patrol the corridors, the footpads went away and the Oomps marched back and forth to no purpose. I mentioned that the blue pamphlet said that experienced persons could visit Pussycat Palace alone in perfect safety. They told me the pamphlet was a bit outdated; that these 'experienced visitors' always tipped the tour clerk five or ten sols, which somehow seemed to mitigate the nuisance."

"Ah well," said Jardine. "Nine sols won't break us. Let's ignore the whole matter and have our supper."

Syrene had dropped below the horizon, leaving a few long clouds glowing scarlet close above the ocean. Barefoot bare-chested boys brought tall lamps to the tables and the Bold Lions dined to lamplight as dusk fell over Yipton.

The courses were nicely presented, though lacking in zest, in the patterns of cosmopolitan cuisine, where the basic intent was not so much to please the discriminating palate as to offend no one. Portions were carefully metered and something short of lavish. The Bold Lions were not particularly pleased with the repast, but could find nothing definite to grumble about. They were served, first, a pale ambiguous broth, then molluscs fried in a light batter, with a salad of greens, salpiceta nubbins, and sea lettuce; then dishes of steamed eel on a bed of pilau, and finally a dessert of coconut meringue in clotted coconut cream, with tea and plum wine.

Cloyd sat back in his chair. "I have just consumed the rations of an Ancient Gladiator."

"That may be true for me as well," said Jardine. "And I am now ready to fight Fader and his footpads."

Uther looked around the panorama. "Let us be fair. Once we ignore the Chife, the place is fascinating, weird, charming in spots, odd everywhere else, distinctive in every way; we have traveled five thousand light-years from Araminta—but I think I've had enough. I'm going home tomorrow, and the chances are very good I'll never be back!"

"What!" cried Kiper. "Do I hear correctly? When we haven't even visited Pussycat Palace yet!"

Uther spoke somewhat primly: "I am sure that a single occasion will suffice."

"Poof!" said Kiper loftily. "You can't hope to be a true connoisseur of pit-a-pat by dashing in and dashing out like a frightened bird! Take Cloyd or Arles, for example. Do they take shortcuts or scamp the job? Never! 'Only too much is enough!' That's the slogan they march under."

"They can march as they like, and take Tours 100 through 200 inclusive, and live in the basement of Pussycat Palace, where the girls wash their stockings. It's far too rich for my blood."

Shugart as usual was judicious. "I'm half inclined to agree—but only half. Let's wait and see how we feel in the morning."

"In full candor," said Arles, "I'm also about half ready to leave. Even a bit more: say about two-thirds ready. The Chife is not at all to my taste."

Cloyd shook his head in wonder. "It sounds as if the festivities might be breaking up early. Dauncy, what of you?"

"I'm with Shugart. Let's see how we feel in the morning. But I suspect that anything more than today might be anticlimax."

"Kirdy, what's your feeling on this?"

Kirdy turned a dubious glance toward Glawen. "I suppose we could profitably stay on a day or so, just relaxing out here on the terrace."

Jardine said: "Let's drop the matter for now. We all may have new ideas in the morning."

"Good enough!" declared Kiper. "Tonight it's the grand foray on Pussycat Palace."

Kirdy put down his teacup and straightened in his chair. "Pussycat Palace—not for me. It's just too much for one day. I'm giving it a miss."

Shugart surveyed him in wonder. "I have known a hundred marvels at Yipton, but this is the greatest sensation of all!"

"Enjoy it for free," said Kirdy with a humorless grin.

"But why? Answer me that!"

"There's no mystery; I'm just not in the mood."

Kiper spoke aggrievedly: "I thought that was why we were making the trip!"

"Perhaps tomorrow."

"But we might be leaving tomorrow!"

"Tomorrow morning, then. Tonight I want to rest and gather my wits."

Arles said thoughtfully: "I know exactly how you feel. I'm staying behind too."

Shugart jerked back thunderstruck. "I can't believe that I'm hearing correctly! Listen to these prodigies of nature! Can they be the same slavering rip-roaring tried-and-true Bold Lions of yore?"

Arles laughed weakly. "I'm just a bit off my feed. Don't let that deter you others."

Shugart threw his arms in the air. "As you like. I will say no more."

Jardine said: "I've picked up some information around the lobby.

It seems that they'll try to charge ten sols but will take five. Ignore all extras; they are frosting on the cake, so to speak, and quite redundant. Gratuities also are unnecessary; the entire take goes directly to Titus Pompo, who doesn't so much as lift a finger to earn it."

The group removed to the lobby. Kirdy took Glawen aside. "It looks as if the excursion is breaking up early."

Glawen assented. "So it does."

"If the group goes, it takes our cover with it." Kirdy spoke in a terse staccato voice, as if he suspected Glawen of insubordinate tendencies. "We're left out in the open: two obvious Bureau B types. All of which means that we've got to accelerate our program and do what we can tonight."

"I suppose that's the way of it."

Kirdy looked off across the lobby. "Frankly, as of now, I don't see that there's much we can accomplish in safety."

Glawen glanced skeptically sidewise. What was Kirdy trying to tell him, without enunciating the specific words? Glawen said deliberately: "That's what we'll have to decide after reconnaissance."

Kirdy cleared his throat. "We can't go too far too fast, and safety must be the first consideration. Do you agree?"

"More or less. But—"

"Never mind the buts. This is my plan. While the rest of you are at Pussycat Palace, I'll cast about in an unobtrusive manner and discover what's within range of the possible. Then, when you get back, if anything seems feasible, we'll get on with the job."

Glawen sat silent.

"Well?" demanded Kirdy.

"I still don't want to go to Pussycat Palace."

"Go anyway!" snapped Kirdy. "No one must suspect that we're associated except as Bold Lions. We probably shouldn't be talking now. You'd better join the others."

Kirdy arose and went off to examine the grotesques. Glawen sighed and joined the Bold Lions.

A few minutes later Fader appeared. "Is everyone on hand?"

Shugart said: "Two of the group aren't up to it. There'll be just seven."

"I still must charge nine sols, since that was the quoted price, and I turned down another job in order to keep faith with you."

"Seven persons: seven sols, gratuity included. That is all you will get from us," said Shugart. "Take it or leave it."

Fader shook his bronze curls in pain. "You Araminta workers are both hard and crooked; I pity the poor girls at the Palace if your erections are of similar quality. Very well, I yield to your avarice. Give me the seven sols."

"Ha, ha, ha," laughed Shugart. "You shall be paid upon our return. Are you ready?"

"Yes; let's be on our way."

"The Bold Lions are on the prowl!" Kiper called out. "Girls, beware!"

"Kiper, if you please!" said Jardine. "We do not need to advertise our indiscretions. This is by tradition a furtive activity."

"Exactly so," said Uther. "If you insist on calling out slogans, at least identify us as the Theosophical Society, or the Temperance Union."

Arles suddenly bestirred himself. "I'm not altogether well, but I think I'll go along just for the company."

Fader said: "You must pay the requisite fee of one sol."

"Yes, by all means! Let's go."

"Follow me, then! Do not stray!"

Fader led the group along the passages of Yipton and finally brought them to an arched portico faced with lavender tiles. A sign indited in blue symbols read:

PALACE OF HAPPY PLAY

Fader ushered the Bold Lions through the arch and into a reception room furnished with cushioned benches.

"I will wait for you here," said Fader. "The routine is simple. Buy a ticket for ten sols at yonder wicket. This ticket includes amusing extras, for what is called an around-the-world voyage."

"No extras are needed!" said Uther. "We opt for the five-sol ticket."

"That buys what is known as a coastwise trip," said Fader. "In addition, for those who are so inclined, there is a selection of exhibitions, pantomimes, farces and pastiches, priced at various rates. The ticket agent will supply full information."

"That sounds interesting!" declared Arles. "Just what I need for a spruce-up, and perhaps I'll feel my old self in the morning."

The Bold Lions filed past the wicket, bought their tickets, then stepped through a curtain of beaded glass strings into a long hall. At intervals doorways opened off the hall; girls stood in the doorways watching the passing traffic. All were young and well-formed; all wore simple knee-length white frocks.

Glawen chose one of the girls, and went into her chamber. She closed the door, took the ticket, and slipped out of her garment. Then she stood silent, waiting while Glawen awkwardly removed his tunic. Glawen paused, looked into the girl's face, then turned away. He winced, sighed, then donned his tunic once again.

In a worried voice the girl asked: "What is wrong? Have I done something to offend you?"

"Not at all," said Glawen. "It seems that I'm not in the mood for this sort of pit-a-pat."

The girl shrugged and pulled the frock back over her head. She said: "I serve tea and cakes as an extra. The charge is one sol."

"Very well," said Glawen. "If you will share them with me."

Without comment the girl brought a pot of tea and a platter of small pastries. She poured a single cup. Glawen said: "Please, pour for yourself as well."

"As you like." She poured another cup of tea and sat watching Glawen without interest, a situation which at last prompted Glawen to ask: "What is your name?"

"Sujulor Yerlsvan Alasia. It is a North Wind name."

"My name is Glawen, from the House of Clattuc."

"That is an odd name."

"It seems ordinary enough to me. Are you interested in where I come from? Or anything about me?"

"Not really. I must take events as they come."

"So I am an 'event.'"

"Yes, that is so."

"Do all the girls at Yipton come to work here? Or just the prettiest?"

"Almost all work here for a time."

"Do you like the work?"

"It is easy. I don't like some of the men and I am pleased to be done with them."

"Do you have a lover?"

"I don't know what you mean."

"Some young man who loves you and whom you love."

"No; nothing like that. What an odd idea!"

"Would you like to travel, and visit other worlds?"

"I have not thought too much about it. I wonder why everyone asks me that question."

"I'm sorry if I'm boring you," said Glawen.

The girl ignored him. "It is time that you should go, or pay a surcharge. You may leave your gratuity on the table."

"I think not, since it all goes to the Oomphaw."

"As you please."

Glawen returned to the sitting room. Presently, all the Bold Lions were on hand, Kiper arriving last, and it developed that Kiper had been the only Bold Lion to undertake an "around-the-world voyage."

Fader inquired if anyone cared to commission a special pageant; receiving a negative response from Shugart he conducted the group back to the hotel. "Will you be requiring my services tomorrow?" he asked.

"Most probably not," said Shugart. "Beyond doubt you have made today memorable, and I, for one, will never forget you."

"That is good to hear," said Fader. "Your praise has sweetened an otherwise trying day for me." He bowed and departed.

Shugart turned to the other Bold Lions. "Well, what now? The night is still young!"

"I think I will settle myself to another of those excellent rum punches," said Kiper.

Cloyd declared: "For once in his life, Kiper has had a rational thought. As we drink he can describe to us the scenery encountered on his around-the-world voyage."

Glawen, meanwhile, found Kirdy sitting in a quiet corner of the lobby, turning the pages of an old magazine. Glawen slid into a seat beside him.

Kirdy tossed the magazine aside. "How did it go at Pussycat Palace?"

"About what I expected."

"You don't seem all that enthusiastic."

"It's not an enthusiastic environment. The girls are polite enough —'dutiful' is probably a better word—but still, in the end I just drank tea."

"Most fastidious of you."

Not for the first time it occurred to Glawen that Kirdy did not like him very much. "It wasn't that at all."

"The girl smelled bad?"

Glawen shook his head. "This may sound peculiar, but do you remember the old man who gave me the fish?"

"Yes, of course."

"I went with the girl into her room. She took off her clothes and stood waiting. Her expression was like that of the old man. I could not bring myself to touch her."

"That's a bit fanciful, isn't it?"

"I had a nice cup of tea, and she told me her name, which I've forgotten, and the time went easily enough."

"Expensive tea," grunted Kirdy. He turned away and picked up his magazine.

Glawen asked: "How did things go with you."

229

Kirdy composed his face. "Not bad. But, well, not really good. Our plans, if any, need careful thought."

"What happened?"

"I went out to reconnoiter. The section we are interested in lies just around the harbor from the hotel. I went down to the dock and strolled along the harbor road to the breakwater, like any other innocent tourist exploring the precincts of Yipton.

"Once past the hotel a wall of bamboo poles skirts the road, about fifty yards long. A single door opens into this wall. It seemed to be securely locked; still, to make sure, I tried to open it. The door was definitely locked and I continued along the road to the end of the wall, at the eastern seafront. By craning my neck around the wall I could see a dock. I turned around to find an Oomp standing about five feet away: a large fellow in a white cap. He asked me: 'What are you looking for?'

"I said: 'Nothing in particular. Just looking.'

"He gave me a rather peculiar smile, then said: 'You tried that door down the wall. Why?'

"I said: 'Casual curiosity, I suppose. I wondered what might be on the other side. Someone told me that this was where glass was melted and blown.'

"He said: 'That is not so. It is all warehouse area. Do you still want to look inside?'

"I tried to act ingenuous and full of childlike innocence. I said: 'If you think there's anything to interest me—why not?'

"He put on a rather sinister leer, and asked: 'What are you interested in?'

"'I'm an anthropologist by trade,' I told him. 'I'm fascinated by Yip ingenuity in creating a habitat in the empty ocean! Yip glass-blowing and ceramics are especially interesting.'

"'There's nothing along here like that,' he told me. 'The tourist attractions are elsewhere.' So I came back to the hotel."

"Did he ask for your name?"

"The subject never came up."

Glawen ruminated a moment. "It's odd that he failed to ask your name."

"I suppose it is a bit unusual, but it doesn't concern us now. I can find no safe access to that section; we have no choice but to back away."

"You've totally ruled out the roof?"

"Of course! The roof is made of fronds. A person need only put his foot down to fall through."

"Not if he keeps to the rafters and the ridge beams. I can see the roof from the window of my room, but there's a canal just below. What about your room?"

"It is no better. There's a drop of fifteen feet to the roof. The only way down would be by ladder, which we don't have."

"Or a rope."

"We have no rope either."

"I know. Maybe we can improvise."

The muscles of Kirdy's face contorted. "I'm not going out on that roof! It gives me vertigo just to think of it!"

"Let's go look over the situation," said Glawen. "If it seems feasible, I'll give it a try. That's what we've come to do, and here's the one opportunity."

"Very well," said Kirdy grudgingly. "So long as it's understood that I'm not going out on that roof."

The other Bold Lions sat at a table to the side of the terrace, drinking rum punches to the light of Lorca, Sing and an array of flickering lamps. Their voices rose and fell across the night, as they allowed the other tourists to notice what fine fellows they were.

Kirdy and Glawen went quietly upstairs to the fourth floor. Glawen asked: "Do you know which is Arles' room?"

"He's second down the hall. Why?"

"Let's look out your window."

Kirdy's room was dark except for the glimmer from a small hooded night-light. Crossing to the window, the two looked out over the roof: a clutter of hips, jogs, gables and ridges, black and pink in the eerie light of Lorca and Sing.

Kirdy pointed. "That would be the proper area: just about there. But, as you can see, it's quite inaccessible, and this is how we must describe it to Bodwyn Wook, without inconsistency in our reports."

"But I don't agree with you. I think we should give it a try."

"How will you get down to the roof? It's fifteen feet or better."

"As I recall, Arles came to Yipton wearing a fine cloak of stout material."

"True. Rather too fine for the occasion, if you ask me."

"The theft of this cloak from Arles' room will cause consternation but no surprise, and Arles will learn to dress more modestly in the future."

Kirdy gave a dry chuckle. "Arles might even volunteer his cloak, were he asked."

"Possibly, but when one asks permission, one often gets no for an answer. As it is, Arles has not specifically forbidden us the cloak, which is good enough for me."

"Surely his door is locked."

Glawen examined Kirdy's door. "Notice: the jambs are split bamboo and not at all rigid. Are you carrying your big clasp knife?"

Kirdy wordlessly brought forth the knife. Glawen took it to the door into Arles' room. While Kirdy kept watch, Glawen inserted the heavy knife blade between door and frame. He applied gentle pressure; the frame sprang aside, allowing the door to slide past the latch. Glawen entered the room, took up the cloak, retreated, closed the door carefully, and the two returned to Kirdy's room.

Glawen cut away the cincture of silver lace which Kirdy rolled into a tight wad and discarded. Glawen cut the cloak into long strips, which Kirdy tied together, to produce a rope twenty feet long. Glawen tied one end to the window frame and lowered the other end to the roof below. "Now, before my courage gives out—"

"Courage?" Kirdy grunted. "I call it suicidal Clattuc recklessness."

"One last precaution. I might get lost out there. Take the night-light and hold it in the window. If you hear me whistle, move the light in a circle."

"Right. Needless to say, be careful."

"Needless to say. Well, here I go."

Glawen hesitated only long enough to look right and left along the roof, then lowered himself down the makeshift rope. Gingerly he rested his feet on the plaited thatch, putting down his full weight only when he felt solidity beneath them.

Now he must locate a rafter under the palm-frond panels, and never allow his full weight to rest anywhere else. The simplest and most direct route would take him up to the ridge, then eastward along the ridge to the area of Bodwyn Wook's interest.

He found a convenient rafter. Moving with the utmost delicacy, to avoid making crackling or squeaking sounds, which might attract attention below, he moved up the slope. From time to time he looked over his shoulder, thus preserving his orientation with the night-light. He arrived at a hip, which provided less precarious support, and climbed rapidly on his hands and knees.

He reached the ridge and, sitting astride, looked back to the loom of the hotel across a gulf of black shadow. So far, so good. For a moment he sat resting, surrounded by a landscape of irrational shapes colored pale pink and black.

Urgency pressed on him. He set off along the ridge, scuttling like a great rat. His fear was suspended; he felt almost exhilaration.

At last he halted, and surveying the geometry of the roof, decided that he had come far enough. Beneath him now should be the target area. What would happen to him if he were caught? His mind recoiled from the idea.

He located a rafter and slid down the slope a few feet, then set to work cutting a hole in the thatch with his knife.

The knife slid into emptiness. Glawen enlarged the hole and put down his eye. On the floor below, the light of a dozen lamps illuminated a flyer of medium size. A workbench ran down one side of the room, furnished with various items of material-shaping equipment. A dozen men worked somewhat languidly at one job or another; it seemed to Glawen that not all of them were Yips, but he could not be sure.

In order to see from a different angle, he shifted his position and felt the thatch crackle under his weight; in an instant he would be falling. Desperately he thrust down his knee and tried to draw himself back to the rafter. His knee burst through the thatch; he caught a momentary glimpse of men looking up in wonder; then he had drawn away to safety.

Seething with fury and fear, Glawen clambered to the ridge and crawled back the way he had come. There was no time to waste; Oomps would be on the roof within minutes, and the thought of what they would do if they caught him made his skin crawl.

He came abreast of the hotel, and there in the window was the night-light. He slid recklessly down the hip, transferred to the rafter and backed down to the hotel wall.

Where was the rope? Glawen looked through the shadows this way and that. The rope could not be seen, nor, looking up, could he see the night-light.

Apparently, in his haste and confusion, he had not come far enough down the hip before transferring to the rafter. The rope must be hanging a few feet farther on, and he could only grope for it in the darkness.

He went along beside the wall ten feet, twenty feet, thirty feet. No rope. He turned to retreat in the other direction, but thought to hear quiet urgent voices from across the roof; it was too late now to go back; he could only hope that Kirdy had also heard the voices and extinguished the night-light.

Just ahead was the corner of the hotel. He went forward and looked down, and saw the small canal which ran behind the hotel. A few yards farther along, a boat lay moored to the hotel dock: apparently a garbage scow.

The garbage collector was not visible and was evidently occupied inside the hotel. He had covered the garbage piled in the bow with a mat. The canal at this point was about twelve feet wide. Glawen ran along the edge of the roof, until he stood opposite the garbage scow. He levered his legs under him, jumped. Forever he seemed to float through the air, while his trajectory took him across the canal and down upon the mat. He alighted crouching, with no great shock, the boat absorbing most of his momentum. He scrambled across the mat, jumped to the dock, and looked wildly back and forth.

Thump, thump, thump: footsteps.

Glawen pressed against the side of the hotel. Out upon the dock came the garbageman, laden with an enormous sack of garbage. As soon as he turned to relieve himself of the burden he would see Glawen.

Glawen ran soundlessly forward. He seized the garbageman by sack and shoulder, propelled him smartly to the edge of the dock and over into the canal. Then he ran to the kitchen door, looked within. A small pantry was at hand; Glawen stepped forward and ducked into the shadows.

Attracted by the splash and the exclamations the cook on duty and a pair of scullions came out on the dock. Glawen stepped from the pantry, ran through the kitchen, along a short service hall, and out upon the terrace.

He stood composing himself. The Bold Lions sat as before. Unobtrusively Glawen seated himself between Shugart and Dauncy, neither of whom took any notice, their attention given to Arles as he described the amazing events he had witnessed at his exhibition.

Glawen nudged Shugart. "Excuse me a moment; I'm for the washroom. When the boy comes by, order me another rum punch."

"So it shall be."

Glawen departed the terrace, crossed the lobby, ran up the stairs and knocked at the door to Kirdy's room. "It's Glawen! Open up!"

The door eased back a crack; Kirdy looked out. "So there you are! I was truly worried! When I saw Yips on the roof I had to douse the light and pull up the rope, so they wouldn't trace it here."

"So that's why I couldn't find the rope," said Glawen. "It probably worked out for the best."

"I was watching for you, but I didn't see you," Kirdy explained. "And I was sure that you'd find another way into the hotel."

"We'll talk about it later; there's no time now. Where's the rope?"

"Here. I've made a bundle of it."

"Good. Go downstairs and sit with the Bold Lions. I'll get rid of the rope."

Kirdy departed. Glawen tucked the bundle under his arm and

followed. He crossed the lobby, went down to the dock. Standing in the shadows Glawen wedged a chunk of broken concrete into the bundle and tossed it into the harbor, where it sank immediately. He then returned to the terrace and rejoined the Bold Lions, where Kirdy already sat.

Five minutes passed. A pair of Oomps came into the lobby. They paused, looked all around, then came out on the terrace and approached the Bold Lions. One spoke in a soft voice: "Good evening, gentlemen."

"Good evening," said Shugart. "I hope you are not bringing us news of another surcharge or service tax? I assure you that we've been milked quite dry."

"No doubt, no doubt. What have you been doing?"

Shugart looked up in astonishment. "Observe these goblets, some empty, others full or half full of rum punch! I am no detective but I might well assume that the Bold Lions were carousing in typical style."

"What about Bold Lion tricks and pranks?"

"My dear fellow, we have just engaged in tricks and pranks at Pussycat Palace, and, for the moment at least, have no more in mind."

"That is a clear statement. Who was your escort?"

"A certain Fader."

"Good evening to you all."

The Oomps departed. Uther looked after them. "Now, what in thunder were they after, with their talk of pranks? Kiper, did you do something insane? Remember, this is Yipton, and Titus Pompo takes a dim view of mischief."

"Don't blame me; I've done nothing!"

The Bold Lions sat for another hour, then went up to their rooms. Almost immediately there was a great howl from Arles' cubicle.

The Bold Lions and other tourists looked out into the hall. Arles burst from his room, his heavy round face congested with rage. "They've stolen my cloak!"

"Arles, control yourself!" said Jardine. "Talk sensibly! Who has stolen your cloak?"

"Thieves! The Yipton burglars! My best cloak: it's gone!"

"Are you sure? Did you look everywhere?"

"Of course! Even under the bed! It's gone!"

"It's a serious matter for sure," said one of the tourists. "In the morning you must make a stern complaint. As for now, let us all go to sleep."

"In the morning it will be too late!" declared Arles in a passion.

"It's quite late right now," said the tourist. "You can roar all night long and still not recover your cloak."

"Good advice," said Shugart. "We'll see to it in the morning."

Kirdy said: "It won't do any good. The cloak is gone; why make a fuss?"

"Sensible talk," said the tourist. "Goodnight, all. I hope there will be no more hysterical outcries."

"It's a skulking ding-dong outrage!" declared Arles through clenched teeth. "I'm almost afraid to undress for fear someone will take my pants and shoes."

Uther said shortly: "Sleep with your clothes on, then. As for me, I'm tired and I'm for bed."

"Lucky you!" sniffed Arles. "No one has stolen your cloak."

"I shall sleep all the sounder on that account. Goodnight."

Kirdy gave a few last words of advice: "Don't let a simple stolen cloak spoil the excursion for you. Goodnight."

Arles retreated into his room, and the others did likewise.

In the morning Glawen told Kirdy: "The *Faraz* leaves two hours before noon. We should be aboard as soon as possible; once on the ship, they can't touch us. And it would be best if the Bold Lions departed all at the same time."

"Good idea," said Kirdy. "I'll pass the word."

Kirdy made the rounds of his fellows and found almost all of them disposed to depart Yipton. Only Kiper and Cloyd protested, but without vehemence, and in the end decided to go aboard the *Faraz* with the others.

The Bold Lions took their breakfast, settled their accounts at the hotel and descended to the dock.

At the wicket stood four Oomps: stern muscular men with black lips and heads shaved bald. They seemed easy and casual, but Glawen saw that they carefully scanned each person as he or she paid the departure tax. Kirdy whispered to Glawen: "On the far left: he's the one who saw me by the wall. They are looking for me; I know it."

"Ignore them. You did nothing they know about."

"So I hope."

Glawen paid the departure tax, passed through the wicket unchallenged and with a great surge of relief crossed the gangplank to the deck of the *Faraz*, where the Oomps were not allowed to venture.

As Kirdy started to pay his tax the Oomp to the left made a sign and the others stepped forward. "Your name, sir?"

"I am Kirdy Wook. What of it?"

"We must ask you to come with us."

"What for? I'm planning to take the ferry, and I don't want to be delayed over some trifle."

"The matter may well be serious, sir. An offense has been committed and we must find out who is responsible."

Kirdy looked from one to the other. "This is a great mystery: certainly to me. What offense are you talking about?"

"A certain Arles Clattuc has complained in regard to a stolen cloak. We have discovered in your room a wad of silver lace, which Arles Clattuc identifies as the cincture to the stolen cloak. Through careful inspection we have discovered black fibers which Arles Clattuc states to be identical to the fibers which made up the cloth of the cloak. Thus we must detain you until the circumstances are explained."

Glawen turned to Arles: "Tell them now, quickly, that you forgot, that you lost that cloak to Kirdy in a wager. Don't let him be kept in detention!"

Arles growled: "If he stole my best cloak and tore it to pieces, it serves him right!"

Uther said: "It was a joke! We'll straighten it out later! But for now, tell them it was a mistake!"

"Are you all against me?" cried Arles. "So now I'm forced to be kind Arles, good magnanimous Arles, when it doesn't suit me at all!"

"He's a Bold Lion! Does that mean nothing?"

Grudgingly Arles called up to the Oomps: "I remember now; I gave that cloak to Kirdy. He did not steal it after all. I retract the charges."

"Very well, sir. If you'll just step back through the wicket—totally free this time, sir; no taxes—we'll go over to the office and formally rescind the complaint. Are you coming, sir?"

Arles asked dubiously: "How long will it take?"

"Not long, sir, if all goes well."

"Why can't you just take my word from here? That's more convenient."

"It's not the way we do things, sir. You'll have to come to the office."

Arles backed away toward the saloon. "I'm not going ashore. I told you that it was a mistake, and that's enough!" He turned and went into the saloon.

The Oomps turned back to Kirdy. "If you'll be good enough to come along, sir, there are still certain points we want to clear up."

Kirdy looked longingly across to the *Faraz*, then, with an Oomp at each elbow, he walked away with shoulders sagging.

CHAPTER 5

1

Glawen ran up to the bridge of the *Faraz* and made radio contact with Bureau B at Araminta Station. "Glawen Clattuc here. Put me through to the Supervisor, on urgent business."

A few seconds later a rasping voice sounded through the mesh: "Bodwyn Wook here."

Glawen spoke with care; almost certainly the call was being monitored. "There is a ridiculous situation in progress here, and it might even become serious. Kirdy has been taken into custody. The Oomps claim that he stole Arles' cloak."

"That doesn't sound too important. What actually happened?"

"It's possible that one of the Bold Lions played a trick on Arles, and that Kirdy was blamed. I can't understand the motives of the Yips —unless they believe Kirdy to be guilty of some graver offense. Naturally, he is no more guilty than I am, and the situation is an outrage."

"Indeed, indeed!" said Bodwyn Wook in his reediest voice. "I'll get in touch with Titus Pompo at once. Keep handy to this connection, in case I want to get back to you."

"What of the ferry?"

"It must leave on schedule; no help for it, since passengers have connections to make. I'll straighten things out with Titus Pompo."

Half an hour later, with no further word from Bodwyn Wook, the ferry departed Yipton.

Arriving at Araminta Station late in the afternoon, Glawen went directly to Bureau B and was sent into the Supervisor's office.

Bodwyn Wook pointed to a chair. Glawen looked hopefully toward Bodwyn Wook. "Have you had news of Kirdy?"

"No. I can't get through to Titus Pompo. No one else will talk. What happened out there?"

Glawen reported the circumstances as succinctly as possible.

Bodwyn Wook heard of the flyer with little surprise. "I expected something of the sort. Could you determine the type?"

"It seemed to be a Pegasus Model D, like our own, with a few modifications."

Bodwyn Wook grunted. "It seemed like our own because it was our own, built with stolen parts. Go on."

"That's when my knee went through the mat. I managed to get back into the hotel, by a different route; apparently Yips had appeared on the roof and Kirdy had pulled up the rope."

"An anxious moment or two, eh?"

"Yes. But I had some luck and managed to slip back into the hotel. I went up to the room. Kirdy had already made a packet of the rope. I took it down and threw it into the harbor, and it seemed as if we had come through in good shape, although Arles put up a great howl over his stolen cloak.

"In the morning the Bold Lions discovered that they'd had enough of Yipton, and were ready to go home. Kirdy and I were also willing to leave. But when we went down to the ferry, four Oomps were waiting. I went past with the others, but they stopped Kirdy at the gangplank and took him away."

Bodwyn Wook leaned forward in perplexity. "Why Kirdy? How were they able to center in upon him?"

Glawen scowled, then, in a carefully emotionless voice, said: "Kirdy sent me off to Pussycat Palace so that he could reconnoiter. I did not want to go, but he insisted. When I got back—"

"Just one moment! Let me understand this! You say he sent you off to Pussycat Palace? He 'insisted' that you go?"

"Well, yes. As soon as the ferry pulled out from Araminta Station, Kirdy took command. He stated that you had put him in charge by reason of his seniority and experience."

Bodwyn Wook jerked back in his seat. "He was not telling the truth."

"I suspected as much but Kirdy is very sensitive and I did not want to dispute his word. I decided to make the best of the situation, and work with the circumstances rather than against them. As it turned out, I made the wrong decision."

Bodwyn Wook spoke in a dry voice: "It may be not so bad as it sounds. Titus Pompo will ask questions. Kirdy will no doubt reason, and correctly so, that nothing can be gained by holding his tongue, since you have escaped with the information. I am sure that he will save himself any major discomfort by cooperating to the degree required of him. In short, he will tell everything he knows,

239

which is not very much. After that, what happens is anyone's guess.

"We don't entirely understand Titus Pompo's disposition. He may be guided by rage, malice and determination to set a chilling example. More likely, he will temporize and attempt to bargain. Our best option, in any case, is to act at once and decisively, and I have already put the process into motion. We will move early tomorrow. Meanwhile, go home and get some rest. Return in the morning; I might need further information."

Glawen paused by the door. "What of the Conservator?"

"He will prefer to know nothing about what is ostensibly a routine affair. If notified, he might feel obliged to sing LPF music and put a *pro forma* restraint upon us."

"What do you plan to do?"

"The needful. You may go now and get some rest."

Glawen departed and went listlessly to Clattuc House. His father was not in their chambers, and did not arrive home until late.

In the morning the two arose early, made a quick breakfast and repaired to the Bureau B offices, to find Bodwyn Wook already in conference with the captains Ysel Laverty and Rune Offaw. As yet, there had been no word from Yipton, and Glawen was directed to a couch in the shadows at the back of the room. He had slept only fitfully and found his eyelids hanging heavy. He pulled himself up with a jerk and tried to heed the conversation.

Ysel Laverty, thick, solid, with short gray hair, slate-gray eyes and a reputation for ruthless pertinacity, was speaking: "—complain that our reaction was excessive, especially if there are Yip casualties."

"No matter," said Bodwyn Wook. "Power flows to he who takes charge. We shall act first and argue later, if at all. Now we must show our will to act, or lose our credibility forever. And with it, incidentally, the Conservancy. Scharde, what of your preparations?"

"We are at the ready. If we don't defend ourselves, we deserve what we get."

"Then you might as well get to it. We are probably too late already."

Scharde rose to his feet and departed the room, with a glance toward Glawen and a wave of the hand as he passed.

Bodwyn Wook touched a button and spoke into the mesh on his telephone. "I want Namour co-Clattuc here at once. No excuses, no delay."

Rune Offaw asked: "Why do you need Namour?"

Bodwyn Wook slapped the arms of his chair. "Namour is a swash-buckling desperado after the best—or worst—Clattuc tradition. I trust him only so far as I can see him. If he is in my office, I can see him."

A chime sounded, and a voice came from the mesh. "A call from Yipton: Titus Pompo will speak with you."

"It's about time! Bodwyn Wook here."

After a portentous five-second delay the response came, heavy and resonant: "I am Titus Pompo! Speak!"

Bodwyn Wook turned on the video connection. "My screen is blank. Do you see me? I am Bodwyn Wook, Supervisor of Bureau B. Show yourself, so that I may see with whom I am talking."

"My face is my own. You must gratify your curiosity in other ways. Why did you call me?"

"Hide your face, if you like; that's your affair. But when you lay hands on my nephew then it's my affair. I wish to speak to him this moment, to make sure that he has not been molested."

"Your nephew, it appears, would be the burglar-thief. He is in detention until we reckon up his offenses."

"He is a sergeant of Bureau B. He is not a thief."

"Why did he steal the cloak of Arles Clattuc?"

"I will learn the circumstance from Kirdy himself. If a reprimand is in order, it will be applied with reference to our regulations. Under no conditions are you allowed to interfere with a Bureau B agent and an IPCC affiliate. Bring him out, that he may talk to me."

"His conduct is suspicious and may include espionage. We will make our inquiry and act accordingly."

"Titus Pompo, I will warn you once and once only. You are talking dangerous nonsense. All Cadwal is under the jurisdiction of Bureau B. We come and go at discretion and inspect each square inch of this world as we choose."

From Titus Pompo came an oddly melodious laugh which, however, to a sensitive ear faltered by the tenth of a quaver. "Events have passed you by. At the Lutwen Islands we have asserted our independence of both you and the Naturalist Charter. We are not without support in this regard. The progressive faction at Stroma endorses our action, which now must be considered definite and irrevocable."

Bodwyn Wook laughed: a short sharp bark. "As to that, we shall see. Now then, Pompo, Oomphaw, whatever you call yourself: bring Kirdy Wook to the mesh, or we will consider him dead and punish you with great severity."

Titus Pompo said softly: "Have you no fear of punishment in return?"

"For the last time: do you intend to bring Kirdy Wook to speak to me?"

A glum overtone came into the voice. "As a courtesy to Bureau B and Araminta Station, you may have him back in a month, when he has served his sentence."

"I am immediately sending a flyer to Yipton. Within the hour, it will land on the flight strip. Have Kirdy Wook on hand."

Bodwyn Wook broke the connection.

Five minutes passed. Scharde's voice sounded through the mesh. "We're ready to go."

"Good. I notified Titus Pompo that we would pick up Kirdy on the flight strip. Once he's aboard, proceed as before."

"I understand your instructions. We're off."

A few moments later Namour entered the office, clearly wondering what the summons might signify. He nodded politely to Bodwyn Wook, somewhat more casually to Ysel Laverty and Rune Offaw. He dismissed Glawen with a glance. To Bodwyn Wook he said: "Has some great tragedy occurred? The atmosphere is dank with doom and despair; everywhere I see dolorous faces. What is the occasion?"

Bodwyn Wook gave him a cordial salute. "You misinterpret our mood! Glawen has been telling us of Pussycat Palace, and we are not so much glum as rapt in fantasy. I am happy that you were able to drop in on us. It is always a pleasure to see a face like yours: easy, unknown to fear and doubt, both honest and true."

"Thank you," murmured Namour. "I am no less delighted to be here, in this sanctum of virtue and high principle."

"We do our best," said Bodwyn Wook. "Kind words, however, are few. Only criminals seem to recognize our excellence."

"And, so I hope, a few others like myself."

"From time to time." Bodwyn Wook pointed to a chair. "Sit down, if you will. Ysel and Rune are just off about their duties; urgent events are in the wind!"

"Really!" said Namour, looking curiously after the departing captains. "Should I ask what is going on, or would you prefer that I feign disinterest?"

"It is no secret. The Oomphaw is up to some new tricks. He took my nephew Kirdy into custody on trumped-up charges: an act of sheer insolence which I do not propose to take lightly."

Namour pursed his lips. "The Bold Lion excursion seems to have been a general fiasco. I had a quick word with Arles and he tells me that Kirdy stole his cloak and tore it to shreds. He cannot reconcile this act with the Bold Lion code of conduct, and is totally baffled."

"I agree that it would seem an unusual act, especially in connection with a Wook. I am sure that Kirdy will have a sensible explanation. I

242

might mention that both he and Glawen were engaged upon a Bureau B operation. The damaged cloak was used only as a pretext to hold Kirdy."

"Ah! That explains the furor! And you want me to use my good offices, such as they are, in the case?"

"Not at all! Titus Pompo has casually announced his independence: a bit of pip-squeak arrogance which we will nip in the bud, and in fact I dispatched an armed force to bring Kirdy back and to perform a few other routine inspections. All this will put Titus Pompo's nose out of joint, and our relationship will be taking a new tack. While awaiting news, I thought to discuss these new conditions with you."

Namour thoughtfully rubbed his jaw. "I am at your service. But before making definite proposals I would like to consider the matter overnight. So now, if you will excuse me—" Namour started to rise, but Bodwyn Wook waved him back into his seat. "Deliberate to your heart's content, but first let me suggest some topics. Perhaps you will wish to take notes."

"Yes, yes," muttered Namour. "Whatever you like." He availed himself of writing materials.

Bodwyn Wook leaned back in his chair, clasped his hands over his small belly and looked up to the ceiling. "Our goal is a world without Yips. The Lutwen Islands will be the tourist headquarters, a base from which they can enjoy the beauties of the Conservancy. My timetable is ten years."

Namour looked up with eyebrows high. "Are you serious?"

"You have used the right word in a correct context," said Bodwyn Wook. "I am a serious man; I am proposing a serious solution to a problem which is not only serious but critical! Our ancestors have lived a golden dream where frivolity held sway. They saw the cloud on the horizon, but turned their backs, waiting for men like you and me and Glawen, now dozing on the couch, to set matters straight. Ten years is not unrealistic. Am I right, Glawen?"

"Eh? Yes, sir! Ten years exactly."

Namour said ruefully: "It seems that I must alter the tempo of my life."

"And rather more besides," said Bodwyn Wook. "It is no secret that your perquisities include the services of seven, or perhaps eight, Yip girls."

"Just six," said Namour.

"Six, then. Their functions are no doubt needful and various, but at this time the phaseout of Yip employees must be expedited, and you must set an example. Are you writing?"

"Yes indeed. 'Yip phaseout: expedited. Set example.'"

"However—and this will form the matter for item two—special treatment for Yip domestic help of long and faithful service may be allowed. Attrition with non-Yip replacement will be the rule, both at the Station and out among the lodges. Prepare a chart indicating attrition rates, along with a list of what we shall call Special-Class Yips."

"Very good, sir. Chart and list. I see that I will be quite busy. In fact—"

"Not yet! There's more. Item three: recruit new agricultural workers from places with an agricultural tradition, and technical help from technical environments, and not the other way around."

Namour made notes. "That is now clear."

"Your tone is sardonic," said Bodwyn Wook. "A hint now is better than a growl later, after you had committed the blunder, as in the case of the great Yip larcenies. They robbed us up one side and down the other, while you played blindman's buff and pinky-panky-poo with your eight girls."

Namour smiled ruefully. "You have touched a sensitive area. They were deft as devils, and betrayed my trust."

"Item four," said Bodwyn Wook. "Prepare a list of places on nearby worlds which are actively in need of labor, especially those which will provide transportation and other inducements. I understand that you are already quite familiar with the procedure."

Namour gave his head a deprecatory shake. "If nothing else, I now appreciate the problems involved."

"Problems, inconveniences—they are to be expected when a multitude changes its residence," said Bodwyn Wook. "Happily, neither you nor I will undertake the migration."

"It goes without saying that the Oomphaw has other plans, which, so I suspect, involve the Marmion."

"These plans must be put aside. That is the gist of the message he is about to receive."

Namour shrugged. "I fear that you will only exacerbate him."

Bodwyn Wook glared at Namour through malignant yellow slits. "More appropriately, he should worry lest he exacerbate me. I will close his harbor, and he will eat no more fish. With the bamboo dead, there will be no more mats for his roof and the rain will drip in his face. At night he will grope through the dark for lack of power. The Yips will gratefully leave the pestilential place. As each files by, we shall ask: 'Are you Titus Pompo, the Oomphaw?' And if all deny the identity, we shall know that the last person to leave Yipton is Titus Pompo."

"That may well be the way of it," said Namour. "I suppose, as a first step, you will completely cut off his tourist trade?"

"To the contrary! We shall ply Yipton with tourist after tourist, in platoons and shiploads! The Arkady Inn will bulge, they will run back and forth between kitchen and crowded tables, bearing platters loaded with delicacies. The tourists will pay in scrip, redeemable at Araminta Station only for contraceptives, copies of the Cadwal Charter and one-way outward-bound passage."

Namour laughed in genuine amusement. "Bodwyn Wook, I salute you! Still, it is sad that the Yips, who had no hand in writing the Charter, must suffer its worst impact."

"It is even sadder that they covet someone else's property, but that is the perversity of human, or near-human, nature." Bodwyn Wook glanced at the clock. "I have had alarming reports—and this is confidential information—that the Yips have used stolen parts to complete at least one Model D flyer, which can only be intended as an aggressive weapon. We will capture or destroy this flyer if we find it."

"That is interesting news!" said Namour. "You have given me much to think about." He rose abruptly to his feet. "And now I must go; other business weighs on both of us."

"You need not go yet. I have set aside this time for our conference, and you are entitled to every last second. To another matter." Bodwyn Wook laid a large-scale chart on the table. "This is Yipton, as you can see. This is Arkady Inn; here the harbor and the flight strip." Bodwyn Wook tapped the chart with a long white forefinger. "This would seem to be the location of the Caglioro, with the women's dormitories out around here." Bodwyn Wook darted a glance toward Namour. "Where is the palace of the Oomphaw? Point it out to me, if you will."

Namour shook his head. "I know no more than you."

"You have never treated with him in his private offices?"

"We conduct our business, such as it is, in a room off the hotel lobby. I speak to him through a bamboo screen. Whether these are his private offices I can't say. I suspect that he sits at a place from where he can overlook the lobby. Why are you interested?"

"I could list a dozen reasons," said Bodwyn Wook airily. "To start with: sheer curiosity." He looked again at the clock. "We can expect news at any time now."

The minutes went by, while Bodwyn Wook discussed first one topic, then another, with Namour. At last a voice spoke from the mesh: "Scharde Clattuc here. We have picked up Kirdy. He is alive, but in very bad shape."

Bodwyn Wook's voice rang sharp as a bell. "How so?"

"He is in a state of shock. His eyes are open and he seems to be conscious but he does not recognize me, and will not respond to my voice. He has suffered a number of lacerations and small wounds. The Oomps who turned him over to us claim that yesterday afternoon he broke loose and tried to escape their custody. They say that he jumped into a canal and took refuge under the structures, a place infested with 'yoots,' as they call them.[1] When they found Kirdy, he was lying in the slime and the yoots were chewing on him. That is their story."

"Do you believe them?"

"More or less. They look at him with awe and can't understand how he survived. What they did to him before he escaped is anybody's guess."

"How bad is Kirdy? Will he survive?"

"Not good. He is apathetic."

"Very well. Proceed with the rest of the program."

"It is already under way. So far there has been no reaction from below."

"Keep me advised."

Bodwyn Wook swiveled around in his chair and stared out the window. Namour sat silently, now showing no disposition to depart.

Ten minutes passed. Scharde's voice again came from the mesh. "We are departing the Lutwen Islands."

Bodwyn Wook called sharply: "What occurred?"

"With two craft in protective mode, the third and fourth descended and pulled away the roof with grappling hooks, and the floor below was exposed. There was no flyer visible nor any sign of metalworking machinery. In short, there seemed nothing to destroy. But we immediately noticed that the floor was new bamboo, to hide the real floor below. We broke open this floor, and saw the flyer, along with machinery. We lowered a demolition device which destroyed the flyer and everything else in the room. We then departed, and are now on our way home."

"Well-done," said Bodwyn Wook. "You have achieved everything practically possible at this time."

---

[1] Yoot: a two-legged mandoril-rat hybrid, four feet tall, with a rudimentary intelligence. The creatures are peculiar to the Lutwen Islands, and are intensely vicious.

246

2

The operation against Titus Pompo's machine shop was officially described as a routine mission to expedite Kirdy Wook's return to Araminta Station, after a sudden illness. A rumor or two leaked from Bureau B, or perhaps from Namour, but the scope of the raid and its presumably devastating effect upon the Oomphaw's capabilities were never generally made known.

Kirdy spent two weeks in the hospital while his wounds healed, each leaving an ugly little scar, then further time in the infirmary. He remained in a state of deep apathy, apparently aware of his surroundings, feeding himself and obeying instructions, but taking no heed of visitors and speaking no words. At times he gave evidence of internal distress, screwing up his big pink face until he achieved the likeness of a baby. Tears streamed from his eyes and he made high-pitched whimpering sounds, but uttered no words. Such fits gradually became less frequent; coincidentally, Kirdy took somewhat more interest in his environment, watching comings and goings, looking at pictures in magazines, but still he remained silent and ignored visitors.

The school term came to an end. After prodigies of toil and special tutoring, Arles passed his examinations and was duly accorded a certificate of completion. Glawen, along with Wayness, Milo and a few others, was graduated with honors.

Each year the savants currently resident at Vagabond House were fêted at a banquet to which were also invited the graduating class at the lyceum, the Conservator and his family, the Bureau Supervisors and Assistant Supervisors, the six Housemasters and the lyceum faculty and five Special Dignitaries, selected by the Lyceum Faculty Council.

This was the most exclusive and stately occasion of the year, at which the gentlemen of the Houses wore dress uniforms and the ladies appeared in the most splendid confections their dressmakers could contrive. Those who were not invited consoled each other with assurances that the affair was both tedious and dull as ditchwater, and that personally they would never waste the time attending, even had they been invited. Nonetheless there was always avid competition for one of the five "special" invitations.

At the conclusion of the banquet, before the speeches began, Glawen sought out Wayness and took her up to the balcony, where they sat close together, looking down on the notables below.

Wayness wore a long skirt, tight at the waist, flaring at the hem, striped black, green and wine red, a black jacket of some heavy lusterless stuff and a black ribbon in her hair. Glawen's continued half-covert inspection made her edgy and at last she exclaimed: "Glawen, you must stop that! I sit here cringing with nervousness, as if I'm buttoned up crooked, or a big bug is sitting in my hair."

"I've never seen you so elegant before."

"Oh. Is that all? Do you approve?"

"Certainly. Although you seem strange and unfamiliar."

Wayness made a flippant response: "I've never been anything but strange! As for familiarity, I don't dare with Mother so close."

Glawen smiled sadly, and Wayness looked at him sidelong. "Why are you so glum?"

"You know why."

"I don't want to think about it tonight."

"I can't help it. I wonder if you'll ever return."

"Of course I'll return! And if not—"

"If not?"

"Then you can come to look for me."

"Easy enough to say. Across all the thousands of worlds, and all the billions and trillions of people."

"That's encouragement, in a way. If you don't find me, you'll surely come upon someone else exactly like me, or—is it thinkable—nicer than me."

"There's no one in the whole Gaean Reach exactly like you, with exactly that pretty mouth, exactly that tilt of the chin, or that little curl of hair, or the way you smell."

"I hope it's a pleasant smell."

"Of course. I always think of wind blowing across the moors."

"That's just the soap I use. Glawen, please don't be sentimental because I'm going away. I'll get maudlin too and start to cry."

"Just as you say. Kiss me."

"With everyone looking up here? No, thank you."

"No one is looking now."

"Glawen, stop. That's enough. I'm much too susceptible to this sort of thing . . . Look! Just as I told you! Mother is scolding me."

"I don't think she saw us; she's not looking now."

"Perhaps not." Wayness pointed. "There's Arles, sitting rather modestly in the corner."

"Yes, I find it amazing. Spanchetta is furious because she could not promote a 'special.' My father is here, which makes it worse."

"Who is that girl with Arles? I don't think I've seen her before . . . They appear to be on very good terms."

Glawen looked at Arles' companion: a rather showy young woman with flowing orange-pink hair, a fair skin and voluptuous contours.

"That's Drusilla co-Laverty, one of Floreste's Mummers. She is also quite friendly with Namour, if rumor can be trusted. Still, it's none of my affair."

"Nor mine. Although it's rather odd."

"How so?"

"No great matter. Did I mention that Julian Bohost is back from Stroma? He still wants to marry me, and also plans to study the Mad Mountain massacres, not necessarily in that order."

"Too bad he couldn't be here tonight and give a speech."

"As a matter of fact, he had just that in mind, but Father told him that tickets were unavailable. How is Kirdy Wook?"

"I don't know. The doctor seems to think that if he wanted to be well he could be well right now. Kirdy won't talk, although he will read and watch television, and bangs the dinner utensils when he doesn't like his food. The doctor says that the brain—Kirdy's brain, anybody's brain—is run by a kind of committee. Kirdy's mental committee doesn't quite trust his conscious mind with full powers yet, and is holding back a bit. It's just a question of time, according to the doctor."

"Poor Kirdy."

Glawen thought back over the fateful evening at Yipton. He said: "All taken with all, I agree. It's poor Kirdy, for a fact."

Wayness looked at him curiously. "You seem just a trifle sardonic."

"Probably so. I've never told you all that went on that night."

"Do you plan to do so? Pussycat Palace and all?"

"I can tell you all I know about Pussycat Palace in three sentences, if you're interested."

"I am, rather."

"I did not want to go, but I obeyed Kirdy's orders, so that I might seem a roaring full-fledged Bold Lion, afraid of nothing. I drank tea with the girl, and inquired as to the health of her family. She watched me with no more expression than you see on the face of a dead fish. That's all that happened."

Wayness hugged his arm. "Let's not talk any more of such things. Here comes Milo. He seems suspiciously jaunty. I wonder what's happened."

Milo dropped into a seat. "I have news concerning our friend Julian Bohost," he told Glawen. "I suppose you know he's at Riverview House. He still wants to go to Mad Mountain Lodge, and single-handedly quell the banjee wars."

"He may get a nasty bruise from a battle-ax."

"He hopes to avoid violence. If they won't join the LPF, or listen

249

to reason, he'll study them from a distance and write a report."

"I suppose I can't object, especially if he is paying his own way."

Milo turned Glawen an incredulous stare. "You can't be serious! Julian is a politician, and pays for nothing."

"Julian doesn't have any money to speak of," said Wayness.

"As Dame Clytie's representative, he feels that tourist transport is unsuitable, and he wants full official treatment, which means at least a Station flyer with a pilot. Father just heaved a deep sigh and agreed. You will be the pilot, if the idea appeals to you."

"It does if you and Wayness are coming. Otherwise, no."

"We'll go along to assist in the studies. Then it's settled."

"I don't think Julian will be all that pleased."

"No matter," said Wayness. "Julian must learn to take the bitter with the sweet. It should be a memorable event."

3

The party from Riverview House was late. Glawen and Chilke had checked out the flyer with particular care. "We can't let anything happen to Julian," Glawen told Chilke. "He is an important politician and might well be the first Oomphaw of Throy."

"It's a good line of work to be in," said Chilke. "Especially if you're helpless at everything else. What sort of chap is this Julian?"

"You can judge for yourself; he's just now arriving."

The carry-all halted beside the flyer. Julian jumped to the ground, crisp and natty in a broad-brimmed white hat and a suit of blue-and-white-striped duck. Milo and Wayness followed, and took their travel bags to the flyer's luggage compartment.

Julian approached Chilke. "Are we ready to go? Where is our flyer?"

"It's that black and yellow object just behind you," said Chilke.

Julian inspected the flyer in disbelief. He turned back to Chilke: "What you have here is not at all suitable. Can't you provide something a bit more commodious, with better amenities?"

Chilke rubbed his chin. "What leaps to mind is the tourist air-bus, if you're willing to wait a few days. You'd have lots of room and nice people to talk to."

"I am conducting an official survey," said Julian coldly. "I need and I expect both convenience and flexibility."

Chilke gave a good-humored chuckle. "Think just a bit. This flyer is here and ready to go, which is true convenience. It takes you wherever you point it, also up and down. That is flexibility. How much are you paying?"

"Nothing whatever, naturally."

"There's your flyer. You can't do better anywhere for the price."

Julian saw that no amount of hauteur could daunt the ingenuous Chilke, and moderated his tone. "I suppose it will have to do." He took note of Glawen. "Ho, there! The earnest young Bureau B agent! Have you come to see us off?"

"Not exactly."

"You're here in your official capacity? To guard the flyer? To arrest skulking Yips?"

"Where?" asked Chilke. "The chap over by the hangar? That's not a skulking Yip; that's my help. I agree he ought to be arrested, but Glawen won't have time today. He's your pilot."

Julian stood back in surprise and displeasure. He stared at Glawen. "Are you competent?"

"Let me put it this way," said Glawen. "My luggage is aboard the flyer. Yours is being driven off aboard the carry-all."

Julian waved his hat. "Hi! Driver! Come back here!" He turned angrily to Glawen. "Just don't stand there; do something!"

Glawen shrugged. "If one of us has to run after the truck, it might as well be you."

Chilke put two fingers into his mouth and blew a great shrill blast. The carry-all halted and, in response to Chilke's gesture, returned. With a set expression, Julian transferred his bags to the flyer. Once again he turned to Glawen. "I insist upon a skillful and experienced pilot. Are you so qualified?"

Glawen handed over a small folder. "Here are my certificates of proficiency, and my licensing."

Julian glanced skeptically through the folder. "Hm. Everything seems in order. Very well. We are bound for Mad Mountain Lodge."

"We'll be in the air about four hours. This particular flyer is not fast, but it's quite suitable for errands of this sort."

Julian said no more. He stepped up into the flyer, to join Milo and Wayness, who had already taken their places. Glawen paused for a final word with Chilke. "What's your verdict?"

"A bit hoity-toity, I should say."

"That's my impression, too. Well, we're off for Mad Mountain Lodge." Glawen climbed aboard the flyer and seated himself at the controls. He touched buttons, pushed the ascensor toggle; the flyer rose into the air. Glawen engaged the autopilot and the flyer slid away into the southwest.

The rolling Muldoon Mountains passed below; the orchards and vineyards of the Araminta enclave gave way to unsullied wilderness: first a pleasant land of wide green meadows among forests of dark blue allombrosa. Presently they came upon the Twan Tivol River, sweeping down from the north to terminate in the Dankwallow Swamp, the source of both the River Wan and the River Leur: a vast area of ponds, puddles, marshes and morasses, overgrown with purple-green verges, balwoon bush, tussocks of sawgrass, with a few gaunt skeleton trees for accent.

Syrene shone from a cloudless deep blue sky. "In case anyone is interested," said Glawen, "we'll have good weather all the way. Also, if the meteorologists are to be trusted, it's a fine day at Mad Mountain, with no banjees reported in the vicinity."[1]

Julian attempted a jocularity: "This being the case, and with no bloodshed in prospect, the tourists no doubt will be refunded their money."

Glawen responded politely: "I don't think so."

Milo added the comment: "And that's why the place is called Mad Mountain."

"Are you sure?" asked Wayness. "I've been wondering."

"The name obviously derives from the banjee battles," said Julian in rather patronizing tones. "Their futility—madness, if you will— has long been recognized, at least by the LPF. If my scheme is feasible and is acted upon, we shall rename the place Peace Mountain."

---

[1] Banjee: one of the many varieties of mandoril indigenous to Cadwal. The usual banjee is a massive two-legged creature, somewhat andromorphic, if grotesquely so. The banjee is sheathed in chitin, black in the mature male, which stands eight to nine feet tall. The head is covered with stiff black hair except for the frontal visage of naked bone.

The banjees are remarkable in many ways. They begin life as neuters, become female at the age of six years, metamorphose to males at the age of sixteen, growing each year thereafter in size, mass and ferocity, until they are eventually killed in battle.

Banjees communicate in a language impervious to the most subtle analytical methods of the Gaean linguists. The banjees construct tools and weapons, and exhibit what seem to be the glimmerings of an aesthetic sense, which, like the language, evades the understanding of the human mind.

Banjees are intractable and while ferocious are not actively aggressive under ordinary conditions. They are well aware of the tourists who crowd the terrace at Mad Mountain Lodge to watch them pass, but pay no heed. Reckless persons sometimes approach the marching hordes or even the battles in order to secure dramatic photographs. Emboldened by the apparent indifference of the banjees, they venture a step or two closer, then another step, which takes them past some imperceptible boundary into the banjees' "zone of reaction," and then they are killed.

Wayness asked: "If it doesn't work out, what then?"

"'Mad Julian Mountain' might win a few votes," said Milo.

Julian shook his head sadly. "Joke all you like. In the end you'll find that you can't laugh away either progress or the LPF."

Wayness said plaintively: "Let's not talk politics, at least so early in the day. Glawen, you're supposed to know everything; why is it called Mad Mountain?"

"In this case, I do happen to know," said Glawen. "On old maps you'll find the name 'Mount Stephen Tose.' About two hundred years ago, a tourist in his excitement supplied the new name, which everyone began to use, and so now it's Mad Mountain."

"Why was the tourist excited?"

"I'll show you after we arrive."

"Is it a scandal that you're embarrassed to talk about?" asked Wayness. "Or a delightful surprise?"

"Or both?" asked Milo.

Wayness told Milo: "Your mind runs farther and faster than mine. I can't think of anything which fits."

"We'll just have to wait and see. Glawen may surprise us yet."

"I'm sure of it. Glawen is very subtle. Don't you think so, Julian?"

"My dear girl, I haven't given the matter a thought."

Wayness turned back to Glawen. "Tell us about the battles. Have you seen them?"

"Twice. When you're at the lodge they're hard to ignore."

"What happens? Are they as bad as Julian fears?"

"They are spectacular, and in some ways rather grim."

Julian gave an ironic snort. "Please instruct me in the ways that they are other than grim."

"It's mostly in the mind of the beholder. The banjees don't seem to care."

"That's hard to believe."

"The battles would be easy to avoid, if they were so inclined."

Julian brought a booklet from his pocket. "Listen to this article: 'The banjee battles are extremely dramatic and picturesque events; happily they have been made accessible to the tourist.

"'Squeamish folk be warned: these battles are horrifying in their frenzy and in the hideous deeds which occur. Shouts and screams rise and fall; the trumpeting cries of victory mingle with the anguished moans of the defeated. Without surcease or pity the warriors wield their mighty instruments of death. They slash and strike, probe and thrust; quarter is neither extended nor expected.

"'For the Gaean onlooker, the battles are poignant experiences, rife with archetypal symbology. Emotions are aroused to which the contemporary mind cannot even fit a name. No question as to the quality of the spectacle; the encounters reek with color: portentous reds, the black gleam on the bizarre angles of armor and helmets; the alkaline blues and greens of the thoracic cushions.

"'The air at Mad Mountain is heavy with the sense of majestic force and tragic destiny—it goes on in that vein."

"It is a vivid description," said Glawen. "The official guidebook is put to shame, and in fact barely mentions the battles."

"Still, are not the facts in order?"

"Not altogether. There are not so many shrieks and moans, but grunts and curses and bubbling sounds. The females and bantlings stand by unconcerned and are not molested. Still, there's no denying that the warriors tend to hack at each other."

Wayness asked: "Forgive me my morbid curiosity—but exactly what happens?"

"The battles seem absolutely pointless and could easily be avoided. The migration routes run east-west and north-south, and cross just below Mad Mountain Lodge. When a horde is approaching, the first signal is a low sound: an ominous murmur. Then the horde appears in the distance. A few minutes later the first attack squad comes running along the route—a hundred elite warriors armed with thirty-foot lances, axes, and six-foot spikes. They secure the crossing and stand guard while the horde runs past. If another horde is passing, the approaching horde does not wait until the other one has gone by, as logic would dictate, but instead becomes indignant and attacks.

"The warriors bring down their lances and charge, trying to force open an avenue for their own group to pass. The battle continues until one or the other of the hordes has negotiated the crossing. It's a disgrace to go last, and the defeated horde sets up a great howl of hurt feelings.

"About this time tourists run down for souvenirs, hoping to find an undamaged helmet. They prowl through the corpses pulling and tugging. Sometimes the banjee is still alive and kills the tourist.

"The dead tourist is not ignored by the management. His picture is hung in the gallery as a warning to others. There are hundreds of these pictures, of folk from almost as many worlds, and they are a source of fascination to everyone."

"I find the whole business disgraceful," said Julian.

"I think it's distasteful myself," said Glawen. "But the banjees won't stop fighting and the tourists won't stop coming—so Mad Mountain Lodge stays open."

"That is a cynical attitude," said Julian.

"I don't feel cynical," said Glawen. "I just don't feel theoretical."

"I'm sure that I don't understand you," said Julian stiffly.

Milo asked: "So what is your scheme for the banjees—assuming you were allowed free rein?"

"My first thought was a set of barricades which would hold one horde back while the other passed, but barriers or fences are easily broken down or avoided. At the moment I'm considering ramps and an overpass so that the banjees can go their separate ways without coming into contact with each other."

"Be reasonable, Julian. You must know that you won't be allowed any such project. Have you never heard of the Charter?"

"The Charter is as moribund as the Naturalist Society. I don't mind telling you that the LPF is studying its options."

"Consider all the options you like. Plan ramps and overpasses to your heart's content, though how you can call this official business is beyond me. It's Peefer business and Julian business, at Conservancy expense. There, if you like, is cynicism."

Slowly Julian turned his head and surveyed Milo under hooded eyelids, and for an instant the curtain of genteel accommodation was torn.

Milo spoke with an unwonted edge in his voice. "More than anything else you want to set a precedent for Peefer meddling in the environment. The next step would be to invite the Yips to lay claim to the land. The Peefers would build grand estates for themselves in the choicest areas of Deucas. Confine all the wild animals behind fences. I assure you, Julian, it won't work."

Julian gave an indifferent shrug. "You are talking like a wild man. I suggest that you calm yourself. This is a tour of inspection. I will make recommendations. They may or may not carry weight. There is really nothing more to be said." Pointedly he turned away from Milo and addressed Glawen: "What does one do at Mad Mountain when the banjees aren't fighting?"

"Rest, relax, drink San-sue stingers and sundowners, discuss the landscape with your fellow tourists. If you're keen for exercise, you can climb Mad Mountain. The trail is easy and relatively safe, and there are interesting things along the way. If you like souvenirs, you can look along the riverbed for thunder eggs, or go out on the battlefield—naturally, when no one is fighting—and scratch around for oddments. If you are truly adventurous, you might ride a bunter out to the banjee camp at Lake Dimple—once again, when the banjees are not in residence. If you're lucky, you might find a magic stone."

255

"What's a magic stone?" asked Wayness. "And what's a bunter?"

"The female banjees grind chunks of nephrite, lapis, malachite and other colored stones into spheres or tablets and carry them in a net around their necks. When they go through the change, at about sixteen, and become male they throw the magic stones into the bushes or into the lake. So you can search the bushes or wade in the lake and perhaps you'll find a magic stone."

"That sounds interesting," said Julian. "Perhaps I'll give it a try. What is a bunter?"

"It's an ugly beast that can be ridden if it is suitably prepared. It must be fed and soothed and put in a placid mood or it becomes quite unpleasant."

Julian made a dubious sound. "How is this accomplished?"

"The Yip stablemen are skilled at the process, which is rather complicated."

"Ha-hah!" said Julian. "So Yips still do the dirty work."

"There are a few here and there that haven't been phased out."

"And why is that?"

"In all candor, no one else wants the job."

Julian gave a scornful laugh. "The elitists ride the bunters and the Yips clean the stables."

"Ha, ha!" said Milo. "The elitists must pay to ride the bunters. The Yips earn handsome salaries. The elitist returns home and goes back to work. The Yips give their money to Titus Pompo. We, incidentally, are paying our own way. You are the only elitist in the group."

"I am the agent of Warden Vergence, who is entitled to official courtesies."

Wayness thought to change the subject. She pointed to the savanna below. "See those long lank white beasts! There must be thousands of them!"

Glawen looked down from the window. "They are monohorn spring-backs, heading for the Zusamilla Wetlands where they do their breeding." He manipulated the controls; the flyer dropped with a lurch that lifted his passengers' stomachs, then leveled off to drift five hundred feet above the ground, where the springbacks ran in tightly ordered ranks, the herd bristling with thousands of voluted six-foot horns.

"Springbacks have no eyes," said Glawen. "No one knows how or even if they see. Still they find their way from the Big Red Scarp to Zusamilla Territory and back and never get lost. If you approach the herd, one will run out to stab you with its horn, then turn back and run hard to find its old place in the line."

Julian glanced down at the sliding white column, then rather ostentatiously began to read his guidebook.

Wayness asked: "Why do they run in curves and slants instead of going directly? Are they just careless?"

"Quite the reverse," said Glawen. "Notice those little hillocks? The springbacks keep well clear, even if they must swing out to make a detour. Why? On top of each hillock lives a brood of fells. They're hard to see because they merge into the ground color. They sit waiting for some careless beast to wander nearby, to save them the trouble of hunting."

Milo scanned the landscape through binoculars. He pointed: "Near the river in that tall blue grass I see some extremely ugly beasts. They are hard to pick out because their color is as blue as the grass itself."

"Those are monitor saurians," said Glawen. "They change color to match the surroundings. You find them always in tribes of nine: no one knows why."

"They probably can't count any higher," suggested Milo.

"It might well be," said Glawen. "Their four-inch-thick hides are proof against most predators, who tire of chewing on them."

Milo asked: "What's going on over there, under that vamola tree?"

Glawen looked through the binoculars. "It's a bull bardicant, and a big one. He's either sick, or dying, or just resting. The skiddits have found him, but can't decide what to do. They're taking counsel and now they're trying to get one of the pups to climb on top of the bardicant. The pup wisely runs away. Someone else tries. Aha! The tail skewers him and he's gone down the gullet. The other skiddits flee in all directions."

"Excuse me," said Julian. "All this is vastly entertaining and speaks well for your training, certainly in the field of animal identification. But I am anxious to arrive at Mad Mountain Lodge, so that I can get my survey organized."

"Just as you like," said Glawen.

The flyer proceeded: over mountains and forests, lakes and wide rivers; majestic vistas unfolded, one after the other. At noon the land rose to become a wide upland, dotted with small lakes. Far to the west a mountain range of twenty lofty peaks dwindled away to north and south.

Glawen pointed below, to wisps of smoke rising from beside a forest. "There's a banjee camp now. The fires, incidentally, are neither for cooking nor for warmth, but to boil up the glue which they use to fabricate their helmets and armor."

"How far now to Mad Mountain?"

"You can see it ahead: that old volcano with the shattered peak. We're flying over the Plain of Moans. There's Lake Dimple, down to the right."

Five minutes later the flyer settled upon the landing pad to the side of the lodge. The four alighted and climbed a short flight of steps to the terrace at the front of the lodge.

The four entered the lobby: a tall room with red, white and black rugs on the stone floor. Banjee artifacts were everywhere to be seen: battle-axes arranged in a crescent pattern over the fireplace; a dozen weirdly beautiful helmets on a rack; spheres and tablets of polished malachite, cinnabar, nephrite and milk opal, each about three inches in diameter, in a case at the registration desk. The clerk noticed Wayness' interest. "Those are banjee magic stones. Don't ask me how to use them; I don't know."

"Are they for sale?"

"From a hundred sols for the cinnabar to five hundred for the nephrite to a thousand for the milk opal."

The four were assigned rooms; at the same time photographs were made of each.

The clerk explained: "The hall yonder leads to the dining room; it is also the gallery where we display pictures of guests who have been killed by the banjees. If you should be so unlucky, we prefer to hang the 'before' picture rather than the 'after'—especially since the gallery is on the way to the dining room."

"Ridiculous!" said Julian. "Shall we have lunch?"

"Give me time to wash my face," said Wayness.

The four met on the terrace, and went to stand by the balustrade which overlooked the Plain of Moans. Milo asked: "Where is this notorious battlefield?"

"Just down there, almost below us," said Glawen. "See those parallel mounds, or rows, running across the plain? They are detritus cast aside by banjee hordes over thousands and thousands of years. They mark the migration routes. One route goes east to west, another north to south, and they cross just below the lodge. When the hordes collide, they don't act like gentlemen, but hit each other with axes."

"For a fact, it does seem rather pointless," said Wayness.

"It's absurd and disgraceful, and it ought to be stopped," said Julian.

"An overpass should solve the problem nicely," said Milo. "Although, I must say, the routes are remarkably wide."

"Easily a hundred yards across," said Glawen.

Julian stood frowning down at the battlefield. Wayness asked gently: "Did you know that the routes were so wide?"

Julian gave his head a curt shake. "This is my first visit to Mad Mountain, as you must know. Let's have our lunch."

The four were seated at a table, and lunch was served. "Perhaps we can help Julian with his calculations," said Milo. "The overpass should be a hundred yards wide, in order to match the route. The span will also be at least a hundred yards, with a clearance of—how much clearance are you planning, Julian?"

"Really, I haven't given the matter serious thought."

"A clearance of forty feet will allow the banjees to march below without dipping their lances. If Julian designs his ramps with a six percent grade, each approach will be about seven hundred feet long. Julian, how many cubic yards of material do you think you will require for your ramps?"

"I haven't gone anywhere near that far in my thinking. An overpass may or may not be the optimum approach. I am here to discover if a practical solution exists."

Wayness spoke in a soothing voice. "Don't let Milo's foolishness disturb you. You do your surveys and think and plan as much as you like, and we'll keep out of your way. Glawen, what do you suggest for this afternoon?"

"We can walk up Mad Mountain. There are some interesting ruins along the way: a stone platform and what seems to have been a tower. Archaeologists think they were built by an extinct tribe of banjees. You'll also see some blue darters. They pretend to be flowers so that they can catch insects. Tourists who try to pick them run into trouble. First, the blue darter spits on them, then shrieks and finally throws off its decoration, curls up its tail and stings."

"Interesting. What else?"

"You'll probably see rockorchids with glass flowers and creeping arbutus, which moves about planting its own seeds. Farynxes live up the mountain. They hunt in a most ingenious fashion. One hides in the bushes; the other lies on its back and exudes the odor of carrion which presently attracts a scavenger bird. The hidden farynx makes a quick leap and both dine on fowl."

"You still haven't told us why it's called Mad Mountain."

"The story doesn't amount to much. A crotchety old gentleman came tottering down the trail shouting, 'The mountain is mad!' It seems that he had gone up to study the ruins. Along the way he picked a blue darter which spit into his beard, stung his hand, screamed and ran away. He sat down on a creeping arbutus, which squirmed out

259

from under him. He came upon what appeared to be a sick farynx, about to be torn apart by a fine fat corbalbird. From the kindness of his heart, the old man chased away the bird, and both farynxes jumped at him and bit his leg. He limped on up to the ruins and there he found a troupe of poets performing interpretive dances, and this is when he lost touch with reality. He tottered back down the trail, and Mount Stephen Tose has been 'Mad Mountain' ever since."

Milo looked at Wayness. "Do you believe him?"

"I have no choice. But I'd like to see these marvels for myself."

"I've had my lunch and I'm ready at any time," said Milo.

"I'm ready," said Wayness. "Let's go. Julian, we'll be back before too long. Certainly before dinner."

"Just a minute," said Julian. "Glawen was assigned to me as an assistant. I may need him."

Glawen stared in astonishment. "What's this? Am I hearing correctly?"

"You heard correctly," said Milo. "Julian needs someone to run back and forth carrying the end of his tape measure."

Glawen shook his head. "I fly the aircraft and identify animals. I will even try to save Julian's life if and when he does something foolish. My duties extend no further."

Julian swung away with a set expression on his face. He went to the balustrade, looked out over the plain for a moment, then turned back to the others. "I've seen all I need to see, at least for the moment."

"Come along, then, and walk up the mountain," said Wayness.

"That's a good idea," said Julian. "Let me change into my walking gear; I'll just be a minute."

So passed the afternoon. With Syrene low in the sky the four returned down the mountain. They went to sit on the terrace, where they drank sundowners and watched Syrene descend into the far mountains.

Wayness pointed out across the plain. "What is that dazzle out there? It must be Lake Dimple."

"Correct," said Glawen. "When Syrene drops low you can see the reflection. There's nothing much out there but the banjee camp, which isn't worth visiting unless you find a magic stone."

"What are the chances?"

"Fair, unless the banjees are using the camp. Then the probability becomes zero."

"We'd have to ride bunters?"

"It's a very long walk."

"Why can't we take the flyer?" asked Julian.

"A tempting idea, but against regulations, since it causes problems with the other guests."

Julian shook his head in deprecation. "Well, no matter. According to the guidebook, the bunters are irascible beasts, but quite safe if one wears the proper riding habit. This puzzles me. Are the bunters so very conventional?"

"Mainly, they have a vile disposition and would gladly kill us if we gave them the chance. Before anyone rides them, the stablemen prepare them and put them in a good mood."

"And apparently the rider must dress to suit the bunter's notion of what is proper costume."

"The riding habits actually serve a practical purpose. The bunter is pacified by a curious procedure. The Yip stablemen feed the bunter well, then tease it with sticks until the bunter is beside itself with rage. At this point the stablemen throw out a straw puppet dressed in a black hat, white coat, black breeches and a red sash—the riding habit. The bunter savages the puppet, stomping and kicking, tossing it in the air, and finally, when the puppet is thoroughly trounced, the bunter tucks it up on its back, to be eaten later, since it is not now hungry.

"The bunter's rage is discharged and it becomes relatively docile. The Yips drop blinders over its eyes; the rider takes the place of the puppet, lifts the blinders and rides away in comfort.

"To dismount, the rider must drop the blinders, otherwise the bunter thinks its victim is escaping and kills it again. So: if you ride a bunter, remember! Never dismount without dropping the blinders."

"I think I understand," said Milo. "If I want to find a magic stone worth a thousand sols, I ride a bunter to Lake Dimple and search till I find one."

"That is more or less correct."

"And my chances of returning alive?"

"Good to excellent, provided that, first, the bunter is properly teased and baited; second, that you remember to drop the blinders before you dismount; third, that the banjees do not discover you prowling around their camp; fourth, that you are not attacked by other wild animals, such as thuripids or upland fells."

"How do you recover stones which have been thrown into the lake?"

"You can wade out and feel through the mud with your toes. You are not allowed to use mechanical equipment; that becomes 'exploitation.' It's borderline in any case, but the authorities have relaxed a trifle, and classify the stones as 'souvenirs' rather than 'precious minerals'."

"I'm willing to make the effort," said Milo.

"I am too," said Wayness. "Although I'm far from easy in my mind. What if the bunter gets hungry along the way and decides to eat its lunch?"

"Then you must blow its head off. Everyone carries a gun."

"I wish I weren't such a coward," said Wayness. "But I'll be nice to my bunter and maybe it will be nice to me."

"That's how I'd feel if I were a bunter," said Glawen. "In fact, I might carry you far off over the hills, and keep you for a pet."

Julian frowned in displeasure, clearly deeming the remark inappropriate or even presumptuous. He surveyed Glawen through narrowed eyes. "Small chance of that. I'd catch you up before you had trotted half a mile." He spoke with a thin smile although his voice lacked any trace of humor. "Your escapade would earn you no applause; to the contrary."

Glawen, somewhat taken aback, made a rueful response. "Even if I weren't a bunter, I'd like her for a pet."

Julian spoke to Wayness: "Please ignore my overgallant assistant; his pleasantries are a trifle overfamiliar, under the circumstances."

"What circumstances are these?" asked Glawen.

"It is not particularly your affair, but I may say that Wayness and I have an understanding of long duration."

Wayness gave an uneasy laugh. "Flux, Julian! Everything moves, everything shifts. As for Glawen, despite his grim practicality, he has a poet's soul, and you must tolerate his flights of fancy."

"I am, after all, a Clattuc," said Glawen. "We are famous for our romantic excesses."

"I can cite a case in point," said Milo. "I refer to the legendary Reynold Clattuc. He risked his life to save a beautiful maiden from a blizzard out on the Kaskovy Waste. He carried her through the storm to a way station; he built fires to warm her, rubbed her hands and feet and patiently fed her hot soup and morsels of buttered toast. She ate as much as she could, then, relaxing in her chair, found herself compelled to belch, which so outraged Reynold Clattuc's sensibilities that he put her out in the snow again."

"Milo, that story is not altogether credible," said Wayness.

"She must have done something else as well," said Glawen. "I don't think I'd put her out for such a transitory offense."

"What do you think she did?" asked Milo.

"It's hard to say. She might have scolded him for burning the toast."

"Clearly the tradition persists," said Milo. "It's wise to mind one's manners while dining with a Clattuc!"

"I'll be careful," said Wayness. "I would not want Glawen to think me vulgar."

Glawen rose to his feet. "Right now I think that I had better order the bunters made ready for tomorrow. Julian, will you be inspecting the battlefield or do you care to try your luck at Lake Dimple?"

Julian wrestled with himself. In a subdued voice he said: "I've seen enough for the present. I'll go out to Lake Dimple."

Glawen and Milo went off to the stables. Julian watched the two cross the terrace, and gave his head a disparaging shake. He turned to Wayness. "Romantic or not, I find that Clattuc fellow definitely objectionable. I quite resent the way he looks at you. He seems to forget that you're a Naturalist and a goodly cut above Station personnel, no matter what airs they put on. For a fact, you should put him right and quite sharply."

"Julian, I'm surprised! I thought that LPFers endorsed the classless society, with everyone marching arm in arm into the dawn of a new era."

"Up to a point. In my personal life I make very definite distinctions, which I consider to be my prerogative. I represent the highest level of the Gaean race, and I refuse to tolerate or associate with anything other than the very best—in which category I am pleased to include you."

"I also have a high opinion of myself," said Wayness. "I too don't care to associate with lesser folk, by which I mean fools and hypocrites."

"Exactly so!" declared Julian. "We share the same point of view!"

"There is one small difference," said Wayness. "Our categories do not include the same people."

Julian frowned. "Well—perhaps not. After all, we each have our own circle of acquaintants."

"So we do."

In a carefully modulated voice, Julian asked: "Are you still planning to go away to Earth?"

"Yes. There is some research I want to do which can't be managed here."

"What is your subject? You've always been so vague."

"Essentially it's a trifle of folklore I want to track down."

"And Milo is going with you?"

"That is the plan."

Julian's voice became brittle. "What of me?"

"I'm not sure what you mean—although I have a suspicion."

"I thought that we had an understanding. I don't want to be kept waiting indefinitely."

Wayness laughed shortly. "That so-called understanding was Mother's idea, not mine. It's not at all practical. In the first place, I am not in sympathy with your political beliefs."

"It wasn't that way before. Someone has influenced you. Could it be Milo?"

"Milo and I seldom if ever discuss politics."

"It couldn't be Glawen Clattuc. He is even more naive than Milo."

Wayness became exasperated. "Isn't it conceivable that I think for myself? Still, you should not underestimate Glawen; he is quiet, unpretentious, and highly intelligent. He is also competent, a quality which I admire very much."

"You defend him fervently."

Wayness said wearily, "Please, Julian, put me out of your mind. At the moment I have my own problems and I don't care to cope with yours. I am absolutely definite on this."

Julian gave a cold shrug and leaned back in his chair. The two sat in silence, watching Syrene drop upon the mountains.

Glawen and Milo returned. "The bunters will be ready, well-fed and amiable, immediately after breakfast."

"In a far friendlier mood than they are now," said Milo. "Or so I hope. Glawen did not exaggerate; the bunters are not lovable. I don't envy the stablemen their work."

"I hope they're good at it," said Wayness.

"They should be by now," Glawen replied. "They've been here for years—at least since my last visit."

Julian prepared to utter a remark, presumably in regard to the Yips, but Wayness forestalled him. "The sun is almost down, and it's time to dress for dinner."

The four went to their rooms. Glawen bathed and dressed in garments considered proper for informal dining at the lodges: dark green trousers with black and red piping down the sides, a white shirt and trim dark gray jacket. Returning to the terrace, he found Milo already on hand, leaning on the balustrade. Dusk had come to the Plain of Moans, with distances blurred and a dull orange afterglow rimming the sky.

"I've been listening to sounds," said Milo. "I've heard several different kinds of howling, a heavy deep roar, or bellow, and a melancholy wailing sound."

"I like listening from up here, behind the balustrade," said Glawen.

"If the other choice is down there on the plain, I like it here too. Listen! What's that?"

"I don't know. It has a sad voice."

Wayness appeared, wearing a white skirt and a pale tan jacket which perfectly complemented her coloring. "What are you two doing?"

"Listening to noises and sounds," said Glawen. "Come over and help."

"For instance!" said Milo. "Listen to that."

"I hear it. No wonder this is the Plain of Moans." Wayness looked up and down the terrace, where half the tables were already occupied by other guests of the lodge. "Are we dining outside?"

"If you like."

"It's a pleasant evening. Let's go."

The three went to sit at a table. Time passed: ten minutes, twenty minutes, and Julian still had not made an appearance. Milo became restive. He looked over his shoulder toward the lobby. "Has he fallen asleep? I'd better give him a call, or we'll be waiting until he wakes up."

Milo went off to investigate. Presently he returned. "Odd! He's not in his room, nor in the lobby nor yet in the library. Where else could he be?"

"What of the gallery? Could he be looking over the pictures?"

"I looked there too."

"Surely he hasn't gone for a walk—unless he's far braver than I," said Wayness.

"Here he comes now," said Milo.

Wayness asked: "Julian, where have you been?"

"Here and there," said Julian airily. He wore a white suit with a red and blue blazon at the neck and a red sash at his waist.

Milo said: "I looked everywhere for you. Perhaps you'll reveal your hiding place?"

"No large affair, nothing to worry about," said Julian.

"Is it a secret?" asked Wayness.

"Of course not," said Julian curtly. "If you must know, I went out to the stables to look over the situation for myself."

"You can't see much this time of night," said Glawen. "The bunters are already in their stalls."

"I spoke for a few minutes with the Yips. I was curious to discover what they really thought of their jobs."

"And they told you?"

"We had a pleasant conversation," said Julian with dignity. "When they learned I was LPF they opened up. The head groom's name is Orreduc Manilaw Rodenart, or something of that sort. He is a person of quick intelligence, and is surprisingly cheerful. The same applies to the whole crew. I heard not a single surly word. I find their equanimity remarkable."

"They're quite well paid," said Glawen. "Although I suppose the Oomphaw takes all their money."

"That's when you'd hear surly words from me," said Milo.

Julian ignored the remarks. "Like myself, they hope for friendlier times. I truly believe that some sort of accommodation is possible, given goodwill in all quarters. The LPF is willing to take the lead in this regard. I am sure that we could arrange this world for the benefit of everyone concerned."

"Under the leadership of the Peefers? Can we anticipate the anointment of Julian Bohost as Grand Oomphaw of Cadwal?"

Julian paid him no heed. "Surprisingly, Orreduc knew next to nothing of the LPF. I explained our goals and mentioned my own place in the organization, and he was most impressed. It was quite heartwarming."

Wayness had become bored and was happy to discover a distraction. She pointed into the sky, where dusk still lingered. "What in the world is that thing?"

Glawen looked up. "You are looking at a Mad Mountain nightwhisk. It's headed for that cardamom tree yonder."

"It looks like a big bundle of black fluff. Doesn't it have wings?"

"It's mostly air, a mouth, a gut and black plumes. It vibrates fibrils which create lift, and the creature flies. It will now perch in the tree and catch insects."

The night-whisk settled delicately upon the topmost branch of the cardamom tree. Wayness pointed. "You can see its eyes glittering, like little red lights! What an odd creature!"

"They almost became extinct, and all the biologists wondered why. Then someone discovered that the Yips were taking time off from work to climb up to the nests, kill the birds and sell the plumes to the tourists. Bureau B quickly invoked Statute Eleven of the Charter, which addresses willful destruction of indigenous species for profit. Under this law the killing of the night-whisks became a crime punishable by death, and the poaching stopped at once."

"Death?" cried Julian in consternation. "For hunting a bird? Isn't that extreme?"

"It doesn't seem so to me," said Glawen. "No one stands in the slightest danger unless he breaks the law. It is transparently simple."

"I understand!" said Milo. "I will explain to Julian. If I jump off a cliff, I will die. If I kill a night-whisk, I will die. Both acts are discretionary, both are suicide, and a person makes his own choice."

Wayness said virtuously: "I'm not afraid of the law. But then I don't intend to kill night-whisks and sell plumes."

Julian, with a sardonic chuckle, said: "Naturally you do not worry, since no matter what, the law would never be applied to you. Only to some miserable Yip."

Milo asked Wayness: "What of that? Is Julian right? Would Father sentence you to death for poaching?"

"Possibly not," said Wayness. "I'd certainly be sent to my room."

A waiter appeared at the table. He spread a red, white and black-checked cloth, brought candelabra and set the candles alight and in due course served the dinner.

The four spoke little, each occupied with his own thoughts. The candles flickered in the faintest of airs and from the plain came sounds: plaintive, melancholy, ominous.

They sat long at the table after dinner, drinking green tea. Julian seemed in a pensive mood and had little to say. At last, he heaved a sigh and seemed to rouse himself. "At times I am truly frustrated. Here we sit, four persons subscribing to a common morality, and still at odds over rather fundamental problems."

Milo agreed. "It's an extraordinary situation. In some of our minds, the gears are not meshing."

Julian flourished his hand around the sky, encompassing thousands of light-years and stars beyond number. "I can suggest a solution to our problems. Our common morality will be served and any reasonable person will make the necessary adjustments without rancor."

"That sounds like the plan we have been waiting for!" exclaimed Milo. "I endorse morality. I think Wayness is also moral; at least there's been no scandal. Glawen is a Clattuc but not necessarily immoral. In any event, speak! And we will listen."

"My plan, in its broadest terms, is simple. 'Beyond' is out yonder, behind Circe's Couch. Thousands of worlds await discovery, some as beautiful as Cadwal. I propose that a revived and dynamic Naturalist Society send out locators, to discover one of these worlds and there establish a new Conservancy, while Cadwal yields to the inevitable realities!"

"Is that the plan?" asked Milo.

"It is indeed."

Glawen spoke in puzzlement. "Where does morality fit into your scheme? It might be that the divergence you mentioned is here. We are not agreed on the meaning of the word 'morality.'"

Milo said soberly: "For convenience we can define it as 'cosmos, space, time and the Conservancy arranged to the tastes of Julian Bohost.'"

"Come, Milo, be serious!" said Julian. "Must you forever act the clown? Morality has nothing to do with me. Morality regulates the needs and by democratic processes guarantees the rights of all the folk, not just the caprices of a privileged few."

"Superficially that sounds good," said Glawen. "But it would seem something like a special case. It does not address the situation here on Cadwal, where a colony of illegal vagabonds, who should not be here in the first place, far outnumbers the hardworking folk of Araminta Station. If you gave them the vote, they'd blow us away."

Julian laughed. "I will generalize, to clarify my point. In the largest morality, the first axiom ordains equality, which means equal perquisites, equal treatment before the law and an equal share of decision-making power for each member of every civilized race: in short, a truly universal democracy. And that is a truly universal morality."

Once again Milo protested: "Please, Julian! Can't you get your head out of the clouds? This isn't morality; it's Peefer egalitarianism in its most hypertrophied form. What is the point of expounding these windy platitudes when you know them to be, at the very least, impractical?"

"Is democracy impractical? Is this what you are saying?"

Glawen said: "As I recall, Baron Bodissey had something to say on the subject."

"Oh? Was he pro or con?"

"Neither. He pointed out that democracy could function only in a relatively homogeneous society of equivalent individuals. He described a district dedicated to democracy where the citizenry consisted of two hundred wolves and nine hundred squirrels. When zoning ordinances and public health laws were put into effect, the wolves were obliged to live in trees and eat nuts."

"Bah," said Julian. "Baron Bodissey was a man from the Eocene."

"And I am off to bed," said Milo. "Today has been long and eventful, with two major achievements. We have designed Julian's overpass and defined for once and all the term 'morality.' Tomorrow may well be as productive. Goodnight, all!"

Milo departed. For a period the three sat in silence, Glawen hoping that Julian would also go off to bed. Julian showed no disposition to do so, and Glawen suddenly realized that, in fact, Julian was determined to outwait him. Glawen instantly rose to his feet; Clattuc vanity debarred him from so ignoble a competition. He bade Wayness and Julian goodnight and went off to his room.

Wayness stirred in her chair. "I think I'm for bed, as well."

Julian spoke softly: "The night is young! Sit out with me for a while! I'm anxious to talk to you."

Wayness reluctantly settled back in her chair. "What do you want to talk about?"

"I can't believe you meant what you said before dinner tonight. Tell me I'm right."

Wayness rose to her feet. "I'm afraid that you're wrong. Our lives go in different directions and now I'm going to bed. And please don't sit out here brooding all the night."

For a time Wayness lay awake, her mind too active for relaxation, listening to the sounds which drifted across the night and through her window. Finally she fell asleep.

In the morning the four arrayed themselves in riding habits provided by the lodge; then, after breakfast, went out to the stables. Glawen brought along a case containing the guns which all would carry in their saddle holsters, as a safety precaution.

In front of the stables four bunters awaited them, with blinders in place over the optic stalks. The bunters were prepared for riding, each with a saddle clamped into the notch in its dorsal ridge. Each saddle was painted a different color: blue, gray, orange and green, by which the bunters could be identified one from the other.

Wayness looked over the bunters with a dubious droop to her mouth. She had expected sullen, graceless and ill-smelling animals, but these four hulks eclipsed her most vivid imaginings.

Wayness tried to reassure herself. "It is sheer projection, of how I would feel if I were asked to carry tourists on my back."

Wayness renewed her study of the bunters. Their sheer bulk was daunting in itself. Each stood six feet high, on six splayed legs, to the serrated upper edge of its dorsal ridge, and measured from eleven to twelve feet in length, exclusive of its tail: a linkage of bony nodules seven feet long. The dorsal ridge at the front terminated in a head of naked bony segments from which depended a flexible proboscis, of an unpleasant pale blue color. Optic stalks lifted from tufts of black fur; these were now covered over by leather cup-shaped blinders. The skin, mottled liver red, gray and purple, hung in flaps and folds and gave off an unpleasant musty odor. Immediately forward of a hump at the base of the creature's tail the saddles were clamped. A pair of chains attached to the harness constricted the proboscis, and a pole taped to the tail protected the rider, that he might not be lashed or plucked from the saddle.

Wayness asked Glawen: "Are we really sure that all of us want to ride these nightmarish animals?"

"Stay at the lodge, if you like," said Glawen. "There's nothing much to see at Lake Dimple, and nothing to do except look for magic stones."

"I've always been considered at least as reckless as Milo. If he goes, I'll go. Still, I'd prefer to ride something less intimidating."

"For the usual run of tourists, the bunters are just right," said Glawen. "They'd ride the devil himself to Lake Dimple if they were sure the pictures would turn out well."

"A final point, and I think an important one," said Wayness. "After I mount the beast and it starts running, how do I control it?"

"Simplicity itself," said Glawen. "In front of each saddle you'll notice a control board. Each is equipped with three levers, which work cables and electrical contacts to guide the bunter. To go forward, push the left lever forward, then pull it back to center. To increase speed, push the left lever forward again, as many times as you consider necessary. Ordinarily just once is enough; the bunters make no difficulty about running. To decrease speed, pull the same lever back, then return to center. To stop, hold the lever back. To stop fast, hold the lever back and drop the blinders. To turn left, swing the middle lever to the left. To turn right, swing the middle lever to the right. The third lever, on the right, controls the blinders. A warning light indicates that the blinders are raised. Never dismount without pushing the lever on the right forward, which lowers the blinders and turns off the light. The bunter will become passive and will not move; there is no need to tie him. To the extreme right is a box which houses the emergency radio, which I hope we won't need. Finally, do not walk close in front of your bunter. The proboscis is tied down but the creature sometimes manages to spit at you anyway."

"It seems simple enough," said Wayness. "Push, pull, swing right, swing left, don't get spit on. I suppose that one should also take care not to walk under the tail. Julian, do you understand all Glawen's instructions?"

"Yes. I understand very well."

"Appearances are often deceptive," said Milo. "Still, these creatures look neither meek nor sated. Julian's beast is stamping and blowing foam from its nose." He indicated the bunter with the orange saddle. "I call that peevish behavior."

Orreduc, the head groom, smiled placidly. "They are restless for their run. All have eaten their fill and destroyed a goodly puppet; they will carry you to Lake Dimple with the keenest pleasure for all."

270

Julian stepped forward, past the restless orange-saddled bunter. "Let's be off!" He went to the bunter with the green saddle. "This is a likely beast! I shall name it 'Albers' and ride it with aplomb, and all will marvel to see me dashing at great speed across the plain! Orreduc, help me aboard Albers."

"One moment," said Glawen. He opened the case and placed a gun in the holster to the side of each control board. Then he checked over each bunter in turn, inspecting saddles, saddle clamps, controls, control cables, blinders, radio, tail stiffeners and proboscis tie-downs. He said at last: "I can't find anything wrong."

Orreduc came forward. "Are you ready, then? For the lady here is the proper mount; she shall sit the blue saddle for her comfort. The bunter is of good condition; she will enjoy her ride with great zest. It is what we call a soft mount. I will help you to the saddle."

"I am innocent nice little Wayness," she muttered. "I can't believe that this is happening to me." Gingerly she climbed upon the bunter. "So far, so good."

Orreduc turned to Milo. "Here is the bunter for you! The gray saddle is good luck. Shall I help you to mount?"

"I can manage, thank you."

"Excellent! Well done, sir!" To Julian: "You, sir, have taken a fancy to your Albers, and he shall be your mount. As for you, sir"— he addressed Glawen—"you shall ride secure in the orange saddle. This fine fellow will serve you well. He is a bit eager, and the froth means that he is happy and ready for his run. Pay it no heed."

The grooms retreated into the stable. Glawen looked around at his companions. "Everyone ready? Raise your blinders. Now push the lever forward, then bring it back to center."

The bunters moved away from the stables, at first slowly, then at a lunging gallop. The Plain of Moans extended before them, a dun-colored desolation. On the left hand the Mandala Mountains skirted the horizon, fading into the murk to north and south.

The bunters ran without effort. Glawen's steed seemed particularly mettlesome, and he was forced to maintain a close restraint. All the bunters seemed to be running with unusual vigor; Glawen decided that over the recent months they had been insufficiently exercised.

An hour's ride brought them to Lake Dimple: an expanse of water flat and drab, five miles long and two miles wide. The banks were low, muddy and stamped deep with footprints, where animals had come down to the water. An occasional smoketree or a skeleton oak stood stark and alone along the bank; in the shallows grew reeds, mustard yellow with black tassels. By some freakish circumstance a single tall dendron stood fifty yards back from the lake. To the side of the dendron a well-trodden area stained gray with the ashes of innumerable fires marked the site of the banjee camp.

Glawen led the others to a spot near the dendron. "There it is, and as you see, the banjees are off somewhere about their travels. The magic stones are found either in that thicket of cankerberry bush over there or on the bottom of the lake, fairly close to shore. But don't dismount without dropping the blinders."

Wayness looked askance at the lake. "I'm just a bit squeamish in connection with mud."

"In that case, search the thicket, but take care to avoid the thorns. Hold a stick in each hand to push the branches aside. The mud is more squeamish but less painful."

"Perhaps I'll just watch for a while."

"Everybody check their blinders. The right-hand lever should be pushed forward and the cups should be definitely in place over the eyestalks. Milo?"

"Blinders down."

"Julian?"

"They're down, needless to say."

"Wayness?"

"They're down."

"And mine are down."

Without further ado Julian jumped to the ground, followed by Milo. Glawen remained in his saddle, perplexed by the conduct of his bunter, which had not become quiet.

Julian walked in front of his bunter, Albers, who instantly emitted a terrible squeal and, bounding forward, kicked Julian. Glawen seized his gun; at the same time his own mount uttered a cry so shrill and piercing that it seemed to defeat the sense of hearing. It reared high on its back legs, throwing Glawen to the ground. Blowing great bubbles of froth from its proboscis the bunter hurled itself on Milo, kicking and stamping and pounding. Then it seized Milo and tossed him high into the air.

Glawen, dazed by the fall, twisted around and fired his gun, to blow away Albers' head. His own mount, turning away from Milo, once again rose squealing on its hind legs, peering down at Glawen while flailing the air with its other legs in an odd dance of triumph and hatred. Kneeling and sick with horror, Glawen fired the gun, again and again. Explosive pellets mangled the bunter's interior and blew away its head; for a moment it stood erect then toppled ponderously to the ground.

Wayness, crying and sobbing, was trying to jump down from the saddle, in order to run to Milo. Glawen yelled: "Don't move! Stay where you are! You can't help him."

He cautiously advanced on the remaining two bunters, those ridden by Milo and Wayness. The blinders properly covered their eyes; they stood quivering with repressed passion, but, unable to see, could not move.

Glawen told Wayness: "Be ready with the gun, but don't come down to the ground."

Julian lay white-faced and moaning, his legs twisted away from his pelvis at strange angles. He gazed up at Glawen: "You did this to me! You arranged it all!"

Glawen said: "Try to relax. I'll get help as soon as I can." He went to look down at Milo, who was clearly dead. Then he stumbled to Wayness' bunter and called the lodge by the emergency radio.

4

In his first hurried call to Bodwyn Wook Glawen had imparted only essential facts. Bodwyn Wook dispatched Ysel Laverty and a team of investigators to Mad Mountain Lodge, then returned a call to Glawen, who reported the circumstances at greater length.

"I have dozens of suspicions," said Glawen. "I'm sure of nothing. Julian's conduct is especially ambiguous. He went out to the stables and talked politics with Orreduc and his helpers. Julian admitted celebrating the virtues of himself and the LPF and no doubt identified the rest of us as flagrant Chartists and aristocrats, anxious to tyrannize the Yips, and send them off to the Great Spiral Nebula. I don't see how he could have arranged the bunter attack, especially since he was first off his mount and the first to be hurt."

"The plan might have gone wrong. But I am not clear as to his motive."

"It's not overwhelming. He disliked both Milo and me to the point of detestation. At this time he probably included Wayness in his circle of enemies; she had just broken off what he thought to be a definite understanding. Julian was in a black mood, no doubt as to that. A murderous mood? Probably not. But the event would not have occurred if Julian had not incited the Yips and set the wheels in motion."

"You are inclined, then, to exculpate Julian."

"I seesaw back and forth in my thinking. It seems absurd to believe that Julian plotted with Orreduc. On the other hand, when we went to the stables, Julian made a great point of selecting the bunter with the green saddle, whom he named Albers. I wondered at the time what was going on. Whatever the case, Albers proved faithless and savaged Julian without hesitation.

"Conceivably the plot might have called for Julian to jump down from Albers, then jump back aboard and ride off while the rest of us were being trampled and tossed, and for a fact he took Albers some distance apart before he dismounted. If this were the plot, Orreduc swindled Julian. Why? I doubt if Orreduc will tell us. Perhaps to eliminate a possible accuser, if things went wrong. More likely because he cared not a fig for the LPF and here was a chance to kill four bad woskers at a single swipe, including one who used big words and wore a white hat. I might note that Julian accused me of arranging his injury —a strange thing to say unless the idea was already in his mind."

"Interesting but inconclusive," said Bodwyn Wook. "What were you telling me in connection with the blinders?"

"They are proof, definite and final, that Orreduc premeditated the murder. The blinders were slit and the seams loosened. This morning they were carefully wedged in place over the eyes so that they seemed in good condition. But once raised and then lowered, they would flap wide open and the bunter would have a clear view ahead. If we all had alighted together and all of the blinders had failed, we would all have been killed. The bunters would have run away and the verdict would have been 'an accident.'

"But two of the blinders, on the beasts ridden by Milo and Wayness, failed to unfold. I was able to shoot the other two and except for Milo, we're alive today.

"Also, to make the scheme even nastier, I'm sure that the bunters were not properly prepared for riding, which incriminates the assistants as well. I think that the bunters were teased and infuriated, then blindered and brought out in a state of total rage."

"I've sent up a pair of biologists," said Bodwyn Wook. "They will give us a definite answer. Where is Orreduc now?"

"In the manager's office, looking glum. After I called you, I went out to the stables and told Orreduc that there had been a serious accident. I brought him to the lodge, so that he and his assistants could not cook up a joint story, in case they had not done so already. I asked Orreduc if he owned a gun, and he said no. But I searched him and found that he was carrying a handgun. I asked why he had misinformed me; he said that the gun belonged to the stable and was not his personal property. The manager is now keeping an eye on him."

"Perhaps Orreduc will reveal what part, if any, Julian played in the affair. Otherwise, conspiracy will be impossible to prove. Now, then: I have been in touch with the Conservator and Dame Cora. The girl had already called them from the lodge. How is she bearing up?"

"She is sitting quietly, doing nothing. I think she feels she's living a bad dream and wants to wake up."

"The team should be arriving at any minute, and also transport for Julian and the body. The girl, I expect, will want to return as well. Captain Laverty will be in charge; give him what help he needs and then you can come home too."

Glawen went to Wayness' room and knocked. "It's Glawen."

"Come in."

Wayness sat on the couch, looking out the window. Glawen went to sit beside her. He put his arms around her and hugged her close. At last Wayness began to cry. After a few moments Glawen said: "It wasn't an accident. Orreduc had cut the leather of the blinders so that they fell open. He hoped that we'd all be killed."

"Why should he do such a thing? I can't understand it."

"He'll be questioned. Perhaps he'll explain. Julian might have told him that we were here to phase him and his helpers out of their jobs. Julian surely identified us as Chartists of full stripe."

Wayness huddled close to him. "What an awful place this is!"

"There won't be any more Yips and no more bunters," said Glawen.

Wayness straightened up and combed her hair with her fingers. "It's foolish to waste time in vain regrets, and yet—" Once again she started to cry. "Life without Milo will be so very different. If I really thought Julian were responsible, I'd—I don't know what I'd do."

Glawen said nothing. Presently Wayness asked: "What will happen to Orreduc?"

"I expect that justice will be quick and to the point."

"And what of Julian?"

"Nothing can be proved against him, even if he were guilty, which he's probably not."

"I hope that I never see him again."

The flyers from Araminta Station arrived. Glawen conferred with Captain Ysel Laverty, then flew the biologists to Lake Dimple, where they tested the blood of the dead bunters. "No question about it! Their blood is full of 'ariactin' and they were beside themselves with rage."

Glawen and the biologists returned to the lodge. Julian, and Milo's body, had been conveyed back to Araminta Station; Wayness had joined the dismal flight.

While Ysel Laverty questioned the understablemen, Orreduc waited in the manager's office, showing increasing signs of uneasiness. The understablemen told varying stories. All insisted that the bunters had been teased and enraged to an intense pitch.

"And then what? Who threw out the puppets?"

Here the stories took different directions. Each groom disclaimed responsibility for this particular step; each declared that other duties had distracted him at that particular time. "Most odd," said Ysel Laverty to the last of the three. "All of you teased the four bunters, then all of you went away and none of you seem to know who threw in the puppets."

"It surely must have been done! That is part of the process! We are all highly careful workers."

"I don't find any used puppets in the trash bin. It's quite empty."

"That is astonishing! Who could have taken them away?"

"I can't imagine," said Ysel Laverty, and went to question Orreduc. He seated himself at the manager's desk, and signaled to one of his sergeants, who brought in the defective blinders, then went to stand by the door.

Ysel Laverty placed the blinders carefully on the table, one so that the leather flaps overlapped and the other gaping wide.

Orreduc watched in fascinated silence.

Ysel Laverty leaned back and fixed Orreduc with a long dispassionate scrutiny. At last, with a trembling half-smile, Orreduc asked: "Why do you look on me with eyes that peer and stare? It is unusual when a person looks so long at another person, and the second person will always start to wonder."

Ysel Laverty said: "I am waiting to hear what you have to say."

"Come, sir! I am not paid to chat or to say things with different people. The manager will be angry if I am not hard at my work. It is important, if guests should want to ride."

"The manager has given orders that you should answer my questions. Right now, that is your only duty. What do you think of these blinders?"

"Aha, my dear fellow! Look here and here; you will see that the blinders are broken! That is my opinion! These must now be fixed and fixed well. I will take them to the leather shop."

"Come, Orreduc, be serious. You are a murderer. Do you care to answer my questions?"

Orreduc's face fell. "Ask what you will. Your mind is like stone and I am already facing what may be a severe penalty."

"Who prompted you to do this deed?"

Orreduc shook his head, and, smiling, looked off across the room. "I am not sure of your meaning."

"What did Julian Bohost tell you last night?"

"It is hard to remember. I am frightened by your threats. If you were kind and said to me: 'Ah, Orreduc, you are a good person. A mistake has been made; did you know that?' Then you would say: 'Please be more careful the next time these young folk go for their ride!' I would say: 'Of course! And now I remember everything, since my mind is free of fear and I am happy again.'"

Ysel Laverty looked to his sergeant. "Do you have a strong charge in your gun? Because soon we must shoot Orreduc."

"Charge is strong, sir."

Ysel Laverty turned back to Orreduc. "What did Julian say to you?"

Orreduc was now sullen. "He said many things. I paid little heed."

"Why did you decide to kill these four young people?"

"Why does the sun shine? Why does the wind blow? I admit nothing. On the Lutwen Islands live a hundred thousand folk. At Stroma are a few hundred; at Araminta a few hundred more. If every Lutwenese still on Deucas were able to kill four woskers, there would be none left."

"Quite so. Lucidly and reasonably put." Ysel Laverty smiled grimly. "We had hoped to terminate jobs like yours by attrition. You were trusted and might have remained here as long as you liked. It seems to have been a mistaken policy. Because of your act, every Yip on Deucas will be sent home, or perhaps off-world."

"You may send me home or off-world also," said Orreduc ingenuously. "The effect is the same."

"Did Julian suggest the so-called accident?"

Orreduc smiled wistfully. "What if I tell you the exact truth?"

"You are going to die. Tell the truth and you'll save your helpers."

"Kill me, then. I hope that both uncertainty and itching piles annoy you the rest of your days."

Ysel Laverty gestured to his sergeant. "Handcuff him; take him to the flyer and put him in the after compartment. Do the same for the others. Go carefully; they might be armed."

Immediately upon Glawen's return to Araminta Station he took himself to the Bureau B offices and there conferred with Bodwyn Wook. He learned that Julian had been hospitalized with a crushed pelvis and two smashed legs. "He is lucky to be alive," said Bodwyn Wook. "If he planned the event, he made a great botch of it."

Glawen shook his head. "In spite of all, I can't credit Julian with murderous tendencies."

"This is my opinion. The situation is ambiguous, but we can take it no farther."

"He probably talked a lot of extravagant nonsense, and perhaps some sedition as well, but there would be no hard proof."

"That is what we hear from the assistant stablemen, though their testimony is too vague to be useful."

"What has happened to them?"

"Orreduc has been shot. The underlings are on their way to Cape Journal, where they will break a road through the rocks to Crazy Katy Lake and the Mile-High Falls."

"They got off easy."

Bodwyn Wook folded his hands and looked toward the ceiling. "Their guilt is hard to measure. They knew what was going on but made no move to prevent it. By our doctrine, they are as guilty as Orreduc. Yips look at life differently. Even now they don't understand why they are being punished; Orreduc gave the orders; they merely obeyed, so why this cruel fate?

"But I feel no great sorrow on their behalf. The rule is simple: 'When you travel to far places, obey the laws of the land.' The Yips neglected this rule and are now en route to Cape Journal."

Returning to Clattuc House, Glawen called Wayness on the telephone. She seemed wan and despondent, and had little to say.

Halfway through the next morning Wayness telephoned Glawen. "Are you busy?"

"Not particularly."

"I want to talk with you. Can I meet you somewhere?"

"Certainly. Shall I come to Riverview House?"

"If you like. I'll wait for you out in front."

Glawen drove the Clattuc power wagon south along the Beach Road. A gusty wind from the sea caused the roadside palms to dip and sway, and set the fronds to rasping. Surf roared up the beach, to retreat in hissing sheets of spume. At Riverview House, Glawen found Wayness waiting beside the road, her dark green cloak flapping in the wind.

Wayness jumped into the seat beside Glawen. He drove another mile south, then turned off the road and halted where they could look out over the tumbling sea. Glawen asked, somewhat tentatively: "How are your father and mother?"

"Well enough. Mother's sister has come to visit."

"What of your plans? Are you still set upon your visit to Earth?"

"That's what I want to talk about." She sat a moment looking out to sea. "I've said very little about what I hope to do."

"You've said nothing."

"Only to Milo, who was coming with me. Now he's gone. It came to me that if, like Milo, I were to die suddenly, or be killed, or lose my mind, then no one would know what I know. At least, I don't think anyone knows what I know. I hope not."

"Why haven't you told your father?"

Wayness smiled sadly. "He would be astonished and highly concerned. He would not allow me to go to Earth. He would insist that I was too young and inexperienced for so much responsibility."

"Perhaps he would be right."

"I don't think so. But I must tell someone else, just in case something happens to me."

"It sounds like dramatic information."

"You can judge for yourself."

"You're planning to tell me?"

"Yes. But you must undertake to tell no one, unless somehow I am killed and you fear for your own life, or something similar."

"I don't like the sound of this, but I'll do as you ask."

"Thank you, Glawen. First, you must know that I am not absolutely certain of anything, and I may be off on a wild-goose chase. But I feel that I must learn the truth."

"Very well. Proceed."

"When I visited Earth before, I was just a schoolgirl. I stayed with my father's cousin at a place called Tierens, which is not far from Shillawy. His name is Pirie Tamm; he lives in an enormous echoing old house with his wife and daughters, all older than I. Pirie Tamm is a complicated person, an amateur of a dozen arts and crafts and recondite skills. He is one of the few remaining Naturalists on Earth —or, for that matter, the whole Gaean Reach—by reason of his interest in evolutionary biology. He has dozens of interesting friends; Milo and I both enjoyed every minute of our stay.

"One day an old man named Kelvin Kilduc came to call. We were told that he was the secretary, and possibly the final secretary, of the Naturalist Society, now on the verge of becoming totally defunct, since the membership consisted only of Kelvin Kilduc, Pirie Tamm, a few antiquarians and two or three dilettantes. The Society had once been prosperous but no longer, owing to the peculations of a secretary named Frons Nisfit, who had held office sixty years before. Nisfit plundered the accounts, sold all the assets and made off with the proceeds. Nisfit could not be traced and the Society was left with a trifling income from investments Nisfit had not been able to liquidate —about enough to pay for the official stationery and the annual registration fee. And of course the Society held title to Cadwal, through the original Grant in Perpetuity, which was integral with the original Charter.

"Kelvin Kilduc in due course became secretary—an honorary position, which gave him a unique status at dinner parties; he was a walking conversation piece. I don't think he took his position seriously.

"I approached him in the most demure and polite manner imaginable and asked if I might look at the original Charter, since I myself was a Naturalist from Throy. He did not want to be bothered and made difficulties: the Charter was locked in a vault, deep under the Bank of Margravia in Shillawy. I did not persist, although I thought him rather stuffy and self-important.

"Poor Kelvin Kilduc died in his sleep two weeks later, and for lack of anyone else Pirie Tamm assumed the post of secretary to the nearly nonexistent Naturalist Society."

"One moment," said Glawen. "What of the folk on Throy?"

"There is a distinction. They are Naturalists, so called, but not necessarily members of the Society, unless they pay dues and fulfill membership requirements, and no one has done so for centuries. In any event, Pirie Tamm became secretary, and felt obliged to visit the bank in Shillawy in order to make an inventory of the Society's possessions—a task which Kelvin Kilduc had neglected in all his tenure.

"To make a long story short, when we looked into the vault, we found a large number of old records, the few paltry bonds which were still yielding income, but no Charter and, worse, no Grant in Perpetuity.

"Pirie Tamm was baffled. Before he thought, he blurted out that this was most serious; the grant was transferable and required only a bill of sale and new registration for a transfer of ownership.

"In other words, whoever held the original Charter and the attached grant owned all Cadwal: Ecce, Deucas and Throy.

"Pirie decided that the Charter and grant had been among the curios sold by Frons Nisfit. I suggested that we check the records to find if a new registration had been entered. Pirie now realized that we had uncovered a most delicate situation, and he did not know what to do, except ignore the whole thing and hope for the best. He obviously regretted that I knew of the situation, and made me promise to say nothing to anyone—at least until he could somehow regularize the matter.

"I don't know what he did—I suspect nothing, although he did learn that the grant had not been reregistered.

"There were a few clues which Pirie rather halfheartedly tried to run down, without any particular success. At the moment he wants only to let sleeping dogs lie, but he is old and ailing, and when he dies the new secretary will look for the Charter—if there is a new secretary.

"So there you have it. I planned to go to Earth with Milo, and try to find the Charter, before something dreadful happens. Now you know what I know, which is a relief, since if something happened to me, no one would know except Pirie Tamm, and he is a weak reed."

"Now I know," said Glawen. "What will you do when you return to Earth?"

"I'll go back to stay with Pirie Tamm. Then I will join the Naturalist Society and become secretary. In that way, no new secretary will discover that the Charter is missing. Pirie might even cooperate and step down in my favor. I can't imagine that anyone else wants the position."

For a few moments Glawen pondered over what he had heard. "I don't know what to tell you. There's something nagging at my brain, but I can't remember what it is. I wish I could come with you."

Wayness said wistfully: "I wish you could too. But no matter. I'll go to Earth and learn what I can, and perhaps there is some easy way out of the difficulty."

"I hope it's both easy and safe."

"Why shouldn't it be safe?"

"Someone else might be looking for the same thing."

"I never thought of that." Wayness considered. "Who would it be?"

"I don't know. Nor do you. And so it might be dangerous."

"I'll be careful."

"And now . . ." Glawen put his arms around her and kissed her, until finally she drew away.

"I'd better be getting home. Mother and Father will be wondering what has become of me."

"I'll think over what you've said. There's something at the back of my mind that I want to tell you, but it won't come to the surface."

"It will come when you least expect it." She kissed his cheek. "Now, take me back to Riverview House, before any alarms are sounded."

CHAPTER 6

1

Wayness had departed Araminta Station aboard the Perseian Lines' packet *Faerlith Winterflower*, which would carry her down Mircea's Wisp to Andromeda 6011 IV: a junction world where she would transfer to a Glistmar Explorer Route space cruiser for the remainder of her voyage to Earth.

Wayness' departure left a dreary void in Glawen's life. Overnight existence became drab and dull. Why had he allowed her to go so fearfully far away, beyond the reach of human perception? He asked himself the question often, and the answer came always in company with a rueful smile: he had been given no voice in the matter. Wayness had made her own decision, on the basis of her own best judgment. This was a process which, in all justice, could not be faulted: so Glawen assured himself, though without full or fervent conviction.

In some respects, Wayness must be compared to a natural force: sometimes warm and beneficent (and in the last few weeks, breathtakingly affectionate), sometimes mysterious and baffling, but never susceptible to human control.

Glawen pondered this unique individual named Wayness Tamm. If through some extraordinary circumstance he became endowed with divine powers and assigned the pleasurable task of designing a new Wayness, he might well diminish the proportion of sheer single-minded obstinacy and intractable, volatile self-willed independence by a soupçon or two—not enough to disturb the flavor of the mix, but to make her just a bit more . . . Here Glawen hesitated, groping for the proper word. Malleable? Predictable? Subservient? Certainly none of these. It might be that whatever divine being had created the original Wayness had done his job with such consummate skill that no improvement was possible.

To occupy his energies, Glawen undertook several new courses of study, which upon completion would allow him to sit for the IPCC

First Grade examination. A passing score, together with demonstrable competence at weaponry, practical technics, emergency control and hand-to-hand combat, would qualify him as IPCC Agent Ordinary, and would allow him IPCC status and authority across the entire Gaean Reach. Several others at Bureau B had achieved such status. Scharde had proceeded past the first grade to IPCC Agent Second Level, which enabled Bureau B to function as an IPCC affiliate.

Kirdy Wook announced that he also would undertake the IPCC regimen, but seemed in no hurry to attend the classes. He had apparently recovered from his ordeal at Yipton, except for a tendency toward vagueness and a set of abrupt or impatient mannerisms, which everyone expected would diminish with his full recovery. Kirdy still refused, or perhaps was unable, to discuss his experiences. Almost as soon as he left the hospital he resigned from the Bold Lions, and thereafter had nothing to do with any of the group.

For a period Glawen tried to engage Kirdy in conversation, hoping to ease him into a more positive frame of mind. The effort, so Glawen found, was like trying to pick up quicksilver. For the most part Kirdy listened in moody silence, smiling a strange glassy-eyed half-smile, in which Glawen thought to sense traces of both hostility and contempt. Kirdy volunteered no remarks of his own, so that, had Glawen not spoken again, the two would have sat in dead silence. To questions, Kirdy either responded not at all or at verbose length but without any reference to the question.

Kirdy had never been noted for his humor; now he seemed to find levity incomprehensible. Whenever Glawen spoke lightly or attempted a witticism, Kirdy turned him a glance so cold and brooding that the words caught in Glawen's throat.

One day Glawen noticed Kirdy turn aside in order to avoid him, and thenceforth he desisted from his efforts.

Glawen discussed Kirdy and his conduct with Scharde. "Something almost funny is going on. Kirdy knows that if I pass the IPCC examination, I'll jump a whole rank over him at the Bureau. Kirdy's only recourse is also to take the examination. This means not only hard study but also the terrible risk of failure—which in Kirdy's case is real, since he's weak in mathematics and also all the practical demonstrations."

"He'd certainly fail the psychometrics."

"That is Kirdy's dilemma. I can't guess how he'll deal with it— except to pray that I fail so shamefully that I quit Bureau B and go into oenology along with Arles."

"Poor Kirdy. He's been through a lot."

"I agree: poor Kirdy. Which doesn't make him any easier to work with."

From Watertown on Andromeda 6011 IV came a letter from Wayness, written while she awaited connections with one of the Glistmar space cruisers. She wrote: "Already I'm homesick, and I miss you extremely. It's amazing how a person can learn to love and trust and depend upon another person so completely and hardly be aware of what's going on until the other person isn't there anymore. Now I know." And she finished: "I will write again from Tierens, with the latest news on the situation. I hope that by some miracle it will be good news, but I am not too hopeful. In an odd kind of way I'm looking forward to getting my teeth into the problem, if only to take my mind off my troubles."

The summer passed; Glawen's twentieth birthday came and went: the last before his twenty-first: Suicide Day, as it was sometimes known. Glawen wavered between hope and despair. His Status Index was still 22, which could have been worse but also could have been better.

On the following Smollen Arles brought Drusilla co-Laverty as his guest to the Clattuc House Supper, to Spanchetta's evident surprise and disapproval.

Arles pretended not to notice. Drusilla was in an ebullient mood, and ignored Spanchetta completely, which caused Spanchetta to glower even more notably.

During the meal Arles sat with magisterial dignity, speaking little except to Drusilla, and then only in a confidential undertone. He had dressed with care, in a black coat, russet trousers, a white shirt with a blue sash at his waist. Drusilla's costume was less conservative, and even extreme. Her gown was a confection of striped black, pink and orange satin, cut low in front. A black turban with a tall black plume confined her pink-blond ringlets; black elf-points rose two inches above her ears. For sheer bravura the ensemble surpassed even Spanchetta's purple and red costume, and Spanchetta's expression, when she troubled to look toward Drusilla, conveyed total disgust.

Drusilla refused to be inhibited. She laughed loudly, gaily and often, sometimes for no apparent reason. She contributed her opinions to conversations everywhere around the table, chatting and chaffing, beguiling her new acquaintances with nods and smiles, pouts and winks.

Scharde, after watching covertly for a time, spoke to Glawen: "I admit to confusion. Isn't she one of Namour's special chums?"

"I think that's over and done with. Or perhaps it's a seasonal affair, since Drusilla still travels with the Mummers."

"She'd seem a bit past her prime. Floreste likes to keep young blood in the troupe."

"She's Floreste's assistant; she doesn't perform anymore."

"Arles looks like a cat who has just caught a very large mouse. I'm confused even further. I thought that Arles no longer cared for girls."

"So did I. It looks as if there might have been a mistake. Drusilla is female, beyond all doubt."

"So she is." Scharde turned away. "Well, it's none of my concern, I'm glad to say."

"Look at Arles. I think he's about to make a speech."

Arles had risen to his feet and for a moment stood smiling around the table, waiting for conversations to subside. At last he tapped his wineglass with a knife. "Please, everyone! I ask your attention! I wish to make an announcement; be kind enough to listen. Sitting beside me you will notice—how could you have failed to notice?—a ravishing and gorgeous creature whom many of you will recognize as the honorable and distinguished Drusilla co-Laverty. She is as talented as she is charming, and for some years has helped Floreste work his miracles with the Mummers. But all things change! In response to my supplications, Drusilla has agreed to become a Clattuc. Do I make myself clear?"

Arles looked around the table as the assembly politely clapped hands.

"I will confide even more secrets to this company. Today we signed the contract and the union has been recorded by the Registrar. The deed is done!"

Arles bowed as the company called out congratulations. Drusilla raised her arm on high, with her head tilted pertly to the side, and waved her fingers.

Scharde muttered aside to Glawen: "Look at Spanchetta. She can't decide whether or not to have a heart attack."

Arles spoke on. "Needless to say, I am as amazed as you all must be by my good luck. We are leaving at once on a romantic tour which will take us far and wide, to places of myth and mystery! But return we shall, I promise you! In all the Gaean Reach no place compares with Araminta Station!"

Arles seated himself and for several minutes was busy responding to toasts and questions.

"So they're off to places of myth and mystery," mused Scharde. "I wonder where Arles found the money. Certainly not from Spanchetta."

"Maybe Drusilla has come into wealth."

"Not on what Floreste pays her. Mummers' money goes into the Orpheum fund. Drusilla is lucky to get her keep and travel expenses, and whatever extra she can connive."

"Perhaps she operates some sort of business on the side."

"Let us hope that it is a business in which Arles can be of practical assistance."

On the following day Arles and Drusilla departed aboard the Perseian Lines' luxury cruise ship *Mircean Lyre*. Later in the day Scharde told Glawen: "The puzzle is clarified. I had a few words with Floreste and the problem of Arles' wealth has disappeared. He possesses no wealth whatever and Drusilla very little more. So how are they able to take passage to 'places of myth and mystery'? Simple. Drusilla is making a routine trip, arranging bookings for the Mummers: something she does every year. Floreste has arranged cheap fares for Mummer personnel; both Arles and Drusilla qualify. Their expenses therefore are minimal and as for the places of myth and mystery, they are bound for such places as Soum and Natrice and Liliander's Home and Tassadero: worlds on Floreste's usual circuit. All are rather dull for the most part."

"I wonder where they plan to live on their return," mused Glawen. "Do you think Spanchetta will welcome them?"

"Not effusively."

Glawen went to look out the window. "I'd like to go traveling myself. To Earth, by preference."

"Wait till after your next birthday."

Glawen gave his head a dour nod. "As a collateral I'm free to go anywhere I like, especially if I don't come back."

"Don't be so gloomy. You're not an outcast yet. I'm sure I can induce old Dorny to drink himself to death. Descant is another. He won't retire and he won't make a serious attempt to die."

"I can't worry about such things," growled Glawen. "If I'm kicked out of Clattuc House, so be it. Since I can't travel to worlds of myth and mystery like Arles, or even to Earth, I think I'll take the sloop out for a sail. Maybe to Thurben Island. Would you like to come along? We can camp on the beach for a day or two."

"No, thank you. Thurben Island is not for me. If you go, take plenty of water; you'll find not a drop on Thurben. And don't swim in the lagoon."

"I think I'll go," said Glawen. "If nothing else, it's a change."

2

Glawen loaded supplies aboard the sloop, filled the water tanks, recharged the power unit, then, without ceremony, cast off the mooring lines and departed the Clattuc dock.

Under power he steered down the Wan River to the river mouth, then up and over the incoming swells where they crossed the bar, and out upon the face of the ocean. A quarter mile offshore he raised the sails and on the port tack sailed due east: a course which eventually would bring him to the steaming west coast of Ecce.

Glawen put the automatic pilot to work, and sat back to enjoy the gurgle of the wake, the wide blue sky, the surge of the boat over the long low swells.

The Araminta shore became a purple-gray mark across the horizon and soon disappeared. The wind shifted; Glawen altered course to north of east—as close to the wind as was convenient.

The day passed, with nothing to be seen but lazy blue ocean, sky and an occasional wandering seabird.

Late in the afternoon the wind slackened, and died to a flat calm by sunset. Glawen dropped the sails, and the boat moved only to the rise and fall of the swells. Glawen went below, prepared a bowl of stew which he brought up to the cockpit and consumed, along with a crust of bread and a flask of Clattuc claret, while sunset colors faded from the sky.

The afterglow departed and stars appeared. Glawen sat back and studied the constellations. The flow of Mircea's Wisp, along with Lorca and Sing, was below the horizon. At the zenith glittered that collocation known as Perseus Holding High the Head of Medusa, with the two blazing red stars Cairre and Aguin representing Medusa's eyes. In the southern sky he found the circlet of five white stars known as the Nautilus. At the center of the circlet shone a yellow star of the tenth magnitude, much too dim to be seen. This star was Old Sol. Out there, coasting across the void in a great Glistmar space cruiser, was Wayness. How large would she seem at such a distance? The size of an atom? Smaller? The problem became interesting. Glawen went below and calculated. Wayness, standing a hundred light-years away, would appear as large as a neutron at a distance of twelve hundred and fifty yards.

"So much for that," said Glawen. "Now I know."

Glawen returned to the cockpit. He looked around the sky, made sure all was secure, then went below, leaving the sloop to take care of itself.

Morning brought a favoring breeze from the south. Glawen made sail, and the sloop slid nicely across the water into the northeast.

At noon on the following day he sighted Thurben Island: a roughly circular mound of sand and volcanic debris, two miles in diameter, sparsely grown over with gray-green thornbush, a few straggling thyme trees and as many gaunt semaphore dendrons. At the center rose a crag of crumbling volcanic basalt. A coral reef encircled the island, creating a lagoon two hundred yards wide. The reef was broken by a pair of passes, at the north and south ends of the island, allowing access to the lagoon. Glawen lowered the sails offshore and powered the sloop through the southern pass against the outflowing current. Two hundred feet from the beach he dropped the anchor, in water so clear it seemed to magnify details of the bottom: coral drums, seaflowers, armored molluscs. Imp-fish and falorials came to investigate boat, anchor and anchor chain, then moved away to await developments: garbage, a swimmer, or someone falling overboard.

Glawen used the boom to lift the dinghy from its cradle and lower it over the side. With many precautions he stepped down into the dinghy, carrying a coil of line, one end of which he had already tied to the stemhead of the sloop. He started the dinghy's impeller and steered for the beach, letting the line pay out behind him.

The dinghy nosed up on the sand. Glawen jumped ashore and pulled the dinghy high and dry above the reach of the surf. He tied the line from the boat to the gnarled trunk of a thornbush, thus doubly securing the sloop against the effects of a sudden squall.

Glawen was now at leisure. He had nothing to do: no tasks, no routine, no demands whatever upon his time—which was why he had come.

He took stock of his surroundings. Behind him were thornbush, a few thyme trees, a few mock balsams, an occasional gaunt black gallows tree, and a knob of rotting basalt at the center of the island. In front of him, the lagoon, apparently so innocent and placid, where the sloop now rode at anchor. To right and to left, identical ribbons of white sand, flanked by gray-green thornbush thickets and thyme trees, with long slender leaves silver on the bottom and scarlet on the top. Cat's-paws stirred by a puff of breeze ruffled the surface of the lagoon and sparkled in the sunlight, while the thyme trees shimmered silver and scarlet.

Glawen sat down in the sand. He listened.

Silence, except for the whisper of the water moving up and down the beach.

He lay back on the sand and dozed in the sunlight.

Time passed. A land crab pinched Glawen's ankle. He stirred, kicked and sat up. The land crab ran away in a panic.

Glawen rose to his feet. The sloop floated placidly at anchor. Syrene had moved across the sky; nothing else had changed. For a fact, thought Glawen, there was little to do on Thurben Island, except sleep, ponder the seascape or, in a fit of energy, stroll up and down the beach.

He looked right, then left. With no evident difference in either direction, he set off to the north. Land crabs scuttled away at his approach, down the beach to the water's edge, where they turned to watch as he passed. Blue lizards jumped up on their hind legs and with mighty kicks and strides ran to the shelter of the thornbush thickets, where they became bold and chattered angry challenges.

The shore veered away to the east, around the northern end of the island. Glawen arrived at a point opposite the north pass through the reef: a natural channel similar to the south pass, allowing the coming and going of boats into and out of the lagoon. Rounding the curve of the beach, Glawen stopped short in astonishment and shock.

Changes had occurred since his last visit. A rude dock extended into the lagoon. Near the foot of the dock, a pavilion of thatch and bamboo, in the Yip style, provided shelter from sun and rain.

For several minutes Glawen stood stock-still, studying the area. He could make out no fresh footprints in the sand; the premises would seem to be deserted.

Glawen relaxed a trifle, but still tense and wary, he approached the pavilion. Wisps of brown thatch rattled in the breeze; the interior was dry, dusty and devoid of occupation. Nonetheless, Glawen wished that he had brought a gun with him; in situations of this sort its bulk and heft would be most reassuring.

Glawen turned away from the pavilion. He looked out along the dock in perplexity. What sort of purpose could such an arrangement serve? A camp for far-ranging Yip fishermen? Glawen noticed an odd contrivance attached to the dock, thirty or forty feet from the shore: a derrick with an overhead beam, like a gallows, evidently intended to raise objects from a boat and swing them around to the dock—or back in the other direction.

Glawen walked out to the end of the dock, which sagged and creaked under his weight. He looked out through the pass, and found empty blue ocean. To right and left: the placid lagoon; shoreward, the ribbon of beach curving around the island. Below, bamboo pilings descended to the bottom; they seemed about fifteen feet long. Shades and shadows slid across the sand, refracted from wavelets moving along the surface.

Glawen stared down into the water, the skin of his back tingling. He had made a chilling discovery; indeed, at first, he could not believe his eyes.

There was no mistake: on the bottom, near the end of the dock, was spread a grotesque tangle of human bones. Some were sifted over with sand; some were draped with waterweed; others sprawled uncovered, as if naked, with only the moving shadows to clothe them.

Glawen forced himself to study the bones. It was difficult to estimate the number of individuals involved. The lenslike quality of the water distorted perception; the bones nonetheless seemed small and delicate.

Glawen seemed to feel the pressure of someone's observation. He jerked around and studied the shore. Everything appeared as before. There was no sign of living creature, though a dozen unseen eyes might be watching from behind the thornbush thickets.

His nerves were playing him tricks: so Glawen assured himself.

Glawen returned to the beach. He stood a moment in contemplation of dock, derrick and pavilion. A new thought entered his mind: what if someone had watched him arrive, then, when he had departed up the beach, had gone aboard his boat and sailed away? The idea caused Glawen's heart to pound; Thurben was not an island where he cared to be marooned, with nothing to eat but land crabs, which were indigestible, and nothing to drink but seawater.

Glawen returned down the beach at a trot, looking over his shoulder every few yards.

The sloop lay serenely to its anchor, precisely as he had left it. His spasm of near-panic drained away. He was alone on the island. Nevertheless, tranquillity had departed; the beach no longer could be considered a somnolent place on which to idle away a few days.

The time was now late afternoon. The breeze had died completely; ocean and lagoon lay calm and flat. Glawen decided to make his departure on the morning breeze. He pulled his dinghy into the water and returned to the sloop.

Syrene sank; darkness came to Thurben Island. Glawen prepared and ate his supper, then went up to the cockpit and sat two hours listening to small unidentifiable sounds from the shore. Overhead blazed the constellations; but tonight Glawen paid them no heed; his mind was occupied with more somber speculations.

At last Glawen went below to his bunk. He lay staring into the dark, unable to control the ideas which came wandering into his mind. Finally he fell into a restless slumber, on several occasions starting up to what he imagined to be the bump and scrape of someone climbing aboard the boat.

The night, with all deliberation, went its way. Lorca and Sing rose behind the island and climbed toward the zenith. Glawen finally fell asleep, so deeply that the coming of day failed to arouse him. Finally, with Syrene almost three hours into the sky, he awoke, edgy and hollow-eyed.

Glawen consumed a breakfast of tea and porridge in the cockpit. A breeze blew from the north, fair for the voyage home whenever he chose to raise the anchor. The deep blue of the sea was accentuated by pillars and domes of bright white cumulus, lifting over the horizon to the south. The world seemed innocent and clean; the circumstances at the north end of the lagoon were so incongruous to this sunny blue and white world as to seem unreal.

Glawen decided to make another quick inspection of dock and pavilion before departure; he might conceivably discover something he had missed the day before. He stepped down into his dinghy and with the impellers at full power, scudded north up the lagoon, with clouds of darting silver falorials following below.

The dinghy arrived at the north pass. The pavilion and dock were as he found them on the day before. Easing the dinghy up to the beach, Glawen jumped ashore with the painter, which he tied to one of the bamboo pilings.

Glawen stood a moment taking stock of the surroundings. As before, he discovered only silence and desolation. He went out to the end of the dock. The surface of the lagoon was ruffled by the breeze, making the bottom difficult to see clearly, but the bones lay scattered as before.

Glawen returned to the shore and examined the pavilion. Behind a shaded open area at the front were eight compartments, furnished only with heavy floor mats. There were no cooking or sanitary facilities other than an outhouse to the rear of the pavilion.

Glawen decided that he had seen enough; he had not been hallucinating on his first visit. He returned aboard his dinghy and pushed off into the lagoon. As the boat moved away from the dock, Glawen glanced out the pass and saw, about two miles to sea, a pair of lateen sails bellying to the breeze.

The vessel's course, by Glawen's best determination, would bring it to the north pass.

Glawen returned at full speed down the lagoon to his sloop. Under the circumstances, lacking a weapon, he could not risk confrontation, and instant flight might be necessary. Once out to sea he would be safe. Downwind or on a reach the catamaran could catch him in any kind of a wind; in a calm or upwind, his power unit would push him smartly away from the unpowered catamaran.

Climbing aboard the sloop, Glawen slung binoculars over his shoulder and hoisted himself up the mast. Focusing the binoculars on the arriving vessel, he saw it to be a two-masted catamaran sixty or sixty-five feet long—large for a Yip fishing boat—and to Glawen's great relief, its course would take it to the north pass. He stood in little risk of detection: against a background of thornbush and semaphore dendron the slender gray mast of the sloop would be indistinguishable.

Glawen watched until the catamaran disappeared around the curve of the island, then lowered himself to the deck. He stood looking indecisively up the lagoon. Prudence urged that he depart Thurben Island instantly. On the other hand, if he walked cautiously up the beach, keeping to the shade of the thornbush thickets, he might learn the identity of those aboard the catamaran. If he were discovered, he could retreat instantly, take himself aboard the sloop and sail away. So what would it be? Prudent withdrawal or a scouting expedition up the beach? Had he a handgun, the response would have been automatic. Lacking a weapon of any sort, save a knife from the galley, he deliberated ten seconds. "I am a Clattuc," Glawen told himself. "Blood, nature and tradition all indicate the way I must act."

Without further ado he tucked the galley carving knife, with a sharp six-inch blade, into his belt, took himself ashore in the dinghy and jogged up the beach, keeping close under the overhanging thickets of thornbush.

As he progressed he kept a careful eye focused ahead of him, in case someone from aboard the catamaran also should be exploring the beach. But he saw no one, which relieved him of the need to choose between uncomfortable options.

The masts of the catamaran became visible; a few hundred yards farther the dock and the vessel itself came into view. Glawen scrambled up the slope at the back of the beach, pushed through a gap in the thornbush and proceeded behind the fringe of thicket, which now provided him cover. Presently he dropped to his hands and knees and crawled carefully closer, to within fifty yards of the pavilion. Here he dropped flat and surveyed the scene through his binoculars.

Four golden-skinned Yips moved back and forth between boat and pavilion. Already they had brought ashore cushions, rugs and wicker chairs, and now set up a long table. They wore only short white kirtles and seemed very young, although black hoods concealed their heads and faces.

Six other men, of mature years, sat in the wicker chairs. They wore loose pale gray robes and, like the Yips, black hoods which concealed their identities. They sat composed and silent: men of substance or even importance, to judge by their postures and the poise of their heads. They made no communication among themselves; each almost pointedly isolating himself from the others. Glawen was unable to divine their place of origin. None were Yips; none would seem to be Naturalists from Throy and, almost certainly, none derived from Araminta Station.

The air tingled with imminence. The six gray-robed men sat stiff and still, their hoods creating an atmosphere of eerie unreality. Glawen no longer apprehended danger; the four Yips and six hooded men were preoccupied with their own affairs. Glawen watched fascinated, his mind sheering away from speculation.

A bizarre new element augmented the situation. From the boat came a tall heavy-boned woman, broad of shoulder, massive of leg and arm, of a sort totally different from both Yips and hooded men. She wore a black mask rather than a hood, which concealed her nose and eyes, but left her heavy flat cheeks and anvil of a chin bare. The skin of these areas and along her bare arms showed oyster white in color, while a ruff of sandy hair thrust an inch above her broad scalp. The only indications of femininity were two flabby breasts and heavy hips encased in loose short trousers.

The woman strode to the end of the dock, looked around the area. She spoke a few words to the Yips; two of them ran to the boat and returned with wooden crates which they placed on the table. Lifting the lids, they brought out flasks of wine and goblets, which they filled and tendered to the six seated men. The other two brought branches from the thornbush thicket and kindled a fire.

The woman returned along the dock to the boat. She jumped aboard and disappeared into the cabin. A few moments later, a group of Yip girls emerged, followed by the woman. The girls moved uncertainly down the dock, looking dubiously right and left, and over their shoulders at the grim figure of the woman behind them. There were six, at the flower of their youth, with wide topaz eyes, delicate features and soft honey-colored hair, and now Glawen divined the source of the bones on the bottom of the lagoon, and he thought he could guess what was about to happen.

The six hooded men sat watching silently and motionless. The six girls looked around the area, their expressions limpidly innocent, but with uneasiness starting to form. At a terse word from the woman, they sat down in the sand.

The nature of the occasion was now clear to Glawen. As he watched, frozen in position, the events of the afternoon proceeded, with inexorable ease and finesse.

Glawen at last could remain no longer. In the bleakest of moods and sickness of the spirit he retreated the way he had come and returned to the sloop, bringing with him the shore line which he had untied from the trunk of a thornbush.

Syrene dropped into the west and Glawen sat pondering what he had seen, and calculated what best he should do. Had he a weapon the planning would have been easier.

The sun sank; twilight settled over Thurben Island, and presently darkness. Glawen cranked aboard his anchor and on minimum power eased the sloop northward up the lagoon, guided by the white beach, pale in the starlight. Below darted a cloud of phosphorescent falorials, each like a length of heavy silver wire four inches long, casting a moving glow which illuminated the bottom.

Ahead, along the shore, appeared the flicker of the bonfire. Glawen carefully lowered his anchor over the side, so that the chain made no sound. He studied the beach through his binoculars. There was still a degree of sluggish activity. Glawen waited an hour, then stepped down into his dinghy; with the impeller at a quarter-power and the wake the softest of gurgles, he moved at slow speed toward the dock, keeping well offshore. Below darted ten thousand falorials in a moving bubble of green-yellow glow.

The bonfire had burned low. Glawen turned the dinghy shoreward toward the dock. Foot by foot he moved across the dark lagoon, and at last eased up to the catamaran. The hulls touched; holding to the catamaran's gunwale, Glawen listened. No sound. He made the dinghy fast to a shroud, and in all stealth climbed aboard the catamaran. He stood poised. Still no sound. He went to the aft mooring line, cut it with his knife and threw it aside. Crouching, he stole along the deck to the bow and cut the forward mooring line. There were no spring lines; the catamaran floated free. Yeasty exhilaration rose in Glawen's throat; he ran crouching back toward his dinghy.

A thud, a scrape, a massive presence. On the offside hull loomed the woman, who through some sensitivity had discovered that all was not well. By starlight she saw Glawen and took note of the gap between catamaran and dock. Uttering a choked cry of rage, she sprang across the cabin roof and flung herself on Glawen, arms forward, fingers bent into hooks. Glawen tried to dodge back but was caught up among the shrouds, and the woman was on him. She emitted an inarticulate cry of triumph and seized him around the neck.

Glawen sagged limp-legged, his face crammed into her belly, breathing the reek of her body. Wildly he thought: "This cannot be! This is not my fate!" He straightened his knees and drove his head into her jaw. She grunted; her arms slackened. Glawen struck out wildly, and clawed the domino down so that it covered her eyes. She groped and tore it away. Glawen thrust with his knife and buried the blade in her abdomen. She called out in horror and clutched at the handle. Glawen braced himself with one foot against the cabin roof, pushed with all his strength, to send the woman stumbling backward—against the gunwale and over, flat on her back into the water. Glawen, panting and gasping, looked down. The glow of the falorials illuminated her face; she had grown what appeared to be an instant beard of writhing silver wires. For an instant Glawen looked down into her eyes, which stared up through the water aghast at this terrible thing which was happening to her. Glawen saw her forehead; it was marked with a curious black symbol: a two-pronged fork with a short handle, the prongs turned inward toward each other.

Falorial poison immobilized the woman; silver wires grew from every part of her body. Air belched from her lungs; she sank slowly to the bottom.

Glawen looked toward the shore. The sounds, muffled by the whisper of the current through the pilings, had troubled no one.

Glawen, still shaken and a trifle dazed, lowered himself carefully into the dinghy. He tied a line to the stemhead of the catamaran and made the other end fast to the stern ring of the dinghy. Applying power to the impeller, he towed the catamaran south down the lagoon to where he had anchored the sloop.

He transferred the towline to one of the after mooring cleats on the sloop, hoisted the dinghy aboard and set off to the south, towing the catamaran astern.

Back at the pavilion someone at last had noticed the absence of the catamaran. Glawen heard far shouts of consternation, and smiled to himself.

Attentive to the glimmer of surf on his right hand, where ocean swells broke over the reef, Glawen steered slowly southward. Where the line of white foam ended, Glawen found the pass through the reef. He drifted out the channel and gained the freedom of the open sea: forever away from accursed Thurben Island.

Glawen continued to tow the catamaran under power for two hours, then hoisted sail and let the wind blow the boats to the south.

Remembering the smell of the woman when she had grappled him, Glawen removed all his clothes and scrubbed himself well. Donning fresh garments, he ate bread and cheese, and drank half a flask of wine. Now, feeling in a most curious mood, he went up on deck to sit for an hour in the cockpit.

At last he stirred, reefed the sail, checked the towline, made all secure, went below to his bunk and presently fell asleep.

In the morning, Glawen boarded the catamaran. He found nothing to indicate identities, either of the woman or of the six masked men.

Glawen transferred the catamaran's complement of navigation instruments to the sloop; no doubt they had been stolen from Araminta Station originally.

Glawen set the catamaran afire and returned to the sloop. He sailed into the southwest on a fresh breeze. Across the water flames rose high, swirling in and out of black smoke. As the distance increased, the flames slowly became invisible and disappeared, leaving only a slanting wisp of black smoke bending over the horizon.

3

After a day and a night of sailing before variable winds, Glawen raised the coast of the mainland. An hour after Syrene had crossed the zenith he rode the ocean surge over the Wan River bar. An hour later he sat in the Bureau B offices reporting his adventures to the entire upper hierarchy: the so-called Zoo—Scharde Clattuc the gaunt gray wolf, Ysel Laverty the boar, Rune Offaw the slender relentless stoat, and, almost lost in his massive leather chair, the small bald orangutan, Bodwyn Wook.

Glawen finished his recital. "I left them marooned and very unhappy: four Yips and six others, of origin unknown. They are probably registered at the hotel: at least that would be my guess."

"Absolutely amazing," said Bodwyn Wook. "And needless to say, totally intolerable." He looked toward the ceiling and spoke in his most didactic voice: "A number of questions come to mind. Who has organized these entertainments? It is not necessarily Titus Pompo, though obviously he cooperates. How long have they been going on? At least once or twice before, by the testimony of the bones. Who are these six hooded persons? What is their origin? How were they approached and by whom? Who is, or, better to say, who was the woman with the tattooed forehead? No doubt we will soon have answers to some of these questions, but I, for one, will not be satisfied until every layer of this dreadful scandal is unfolded. Finally, what is our optimum short-range response?" Bodwyn Wook leaned back. "Gentlemen, I await your opinions."

After a short pause Rune Offaw spoke. "It will shortly become obvious at Yipton that the catamaran is overdue. There is a good chance, so it seems to me, that Titus Pompo will wish to investigate. He might send another boat, or, just possibly, he might risk sending his other flyer, if in fact it exists. We should be prepared to take advantage of this possibility—which, admittedly, is not great."

"So then, what is your suggestion?"

"I think that we should immediately send out a transport for the marooned men, and also set up an ambush with two or three well-armed flyers. If Titus Pompo sends out his hypothetical flyer, we will either force it down, destroy it or possibly escort it here, to Araminta Station. If a boat appears, we can capture the Yips and sink their boat."

Bodwyn Wook looked around the group. "I can think of no better scheme. Unless there are objections, let us get to it, on the instant."

4

Scharde flew the large Agency tourist transporter to Thurben Island, with four Bureau B operatives in his company. Approaching the island, Scharde reduced speed and descended to an altitude of a thousand feet, then drifted north over the lagoon, at last to hover above the dock and pavilion. Two other flyers and a second transport loaded with three days' supply of food and water had already landed upon the central peak from which they would monitor sea and sky by radar.

Scharde's own radar showed a blank sea and empty air. Using binoculars, he inspected the area below, and discovered the four Yips crouching disconsolately on the beach near the base of the dock. The other six men were not to be seen.

Scharde dropped the transport to a landing close to the pavilion. With his three companions he jumped down to the sand. The Yips looked around apathetically. Scharde motioned to them. "Get into the transport."

They rose with an effort. One of them spoke in a husky whisper: "Give us water."

Scharde told his men: "Let them drink."

Down from the pavilion shambled the six men, haggard and wild-eyed. They had discarded their black hoods, revealing themselves to be middle-aged men of ordinary appearance, evidently from the upper reaches of society. They stumbled toward Scharde crying out for water in cracking voices.

Scharde indicated the transport. "Go on board and you will be given water."

The six men clambered into the passenger compartment, where they were provided water. Scharde took the transport aloft and flew back toward Araminta Station.

Fifteen minutes passed. The erstwhile castaways had drunk their fill, and were now cautiously assessing the situation. One called out to Scharde: "I say there, pilot! Where are you taking us?"

"To Araminta Station."

"Good. I may still be able to make my connections."

"I fear not," said Scharde. "You are all under arrest, on very serious charges. You will be going nowhere."

"What! You cannot be serious! After the privations and agonies we have known?"

"You have no lawful basis for such an act!" declared another. "I am a juridicalist of considerable eminence, and I assure you that you have no case at law. As for myself, I intend to demand a substantial refund, and possibly punitive damages."

"From whom? Araminta Station?"

"From Ogmo Enterprises, who else? The facilities were not as represented."

Another of the group endorsed the remarks. "That is accurate and to the point. I am utterly indignant, and I refuse to be mulcted!"

Scharde inquired: "You too are a juridicalist?"

"I fear that I cannot claim that distinction, although I have several such in my employ. I control a number of financial institutions, including a large bank. I am not accustomed to slackness and poor treatment."

Another member of the group spoke passionately: "The hardships to which I have been subjected are inexcusable! My rights have been violated and the Araminta authorities must bear full responsibility!"

"I fail to follow your reasoning," said Scharde.

"It is simple enough. I was inveigled by the proffer of a gracious reception and pleasant entertainment upon this world Cadwal; instead I have met only hardship, thirst, anxiety and discomfort. Someone must pay the penalty."

Scharde said with a laugh: "I suspect that the penalties to be paid will be paid by you."

Another cried out: "I am a Third Degree Acolyte at the Bogdar Kadesh; your imputations are outrageous. Our task is to promulgate the Right, not exemplify it in every trifling detail of our life. I strenuously reject your sly hints, and I must insist upon the respect due my cloth!"

"Just so," said Scharde.

At Araminta Station the castaways, despite a tumult of protests, were locked in an old stone warehouse, then, one after the other, brought to Bodwyn Wook's office for questioning. Present at the inquiry were Scharde, Egon Tamm the Conservator and Glawen.

The four Yips were first to be questioned; one at a time they were brought into Bodwyn Wook's office. Each told in effect the same story. All were Oomp cadets, specially selected to assist at the Thurben Island excursions. This last event had been the third in a series which had started about a month previously. They knew the dead woman only as "Sibil." She had participated in the second outing but not in the first. The four Yips disliked and feared Sibil: her demands were exacting and she tolerated none of the languid negligence which was their ordinary habit. Smartness and punctilio were Sibil's incessant concern: so reported the Yips, and each had a wincing tale to tell of blows and buffets.

The last Yip to be questioned was Saffin Dolderman Nivels: so he identified himself, and answered questions as if participating in a friendly and casual conversation. "I am truly happy to know that Sibil is dead," said Saffin. "She unnerved everyone, and did not make for happy times at the outings."

"Not even the girls enjoyed themselves," suggested Scharde.

"Ah well, it was not expected that they should," said Saffin. "Still, all in all, the excursions will go better with Sibil under the dock instead of on the beach. It will be instructive to look down at her bones."

Bodwyn Wook smiled thinly. "Saffin, you live in a strange and wonderful world."

Saffin nodded politely. "So it seems to me, as well. Of course, I know no other, which is a pity. I am the sort of man who dresses his fish not only with dragon-fire sauce but also sweet persimmon chutney."

Egon Tamm said: "The excursions occurred at two-week intervals. Was this the intended schedule for the future?"

"I don't know, sir. No one troubled to notify me." Saffin looked from face to face, smiling a vague smile. He rose tentatively to his feet. "Now, sirs, if your questions are finished, I and my comrades will go our ways. It is nice to talk with you, but duty calls with an iron voice, and we must not shirk the summons."

Bodwyn Wook chuckled. "Porlock the sociologist claimed that the Yips lacked all sense of humor. He should have heard your mordant jokes. You are a murderer and worse. You will be going nowhere except back to jail."

Saffin's face sagged in dejection. "Sir, I feared that you would take that line! But you have made a misjudgment! Such tasks as you mention are not to our liking, but what of that? For a good cadet, obedience rules the day!"

Bodwyn Wook nodded sagely. "You had no choice but to commit these ghastly crimes?"

"None whatever! I will vouch for it!"

Scharde suggested: "You might have resigned from the Oomps."

Saffin shook his head. "That would not have been a good plan."

"Not so," said Bodwyn Wook. "You will find that it would have been a very good plan indeed: in fact, the wisest plan of your entire lifetime."

Saffin spoke glumly: "In all justice, you should consider our need. When the rich woskers come with gleaming teeth, must we spurn their money?"

Bodwyn Wook ignored the question. "Did the rich woskers give their money to Sibil?"

"Never to Sibil, never to me! Not so much as a dinket for a job well done!"

"Did Sibil talk with the woskers? Perhaps they asked about her tattoo? Or might she have mentioned something to you?"

Saffin disdainfully flicked out his fingers. "To me Sibil spoke only commands which I must obey on the run. The second group were her friends and she talked with them, but only in regard to their conduct."

"How so?"

"They were peculiar people, in many ways, and would not touch the girls, but Sibil made threats and insisted that they fornicate, and they did their best to obey, for fear that she would carry out her threat."

"And what was the threat?"

"She said that they must fornicate either with the girls or with Sibil herself; they could choose at will. All made haste to use the girls."

"No doubt the wiser alternative," said Bodwyn Wook. "I might well have made the same choice. How else were these folk peculiar?"

Saffin could impart only vague impressions. "They were quite odd, but it was all the same to Sibil, and now that I think of it, there was talk of another excursion: a party of four female ladies and four men. I wondered what activities Sibil had in mind."

"Perhaps she meant to employ your own expert services."

Saffin blinked. "That is not considered my line of work."

"We shall never know, and speculation lacks all utility. What more can you tell us?"

"Nothing whatever! Surely you are now convinced of my innocence. Am I free to go?"

300

Bodwyn Wook gave an incredulous snort. "Do you not understand the awful deeds you have done? Do you feel no guilt? No shame?"

Saffin said earnestly: "Sir, you are old and wise, but you cannot apprehend every small and delicate phase of the cosmos!"

"Agreed! What, then?"

"Perhaps there is some trifling detail known to me but quite outside your range of expertise."

"Once more, agreed! Certain niceties of your work with the girls surpasses anything I might have hoped to achieve."

"All this being the case, would you think me disrespectful if I explained the rules by which you and I and all of us must control our conduct, if we wish to facilitate our lives?"

"Speak!" declared Bodwyn Wook. "I am always willing to learn."

"'Now' is 'now'! That is the liberating slogan! You must repeat it to yourself! 'Past' and 'bygone times'—these are vapid mental constructions, nothing else. What has happened is gone! It is vanished! It has become the abstraction of nothing! The so-called 'events of the past' might as well never have been, and it is the best part of expedience, and easier for all of us, to regard them in this light! Believe me, sir, not just this once but a thousand times over! Never succumb to bad habits! Brooding upon memories, wistful longing for some imaginary heyday: these are sure signs of ingressive senility. The proper way is to take life as it devolves: one must never grope to support himself on the smoke-wisps of what has already happened. 'Now' is 'now'! All else is footling and useless. In practical terms, 'now' is when I wish to leave this dreary chamber, which smells of generation after generation of wosker, and once again rejoice in the open air and sunlight."

"And so you shall," declared Bodwyn Wook. "I have been profoundly moved by your eloquence! You have earned yourself a stay of execution, if my colleagues will only agree!" He turned to the others. "Saffin has uttered some home truths! I now recommend that, rather than hanging these villains from a tree, or locking them forever in a dark dungeon, we allow them a kindly and useful future. First, they shall go out to Thurben Island, and while they enjoy the sunlight and open space they shall destroy the dock and pavilion, and restore conditions to the wild state. Then it shall be on to Cape Journal, where the vast open space and the wild winds will satisfy even Saffin's untamed spirit! The pleasure of devoting his life to useful toil is an added bonus—icing on the cake, so to speak."

"I, too, was affected by Saffin's philosophy," said Egon Tamm. "Your program is optimum, as Saffin will surely agree."

"Quite so," said Bodwyn Wook. "Saffin, you are a lucky man. Still, for the moment, you must return to the jail."

Saffin was led away protesting. Bodwyn Wook sat back in his chair. "It is difficult to sentence someone with so limpid a gaze and a smile so artless . . . Ah well, Saffin himself would be the first to decry sentimentality. What have we learned?"

"There have been some interesting bits and pieces," said Scharde. "Of course, they raise more questions than they answer."

"I am puzzled by Sibil," said Egon Tamm. "If I were conducting such excursions, I would employ a hostess who was charming and gracious—certainly not Sibil."

"It is a puzzle," said Bodwyn Wook. "But we must proceed. Scharde, I believe that you have had a few words with your principals?"

"I can supply some small information. They are all middle-aged persons of genteel background. All describe themselves as persons of importance. Each is outraged by his confinement and several have uttered threats. All are aggrieved and believe themselves victims of a swindle."

Bodwyn Wook heaved a sigh. "I suppose we must listen to their complaints. Perhaps we will glean a morsel or two of information."

The six participants at the Thurben Island excursion, one after the other, were brought into the chamber and subjected to interrogation. Like the Yips, all told the same story. They had learned of the excursion by way of brochures, issued by Ogmo Enterprises, which they had obtained at their travel agencies. Each described his interest as no more than casual curiosity, although each had paid the travel agent a thousand sols along with fares for passage to Araminta Station. None had met anyone connected with Ogmo Enterprises until their arrival at Yipton. At this point Sibil took them in hand. All reaffirmed their status, as persons of wealth and social position; none considered themselves sexual deviates or anything other than ordinary folk out for "a bit of a lark" or "just to candy a few apples." Another became indignant. "Me? A sexual pervert? You must be insane!"

Each of the six attempted to conceal his identity by means of a false name, in order that scandal or ugly rumor might be avoided. "It would not be useful to raise a great foofaraw; that is the long and short of it!" stated one, who described himself as a rancher. "My spouse would be greatly exercised."

"She need not know," said Bodwyn Wook. "Unless you want her present at your execution. It makes no difference to us whether we hang you under your right name or not."

"Eh? What are you saying? You cannot be serious!"

"I am not a frivolous man. Do I appear to be laughing?"

"No."

"That will be all for now, sir."

The rancher departed on hesitant feet, looking over his shoulder for some sort of reassuring signal, which was not forthcoming.

Another of the group, a self-styled "financier and banker" who gave his name as Alvary Irling, complained even more bitterly, and threatened legal action if his demands were not met. Bodwyn Wook asked: "How can you institute such charges if you are dead?"

"Dead? How should I be dead?"

"Execution for murder is acknowledged to be a cause of death, except in freak cases."

"That is nonsense!" declared Alvary Irling in a contemptuous voice.

"Nonsense, is it?" roared Bodwyn Wook. "Do you see yonder shardash tree? Perhaps before the day is out you will be dangling from that overhanging limb, where we can enjoy the spectacle!"

Alvary Irling said coldly: "I wish to consult my attorney."

"Your request is denied! He could only complicate a simple process, unless we hanged him as well, for conspiring to impede justice."

"If this is humor, I find it grotesque. I am an important man of many affairs, and this detention is causing me great inconvenience."

Still fulminating, Alvary Irling was taken back to the makeshift jail. Bodwyn Wook gave his head a shake of vexation. "I see no reason to waste any more time on this disgusting affair. The Conservator, of course, has the final word in matters of this sort."

"There can only be one judgment," said Egon Tamm. "First, execution of these six, then identification of the organizers and similar treatment for them, no matter where they are to be found."

"You will hear no disagreement from me," said Bodwyn Wook. He took notice of Scharde. "Am I wrong, or do you have other ideas?"

"Allow me to link together a few facts," said Scharde. "First: we know that sooner or later the Yips will try to swarm ashore into Marmion Province; if they succeed, it's all over for the Conservancy. At the moment we might or might not be able to turn them back; certainly our equipment is inadequate, and we can't get what we need because we lack money. Think a moment. We have in custody six wealthy criminals. If we kill them we have six carcasses. If each of them pays over a large indemnity—say, a million sols each—we have six million sols: enough to buy us two armed flyers and a permanent gun station over the Marmion Straits."

Bodwyn Wook spoke in a sour voice: "It is neither neat nor nice nor appealing."

"But very practical," said Egon Tamm. "Further, I do not need to consult those damnable Peefers. You won't get six million sols any other way—at least, not from Throy."

"Very well; it is so decided," said Bodwyn Wook. "I suggest that we add a thousand-sol surcharge, to finance our investigation of Ogmo Enterprises." He spoke into the mesh. "Bring in the six prisoners, all together."

The six Soumjians, still wearing the gray robes which had been their costume at Thurben Island, filed sullenly into the chamber, and were ranged in a line against the wall. Impelled by a mischievous caprice, Bodwyn Wook summoned his bailiff. "There they stand: six rascals in a row. Make a good photograph for the record, and note the names carefully." He addressed the prisoners. "Make sure that you announce your correct name to the bailiff; if you try to deceive us, we shall promptly discover the truth and it will be the worse for you."

"Come now!" rasped the man who called himself Alvary Irling. "What difference does it make what name we use?"

Bodwyn Wook ignored the question. "Your crimes are horrid. You might properly display some measure of shame, but remorse is clearly too much to expect. Therefore I read you no homilies; you would only find them dull. You will be more interested to learn that we have passed judgment and decided upon your penalty. Stop! No remarks! You must listen to me! Each of you deserves the instant extinction visited upon a noxious insect. I for one would take pleasure in watching you dance all together from the shardash tree, perhaps to the music of a string quartet, and it may come to that yet.

"Now, then: despite the revulsion caused by your mere presence in this room, we find that we need money more than carcasses. Not to mince matters, you may evade death by paying a fine of a million plus a thousand sols each."

For a moment the six stood in silence, as their perspectives shifted and they felt the full impact of this new calamity. One after the other began first to murmur, then to give full voice to his distress. "A million sols? You might as well ask for the moons of Geidion!" "To pay over a millions sols would ruin me!" And: "If I sold everything I could barely realize a million sols!"

Finally Bodwyn Wook lost his patience. "Very well. Those who choose to pay, go to yonder side of the room. Scharde, perhaps you will be kind enough to hang the others."

One of the men shouted in terror: "I would pay, but I could not realize such a sum on short notice!" "Nor I!" cried another. "A million sols is not what we casually carry about in our pockets! Can you not reduce the figure to, let us say, ten thousand, or even nine thousand, sols?"

"Aha!" said Bodwyn Wook. "Do you think to haggle? You shall pay the sum demanded and not a dinket less."

Scharde spoke quietly to his colleagues: "I notice that Alvary Irling, who is the banker, stands aloof and silent. Presumably he will pay the fine. It occurs to me that he might well extend loans to each of his companions and pay over to us the full sum of six million and six thousand sols. Upon his return to Soumjiana, he could deal in an ordinary manner with the debts."

"The concept lacks merit," declared Alvary Irling. "It is not my business to collect your ransoms for you."

"To the contrary!" said Bodwyn Wook. "It is a noble and expeditious idea, and simplifies the entire transaction."

"Perhaps from your point of view. I am a banker, not an altruist."

"Has it ever been any different?" asked Bodwyn Wook. "The terms are mutually contradictory."

"I know nothing of these persons; they show me no collateral, and I have no assurance of repayment."

"Sit down at the table and make out promissory notes. For you it should be all in a day's work, with even the possibility of profit to enliven your task."

"This is irregular, inconvenient and bad business practice," grumbled Alvary Irling. "A thousand difficulties lie in ambush ahead."

"Not at all," said Bodwyn Wook. "Prepare a draft upon your bank to the sum of six million and six thousand sols, and we will transmit it through the ordinary channels. As soon as the money is in our hands, the doors of the jail will open before you."

Scharde asked: "What is the name of your bank?"

"I am the Bank of Mircea."

"A solid institution!" said Bodwyn Wook. "Under happier circumstances it would be a pleasure doing business with you. Before you leave us, I may consult you in regard to my investments."

5

Glawen stood by the Hotel Araminta registration desk, considering the persons present in the lobby. A large contingent had just arrived aboard the Perseian Lines' packet *Sublume Overdyne*; was it possible that some of these apparently polite and well-behaved folk held

305

vouchers which would entitle them to a "Perfection of Joy" excursion on Thurben Island?

He studied first one group, then another. They need not be exclusively male; according to Saffin, Sibil had planned to entertain a party of four men and four women. Anyone traveling to Yipton might be considered a suspect.

These persons should not be hard to isolate. Visitors to Yipton already were examined to ensure that they carried no hard currency; the search might well be extended to include Perfection of Joy vouchers.

And then? Glawen turned away. These decisions happily were not his to make.

Glawen went to the manager's office and carefully studied the guest register, making such notes as he thought necessary.

The work required two hours. When he had finished he left the hotel and set out for the Old Arbor. Here he would meet his father, who had been making similar investigations at the spaceport terminal.

As Glawen passed the airstrip hangar he was hailed by Chilke. "Where are you bound for?"

"The Old Arbor."

"I'll stroll along with you, if there's no objection."

"None whatever."

The two walked along the beach road, then turned up Wansey Way. "I've been wanting to consult with you," said Chilke. "There's something gnawing at my mind."

"If there's something wrong, I didn't do it."

"It's something wrong I once did. Your father let fall a few words about Thurben Island and he mentioned a big bad-tempered lady by the name of Sibil."

"I remember her very well."

"According to Scharde, who took the information from you, this Sibil wore a black tattoo on her forehead: a two-pronged fork with the points turned in toward each other."

"That's my impression. I had only one good look, but it sticks with me."

"All this is very odd," said Chilke. "I can't begin to understand what is going on."

"How so?"

After a moment Chilke said: "I seem to recall telling you, a few years back, how I happened to arrive at Araminta Station."

"So you did, although I don't remember the details, I'm ashamed to say. Namour was involved, as I recall. You worked on a ranch where the lady in charge wanted to marry you."

"That's close enough. Do you recall how I described the lady?"

"Not really. I think you said she was tall and big and somewhat portly."

"That's true, so far as it goes. Also she had white skin, and a tattoo on her forehead: a two-pronged fork, with the points bent in toward each other."

"And you suspect that she might be Sibil?"

"Not having seen Sibil, I can't say. But I know something for sure: it wasn't just coincidence that brought me here to Araminta Station. But if not coincidence, then what, and why? Namely, why me, Eustace Chilke? If I asked Namour, he'd laugh in my face."

"No doubt you're right. It staggers me to think of the things Namour knows and keeps to himself."

Chilke laughed. "Namour is a marvel. But I'm interested in what this Sibil lady looked like, other than that she was big, mean and tattooed."

"You've covered the main points. She had a man's shoulders, big heavy hips and a big belly, all muscle, but no bust to speak of: just two shrunken bags which she tried to ignore. She had a long jaw, sunken cheeks, a long low nose that might have been broken once upon a time in a fight. Her skin was white as chalk, and her mouth was just a gray mark. Her hair? It was sandy brown and stiff, like a scrub brush. All taken with all, I'd call her middling-ugly, and she smelled bad to boot."

"That doesn't sound much like Madame Zigonie, tattoo and big arse regardless. She had a round face with round cheeks and a fine bust, not to mention reddish-black curls."

"The hair could have been a wig."

"I don't think so. I'm satisfied Sibil was someone else. You should try to find out where ladies wear that kind of tattoo."

"That's a good idea. We'll call IPCC Information; we're affiliates, as I guess you know."

"That makes you a full-fledged IPCC agent. People take that rank seriously around the Reach." Chilke came to a halt. "I've learned what I wanted, so I'll get back to work."

Glawen went on to the Old Arbor. Scharde had not yet arrived. He seated himself at a table to the side, in the dappled shade of the foliage. He ordered a dish of salted fish and a flask of the Diffin Soft Green Elixir, and settled himself to wait.

Time passed. Glawen ordered another flask of wine and, leaning forward, tilted the goblet back and forth, sending films of light swirling through the pale green liquid.

An expanse of russet satin obtruded across his vision. Slowly he raised his eyes, knowing full well what to expect: a black vest embroidered with purple birds in green vines, a thick white neck, a large face from which black eyes glittered like fire opals and, surmounting all, a great tumble of dark curls, constrained by some mysterious means in a quasi-cylindrical shape, although recently Spanchetta had taken to wearing roguish little curls down over each ear.

Spanchetta inspected Glawen with heavy jocosity, only partially masking dislike and disapproval. Glawen stared back like a bird hypnotized by a snake.

Spanchetta asked: "Is this how the Bureau B types toil away the hours? I see that I am attached to the wrong bureau. I too enjoy my rest."

"You are making a mistake," said Glawen politely. "I am here by order of my superiors. Despite appearances, I am hard at work."

Spanchetta gave a curt nod. "Since you have nothing better to do, perhaps you will provide me some information."

"I will do my best. Do you care to sit?"

Spanchetta settled into a chair across the table. "Explain, if you will, the secrecy which now pervades Bureau B. Everyone knows that something is in the air, but no one troubles to elucidate. Why, then, pray tell me, all this furtive activity?"

Glawen smilingly shook his head. "You put me at a disadvantage. I cannot properly answer you."

"Certainly you can! Did you not hear my question? Have you lost the use of your tongue?"

"Assume," said Glawen, "that these secrets existed. Assume that for some reason they had been confided to me. In such a case, I would not be allowed to reveal my knowledge to everyone who casually put a question to me. This is a hypothetical case, of course; still, if you wish to set your mind at ease, why not make your inquiries of Bodwyn Wook?"

Spanchetta made a contemptuous sound. "You are very verbose; uncharacteristically, I must say. It is more than noticeable. How much wine have you consumed, as you sit here working?"

"Not a great deal. May I order a flask for you?"

"Thank you, no. I must shortly return to my own work, and it would not do to stagger into my office singing and dancing, as seems perfectly acceptable at Bureau B."

In order to change the subject, and for lack of a better topic, Glawen asked: "How goes it with Arles? Have you had news? Or are his activities also classified 'secret'?"

Before Spanchetta could blurt a response, Scharde approached the table. He seated himself and looked quizzically at Spanchetta. "Are you just coming or just going? Or will you join us in a cup or two of wine?"

Spanchetta hesitated, then with great dignity acquiesced to the invitation. "I have been trying to learn the meaning of the muted whispers and furtive signals which are prevalent every time two or more Bureau B people get together. Glawen has found a clever means to evade questions; he proposes all sorts of hypotheses and conundrums, and while I am puzzling out the answers, he changes the subject. Perhaps you have a wider range of discretion."

"I hope so. In sheer point of fact, there is much to preoccupy us nowadays, what with events on Stroma and Titus Pompo ever more of a nuisance. We are about to lose patience with him."

Glawen said blandly: "Just as you came up, Spanchetta was about to report the latest news of Arles."

"That is not quite accurate," said Spanchetta with a sniff. "I have had no news."

"Ah well, Arles is probably engrossed in his own affairs," said Scharde. He poured a goblet for Spanchetta. "I still wonder that you encouraged him to marry a collateral, and a Laverty at that."

Spanchetta replied in a plangent voice. "I did not encourage the match. Indeed, I was astounded that Arles should take such a step without consulting me. He suspected, perhaps, that Drusilla, with her ambiguous antecedents, would not have been my first choice."

"The hay is in the barn now," said Scharde.

"Precisely so." Spanchetta drank half the contents of the goblet at a gulp. She set it back down with a thump. "In any event, you are a fine one to cavil, when I recall how you misled and mistreated poor Smonny, and drove her to distraction."

"It was a tragic case," said Scharde. "Still, I suspect that she ended up in good shape. She was a woman of great persistence. It's odd that you never heard from her."

"Not altogether. Simonetta was a sensitive and truly delightful girl."

"Something of a hellion, so I recall. Spanny and Smonny: the two of you made quite a pair."

Spanchetta disdained comment. She drained the goblet and rose to her feet. "Not being employed in Bureau B, I find that I must go to work, none the wiser—naturally enough—for all my questions."

Spanchetta marched away and departed the Old Arbor. Scharde brought out a notebook. "I have been to the ferry terminal, which made me a few minutes late. But no matter; I noted down a most informative list. These are just names, but we can match them against the spaceport list and the hotel list and discover the home worlds."

"Something occurred to me while I was at the hotel. A new shipload of tourists arrived this morning. Some of them might be carrying Perfection of Joy vouchers."

"True," said Scharde. "I'll mention the matter to Bodwyn Wook; maybe he'll want to look into the possibility. For now, let's compare our lists."

6

Upon leaving the Old Arbor Glawen went directly to the Bureau B offices, where he was intercepted by Hilda, the thin and astringent secretary. Hilda distrusted all Clattucs for what she felt to be their "fleering and domineering" habits; she regarded Glawen with particular suspicion, since to the typical Clattuc qualities he added another dimension of crafty and almost sinister politeness which could only be contrived. No question about it! Glawen was a master of intrigue; how else had he progressed so far and so fast in the good opinion of the Supervisor? Therefore, to Glawen's request that he be immediately allowed access to Bodwyn Wook, Hilda stated that Bodwyn Wook did not wish to be disturbed, and had issued orders to this effect—which, in a certain sense, was the case.

After Glawen had cooled his heels for an hour, Bodwyn Wook looked into the outer office and saw Glawen sitting in a chair.

Bodwyn Wook jerked to a halt. "Glawen! Why are you sitting so placidly? Have you nothing better to do?"

"I have indeed, sir, but your secretary prefers that I sit here in this chair."

Bodwyn Wook raked Hilda with a cold stare. "What foolishness is this? Surely you must know that Glawen is to be sent in the moment he shows himself?"

"Your orders were explicit."

"No matter! Interpret them with a more flexible intelligence henceforth! You have wasted everyone's time! Come, Glawen."

Bodwyn Wook led the way into his office and dropped into his great black chair. "What have you learned?"

Glawen placed three sheets of paper on the desk. "My father and I sorted through records at the spaceport, the hotel and the ferry. These are the names which match up with the three excursions."

Bodwyn Wook studied the lists. "The first party would be this group from Natrice: Sir Mathor Borph and Sir Lonas Medlyn from Halcyon City; also SS. Guntil, SS. Foum, SS. Nobile, SS. Koldach, SS. Rolp and SS. Buler from Lanklands. SS.? These honorifics mystify me. What does 'SS.' indicate?"

"I don't know."

Bodwyn Wook put the Natrice sheet aside. "The second party: six folk from Tassadero, which I believe to be a planet of Zonk's Star. Zonk, of course, was Zab Zonk the Pirate, infamous up and down the Wisp. Hmm. I see no reference to Sibil."

"We think that she might be 'S. Devella of Pogan's Point.'"

"These other men derive from Lutwiler Country. What signifies this word in parentheses: 'Zubenites'?"

"I looked up Tassadero in the reference guide. Fexelburg is the spaceport: a 'modern, progressive city,' according to the guide. Lutwiler Country is out on the Eastern Steppe, and is populated by members of the Zubenite sect."

Bodwyn Wook looked at the third list. "These are the gentlemen from Soum, whom we have in custody. There seem to be no surprises here." Bodwyn Wook put the lists aside and leaned back in his chair. "We seem to make some small progress. Let me explain my thinking. The excursions depend upon three elements: Titus Pompo, the customers and the organizer, sometimes known as Ogmo Enterprises. He is now the only unknown element in the case, but we cannot let it rest there. He is possibly the worst scoundrel of the lot; also, he may well be someone already known to us. I will not, at this time, hazard any guesses or put forward any names, not even in idle speculation. Suffice to say, he must be tracked down, identified and taken into custody. What do you say to that?"

"Nothing, sir. I agree."

"Quite so." Bodwyn Wook raised his eyes to the ceiling. "I will point out that, in order to conduct an investigation, one needs investigators. Your name has been mentioned in such a connection. You would be required to travel off-world, to Natrice, Tassadero and Soum, and on each of these worlds make appropriate inquiries. Does the program interest you?"

"Yes, sir."

"This person—for lack of a better name I shall call him Ogmo—has certainly left traces. He has dealt with travel agencies and issued a brochure. Money must have been paid to the travel agencies, then transferred to Ogmo. Such transactions must have left further traces: all of which, if properly followed, should lead to Ogmo. Do I make myself clear?"

"Yes, sir."

"Good. Aside from these general points, I can offer no further guidelines. You and your colleague must use your notable ingenuities and develop your own lines of inquiry. Now, then: do you have questions?"

"Yes, sir, I surely do. You used the word 'colleague.' I have already had one bitter experience of working with a colleague, namely Kirdy, and I don't want to repeat the mistake. All in all, I am sure that I can work to better effect alone."

Bodwyn Wook frowned and cleared his throat. "I fear that, in this case, we must regretfully give second priority to your personal preferences. For various reasons, all of considerable importance, I think it best that you work with an associate."

Glawen sought for words, framing and discarding a number of remarks, while Bodwyn Wook watched him with owl-like imperturbability. Finally Glawen asked: "And whom do you have in mind as this associate?"

"Working with an associate is not the end of the world," said Bodwyn Wook bluffly. "Perhaps your previous experience with Kirdy was not fully successful, but we must learn from our mistakes. You will definitely be in charge, and I'm sure that extra eyes, extra hands and the extra force of a keen Wook mind will often prove of value. And—as I indicated—there are other reasons why the arrangement is important."

"You mean that I must work with Kirdy—again?"

"Responsible work is essential to Kirdy's recovery. He must bring his mind down from the clouds and focus it on reality." Bodwyn Wook spoke into his communicator. "Is Kirdy on hand?"

Kirdy entered the office. His eyes fell upon Glawen, and instantly seemed to become round and glassy.

"Here you are, the two of you: back together again!" So called out Bodwyn Wook in fulsome tones. "Since that Yipton dustup Kirdy has been a bit off his feed, but now he's as right as rain, and ready for action. What he needs is stimulation and good hard work, to exercise the talents which are his Wook birthright. This investigation is exactly the proper prescription and an opportunity which we can't neglect! Especially since the two of you have worked together before."

Kirdy smiled: a slow cool twisting of the mouth. "So we have."

Glawen said anxiously: "For this reason alone, Kirdy might not be comfortable working as my subordinate. It might be better if—"

"Nonsense!" declared Bodwyn Wook. "By this time you two know each other's foibles and fancies, and you should be able to cooperate in full harmony."

Kirdy nodded ponderously. "I find this truly a wonderful opportunity."

"Then it is settled," said Bodwyn Wook. He spoke into the communicator: "Hilda, if you please!"

Hilda entered the office. Bodwyn Wook said: "Prepare travel credentials for Glawen and Kirdy. I now promote them both to the rank of sergeant; use that designation."

"Wait!" cried Glawen. "If I am required to deal with off-world police, I would prefer higher credentials, if only for this particular assignment. I suggest the rank of captain, at the very least."

"The point is well-taken! Hilda, that shall be the way of it!"

Hilda sniffed and cast a sour glance toward Glawen. "What of Kirdy? Is he only to be a sergeant? He might also have to deal with policemen."

Bodwyn Wook made an expansive gesture. "Just so! Both, during this assignment, are to be captains of the Cadwal Police! Probably the youngest captains in the history of Bureau B!"

Hilda said: "Glawen doesn't even command full Agency status, and the way things look, he never will. Isn't this something of an extravagance, making him a captain?"

"Not at all," said Bodwyn Wook. "Neither law nor common sense debars a collateral from whatever rank he is able to earn."

Again Hilda sniffed. "I've heard it said that for three diseases—pride, pomp and Clattuc birth—a strong dose of humility is the best medicine."

"Aha!" cried Bodwyn Wook. "These trifles of folk wisdom often conceal nuggets of pure truth! . . . What is that you are saying, Glawen?"

"I cited another nugget of folk wisdom. It's just as well that it went unheard."

Kirdy spoke in a flat voice: "He said: 'A cow that has never been bred yields very sour milk, if any.'"

Bodwyn Wook rubbed his chin. "Quaint, yes; relevant, no. Hilda, you are going?"

"I have work to do."

"Call the travel office and discover the next departure for Soumjiana on Soum."

"I can tell you at this moment," said Glawen. "The *Sagittarian Ray* departs at noon tomorrow."

"Very good. Captain Clattuc and Captain Wook, go at once to the travel bureau and procure passage vouchers, then pack for the voyage. I urge that you make do with one small valise apiece. Tomorrow morning come here for your credentials, money and final advisements."

Glawen and Kirdy departed the office. In silence they descended the stairs. On the ground floor Glawen said: "Let us sit a moment in the rotunda."

"Why?"

"I have something to say to you."

Kirdy turned aside and followed Glawen to a bench near the central fountain. Glawen seated himself and indicated that Kirdy should also be seated.

Kirdy stiffly refused. "I will stand. What do you want of me?"

Glawen spoke in a neutral voice. "We must resolve the issues that lie between us, here and now. They can wait no longer."

Kirdy laughed: a husky grating sound. "I am in no hurry. I can wait—until the proper time."

"The proper time is now."

"Really?" Kirdy chuckled. "Is it for you to call the tune to which I must dance?"

"It is for me to ensure that this mission goes smoothly. Under present conditions, it is not possible."

"That is a fair statement. What, then, must we settle?"

"Your antagonism. It is not justified."

Kirdy frowned in puzzlement. "You are not talking sensibly. After all, it is my antagonism, not yours. How can you know on what basis it is founded?"

"Your sufferings at Yipton were severe. I did not share them, and for this reason you are resentful. Am I correct?"

"In some degree."

"Your own blunders and bad judgment brought on your troubles. It is not rational to blame me. It is the work of your subconscious mind, which does not want to admit a fault. You must bring yourself under control."

Kirdy laughed once more. "Spare me your platitudes. I will use the mental processes I find most convenient."

Glawen studied Kirdy's face. The large blunt features, once so easy, pink and mild, now seemed to be formed from rigid cartilage. Glawen asked uneasily: "Why not use your ordinary old conscious mind? That seems a good plan to me."

"Ah, little do you know! That mind was smashed into twittering little gobbets; they fly blindly back and forth through my head like

314

bats in a dark room. I find them a source of annoyance, since another mind is now in charge, and the annoyances will be" —here Kirdy pinched his thumb and forefinger together— "so. And thus . . ." Kirdy stopped short.

"And thus what?"

"Nothing."

"Do you want advice?"

"I will listen, whether I want it or not. I thereby learn!" Kirdy gave Glawen a knowing leer. "Advise on, Glawen! Let us learn how you would assist me in my career."

"First, why be in such a hurry to expunge your old mind? Maybe it will join together again. Second—"

"I already know the second. Stay at home. Rest, enjoy life, read some amusing books. Let Glawen advance his career in peace."

"Call it what you like, but the facts are real. We cannot work together if every time I turn my back you pick up an ax. That makes for uncomfortable conditions."

Kirdy considered. "Only from your point of view."

"But you fail to grasp the central point! You have no reason for this attitude!"

Kirdy looked off across the rotunda and spoke in boredom: "Oh, I have reason! Several reasons! Many reasons! You will never know them! Perhaps they could not be put into words! Perhaps they are even irrational. If so, who cares? I feel them, nonetheless."

"If you recognize these reasons as irrational, can you put them aside?"

"If necessary."

"Do you agree that it is necessary?"

"I will give the matter thought . . . Where are you going?"

"Back up to Bodwyn Wook's office."

"I will come with you."

Hilda wordlessly ushered the two back into the inner office. Bodwyn Wook looked up in irritation. "What is it now?"

"This situation is impossible," said Glawen. "Kirdy is not in good mental health! He won't even promise not to kill me!"

"Of course he won't!" snapped Bodwyn Wook. "Why should he? Have I promised not to kill you? Has Hilda? Has anyone? You are on the verge of hysteria!"

Glawen strove to keep his voice calm. "Let me put it this way. A team cannot function if its members do not trust each other. Kirdy is not sane and I don't see how I can work with him."

Bodwyn Wook turned to Kirdy: "Let us settle this once and for all. Are you sane or not?"

"I consider myself sane."

"Can you work with Glawen?"

"The question more properly should be: 'Can he work with me?'"

Glawen started to speak, but Bodwyn Wook waved his arms high in the air. "Glawen, you may go! I will talk to Kirdy and put this affair into perspective. Not another word! I will see you in the morning."

Glawen marched from the room, through the outer office and down the stairs. In the rotunda he walked back and forth, inclining first toward one desperate plan, then another. At last, cursing under his breath, he went into the travel office and picked up his vouchers for passage aboard the *Sagittarian Ray*.

During the evening he kept his problems to himself, and Scharde asked no questions. In the morning, Glawen walked down to the Bureau B offices and along the way met Kirdy, turned out in a spanking-new Bureau B uniform, with the captain's red piping prominent. Kirdy looked Glawen up and down in disfavor. "Why are you not in uniform?"

"Because I don't choose to be, and because it is not at all appropriate to the mission."

"That is not for you, but for me, to determine." Kirdy turned away and strode off to the Bureau B offices, with Glawen coming behind more slowly.

Arriving at Bureau B, Glawen reported to Hilda, who placed a folder containing his documents in front of him. Glawen glanced though them; all seemed in order. "Now, then, where is my money?"

With hands trembling in reluctance, Hilda tendered him a packet. "Count the contents. You will find a thousand sols. It is a great deal of money. Be very careful with it; you will be issued no further sums."

Glawen counted the money, tucked documents and packet into the inner pocket of his jacket. Hilda watched with cold amusement. "If you carry your money in that pocket, it will be stolen immediately. Have the seamstress sew pockets on the inside of your trouser legs. This is where you should carry your funds."

"These pockets are already in place, but I delayed using them," said Glawen. "I feared that removing my trousers in your presence might offend you."

"Pish," sneered Hilda. "What do I care, one way or the other?" She jerked her head toward the inner office. "You may go in; the Supervisor is expecting you."

Glawen went through the door to find Bodwyn Wook standing by the window. "Sir, it is I, Glawen."

Bodwyn Wook turned and slowly came to his desk. He seated himself and at last deigned to take note of Glawen. "You are ready to go?"

Glawen looked at him sharply; was he mistaken, or did Bodwyn Wook's demeanor seem constrained? Glawen said firmly: "No, sir. I am not ready to go. I can only reiterate that Kirdy is incapable of conducting sensitive work. I just met him dressed in a new uniform, advertising to all the Reach that he is employed by Bureau B. What is worse, he chided me for being out of uniform."

"Ah yes! Poor Kirdy is perhaps a trifle distrait. I rely on your sturdy common sense to even the balance. You have received your documents? And your money? Also your rectification pills?"

"I picked up a kit at the pharmacy."

"Throw away the stuff called Erythrist; it's useless, especially against Soumian itch. They'll give you a specific at the Soum spaceport; you'll get it as you pass through the wicket. So then: you are all ready."

Glawen began to feel desperate. "Sir, I cannot work with Kirdy under present conditions."

"Come, now, Glawen! We must take the long view. The experience will not only help Kirdy but may well expand your own capacities."

"What, then, is my mission? To investigate the Thurben Island case or to provide therapy for Kirdy?"

Bodwyn Wook's voice sharpened. "Come, Glawen! Your anxieties are fast becoming tiresome. Does your question truly need an answer?"

"I'm sorry to annoy you, sir, but perhaps it can't be helped. Does Kirdy carry his own money?"

"He has been issued a substantial sum."

"How much, exactly?"

"Two thousand sols, if you must know. It is a great deal of money, but bribes might be necessary."

"But I was issued only a thousand sols."

"That should be sufficient."

"You have made it absolutely clear that I am in charge?"

"Well—I believe that was more or less implicit."

Glawen heaved a deep breath. "Be good enough to write me an exact definition of my authority, stating that Kirdy must obey my orders in every detail."

Bodwyn Wook performed a small airy gesture. "In this business we must deal with practicalities. I left the subject of authority a trifle vague. As you know, I want to augment Kirdy's self-esteem in every possible way. In fact, I might even have hinted that he was in charge of the operation."

Glawen threw documents and money down on the desk. "In that case, my presence can only have an adverse effect upon the mission. The effort Kirdy puts in trying to murder me, and my efforts trying to avoid death, are both counterproductive. With enormous relief I definitely withdraw from the operation."

Bodwyn Wook's eyes snapped with anger. "You are singing a brassy song! I advise you to moderate your legato."

"Even better, I shall do my singing elsewhere. I bid you good day." Glawen bowed and strode furiously for the door. In a sullen voice Bodwyn Wook called out: "Come back here! Can't you take a joke? You are as humorless as Hilda. You shall have your memorandum."

"I want much more than that. You must clearly inform Kirdy of my authority, and you must reduce his rank to sergeant."

"I can't do that! I have already confirmed the appointment."

"Explain that you have made a mistake. Further, I will take custody of his two thousand sols. He shall carry only a hundred sols pocket money. Next, instruct him to change from his uniform into less conspicuous clothes."

"All this is impossible! The ship leaves in an hour!"

"There is time. If necessary, the ship can wait. In any case I will not be aboard unless I am relieved of Kirdy's therapy. I would a thousand times prefer to go alone."

Bodwyn Wook shook his head. "You are a willful young devil! If insolence were bricks and insubordination mortar you could build a great palace for yourself."

"Not so, sir! You would never have given in so easily if I were not right!"

Bodwyn Wook laughed. "Don't try to psychoanalyze your supervisor; that is the most flagrant act of all! Hilda! Where is Kirdy?"

"Here in the outer office."

"Send him in."

Kirdy entered the office. Bodwyn Wook rose to his feet. "I tried to handle this affair by mishandling it. I was wrong, and now I must put things right. There is no animus in my judgment; I am fond of both of you. But there can only be a single commander to any operation, and it will be Glawen. Kirdy, you will obey Glawen in all lawful orders. I must reduce your rank to sergeant, temporarily, I hope, and you must change from the uniform, since essentially this is a secret investigation. If you have grievances against Glawen, you must here and now put them aside, or resign from the mission. What is it to be?"

Kirdy shrugged. "Whatever you say."

"I will take that to signify acquiescence. Finally, I will take custody of the money Hilda issued to you this morning."

Kirdy stood motionless, his face white, only his eyes alive. Slowly he reached into his pocket, brought out the packet of money and placed it upon the table.

Bodwyn Wook said: "You must not consider this a defeat or a setback; your career is open before you. What have you to say?"

"I have heard your commands."

"Will you try to work on amicable terms with Glawen?"

"I will work with him, for the good of Araminta Station. My feelings are my own."

Glawen said: "You are certainly not the ideal associate, but it seems that we must work together. Let us be altogether forthright. You are now convalescent but you still suffer a disability which you described to me yesterday. Will not this disability make full cooperation difficult for you?"

Kirdy stood silent. Bodwyn Wook and Glawen stared at him, as did Hilda from the back of the room, all prepared for the qualified or ambiguous reply which would irrevocably remove Kirdy from the operation.

Kirdy said tonelessly: "Yes. We shall work together."

Glawen spoke curtly: "Then go change into ordinary clothes and go directly to the spaceport. I'll see you aboard the ship."

Kirdy departed. Glawen waited ten seconds, then came forward, took the money from the table. "We will do our best." He left the room.

Bodwyn Wook sighed. "Clattuc or not, he's got plenty of good Wook blood in him. I truly admire that proud young rascal. He's quick-minded and hard as nails, but there's a sweetness about him that makes all right. I could wish he were my own son."

Hilda gave a soft snort. "I'm long past the age of wishing. Still, once in a while, I wish. If there had been a Glawen when I was young, things might have gone differently for me."

CHAPTER 7

1

Glawen, stepping up into the hulk of the *Sagittarian Ray*, felt a pleasant excitement; never before had he traveled off-world. Kirdy, on the other hand, had toured far and wide with Floreste's Mummers, up and down Mircea's Wisp. The worlds of the present itinerary, Natrice, Soum and Tassadero, were of no novelty to Kirdy, and his mood, as he boarded the spaceship, was glum. Several times he paused to look back over his shoulder as if ready to abandon the entire venture.

A steward conducted the two to their cabins. Glawen delayed only long enough to slide his luggage into a rack and hang up his cloak, then went out upon the promenade, which gave him a view of the spaceport observation deck. There stood his father and Bodwyn Wook, who had come to see them off and to issue final instructions. Bodwyn Wook had been emphatic on several points: "Never mind that you are a Clattuc and snort fire through your nostrils! This is a delicate case and wants delicate handling. Neither curt language nor sarcasm speeds the efficiency of off-world police; they have not had your advantages, so deal with them gently. In fact, obey all local laws, whether you understand them or not! You are Bureau B agents, with IPCC affiliation, but local police often neglect such niceties."

Scharde augmented Bodwyn Wook's remarks. "On Tassadero you will wear local clothes as a matter of convenience. Hawkers will meet you at the spaceport, and urge you to buy from their barrows. Despite their outcries, insults and ridicule, wait till you arrive in Fexelburg, then go to a shop with posted prices. Otherwise, you will be swindled. The spirit of Zab Zonk the Pirate survives in many forms on Tassadero."

Bodwyn Wook issued a further warning: "Avoid politics everywhere! The factions are particularly angry on Natrice, which will be your first stop. There is little chance that you would become embroiled; still, guard your opinions!"

"I hope I can keep all this straight," said Glawen. "On Natrice, avoid politics. On Tassadero, dress to the fashion, but do not be swindled. What should we fear on Soum?"

"Marriage," said Scharde. "If you take a girl to bed, insist that she first sign a specific repudiation of marital intent. These forms are available at kiosks and sweetshops."

"I suggest that you go aboard," said Bodwyn Wook. "The ship might leave while you stand here listening to our final instructions."

Standing by a window along the promenade, Glawen waved toward Scharde and Bodwyn Wook, but they failed to see him. Glawen swallowed the lump in his throat and pretended that he felt no forebodings or fears.

A few late arrivals came running from the terminal and thankfully boarded the ship. Imminence grew heavy in the air. A chime sounded. Glawen felt the dull impact of ports thudding shut. A thin whine from no apparent source rose in pitch and passed beyond audibility. Without sensible acceleration the ship rose from the soil of Cadwal into the sky.

Glawen looked along the promenade. Kirdy was nowhere to be seen. Glawen turned back to the outside view. Kirdy had known terrible events, and deserved whatever compassion as might conveniently and practically be extended.

Cadwal became a ball, bright in the lemon-white shine of Syrene. Far to the south Throy was a black-green wedge. Glawen tried to find the site of Stroma, without success. Wistful thoughts of Wayness entered his mind; when would he see her again? And what would she have to tell him?

Kirdy came slouching along the promenade, face somber, eyes unfocused. Glawen saw that he would walk wordlessly past. Despite his previous pang of sympathy, he was now a trifle nettled. He called out: "Kirdy! Over here! Look at me! I'm Glawen!"

Kirdy halted, pondered a moment, then joined Glawen by the window.

"Let me propound a syllogism," said Glawen. "'The world is real. I am part of the world. Hence I am real.'"

Kirdy reflected. "I am not sure that the logic is totally rigorous. You should have phrased the first premise thus: 'The world is made of real parts.' Or: 'Every part of the world is real.' And next: 'I am one of these parts.' In the latter case you leave unresolved the question as to whether an aggregation of real parts necessarily constitutes a real whole."

"I'll give the matter some thought," said Glawen. "Meanwhile, you and I are both aboard the ship. We cannot avoid each other—at least not altogether. These are the facts."

Kirdy only shrugged and looked off along the promenade.

With great politeness Glawen asked: "Do you still enjoy the view? I suppose you have seen it many times."

Kirdy glanced out the window, as if only just now taking note of the spectacle. "As you say, I've seen it before. It doesn't change much. Sometimes Lorca and Sing hang out there like a pair of carrion birds, sometimes not. Floreste never liked to see them; he thought they brought bad luck. He had dozens of such quirks and fancies, which we ignored at our risk."

Glawen asked: "How long were you with the Mummers?"

"Seven years. I started when I was ten. I was one of the original Tumble-bugs."

"It must have been a great adventure."

Kirdy grunted. "Floreste kept us hard at it. Half the time we never knew where we were, although we usually made the same run: Natrice, Soum, sometimes out to Protagne or Tassadéro or New Calvary, or even Mildred's Blue World, then back to the Wisp and Old Lumas, and once or twice down to Caffin's World. We never went much farther."

"Why was that?"

"We'd go as far as Floreste could promote cheap transportation; he's an avaricious old devil—not for himself, mind you, but for his new Orpheum."

"Which of these worlds did you like the best?"

Kirdy replied in a measured monotone. "Floreste fed us better on Soum. Natrice was dull and very moral, especially out along the Lanklands, where food was the worst. We were served cakes of shredded nettles and a sour black lizard soup. The only sweets were shriveled little pellets like raisins, which I learned were dried insects. Floreste would only go to the Lanklands when he couldn't fill our schedule in Poinciana or Halcyon or Summer City. The Sanart Scientists have a law which bars heterosexual pageants to heterosexual audiences. Floreste ignored the law but no one bothered him, since his shows were so innocent, particularly among the Sanart Scientists."

"Sanart Scientists?" Illumination came to Glawen's mind. "So that's where the 'SS.' in front of names comes from."

"They'll all SS. this or SS. that," said Kirdy. "It's a mark of dignity."

"What of the ladies? Are they dignified too?"

"They'd like to be, I'm sure. But they're Vs. this and Vs. that."

"Which means what?"

Kirdy shrugged. "Floreste said it meant 'Vessel,' but he might have been joking. They wear long black gowns and funny black hats. Floreste said it was because ladies were inherently frivolous. The Scientist ladies looked more woebegone than anything else. I'm told that each morning at dawn everyone bathes in cold water."

"I'd be woebegone too," said Glawen.

Kirdy gave an abstracted nod. "We heard strange stories about the Sanart Scientists."

"The strangest of all is that six Sanart Scientists went out to Thurben Island, along with Sir Mathor Borph and Sir Lonas Medlyn from Halcyon."

"Those last two are Patrunes, which means 'aristocrats.' Ordinarily they're not on good terms with the Sanart Scientists, but I guess on Thurben Island all cats are gray. Ah, me. It's none of our business, after all."

Glawen turned him a puzzled glance. "Certainly it's our business, if it helps us identify Ogmo."

"Don't you really think it's a lot of wasted energy? This is just one of Bodwyn Wook's famous flaming uproars. The old baboon fears he'll be ignored otherwise. The Thurben Island parties are stopped; what more does he want?"

"He wants to capture the villains responsible, so that they won't do it again. It's a fine idea."

"I'm not so sure," said Kirdy. "Get rid of one villain; two others jump up to take his place. This Ogmo business is a sheer mare's nest, a tangle of false starts and folly. And whom do we find skulking and hiding and dashing about in a lather of sweat and discomfort? Is it Bodwyn Wook? Not on your life. It's a pair of young varlets, Glawen Clattuc and Kirdy Wook."

Glawen said dolefully: "That is our lot in life."

"Bah!" said Kirdy. "Why should we bother? The same stuff goes on at Yipton, if someone cares to pay the price."

"I suspect that you are right," said Glawen. A soft voice from the nunciators announced lunch. "In any event, this is our assignment and I'd prefer to do it properly than otherwise. What about you?"

Kirdy merely turned Glawen a stony glance, which Glawen pretended not to notice.

The two went aft to the dining saloon and seated themselves at a table. A pop-up screen displayed the bill of fare; Kirdy glanced at it, then looked away.

Again Glawen raised his eyebrows. Kirdy was full of surprises. Glawen asked: "What looks good to you?"

"I'm not particular. I'll have whatever you're having."

Glawen was reluctant to make himself responsible for the quality of Kirdy's meals. "You'd better order for yourself. I don't want to be blamed if you don't like what you get."

"I'll just have some bread and stew."

"That's simple enough, although here it's called ragout."

"I don't care what it's called."

Glawen put through the order. Kirdy was served the ragout, but found it not to his liking. "I wanted plain stew. This is doused up with some strange extragalactic sauce. I wish you had ordered stew, as I asked."

"After this, you take care of your own meals. Why should I order your stew in the first place?"

Kirdy shrugged but offered no explanation. Glawen watched him surreptitiously. He asked cautiously: "These bits and pieces of your conscious mind—are they starting to come together?"

"I don't think so."

"Too bad. Bodwyn Wook is hoping that this trip, with new scenery and new experiences, will straighten you out. What is your opinion of that?"

"He's wrong, but he is the master, and must be obeyed."

"That's one way of looking at it," said Glawen.

Kirdy went on in a bleak voice: "Everything considered, I'd just as soon be home. I don't know anything about this Ogmo business. Perhaps it is right; perhaps it is wrong. Your company is forced on me, despite my reluctance; each time you speak my fist balls up so that I may smash it in your face. It may be a good and proper act; still I am a careful man and I desist, because I would forfeit your assistance out here among these strange people and strange noises. I would be left alone. Alone, alone, as if groping in the dark."

Glawen managed an uneasy grin. "You premises are distorted but your analysis is correct. If you smashed my face, I would not only smash your face but I would have nothing more to do with you. So, continue to desist." And he added: "Especially since I am your appointed master and this is my order."

Kirdy pursed his lips. "True! That is a good point."

As the voyage progressed, Kirdy became ever more dependent, a situation Glawen found both irking and bizarre. Kirdy's favorite topics were the old times, when he and Glawen were children. In painstaking detail he recalled incidents which Glawen had forgotten, then derived meanings and portents which Glawen usually found both farfetched and inaccurate.

After a few such episodes Glawen tried to shift the focus of Kirdy's attention forward in time. And finally one morning as they sat over breakfast Kirdy spoke of his experiences at Yipton. "I amaze even myself. They thought me a compliant lout, a creature wadded together of mush and putty, with bird droppings for brains."

Kirdy paused to reflect, showing a smile of bitter irony to some startled folk at a nearby table. "So they gave me the first dose of stuff, and even identified it. 'Now for a little taste of nyene,' said the Yip: a scurrilous little toad who might well have been Titus Pompo himself. 'This will bring you close upon basic truths and you will see the flow of existence from both the underside and the top perspective together; it makes, so I am told, for an interesting view.'

"It was then that they learned my mettle. I kicked out and crushed the jaw of one. I struck another with my fist and smashed the bones of his head, so that his eyes rolled around like a comical toy. I looked to Titus Pompo—I shall call him that—but he dodged behind the table. I turned the table over upon him and jumped up and down trying to crush him; then I discarded the table that I might more easily tear him limb from limb, but more of the Oomps were coming so I jumped from the window and into the canal.

"They never found me, for I slid through the slime into the space under the pilings, and there I lurked, where none dared come for me." Kirdy chuckled: a low gurgling sound which caused Glawen's stomach to knot. "So I was at liberty, in the realm of the yoots. Aha! Those were the times! How shall I describe them? The place is stink and slime. The yoots—so the Yips call them—use this space as their own kingdom. How does one deal with the yoots? Through kindness and logic? What mean these in the crawl spaces under Yipton? Unreal! I horrified them with my deeds, so that they fled at the sound of my voice, sweetly calling to them. I ate their young and took the fish they had caught and ate these as well, and here was the secret—the truly great secret! The fish freely ingest the trapperfish which give off nyene as their poison, which in turn is rendered ineffective by the counterstuff of the fish, which the yoots call glemma.

"As soon as I took in the glemma a change came over me; I was no longer the raving wild thing and the yoots lost their dread and began to creep in on me. They fear the sight of their own guts, so I disemboweled some of them, but I was allowed no peace. I thought then I would swim in the canal by night, and take a boat, and make for the Marmion. I put this plan into effect, but I was captured and brought again to Titus Pompo, if indeed it was he.

"This time they took great pains with me, and tied me so I could

325

not stir. 'Now we shall see!' said Titus Pompo. 'Shall we taste some good nyene?'

"So I was dosed, but the stuff failed to act. I feigned madness, so that they gave me over to my own people, and I returned to Araminta Station. And then—my prospects had changed. I had discovered new goals." Kirdy stopped short.

Glawen prompted him: "And what are the new goals?"

Kirdy gave Glawen a crafty side glance. "I can trust no one. This I now know. Of all the realities, it is most certain: the purest, sweetest and only truth. I am I. All else is stink, slime and crawl space."

Glawen had no immediate response to make. Presently he said: "If your goals are creditable, who should they be secret?"

"No matter. I will not think along these lines just now. One day you will learn the scope of my concept."

Glawen said coldly: "I doubt if I will be interested."

Kirdy eyed him with a blue gaze, cold and opaque, which at one time had seemed so candid and mild. "You must not be sure of anything. Change is everywhere. I even notice changes in myself. At one time I was hard and impermeable. I saw with total penetration, as I had never seen before. I defined the deceit behind every pretense. I saw people in bitter fact for animals prancing and sidling in ridiculous clothes. Before, such messages came to my subconscious, which kindly barred them from my frontal mind. Now this subconscious is my frontal mind and the new clarity of my view is uninhibited. All is lucid. Even you, Glawen! Your postures hide nothing from me."

Glawen laughed shortly. "If they offend you, I suggest that you return to Araminta Station by the first ship out of Poinciana. I can manage well enough alone. Is that posture clear enough, or should I make it even more clear?"

"Unnecessary."

"Well—what will you do? Return to Cadwal?"

"I will consider the matter."

2

The *Sagittarian Ray* decelerated from intersplit, passed to the side of the blue star Blaise—the "Blue-eyed Devil"—and descended upon Natrice. Looking down from the promenade, Glawen saw a world of modest size, half in, half out of the blue glare of Blaise. Small polar ice caps showed as dazzling white blotches; other aspects of the topography were blurred by a dense atmosphere and high mists of ice crystals which reflected most of Blaise's harmful actinics.

In the great saloon of the *Sagittarian Ray* the stewards had set up a large geographic globe representing Natrice. Glawen, studying the globe, had learned that the hemispheres were roughly symmetrical. A narrow equatorial sea, the Mirling, girdled the globe, with a coastal plain flanking each shore. To north and south the landscape tilted and folded to become first temperate uplands, then tall mountains, then tundra to the ice caps. In the north hemisphere, the regions beyond the coastal plain were the Lanklands; the corresponding areas to the south were the Wild Counties. The population of Natrice, through historical circumstances, was not large. A few small cities faced each other across the Mirling, of which the largest was Poinciana, also the site of the spaceport. Next in importance was Halcyon, almost directly across the Mirling.

The first permanent settlers had arrived while Natrice still lay "Beyond"—which meant past the recognized boundaries of the Gaean Reach. These folk were retired pirates, slavers, fugitives and desperados of every stripe, along with a leavening of ordinary criminals. They were united by a desire to enjoy their wealth in peace, secure from the persecutions of the IPCC. To this end they established comfortable estates along the shores of the Mirling, using an architecture in perfect harmony with the environment. Wide low domes of foamed concrete created vast areas of cool dim space, rich with muted colors. The mansions were surrounded by shaded pools and wonderful gardens; the fascinating native flora coexisted with equally remarkable imports. There were palms of every description, yellow umbrella trees, black sky-spikes; salmatics with drooping branches and heart-shaped blue-green leaves; sweet limes with dark green foliage, perpetually in bloom and yielding exquisite fruit; jasmine, hinano, kahalaea; ramifolia standing high on ten crooked legs; batter-brain, with branches terminating in clublike knots; sky grass, with pink, blue, green and violet stalks, used to border paths; silver fern and black fern, crying out when touched together; lattice dendrons dangling hundreds of carmine flower-gongs; rose-wisteria hybrids; balloon vines and flameflowers from Cadwal; red, black and white-striped golliwog barrels.

In such surroundings the cutthroats, tomb-robbers, slavers and scoundrels became the Patrunes of Natrice. They conducted their lives in full propriety, taught honor, duty and virtue to their children and distanced themselves from old associates, who tended to borrow money, or reminisce, or even ask advice on how best to commit some atrocious crime. To avoid these episodes, the Patrunes adopted the

327

manners of aristocrats and trained their children in patrician aloofness, and so the centuries passed. The Patrunes became aristocrats indeed, with their origins now the subject of humorous conjecture, or even rueful pride.

When the Gaean Reach enveloped Mircea's Wisp, a surge of immigrants moved into Natrice, not at all to the satisfaction of the Patrunes. Most numerous were the Sanart Scientists: an order of naturopathic philosophers who settled the Lanklands. They arrived from everywhere across the Gaean Reach in a continuing flood, which at last prompted the Patrunes to close the Poinciana spaceport to further immigration. The Scientists paid no attention to the proscription and opened their own spaceport on an upland meadow; the influx continued, with the Patrunes powerless to interfere. Finally the tide dwindled and stopped, apparently because all the Sanart Scientists of the Gaean Reach had now arrived on Natrice, in numbers of over a million. They framed small acreages, smelted enough metal and cut enough timber to meet their needs, and in general kept to themselves, making no attempts to disseminate their creed, which was considered a self-evident truth.

In this assumption they were possibly correct, since the Sanart philosophy was disarmingly simple. Gaean man, so they asserted, was constituted a natural creature built of natural stuffs; his health, goodness, strength and sanity depended upon full synchrony with the "slow sweet harmonies of nature," as they expressed it. These few words summed up the Idea, from which the Sanart Scientists derived other more or less elaborate corollaries. They rejoiced in elemental processes: thunder, lightning, the flow of water, the warmth of sunlight, the rich substance of the soil, the flux of the seasons. Natural pleasures and natural foods were deemed good and worthy of enjoyment. Synthetic foods, artificial entertainments, unnatural habits, abstract aesthetics—these were considered bad and to be avoided, or even, in some cases, expunged. Loyalty, fortitude, persistence and austerity: all were good, all contributed to Truth and the Idea. Intemperance, overindulgence, indiscriminate tolerance were bad, along with gluttony, waste, excesses of luxury and sensuality.

The Idea was never urged or advocated. It was a concept of natural power, though still a human thought on a human scale. Above all else, the Sanart Scientists despised mysticism. They abhorred priests and their religions, which the Scientists considered so stultifying and preposterous as to verge upon criminal foolishness.

Almost equally to be deplored was the hedonism and idle luxury enjoyed by the Patrunes, who were parasites upon the yield of invested wealth. The ordinary tendency of the Sanart Scientist would be to shrug stonily and turn away, perhaps with a grim smile. Let the Patrunes wallow in their debasement as they liked—were it not for a disturbing circumstance: their frivolities and delightful revels set a bad example for impressionable young folk when for one reason or another they wandered into town. They would return to the Lanklands full of silly nonsense no longer in full accord with the Idea. Some "went bad," and tried to implement their new notions. When reproached or corrected, certain of these "bad ones" became defiant and left the Lanklands altogether. The situation was not improving; rather, the new notions were infecting ever more young folk of the Lanklands like a vile disease.

Every three years district delegates met at a World Synod. At the last few of these, strong language had been used in connection with the Patrunes, who were identified as the source of the troubles. The most intemperate voices urged forthright action to rid Natrice of its "degenerates, whose lives are like septic sores!"

The proposals, when put to a vote, were always defeated, but by decreasing margins. An uneasy tension was abroad in the Lanklands.

Along with the Sanart Scientists a miscellany of other folk had come to Natrice, bringing new skills, new talents, new enterprises. Upon gaining wealth, the newcomers, to the disgust of the Scientists, put on airs and attempted the Patrune life-style, but the more they exerted themselves the more sedulously were they snubbed by the Patrunes, until at last they made the best of their inferior status.

The *Sagittarian Ray* landed at the Poinciana spaceport. Glawen and Kirdy disembarked directly into a canopied carry-all which whisked them across the field, through the noonday glare of Blaiselight to the terminal. At a tourist information booth they were recommended to the Hotel Rolinda. "This is a resort of the highest style," stated the tourist adviser, a fashionable young gentleman who had carefully draped his body in loose white garments, after the casual Patrune style. "The Rolinda is absolutely modern and adheres to the highest cosmopolitan standards."

Kirdy made a soft sound of melancholy recollection. "Floreste favored Mirlview House for the Mummers."

"Definitely and distinctly inferior," declared the adviser. "The emphasis is upon achieving tolerable results with minimal effort. It is the resort of the Sanart Scientists when they visit the city; need I say more?"

"The Mirlview was indeed somewhat severe!" mused Kirdy. "Still, those were wonderful times! In those days I had so much to learn, and so much yet to undergo." His voice dwindled away.

"Quite so," said the adviser. "I cannot in good conscience recommend the Mirlview. Persons of judgment and high connection inevitably select the Rolinda. True, it is expensive, but what of that? If disbursing a dinket or two causes a person pain, he should best stay home, where his frugalities will not offend members of the travel industry. Are you in agreement?"

"Of course," said Glawen. "I am a Clattuc and Kirdy is a Wook. For us the best is none too good; we use both jam and butter on our bread."

"Indeed."

"Absolutely. How do we arrive at the Rolinda? Must we walk through the heat?"

"Of course not. The hotel will place a luxury vehicle, with a cooled interior and a selection of ales and beers, at your service."

"As a compliment to their guests?"

The adviser raised his eyebrows. "My dear sir!"

"There is a charge, then."

"A substantial charge, I assure you. There is an omnibus. It is used by the overly thrifty, the penurious, Sanart Scientists and vagrants. It is fast, convenient and cheap, but has no other advantages. If, like myself, you are cursed with a streak of wayward insouciance, you might try the omnibus, just for a lark. It may be boarded directly in front of the terminal."

"It will serve us well enough. One more question: which are the principal tourist agencies?"

"I would unhesitatingly suggest, as the most prestigious, the Phlodoric Agency and Bucyrus Tours. You will find both offices along the Parade at the Hotel Rolinda, for your easy convenience."

"And persons traveling off-world would normally use these agencies?"

"That is correct, sir."

Glawen and Kirdy boarded the omnibus and were conveyed to the Hotel Rolinda: a complex intermesh of four low near-flat domes arranged to leave a space eighty yards in diameter at the center. In this space grew a garden which was shaded from the most ardent Blaiselight by a high shell of gray glass. To right and left rose a pair of slender gray glass towers, housing accommodations for the guests.

The omnibus approached the hotel, halted under a gray-glass portière; Glawen and Kirdy alighted into cool wafts of chilled air. They passed through a curtain of scented mist into a dim space of such large dimension that it could not immediately be apprehended. A white ceiling, low at the side walls, curved gently to a height of thirty feet at the center. The business desk ranged along the wall to one side; to the other a dining area flanked the jungle garden.

Glawen and Kirdy crossed to the desk, where they were assigned rooms on the nineteenth level of the north tower. The rooms, so they discovered, were furnished comfortably in a style which was bland and neutral but in any case rendered unnoticeable by the view through the gray-glass walls.

Glawen stood looking out across the landscape, so different from any he had known before. Hundreds of low white domes were strewn irregularly and seemingly at random over the ground out to the edge of his vision, each surrounded by masses of dark foliage. To the south, then away to right and left, spread the placid Mirling, showing a silken blue surface to the Blaiselight. An intriguing and unusual panorama, thought Glawen, if perhaps somewhat overstark, overbright and too insistently blue and white.

Glawen turned away from the view. In a bathroom of monolithic gray-blue glass, illuminated by some mysterious means from within its own substance, Glawen bathed: first in a gush of scented foam, then a rinse of scented water. Returning to the bedroom he discovered that loose white garments in the mode of Poinciana had been laid out for his use. He dressed, then went out into the hall and knocked on Kirdy's door.

There was no immediate response. Glawen was on the point of turning away when the door swung open. Kirdy looked out, sandy hair tousled, his large ruddy face set in surly lines. "Why all the disturbance?" He took note of Glawen's garments and stared in suspicion. "Where are you going?"

"Down to the lobby. I want to ask some questions. Join me when you are ready, and we'll have lunch."

Kirdy made a peevish face. "You should have warned me that you were going out. I planned to eat in my room."

"Eat wherever you like. Come down when you're ready. If you don't see me, sit down and wait; I won't be leaving the hotel. I don't think."

"Oh, devil take all! Wait for me, then. I'll be fifteen minutes or so. Where did you find the clothes?"

"They were laid out while I was bathing. But I'm not waiting. I have work to do. If you don't see me, sit down and watch the ladies walk back and forth."

Kirdy growled: "Always you make things difficult! Why can't you

331

be sensible for a change? You must learn to take me and my opinions into account."

"That is absurd," said Glawen. "It's you who must be sensible. We're here on serious business!"

Kirdy's throat suddenly pulsed and seemed to swell. He spoke in a voice rumbling with the sound of doom. "I feel an absence of respect. You have no care for my feelings. Your eyes fleer half closed in scorn. You ignore my words as if I had not spoken, and give glib evasions. You make flippancies of me and my great studies. I am not a person to be taken lightly, as I have demonstrated on several occasions. You may learn as much in your turn."

Glawen stared blankly, at a loss for words. He became angry. Crazy or not, Kirdy must be brought up short. An instant later he reconsidered. Anger would only amuse and reinforce Kirdy in his present phase. Glawen spoke coldly. "Your manner is unacceptable. It is clear that we cannot work together. Both of us will take pleasure in your return to Cadwal. I will continue the investigation alone."

Kirdy's mouth twisted into a crooked smile. "Aha, Captain Clattuc! That's what you wanted from the start!"

"Think whatever you like. Bodwyn Wook asked me to bring you along; that is why you are here, in the hope of straightening you out."

"And you blame me for my difficulties? That is generous of you."

"Wrong. I am committed to Bodwyn Wook, and I will continue to put up with you, but only if here and now you decide to straighten out. That means you must act like a normal person. I refuse to cope with your surly fits any longer."

Kirdy glared, opening and closing his hands. Glawen watched him closely, prepared for anything. "Make up your mind," said Glawen.

Kirdy temporized. He spoke in grumbling tones: "What you ask is easier said than done."

"I suspect it's not so hard as you make out. Proper behavior should be second nature to a Wook. You know how to act; why don't you simply do so?"

"As I told you, it's easier said than done."

"Hard or easy, I don't care. Do it or go home."

"I can do only the best I can."

"That means you'll do only as well as you want to, which isn't good enough. Make up your mind. Sane behavior, or the first ship home."

Kirdy shut the door with a thud. Glawen turned away and went down to the lobby. At the moment Kirdy was furious, but—so Glawen believed—in a sane and normal fashion. In a few minutes he would cool off and take stock of the situation. Glawen imagined him standing by the gray-glass wall, big face creased in thought. Perhaps the fragments of his old conscious mind might come together, taking strength from necessity, and renew a normal dominance over the subconscious mind. Perhaps the crafty subconscious would feign normalcy and try to deceive Glawen. Too bad, thought Glawen, that Bodwyn Wook himself wasn't on hand to deal with the problem.

At the front desk Glawen inquired the whereabouts of the Phlodoric Agency and Bucyrus Tours. The clerk indicated a broad passage leading off around the central garden, with shops to the side. "You will find these places along the Parade. Both are of good repute and deal often with folk of the highest connection, including, needless to say, Patrunes. Sirrah Kyrbs manages the Phlodoric Agency; Sirrah Fedor is equally efficient at Bucyrus Tours."

Glawen visited first the Phlodoric Agency. He identified himself to Sirrah Kyrbs, and was taken hurriedly into a back office, lest some highly connected patron notice his presence.

Sirrah Kyrbs, a portly gentleman of early middle age, carefully attired, groomed, perfumed, shorn and shod, accorded Glawen a formal if somewhat stiff courtesy. "Sir, I am naturally curious as to the reason for your visit."

"I will explain presently, but first let me ask you this: have you had dealings with Ogmo Enterprises?"

"Ogmo Enterprises? I think not. But let me consult my files." Sirrah Kyrbs touched buttons on his office computer, discovering no pertinent information. "Sorry. I can't help you there."

"What of the Perfection of Joy excursion to Cadwal?"

Sirrah Kyrbs shook his head in bemusement. "The same applies."

"Thank you, sir." Glawen took his leave.

At Bucyrus Tours Sirrah Fedor provided no more information than had Sirrah Kyrbs. Glawen returned to the lobby, where he found Kirdy, neatly dressed and apparently in full command of his faculties, sitting quietly to the side of the room.

Glawen went to join him. Kirdy jumped to his feet. "Where have you been?" His voice, thought Glawen, was emotionally neutral, if a trifle tense. The question? It might be considered either fretful complaint or reasonable curiosity. Glawen decided to give Kirdy the benefit of the doubt.

"I looked into the two travel agencies. Neither admits dealings with Ogmo Enterprises, nor yet has booked any Perfection of Joy excursions. Both managers would seem to be honest."

"So where does that leave us?"

"Let's have our lunch and we'll talk things over."

The restaurant bordered the jungle garden, which under the gray-glass dome, occupied an area well over two hundred feet in diameter. Vegetation of a thousand sorts grew high and low, displaying leaves of every quality. At the center a crag of rough black basalt reared fifty feet above the jungle floor. A stream of water gushed from a spring near the pinnacle and descended, leaping and bounding and creating a pleasant sound. Paths from the restaurant penetrated the edges of the jungle garden, leading to tables hidden in the foliage.

Glawen and Kirdy sat at the edge of the garden and were served a lunch of high quality. Kirdy, considering the prices, shook his head in melancholy recollection. "Floreste would feed the Mummers a week on what our lunch will cost us. In those days, we didn't know the difference—or perhaps did not care. We were truly a harum-scarum group; there was always some kind of high jinks afoot. I don't know if I could go back to that sort of life. It has its attractions, of course. The girls were all so pretty, and so close at hand, and yet so unavailable —Floreste saw to that. He was not at all permissive; if you loved, you loved in vain—at least until the end of the tour. Then, of course, you could do what you wanted—if it wasn't already too late. All in all, they were good days."

"They are days long past," said Glawen. "Let us discuss our situation. It is clear that—"

Kirdy interrupted. "I've given the matter careful thought. I understand your point of view. For the investigation to proceed, obviously we must work in harmony. It is not necessary that I like you or that you like me. But we must agree on a system which allows us to work together."

"Quite so," said Glawen. "We shall use the ordinary and traditional system. I am the person in charge; you are the assistant. There is no scope for fits of temperament. I don't want any more emotional spasms or threats; they distract me from my work. So—there you have it. The old-fashioned system, or none at all, which means that I go my way and you go back to Cadwal."

"I understand and agree."

Glawen remembered his fears of the crafty subconscious and feigned normalcy. As if from casual curiosity he asked: "At this moment you seem quite the old Kirdy. Have you assembled the pieces of your old mind, so to speak? Or has your second mind adapted to real conditions?"

Kirdy showed a small tight smile. "Real conditions? That is an ambiguous term, which amuses at least one of my minds. In all candor, I have had what amounts to an enlightenment. All this time I have theorized that my conduct prior to the Yipton affair was governed by what I shall call Mind A and after Yipton by Mind B. I have just now learned that this was not quite correct. In truth, Mind B has been dominant for many years, with Mind A the intercessor in charge of what you just now called 'real conditions.' I think this is the general rule with everyone: you, me, Bodwyn Wook, Arles, Namour: everyone. Mind B is the citadel; Mind A is the herald that runs out the gate to deliver messages here and there, and occasionally brings back news of the outside world."

"I know nothing of the subject," said Glawen. "You may well be right. At the moment I want your full cooperation: no threats, no sulks, no peevish complaints. Are you able to control yourself to this extent?"

"Naturally," said Kirdy coldly. "I can do anything I see fit to do."

"And you will do it?"

Kirdy's face tightened: a signal which Glawen found disturbing. "I'll do my best," said Kirdy shortly.

"Sorry," said Glawen. "As I have mentioned before, that's not good enough. I want 'yes' or 'no,' once and for all, without reservations or escape routes."

"In that case, yes." Kirdy's voice again was dead and mechanical. Glawen heaved a deep sigh. He could do no more, except hope to finish the investigation at speed and as speedily return to Araminta Station.

The two finished their lunch in silence. Glawen rose from the table. "I must ask a few more questions at the travel agencies. You can come with me or wait in the lobby, as you like."

"I'll come with you."

The two walked down the Parade to the Phlodoric Agency. Sirrah Kyrbs, sitting at his desk, looked up with a slack face. He rose and greeted them with a stiff bow. "May I be of service?"

"I hope so, sir. This is my colleague, Sergeant Kirdy Wook. I have a few more questions, if I may again impose upon your patience."

"I will surely respond as the law directs, within such limits as may be dictated by discretion."

"You need have no fears. Your information will be kept in strict confidence."

"Ask on."

"Is the name 'Sir Mathor Borph' known to you?"

"Naturally. Sir Mathor is one of our valued patrons."

"What of Sir Lonas Medlyn?"

"I know the name. His family is perhaps less estimable than that of Sir Mathor."

"I understand that both Sir Mathor and Sir Lonas recently traveled off-world. No doubt you made the necessary arrangements?"

"Sir, I may not, in all responsibility, discuss the affairs of our clients."

"I fear that to some extent you must put aside your scruples," said Glawen. "This is an official police inquiry. It is your duty, and it also serves the best interests of your firm, to assist us. Additionally, your remarks will be regarded as confidential."

"Hm. How do I advance the interests of my firm by engaging in unwise volubility?"

"I need not describe the coercive powers of the IPCC. But, obviously, Phlodorus could not survive if transport companies refused to honor tickets issued by the agency."

"Hm. Allow me to see your credentials."

"Certainly." Glawen produced his documents, and Kirdy did likewise. "You will notice that we are full IPCC affiliates."

Sirrah Kyrbs shrugged and returned the documents. "The IPCC is not held in high esteem on Natrice: no doubt a survival from the attitudes of the first settlers. Indeed, we lack a permanent IPCC office here on Natrice. Well, no matter. It is neither here nor there. I will try to answer any reasonable question."

"Thank you. I take it you did sell tickets to Sir Mathor and Sir Lonas?"

"It is hardly a secret. Several months ago Sir Mathor and Sir Lonas took passage for Cadwal, aboard the Perseian Lines' *Alphecca Sword-stone.*"

Glawen nodded. "So far, so good. Now, what of six Sanart Scientists? Their names would be—"

Sirrah Kyrbs made a small gesture. "I know the group, and I am surprised that they chose to travel on what would seem a frivolous occasion. These persons, as you may know, often adhere to fixed opinions."

"And they also purchased their tickets through you?"

"Not in person. I sold a block of six tickets, in their names, to a young lady who described herself as their representative."

"This young lady: how did she identify herself?"

"She did not trouble to do so. I took her for an off-world person, of no great connection—definitely not a Sanart Scientist."

"Was she a guest here at the hotel?"

"I think not. She wanted the tickets at once, so that she need not make another trip to pick them up."

"You have no clue, then, as to her identity?"

"None. She paid the account in cash and I dismissed the matter from my mind, except for a moment of amusement when I thought of the Scientists and the Patrunes traveling together to the same destination, and I wondered if they would speak."

"A curious situation," said Glawen.

"We see many such in our business, and it is not our place to speculate upon who goes where with whom, if you catch my meaning."

"Oh, definitely."

"I can tell you no more. If you require further information, I suggest that you consult the principals."

"That is an excellent idea," said Glawen. "I should have thought of it myself. Where will I find Sir Mathor and Sir Lonas?"

Sirrah Kyrbs gave a small grimace. "I had the Scientists in mind. The Patrunes can vouchsafe no information whatever; they bought only their own tickets."

"All is grist for the mill," said Glawen. "We will put a few casual questions to Sir Mathor, and perhaps he will be able to clear up the entire affair."

Sirrah Kyrbs cleared his throat, looked all around the room, clasped his hands behind his back and leaned toward Glawen. "I confess to curiosity. What is the nature of this so-called affair?"

"It is, in essence, a complicated blackmailing scheme. The Patrunes might have been victimized had we not taken decisive steps."

"I see. Although the Patrunes, of all folk, would be difficult to blackmail. They are a law to themselves—which is one reason the IPCC is not represented on Natrice. The Patrunes mete out their own justice, regardless of all else. Since the Sanart Scientists do the same, you can understand that friction and hostility often occur."

"Where would we find Sir Mathor and Sir Lonas?"

"Sir Mathor naturally inhabits the historic Borph estate out of Halcyon, across the Mirling. Sir Lonas, so I understand, is his boon companion and aide, and shares his residence."

"And how do we go to the Borph estate?"

"It is simple enough. You fly the Mirling to Halcyon, hire a cab and ride thirty miles or so along the shore. The flyer leaves every half hour, so if you make the connection, the trip will require about an hour and a half, or two hours at the most. It is probably too late to attempt the trip today."

"That is my opinion also," said Glawen. "Now: one final word. We want to find Sir Mathor at home when we call, and if he knew we were coming he might make himself unavailable. You have no plans to call Sir Mathor, thinking to do him a favor?"

Sirrah Kyrbs smiled grimly. "I intend to isolate myself as far as possible from this business."

"That is prudent."

"I will go so far as to advise you. You will need a hat, against the rays of Blaise, and because it is proper outdoor wear. You will find a selection of hats in your room. The broad-brimmed white skimmer is appropriate for daytime journeys."

"Thank you, both for the advice and the information."

3

Glawen and Kirdy passed the remainder of the afternoon in idle pursuits. They wandered through the shops along the Parade, watched the activity at the hotel swimming pool, inspected the periodicals in the reading room and late in the afternoon retired to the saloon-lounge for a sundowner. An hour later they went up to their rooms to change clothes for dinner: a convention rigorously enforced at the Hotel Rolinda.

Glawen found proper garments laid out for him, the hotel valet having looked through his luggage to discover nothing suitable. Glawen surveyed the garments: trousers of glossy black woven floss, a dark saffron blouse, a deep scarlet coat with black facings, short in front, swallow-tailed in back, a two-inch black headband with a pair of modish ornaments of fine silver wire trembling above, like insect antennae.

When Glawen had dressed, he stood an indecisive moment, then abruptly left the room and descended to the lobby. He seated himself where he could watch the ever-fascinating movement of the other guests, and composed himself to wait.

Twenty minutes passed before Kirdy appeared, looking uncomfortable and somewhat gauche in the formal garments, as if they were a size too small. His mouth was compressed, presumably by reason of annoyance at Glawen's failure to consult Kirdy in regard to his movements.

Glawen made no comment. He rose to his feet and in stiff silence the two crossed the vast expanses of the lobby and went out into the garden restaurant.

Tonight they were seated at a table ten yards deep into the foliage, in illusory but convincing and totally pleasant isolation. A blue-green luminosity pervaded the area, apparently deriving from the foliage itself. Glawen theorized that a fluorescent substance had been mingled with the vegetable saps and serums, then stimulated to luminosity by radiation from a high source.

Glawen and Kirdy sat on intricately patterned brown, black and white cushions in fan-backed chairs of woven rattan, of a style originated thousands of years before in the ancient Orient of Old Earth, and the rattan squeaked and creaked to their movements. A cloth of black, brown and white covered the table; the implements were carved from wood. Red orchids dangled overhead; to the side a cluster of white lobelia blooms glowed with an ivory-white light. Music, of that style known as Old Gitanesque, barely audible, waxed and waned as if carried by a breeze from a site of distant revelry.

Kirdy found the restaurant and its appurtenances impressive. "Competent brains have been at work! They have created a romantic and dramatic ambience! All tinsel, fakery and nonsense, of course—but well done!"

"That's how it seems to me," said Glawen, wondering what this new aspect of Kirdy might signify, if anything. "But it's genuine fakery, and not imitation."

"Exactly so!" declared Kirdy in a large rich voice. "Through human dedication the place is transformed from a mishmash to a thing in itself! I will go so far as to call it a true work of art, since it answers all the critical questions. It is artificial, and uses natural elements to transcend Nature—which is the very definition of art. Do you agree?"

"I see no reason to disagree," said Glawen. This particular version of Kirdy seemed rather like that pompous, philosophical Kirdy of five years before. "Of course, I've heard other definitions. Everyone seems to have a definition or two tucked away for occasions such as this."

"Indeed? What is yours?"

"For the moment it slips my mind. Baron Bodissy uses 'art' as a synonym for 'claptrap'—but I may be quoting him out of context. He'd probably endorse your notion of the restaurant as an art form. For a fact, I don't see why it doesn't qualify."

Kirdy had lost interest in the idea. He gave his head that now-familiar shake of wistful recollection. "When I was a Mummer I never guessed that places like this existed. Floreste knew, but he kept us Mummers in the dark."

Ha, thought Glawen. Kirdy's analytical phase had been superseded by what Glawen thought of as "the autobiographer."

"We hardly knew which planet we were on," mused Kirdy. "The

hotels always smelled strangely, of indecisive antiseptic, and were either too hot or too cold. The food was always bad—although here on Natrice, we'd sometimes play a party at one of the Patrune houses and they always fed us fine delicacies. Ah! Those were good feasts!" Kirdy grinned at the recollection. "At places like Mirlview House, things were far different. We'd be served fried porridge with boiled greens, or steamed dogfish with curds, or pickled squash and tripes. At least no one was tempted to overeat—not even Arles, who spent all his pocket money on sweets. Still, we had merry times." Kirdy looked at Glawen in speculation. "You never were a Mummer: I wonder why."

"I have none of the right skills."

"No more did I, or Arles. Floreste made us into Primordials and Ogres and Thunder-demons, where no great skill was required. Yes, those were good times! No doubt it's much the same now. Different faces, different voices, but the same larks and laughter." Kirdy's expression became remote and soft. "Of course I couldn't perform worth a whisker anymore."

Kirdy continued with his memories until Glawen became bored and changed the subject. "Tomorrow should be an important day."

"I hope we learn more than we did today."

"Today wasn't a total loss. We discovered another actor in the drama."

"Oh? Who is that?"

"A young off-world woman who buys tickets to Cadwal in blocks of six."

"You should call her an 'actress' in the drama, not an 'actor.'"

"I want to know her name; her gender can wait. Who can she be? Perhaps Sir Mathor will know."

Kirdy grunted. "Sir Mathor won't tell you whether it's day or night —that's my guess. IPCC means nothing to the Patrunes; they make their own law."

"We shall see," said Glawen.

In the morning Glawen dressed with care, using his own garments rather than the casual local wear furnished by the hotel.

Kirdy knocked on the door; Glawen admitted him. Kirdy had dressed in the local garments and looked at Glawen in perplexity. "I can rely on you always for perversity! Will you kindly explain why you act this way?"

"Are you referring to my clothes? Perversity has nothing to do with it."

"Do you plan to explain?"

"Certainly. The Patrunes have no great opinion of the locals; we'll get more serious attention if we approach Sir Mathor in our own clothes."

Kirdy blinked and reflected. "Do you know, I think you are right. Give me two minutes, and I'll change."

"Very well," said Glawen. "This time only I'll wait for you. But hurry."

Immediately after breakfast, Glawen and Kirdy rode the omnibus to the airport. They boarded a flyer and were whisked off over the Mirling, to land at Halcyon after a flight of half an hour.

The time was now midmorning. A milky overcast swathed the sky; Blaise, a great blue pearl, seemed to swim with films of prismatic light: orchid, rose, pale green.

At the exit from the Halcyon airport Glawen and Kirdy found a cab rank where vehicles controlled by internal computer systems were on hand for those persons requiring transportation.

A placard provided instructions:

1. Select a vehicle. Board this vehicle and be seated.
2. The control mechanism will request that you state your destination. Respond in this fashion: "The residence of such and such a person" or "The offices of such and such an enterprise." Usually this will suffice.
3. A fee will be quoted; drop coins into the proper slots. Pay for waiting time in advance. The vehicle will refund any surplus.
4. You may issue the following orders: "Go faster." "Go slower." "Stop." "Change destination to such-and-such a place." Other directions are unnecessary. Vehicle will proceed at what it calculates to be the most appropriate speed along the most expeditious route. Please do not abuse the equipment.

"That seems simple enough," said Glawen. He selected a low-slung two-seater protected from the Blaiselight by a bubble of dark green glass. Kirdy, however, hung back and frowned down at the vehicle. "This is not wise."

Glawen looked at him in wonder. "Why not?"

"These cars cannot be trusted. They are guided by brains taken from cadavers. That is what we learned from unimpeachable sources when we were Mummers. Nor were the brains necessarily the freshest."

Glawen gave an incredulous laugh. "Where did you hear that?"

"I had it on good authority; I forget just where. Perhaps Arles, who is seldom fooled."

"In this case, he must have been joking. These are obviously guided by simple computers."

"Are you sure of your facts?"

"Of course."

Kirdy still hung back. In exasperation Glawen asked: "Now what is the trouble?"

"In the first place, that car is too small. The seats are cramped. I feel that we should hire a proper cab with a proper driver, who will do exactly as we wish. These vehicles are impervious to human desires; they do as they think best, even if it means tipping us into the sea."

"I'm not worried," said Glawen. "If it starts to misbehave, we merely need say 'Stop!' Here is a four-seater; you can have two seats to yourself. Either get aboard or wait here for me, just as you like."

Kirdy muttered under his breath and gingerly climbed aboard the four-seater. "This is an absurd system. Everything is absurd. The whole Gaean Reach is topsy-turvy, including you, with your weird ideas and codfish grin."

Glawen's smile, which he had thought to be friendly and affable, froze on his face. He boarded the vehicle. A voice issued from a mesh on the front panel: "Welcome, sirs and ladies!"

"You see!" said Kirdy in a voice of vindication. "The thing doesn't even know what sort of people we are!"

The voice said: "Two persons are aboard. Are there more to come?"

"No," said Glawen.

"What is your destination?"

"The residence of Sir Mathor Borph, about thirty miles east along the shore road."

"The exact distance is 29.68 miles," said the voice. "One-way fare is three sols. Round-trip fare is five sols. One or the other fee is now payable. Waiting time is one sol per hour. You may deposit as much money as you wish. A refund of the excess fee will be made."

Kirdy muttered: "Instruct the thing to drive carefully."

The vehicle asked: "Are you ready to depart? If so, say 'Ready.'"

"Ready."

The vehicle slid out into the road and made several turnings. "It never understood our directions!" said Kirdy in disgust. "It is clearly confused."

"I think not," said Glawen. "It is taking us to the shore highway by the best route."

A moment later the car swung out upon a broad avenue paralleling the coast and immediately accelerated to a speed which caused Kirdy to protest.

Glawen paid him no heed and gradually Kirdy relaxed, although there were still aspects to the mission which he could not approve. "Sir Mathor does not know that we are coming. It is considered rude to call without an appointment."

"We are Bureau B agents; we don't need to be polite."

"Nonetheless we should have notified Sir Mathor in advance; after all, he is a Patrune. Then, if he did not want to see us, he could have told us not to come."

"I want to see him regardless of his wishes. I came to Natrice for that purpose."

"He may be very terse—even rude."

"To a Clattuc and a Wook? Not likely."

"He may not know of our pedigree."

"If necessary, you may inform him, but in a kindly manner, so as not to hurt his feelings."

"Bah," growled Kirdy. "I never know when you are serious."

"That would seem to indicate good mental health. This trip may be sound therapy after all."

Kirdy had no comment to make. The two rode in silence through a landscape of mixed tropical vegetation, cultivated groves, areas of rampant jungle with trees standing three hundred feet tall, overshadowed by giant dendrons holding parasols of maroon foliage another two hundred feet higher. At intervals gaps in the foliage allowed glimpses of the Mirling, lavender-blue under the hazy Blaiselight. Occasional side roads led seaward to the estates of one or another Patrune, each guarded by a high wall.

The vehicle presently veered from the highway into one of the side roads and halted under a portière. "This is the specified destination. Do you wish to return at once?"

"No. Wait."

"Waiting charges are one sol per hour, payable in advance. Excess payment will be refunded."

Glawen pushed five sols into the receptacle.

"The car will await your orders for five hours. Please specify a code name to ensure your priority of use."

"Spanchetta," said Glawen.

"For five hours this vehicle is reserved to the use of Spanchetta," intoned the car.

Kirdy looked at Glawen in disfavor. "Why did you give out that name?"

"It was the first name that entered my mind."

"Hmmf," sniffed Kirdy. "I hope that we will not be obliged to prove our identity."

"I'm not worried. Now: listen carefully. These are your instructions. Do not intervene in the conversation unless I ask you a direct question. If I make an inaccurate statement, do not correct me, because I may have a purpose in mind. Show neither antagonism nor cordiality; maintain a proper detachment, even though we are showered with abuse. Do not admire any ladies who may be present. In general, behave like a genuine Wook of Wook House!"

"I am inclined to resent these instructions," muttered Kirdy.

"I don't mind in the slightest. Resent all you like, so long as you do as I ask."

"I don't know if I can keep them all straight. Behave like a Wook, shower no abuse, admire the ladies—"

"I'll go over it again," said Glawen. He repeated his instructions. "Is it all clear?"

"Naturally," said Kirdy. "After all, I am not a sergeant at Bureau B for nothing."

"Good." Glawen went to the portal and pressed a button. A voice said: "Sirs, please state your names and your business."

"We are Glawen Clattuc and Kirdy Wook, of Bureau B, at Araminta Station on Cadwal. We wish to consult Sir Mathor Borph on a matter of importance."

"Are you expected?"

"No."

"A moment, if you please. Your names will be announced."

Three minutes passed. Kirdy began to fidget. "Clearly—"

The portal slid aside. A tall man of impressive muscular development, dark-skinned, with white hair and pale gray eyes, stood in the opening. He inspected the two visitors with dispassionate care. "You are natives of Cadwal?"

"That is correct, sir."

"What is your purpose here?"

"Are you Sir Mathor?"

"I am Sir Lonas Medlyn."

"Our business is primarily with Sir Mathor."

"Are you business agents, or solicitors, or religious evangelists?"

"We are none of those."

"Come, if you please."

Sir Lonas moved off along a path paved with tablets of white shell-stone. Glawen and Kirdy followed: under flowering trees, across a pond by a low bridge and up to a cluster of wide low domes. A door slid aside; Sir Lonas ushered the two into a circular foyer, and signified that they were to wait. He disappeared through a portal. Glawen and Kirdy looked in awe about the foyer. A dozen nymphs carved in marble stood on pedestals around the periphery of the room; the alabaster floor was innocent of ornamentation. From the ceiling by a thread of silver wire hung a sphere of crystal two feet in diameter, of hypnotic clarity.

Sir Lonas returned. "You may come." He led the two into a space wide past any quick or intuitive sensation of its scope. At the far end of the room glass panels looked out across a terrace to a swimming pool, shaded under a high flat shell of gray glass. Shining through this glass, the light of Blaise was refracted around the sea-blue central disk into concentric rings of color: carmine, bitter green, purple, dark blue, light acid blue, burnt orange, pink. A dozen folk of various ages splashed in the pool; as many more sat grouped in the shade of parasols.

Sir Lonas went out to speak to Sir Mathor: a man of early maturity, tall, with short gray-blond hair, regular features and good physique, who at once jumped to his feet and came into the great parlor. He halted a dozen feet from Glawen and Kirdy, to give each a measured inspection. Glawen thought to perceive a person confident, easy of disposition, somewhat self-indulgent but without obvious or ostentatious quirks of character. Sir Mathor, indeed, while handsome, alert and equipped with perfect social poise, seemed on the whole quite ordinary.

Sir Mathor, in his turn, took no pains to hide his surprise at the quality and style of his visitors. He asked: "You are from Araminta Station on Cadwal? A remote place, well past the back of beyond. What brings you here?"

"I mentioned to Sir Lonas that we are representatives of our Bureau B," said Glawen. "I am Captain Glawen Clattuc; this is my associate, Sergeant Kirdy Wook. Here are our credentials."

Sir Mathor waved them aside. His manner was still puzzled, if somewhat amused. "You are clearly a young man of candor; I have no doubt you are telling the exact truth. I merely wonder what you want of me."

"Unless someone assumed your identity, you and Sir Lonas recently visited Araminta Station. We wish to inquire into the circumstances of this visit. May we sit, or do you prefer that we stand?"

"Sorry, indeed! A shocking lapse of courtesy! Sit, by all means!" Sir Mathor pointed to a sofa; Glawen and Kirdy seated themselves, but Sir Mathor paced slowly back and forth in front of them: three steps in each direction. Finally he came to a halt. "My recent visit to Araminta Station, you say. Are you sure of your facts?"

"You may be confident as to our professionalism, sir. We are, as a matter of fact, IPCC affiliates. You used a fictitious name at Araminta Hotel, but this is neither unusual nor actionable, and certainly is not the reason for our visit."

"Most extraordinary," said Sir Mathor. "I am totally perplexed."

"That is quite all right, sir," said Glawen. "It is only necessary that we understand the situation. I hope that you are willing to discuss the matter with us in full detail."

Sir Mathor threw himself into a low deeply cushioned chair. He leaned back, thrust out his legs. He looked to the side, where Sir Lonas stood quietly, hands clasped behind his back. "Lonas, would you be kind enough to bring us refreshment: perhaps some of that excellent Yellow Frost? I'll have the same."

Sir Lonas nodded and moved away. Sir Mathor turned his attention back to Glawen and Kirdy. "Now, then: suppose you tell me exactly what sort of information you are after."

"About two months ago you went to Yipton and thence on an excursion to Thurben Island. There you engaged in activities which are illegal: both on Cadwal and across the Gaean Reach."

Sir Mathor threw back his head and laughed: a musical metallic sound conveying no trace of humor. "And you have come to take me into custody?"

Glawen shook his head. "We are not quite that naive, Sir Mathor. Still, there is nothing to laugh about. These crimes have ugly names."

"Yes, yes. Ugly words often describe healthy processes." Sir Mathor watched as Sir Lonas served around goblets of frozen punch. He spoke as if casually: "Tell me this: have you discussed this affair with other parties to the excursion?"

Glawen responded politely: "Proper procedure requires that I ask my questions in an orderly fashion. Still, I might ask: what difference does it make?"

Sir Mathor's composure at last showed a crack. "A great difference indeed! If you want information: yes, I will give it to you, so long as you do not approach these other folk. Not just yet."

"I suggest that you tell me the facts. Start with how you became aware of the excursion."

Sir Mathor heaved a sigh. "I'd feel happier talking to you if I knew your objectives. It seems to me—now I am just musing—that if you were only anxious to punish the folk on the excursion you would have immediately lodged a case with the IPCC. Extortion? Blackmail? This doesn't seem to be your game, which of course is sheer wasted effort in any case. What, then? Who are you after?"

Glawen said: "Please don't discover mysteries where none exist. We are outraged by the affair. We would like to punish everyone involved, particularly those close to home. In all candor, you do not seem the sort of person who would want to identify himself with such a sickly episode."

"You are quite right. I have far more urgent matters on my mind." Sir Mathor paused and tapped his chin with his fingers. "I'm not quite sure how to handle this matter." He hitched himself up in the chair. "You may or may not be aware that here on Natrice we are fighting a quiet but desperate war with an enemy who outnumbers us twenty to one. If it comes to violence we will suffer enormous damage. It is no exaggeration to say that our very survival is at stake—and we will use any weapon which comes to hand."

"Ah," said Glawen. "I am beginning to understand. You refer to the Sanart Scientists?"

"I refer to one of their factions: the so-called Ideationists. These folk are fanatics who make a virtue out of severity. In the past they have attacked us financially, philosophically and verbally, none of which troubles us. Recently gangs of anonymous raiders have come down from the Wild Counties and attacked us by night, killing and depredating.

"There is our predicament. Our enemy is motivated by his 'Idea,' which is not inherently ignoble. Its virtues are self-evident; where is a force more violent than that which is generated by a surfeit of virtue? How does one fight virtue? With depravity? Is depravity, after all, any better than virtue? Arguable. At the very least, depravity allows the practitioner a variety of options. Personally, I advocate neither extreme. I merely want to live my life out in placid self-indulgence. Yet here I sit, at this moment, caught up by these Sanart passions. They want me to embrace their Idea. I resist; I am forced into an uncomfortable posture of self-defense and worry. The sweetness of my soul has gone rancid; I am pushed willy-nilly into a condition of hatred.

"So then: what does one do? He sits himself in his chair to think— as I do now. He stimulates his mind with Yellow Frost—as I do now." Sir Mathor drank from his goblet. "I say: are you gentlemen not drinking?"

"It is neither proper nor wise to drink on duty," said Glawen. "At best it lends a false air of good fellowship to the inquiry. At worst the drink will contain drugs or poison. This is not just a neurotic obsession;

347

I would be interested to watch while you or Sir Lonas drank from these goblets."

Sir Mathor laughed. "Whatever the case, we ponder how we must deal with the Sanart Scientists. We do not want to destroy them. We will be happy if they moderate their fervor and allow us to live our shiftless, idle, ignoble, but thoroughly enjoyable lives.

"To this end we have chosen a scheme to confuse and demoralize our enemies, so that in the end they too may learn the evils of frivolity and the wicked enticements of lassitude. We hope to achieve this goal by demonstrating the hypocrisy and secret immorality of the most flagrant Ideationists.

"Knowing this much, all must now be clear to you. We selected the six most ardent Scientists: I arranged that they received passage vouchers to Cadwal, along with the notice that the Conservator wanted to merge the Idea into Conservationist ideology; would the six eminent Scientists care to attend a colloquium, all expenses paid, on Cadwal?

"Needless to say, the six Scientists accepted, and the rest you know."

"And on Thurben Island the Scientists behaved as you hoped?"

"They were superb. We dosed them well with anti-inhibitors; all restraint was gone. They did spectacular deeds, which were carefully recorded.

"And so, in a state of confusion, the six Scientists returned to the Lanklands. There were aware that something untoward had happened and none could remember the details of the colloquium, and all were assured that the strong wines of Cadwal had made them drunk. On the return trip they could talk only about the dangers latent in the grape, and each wanted all the others to apologize. As for the record, we have arranged for its showing at next week's Synod. The impact will be tremendous."

"The delegates may well guess the truth."

"Most will prefer to believe the scandal. Even among the skeptics, the images will linger forever and contradict a million homilies."

"He is right," declared Kirdy in a deep voice.

"The Patrunes will be allowed to show such material at a Synod?" asked Glawen.

Sir Mathor smiled at some private thought. "I can tell you this: firm arrangements have been made. The record will be made abundantly public. The matter even now is out of our hands." Sir Mathor relaxed back in his chair. "So now you know all."

"Not quite all. At the very start, how did you learn of the Thurben Island excursions?"

348

Sir Mathor frowned thoughtfully. "I hardly know. Small talk at a party, something of the sort."

"I don't see how that is possible. Your excursion was the first. Two others followed."

"Indeed? I stand corrected. It makes no great difference now; it's all in the past."

"Not quite. The folk who organized the excursions are still at large."

"I'm afraid I can't help you there."

"Surely you remember who arranged the parties?"

"I bought the tickets from the agency. Later I spoke to a very personable young woman, and she made arrangements with me. Later still a man telephoned to say that he had delivered the invitations and the tickets and that the six Ideationists had accepted."

"What was his name? What did he look like?"

"I really can't say; I never saw him."

Glawen rose to his feet; Kirdy did the same, somewhat more slowly. Glawen said: "For now, that is all we need. Perhaps you will hear no more from us, but that is for my superiors to decide."

"They knew you were coming to see me?"

"Of course."

"Where are they staying?"

"They are at Araminta Station."

"Oh! So now: what are your plans?"

"As I explained, our main concern is to identify the principals of Ogmo Enterprises. You do not seem inclined to help us, so we must continue our inquiries elsewhere."

Sir Mathor pulled thoughtfully at his chin. "Really. And where is 'elsewhere'?"

"I can't undertake to answer your questions, sir."

"I suspect that you intend to inquire of the Ideationists as to the man who brought them their tickets."

"Certainly. Why not, if it will identify this man for us?"

"For several reasons," said Sir Mathor in a voice of sweet reason. "First of all, I do not want him identified; I would be both embarrassed and inconvenienced. Secondly, I cannot trust your discretion, with the Synod coming up so soon." He pulled himself to his feet and turned his head. "Eh, Lonas? Am I not right? They shouldn't do this, should they?"

"I should certainly think not."

Sir Mathor said to Glawen and Kirdy: "Gentlemen, I feared from the very first that it might come to this. Mind you, I hoped and proposed possibilities to myself; I weighed this against that even as we sat talking. Always I reverted to the bitter facts. Lonas, where has your thinking taken you?"

"The facts are bitter."

"See to it, quickly and quietly, so as not to disturb our friends. Gentlemen, in an instant you will be wandering the land behind the stars. If only you could send back news of these blessed regions! But no doubt you will be dazed by the beauty of it all." Sir Mathor's voice was soft and soothing. Sir Lonas came forward, one long stride, another.

Kirdy gave a sudden hoarse yell: a sound of choked raving fury. While Sir Mathor stood aghast, Kirdy struck with his massive fist; it hit with the impact of a club. Sir Mathor's face went queerly askew, his eyes rolling up to show only the whites. A metal object dropped from his hand: a small gun. Glawen scooped it up as Kirdy turned on the startled Sir Lonas, who stood a foot taller than himself and outweighed him a hundred pounds. Kirdy seized Sir Lonas' coarse black hair, pulled the great head to one side and chopped at the neck. Sir Lonas stumbled into a chair and fell heavily backward, kicking out in a frenzy as Kirdy, moaning and keening, tried to find a way to jump on the thrashing body. Sir Lonas twined his legs around Kirdy's waist; Kirdy hammered at the stern handsome face, but now Sir Lonas bore Kirdy down to the floor and began to strangle him. Glawen stepped forward and fired a pellet into the back of Sir Lonas' head.

Kirdy jumped panting to his feet. Glawen looked out across the terrace. No one had heeded the events in the parlor.

Kirdy peered down at Sir Mathor. "He's dead," he said in wonderment. "I broke open his head. My hand hurts."

"Quick," said Glawen. "We must drag them over here, into this side room."

The strength of both was needed to pull Sir Lonas across the floor, each to an ankle. Glawen straightened the rumpled rug and picked up an overturned chair. "Let's go."

The two ran from the house, and climbed aboard the waiting vehicle. It spoke: "State the name in which this car is reserved."

Kirdy looked anxiously at Glawen. "Do you remember? I've forgotten. It was something odd."

For a terrible instant the name eluded Glawen as well. He cried out: "Spanchetta!"

The vehicle took them back to the Halcyon airport, where they were forced to wait twenty nerve-racking minutes before the flyer departed for Poinciana.

As they flew above the Mirling, Glawen considered what had happened. Neither he nor Kirdy had attracted attention on the route to the Borph estate; there could be no reason to associate them with the two deaths. Indeed, the Patrunes would be sure to blame a gang of Sanart terrorists. Still, on the day previously they had mentioned the names "Sir Mathor Borph" and "Sir Lonas Medlyn" to someone. Who? The manager at the Phlodoric Travel Agency. As soon as the news of Sir Mathor's death reached his ears, he would inevitably reach for the telephone and call the police. "I have an incident to report, which may or may not be relevant to your case." So the conversation would begin, and within the hour the police would take Glawen Clattuc and Kirdy Wook, of Araminta Station, Cadwal, into custody. On Natrice, Patrunes defined the law and its application. "IPCC affiliation" would be contemptuously ignored.

Another thought augmented Glawen's apprehensions. The police might well derive information from the hired vehicle. They would be informed that a pair of suspicious characters were in all likelihood on the flight to Poinciana, and Poinciana police might even now be waiting for the flight to arrive.

The flyer landed at the airport; the two passed unmolested through the terminal. Glawen saw no evidence of police activity.

Kirdy's thinking appeared to be running parellel to Glawen's. He touched Glawen's elbow and pointed. "Look yonder."

Glawen turned. At the adjacent spaceport he discovered the familiar hulk of the *Sagittarian Ray*, from which they had alighted only the day before.

"Yes," said Glawen. "Your instincts and my logic lead to the same conclusion."

"The passage yonder takes us into the space terminal," said Kirdy.

Without further deliberation, the two rode a slideway into the space terminal, and went to the counter of the ticket agency. Glawen asked the clerk: "When does the *Sagittarian Ray* depart?"

"In just about an hour, sir."

"And what is its next port of call?"

"Soumjiana on the planet Soum."

"That is convenient. Are accommodations still available?"

"Definitely, sir, in either first or second class."

"We will want two single cabins, second-class."

"Just so. I will need three hundred sols and your identity cards."

Glawen paid over the money. The two displayed their papers and received the passage vouchers.

They moved away from the counter. Kirdy said in a grumbling voice: "Our luggage is still at the hotel."

"Do you want to go get it?" asked Glawen. "There is time enough and the bodies probably haven't been found yet."

"What about you?"

"I think I'll go aboard the ship."

Kirdy gave his head a nervous shake. "I'll go aboard the ship too."

"Come along then . . . And yet—" Glawen hesitated.

"Now what?"

"There is also time to make a telephone call."

"What of that? Who would you be calling?"

"One or another of the Ideationists. SS. Foum, for example. I'd like to learn who brought him his ticket."

Kirdy grunted. "Do you think he'd tell you over the telephone? He'd ask all kinds of questions, and in the end tell you nothing."

"I also could warn him of the plot, which, all in all, seems a trifle unfair."

"I never quite understood this plot," said Kirdy. "Still, on the whole, the controversy seems none of our concern, one way or the other."

Glawen heaved a sigh. "I must agree with you there. In fact, the longer I think on the matter, the more I agree."

"Then let's go aboard the ship."

4

The stars along Mircea's Wisp, for all the drama of their glittering flow, were themselves of average size and luminosity. No exception was Vergaz, the pink-white sun in the sky of Soum.

The *Sagittarian Ray* slanted down upon Vergaz, oriented itself first to the orbit of Soum, then to its plane of diurnal rotation, and finally landed at the Soumjiana spaceport. Cargo and passengers, including Glawen and Kirdy, were discharged, and the *Sagittarian Ray* went its way down the Wisp toward the terminus at Andromeda 6011 IV.

At the space terminal Glawen inquired regarding connections to Tassadero by Zonk's Star, a lonely and isolated system to the side of the Wisp. He learned that a pair of small packets serviced the route: the *Camulke*, leaving in four days' time, and the *Kersnade*, scheduled to depart in something over a month. Neither date was altogether convenient, if it became necessary to travel to Tassadero—unless the inquiries on Soum could be completed within four days. This possibility did not seem utterly remote, and Glawen reserved passage aboard the *Camulke*, to Kirdy's instant dissatisfaction. "Why in blazes do you insist on this frantic haste? Do you never consider the wishes of anyone else? I say, let's work at leisure and enjoy our stay! The sausages are specially good at Soumjiana."

Glawen politely rejected Kirdy's protest. "For all we know, time may be a critical factor in the case. If so, Bodwyn Wook would not take kindly to our loitering and eating sausages, especially at Bureau expense."

"Bah," muttered Kirdy. "When Bodwyn Wook and I go off together, he must learn to trot along at my pace."

Glawen laughed. "Surely you don't intend me to take you seriously."

Kirdy only grunted and watched from the corner of his eye while Glawen completed his business at the reservation counter.

While they awaited the vouchers, Kirdy asked in a silken voice: "What if we can't finish the work in four days?"

"We'll worry about that when the time comes."

"But just suppose."

"Much would depend on circumstances."

"I see."

The time was midmorning. Glawen and Kirdy rode into Soumjiana by elevated transit car, through a district of industrial facilities and small workshops, uniformly fabricated of foamed glass, stained pale blue, watery green, pink or occasionally a pallid lemon yellow. To right and left the city spread away across a flat plain, accented only by lines of slim black trees which marked the routes of important boulevards.

In geological terms, Soum was an old world. The mountains had long been worn down to nubbins; innumerable small rivers wandered this way and that across the land; the seven seas knew only the most lackadaisical storms.

The Soumians, like their world, were of a mild and equable temperament. A certain school of sociologists, calling themselves the Circumstantial Determinists maintained that the placid environment had shaped the psyche of the Soumians. Another group, who called themselves merely sociologists, pronounced the theory "arrant mysticism and total nonsense." They pointed out that over the centuries folk of a hundred different racial stocks had come as immigrants of Soum, each necessarily adapting to the customs of all the others and in the process learning tolerance and compromise: faculties now integral with the Soumian personality. Women and men enjoyed equal status and tended to dress alike; there was little mystery or glamour to sexuality. Such being the case, sex crimes were uncommon, along with fits of

353

murderous jealousy, while grand amours and romantic adventures were little more than the subject of wistful speculation—unless one could afford services like those offered by Ogmo Enterprises in the Perfection of Joy brochures.

Arriving at the center of Soumjiana, Glawen and Kirdy took lodging at the Travelers Inn, overlooking the Octacle, as the great eight-sided central plaza was known.

Kirdy seemed restless and somewhat out of sorts. Glawen took time to explain his plans in detail. "We have a list of the travel agencies used by the Soumians who were taken on Thurben Island. We'll visit these places and try to identify the connecting link with Ogmo Enterprises. Perhaps we can turn up an address or a bank account or even a person with a name and a face."

"Possibly."

"If we work briskly, we should easily be able to finish here inside of four days—assuming, of course, that we find it necessary to go on to Tassadero, which I hope will not be so."

Kirdy was still not reconciled to the schedule. "Four days may not be enough. Of all the places the Mummers played, this was our favorite. Everyone liked the sausages from the little sausage grills. You'll see them everywhere around town and especially out on the Octacle. At one of these grills, the sausages were particularly tasty, and I am anxious to discover its location. Floreste never allowed us more than two apiece, which everyone considered extremely unkind and avaricious of him. Two sausages were just enough to tantalize a person. I am determined to locate the best and my most favorite sausage grill. It may well take more than four days. If so, what of that? At last I will get my fill of those wonderful sausages!"

Glawen opened his mouth to speak, then closed it again. What was there to say? He started over again. "Kirdy, do you hear me?"

"Of course I hear you."

"We are not here to search out sausages, not even if they were nectar and ambrosia and attar of roses, all mixed together. If you must look for sausages, I cannot stop you, but I will not join you."

Kirdy's eyes gleamed blue. "This is not sensible! We must stay together!"

"It seems sensible to me. You track down the wonderful sausages; I'll look for Ogmo Enterprises and we'll both be happy."

"Bah. In the first place, four days is not long enough."

"For me or for you?"

"For me. I don't want to be hurried, and run from one grill to the next, eating sausages with both hands."

354

"Quite all right; stay as long as you like."

"Oh? And what of you?"

"As soon as I finish, I'm leaving."

Kirdy's big pink face became aggrieved. "That is not a pleasant attitude."

Glawen became vexed, despite his best intentions. "Ha! You and your sausage quest. I can't take it seriously. Don't you remember what we're here for?"

Kirdy smiled sourly. "I remember well enough. But I'm no longer interested. What difference does it make now? It's all in the past. Now is now, and now is when I am alive."

. "It is absolutely pointless becoming angry with you," said Glawen. "Come, it's time for lunch. Eat sausages if you like; it seems a harmless addiction. Come to think of it, I like sausages too."

At intervals around the Octacle small sausage grills wafted savory odors into the air. Kirdy insisted upon buying and devouring two sausages at each of four different grills. At each place he said: "Quite good, but not the sausage I'm looking for." Or: "A bit too much pepper spice here, don't you think?" And: "These sausages have good character, but they lack a certain something. But let's try that grill over yonder; it might just be the one I'm looking for."

At each location Kirdy consumed the sausages with full deliberation, nibbling a bit at a time, while Glawen watched in mingled annoyance and amusement. Kirdy apparently hoped to circumvent Glawen's plans by wasting so much time that Glawen would be forced to postpone his departure. But while Kirdy ate sausages Glawen located the travel agencies he wished to visit on a map of the city. Almost all were located on or near the Octacle. When Kirdy started for the fifth grill, Glawen pointed to one of the travel agencies, only a few yards distant. "Lunchtime is over. I will be in there. Eat sausages or go back to the hotel: just as you like."

Kirdy became angry. "I have not finished my lunch yet."

"Too bad. There's work to be done."

Kirdy turned away from the sausage grills and followed Glawen to the travel agency.

So passed the afternoon, the whole of the second day and the morning of the third, with Kirdy wasting as much time as possible and Glawen finding a grim and, so he well realized, unreasonable pleasure in thwarting Kirdy's dilatory tactics. During this period Glawen visited each of the travel agencies on the list. At each the results were similar. Each had transacted its business with a personable young woman wearing garments of off-world style. Her most striking attribute, from the Soumian perspective, was her unabashed femininity, the recollection of which brought small smiles to the faces of the men and contemptuous sniffs from the women. She was described as of middle stature, with a lavish figure and hair defined as black, brown, auburn, red, blond and silver-white, the color apparently being adjusted to either her mood or her costume. She was further characterized as "off-world exotic," "schlemielish" (an adjective beyond Glawen's comprehension), "hoity-toity," "pretensive: all bust, bottom and eyelash," "a bit pushy," "off-caste refined, if you know what I mean." And: "Mysterious! I asked her name and she said she was the 'O' in 'Ogmo.' Does that make sense? I ask you!" "I took her for no better than she had to be; definitely larky." And: "She came on like an actress, all poses." And: "I asked her where these Perfection of Joy parties took place; she said: 'On Cadwal.' I asked if all the girls on Cadwal were as pretty as she was. She just smiled and said it wasn't her kind of place, being much too old-fashioned."

In each of the agencies, Glawen inquired as to the financial arrangements. "When you sold vouchers for these Perfection of Joy excursions, you received money. What happened to this money? Did the young lady pick it up?"

In each case the answer was the same. "We transferred the money to the Ogmo account at the Bank of Mircea. These were our instructions; we followed them explicitly."

"Have you seen the young woman on any other occasions?"

"No, sir."

"Do you know where the offices of Ogmo Enterprises are located?"

"No, sir."

Glawen could not avoid a sensation of disappointment. The most promising leads of the investigation had dwindled to nothing. He had learned only of a young woman who had come and gone, leaving no indication of her identity, although her personality and even her appearance had taken on a murky reality.

Kirdy ate his usual lunch of sausages, and made his usual attempt to prolong the lunch hour, and his lack of success, as usual, provoked a series of surly protests. Glawen paid no heed and with Kirdy as usual sauntering two steps behind, he crossed the Octacle to the Bank of Mircea—by coincidence, that bank controlled by Alvary Irling, still in custody at Araminta Station.

At the bank Glawen was forced to argue and threaten and flourish his credentials up four tiers of ever more elevated functionaries before he finally gained access to an official with both the authority and the will to dispense information. Kirdy meanwhile waited in the lobby, intently watching Glawen's every move, apparently suspecting at some level of his mind that Glawen might try to give him the slip.

The bank official listened carefully to Glawen's request, then shook his head. "I can't help you. Ogmo Enterprises is a blind account. Money can be deposited by anyone, then it simply disappears, so far as we are concerned. Withdrawals can be made only by using the proper code. The account is secret and anonymous; it could only be more so if it did not exist at all."

"You could not locate the account, if you were of a mind to do so?"

"A cybernetic genius might locate the account by depositing funds to the credit of Ogmo Enterprises and tracing the computer's activity. He might be able to learn the code; as to this I'm not sure. But he could not identify the account holder."

"What if he were ordered to do so by, let us say, Alvary Irling, sparing no expense?"

The official inspected Glawen with an expression combining both curiosity and calculation. He spoke in a noncommittal voice: "You use that name with easy éclat."

"Why not? He is currently our guest at Araminta Station. Should I be inclined to make the suggestion, he would discharge you on the instant."

"Really." The official straightened the papers on his desk. "You wield great influence. Interesting. Please ask him to promote me to first executive director at a large salary."

"I might well do so if you provided the information I need."

The official regretfully shook his head. "I am helpless. It is not just a matter of bank regulation. The code is known only to the depositor. His name does not appear in the bank records."

Glawen departed the bank, with Kirdy following close behind. They returned to the Travelers Inn, Glawen in a gloomy mood.

In the hotel lobby Glawen flung himself down into a chair. Kirdy, smiling a cryptic smile, stood looking down at him. "Now what?"

"I wish I knew."

"Don't you want to make more inquiries?"

"Of whom? What should I ask?"

Kirdy gave an indifferent shrug. "There is much more to learn. Soum is a large world."

"Let me give the matter some thought."

"Think away." Kirdy went off to look at a bulletin board. He uttered a cry of glad surprise and came bounding back across the lobby. "We can't leave Soum! Impossible that we should leave now!"

357

"How so?"

"Look at the poster!"

Without great interest Glawen went to look at the bulletin board, where he discovered a placard printed in lively colors:

The famed impresario
Master Floreste
brings his talented troupe
The Waifs of the Wisp
back to Soumjiana!
Advance patronage is advised.

"They won't be here for a month or more," said Glawen. "We'll be gone tomorrow."

"Tomorrow?" cried Kirdy in shock. 'I don't care to leave tomorrow!"

"Stay as long as you like," said Glawen. "Just don't bother me with any more foolish complaints."

Kirdy stared at Glawen, the muscles of his face cording. "I advise you to watch your language! You are not speaking to a child!"

Glawen sighed. "Sorry, I did not mean to offend you."

Kirdy gave a nod of measured dignity. "I have a suggestion to make."

"So long as it involves neither sausages nor the Mummers, I'll listen."

"This investigation is obviously a pack of nonsense. I suspected as much from the start. I feel that we should spend another week or two here on Soum, attending to certain business, then take the first ship back to Cadwal."

"You go if you like," said Glawen. "It's my duty to complete the investigation as best I can. That means Tassadero tomorrow."

Kirdy compressed his lips and looked off across the lobby. "Duty is all very well, if it is necessary. But this is foolish duty and needless."

"That is not for you to decide."

"Of course it is for me to decide! Who else should I trust in this regard? You? Bodwyn Wook? Arles? Estimable fellows all, but I am I! If I think a certain 'duty' is needless, I refuse to trouble myself. It is undignified parading around for no purpose. My dignity will not allow me to make a fool of myself. That is how it always has been and always will be."

"Quite all right," said Glawen shortly. "Make decisions how you like, but don't trouble me with them. Tomorrow I leave aboard the *Camulke*. Go or stay as you like."

5

Zonk's Star, a white dwarf of negligible luminosity, moved inconspicuously alone through a black gulf to the side of the Wisp, with a single small planet, Tassadero, huddling close.

Three races resided on Tassadero: the Zubenites of Lutwiler Country, numbering about a hundred thousand; half as many nomads roaming the Great Steppes and the Far Regions; and three million inhabitants of Fexel Country, which included the city Fexelburg. These three peoples retained their separate identities, prompting an unusually ebullient notice in the Planetary Index:

The folk of Tassadero are socially and psychologically immiscible, and perhaps genetically as well. Each race considers the other two physically repulsive, and they interbreed about as often as might an equal number of hummingbirds, flatfish and camels.

The Fexels are of ordinary Gaean stock; the average tourist will find them the least unusual of the three races. They cultivate a sophisticated life-style perhaps a trifle overzealously; some observers may find their zest for novelty and fads less than refreshing.

From the Fexel perspective, the Zubenites are religious fanatics of uncertain pedigree and unsavory habits, while the nomads are dismissed as mere barbarians. In their turn, the nomads deride the "flutter-fingered fops, intellectuals and popinjays" of Fexel Country. The nomads claim descent from the pirates who long ago launched their forays from Tassadero. Zab Zonk was the pirate king and his tomb, said to house a great treasure, has never been discovered. Every year thousands of "Zonkers" arrive from off-world and spend weeks or months searching the steppes and the Far Regions for the elusive tomb. The Zonkers bring with them, be it noted, a treasure of their own, in the form of foreign exchange.

A few other items may interest the tourist, jaded and bored after his failure to find Zonk's treasure. He may inspect the so-called "rivers of purple ooze" or enjoy winter sports at Mount Esperance. This is a dead volcano twenty thousand feet high, with slopes affording spectacular ski runs twenty miles long.

Glawen, sitting in the saloon of the *Camulke*, put aside the Planetary Index. Kirdy stood by the observation window, looking morosely off across space toward the bright flow of the Wisp.

Glawen's last attempt at conversation had brought only an uninterested monosyllable in response; he decided against asking Kirdy's opinion of Fexelburg and picked up the official publication of the Fexel Tourist Information Agency, a handsome volume entitled *Tourist Guide to Tassadero*. One entry described Zonk's treasure in fulsome detail. The text went on to assure the interested treasure-hunter: "The authorities further guarantee that whoever finds this valuable hoard will realize its total value; he will be assessed no taxes, duties, deductions or special imposts."

Kirdy had turned away from the window. "Listen to this," said Glawen. He read the paragraph aloud. While he read, Kirdy turned back to the window. "What do you think of that?" asked Glawen.

"Most generous and truly kindly of the authorities—I don't think." Kirdy spoke without turning his head.

"It also says here: 'Persons are warned not to buy maps purporting to reveal the exact location of the treasure. It is amazing how many of these maps are sold! If one is offered such a map, he should ask the vendor: "Why, instead of selling me this map, do you not go to the stipulated location and possess the treasure for yourself?" The vendor will be prepared for the question, but no matter how convincing his response, do not buy the map, as it will doubtless prove to be bogus.'"

"Ha!" said Kirdy. "Arles bought such a map, from an old man who claimed to be dying and wanted some fine young fellow like Arles to enjoy the treasure. This sounded reasonable to Arles, but Floreste would not let him go out on the North Steppe to collect the treasure."

"That seems a bit unfair. Arles could have put the wealth to good use. He might even have bought a space yacht for the Bold Lions."

"That was his stated intention."

Glawen returned to the tourist guide. He learned that the "rivers of purple ooze" were in fact colonies of purple jellyfish which slid across the steppe in columns four hundred yards long and thirty yards wide. According to the tourist guide, the "rivers of ooze" were spectacles to excite even the most blasé: "These wonderful phenomena are notable for the mystery of their being! They thrill us with their eerie beauty! But again, warnings must be cited! All is not gorgeous. The odor exuded by these great worms is quite acrid. Fastidious folk are advised to study the creatures from an upwind vantage."[1]

Glawen, reading further, came upon an article entitled "Zab Zonk: In Song and Story," in which Zonk's exploits were chronicled and the dimensions of his fabulous treasure were calculated.

So far, we are dealing with what seems at least an approximation of fact [wrote the author]. Have others been as judicious? Decide for yourself, from this sampling of Zonk lore. Here is his preferred toast:

"I cry glory to Zonk, High, Full and Mighty Emperor of the Magnitudes, of Life and Death, of Now and Then, of Hither and Yon, of all things Known and Unknown, of the Universe and all the Elsewheres! Glory to Zonk! So be it. Drink."

When signing his name, Zonk was more modest, and his handwriting was oddly delicate: "ZONK: First and Last Over-man."

From sources unknown but very remote comes this apostrophe:

"ZONK: Avatar of Phoebus, Sublimation of all Melodious Beauties, He who Partakes of Uiskebaugh and Performs the Seventeen Signals of Love!"

When measured against such vistas, truth must defer, with neither apology nor regret, to the far more amiable arrangements of legend.

Kirdy turned away from the window and seated himself in a chair with his legs outstretched, his head back and his gaze fixed on the ceiling. Glawen put aside the book. "What is your opinion of Tassadero?"

Kirdy responded in a monotone: "Fexelburg is not too bad. The backcountry is dreary for a fact. The 'ooze rivers' give off a fearful chife. I don't much like the food anywhere. In the towns they douse everything with strange spices and odd vegetables, and I don't believe they like it themselves, but they have to eat it because it is the new trend. One never knows what to expect and can't recognize it after it arrives." Kirdy gave a dreary chuckle. "The ranchers eat well enough but Floreste ruined our visit for us. That was when we saw the purple ooze."

"What did Floreste do?"

---

[1] In his monograph *The Purple Sliders of Tassadero* the biologist Dennis Smith uses more direct language: "They give forth a majestic stench, which, beyond cavil or question, is a thing of truly epic scope. The tourist officials fail to mention a curious side effect of this stench: it penetrates the skin and hair of dainty ladies and dignified gentlemen alike, and cannot be eradicated, nor stifled, nor disguised. The stink persists for several months. Sometimes it is argued that the tourist bureaus of Tassadero should be censured for their ambiguities."

"The rancher invited us out to his ranch and fed us royally. His wife and children wanted us to demonstrate one or two of our acts, which we were quite willing to do, but Floreste, avaricious old bastard, demanded a fee. The rancher just laughed and sent us back to Fexelburg. Everyone was fearfully vexed with Floreste. I was on the point of resigning the troupe then and there." Kirdy gave a sad laugh. "Now I wish I had stayed on. There were no worries, no fears! Everyone knew what he must do. Sometimes, when Floreste wasn't watching, we could sneak in and play with the girls. Some of them were sheerly beauties! What jolly times we had!"

Glawen asked: "Did you ever play in Lutwiler Country?"

"Lutwiler Country?" Kirdy frowned. "Wouldn't that be the Zubenites? We never went near them. They don't approve of such frivolity, unless it's free."

"Strange!" said Glawen. "Why should they trouble with Thurben Island?"

Kirdy's interest, never too focused, became diffuse, and he returned to staring at the ceiling. Glawen gave silent thanks that the investigation was approaching its end.

In due course the *Camulke* landed at the Fexelburg spaceport. Glawen and Kirdy disembarked and were briskly passed through the entry formalities, by officials dressed in unusually natty red and blue uniforms.

The official at the alien registration counter looked critically from Glawen's and Kirdy's documents to their garments. He asked with polite incredulity: "You are officers accredited to the Cadwal police?"

"That is correct," said Glawen. "We are also IPCC affiliates."

The official was not impressed. "That means little to us. We are not great champions of the IPCC here at Fexelburg."

"Why is that?"

"Let us say that our priorities are different. They are long on regulation and short on flexibility. In practical cases we have yet to find them useful."

"That's surprising! The IPCC is generally well-regarded."

"Not in Fexelburg! Party Plock is the adjutant, or adjudicator or double commander, or some such title, and a full martinet to boot. In these parts we must be ready for anything; after all, Tassadero is for the most part savage steppe! Flexibility is the watchword and devil take the rulebook. If Triple Commander Partric Plock and his cookie-pushers demur, it can't be helped. At Fexelburg first things come first."

"That sounds reasonable. I'll be interested to meet this dragoon Plock."

The official turned a sour side glance at Glawen's garments. "If you go there dressed as you are, they'll bar you at the door and call you 'clown' besides."

"Aha!" said Glawen. "I finally understand your disapproval. These are the only clothes we own. Our luggage was lost and we have not yet made replacements."

"The sooner the better! I suggest that you put yourself into the hands of a capable haberdasher. Which is your hotel?"

"As yet we have made no choice."

"Allow me to suggest the Lambervoilles, which offers full prestige and high style. In Fexelburg we are ultramodern in all respects, and you will find nothing dowdy or disreputable."

"That is certainly reassuring."

"Remember: first things first! Before you attempt the Lambervoilles, dress for the public esteem. The Nouveau Cri Salon is just across from the Lambervoilles; they will turn you out in decent style."

"What is the most convenient transportation?"

"Leave the terminal; board the tram car. Presently you will pass a heroic statue of Zab Zonk at the murdering of Dirdie Panjeon. Alight at the next stop; you will see the Lambervoilles on the right hand and the Nouveau Cri on the left. Is all clear?"

"Quite clear and we thank you for your advice."

The two departed the terminal. They boarded a glistening glass and black metal tram and were carried swiftly toward the center of Fexelburg. The local time was midmorning; Zonk's Star, a large pale disk, rode halfway up the sky. To right and left spread the suburbs of Fexelburg: rows of small bungalows constructed to a jaunty architecture, each flaunting some studiously novel trick of decoration to set it apart from its neighbors. Slender black native frooks, a hundred feet tall, lined the boulevards.

The tramway swung out into a main thoroughfare, leading into the heart of Fexelburg, with private vehicles moving at speed to either side of the central tramway. The long, low, unnaturally sleek vehicles were apparently designed for ostentation rather than utility; each was enameled in vivid colors and often flew an ensign from a jack staff, displaying the insignia of the owner's automobile club. In each vehicle, at the top of the control bar, a cluster of keys allowed the driver to play tunes to his mood as he drove, often very loudly, so that the occupants of other vehicles and casual pedestrians might also enjoy the music.

At the very least, thought Glawen, the city Fexelburg pulsed with frenetic energy.

Kirdy was still unhappy and rode with the corners of his mouth pinched in, as if at a bitter taste. Glawen wondered if he still resented leaving Soumjiana before his survey of the sausage grills had been completed. Or perhaps he had no liking for Tassadero.

The tram passed a large statue, depicting Zab Zonk in the act of executing a faithless mistress. Glawen and Kirdy alighted at the next stop, across a small plaza from the Lambervoilles Hotel, which, like every other enterprise of Fexelburg, advertised its presence with a large animated sign. Kirdy pointed to the sign with an air of excited discovery. "There it is! The Lambervoilles! Floreste always took us to the Flinders Inn, where the nomads stay."

"Floreste perhaps sees himself and the Mummers as nomads."

"Come!" said Kirdy sternly. "This is not the time for jokes."

"A thousand apologies."

Glawen and Kirdy crossed the boulevard, dodging and running to avoid the vehicles which sped past, careless of pedestrians, each driver playing a lively tune on the keys of his control bar.

A few yards around the plaza a garish animation advertised the Nouveau Cri Haberdashery. The sign depicted a man in a fusty black suit entering a doorway and immediately emerging dressed in stylish new garments. He entered again, to reappear in a different costume. Again and again the man in the black suit passed through the doorway, coming out each time in a new ensemble.

Kirdy came to a sudden halt. "Where are you going? The hotel is over here!"

Glawen looked at him in wonder. "Don't you remember what the official at the spaceport told us?"

Kirdy scowled. He had hoped to go directly to the Lambervoilles where he might indulge himself in a warm bath and perhaps doze off for an hour or two. "We can buy clothes later."

Glawen paid no heed, and continued around the plaza toward the Nouveau Cri, leaving Kirdy staring disconsolately toward the Lambervoilles. Kirdy suddenly became aware of Glawen's absence. He uttered a startled yell, and ran angrily in pursuit. "You might say something before you make one of those furtive departures!"

"Sorry," said Glawen. "I thought you had heard me."

Kirdy merely grunted. The two entered the haberdashery. A clerk no older than themselves came forward, halted, stared at their clothes, then spoke in a voice of supercilious politeness: "Sirs? What might be your wishes?"

"We want a change or two of clothes," said Glawen. "Nothing too elaborate; we'll be here only a short time."

"I can provide you both suitable outfits. What categorical dimension will you be occupying?"

Glawen shook his head in puzzlement. "These terms are not familiar to me."

Kirdy said shortly: "It is a roundabout way of asking whether we consider ourselves gentlemen or pariahs."

The clerk made a delicate gesture. "You are off-world persons, I see."

"That is true."

"So then: what might be your walk of life? It is important that your clothes reflect your social perspectives. That is a truism of the clothing industry."

Glawen spoke haughtily: "Is it not obvious? I am a Clattuc; my friend is a Wook. That should answer your question a dozen times over."

"I suppose it must," said the clerk. "You seem quite definite. Well, then: to the selection. As gentlemen, you will wish to dress as gentlemen, without compromise or false economies. Let me see. For an absolutely minimum wardrobe, you will need a pair of morning suits or, better, three: casual, business and ceremonial. Next, a suitable costume for a formal luncheon. Sportswear for afternoon recreation, which may be used for riding in a vehicle, although full and legitimate driving regalia is preferred. For afternoon social events in the company of charming ladies: what we call our pale gray bird-basher. Late afternoon social, of two levels, and dinner gear: formal and informal. All with proper accessories, and a range of hats, at least two dozen."

Glawen held up his hand. "All this for a week's stay?"

"A wardrobe from the Nouveau Cri will win compliments across the breadth of the Gaean Reach, certainly during the reign of this season's fashion, which is quite distinctive."

"The time for realism has arrived," said Glawen. "Fit us each with an all-purpose suit that will get us into the Lambervoilles, and maybe a casual outfit or two. We won't need anything else."

The clerk cried out in a fluting voice of distress: "Gentlemen, I will do as you require, but consider my personal example. I honor my body and treat it with the generosity it deserves. It is washed with rainwater and pear-oil soap, then laved with Koulmoura lotion, with tincture of calisthene for the hair. Then I don the freshest of fresh linen and an absolutely proper choice of garments. I deal nicely with my body; it serves me well in return."

"It seems a pleasant association," said Glawen. "Still, my body is less demanding, and Kirdy's body simply doesn't care. Give us the garments I have ordered, not too expensive, and we'll be happy, bodies and all."

The clerk gave a sniff of contempt. "I understand your needs at last. Well, I can only do my best."

Arrayed in their new garments, Glawen and Kirdy went confidently to the Lambervoilles Hotel and discovered no difficulty either with the doorman nor yet the grand officials at the central desk, where they were assigned chambers high in the central tower overlooking the plaza. As they rode up in the elevator, Kirdy announced his intention first to bathe, then go to bed."

"What?" cried Glawen. "It's not even noon!"

"I am tired. The rest will do us good."

"It may be good for you. Not for me."

Kirdy emitted a whimper of sheer frustration. "So what, then, do you propose?"

"You do as you like. I am going down to the restaurant for lunch."

"And I am to be left alone in hunger?"

"If you are asleep, you will never notice."

"Of course I'll notice, asleep or awake. Bah! As always, you insist on your own way. Do my inclinations mean nothing?"

Glawen laughed a sad tired laugh. "You know better than to ask a question like that! We were sent here to investigate, not to sleep. And you must be as hungry as I am."

Kirdy muttered: "I warn you, the food is bizarre. They will feed us worms and feathers in a sauce of minced gangaree, with ginger and musk on the side. They put ginger in everything; that's the fashion on Tassadero."

"We'll have to be on our guard."

The two descended to the restaurant. Signs and placards urged important new dishes upon them, but Glawen finally ordered from a bill of fare labeled "Traditional and Dietetic Cooking for the Elderly and the Diseased," which yielded them food more or less congenial to their tastes.

During the meal Kirdy again proposed that they return to their rooms for a period of total relaxation. Glawen again urged him to do as he liked. "I have other plans in mind."

"No doubt connected with this rather pointless investigation?"

"I hardly consider it pointless."

"What do you expect to learn? The tourist agencies all sing the same song. They'll tell you ruddy chuck-all."

"We'll never be sure if we don't ask."

"I've had my fill of tourist agencies," grumbled Kirdy. "They sell you doughnuts and charge double for the hole."

"In any event, we can interview the Zubenites who went out to Thurben Island, since we know their names."

"They will reveal nothing. Why should they?"

"Perhaps because we ask them nicely."

"Ha-ho! A forlorn hope, if ever I heard one! On this world, as on other worlds, folk exert themselves only to be vexatious." Kirdy shook his head in bitter despair. "Why is it thus? There are never answers to my questions. Why, indeed, am I alive?"

"Here, at least, the answer is self-evident," said Glawen. "You are alive because you are not dead."

Kirdy darted Glawen a suspicious glance. "Your remark is more subtle than perhaps you intended it to be. For a fact I cannot conceive of any other condition, which may well be a compelling argument in favor of immortality."

"Possibly so," said Glawen. "I, personally, find it easy to conceive of this other condition. I can readily imagine myself alive and you dead. Does this weaken your argument in favor of immortality?"

"You have missed the whole point," said Kirdy. "One thing is sure, at least: the Zubenites will tell you nothing if they think it will get them in trouble. Incidentally—speaking of trouble—have you noticed the two men sitting at the table yonder?"

Glawen glanced in the direction Kirdy had indicated. "I notice them now."

"I suspect that they are police detectives, and they are watching us. I don't like that sort of thing. It makes me uneasy."

"You must have a bad conscience," said Glawen.

Kirdy's face became even pinker than usual. For an instant he turned the full glare of his china-blue eyes on Glawen, then swung half-around in his chair and gazed moodily off across the room.

"That was just a joke," said Glawen. "But you failed to laugh."

"It wasn't funny." Kirdy continued to brood.

For a fact, thought Glawen, he doesn't like me very much. He sighed. "The sooner we are home the better."

Kirdy made no reply. Glawen looked again at the two men who might or might not be police detectives. They sat at an inconspicuous table by the wall, conversing in low tones. Both were middle-aged and otherwise much alike: stocky, dark-haired, sallow, heavy of jowl, with clever darting eyes. They wore garments which the Nouveau Cri clerk might have defined as "all-purpose semiformal business wear, at a categorical level of the middle professional service class."

"I believe that you are right," said Glawen. "They look like police officers to me. Well, it's nothing to us."

"But it's us they are watching!"

"Let them watch. We have nothing to hide."

"Fexelburg police are almost hysterical in their suspicions. Unless you're a tourist spending lots of money, they wonder about you. Floreste deals with them carefully. It might be wise to request their cooperation."

"You may well be right."

As they left the dining room, the two men arose, followed them into the lobby and approached. One of the two spoke: "Captain Clattuc? Sergeant Wook?"

"Correct, sir."

"We are Inspectors Barch and Tanaquil of the Fexelburg police. May we have a few words with you?"

"Whenever you like."

"Now is convenient for us. This way, if you please."

The four seated themselves in a quiet corner of the lobby. Glawen said: "I hope that we have broken none of your laws? We were absolutely assured that our garments were proper for lunching at the Lambervoilles."

"Sufficiently so," said Barch. "In actuality, we are approaching you from motives of sheer curiosity. What might the police of Cadwal want on Tassadero? We can find no easy explanation; perhaps you will take us into your confidence."

"That has been our intention," said Glawen. "But, as you must know, we have only just arrived, and there seemed no need for haste."

"Of course not," said Barch. "Tanaquil and I simply happened to be at loose ends and thought to take advantage of the occasion. I take it you are here on official business?"

Glawen nodded. "It might be simple, or it might be difficult, depending upon circumstances. I hope that we can count upon your cooperation, if necessary?"

"I would certainly expect so, to whatever degree we find possible. What, precisely, is the nature of your business?"

"We are investigating a series of criminal entertainments which were offered to off-world groups on one of our ocean islands. These groups were recruited at various worlds along the Wisp, including Tassadero, which is why we are here."

"Most unusual! Tanaquil, will you ever cease to be amazed by the weird convolutions of criminal behaviors?"

"Never, and I assure you of this!"

Barch turned back to Glawen. "And who were the participants in this ugly business from Tassadero?"

"This is where I must ask your special discretion. Our main purpose is to identify the organizer of the scheme, and so we must deal carefully with the participants, at least until we find out what they know."

"So much is clear. I think that we can guarantee full and total discretion. What do you say, Tanaquil?"

"I am of the same opinion."

"In that case I will speak freely," said Glawen. "We learned that six Zubenites from Lutwiler Country went to Thurben Island and there were involved in absolutely remarkable activities."

Barch gave an incredulous laugh. "Zubenites? That is astonishing indeed! Are you sure of your facts?"

"Quite sure."

"Extraordinary! Zubenites are not prone to erotic excess, and that is an understatement! Tanaquil, have you ever heard the like?"

"I am in a state of shock! What will they do next?"

Barch said by way of explanation: "We are fairly well acquainted with the Zubenites, who come in from Lutwiler Country to do their marketing. They are considered stolid folk, the next thing to torpid; hence our perplexity."

"Nevertheless, Zubenites were involved. They might have been subjected to a form of coercion, and for this reason, I hope that they will agree to tell us what we want to know."

"Which is?"

"Who sold them the tickets? How were the tickets delivered? Who took their money? Some member or members of Ogmo Enterprises were Cadwal residents; who might these persons be? In short, we want to find out what went on."

"It seems straightforward enough. Am I correct in this, Tanaquil?"

"I think so. Still: a cautionary point! I doubt if the Zubenites will choose to be informative, if for no other reason than sheer inertia."

"That would be my own guess," said Barch. "What, then, are your options? They are sadly limited. You cannot threaten criminal proceedings; no such law exists in Lutwiler Country."

"What of your own authority? Here is where your cooperation might be indispensable."

Barch and Tanaquil both laughed. "In Lutwiler Country? Or in Varmoose Country? In any of the Far Countries?" Barch jerked his thumb toward a nearby table. "See that old lady in the fancy green hat?"

"I see her very well."

"She has exactly the same authority in Lutwiler Country as I. In short, none. We keep the peace in Fexel Country, but no farther; in the absence of both means and inclination, we refuse to spread ourselves thin."

Tanaquil held up his finger. "We make one exception! Tourists base themselves at Fexelburg for their explorations and treasure-hunting; we regard them as our responsibility. If nomads molest a tourist caravan, we punish the nomads severely. But that is hardly police work, and it happens rarely nowadays."

"Quite so," said Barch. "The tourist trade is important to us, and the nomads ingest this knowledge with their mother's milk."

"What of the Zubenites? Surely they live by some sort of law."

Barch smilingly shook his head. "They live in the shadow of Pogan's Point, and the Monomantic seminary exerts all necessary authority. Away from Pogan's Point and across the steppes the only justice is what happens when you get caught. Those are the rules of life on Tassadero."

"In bad situations I suppose that the IPCC will impose order," suggested Glawen. "After all, Gaean law operates everywhere, including Lutwiler Country. We are IPCC affiliates ourselves, incidentally."

Barch shrugged. "The IPCC at Fexelburg is unpredictable. Commander Plock is sometimes a bit hard to deal with. He is, let us say, set in his ways."

Tanaquil spoke. "A certain person, whom I will not identify, has even used the word 'arrogant' in this connection."

"I'm sorry to hear this," said Glawen. "Since we are IPCC agents, we must pay the office a courtesy call, and we will certainly keep your remarks in mind."

Barch said thoughtfully: "There is another matter, rather delicate, upon which I must take advice. Please excuse me a moment, while I telephone my superiors."

Barch crossed the lobby to a telephone.

Kirdy asked Tanaquil: "What is suddenly so delicate?"

Tanaquil rubbed his chin. "The Zubenites can be surly when they are ruffled. The folk at the Monomantic seminary are downright strange. We take pains never to cause annoyance, since we don't want them becoming obnoxious and taking revenge on the tourists."

"How would they do that?" asked Glawen.

"There are ways: petty annoyances for the most part. For instance, dozens of tourist caravans search Lutwiler Country for Zonk's Tomb, or pass through on the way to the Far Countries. The Zubenites need only put a gate across the road and charge toll, or require that each tourist must climb up Pogan's Point to the seminary to have entry documents signed, and return the next day for countersignature, at a fee of twenty sols. Or they might insist that the tourists learn Mono-mantic Syntoraxis, or any of a dozen other nuisances, and soon the tourist trade, at least through Pogan's Point, would be a thing of the past."

Inspector Barch returned. "My superiors agree that we should offer every assistance. They hope that you will keep us informed of your activities and also of your eventual findings. They advise that you use the utmost tact in your dealings with the Zubenites. The Monomantic seminary is the philosophic center of the Zubenites; you might say that it is the seat of government, such as it is. So far as we are concerned, we are out of the picture. We interfere with the Zubenites as little as possible, for very good reasons."

"So, if they refuse to answer my questions, I cannot threaten them with reprisals from the Fexelburg police?"

"It would be foolish, inadvisable, useless and a waste of breath."

"That seems definite enough."

Barch and Tanaquil rose to their feet. Barch said: "It has been a pleasure talking with you. We wish you the best of luck in your inquiries."

"Those are also my sentiments," said Tanaquil.

The police inspectors departed. Glawen watched them cross the lobby. "They have made themselves clear," he told Kirdy. "They really don't want us meddling with the Zubenites, but they can't stop us, so they'll cooperate. That means they want to know what we are doing at all times."

"I thought that they seemed decent enough," said Kirdy.

"That is my impression too," said Glawen. He rose to his feet.

Kirdy asked in sudden suspicion: "Where are you going?"

"Just over to the desk."

"What for? Is something wrong? We've just arrived; are you complaining already?"

"I am not complaining. I want to locate the IPCC office."

Kirdy groaned and uttered a vulgar oath, to which Glawen paid no heed. He went to the desk and a moment later returned. "It's just five minutes' walk around the plaza. I'm curious to look in on this 'doctrinaire, arrogant' group."

"Can't you ever relax?" demanded Kirdy. "Not even for an hour?

It's time for a proper nap; we've exerted ourselves enough for one day."

"I'm not tired."

Kirdy spoke with finality: "I must rest for a bit and I am going to my room."

"Pleasant dreams," said Glawen.

Kirdy stalked off across the lobby, but Glawen noticed that he went only a few steps, then flung himself angrily down into a chair. When Glawen turned to leave, Kirdy jumped to his feet and followed. He caught up with Glawen just outside the main portal. "Aha!" said Glawen. "You weren't able to sleep?"

"Something like that," said Kirdy grimly.

The two walked around the plaza. Kirdy compared the area unfavorably with the central square at Soumjiana. "Look! Right and left, in all directions! You will find not a single sausage grill!"

"Sausages are not in style this season."

"That must be the answer. Ugh! What a dreary place! I have never liked Tassadero. Zonk's Star is a sorry excuse for a sun!" Kirdy squinted contemptuously up toward Zonk's Star. "It is infested with mildew. Such light cannot be healthy."

"It's just light. Not much of it, of course."

"Perhaps, perhaps not. I have had it on good authority that Zonk-light includes a peculiar vibration found nowhere else. It rots the teeth and does odd things to the fingernails."

"Where did you hear this?"

"Floreste learned this and much more from a scientist who had studied the subject in depth."

"I saw no such information in the tourist brochure. They said: 'Zonk's Star floats through the sky like an enormous pearl, shimmering and wavering through a hundred subtle colors. The distances at Tassadero are particularly charming' or words to that effect."

"That's pure bosh! They are howling liars, these tourist blokes."

Glawen had no comment to make. The two arrived at the IPCC offices. Upon entering, they found themselves in a large room furnished with four desks and a line of heavy settees, durable if lacking in style. At the moment the room was empty of staff except for a young woman working at a desk. She was tall, slender, with short ash-blond hair, and a look of easy competence. She wore the regulation uniform which made no concessions to gender save in cut: dark blue blouse with red piping, dark blue breeches and black ankleboots. Two white stars at each shoulder indicated her rank. She measured Glawen and Kirdy with two swift glances and spoke in a crisp neutral voice: impersonal but far from unpleasant. "Sirs? Do you have business with us?"

"Nothing urgent," said Glawen. "I am Captain Clattuc and this is Sergeant Wook; we are affiliates from Araminta Station on Cadwal; we thought it proper to let you know that we were in the neighborhood."

"A very good idea! I'll turn you over to Commander Plock, who will want to meet you. Will you come this way? There is no great formality around here."

She took the two to a side office and spoke through the doorway. "Off-world visitors, Commander: Captain Clattuc and Sergeant Wook, from Cadwal."

Commander Plock jumped to his feet: a tall man, broad of shoulder, narrow of hip, with short thick black hair, glowing hazel eyes and features of jutting bone and corded cartilage. Odd! thought Glawen; Plock looked anything but a slave to regulation.

Plock pointed to chairs. "Be seated, if you will. You are Captain Clattuc and this is Sergeant Wook, correct?"

"Correct, sir."

"This is your first time on Tassadero?"

"For me it is," said Glawen. "Kirdy has been here before, with Floreste's Mummers."

"And what are your impressions, so far?"

"Fexelburg is a lively place, certainly. The folk dress with great care and the car drivers are all dedicated musicians. The police would seem to be extremely alert. Even suspicious. Almost as soon as we arrived at the hotel, Inspectors Barch and Tanaquil were on hand to pay their respects."

"Almost insulting," said Plock. "On your next visit use more expressive titles: 'Plenipotentiary High Exterminator Clattuc,' 'Supreme Warlord of the Araminta Armies Wook': something of the sort. Then they will send a more dignified delegation out to learn your business—which I assume is of a professional nature?"

"I'll be glad to explain, if you have the time."

"If Barch and Tanaquil took the time, I guess I can do the same. Proceed."

Glawen explained the circumstances which had brought Kirdy and himself to Tassadero. Like Barch and Tanaquil, Plock was puzzled. "Why the Zubenites? I'd expect such antics of the Fexels. Announce a fashionable, very expensive, new way to fornicate and they would fight to thrust their money at you."

"This is more or less what I heard from Barch and Tanaquil. They were cordial enough and spoke of full cooperation, but I don't think it means much. They want us to stay away from Lutwiler Country—

that is the impression I get. Lutwiler Country is dangerous, so they say, without law of any kind."

"Gaean law operates everywhere," said Plock. "Barch and Tanaquil know this as well as I do."

"I said something to this effect, but they paid no great attention."

"For a fact there is no local law in Lutwiler Country. Justice lacks refinement, and operates at a basic level. In Lutwiler Country I use the title 'executive adjudicant' because I am forced to be policeman, judge, prosecutor, defender and public executioner all at once, without so much as changing hats."

Kirdy asked: "What crimes take you out on the steppes?"

"Almost anything you can imagine. Every few years a nomad turns bandit and becomes rather nasty. He burns ranch houses, kills tourists, kicks dogs, throws babies into the purple ooze and generally makes a fuss. The IPCC is then called upon to abate the nuisance. That means lonesome days and bitter nights out on the steppe, looking for fire with my infrared sensor. When I find the bandit, I chat with him a few minutes, then I find him guilty and shoot him. That is the way things go in the Outer Countries, including Lutwiler."

"Inspector Barch said the Fexelburg police will guard tourists, if necessary."

"Just so. They wanted us to take on the job; we told them that if they fitted out caravans and sent tourists out into the Far Countries, then protection became their responsibility. If we had to deal with it, tourists would not be allowed out of Fexelburg unless they hired their own armed escort."

"The IPCC is not popular with the Fexelburg police."

Plock threw back his head and laughed. "We've had our difficulties. The upper echelons do well for themselves. A year or so back a certain Rees Angker formed a 'citizens' watch' to look into police peculation. He disappeared one night and was never seen again. The citizens' watch got the message and disbanded. We offered to investigate, but the Fexelburg police refused our help. When we persisted, they ordered us to close down our office, as it was not needed. We agreed and prepared to move out. There was an incidental technicality: our business, the protection of interstellar commerce, became impractical without a local IPCC presence. For this reason there would be no more ships arriving at Fexelburg spaceport and they might as well close it down, starting the day after our departure, and we were already packing to leave. Ah! What satisfying outcries! We were assured that it was all a mistake, that we were both needed and loved! They sold us this building at half its value where before we paid an exorbitant rent, and we were exempted from all taxes. So it worked out well."

"And that was the end to it?"

"Not quite. We demanded the resignation of the Chief High Commander of Police and the two High Commanders responsible for the disappearance of Rees Angker. Presto! It was done! They graciously renounced their titles, but operated as before. One day someone—don't ask me his name—flew these three gentlemen out into Varmoose Country and put them down on Wasty Steppe, exactly halfway around the planet. Each was given a handkerchief, a small bottle of mouthwash and a change of underwear, and allowed to go his way. Doubtless they carved out interesting new careers for themselves. So then: are the Fexelburg police now foursquare and incorruptible? I think not. They still do as they like, but rather more discreetly, since they know that we are watching."

"Well, it seems that we must take our chances with Lutwiler Country," said Glawen. "What is the best way to go?"

"If you hire a car, the driver will scorch like a maniac and never stop playing tunes. The omnibus makes three trips a day in each direction. You can go out in the morning, make your inquiries—which I suspect will be futile—and return in the evening. The depot is just around the plaza, in front of the AD&A travel agency. It might be a good idea to get your tickets now, as the buses tend to fill up."

Glawen and Kirdy rose to their feet. "One last word, and most important," said Plock. "The IPCC, unlike the Fexelburg police, goes anywhere, especially to help one of its own. I advise you to work out a fail-safe system of some sort, where one of you is always within reach of a telephone. Then, if anything goes wrong, use this system to notify us, and we will do our best to put things right."

"There are telephones in Lutwiler Country?"

"Hm," said Plock. "Not many. At Flicken Junction, halfway along the route, and also at Pogan's Point, but nothing in between."

"We'll work something out," said Glawen. "Thank you for your advice."

Glawen and Kirdy continued around the plaza searching in vain for the AD&A travel agency. Finally they put inquiries to a passerby, who gave them a quizzical look and jerked his thumb over his shoulder. "You're standing directly in front of the place."

"Oh! Excuse our stupidity!" Turning, Glawen studied the sign which advertised the premises of the Alien Dance and Arts Travel Salon.

Kirdy stared up the sidewalk. "That man took an offensive tone with us. I am tempted to speak with him and perhaps kick his stomach."

"Not today," said Glawen briskly. "We don't have the time."

"It wouldn't take all that long."

"His mind is now on other matters; he wouldn't understand his punishment. Come; let us look into the AD&A, as they call it."

The two passed through doors strikingly fabricated from concentric bands of purple and black glass, with a central starburst formed from crimson and blue-green shards. They stood ankle-deep in black carpet, at the center of a large waiting room. Vivid posters decorated the walls; directly before them was a business counter and a window with a sign reading "Omnibus Tickets."

A poster to the side depicted a large glossy omnibus halted on the road in the middle of a beautiful bucolic countryside. The omnibus seemed almost empty; from the window leaned a smiling tourist couple conversing with a pair of charming bright-eyed children who stood beside the omnibus. The small girl was depicted in the act of offering a bouquet of wildflowers to the lady tourist; the boy pointed excitedly across the fields to a column of purple ooze in the distance. A caption read:

Explore wondrous Tassadero by omnibus!
Safe! Comfortable! Convenient!
Buy your ticket here.

The window was closed. Glawen went to the counter. A young woman sat working the keys of a business machine and paid him no heed. In a courteous voice Glawen asked: "Can you sell me an omnibus ticket?"

The young woman glanced at Glawen, running her eyes up and down his garments. "At the window, sir. Can't you read the sign?"

"The window is closed."

"I know. I closed it myself."

"You will open it yourself?"

"Yes."

"When?"

"In eleven minutes."

"You will then sell me a ticket?"

"I will do my very best, sir."

"In that case I'll wait."

"As you like, sir."

Glawen wandered off to look at the travel posters. A large number

376

of these dealt with Zab Zonk, the episodes of his career and his unclaimed treasure.

VISIT VIVID TASSADERO

read the heading on one poster, which depicted Zonk decapitating an adversary with a ruby-encrusted blue metal scimitar, while in the background maidens peered with awe and delight into cases overflowing with gems.

A smaller caption at the bottom of the poster read:

Will it be you who finds this treasure?

Another poster showed Zonk with a group of adoring maidens in postures of abject submission, while Zonk indulgently caressed the head of a particularly choice blue-eyed blond. The caption read:

Zab Zonk enjoys his wealth, and well he should.
Who will enjoy it next?
Come to Tassadero and give it a try!

Another poster displayed a tourist opening a door upon a room full of luminous jewels. The caption read:

The immured treasures of Zab Zonk
might be yours alone!

Among the pamphlets on a table Glawen noticed a brochure bound in purple velvet with a drawing in gold ink of a nude girl, standing half turned away, looking over her shoulder as if out of the picture. The title read:

PERFECTION OF JOY:
It is attainable.

"Well, well," said Glawen, "what have we here?" He started to take the brochure to the counter, but at this moment Kirdy uttered a poignant cry mixed of surprise and gladness. "Come here at once! Look at this!"

Glawen put the brochure in his pocket and joined Kirdy by the wall. With a trembling forefinger Kirdy tapped a poster. "The Mummers are in town! We must go find them at once! Look! Here are their pictures! There is Arles, and there Glostor and Malory and Favlissa and Mullin and Dorre; I see them all! And Floreste himself! Ah, good old Floreste!"

"The last time you mentioned Floreste he was 'an avaricious old bastard'!"

"No matter! What a wonderful coincidence! Just when things seem utterly dismal, something like this turns up!"

Glawen examined the poster, which, along with photographs of Floreste and the Mummers, listed some of their programs and their schedule for the coming weeks. "You did not read the date correctly. They will not be here for another two days. They are now playing a town called Diamonte."

"Then we shall go to Diamonte! It is the only thing to do! Think how surprised they'll be to see us! Think of the festival we'll all enjoy!"

"Kirdy, step over here, if you will." Glawen led the suddenly scowling Kirdy to a quiet part of the room. "Listen closely, and listen carefully," said Glawen, "so that I need not repeat myself. We are not visiting the Mummers at Diamonte or anywhere else. Tomorrow I am going to Pogan's Point to find out something about Sibil, who gave Pogan's Point as her address. It may be a bit chancy, if the others out there are anything at all like Sibil. For this reason I want you to remain at the hotel, either in your room or in the lobby. I expect no trouble, but if I am not back tomorrow evening then you must get in touch with Plock at the IPCC. Is this all perfectly clear?"

Kirdy looked off across the room toward the poster. "It's clear enough, but—"

"No buts about it. If all goes well, we will be leaving for home the day after tomorrow on the *Camulke*. When the Mummers return to Araminta Station you can see them as much as you like. But not now. This is most definite. Come along; I must buy my ticket and I want to ask some questions of the manager."

The ticket window was open. Glawen bought a round-trip ticket to Pogan's Point, then asked the young woman who now serviced the ticket window: "What is the manager's name?"

"Arno Rorp. He's in the side office."

Glawen went to the side office and finding the door open stepped inside. At a desk sat a thin suave gentleman of middle age with smooth gray hair immaculately coiffed, and a mustache even more neatly trimmed. Glawen introduced himself, displayed the Perfection of Joy brochure and asked how it had arrived at the Alien Dance and Arts Salon.

Arno Rorp looked wryly down at the brochure. "Frankly, this is not the sort of material we normally handle. But—well, I was persuaded. For a fact, it seems little more offensive than many of our Zonk posters."

"How many of these brochures were you allotted?"

"Three dozen. Most went to the idly curious, but they've generated some small custom, from a rather unlikely source."

"The Zubenites?"

"Quite so. How did you know? But I forget; these excursions take place on Cadwal."

"No longer," said Glawen. "Who approached you originally?"

"In connection with the excursions? A rather engaging young woman, off-world, not out of the top drawer, I should say."

"Did she leave a name?"

"Ogmo Enterprises, nothing more."

"Did anyone else appear, representing Ogmo Enterprises: a man, for instance?"

"Never."

"Please step over here a moment." Glawen took Arno Rorp to the poster advertising Floreste and his Mummers.

"Ah, yes," said Rorp. "The Mummers. They put on a most entertaining show."

"Look at these photographs," said Glawen. "Are any of the faces known to you?"

"Yes indeed," said Rorp. "Most odd! This is the young woman who brought in the brochures." He squinted at the caption. "Drusilla. So that's her name."

Glawen took the poster from the wall. "I want you to write your signature on her photograph. Then in this blank space, write: 'My signature designates the person who distributed Perfection of Joy brochures.' Then sign your name again."

"Hm. Will this act involve me in lawsuits, angry correspondence, physical violence?"

"Not at all. Trouble comes when you fail to cooperate with the police."

Arno Rorp winced. "Please say no more." He wrote as directed.

"Most likely you will hear no more of this," said Glawen. "In the meantime, please do not mention my inquiries, in case you see this young woman again."

"As you wish, sir."

Glawen and Kirdy set off across the plaza toward the hotel, with the great bland disk of Zonk's Star now low in the west. Zonklight had a curious quality, thought Glawen: pale and soft, yet fluent as if with the ability to seep around corners and flood into crevices. It also seemed to enhance dark colors: the maroons and umbers, dark greens and indigos, while shadows were blacker than black.

Kirdy showed no disposition to speak; glancing sidelong, Glawen saw Kirdy's face to be set in strong stern lines. Glawen said: "Finally Ogmo Enterprises has a name."

Kirdy gave a noncommittal grunt.

"I suppose it's no great surprise," said Glawen. "I've long had a feeling that events were leading in this direction."

"Of course," said Kirdy indifferently. "I thought you knew all along."

"Did you?"

Kirdy shrugged. "The affair is over and done with. I say, let it rest in peace."

"That's not the way things happen," said Glawen. "It's also another reason why I don't want you fraternizing and gossiping with the Mummers. They must not know of our investigation."

"I still don't see what difference it makes."

"You can't be that dense. If Drusilla knows that we can link her with a set of crimes, she'll simply disappear, and we'll never know what she can tell us about her confederates. Don't forget that she is married to Arles."

Kirdy gave a contemptuous snort. "Are you accusing Arles as well?"

"Accusations can wait until we return to Araminta Station."

A few steps farther Kirdy made a tentative suggestion: "We could visit the Mummers but still keep a close tongue in our heads."

Glawen sighed. "If you think that I am mishandling this investigation, make a report to Bodwyn Wook. Until then, you are under my orders, and I have made them absolutely clear. If you disobey, I will instantly expel you from Bureau B."

"You don't have the authority."

"Just test me out, and see for yourself. You are not so disoriented as to misunderstand the meaning of an official order."

"I don't like official orders."

"Too bad."

"Not really. I've always done what I wanted, official orders or none."

The two walked on in silence. Arriving in the lobby of the Lambervoilles, Glawen made an amicable suggestion: "Let's look into the lounge and try out the virtue of the local ale."

Kirdy asked a sarcastic question: "Is that an official order?"

"Not at all," said Glawen. "I would like to hear your appraisal of the case as it now stands."

"Why not?" asked Kirdy. "Talk is cheap."

The two went into the lounge and took seats in deep leather chairs before a fireplace, and were served ale of good quality in tall glass beakers. "So then," said Glawen. "Who is guilty and who is innocent? Have you formed any opinions?"

"First of all, I wonder why you want to go out to Pogan's Point. You have learned who distributed the brochures."

"So far, so good," said Glawen. "But I have an uncomfortable feeling that we have only seen the tip of the iceberg. For instance, Sibil wore a tattoo on her forehead."

"What of that? I've heard of ladies with port and starboard running lights tattooed on their bottoms."

"No matter. These women with tattooed foreheads are mysterious."

"There are more than one?"

"Yes. One such woman had strange dealings with Chilke. Something is going on which neither he nor I understand. Namour may be involved, and I'd like to find out why, how, when and where."

"Bah," muttered Kirdy. "The folk at Pogan's Point don't know Namour."

"Probably not. I can't so much as guess what they know—but I want to find out. And tomorrow is an excellent opportunity."

"We could put the time to better use," grumbled Kirdy.

"How?"

"By visiting Diamonte and the Mummers, of course!"

Glawen said in a strained voice: "I've already explained three times and given three sets of explicit orders that I don't want you to visit the Mummers. You know my reasons. Don't you remember?"

"I remember your words, but they carry no great conviction."

"In that case, why should I trouble to explain anything to you? Now, for possibly the fourth and certainly the last time, I issue these clear, definite and direct orders: Do not communicate with the Mummers! Do not go near them! Do not speak to, listen to, look at, signal to, send messages to the Mummers, their representatives or any members of their entourage. Do not attend any performances. In short, have nothing whatever to do with the Mummers! Have I forgotten anything? If so, include it as part of the orders. I can't be any more definite. Am I correct in this?"

"Eh? Yes indeed. I'll have more of this excellent ale."

"Tomorrow," said Glawen, "I will be leaving early for Pogan's Point. You must sit in the lobby or in your room, but make sure the desk clerk knows where you are. If I am not back tomorrow evening, communicate with the IPCC. Did you hear me?"

Kirdy smiled: a curious smile, thought Glawen, full of poise and wisdom. "I heard your words. I understand them at all levels of my mind."

"Then I will say no more. I am going out now to a bookshop and buy some books, so that I may learn something about the Zubenites. Either come with me, or wait here or go up to your room and sleep."

"I'll come with you," said Kirdy.

CHAPTER 8

1

Glawen arrived early at the Alien Dance and Arts Travel Salon, to find the eastbound omnibus already on hand and apparently packed to capacity, with rows of pallid big-eyed faces peering from the windows. Glawen surveyed the scene with displeasure. This bus and its contents in no respect resembled the bus of the travel poster. Glawen congratulated himself on his foresight in securing a reserved seat, inasmuch as the bus seemed not only loaded but overloaded.

There was no help for it, he thought, and boarded the bus by the entry at the front end. For a moment he stood looking down the ranks of passengers, all dressed alike in gowns of fust and all burdened with parcels.

The driver was not accustomed to such indecision; he held out his hand and spoke crisply: "Give me your ticket, if you please. That is the rule, if you want to ride. If you do not, please descend from the bus."

"I definitely want to ride," said Glawen. "In fact, my seat is first-class reserved. Here is my ticket; please show me to my place."

The driver gave the ticket a cursory glance. "Yes, all is correct. This is a valid ticket."

"And which is the first-class section?"

"The entire accommodation is first class. You have reserved for yourself the privilege of sitting where you like."

"That is not my understanding! The ticket designates a seat for my use; someone else is sitting there now."

The driver gave Glawen a questioning look. "The 'privilege' is for everyone, not just for you alone! There are no elitists on the steppes!"

"All very well," said Glawen. "Still, I hold a ticket, which presumably guarantees me a seat. Where shall I sit?"

The driver glanced over his shoulder. "Offhand, I can't say. Why not try the rear bench."

Glawen went to the back of the bus, and thrust himself into a crevice between a pair of stout Zubenites. For convenience they had piled their parcels on the seat and resisted Glawen's intrusion, sprawling their legs apart and slumping their soft torsos as flaccidly as possible, but Glawen only thrust and squirmed the more vigorously, eliciting mournful mutters from the Zubenites. At last, with poor grace, they transferred a few of their parcels to the rack provided for the purpose. Seeing how the land lay, Glawen abandoned tact and thrust himself all the way back into the seat. The Zubenites groaned as if in pain. One cried out: "Mercy, dearest brother! Take pity on our poor natural bones!"

Glawen spoke in a severe voice: "Why is that bundle on the seat beside you? Put it up on the rack and we'll all have more room."

"It would be wasted effort, since I travel only to Flicken. Still, if you insist, it seems that I must oblige you."

"You should have put it there in the first place."

"Ah, dear brother! That is not the proper way."

Glawen saw no need to argue the point. He took stock of his fellow passengers, who seemed equally divided between men and women, though often the distinction was hard to make. All wore the same garment: a hooded smock, baggy breeches tucked into long black stockings, long pointed black shoes. The hoods were thrown back, revealing stubbles of coarse black hair. Faces were large, round and white, with large moist eyes and long noses flattened at the tips. Glawen found no mystery in the lack of crossbreeding between Zubenite and the other races of Tassadero.

The driver found no reason to wait for more passengers. He started up the omnibus and drove out of Fexelburg, along a road which led eastward across the steppe.

The scenery quickly became uninteresting. With nothing better to do, Glawen began to watch his fellow passengers, with some casual notion of analyzing their thought processes from a study of their unconscious mannerisms. He met no success; the Zubenites sat staring torpidly into space, not even troubling to look out the windows. Perhaps, thought Glawen, they were all pondering the subtle disciplines of Monomantic Syntoraxis.

Probably not. Unless he was greatly mistaken, these folk were neither High nor Low Adepts, but small farmers, lacking all interest in philosophy.

On the previous evening, Glawen had glanced through the *Syntoractic Primer* and now he thought to put his theory to the test. He spoke to the Zubenite on his right: "Sir, I notice what might seem to be an ambiguity in the arrangement of the Natural Doctrines. Tesseractic

384

Conjunctions properly should precede Doctrine of Thresis and Anathresis. Have you formed an opinion on this topic?"

"Dearest brother, I cannot speak to you today, since I do not know what you are talking about."

"That answers my question," said Glawen. He gave his attention to the landscape: a plain which seemed to extend forever, given accent and perspective by solitary frooks, standing at distant intervals. Far to the north a line of low hills melted into the haze. Somewhere out there was Zonk's Tomb, if the legends were to be believed. Glawen wondered if Inspectors Barch and Tanaquil on their holidays participated in the great treasure hunt. Most likely not, he decided.

In due course the bus arrived at Flicken: a village already deep in Lutwiler Country, consisting of a few drab cottages, a mechanic's shop and Keelums' General Store, which advertised:

Supplies for the Treasure-hunter
Food and Lodging Available

The bus halted in front of the store long enough to discharge passengers, including the portly Zubenite sitting next to Glawen. As he lifted his parcel from the rack he turned Glawen a reproachful look, as if to say: "Now, at last, do you understand the nuisance you have made of yourself?"

Glawen returned a cool and measured nod of farewell, but received no acknowledgment of the courtesy.

The bus proceeded east and, as Zonk's Star reached the meridian, entered a region cultivated to garden crops and cereals. Ahead rose the great black crag of Pogan's Point and a few minutes later the bus entered the town which spread away from the base of the crag. Peering from the window, Glawen glimpsed the seminary, a massive stone structure built halfway up the crag.

The bus entered the town's central square and halted beside a ramshackle depot. Glawen alighted from the bus and again looked up at the Point, which he conjectured to be the neck of an ancient volcano and certainly the most notable object he had seen all day. A narrow road sidled up the crag, angling back and forth, finally arriving at the seminary. Glawen's first impressions were reinforced. The seminary, a huge block of stone three stories high, loomed over the town like a fortress. It was surely not a place where frivolity and joyous revels interfered with the study of Monomantic Syntoraxis.

Glawen went into the depot: a single large room with a counter at the far end. At one time or another the walls had been painted yellow-green, which someone, presumably the stationmaster, had found unpleasant and had covered over as best he could with posters and placards, making a small personal assertion against the dismal atmosphere of Pogan's Point.

The bus driver had brought in a bag of papers, journals and periodicals, which he had turned out on the counter; the depot evidently served the community as a post office. The stationmaster stood looking through the papers: a thin-faced man of middle stature and middle age, with graying russet hair and bright hazel eyes. His most distinctive feature was a fine bristling russet mustache which, like the posters and placards, defied the dismal surroundings. He wore a red cap and a blue jacket with brass buttons to signify his official status, but Glawen suspected that had the costume not amused him he would never have worn it. He was obviously no Zubenite.

Glawen approached the counter; the stationmaster gave him a quick side glance. "Well, sir? What can I do for you?"

"I want to discover for certain when the bus returns to Fexelburg."

"The noon bus is gone. The evening bus leaves in just about five hours, close on sundown. Do you need a ticket?"

"I already hold my return, but I want to make sure that my seat comes with the iron-clad reservation I paid for."

"No doubt about it, sir! The seat is reserved for you, but neither I nor the driver feels inclined to explain to the Zubenites. They have barely the wits to come in out of the rain, but they are quick as weasels when they spy an empty seat on the bus. It may be that this is where they keep their brains."

"Since I am a stranger here, I must reserve judgment, along with my seat on the bus."

"You need not worry as to your seat. The night bus is never crowded."

Glawen brought out his list of the Zubenites participating at the second Thurben Island excursion. "Are you acquainted with these names?"

The stationmaster read the names aloud, pursing his lips as if at an astringent flavor. "Lasilsk. Struben. Mutis. Kutah. Robidel. Bloswig. These are all seminary persons: High Ordinates, they call themselves. If you are here seeking Zonk treasure, seek elsewhere. Go near the seminary, you'll get short shrift, if not worse."

"I am not treasure-hunting," said Glawen. He indicated the list. "I want to talk with these people, or at least some of them. How should I go about it?"

"They will not come down here: I can assure you of this."

"In short, I must go up to the seminary."

386

"But"—here the stationmaster held up his forefinger to emphasize his remarks— "if you intend no more than an hour or two of cozy gossip, with inquiries as to their health and maybe a casual reference or two to Zonk and his tomb, I advise you to sit in that chair and stir not an inch until you board the evening bus; then ride happily and safely back to Fexelburg."

Glawen looked dubiously out the window up at the seminary. "You make them sound like a family of ogres."

"They are philosophers. They are bored with tourists pestering them. They have explained a thousand times that if Zonk's treasure were near at hand, they would have found it long since. Now they refuse to answer the door. If anyone knocks more than three times they pour a bucketful of slops down on him, or her."

"That would seem to discourage almost any polite caller."

"Not always. One pair of tourists dodged the slops and knocked again. When the door was opened, they said that they were architectural students who wanted to look over the construction of the seminary. The Ordene said: 'Of course! But first you should know just a bit about our way of life, which dictated the internal arrangements.' 'Of course,' said the tourists, expecting a brief five-minute discussion. 'We'll be glad to learn.' At this they were taken away, dressed in gray robes and taught Syntoractic Elementaries for a year. Finally, they were allowed to look through the seminary. By this time all they wanted to do was leave; they came running down the hill waving their arms in the air. They bought tickets on the bus to Fexelburg; I asked them if they wanted a return ticket; they said no, they weren't coming back."

"They seem very dedicated philosophers," said Glawen.

"Some other tourists marched up the back side of the hill, hoping to find a cave or a passage. They never came down again; somebody said that they fell in the seminary garbage pit. For all I know there have been others; I don't count tourists."

"Don't the Fexelburg police protect tourists?"

"Certainly. They warn them away from Pogan's Point."

"I don't care about Zonk or his treasure. I want information about another matter. But I don't care to risk either the slops or the short shrift. Is there a telephone connection to the seminary?"

"So there is. Let me call for you, and I'll see how the land lays. What is your name?"

"I am Captain Glawen Clattuc of Araminta Station on Cadwal."

"And your business?"

"I prefer to explain that in person."

The stationmaster spoke into a telephone, waited, spoke again. He looked at Glawen. "They don't care about your preferences; they want to know your business."

"I need information in regard to Ogmo Enterprises."

The stationmaster spoke into the telephone, then told Glawen. "They don't know what you are talking about."

"Recently the six persons on that list visited Cadwal. I want to learn who supplied them the tickets. That is my only concern."

The stationmaster transmitted the information, listened, put down the telephone and slowly turned to Glawen. "I am truly surprised."

"How so?"

"They have agreed to speak with you."

"Is that so amazing?"

"In a way. They deal with very few outsiders. Go up the road, knock on the door. When you are met, ask for the Ordene Zaa. Go gently, my friend! These are odd folk!"

"I will ask my questions as politely as possible. If they don't care to answer, I will leave. There is no other option open to me."

"That seems a reasonable program."

The stationmaster accompanied Glawen to the door. Together they watched a group of Zubenites hunching across the square.

Glawen asked: "How can you distinguish men from women?"

"That is a favorite question of the tourists! I always tell them: 'Why bother to find out?'"

"You haven't made friends with any of the local ladies?"

"Pshaw! That would be what is called an exercise in futility. They think no more of me than if I were a nanny goat." He pointed across the square. "There is the start of the road up the hill."

2

Glawen crossed the square, bending his neck to a chilly wind from the north. Where the road left the square, a sign read:

MONOMANTIC SEMINARY
Warning! Keep out!

Glawen ignored the sign and started up the road. Back and forth he trudged: a hundred yards to the left, a hundred yards to the right, with each traverse broadening the vista across the steppes of Lutwiler Country.

The seminary loomed across the sky. The road made a final turn and swung back to pass before the front of the structure. Glawen halted to catch his breath where three stone steps led up to a small porch and a heavy timber door. In the wan light of Zonk's Star, the panorama was that of a world notably different from his own, in perspective, in the flux of color and light and most of all in mood. At his feet the town was a clot of brownish-red, umber or dull ocher structures with black roofs huddled around the square. Beyond were the cultivated lands, with windbreaks of frooks and sorcerer trees, and then the steppes, fading at last into the murk.

Glawen turned to the seminary. He squared his shoulders, settled his jacket and looked up the face of the building. The tall narrow windows seemed blind and vacant, as if no one troubled to look out at the view. A most cheerless place in which to study, thought Glawen, with the single advantage: there would be no frivolities or entertainments to distract the students. He stepped forward, raised and let fall the brass door-knocker.

A moment passed. The door opened; a burly round-faced man, somewhat taller than Glawen, with round close-set eyes, looked forth. He wore a gown of gray-brown fust and a cowl leaving only his face exposed. He gave Glawen a scowling inspection. "Why do you think we post signs? Are you illiterate?"

"I am not illiterate, and I read your sign."

"So much the worse! We don't take kindly to intruders!"

Glawen controlled his voice. "I am Captain Glawen Clattuc. I was told to knock at the door and inquire for the Ordene Zaa."

"Were you indeed? And what is your business?"

"I have already explained it over the telephone."

"Explain it again; I don't admit every popinjay who comes skulking around in search of treasure."

Glawen drew himself up. "I am not acquainted with your methods. What is your name?"

"That is not germane, at the moment."

Glawen read names from the list. "Are you one of these?"

"I am Mutis, if you must know."

"Then you were present at the Thurben Island excursion?"

"What of it?"

"Who provided you your tickets?"

Mutis held up his hand. "Put your questions to the Ordene and see how she answers you."

"That was my request in the first place."

Mutis ignored the remark. "Stand where you are." The door closed in Glawen's face.

Glawen turned, descended the steps and went out into the road, where he paced back and forth. He stopped short. A childish act, he told himself. It was beneath his dignity to so much as notice Mutis' conduct. He returned to the porch, but stood with his back to the door, looking off across the steppe.

Behind him he heard the door open and turned. The expression of easy condescension he had prepared for Mutis was wasted. In the doorway stood a person of lesser stature, far more slender than Mutis. Man or woman? Glawen was disposed to guess woman. Her age? Judgment was difficult, by reason of the austere seminary garments. Glawen assumed early, or perhaps middle, maturity. Even swathed in the folds of her white gown she seemed thin; the cowl exposed only dark luminous eyes, a short thin nose, skin almost as white as the cowl, a mouth colorless and severe. Her racial stock was clearly different from that of the Zubenites Glawen had observed on the bus. Standing in the doorway she examined Glawen from head to foot, with rather more careful attention than he thought needful. At last she spoke, in a husky voice: "I am the Ordene Zaa. What do you want of me?"

Glawen responded with formal politeness: "I am Captain Glawen Clattuc, from Araminta Station on Cadwal. The Conservator has sent me here to make certain inquiries. That is the reason for my presence."

Zaa's face showed no change of expression, nor did she show any disposition to allow Glawen entry into the seminary. "I can only repeat my question."

Glawen acknowledged the remark with a punctilious nod of the head. "I am an officer of the Station Police, and I am affiliated with the IPCC. If you wish, I will show you my credentials."

"No matter. It is all the same, one way or the other."

"I cite these facts so that you will not mistake me for a casual visitor. My inquiries concern the recent Thurben Island excursion made by six of your people." Glawen read off the names. "I am not interested in these six men; I want only to learn the identity of the person or persons who arranged the event."

Zaa stood silently in the doorway. Glawen realized that he had asked no question. The cool stare was unnerving. He must take care, he told himself, neither to become impatient nor yet to lose his composure. He spoke as before, formally polite: "Can you provide me the name of this person?"

"Yes."

"What is this person's name?"

"This person is dead. I do not know whether dead people make use of names."

"What was the person's name while he or she was alive?"

"The Ordene Sibil."

"Do you know how the Ordene Sibil learned of the excursions?"

"Yes, and to anticipate your question, I see no reason to divulge this information."

"What are the reasons for your reluctance?"

"They are complicated and would require a certain amount of background knowledge before you could understand them."

Glawen nodded thoughtfully. In his most cordial tones he said: "If you care to step outside, we can sit on the steps, which will spare you the fatigue of standing. Then, if you choose, you might provide me a brief outline of this 'knowledge'—enough, at least, for our present purposes."

The Ordene Zaa said evenly: "I suggest that you keep a very tight check on your impertinence. I detect in you both vanity and aggressiveness; you have made a poor impression."

"I am sorry to hear that," said Glawen. "This certainly was not my intention."

"I see no reason to sit on the steps and there repeat the remarks I have already made. Consider them carefully and well. If you wish further information, you may enter the premises, but you do so by your own volition, not by my invitation. Is this clear?"

Glawen frowned. "Not altogether."

"The statement seems clear enough to me," said Zaa.

Glawen hesitated. Zaa's remarks, by their tone as much as by their content, hinted of inconvenience, the responsibility for which he would be taking upon himself. He opened his mouth to ask for details, but the doorway was empty; Zaa had turned away.

Glawen stood looking indecisively through the doorway. What harm could come to him? He was a police official; if he were detained or molested, Kirdy would notify the Adjudicant Plock. He took a deep breath and stepped through the doorway into a high-ceilinged vestibule with stone walls and floor, unoccupied except for himself.

Glawen waited a moment, but no one came to speak with him. To the side a short vaulted passage led into what would seem a conference room: like the vestibule, high-ceilinged and paved with square tiles of black stone. Three high windows, tall and narrow, broke the far wall; pallid beams of Zonklight slanted down upon a long table of wooden planks, scrubbed so diligently over so many years that the hard grain stood out in relief. Heavy wooden chairs surrounded the table;

benches skirted the walls. At the back of the room, in the shadows, stood Zaa.

Zaa pointed to a bench. "Sit; enjoy your rest. Say quickly what you wish to say."

Glawen made a polite gesture. "Perhaps you will join me?"

Zaa looked at him blankly. "At what?"

"I do not like to sit while you stand."

"You are gallant, but I prefer to stand." She pointed to the bench again, in a manner Glawen found somewhat peremptory.

Glawen bowed with dignity, and settled upon the end of a bench. Hoping to bring an element of civility to the conversation, he said: "This is a remarkable building! Is it old?"

"Quite old. Exactly why have you come here?"

Patiently Glawen repeated the reasons for his presence. "As you see, it is not complicated. The promoter of these excursions is a criminal who must be brought to justice."

Zaa smiled. "Is it not possible that our concepts might differ?"

"Not in this case. The details would sicken you."

"I am not easily affected."

Glawen shrugged. "Justice to the side, your interests may best be served by answering my questions."

"I am unable to follow your logic."

"Our present investigation is focused upon Ogmo Enterprises. If the IPCC becomes involved, the investigation will widen to the seminary, by reason of Sibil's participation—quite likely to your embarrassment and certainly to your inconvenience, since the hearings will be held at Fexelburg."

"And further? I wish to hear the full compendium of threats and horrors."

Glawen laughed. "These are neither—only predictable circumstances. But further, since you ask, the six High Ordinaries may well be indicted as accessories, as no doubt they deserve to be. As of now, this aspect of the case exceeds my instructions."

Zaa seemed amused. "Let me make sure that I understand you correctly. If I do not answer your questions, the IPCC will enter the case, cause me inconvenience and indict six High Ordinaries. Is that the gist of your statement?"

Glawen gave another uneasy laugh. "You have cast my remarks into the crudest possible mold. I pointed out some possibilities which you can avoid, if you choose to do so."

Zaa came slowly forward. "You are aware that this is Lutwiler Country?"

"Of course."

"The local laws are designed to work for our protection. They concede us the right to deal brusquely with intruders, criminals and pests. Adversaries confront us at their own risk."

Glawen spoke with confidence. "I am a police officer performing my routine duties; what should I have to fear?"

"First of all, the usual penalties meted out to blackmailers."

"What!" Glawen jerked up in shock. "How did you come by this idea?"

Zaa appraised him for a moment, and Glawen thought that she might be enjoying herself. "Today I was warned of your arrival and told of the demands you would make."

Glawen's jaw dropped. "This is absurdity! Who notified you?"

"Names are not in the least relevant."

"They seem so to me—especially since the information is false."

Zaa gave her head a slow silken shake. "I think not. You have betrayed your position with your own words."

"How so?"

"Are you truly so ingenuous? Or do you still think to befuddle me with your smirks and artful mannerisms?"

"Madame, you misinterpret me completely! I attempt nothing of the sort! I assure you of this with all my heart! If you have read such an intent into my conduct, you are mistaken."

"Address me as 'Ordene,' if you please."

Zaa's voice was colder than ever, and Glawen realized with a pang that he had put his case with tactless fervor. "In any event, I am neither ingenuous nor a blackmailer."

"This is demonstrably untrue. With careful malice you threatened me with an IPCC investigation. With obvious satisfaction you described the anguish and humiliation to be visited upon me and recited the harms to be done to the High Ordinaries."

"Stop!" cried Glawen. "The longer you talk, the worse these imaginary misdeeds become. Face facts! The crimes were committed! Someone must investigate them. I make no demands upon you. If you decide not to answer my questions, I will bid you good day and you will never see me again."

Zaa seemed to come to a decision. "Yes! We shall contract together! The terms shall be these: I will supply in full measure the information you want; in return you will render certain services for me."

Glawen rose to his feet. "What kind of services? When, where, why and how?"

"There will be opportunity to discuss details provided we can agree in principle. If you are favorably inclined I will consult with the other Ordenes."

"It is pointless to consult with anyone, because first I must know what you want of me."

Zaa said stonily: "I cannot even broach the subject until I reach a consensus."

"Can you do so at once? Time presses on me; I must leave here inside an hour or two."

"I will act with all haste—if you agree to my proposal in its broad principles. I must have an unqualified answer."

Glawen shook his head. "This comes much too suddenly upon me. I can't agree to terms so vague."

Zaa said coldly: "You must decide whether you want the information you came here for, or not."

"I want the information, certainly. But what are these services? How much time will be needed? Is travel involved? If so, where? If you want me to injure or threaten someone, or take risks, I decline altogether. In short, I insist upon learning full details before I agree to undertake these services."

Zaa seemed pleased rather than otherwise. "So shall it be! It is a prudent posture to take and I commend you for it. I accede to your wishes, and the contract shall be on your terms."

Zaa turned and made a gesture. From a shadowed passage came Mutis. Zaa gave him a terse order, which Glawen failed to hear. Mutis turned away and disappeared into the gloom of the passage.

Glawen found the episode disquieting. "What is the reason for that?"

"You have insisted—wisely so—upon full knowledge of what we want of you. In this regard, the indispensable first step is an understanding of our order and our basic precepts, which you will find not only fascinating but helpful and a source of strength. I have sent for someone who will instruct you, at least in basic principles."

Glawen forced himself to speak quietly and in mild tones. "Ordene Zaa, with all due respect, your program is neither feasible, nor practical, nor at all to my liking. As a matter of fact, last night I looked through a book, a primer of Monomantics, and I already know something of your ideas: enough to last me for quite a while."

Zaa nodded and smiled. "I know the book. It is, let us say, an introduction to an introduction. It definitely will not serve the purpose."

Glawen spoke with resolution: "Ordene Zaa, I have neither time nor inclination for your studies. Give me my information, then explain what you want me to do for you. If at all feasible, I will do it. But I want no instruction nor any demands upon my time. In fact I must catch the evening bus back to Fexelburg, or my colleague will be worried and notify the IPCC."

"Really? In that case, there will be a telephone call and you will be allowed to reassure them that all is well."

"Haven't I made myself clear?" asked Glawen.

Zaa paid no heed. "Instruction is essential. Otherwise, your understanding will not be complete, and this is a term of our contract."

Into the chamber came Mutis with two others: the first as burly as Mutis himself, the second a person of distinctly slighter physique: a youth or a young woman.

Zaa spoke to the three: "This is Glawen, who will be taking instruction with us for a period. Lilo, you will bring him through the Primers and probably the first Compendium." To Glawen Zaa said: "Lilo is an excellent instructor, perceptive and patient. Mutis and Funo are both High Ordinaries, and House Monitors. Both are wise and dutiful, and you must heed their advice at all times."

Glawen cried out angrily: "Once and for all, I want no instruction in Monomantics, or anything else. Since you apparently do not plan to give me the information I came for, I will leave."

"Do not be discouraged," said Zaa. "If you study diligently, we shall not think the trouble in vain. You will now be prepared for study."

Mutis and Funo moved forward. "Come!" said Mutis. "We will show you your chamber."

Glawen looked at Zaa and again sensed the emotion on her face. She took pleasure in his humiliation. He spoke soberly: "So you seriously plan to keep me here against my will?"

Zaa had once again masked herself. "It is not a frivolous decision," she said. "The terms of our contract are explicit."

Glawen moved toward the passage. "I am leaving. Interfere with me at your own risk."

Mutis and Funo stepped slowly forward; Glawen pushed them aside and strode through the passage into the vestibule. Mutis and Funo followed without haste. Glawen went to the door, but could find no latch or release. He shoved and tugged, but it refused to swing open.

Mutis and Funo came slowly forward. Glawen stood with his back to the door, prepared to fight as best he could.

Lilo intervened. "Do not struggle; they will hurt you badly, and make you meek through pain. Do not give them the chance!"

"How do I get out of here?"

"You cannot. Do as you are told. Come with me. I assure you it is the best way."

Glawen assessed the two House Monitors. He was clearly outmatched. Why embroil himself; when he failed to return, Kirdy would transmit his message to Plock at the IPCC office, who would take such steps as were necessary.

"Come," said Lilo. "They need not so much as touch you."

"Lucky Glawen," said Mutis.

Glawen spoke between clenched teeth: "This is intolerable! I have important business elsewhere!"

"It must wait!" said Funo in a voice oddly shrill for a person so large and muscular. "You heard the Ordene. Now, hurry along with you before we lose our patience!"

"Come," said Mutis, inching forward, his loose pink mouth open and pulsing like a polyp.

Glawen stepped warily around him. Lilo took his arm and led him along the passage.

3

Glawen sullenly followed Lilo up a flight of dank stone steps to the second floor, then along a corridor. Watching the swing of Lilo's hips, Glawen decided that Lilo was female. Behind padded Mutis.

Lilo halted at the bottom of a second staircase and waited while Mutis stepped ahead and by some means set aglow a line of dim lamps to illuminate the stairs. Lilo told Glawen: "We will now climb these steps, but be careful, as they are very dangerous, especially when the lights are not shining."

"Let him find out for himself," said Mutis with a small hard smile. "He's in line for a bump or two."

Lilo started up the stairs. Glawen stopped short, quivering with a sudden surge of panic. Lilo paused, looked over her shoulder. "Come."

Glawen still hesitated. Mutis and Funo stood watching him, round white faces impassive. Glawen tensed, thinking to leap upon them, take them by surprise, and somehow make his escape. Rationality prevailed. Mutis and Funo were not to be surprised so easily, and in any event, Kirdy would be notifying the IPCC of his absence before the evening was out.

Lilo spoke again: "Come, Glawen."

Glawen swung about and marched grimly up the staircase, two steps behind Lilo. An odd staircase for so massive a structure, he thought. It was steep, irregular, devoid of railings, and twice changed direction at eccentric angles. Lilo had described it as dangerous, especially in the dark. It might well be so.

Lilo led him out into a long bleak hall and took him to a chamber lined with bins and racks. "This is a small preliminary step, but it is essential. You must be cleansed and dressed in a proper garment, that you may conform to the standards. You may now remove and discard your alien wear, which is not suitable for the seminary. You will not be using it again."

"Of course I will be using it again," said Glawen between clenched teeth. "This is sheer madness! Has the world gone insane? I don't want to be here, and I don't intend to stay here!"

"As to that, Glawen, I cannot say. I can only obey the Ordene. You will find that it is the easiest way."

"But I don't want to obey the Ordene."

"So it may be, but seminary rules are exact. And who knows? When you discover the excellence of Syntoraxis, your attitude may change! Consider that!"

"It is a most remote possibility. What I have seen so far I abominate."

Lilo said coldly: "For now, you may use that booth, for your privacy."

Glawen stepped into the booth, removed his outer garments and emerged, to find Mutis waiting for him.

Mutis pointed to a stool. "Sit!"

"What for?"

"So that I can remove that septic louse-mat from your head. Here we live in a state of civilized cleanliness."

"Never mind the haircut," said Glawen, restraining his outrage with an effort. "When I leave here I don't want to look a freak."

"Sit." Mutis and Funo seized his arms and thrust him down upon the stool. "Now, then!" said Mutis. "Sit quiet and give us no trouble or it's the owl-trap for you, and the wind blows cold of nights."

Lilo said tonelessly: "Do as he orders. It will be for the best."

Silently vowing a dozen revenges, Glawen sat like a stone while Mutis, with rude efficiency, clipped away his hair.

"Now, then!" said Mutis. "Off with your breechclout, or whatever you call it, and into the bath!"

Glawen was forced to wash in acrid "decontaminant fluid," then shower in cold water, and at last was allowed to dress in standard seminary garments which he selected for himself from bins.

Mutis had now gone off about his affairs. Lilo told Glawen: "I will now take you to your chamber, for a period of meditation."

"One moment." Glawen made a bundle of his old clothes, which he tucked under his arm. Lilo watched without comment. "Come."

She led him along the corridor, meanwhile reciting a list of admonitions for Glawen's guidance. "For a certain period, you must refrain from visiting the town or walking about the countryside. Dismiss all such inclinations; they will be strongly disapproved."

"I won't be here long enough to feel the need. Or so I hope."

Lilo spoke more quickly. "In that case, you will find no reason to attempt the stairs, since they are extremely dangerous."

"They sound not only dangerous but ominous," said Glawen.

"You are perceptive! So, be guided! Remember, the earnest student finds life easier than one who frets and shirks. Plainly, you are not one of this latter sort; am I correct?"

"I am a Clattuc of Clattuc House! Does that answer your question?"

Lilo glanced at him sidewise. "What is a 'Clattuc'?"

"This will be made clear: sooner, I hope, than later."

Lilo was silent for a period, then asked, almost wistfully: "You have traveled far and wide across the Reach?"

"Not as far as I might like. In fact, I have visited only a few worlds along the Wisp."

"It must be interesting to travel," said Lilo. "I have only a few memories of the crèche at Strock, and then the seminary." She halted before the door. "This is to be your chamber." She opened the door, and waited. Glawen stood back obstinately. Lilo said: "Truly, you gain nothing by inflexibility. Mutis loves nothing more than intransigence."

Glawen sighed and entered the room. Lilo said: "We shall talk more later. I am pleased that the Ordene selected me to be your instructor; usually the task falls to Bayant or Hylas. Meanwhile, for your convenience and protection, I will lock the door."

"Protection against what?"

Lilo made a vague gesture. "Sometimes, when students finish their work they hope to gossip with others who might prefer to rest or meditate. By locking the door I will spare you this nuisance."

The door closed. Seething with fury all the more poignant for his feeling that he had been swindled and fuddled and fooled, Glawen took stock of the chamber. The dimensions were adequate: twenty feet to the far wall and a width of about twelve feet. The chill of the stone floor was relieved by a mat of woven withe; the walls were washed a nondescript buff. A wooden table and chair stood against the far wall under a high window. To the left was a crude cot, to the right a tall wardrobe and storage case. A door opened into an austere bathroom.

Glawen threw his bundle of clothes upon the cot and went to sit in the chair.

The room was chill; Glawen still felt half numb from the shower. His teeth began to chatter, which caused him new annoyance. He rose to his feet, swung his arms, walked back and forth, jumped up and down and presently felt more comfortable.

Glawen looked up at the window. A center vertical post divided the opening into halves, each too small for egress. Each segment of glass could be swung open to provide ventilation if need be; both segments were now closed against the vertical center post.

Glawen climbed up on the table and looked out the window. He was provided a view across the steppe and down along the eastern fringe of the town, where stood a scattering of ramshackle cottages. Zonk's Star could not be seen, but judging from the dim light and the length of the black shadows, the time was close upon sunset. The omnibus might already have left for Fexelburg, and to his sorrow he was not aboard.

Glawen stood on tiptoes and looked down. The wall dropped a hundred feet sheer to the rocky hillside. Glawen opened one of the windows and tested the rigidity of the center post. He pushed, pulled; the post failed so much as to quiver. He closed the window against the cold wind. What had been Mutis' remark? Something about the "owl-trap"? Glawen shivered at the thought. He jumped down from the table and resumed his seat in the chair. Assuming that Kirdy followed instructions promptly and efficiently, Glawen could expect rescue as early as this very evening—though a more realistic hope would be tomorrow.

Glawen stretched out his legs and tried to take a balanced view of the circumstances. It was an adventure he surely would never forget. He managed a wry chuckle. The effrontery of Zaa and her cohorts was so brazen as to transcend ordinary logic or even reality. They were using the techniques of mind control: first, destroy the victim's confidence in what he considered the proper patterns of existence, then substitute an alternate system which functioned well. Whether purposeful or not, these seemed to be Zaa's tactics. "It will not be one of my proudest cases," Glawen told himself.

Another matter came to mind: if Zaa were to be believed—and why not?—she had been notified by telephone of his coming. Who had been aware of his plans? Kirdy, Inspectors Barch and Tanaquil, the

Adjudicant Plock. Why would any of these persons betray him? The mystery was profound.

Glawen rubbed his chin, in order to stimulate his thinking. Zaa had dealt with him, a police officer, with total disregard for the consequences; clearly she felt no fear of the Fexelburg police. Was it enough to say that this was Lutwiler Country, where Fexelburg police lacked jurisdiction, or—more likely—deliberately chose not to involve themselves?

It suddenly occurred to Glawen that at no time had he suffered violence. He had been subdued by nothing more than hints and subtle menaces, and now he found himself locked in a room with his head shaved bald. He straightened in the chair, quivering with shame.

Glawen gritted his teeth and assured himself. "What is done is done! I have been taught a good trick, if nothing else."

But a single question loomed larger than all the others together: why?

Glawen became aware that the room had gone dark. He climbed on the chair and looked out the window. Night had come to Lutwiler Country. Mircea's Wisp streamed at a slant across the sky. Glawen resumed his seat. He had noticed no source of light nor any light switch. He settled himself to wait.

Ten minutes passed. There was a sound in the hall and the door opened, to reveal Lilo's slender silhouette.

Glawen spoke coldly: "Is there neither light nor heat in this room?"

"There is light, certainly." Lilo touched a button beside the door, to bring illumination from light-ribbons along the ceiling.

Lilo entered the room. Quietly and thoughtfully she closed the door and came across the room. Glawen saw that she carried half a dozen books. She took them to the table and put them down, still with the half-abstracted air. Glawen watched silently as she arranged the books in a neat row along the back of the table. Sensing Glawen's altered mood, Lilo turned her head and studied him warily. "These are the study materials you will need. As you know, I am to be your instructor, for a certain period at least. Of course the most important work will be done by you yourself: that's where true progress is made. The texts are dense, but they yield to careful study."

Glawen said stonily: "I have no interest whatever in Monomantics."

Lilo spoke earnestly: "Your interest surely will grow, when you discover the advantages of study. Now, then! We must make a start, so that they won't think us slackards."

Lilo selected one of the books and with feline delicacy settled herself upon the cot. "This is the Index of Primes. They should be memorized,

400

even if their thrust is not immediately clear. I will read them to you, and you must listen with both ears, to receive their force and their sound, even if you don't understand. 'One: Duality is the stuff of grind and abrasion; it shall merge to Unity. Two—'" Glawen watched her with eyes half closed as she read, wondering as to what vagaries of fate had brought her to Pogan's Point seminary. She was, he thought, a well-meaning creature, with perhaps more warmth and sympathy to her nature than might be useful to her. She darted him a quick look: "Are you listening?"

"Of course! You have a soothing voice. It is the only pleasant thing I have encountered here."

Lilo looked away. "You should not think in such terms," she said severely. Glawen saw that she was not displeased. Lilo went on: "You have heard the Index, which we will repeat every day until you have it thoroughly committed. Now, to the sweep of our studies. Here, in green type, is Precepts, Laterals and Fluxions and in the same volume, but printed upside down in red, are Useful Terminators. These are immensely important, but at the moment you had better start with Facts and Primordials, which gives a sensible footing to what comes after. And of course you have your Primary Concepts." She handed Glawen the book. "This must come first."

Glawen looked into the pages. "It seems difficult—far beyond my scope, even if I were interested, which I am not."

"Interest will come! Syntoraxis is essentially a progression of axioms, each deriving from the so-called Fundamental Verity. Very crudely, the Verity commands the unity of all things. Fundamental Verity is a node of intellectual force: a substance known as *sthurre*. To attain the pinnacle is hard, but possible. Nothing must blur the clarity of our vision. Pogan's Point here in Lutwiler Country is exactly the right environment. There is nothing to impede our progress. The seminary has no distractions; it is neither harsh nor pleasurable—"

"It is cold, though."

Lilo paid no heed. "—allow nothing to distract us, especially a foolish indulgence in transient frivolity. Pain can be ignored; pleasure is more insidious."

"And far nicer, don't you think?"

Lilo compressed her lips. "That idea lacks both merit and consequence."

"For Mutis and Zaa, perhaps. Not for me. I grieve for pleasures I've missed, but I spare not a thought for the pain I have neglected to suffer."

Lilo said sternly: "You must not be flippant! Such ideas are debilitating and disturb the flow of logic. As the Primer tells us, the erratic impulses of evolution have caused anomalies which we have been trying to correct. Our goal is the imposition of order on chaos. Remember 'Three' in the Index? 'Unity is purity! Energy is direction! Duality is collision, disorder and stasis!'"

Half amused, Glawen studied Lilo's features, which, like those of Zaa, were fine, delicate and accented by large dark eyes. Lilo asked: "Are those ideas firmly in your mind?"

"Absolutely."

"Duality is to logical unity what death is to life. The chapter 'Opposites and Apposites' analyzes the subject in broad outline and is adequate for the beginner's needs."

"What do you mean by 'Duality'?"

"That should be clear even to you! Duality is the source of the Great Schism which drove us apart from the Polymantics. In any event, they were dominated by the masculines, which again caused polarities. In the Progressive Formula, which we endorse, sexual polarization is either ignored or avoided."

"And what do you think of that?"

"There is no need for me to think. The Monomantic Creed is correct."

"But how do you feel, in personal terms?"

Lilo again compressed her lips. "I have never thought to analyze the subject. Introspection is not a productive employment."

"I see."

Lilo darted him a sidelong glance. "What of yourself?"

"I like Duality."

Lilo gave her head a shake of disapproval, though seeming to smile. "I suspected as much. You must accept Unity." She darted him another quick glance. "Why do you look at me like that?"

"I wonder how you think of yourself. Female? Male? Unified? Type unknown? Or what?"

Lilo looked off across the room. "These ideas are not considered appropriate for discussion. An irrational evolution has blighted us with dualism; we thrust it aside with all the force of our philosophy!"

"You did not answer my question."

Lilo sat looking down at the Index. "How do you regard me?"

"You are properly female."

Lilo gave a slow reluctant nod. "I am physiologically female, that is true."

"If you let your hair grow you might even be considered pretty."

"What an odd thing to say! It would mean conscious duality."

Impelled in equal part by mischief, malice and feckless Clattuc gallantry, Glawen went to sit beside Lilo on the cot. She looked at him with startled eyes. "Why are you doing that?"

"So that we can study Duality together and learn how it works. It's far more interesting than Monomantics."

Lilo went to sit in the chair. "That is the most extraordinary suggestion I have ever heard!"

"Are you interested?"

"Of course not. We must give our attention wholly to the approved regimen." A musical tone sounded. "It is time for supper. Come; you and I will go together."

In the refectory Glawen and Lilo were served bread, beans and boiled greens from a row of iron pots. They went to sit at a long table. About thirty other members of the order hunched over their platters. Glawen asked Lilo: "Is anyone here your special friend?"

"We love each other and all of humanity with the same deep fervor. You must do the same."

"I find it hard to love Mutis."

"At times Mutis is inclined to be arbitrary."

"But you love him, nonetheless?"

After a moment Lilo said: "All of us must generate our share of universal love."

"Why waste any on the likes of Mutis?"

"Ssst! Quiet! You are a noisy person. In the refectory silence is the rule. Many of us set aside this time to ponder, or to clarify some apparent paradox, and no one wants to be disturbed."

"Sorry."

Lilo looked down at Glawen's plate. "Why aren't you eating?"

"The food is revolting. The beans are spoiled and the greens are burned."

"You will be hungry if you do not eat."

"Better hungry than sick."

"Come, then; there is no point sitting here in idleness."

Once more in the chamber Lilo primly seated herself in the chair, and Glawen sat on the cot. Lilo said: "We should now discuss the Primordials."

"Let's talk about something more interesting," said Glawen. "What services does Zaa expect of me?"

Lilo gave a nervous flutter of the hand. "I would not care to venture an opinion."

"Who telephoned to tell her I was coming?"

"I don't know. Now, in regard to the books, I will leave them at your disposal. Since they are valuable, I have been instructed to secure a receipt." Lilo rose to her feet and extended a sheet of paper. "You must affix your symbol and your name to this."

Glawen waved aside the receipt. "Take the books away. I don't want them."

"But they are indispensable for your studies."

"This travesty must come to an end, the sooner the better. I am Captain Glawen Clattuc, a police officer. I am conducting an investigation. When I complete my inquiries I intend to leave."

Lilo stood frowning down at the receipt. "Still, you must sign this paper; these are Zaa's instructions."

"Read what is written on the receipt."

In an uncertain voice Lilo read the document. "'I, Glawen, acknowledge receipt of six books, here listed by title'"—Lilo read the titles—"'which I will use carefully and diligently as my studies dictate. I will pay the usual royalty to the Monomantic Institute for this usage, and also a reasonable charge for sustenance, accommodation and other sundries.'"

"Give me the pen," said Glawen. At the bottom of the page he wrote: "I, Glawen Clattuc of Clattuc House, Araminta Station, Cadwal, Captain of Police and affiliate of the IPCC, will pay nothing whatever. I am here in my capacity as a police officer, and will depart as soon as convenient. Any claims for reimbursement of any kind must be made to the IPCC office at Fexelburg."

Glawen returned the paper to Lilo. "Take the books. I do not intend to use them."

Lilo took the books and went to the door. Glawen jumped up and stood in the doorway. "Never mind the lock. Since I am not studying, I will take my chances with distraction."

Lilo went slowly out into the hall, where she paused and looked back with a troubled expression. She said at last: "It's better that I lock the door."

"I don't like it. It makes me feel a prisoner."

"It is for your convenience, and safety."

"I will take the chance."

Lilo turned and went off down the hall. Glawen watched as she disappeared down the purportedly dangerous staircase. For an instant he was prompted to follow, but decided against precipitating a confrontation. Let Plock from the IPCC deal with these extraordinary folk.

On the other hand, no harm could come of taking precautions. He looked up and down the hall, and saw no one. He ran to the wardroom where Mutis had cut his hair. From a shelf he took six clean bed sheets and returned to the door. Once again he looked out into the hall. It was still empty. He returned to his chamber as quickly as he had come. Standing on the chair he lay the sheets on top of the tall wardrobe where they could not be seen. After a moment's thought he also concealed the bundle he had made of his clothes.

Half an hour passed. Mutis opened the door and looked into the room. "Come with me."

Glawen spoke in a cold voice: "Have you no manners? Knock at the door before you enter!"

Mutis gave him a dull uncomprehending stare and signaled with a sweep of his heavy hand. "Come."

"Come where?"

Mutis scowled and stepped forward. "Need I make myself any more clear? The word was 'Come'!"

Glawen slowly rose to his feet. Mutis seemed to be in an ugly mood. "Hurry!" growled Mutis. "Do not keep me waiting. So far you have come off easily."

Glawen sauntered from the chamber. Mutis pressed close behind him. "Have I not said: 'Hurry'?" He drove his fist into the small of Glawen's back; Glawen jerked his left elbow into Mutis' neck; he turned to see the flat small-featured face contorting, so that the mouth was a small pink circle. Mutis lurched forward; Glawen tried to strike out and jump back, but too late; Mutis overpowered him and bore him to the floor. Glawen rolled and kicked, to catch Mutis in the ear. He jumped to his feet and stood panting, but now the hall was full of confusion and hooded figures in flapping gray gowns. Anonymous hands seized Glawen and pulled the hood down over his eyes so that he could not see. He heard Mutis speaking in a furious babble, and a shuffling rustle, as if Mutis were trying to push toward him.

Glawen was half led, half pushed down two flights of stairs. Here there was further confusion: exclamations and questions. Mutis at last gave sullen instructions: "To the old place; those were the orders."

Glawen heard murmurs of doubt and soft comments which he could not comprehend. He tried to throw off the hands which gripped him so that he could raise the hood, but without success.

Mutis spoke: "I will now take him in charge. He is docile; I need no more help."

"He is quick and strong," said a voice hard by Glawen's ear. "We will come too, and prevent violence."

"Ah, bah!" grunted Mutis.

Glawen was taken along a corridor which smelled of wet stone, ammonia and an aromatic odor as of fungus crushed underfoot. He heard a creak and a scrape, and he was thrust forward.

Hands released their grip; he was free. Once more he heard the creak and scrape, and the thud of a closing door, then silence.

Glawen pulled the hood from his face. He could see nothing. He stood in absolute darkness.

After a moment Glawen moved back toward the door and found the wall. Echoes, or perhaps another subtle perception, informed him that he stood to the side of a large room: a subterranean place, to judge by the odor of wet rock. The only sound was a soft tinkle of running water.

Glawen stood motionless for five minutes, trying to gather into coherent form what remained of his composure. "I seem to have made a number of mistakes," said Glawen to himself. "Conditions are truly going from bad to worse."

He felt the wall behind him, encountering natural stone: uneven, damp and smelling of mold. It would seem that he stood at the very core of Pogan's Point.

Glawen started a cautious exploration, testing the floor as he went, half expecting to come upon the lip of a chasm: a trick which might well be expected from the Monomantics, so that when Plock came to look for him, the Ordene Zaa in tones of injured innocence could say: "The crazy Captain Clattuc? We could not restrain him! He chose to enter a cave and fell into a chasm! We had nothing to do with it!"

But Glawen found no chasm. The floor seemed level. Glawen groped ten paces to the left of the door, then returned and tested ten paces to the right. The apparent curvature of the wall—assuming that the chamber was circular—would indicate a diameter of about sixty feet. The circumference would then be, roughly, about two hundred feet. Glawen went back to the door and prepared to wait. Sooner or later, someone must come to see to his needs. Or perhaps no one would come—ever. Glawen wondered if this might have been the fate of the missing tourists, who had sought too zealously for Zonk's Tomb. It was not a cheerful notion. He had kicked Mutis in the ear, but he could not die happy on that account alone.

Half an hour passed. Glawen became uncomfortable leaning against the wall and seated himself on the floor. His eyes grew heavy and despite the cold hard stone he began to doze.

Glawen awoke. Time had gone by: several hours at least. He felt cold and cramped and miserable. His mouth was unpleasantly dry.

He listened. No sound but the plash of running water, coming generally from the right. He heaved himself to his feet and felt for the door. A sudden idea entered his mind; perhaps it had never been locked! What a fine sardonic joke to play on the foreign policeman: to put him in a dungeon and leave him to starve—behind a door which had never been locked!

Glawen tested the door. It felt dismally solid. He groped along the panel and around the frame, but found neither latch nor hinge nor draw chain, Glawen drew back and gave the door a great buffet with his shoulder. The door failed to move. Glawen uttered a despondent grunt.

An hour passed, or perhaps two; Glawen found himself unable to judge. In any case the wait had become most tedious, and he could hope for little better the rest of the long night; almost certainly he would be confined until morning, while everyone else enjoyed the comfort of their warm beds.

Glawen heaved a sad sigh, and took command of himself. Fury at this point was a futile exercise.

His mouth was thick with thirst. Keeping always in contact with the wall, he crawled on hands and knees to the right, and after about twenty yards came upon a rill of cold water. He cupped up a handful and tasted. The water was harsh with minerals and barely potable. Glawen drank a few mouthfuls, enough to assuage his thirst, and rising to his feet groped around the wall and back to the door.

An unknown period of time passed. Glawen sat by the door, his mind numb.

From high up on the wall came a sound. Glawen lifted his head. The sound was repeated; he identified it as the squeak of a door moving on dry hinges. The sound was joined to a crack of light which revealed the outlines of a balcony, twenty feet above the floor.

A figure shrouded in white came out on the balcony, carrying a lamp. Glawen sat motionless; the play of light and shadow confused his perceptions; he felt only a passive interest as to who or what had come to overlook the chamber.

The person in white fixed the lamp into a socket, then with a swift motion threw back the hood of the gown. In the yellow lamplight Glawen saw a thin face with large dark eyes, a thatch of tawny-copper hair and fine, clearly defined, features. The hair clasped the face like a copper casque, almost covering the ears, clinging to the forehead and swirling up in curls at the nape of the neck. With dull surprise Glawen saw this person to be the Ordene Zaa. Her gown was of a softer fabric than that which she had worn before and fitted her with rather more grace.

Zaa looked down at Glawen, her expression inscrutable. She spoke in a light, almost airy, voice: "With great skill you have contrived an uncomfortable plight for yourself."

Glawen responded in measured tones: "My conduct has been quite correct. You have wrongfully placed me into this plight, for reasons quite beyond my understanding."

Zaa shook her head. "In terms of local realities, my conduct is correct. Yours is based upon naive theorizing; already it has been proved useless."

"I do not care to argue," said Glawen. "It would seem as if I were complaining."

Zaa looked down with amusement. "You seem to have an unusually serene disposition."

Glawen perceived that Zaa was playing with him as a cat with a mouse, and made no comment.

Zaa prompted him: "Is it by reason of stoicism? Or a resolute philosophy of elaborate parts?"

"I couldn't say; I am not much for introspection. Perhaps I have simply gone numb."

"A pity. If Mutis has a fault, it must be that he does not forgive lightly, and I believe that his head still rings from the force of your kick. But we cannot dwell upon past wrongs; we must look to the future. What do you say to that?"

"I say, give me my information and I will be away from this dismal place without a moment's delay, and never so much as look over my shoulder. This is your most sensible option."

Zaa smiled. "Only from your point of view."

"From yours as well. If you harass a police officer you make trouble for yourself."

"You forget that this is Lutwiler Country. Your authority is meaningless."

"The IPCC does not concede this point of view."

"Do not let this theory influence your conduct," said Zaa. "I am in control of the seminary: such is the nature of local Truth. You must accede to my program, not I to yours. If this is unclear, then plainly you are in need of cerebral therapeutics."

"Your statement is clear. I need no therapy."

"I am not altogether convinced, after hearing statements from Mutis and Lilo. In the one case you made erotic suggestions—"

"What? I did no such thing!"

"—in the other you were brutally offensive and inflicted pain upon Mutis, whose ear still smarts and throbs."

"These accusations are absurd!"

Zaa shrugged. "The gist of the matter is definite enough. Mutis describes you as intractable. Lilo is troubled by your tactics, and wonders where she has gone wrong."

Glawen managed a laugh. "I will tell you the facts. Mutis struck me in the back before I struck him. He provoked me to a fight—probably by your orders. As for Lilo, perhaps I was a trifle gallant, out of sheer boredom, just to add a bit of sparkle to her life. My conduct was certainly not lewd. The sexual obsessions are in her head, not mine."

Zaa gave another indifferent shrug. "It may well be, and why not? You are strong and confident; an impressionable young woman might find you appealing." Zaa looked around the chamber. "These accommodations are not luxurious, but they are inexpensive: in fact, free. Since you insist upon paying nothing for your lodging, this cave must suffice."

"You would use an agreement to pay as proof that I stayed here of my own accord. That is not the case. I am here as a prisoner."

"Have you forgotten our contract?"

"Contract?" Glawen looked blank. "The terms were so vague as to be meaningless. Neither this so-called contract nor any other contract has force between a captive and his captor."

Zaa laughed—a light tinkle, as of glass wind chimes moved by a breeze. "In Lutwiler Country such contracts have peculiar and particular force, especially in regard to the duties of the captive."

Glawen had no comment. Zaa went on. "Do you recall our agreement?"

"You offered all your information in return for certain services not specified: a bargain to which I could not agree. You then tried to teach me Monomantic Syntoraxis as your end of the contract. It is a fine joke, but do you wonder that I no longer take you or your contract seriously?"

"That is a mistake. The contract must be taken seriously."

"In that case, this is my suggestion," said Glawen. "Let me out of this hole, give me the information I need, then explain what you want of me. If it is something I can do, and is not criminal, immoral, harmful, hurtful or even disgraceful, and won't take too long or cost too much, I will do it."

Zaa reflected. "That is a disarmingly simple plan."

"I am happy that you like it."

"Ah! I am concerned less for your happiness than your sincerity."

Glawen considered the word. "I am sincere in regard to my undertakings."

"Hm, perhaps so. But I must be certain. I am almost afraid to test you out. One moment; we will discuss the matter further."

Zaa stepped back from the balcony; the door closed. A few moments later the lower door swung aside. Zaa entered and the door closed behind her. "It is easier to talk at this level."

"True." The substance of Zaa's white gown was sheer; she seemed metamorphosed from the epicene creature Glawen had first encountered; in the lamplight the sharpness of her features became delicacy; the cap of copper-red hair gave her face a piquant cast; her dark eyes were soft and luminous. A waft of subtle perfume crossed the five or six feet between the two.

Zaa looked about the chamber with a vague expression. "Have you familiarized yourself with this place?"

"In the dark? I am a Clattuc, but I am not insane."

"Look about you now. It is a void at the very heart of the Point."

"It is a dreary place, certainly."

"Notice the dais against the wall yonder. The bundle on top is a pad and a blanket, which visitors may use for a bed."

"What fee do you ask?"

"None. You may sleep free of charge where Zab Zonk lay in his white jade catafalque, shaded under swagged curtains of moonstones and pearls."

"It is peculiar accommodation for indigent guests."

"Do you find it so?"

"The atmosphere is picturesque if a bit macabre. The appointments are minimal."

Zaa looked around the chamber. "It is austere, beyond a doubt. Better facilities are more expensive."

Glawen ignored the silken jest. "Do the Fexels know that you have found the tomb?"

Zaa languidly stretched her arms to either side, and glanced at Glawen over her shoulder. Glawen watched in fascination. "Naturally," said Zaa. "Why else do they oblige us at all times and indulge our whims? Because thousands of tourists spend fortunes straggling across the steppes, hoping to find the tomb. We keep the secret, and the Fexels leave us in peace."

Glawen looked thoughtfully toward the dais. Strange how casually he had been entrusted with so precious a secret! Zaa had not even suggested discretion. How could she be sure that he would keep this rather sensational information secure, once he left the Point? Evidently she took his good faith for granted. Remarkable! Zaa did not seem a trusting woman. Other ideas entered Glawen's head; he pushed them and their implications to the side.

He asked Zaa: "What of the fabulous treasure?"

"The catafalque was smashed. Zonk's bones could not be found. There was no treasure." Zaa turned and walked slowly across the chamber. She stopped and looked over her shoulder. "Are you coming?"

Glawen followed, feeling as if he were walking through a dream. Great events hung in the air; what might be their import? He could not guess; his mind veered this way and that in the effort to avoid thought of any sort.

Zaa stopped by the little rill which trickled across the floor. She looked back at Glawen. "You have noticed this stream?"

"Yes. On the chance that it was not connected to your drains, I went so far as to taste it."

Zaa nodded gravely. "The water is mineralized but it is potable. Look now, how the water drains into a tunnel. Other persons, even more afflicted with mental disorder than yourself, thought to curtail their therapy by crawling down the hole. It is not a good plan. The tunnel narrows and the adventurer cannot return. If he manages to squeeze past the narrow place, he falls into a deep dark pool. The water is cold and after a few moments of splashing about, he drowns, and his tissues quickly become mineralized. It is said that a very thin person once crawled down the tunnel at the end of a rope, in search of treasure. He found nothing of value, but when he shone his lamp into the pool, he saw a number of white shapes at the bottom, disposed in various postures. Some of these petrifactions date back to the time of Zab Zonk; indeed, one may well be Zonk himself, though we have never troubled to make sure."

Glawen said in subdued voice: "The pool would be a tourist attraction in itself."

"No doubt! We want nothing to do with tourists! The confusion, noise and litter would sorely try our patience. The tomb will never know change, nor the pool. Think! A million years from now explorers of some alien race may chance upon the pool. Imagine their amazement as they peer down through the water!"

Glawen turned his back to the tunnel. "It is an interesting thought."

"Quite so. Here in the tomb one feels the flux of time. In the stillness, I often think to hear the murmur of those far future voices, as they explore the tomb." Zaa dismissed the subject with a flippant wave of her fingers. "But it need not concern us. We are the things of Now! We are alive! We are aware! We ordain! We ride our personal worlds across the universe as if they were great rumbling chariots!"

After a moment Glawen said, somewhat more cautiously: "I am surprised that you have confided so much information, particularly in regard to Zonk and his tomb."

"Why not? Information is what you came for! Am I not correct?"

"Correct! And yet—"

Zaa wandered to the dais. She seated herself on the edge and looked up at Glawen. "And yet?"

"Nothing in particular."

Zaa said: "Either you must sit or I must stand; I cannot talk with my head tilted back."

Glawen gingerly seated himself at a discreet distance, and appraised Zaa from the corner of his eye. The lamplight blurred her features and gave her face an odd end-of-nowhere charm.

Zaa spoke softly: "As I mentioned, Lilo is convinced that you are charged with a immoderate and rampant eroticism, so that you fairly sweat with lust."

"Lilo's hopes or fears—whichever it may be—exceed reality by a factor of fifty to one," said Glawen. "She is too excitable for her own good, and no doubt is a victim of fantasies. On the other hand, if the only men she sees are beasts like Mutis and Funo, I can appreciate her yearnings."

"Funo, so it happens, is a woman."

"What! Are you serious?"

"Of course."

"Ha! I wonder that poor Lilo is as sane as she is."

"Do you consider Lilo sexually stimulating?"

Glawen frowned off across the room. The situation was becoming ever more rife with delicate possibilities. Time was the important factor! Surely by now Plock must be in receipt of his message, and surely would not delay at undertaking his rescue.

Meanwhile, Zaa seemed relaxed and might well be inclined to provide more information. If he exercised his gallantry to the fullest, she might become more relaxed than ever. Glawen winced. Zaa undeniably seemed less grotesque and more nearly human than before but there was still about her the unnerving suggestion of a white reptile: a walking lizard, or a white-skinned newt with red hair. Glawen winced again. He must expunge these ideas from his mind; if Zaa suspected their presence she might become not only cold but spiteful.

So much passed through Glawen's mind in no more than two seconds. What had she asked? Did he find Lilo sexually stimulating?

Glawen said: "I will be absolutely candid. Men are stimulated in a different manner from women, as you must know."

"I have never troubled to explore the subject."

"Well, it is true. In the case of Lilo, the gray gown simply swallows her figure, which needs all the help it can get. Her hairless scalp is far from appealing, and I've seen corpses with a healthier skin color. On the positive side, she has good features and beautiful eyes. She is graceful and there is a certain wistful charm to her manner. As I think back, I can't believe that I alarmed her; she seemed to come to life under the attention."

"These feelings perhaps disturbed her, causing both guilt and confusion, which she attributed to you and, as I see now, perhaps exaggerated. It seems, then, that you find her gauche?"

"Gauche, prim, resolute: whatever. If she were to grow hair, dress nicely and get some color in her skin, she would seem passably attractive."

"Interesting! As of now: you find her unappealing?"

Glawen wondered how best to phrase his remarks. "Spacemen encounter all kinds of women. I have heard them say that at night all cats are gray."

Zaa nodded thoughtfully. "Lilo of course is totally innocent. Her life to date has been formally Monomantic and unified, and for certain reasons we are interested in her instinctive response to the proximity of a personable young man such as yourself."

"So this is why Lilo became my instructor."

"In part."

"Surely I am not the first man of her acquaintance?"

Zaa gave a sad laugh. "I see that I must explain. The Monomantics espouse Unity as their goal. The Polymantics accepted Duality, but they were dominated by masculines. The Monomantic rebellion was led by heroic females, who insisted upon sexual equality, and thought to create a race in which sexuality was not a coercive force. In the biological workshops at Strock, many roads were tried, but the efforts always fell short. The Zubenites of Lutwiler Country were at first considered a glorious success, because they proved at least partially intra-fertile. To this degree Duality has been conquered; we have perfected Monomantics in many phases. The doctrine asserts that 'man' and 'woman' are archaic and essentially incidental words. Mutis is a man; Funo is a woman. They may not even be aware of their differences, which are not functional. Mutis is impotent; Funo

413

produces no eggs. So it is among the Zubenites. Their survival as a people is barely tentative."

Glawen kept a closed mouth upon his opinions.

"Still, our efforts have been at least theoretically successful. Duality has been discredited and sent reeling; it can no longer be considered an inspirational philosophy. Do you agree to this?"

"I have never taken a position, one way or the other."

"Unity is now the rule. Men and women are equal in all respects. Women have been freed from the ancient curse of childbearing. In their turn, men no longer suffer the glandular pressures which distracted their energies and sometimes prompted them to illogical gallantries. What do you say to that?"

"It's an interesting point of view." Glawen cautiously went on to say: "I have no difficulties with my glands, and I certainly would not care to attempt Unity."

Zaa smiled. "I may inform you that a new theory has won strong supporters, among them myself. The Zubenites are not altogether satisfactory; they will not copulate, for one reason or another, and the population will not sustain itself. Younglings are brought in from Strock or the folk would not survive."

"Lilo does not seem the typical Zubenite woman—nor, for that matter, do you."

"Lilo has an interesting history. To facilitate our work at Strock, we brought in a brilliant young geneticist from Alphanor, not altogether by his own volition. Out of boredom he began to perform secret experiments. It seems that in the case of Lilo he used a sample egg of high quality and his own sperm. He bred her in a special culture dish; the zygote was nurtured in a tub to itself, without sequestrators or hormone suppressants, and fed special nutrients. In his regular work, because of his resentment and general cheerlessness, he defaulted upon his duty and produced a thousand one-eyed creatures with one leg, blue spots and enormous genital organs, which he conceived to be a ludicrous joke. In another vat he wasted three dozen prime eggs by impregnating them with the sperm of a raccoon which chanced to be on hand. The joke escaped detection until the infants began to grow tails, and then of course the truth was made known and the geneticist was discharged with prejudice.'

"Lilo almost shared the fate of the teratoids, but someone noticed that she was developing along more conventional lines, and so she survived. But how her rather striking excellence was achieved we never learned, since the geneticist was no longer alive."

"That is an interesting tale," said Glawen.

"As of now, Lilo is similar to a female of the old Duality. Not wishing to embarrass her, we have not shared this information with her. It seems that she has received the news by another means."

"All this aside," said Glawen, "my first concern is for myself. How much longer do you intend to keep me confined in this hole?"

"I see that I must be totally candid," said Zaa. "In our efforts to expunge Duality, we have overachieved: this you know. We can produce Zubenites at will, but they have many negative characteristics and changes are necessary. Must we amend Monomantics and risk a new sexuality? The theory which I mentioned suggests that this may be necessary, through the inherent nature of protoplasm. From Strock comes nothing but dismal news. The processes are failing. Zygotes die faster than they can be produced; the younglings are sickly and abnormal.

"To survive, it appears that we must return to primitive techniques. Ah, but now? The men are like Mutis, incapable of the task, while the women are like Funo; they would go into convulsions at the idea.

"Now, then! This is not true in every case. A few women ovulate, and are still receptive. It is the men who are helpless. They are a poor lot, dull and limpish."

Glawen said nervously: "They might surprise you! Dress the ladies in pretty costumes; let them grow their hair and play in the sun so that they take on some color. Instead of philosophy, they should learn to dance and sing and set out fine banquets with good wine! The men would soon come around."

Zaa made a sound of disgust. "We have heard that story before. A certain man claimed full knowledge in the field of human emotions. He stated that our problems were mental, no more; that we should undergo a series of what he called sexual therapy sessions. We tested his theories at great inconvenience and even greater expense! We discovered only that this man's avarice far exceeded his performance."

Glawen pretended only idle interest. "It seems that you are referring to the Thurben Island affair."

"Obviously. Isn't one such event enough?"

"This avaricious savant accomplished nothing for you? What were his credentials?"

"The results were at best ambiguous. He urged us to continue the program, and our Ordene Sibil remained to observe and to learn, but her news is unclear."

"And the savant: what is his name?"

"I hardly remember; I made none of the arrangements. Floreste:

415

that is his name. He directs a troupe of clowns and charlatans; he is mad for money!"

Glawen heaved a sigh. Zaa, he reflected, was remarkably free and open with her information. He wondered what undertakings she would demand before allowing him to go his way—although Plock would surely be arriving at almost any moment.

Zaa said in an offhand voice: "It was Floreste, incidentally, who notified me of your coming. He does not want you returning to Cadwal. You would disrupt his plans, so he tells me."

Glawen spoke in puzzlement: "How could he know anything of my movements?"

"No mystery there. Your associate remained at Fexelburg; am I right?"

"True: Kirdy Wook."

"It seems that Kirdy Wook called Floreste as soon as you boarded the bus and asked if he might rejoin the troupe. Floreste agreed, and Kirdy is with him now. Whatever your arrangements, insofar as they concern Kirdy, they are not in force."

Glawen sat as if stunned.

Zaa went on. "Now: in connection with our own arrangements, and here I refer to the so-called contract: when you first arrived, I was favorably impressed. You are healthy, intelligent and well-favored; you are evidently normal in your sexual functions. I decided that you should attempt to fertilize the ovulating women, and create a cadre of what I shall call Neo-Monomantics. I put Lilo in close association with you, half expecting that some kind of situation might develop. But acting from what seems to be sheer mischief you startled Lilo and put her into a dither. Of course all is not lost; she is at once fascinated and frightened by what she thinks is involved. I will make sure that her hair grows and that she brings color to her skin. Others will do likewise."

Glawen cried out aghast: "All this will take months!"

"Of course. You must now think in these terms—or even longer. In the meantime, you may experiment with me. I am fertile; I am a true woman and I am not afraid. To the contrary."

Glawen asked huskily: "These are to be the 'services' called for in your contract?"

"That is correct."

Glawen found himself unable to think rationally. One thing was clear: in order to escape he must first win clear of Zonk's Tomb. He looked sidelong at Zaa. "I don't consider the environment particularly congenial."

"It is as good as any other in the seminary."

"The dais is not all that comfortable."

"Put down the pad."

"That is a sensible idea."

Glawen spread the pad. He looked around to find that Zaa had stepped from her gown. Silhouetted against the lamplight her form was not unpleasing. Zaa came close and unclasped his gown. Glawen found himself stimulated despite the unusual circumstances. The two dropped down to the pad, where the lamplight revealed more detail than before. Glawen told himself desperately: "I will not notice the white skin nor the blue veins, nor the knobby knees, nor the sharp teeth; I will ignore the weird circumstances and the ghosts watching with wide blank eyes."

"Ah, Glawen," breathed Zaa. "I suspect that Duality has never truly left me behind. I am Ordene but I am a woman!" She threw back her head and the red wig rolled away to reveal her narrow white scalp and a tattoo on her forehead.

Glawen gave a choked cry and disengaged himself. "It is beyond my capacity! Look at me! See for yourself!"

Wordlessly Zaa rearranged the wig and resumed her white gown. She stood looking at Glawen with a queer twisted grin. At last she said: "It seems that I too must grow my hair and exercise my body in the sun."

"But what of me?"

Zaa shrugged. "Do as you like. Study Monomantics. Perform gymnastic exercises. Explore the deep pool. I have given my information unstintingly! Until I am satisfied with your services, and until my primitive female rage is soothed, you shall never leave Pogan's Point."

Zaa went to the door, tapped three times. It swung open; she passed through and the door closed.

4

Glawen sat on the edge of the dais, legs sprawled out, gaze fixed on nothing in particular. This moment, he thought, must be considered the very nadir of his life—though the situation had the potentiality for becoming worse.

Time passed, of duration unknown: more than an hour, less than a day. Someone came out on the balcony and lowered a basket on a string, then departed, leaving the lamp in place.

Without haste and with no great interest, Glawen went to investigate. The basket held several pots, containing bean soup, stew, bread, tea and three figs. Evidently he was not to be starved.

Glawen discovered that he was very hungry. He had eaten nothing in the refectory except a bite or two of bread; how much time had passed since then? More than a day, less than a week.

Glawen finished all the food and replaced the pots in the basket. He now felt somewhat more energetic and looked around the tomb. The ceiling, fifty feet above, was a vault of unbroken stone. The spring seeped into the room through a fissure halfway up the wall.

Glawen went to look at the tunnel where the water left the chamber. The opening was roughly circular, about three feet in diameter. Glawen could see that the tunnel trended downward after leaving the tomb. From far away he heard a steady gurgle, of water falling into water. Glawen turned away with a shiver. One day he might want to seek out the pool, so dark and cold, but not yet.

Glawen went back to sit on the edge of the dais. What now? Something must happen, he told himself. A person simply did not live away the days and weeks and years of his life immured in a cave. Still, there was no immutable law of nature which stated the contrary.

Time passed. Nothing happened, except that after a long interval the basket was drawn up and another basket lowered.

Glawen ate, then arranged himself on the pad, pulled the blanket over himself and slept.

A time certainly to be measured in days and weeks went by, with two food baskets apparently representing the interval of one day. Glawen noted the succession by scratching a mark for each two baskets on a flat stone. On the eleventh day Mutis appeared on the balcony, and lowered fresh garments and a fresh sheet. He spoke in a gruff voice: "I am instructed to ask if there is anything you want?"

"Yes. A razor and soap. Paper and a stylus."

The items were lowered in the next basket.

Thirty days passed by, and forty, then fifty. The fifty-second day, if Glawen's reckoning was accurate, was his birthday. Was he now Glawen Clattuc, full-status Agent of Araminta Station? Or Glawen co-Clattuc, collateral and excess population, with no status whatever?

What could be happening at Araminta Station? By now someone must be making inquiries as to what had happened to him. What would Kirdy tell Bodwyn Wook? The truth? Not likely. Still, no matter what else, his father Scharde would never abandon the search. His route should be simple to follow, but what of that? Even if Scharde arrived at the seminary, and was invited by Zaa to make a search, and thus discovered Zonk's Tomb, Glawen knew that before such a time, another body would have joined the white conclave at the bottom of the pool.

Meanwhile, Glawen tried to maintain both his physical fitness and his morale. He spent much time each day at calisthenics, running endless laps around the room, jumping up and kicking at the wall in a contest with himself, walking on his hands, turning handsprings. The exercise became an obsession: an ocupation which he used as a substitute for thinking; every day he crowded more and more effort into his waking hours.

Sixty days passed. Glawen found difficulty in remembering the outside world. Reality was the volume and extent of Zonk's Tomb. Lucky Glawen Clattuc! Thousands of tourists came to Tassadero in search of this hole in the rock which he knew so well! And it came to him, in a sudden instant of clarity, that Zaa had been totally generous with her information not because she trusted him, but because when he had performed all the services of which he was capable, his silence would be ensured by the most definite and final of means. When Zaa so casually had identified the cave as Zonk's Tomb, she had as much as assured him that she planned his death.

On the sixtieth day, the lower door opened. Funo stood in the doorway. "Come."

Glawen gathered up his papers and followed. Funo took him as before up two flights of stairs and to the room he had occupied before. The door closed. Glawen climbed up on the chair: his bundle of clothes and the spare sheets were as before.

There were sounds at the door. Glawen jumped down, just as Mutis threw open the door. "Come! You must bathe yourself."

Glawen submitted to a sanitary shower and a rinse of cold water. Mutis ignored Glawen's new growth of hair. "Dress in proper garments, then go to your chamber."

Without comment Glawen obeyed. Upon his return to the chamber the door was closed and presumably locked. On the table Glawen discovered his usual supper, which he ate without appetite. Presently Mutis came to take the empty pots.

The time was now evening. The misty lavender afterglow had left the sky; through the windows came starlight from the far flow of Mircea's Wisp.

Half an hour passed. Glawen remained at the table, sorting through the papers he had brought with him. The door opened; Lilo came slowly into the room, looking neither right nor left. Glawen assessed her with interest. She wore white trousers, a tan-gray blouse and sandals. The entire effect of her being had altered; she was barely recognizable as the pale big-eyed creature Glawen had met before. Her hair had grown into a crop of loose chestnut curls, framing a face which now seemed thin and fragile rather than gaunt and which—perhaps through time spent in the open—had taken on a dusky tan color. She seemed pensive and composed; Glawen could divine nothing more of her mood.

Lilo came slowly forward. Glawen rose to his feet. She halted and asked: "Why do you stare at me?"

"From surprise. You seem a different person."

Lilo nodded. "I feel a different person—someone with whom I am not yet familiar."

"Are you pleased with the change?"

"I'm not sure. Do you think I should be?"

"Certainly. You seem normal—almost. In any city no one would look twice at you—except perhaps to admire you."

Lilo shrugged. "It was a change which I was ordered to make. I was afraid I would seem grotesque or garish or vulgar."

"Small chance of that."

"Do you know why I am here?"

"I can guess."

"I am embarrassed."

Glawen gave a short laugh. "Embarrassment is a luxury now beyond my reach. I have forgotten that such an emotion exists."

Lilo spoke in a troubled voice: "It is not necessary to think such thoughts. What must be done must be done. And so I am here."

Glawen reached out and took her hands. "I suppose Mutis is watching through a spy hole."

"No. The walls are solid rock. Spy holes are not possible."

"I'm glad to hear that, at least. Well, then, let's get on with it."

Glawen led her to the cot. Lilo hung back. "I think I'm frightened."

"There's nothing to fear. Just relax."

Lilo followed Glawen's instructions, and the event went without unforeseen incident. Glawen asked: "So now what is your opinion of Duality?"

Lilo pressed as close to him as possible. "I don't know how to explain. I am probably thinking wrong thoughts."

"How so?"

"I don't want to share you with the others."

"Others? How many others?"

"About twelve. Zaa will come tomorrow, if all has gone well tonight."

"You are expected to report to her?"

"Naturally. She is waiting in her office."

"Will you tell her once again that I am an erotic maniac?"

Lilo was puzzled. "I never told her that in the first place."

"You weren't upset and outraged by my erotic hints and proposals?"

"Of course not! I never noticed any, in the first place."

"Why should Zaa assure me that I had disgraced myself?"

Lilo considered. "Perhaps she misunderstood. Maybe she was, well"—Lilo breathed a word in Glawen's ear—"jealous."

"She seems to have overcome her emotion."

"From necessity. I am first because she wants to make sure that you function properly."

"Does she plan to lock me into the tomb again?"

"I don't think so—so long as you perform well. If not, Mutis will strangle you with a rope."

"In that case—shall we try again?"

"If you like."

Lilo at last left the chamber. Glawen waited five minutes, then crossed the room and tried the door. It was locked.

The time had come. He dressed himself in his own clothes, and went to lie on the cot.

An hour passed. Glawen went to press his ear against the door. He heard nothing and instantly went to work, with a feverish intensity of purpose.

The cot was a construction of wood, designed for easy erection and dismantling, with meshes of rope to support the mattress. Glawen removed the ropes. The strong wooden side timbers were now at his disposal.

Glawen loosely rearranged the cot, so that if anyone chanced to look into his room, nothing would seem disarranged. One at a time he took the spare sheets into the bathroom, ripped them into six-inch ribbons, tied them to make up a rope a hundred and twenty feet long, which he thought adequate to his needs.

Again he listened at the door. Silence.

With a timber from the cot and rope, also from the cot, he climbed on the table and opened wide the two casements. He examined the center post which barred his passage. There were several ways to remove it; the simplest method was to break the weld at the bottom.

He tied the end of the timber to the bottom of the post, with many turns and loops of the rope, so that the timber functioned as a lever for the exertion of torque. Cautiously he swung the end of the timber out into the room, applying torque to the post. The rope, as he had expected, tightened and stretched; he readjusted the bindings, and once more applied leverage. With a wrench and a sharp snap the welds broke.

Glawen sighed in satisfaction. He bent the post back and forth until it broke; the entire window was open for his passage.

In a fury of haste, Glawen made his rope of torn sheets fast to the timber, which he now used as a toggle across the window opening. He threw the rope out the window, clambered through into the darkness and let himself slide down the rope.

His feet touched the rocky slope. "Goodbye, seminary," said Glawen, almost choking on his exultation. "Goodbye, goodbye, good-bye!"

Glawen turned and picked his way down the hill, in glorious freedom. In due course he crossed the square into the village.

The depot was closed and dark; an omnibus stood nearby, with the entry door ajar. Glawen looked within, to discover the driver asleep across the back seat. Glawen prodded him awake. "Do you want to earn fifty sols?"

"Naturally. That's all I am paid each month."

"Here you are," said Glawen. "Drive me to Fexelburg."

"Now? You can ride for the price of a ticket in the morning."

"I have urgent business in town," said Glawen. "In fact, I even have a ticket."

"You're a tourist, I take it."

"Correct."

"Did you go up to the seminary? You'll find nothing there but surly treatment."

"That's how it seemed to me," said Glawen.

"I see no reason not to oblige you. Urgent business, you say?"

"Yes. A telephone call I forgot to make."

"A pity. But perhaps it will all come right. And meanwhile I profit by your mistake."

"Unfortunately that is the way the world goes."

5

The omnibus moved through the night, under a sky spread with constellations strange to Glawen. Tonight the wind blew in gusts, sighing around the bus and bending the lonely frooks, where they could be seen in the starlight.

The driver was Bant, a large young Fexel of good disposition and a tendency toward garrulity. Glawen responded to his remarks in monosyllables, and Bant presently fell silent.

After two hours of travel, Glawen asked: "What of the early morning transport from Pogan's Point? How will that be arranged?"

"I have been wondering along the same lines," said Bant. "I foresee no real problem. In the simplest case, there will be no transport whatever, and the problem becomes moot. But I have arrived at a plan which should please everyone. In an hour or two we will arrive at Flicken, where I will telephone Esmer, the relief driver. I will offer him five sols to bring out the old green Deluxus Special to service the morning trade. Esmer will be happy to earn an increment; the customers will be content; I cannot see where a single tear of anguish need be shed—certainly not by me."

"That is an ingenious solution. How long before we arrive at Flicken? I also want to make a telephone call."

"I estimate another hour or an hour and a half. I am driving slowly because of the wind. The gusts make steering unpredictable at high speeds. What is your opinion on this?"

"I believe that safety is important. It is better to arrive alive than dead."

"This is exactly my point," said Bant. "I have explained this to Esmer: what is the value of thirty minutes, more or less, to a corpse? He is already late and no longer in a hurry. The time is more useful on this side of the veil, such is my belief."

"And mine as well," said Glawen. "In regard to the telephone at Flicken, the time is late; will it be available for our use?"

"Without a doubt. Keelums will be in bed upstairs but the sound of a sol or two will bring him down quickly."

The conversation languished once again. Glawen could not wrench his thoughts away from the seminary. He wondered when his departure would be noticed. Certainly at dawn, and quite possibly earlier. Perhaps someone had already looked into his vacated chamber. Glawen grinned at the thought of the consternation which his absence would evoke, with the location of Zonk's Tomb no longer a secret. He had been pondering the situation since leaving Pogan's Point, and now he could not get to the telephone fast enough.

Far ahead appeared a cluster of dim lights. Bant pointed. "Flicken."

"Why the lights? Is someone up and around?"

"I believe that it is a matter of civic pride."

"What time might we expect to arrive in Fexelburg?"

"If we take a bowl or two of soup to ward off the chill and perhaps a slice of meat pie—let us say, a total stop of half an hour, which will include our telephone calls—we should arrive about dawn. At this time of year the nights are short."

At dawn Glawen's escape would be known, if not much sooner, and as if in response to the thought, Glawen felt a sudden eerie waft of emotion, seeming to come from the direction of Pogan's Point: a rage and hatred so intense as to seem a palpable projection. Rightly or wrongly, Glawen felt assured that at this moment his absence had been discovered.

The bus rolled into Flicken and halted in front of the general store. Bant alighted and went to the door, where he pulled on the bell cord. "Keelums!" he called. "Arouse yourself! Sleep some other time! Keelums! Are you awake?"

"Yes, I'm awake," croaked Keelums from an upstairs window. "It's Bant, is it? What do you want?"

"Some hot soup and the use of your telephone. This gentleman will offer you a sol for the privilege, and if he doesn't I will. Of course, if you are proud, you need not accept."

"Oh, I am proud enough! Especially after I take the money. Soup, is it?"

"And some meat pie, and a taste of the raisin pudding. Open up! The wind howls and bites at my poor shanks!"

"Be patient! Allow me to pull on my robe."

The door opened. Glawen entered the store, followed by Bant. "Where is the telephone?" asked Glawen.

"Over on the desk, but first, before we forget, the sol."

Glawen paid over the money and went to the telephone. He called the IPCC office at Fexelburg, and was finally connected with the Adjudicant Partric Plock at his residence. To hear the cool calm voice brought Glawen such relief that he became almost limp. "Yes?" asked Plock. "Who is calling and what do you want?"

Glawen identified himself. "I think you will remember me. Two months ago I went out to Pogan's Point to make inquiries at the seminary."

"I remember you very well. I thought you had gone home to Cadwal long ago."

"I was betrayed by my colleague, who chose the join Floreste's Mummers in preference to notifying you that I had not returned. I have been held captive for two months in Zonk's Tomb, which is a cave in the Point. I have just escaped, and I am calling from Flicken. That is the gist of things, but there is more."

"Go on."

"The Fexelburg police know all there is to know about Zonk's Tomb. They suppress the knowledge and, in effect, allow the Monomantics at the seminary a free hand so long as they also keep the secret. I suspect that as soon as the Ordene Zaa discovers that I am gone, she will notify the Fexelburg authorities, who will then try to intercept me along the road."

"I am sure that you are right," said Plock. "As a matter of fact, we have been waiting for some such unambiguous pretext for cleaning out the Fexelburg police force. Let me think a moment. You are at the Flicken general store?"

"Yes."

"How did you get there?"

"I hired the omnibus."

"When do you expect that your escape will be known?"

"A few minutes ago I had a strange telepathic sensation; it was to the effect that my escape had been discovered. In any event, they'll know by dawn, at the latest."

"I will be flying out to Flicken at once, with a force of men. We will arrive in about half an hour. In case the Fexelburg police have preceded us, and are already on the way, send your driver on to Fexelburg, but you remain at Flicken. The police will be coming along the road and even if they are flying, they will be delayed if they notice the bus. Do you understand my thinking?"

"Perfectly."

"We will be there as soon as possible."

Bant now used the telephone to make his arrangements with Esmer. He then turned to Glawen. "It is time for us to be on our way, if we wish to arrive by dawn."

"The plans have been altered," said Glawen. "You are to continue into Fexelburg alone."

Bant's round face showed surprise. "You are staying here?"

"Yes."

"Isn't that unreasonable? You want me to continue into Fexelburg with the omnibus totally empty?"

"So long as the fifty sols are not unreasonable, nothing else matters."

"A truer word was never spoken! In that case, goodbye. It has been a pleasure dealing with you."

The omnibus departed. Glawen went back into the store, where he gratified Keelums with another sol. "I am to wait for some friends who will be here shortly. You may go back to bed. If we need anything, we will call you."

"Just as you like." Keelums went off upstairs to his bed. Glawen turned down the lights and, seating himself by the window, waited in the dark.

Through his mind flashed images from the past two months, in rapid sequence, while he sat looking off into the night. The ultimate joy of his life had come when his feet had touched the rocky hillside. What if Mutis and Funo had been waiting and smiling? His mind veered away from the idea. Would the recollections ever lose their vivid emotional bite? He thought not. Even now his skin crawled to think of the grotesque deeds done to him, Glawen Clattuc. Even so, why should he be surprised? The cosmos took no notice of human rationality, or human anything whatever. As he sat brooding, another curious mood came to trouble his mind: a waft of rending grief and woe, a sadness not to be contemplated, and perhaps beyond understanding.

Glawen stared out into the night. What was happening to him? He had never before experienced such influences; could they be real? Perhaps his time immured in Zonk's Tomb had brought him a new and unwelcome sensitivity.

The mood waned, leaving a feeling of chill and desolation. Glawen jumped to his feet and walked back and forth, swinging his arms.

Twenty minutes passed, and half an hour. Glawen went out to stand in front of the store. Down from the sky came a large black flyer, emblazoned with the nine-pointed insignia of the IPCC. It landed on a plot of empty ground behind the store; Plock alighted, followed by five uniformed personnel: a pair of full agents and three recruits.

Glawen went to meet them, and all trooped into the store, to disturb Keelums anew. Glawen ordered soup for the new arrivals. Then, at Plock's instructions, Glawen called the Fexelburg Central Police Station. "This is Captain Glawen Clattuc. Connect me at once with Superintendent Wullin, on an important matter."

The response was sardonic. "At this time of night? Have you had some sort of insane dream? Superintendent Wullin would not desist in his snoring for the Avatar Gundelbah himself. Try tomorrow."

"The matter is most urgent. Connect me with Inspector Barch. Tell him Captain Glawen Clattuc is calling."

Inspector Barch came to the telephone. "Captain Clattuc? I'm surprised to hear from you! I thought that you had gone home long ago. Why do you call while I try to sleep?"

"Because I have information of great importance, and because I am in a state of fury and outrage, both justifiable."

"Apparently you have had some interesting adventures."

"Yes, quite." Glawen gave an account of his adventures, stressing

426

his outrage, and the need for official response without a moment's delay. "I can hardly overstate the insolence of these freakish people, and their cynical mistreatment of a police officer."

"You have used the correct word," said Barch. "'Freakish' describes them in all adequacy. For this reason, they have been treated perhaps too casually in the past."

Glawen spoke on. "I was held for two months in a cave which they assured me was Zonk's Tomb. Naturally I discovered no treasure. But the mystery is at last put to rest!" Even as Glawen spoke, he reflected that Barch must have known of his imprisonment. The idea made cordiality difficult.

Barch, however, seemed to have no such trouble; if anything, he was amused. "You have had an unhappy experience. Still, realities are as they are, and as you know, Lutwiler Country is outside our bailiwick."

"And you propose to take no action?"

"Not so fast! Here on Tassadero, nothing is simple. Things are done in a certain way, and two plus two often totals seven, or perhaps thirty-seven, depending on who is in charge of the reckoning."

"I don't understand this kind of talk," said Glawen. "I want simplicity, and I want action. Perhaps I should notify the IPCC, since you are worried about your jurisdiction. The IPCC acts anywhere across the Gaean Reach."

"Exactly so, and this is why their efforts are so inept," said Barch. "The local IPCC are all cookie-pushers. If action is what you want, you have come to the right place. You are at Flicken?"

"Correct, at Keelums' General Store."

"Stand by the telephone while I call Superintendent Wullin. He'll surely order a big raid on the Monomantic seminary. But don't call the IPCC; they'll only interfere."

"Whatever you say."

A few moments later Barch called back. "The Superintendent asks that you wait where you are at Flicken. He has decided to take definite action."

"What kind of action?"

"It will be stern and definite, I can assure you of this! We'll discuss the options later. Above all, do not talk to anyone about your experiences."

"I don't see why not. In fact, I'll talk to whoever is interested, since I have undoubtedly located Zonk's Tomb and there is not so much as a counterfeit dinket to be found. This news should be disseminated rapidly, as a service to tourists."

"That's an altruistic point of view," said Barch. "Is there anyone to whom you have already told your story?"

"No, it's still too early."

"We'll be out right away."

"You'll need a large flyer."

"What for?"

"There are thirty Monomantics at the seminary. I am bringing charges against them all and I want every one of them in custody."

"I don't know if we can do that today," said Barch.

"Then don't bother to come. I'll call the IPCC."

Barch's voice became a trifle strained. "I suggest that today we arrest only the ringleaders. Then we can make up our minds as to the others. Most of them are just simpleminded religious fanatics. We'll have to sort them out as we go. Anyway, wait there; don't move and don't talk to anyone; you might compromise your case."

"That seems farfetched. Inspector Barch, are you dragging your feet on this case?"

"Of course not! Never! Not at all! I'll be there in a very few minutes and explain everything."

The telephone went dead. Glawen turned away, half smiling. "Barch's patience is very elastic."

"Only until he arrives. Now we must decide how to dispose ourselves. It's important that we catch the rascals red-handed, so to speak."

"Not too red-handed, I hope."

"That will be our goal."

Half an hour passed. The first silver fringes of dawn showed around the horizon; a half light the color of milky water illuminated the landscape. Down from the sky came the flyer from Fexelburg, to land directly in front of the store. Four men jumped briskly to the ground: Inspectors Barch and Tanaquil, with two others of ordinary rank.

Glawen waited by the front of the store. The four policemen sauntered toward him. Barch raised his arm in an affable gesture. "You will remember Inspector Tanaquil, of course."

"Of course."

"You have had some unusual adventures," said Barch.

"True," said Glawen. "To my great discomfort. But I am puzzled."

"How so?" asked Barch.

"That flyer is only a four-seater. There are five of us here, and we will want to take at least five or six persons into custody at the seminary."

"Well, Glawen, if the truth be known, it's not all so easy as it first seemed. The Ordene notified us some time ago that you had escaped from her custody. As I mentioned, in Lutwiler Country, we tend to let the Ordene Zaa do things as she thinks best. She has brought serious charges against you and wants you back at the seminary."

"You must be joking," said Glawen. "I am an officer of the IPCC."

"I joke very seldom. So there is one of the options I mentioned. Wullin was annoyed when I awoke him for orders, and he provided us a second option, which you may well prefer. It is called the Fexelburg hammock, and all things considered, I think this is the option we shall use."

"Your manner verges on the offensive," said Glawen. "I know nothing of your hammock, nor do I want to know."

Barch only laughed. "I shall explain it anyway. We use it when four officers and a rascal must ride in a four-seat flyer. The rascal uses the hammock." He signaled to his underlings. "Show us how quick you are with the hammock. It's cold out here and I'm quite willing to get home to my breakfast."

"Come to think of it," said Glawen, "I am too. You can't imagine the terrible food at the seminary."

"I'm afraid there'll be no breakfast for you today."

The patrolmen approached Glawen with a length of rope. "Don't bother," said Glawen. "I prefer to wait for the omnibus."

"Come, Glawen! Just a bit closer to the flyer. You don't care to walk? No matter. We'll drag you. Ferl, get busy with the rope. Now, then—"

Two men seized Glawen and marched him to the flyer. There Ferl dropped a loop around Glawen's ankles, a half hitch around his arms and chest and another half hitch around his neck. The other end of the rope passed through the cargo hatch into the flyer, where it could be cast off at an appropriate moment, somewhere over the steppe.

"You have forgotten something," said Glawen.

"Eh? What is that?"

"I am an IPCC officer."

"I bear you no special malice on that account," said Barch. "Gentlemen, are we ready? Then let us be up and away."

Plock appeared from the far side of the flyer, carrying a gun pointed in the direction of the four policemen. "What seems to be going on?"

"Oh, my," said Barch. "It's Party Plock."

Plock looked from face to face. "Do I recognize Inspectors Barch and Tanaquil?"

"You do," said Barch, in a voice suddenly subdued. "It appears that Glawen, so callow and innocent, has played us a trick."

"A harsh cruel trick," said Inspector Tanaquil.

"Something of the sort," said Plock. "Still, if you recall, he warned you, and warned you again, that you were molesting an IPCC officer."

Barch spoke in doleful tones: "I conceived it to be no more than youthful vainglory."

Two of Plock's men came up from behind and searched the Fexels, taking their weapons. A third released Glawen from the "Fexelburg hammock."

Glawen said: "I am disappointed with Inspectors Barch and Tanaquil. They truly meant to kill me. Strange. They were so friendly at Fexelburg. I have a great deal to learn about human nature."

"Orders are orders," said Barch. "They must be obeyed."

"Who gave you these orders?" asked Plock.

"Allow me the dignity of faithful silence, Commander Plock."

"Out here in Lutwiler Country, I must be called Chief Adjudicant Plock."

"Just as you like, Chief Adjudicant."

"I am afraid that I must press you for an answer. You can die your death either here, faithless and undignified, or totally silent, totally dignified, inside a crawl of purple ooze."

"Has it come to that?"

"This is Lutwiler Country. You tried to murder an IPCC agent in cold blood. You know the rules."

"Yes. I know the rules."

"I will tell you this. You shall not eat your breakfast this day, but console yourself. Tonight many of your superiors will not be dining at their favorite resorts. We cookie-pushers are ready to clean out the Fexelburg police force. Once more: who gave you the orders?"

"Wullin, naturally, as you well know."

"No one higher up the ladder?"

"I wouldn't dare call them at that time of night."

"Wullin might, and Wullin will tell me before he dies."

"Why bother to ask him? Everyone is in it together."

"In a week they will all be gone. You are the first, if it is any consolation to you." Plock fired his gun four times and four corpses lay in the road.

Plock went into the general store and summoned the white-faced Keelums. "I assume that you have a power wagon of sorts?"

"Yes, sir, that I do, and quite a good vehicle, which we use to bring in stuffs from Fexelburg."

"Here is ten sols. Bring out your power wagon, load these four dead hulks aboard, take them out on the steppe and drop them off where they will give no offense. As you see, we are IPCC officers, and this is your command: say nothing of this matter to anyone."

"No, sir! Not a word to anyone!"

"Then be quick, before the whole village is up and about."

Plock returned to the road. Glawen, sorting through the weapons taken from the Fexelburg police, selected a small handgun for his own use, which he tucked into the pocket of his jacket.

"Our business here is done," said Plock. "Are you of a mind now to visit Pogan's Point?"

"I am ready," said Glawen.

"The police flyer will be useful," said Plock. He spoke to the two full agents. "Kylte, Narduke: the two of you follow us in the extra flyer to Pogan's Point."

<h1 style="text-align:center">6</h1>

Zonk's Star, rising in the east, brought the pallid light of morning to Lutwiler Country. The two flyers slid across the steppe, following the road which Glawen had traveled by bus the night before.

Glawen sat relaxed and half asleep, until he was aroused by Plock: "Pogan's Point ahead."

Glawen sat up straight and tried to become alert. Ahead the black crag of Pogan's Point reared high into the air. Glawen pointed. "Look! Halfway up you can see windows glittering in the sunlight! That's the seminary."

The flyers circled the crag and landed in the central square of the village. The occupants alighted and, wasting no time, started up the zigzag road which led to the seminary. Only Maase, youngest of the recruits, was left to guard the flyers and maintain contact with the office at Fexelburg.

Back, forth, back, forth, trudged the six men and finally arrived at the front of the seminary. Plock rapped at the door with the door-knocker: once, twice, a third time, eliciting no response. He tried the door, but found it locked. At last the door moved slowly ajar, with a dour creaking of the hinges. Mutis peered through the opening. He looked around the group, giving Glawen no sign of recognition. He growled: "What do you want with us? This is the Monomantic seminary; we know nothing of Zab Zonk or his treasure. Be off with you!"

Plock pushed the door back against Mutis' outraged protest. "What are you doing?" cried Mutis. "Stand back, or it will be the worse for you!"

The IPCC agents entered the vestibule. "Bring the Ordene Zaa here in double-quick time!"

"Who shall I say is calling?" demanded Mutis sullenly.

Glawen laughed. "Come, Mutis! You know very well who is calling, and why. This is an IPCC squad, and you are in deep trouble."

Mutis departed and presently returned with Zaa. She halted in the entrance to the stone passage and surveyed the group. Today she wore the garments in which Glawen had seen her first. She took note of his presence and stared at him a full three seconds. Glawen said: "If you recall, I warned that you could not molest an IPCC officer and escape without punishment. The time has come and you will see that I am right."

Zaa spoke sharply to Plock: "What is your business here? State it quickly, then leave!"

"Glawen has hinted of our business," said Plock. "We are in no hurry, since we intend to do a thorough job."

"What are you talking about? Do you realize that this is the Monomantic seminary?"

"You reassure me!" said Plock. "This is the correct address and we are not making a dreadful mistake. As of now, you and all other residents of the seminary are under arrest, for offenses committed against Captain Glawen Clattuc. You may instruct them to assemble outside."

Zaa made no move to obey. She said stonily: "Your jurisdiction does not prevail. We are the law of Lutwiler Country. You must leave here or stand in defiance of the law."

Plock lost patience. "Quickly now! If you do not obey at once my men will tie you securely and carry you outside." Zaa shrugged and, turning her head, spoke to Mutis. "Call general assembly outside." Zaa started to leave the room. Glawen asked: "Where are you going?"

"It is no concern of yours."

"Answer the question, if you please," said Plock.

"I have some private affairs to which I wish to attend."

Plock spoke to one of his subordinates: "Go with her and make sure that she destroys no records."

"I will wait," said Zaa.

The Monomantics filed downstairs and out the door, to stand blinking in the morning Zonklight.

Plock asked Zaa: "Is this all?"

Zaa looked at Mutis: "Is everyone down?"

"Everyone."

Plock spoke to the group. "Crimes have been committed on these premises. Their full description is not yet clear, but they are certainly serious. Each one of you shares the guilt. It is irrelevant that you took no active part in the crimes, or that it was none of your concern, or that you were preoccupied with your studies. All are accomplices, in greater or lesser degree, and all must pay the penalty."

Glawen had been looking from face to face with growing perplexity. He said: "It seems to me that one person, at least, is not here. Where is Lilo?"

No one replied. Glawen addressed his question to Zaa directly: "Where is Lilo?"

Zaa showed a small cold smile. "She is not here."

"I can see that. Where is she?"

"We do not discuss our internal arrangements with strangers."

"I don't want discussion: just an answer to my question. Where is Lilo?"

Zaa gave an indifferent shrug and looked off across the steppe. Glawen turned to Mutis. "Where is Lilo?"

"I am not authorized to give out information."

One of the Monomantics, a young man standing a little apart, turned sharply away, as if in disgust. Glawen asked him: "Tell me: where is Lilo?"

Zaa swung sharply about. "Danton, you will give no information."

Danton replied in flat intonations: "With all respect, these are police officers of high rank. I must answer their questions."

"Quite right," said Glawen. "Answer my question, if you will."

Danton darted a side glance toward Zaa, then spoke: "About midnight they noticed that you were gone. In our rooms we all heard the cries of rage, and wondered what had occurred."

"This was about midnight, you say?"

"Something after midnight. I do not know the exact hour."

Somewhat past midnight, sitting in the dark at Flicken, Glawen had felt his mind picked up and tumbled in a wash of rage and hatred: perhaps as telepathic projection from the seminary, though coincidence could not be ruled out. "Then what happened?"

Zaa spoke again: "Danton, you need say no more."

Danton, however, spoke on in a dreary monotone. "There was a great uproar. Lilo was blamed. They chided her for bringing you extra sheets, and would not listen to her denials. Mutis and Funo put her in the owl's cage. Last night the winds blew harsh and bitter. This morning she was dead. Mutis and Funo took the body around the hill to the garbage pit and threw it away."

Glawen winced. He dared not look at Mutis lest the roil in his stomach cause an undignified reaction. When he felt that he could control his voice, he swung about and spoke to Zaa: "Lilo had nothing to do with the sheets. I took them two months ago, the first time I occupied the room. I would have been gone at that time if you had not put me into the tomb. Lilo knew nothing of my plans."

Zaa made no comment.

Glawen spoke on. "You murdered the girl for no reason whatever."

Zaa was unmoved. "Mistakes are made everywhere. Each instant, across the Gaean Reach, a thousand such events are taking place. They are implicit to the conduct of coherent civilization."

"So it may be," said Plock. "This is the function of the IPCC: to minimize these so-called mistakes. In the present case, judgment is clear and simple, despite the complexity of your motives. You imprisoned Glawen Clattuc; when he escaped, you murdered an innocent girl. If rumor can be believed, as often it can, you have murdered an unknown number of tourists. Am I correct in this assumption?"

"I have nothing to say. Your opinions are fixed."

"It is true," said Plock. "I have formed my judgment." He addressed the entire group. "This place is a pest house, and must be vacated now. Gather your personal belongings and return here at once. You will be taken to Fexelburg, and a disposition made of your individual cases. These instructions, incidentally, do not apply to Funo, Mutis, nor the Ordene Zaa. You three may now come with me around the road to the garbage pit. You will need no personal belongings."

Mutis looked uncertainly toward Zaa, his face sagging. Funo stood stolidly, thinking her private thoughts. Zaa said sharply: "That is absolutely absurd. I have never heard such nonsense!"

"Lilo perhaps thought the same, when you ordered her to her death," said Plock. "These ideas always seem implausible when they apply to yourself. But it makes no great difference."

"I wish to make a telephone call."

"To the Fexelburg police? You may not do so. I prefer to take them by surprise."

"Then I must write some letters."

"To whom?"

"To the Ordene Klea at Strock and other Ordenes."

Glawen kept his voice casual. "Such as who?"

Zaa said curtly: "I will not write, after all."

"Would one of your Ordenes be Madame Zigonie, who lives at a country place on the world Rosalia?"

"We are wandering far afield. I will tell you no more. Do your filthy work and be done with it."

Plock said: "That is a practical suggestion, and we shall not wait upon ceremony." He fired his gun three times, with precision.

"The work is done," said Plock, for a moment looking down at the three bodies.

How quick it went! thought Glawen. Funo no longer thought private thoughts; Mutis felt no more indecision and Zaa's knowledge was irretrievably gone.

Plock turned to the awed Danton: "Take these bodies to the garbage pit. Use a barrow, or a cart, or make up a trestle: as you choose. Pick out two or three sturdy fellows to help you. When you are finished, join the others down the hill."

Danton started to obey Plock's order, but Glawen halted him. "The stairs between the second and third floors: why are they dangerous?"

Danton glanced toward the corpses, as if to assure himself that none could hear him. "When a stranger was brought to the third floor, and held against his will—which happened more often than you might think—Mutis strung a trip wire across the steps near the top of the flight, and this wire was charged with electricity. If someone tried to use the steps, he would end up in a huddle of broken bones at the bottom. Mutis and Funo would then carry him, alive or dead, to the garbage pit and throw him away."

"And no one protested?"

Danton smiled. "When one studies the Syntoraxis with great concentration, he seldom notices anything."

Glawen turned away.

Plock said to Danton: "You may now dispose of the corpses."

7

The vacant seminary seemed to echo with a thousand whispers just below the threshold of perception. Glawen and Plock, with Kylte and Narduke, stood in the first-floor conference room. Plock spoke in an unwontedly thoughtful voice: "Since I am not a superstitious man, the twittering of so many ghosts disturbs me."

"Neither Zab Zonk nor his ghost troubled me," said Glawen. "For a fact, I might have welcomed the company."

"In any case, we must risk the upper floors. There might be some

Monomantics so engrossed in their studies that they failed to hear the commands."

"You three go. I want no more of the upper floors. When you look into the kitchen, turn off the fires, otherwise the soup will burn even worse than usual."

Plock and his two associates climbed the stairs. Glawen meanwhile explored the first floor. He found Zaa's private apartments and her office: a large room with plastered bone-white walls, furnished with lamps of a peculiar contorted design, a heavy black and green rug and furniture upholstered in dark red plush. A peculiar room, thought Glawen, reflecting the tensions which obviously had pulled Zaa in a dozen different directions. Shelves held a variety of books, all of a secular nature. Glawen searched the desk but found no records, addresses, files of correspondence or any other material of interest to him. Yet it seemed that Zaa had been anxious to destroy certain items of information. What and where? Or had they misjudged her intentions? In a drawer of the desk Glawen found a strongbox, unlocked, containing a large sum of money. He took the box from the drawer and below found a photograph of a dozen women, standing in what appeared to be a garden. The environment would seem to be not that of Tassadero. One of the women was Zaa of ten or even fifteen years ago. Another of the group was Sibil. The others were not known to Glawen. They must include Klea, now at Strock, and possibly Madame Zigonie of Rosalia. The individuals were not identified, either by code or legend or handwritten designation. Glawen tucked the photograph into his inner pocket; it was not information which would interest the IPCC to any large extent.

Glawen turned his attention to Zaa's private apartments and, holding his revulsion under tight rein, he continued his search for documents: letters, address books, journals, photographs. As before, he found nothing of consequence: no reference to Madame Zigonie of the world Rosalia, nor any other name he recognized.

Plock and the others came down from the upper floors. Glawen took them to Zonk's Tomb, where the lamp still cast a yellow glow around the chamber.

Glawen opened the door but could not bring himself to enter the chamber more than a step or two. "There it is," he said. "Just as I left it: platform, stream, tunnel and all."

Plock surveyed the extent of the tomb. "I see no treasure."

"I found none, and with nothing better to do I looked quite carefully. I found no trapdoors, no loose stones, no sliding panels and no treasure."

"It's none of our affair, in any case," said Plock. "I have now seen Zonk's Tomb and I am ready to leave, at any time."

"I've seen all I care to see," said Narduke.

"I have lost nothing here," said Kylte.

"I also have seen enough," said Glawen. "I am willing to leave."

Glawen took the group to Zaa's office and poured the contents of the strongbox out on the desk. Plock counted the money. "I make it roughly nine thousand sols, give or take a dinket or two." He reflected a moment. "In my opinion," he told Glawen, "the Monomantics owe you a large debt of damages, which is hard to evaluate. Let us place an arbitrary value of a thousand sols a month on your time, with another thousand sols for mental anguish. In one minute we arrive at a disposition which could require months of the court's time, and who knows what might happen to these funds in the interim? It is better to collect now when the money is at hand. Here is the award: punitive damages in the amount of three thousand sols against the Monomantic seminary."

Glawen tucked the money into his pocket. "It is a better end to the affair than I expected. I can put the money to good use."

The four men left the seminary and descended the hill to the village.

CHAPTER 9

1

Toward the middle of a gloomy winter afternoon, the spaceship *Solares Oro* broke through the overcast above Araminta Station and settled to a landing close beside the space terminal.

Among the debarking passengers was Glawen Clattuc. Immediately after passing through the formalities of entry, he found a telephone and called Clattuc House. Today was that day of the week known as Smollen; the Clattucs would be preparing to assemble for the weekly House Supper. However, instead of his father, the synthetic voice of the Clattuc switchboard responded to Glawen. "Sir, to whom do you wish to speak?"

Odd, thought Glawen; he had directed the call to the chambers shared by himself and his father. "To Scharde Clattuc."

"He is not now on the premises. Will there be a message?"

"No message."

Glawen called Wook House. He was told by the majordomo that Bodwyn Wook had descended to the House Supper, and could be disturbed only in the event of the most urgent emergency.

"Please give him this message immediately. Tell him that Glawen Clattuc will come to Wook House very shortly, in fact as soon as I stop by Clattuc House and have a few words with my father."

"I will give him your message, sir."

Glawen went out to the cab rank in front of the terminal and approached the first in the line of waiting taxis. The driver showed no interest in his luggage, but watched with benign approval as Glawen loaded it into the bin at the back of the taxi. He was of a sort unfamiliar to Glawen: a swarthy young man with pretensions to fashion, sharp-featured, with clever eyes and an unruly bush of dark hair—evidently part of the new labor force which had been imported to replace the Yips.

Glawen seated himself in the passenger's compartment. The driver, putting aside the journal he had been reading, looked over his shoulder with a cordial smile. "Where will it be, sir? You just name the place; we'll get you there, in grand and glorious style: have no fear on that score! My name is Maxen."

"Take me to Clattuc House," said Glawen. In the old days the Yip driver, if not quite so affable, would have been on hand to load his luggage.

"Right, sir! We're off to Clattuc House!"

Watching the familiar landmarks pass by, Glawen felt as if he had been away from home years beyond number. Everything was the same; everything was different, as if he were seeing with a fresh vision.

Maxen the driver looked over his shoulder. "Your first time here, sir? From your clothes I'd put you as a Soum, or maybe from Aspergill down the Wisp. Well, I'll give you a hint. This is a remarkable place. I might even call it unique."

"Yes, perhaps so."

"Personally, I find folk a bit strange. The population is seriously inbred, that goes without saying, which seems to make for considerable, shall we say, eccentricity? That's the general feeling."

"I am a Clattuc of Clattuc House,' said Glawen. "I've been away for a period."

"Oh-ah!" Maxen made a rueful face. Then he shrugged and chuckled. "Just so. You won't find many changes. Nothing ever changes here; nothing ever happens. I'd like to see them put in a jolly fine dance hall, and a row of casinos along the beach. Also, why not some fried fish shacks along Beach Road? They would not go amiss. The place needs a bit of progress."

"It may well be."

"You're a Clattuc, you say? Which one of the tribe are you?"

"I am Glawen Clattuc."

"Glad to know you! Next time I'll recognize you from the start. Here we are at Clattuc House: too grand for the likes of me, I fear."

Glawen alighted, removed his luggage from the bin while Maxen sat drumming his fingers on the wheel. Glawen paid the standard fee, which Maxen accepted with raised eyebrows. "And the gratuity?"

Glawen slowly turned to stare into the driver's compartment. "Did you help me load my luggage?"

"No, but—"

"Did you help me unload it?"

"By the same token—"

"Did you not tell me that I was inbred and eccentric, and probably weak-minded?"

"That was a joke."

"Now can you guess the location of your gratuity?"

"Yes. Nowhere."

"Quite right."

"Hoity-toity!" murmured Maxen, and drove quickly away, elbows stylishly high.

Glawen entered Clattuc House and went directly up to his old chambers, at the eastern end of the second-floor gallery. He opened the door, took a step forward and stopped short.

Everything had changed. The solid old furniture had been replaced by flimsy angular constructions of metal and glass. The walls were hung with strange decorations pulsing with strident colors and astonishing subject matter. The rugs had been replaced with a garish yellow carpet; even the air smelled differently.

Glawen stepped slowly forward, looking in wonder from right to left. Had his father gone mad? He entered the parlor, and here he discovered a buxom young woman standing before a tall mirror, apparently making final adjustments to her coiffure before going down to the House Supper. Looking at the reflection, Glawen recognized Drusilla, spouse to Arles and still-active member of Floreste's Mummers.

Drusilla took note of Glawen's reflection and looked around in mild curiosity, as if the image of a strange man in her mirror was neither a novelty nor cause for any great distress. After a moment of puzzled peering, she recognized her visitor. "Isn't it Glawen? What are you doing here?"

"I was about to ask the same question of you."

"I don't see why," said Drusilla with an arch pout.

Glawen explained patiently: "Because these are my apartments, where I live with my father. Now I find a beastly yellow carpet on the floor, a bad smell and you. I can't imagine the explanation."

Drusilla laughed: a rich contralto gurgle. "It's quite simple. The rug is the color known as Dizzy-flower; the smell is no doubt Gorton. I am my own unique and delightful self. I take it you have not heard the news?"

A clammy sensation gathered along Glawen's back. "I just got off the ship."

"All is explained." Drusilla put on a solemn face. "Scharde went out on a patrol mission. This was months ago. He never came back and it is certain that he is dead. I'm sure this is a great shock for you. Are you well?"

"Yes. I am well."

"Anyway, the chambers were empty and we moved in! Now, will

440

you please excuse me? Rest as long as you like, but I must go down to supper or face a stern dressing-down."

"I'm leaving too," said Glawen.

"Already I'm a bit late," Drusilla explained. "I will thereby annoy Arles, which is the inexcusable crime around here."

Glawen followed Drusilla downstairs to the foyer, where he halted, leaning against the balustrade. It was not possible that his father, his dear father, was dead, lying somewhere with limbs askew, eyes staring blankly at the sky, seeing nothing! Glawen's own legs became loose; he dropped upon a bench. In all his recent thinking, he had considered nothing so farfetched as this. Even in regard to the chambers, all logic and order seemed to be discarded; Arles and Drusilla had no right occupying them under any circumstances!

The chambers of course were a trivial matter, if his father was truly dead. He became aware of an approaching presence, and looked up to find Spanchetta bearing down on him. She halted and stood with one hand on her hip, the other playing with the tassel of her purple sash. As always, she had bedecked herself in striking garments, and this evening she had enhanced the effect of her costume with three white plumes waving high above her magnificent mound of curls.

"Drusilla mentioned that you were here," said Spanchetta. "It seems that she told you the news."

"In regard to Scharde? Is it certain?"

Spanchetta nodded. "He was flying close by Mahadion Mountain during a storm and was struck by lightning; at least that is the theory. Drusilla told you nothing more?"

"Only that she and Arles have moved into my chambers. They will have to move out again, and at once."

"Not so. Unfortunately for you, Arles and Drusilla produced their son, Gorton, before your cutoff date, and he took precedence over you. You came in with a 21 and failed to gain Agency status. You are now a collateral and have no right to the chambers, and indeed are trespassing in Clattuc House at this very moment."

Glawen stared up at Spanchetta in numb astonishment. She performed a swaggering little side step, and said: "Perhaps this is not the time to talk of such things, but your lineage was ambiguous in the first place, and you have no cause for complaint."

Through the murk of Glawen's thoughts came the ironic reflection: Spanchetta at last is having her revenge on Scharde—long delayed and somewhat vitiated by Scharde's death, but revenge nonetheless, and sweeter than none at all.

Spanchetta turned back toward the dining room. She spoke over her shoulder: "Come, Glawen; you must learn to deal with reality; even as a child you were given to moping. You will find lodging adequate to your needs at the compound, and no doubt you will be assigned good and productive work."

"You are right," said Glawen. "I must not mope." He rose to his feet, marched across the foyer in long strides almost at a run, and out the front door. Halfway down the avenue, he halted on sudden thought and returned to Clattuc House. In the majordomo's office off the foyer he asked the footman on duty: "Where is my mail? I should have letters."

"I don't know, sir. There is nothing for you here."

Once again Glawen departed Clattuc House. He made his way to Wook House. The footman on duty at the door, upon hearing Glawen's name, became instantly polite. "Sir Bodwyn is at House Supper, but he wishes to be notified immediately upon your arrival. One moment, sir."

The footman spoke into a mesh, and listened to the responding voice. To Glawen he said: "Sir Bodwyn asks that you join him at the table."

Glawen looked down at his travel-worn clothes. "I don't think that I am suitably dressed."

"I mentioned as much, but a place has nevertheless been laid for you. Follow me, please."

Bodwyn Wook stood waiting in the hall. He gripped both of Glawen's arms. "You have heard about Scharde?"

"It's true, then?"

"He set off in a flyer and never returned. That is all that is known for certain. He may be alive. More likely he is dead. Needless to say, I share your grief. Tell me, in three words, what have you learned?"

"From Spanchetta I learn that I am lucky to be a collateral. Elsewhere I discovered that Floreste organized the Thurben Island parties. On Tassadero he arranged to have me killed. I escaped, as you see. You will be interested in the full story. Is Floreste now at Araminta Station?"

"Indeed he is: home from tour and seething with grand new schemes."

"You must take him into custody at once, at this very moment, before he learns that I am back."

Bodwyn Wook laughed softly. "Rest easy! Tonight Floreste is totally at our disposal! In fact, he sits at table not twenty yards from where we stand! He drinks our best wine with verve and charms the ladies as they never have been charmed before. You will be seated directly across the table. It is a delicious situation. What of Kirdy? He is vague and I can get nothing from him."

"Kirdy betrayed me. He cannot use mental disorder as an excuse. I don't know the full story, but in effect he sent me off to what would have been my death, had I not escaped. I cannot feel kindly toward Kirdy."

Bodwyn Wook gave his head a sad shake. "It is another tragedy. They pile one on the other, and never seem to stop. Let us go to the table."

The two entered the dining room, and took their seats at the table. Glawen was placed next to Bodwyn Wook, with Ticia at his other side. Almost directly across the great round table sat Kirdy, with Floreste beside him. Each was caught up in conversation and for a few moments neither took note of Glawen.

Bodwyn Wook murmured in Glawen's ear. "This is what Floreste himself might consider a moment of high drama. The tension builds as the two sit there all unknowing."

Glawen nodded. He studied Kirdy with care, revulsion twisting at his viscera. At the moment Kirdy seemed in full command of himself, without oppression of the spirits or the morose introversion of the Kirdy who had accompanied Glawen on his mission; to the contrary, he seemed to demonstrate the heartiness and boyish simplicity which, with his big pink face, china-blue eyes and easy grin, had in the old days made him reasonably popular.

Glawen watched him in fascination. This hardly seemed the same Kirdy he had last seen in Fexelburg. Now Kirdy bent to eat a morsel of poached fish, then, raising his head, patted his mouth with a napkin. His gaze fell upon Glawen and he became still. Slowly his shoulders sagged and he looked down at the table, the jocundity gone from his face.

Bodwyn Wook muttered in Glawen's ear: "There you see neither madness nor mistake. What is plain and evident is pure and unabashed guilt. I need no more to convince me. It is shameful. I must look into his pedigree."

"He has changed since I saw him last. Floreste's therapy has been remarkable. Look! He is now giving Floreste the news. Another supper ruined."

At Kirdy's muttered remark, Floreste jerked up his handsome head and glanced as if casually around the table, sliding his gaze past Glawen. Then he swung half around in his seat and chatted vivaciously with Dame Dorna Wook, who sat to his left.

Glawen waited for a pause, then called across the table. "Master Floreste, I see you are back from your tour."

Floreste darted him a quick cold stare. "Yes, as you see."

"It was a success?"

"About the ordinary. As always, we do our best, and hope for the best. Our creed is optimism."

"It seems that we have a mutual acquaintance on Tassadero."

"Really? That is no great surprise. I meet thousands of folk every week, or so it seems, and of course I remember none of them, save—ha, ha!—only the most charming."

"And you consider the Ordene Zaa charming?"

"Ordene Zaa? And who might that be? And who cares? At the moment I am interested only in this exquisite fish."

"In that case, I will say only that she sends her compliments. Her present circumstances are not at all happy. Were you aware of her troubles?"

"No."

"She became involved in a set of remarkable crimes, which engaged the attention of the IPCC. They may even call on you to verify some of her allegations. Or they may refer the matter to the local IPCC affiliate, which of course is Bureau B."

"Certainly it is nothing to concern me." Floreste turned back to Dame Dorna, and continued his conversation.

Ticia, who had already taken critical note of Glawen's garments, spoke to him in a crisp voice: "Am I mistaken or have you gone out of your way to make our local genius uncomfortable?"

"You are mistaken. I have not gone a single hair's breadth out of my way."

"This 'Ordene Zaa': is she one of Floreste's lovers, or something of the sort?"

"Nothing would surprise me. Both are remarkable people."

"Hmmf. You've been away, haven't you? I don't recall seeing you about for a while."

"Yes, I've been away."

"It is bad news about your father. Come to think of it, you're now a collateral! Yet here you sit, large as life, at our House Supper, where collaterals are roundly snubbed."

"Are you planning to snub me?"

"Henceforth, yes. I can't very well do so tonight, since we are sitting beside each other, and it is all too easy for you to claim my attention."

"I am not overly sensitive," said Glawen. "Snub me all you like."

"I hardly need your permission," said Ticia. "Indeed I snub almost everyone; it makes my favor ever so valuable."

Bodwyn Wook told Glawen: "Pay no heed to the little fool; already she is losing her looks; in another ten years she'll be all teeth, nose and clavicle like her aunt, Dame Audlis."

Ticia said: "Tonight, Uncle Bodwyn, your wit is more entertaining than ever. You are becoming quite the *enfant terrible* in your old age."

"Quite so, Ticia. I am much too mordant, and your stance is correct. Propriety must be maintained and collaterals must not be allowed to trade on old associations. Glawen, I can wait no longer to hear your story. Let us finish our supper in the side room."

Bodwyn Wook and Glawen departed the room. In the corridor, Bodwyn Wook asked: "There is no doubt whatever as to Floreste's guilt?"

"None."

"In that case, I will have him taken up and conveyed to the jail. I must wait till after supper, however, lest I offend Ticia's standards of gentility. What of Kirdy?"

"He betrayed me, you and the bureau. He was subject to mental stress, which was perhaps too much for him. I can't evade the feeling that he knew very well what he was doing. But I would prefer that you form your own opinion."

"My opinion was formed at the dinner table. Indeed, you are dealing too generously with Kirdy. He dealt you a last blow of which you are not aware. When he returned to Araminta, he assured me that you were dead, on absolute and definite authority. I therefore canceled the rescue mission which was on the verge of departure. He lied to me; he knows it and I know it. It could have meant the difference between life and death for you. I am not happy with Kirdy. He will face an inquiry, and at minimum lose Wook status."

"He seems much saner now than when I left him at Fexelburg."

"Come now; let us ingest the rest of our supper. We shall talk as we eat."

2

Glawen and Bodwyn Wook dined in a small parlor off the central gallery. In language as terse as possible Glawen told of his investigations and the difficulties he had encountered in the process. "As I sit here and think back over what happened, I feel a dozen emotions. The strongest is relief that it is all over. There were good moments, of course: when my feet hit the ground outside the seminary. Even tonight I took a certain cruel pleasure watching Kirdy and Floreste across the table."

"And now come the tiresome details. Floreste will demand leniency. His victims were only Yips; they were the raw material of a new artistic technique; he is everywhere recognized as a genius and must not be bound by ordinary regulations. Dame Dorna may very well endorse such arguments; she dotes on him and is a member of the Fine Arts Committee."

A footman entered the room. "Your instructions have been followed, sir."

Bodwyn Wook nodded with satisfaction. "As I expected, Floreste and Kirdy, pleading fatigue, left the supper early. They were accosted at the door and taken into custody. The dignity of the House Supper has not been compromised. Well, then, enough of that. May I pour you some more wine? This is our best Chariste and excels anything else of its type produced at the station."

"It is indeed very good."

For a period the two sipped the wine. "Now, then," said Bodwyn Wook, "we must give some thought to your personal problems."

"I have already done so. I intend to find what has happened to my father."

"Hm, yes. Well, I can't hold out much hope. We searched with great care. We found nothing and heard no distress signals. There are dozens of possibilities; we've tried to analyze them all, with the same result: nothing."

Glawen sat swirling the wine around in his goblet. Presently he said: "That is suggestive in itself, don't you think?"

"Suggestive of what?"

"I don't know. It must mean something. First of all, in the case of a crash, we would expect to find the wreckage."

"Not necessarily. He might have gone down into a forest or a lake."

"Still—one wonders. According to Spanchetta, his flyer was struck by lightning near the Mahadions."

"That is one theory, and it's as good as any—or as bad as any, if you prefer."

"I'll talk to Chilke tomorrow." Glawen hesitated, then said: "I might as well know the worst right now. How will I be affected at Bureau B by my new status? Or am I out entirely?"

"Ha-ha!" said Bodwyn Wook, drinking from his goblet. "So long as I am Superintendent Bodwyn Wook you are Captain Glawen Clattuc. Your abilities, which I consider notable, transcend any question of

446

formal status. And in this connection, I can't help but feel that something rather odd is going on."

"How so?"

"I can't be sure just yet. On the surface, everything seems proper. But I wonder if all is as it seems."

"I'm afraid that I don't understand you."

"Let us go back to a time three weeks before your birthday. You were at Pogan's Point. At this time Erl Clattuc was killed in a landslide at Cape Journal, and your index dropped to 20.

"Then what? Strange events occur! The Mummers return to Araminta Station, with Arles, Drusilla and Gorton. You are once again 21. Had Scharde the option, he would have gone into retirement and set things right—but Scharde has now been gone almost two months.

"What if Scharde does not return before your birthday? What if he fails to return at all? At any time, the Clattuc House Election Board —chaired, incidentally, by Spanchetta—can meet and declare Scharde dead, which is a fair supposition. If this occurs before your birthday, you revert to 20 and regain the Agency status which Scharde intended that you should have.

"Spanchetta pointedly refused to call the meeting until two weeks after your birthday, when you were irrevocably a collateral and expelled from Clattuc House. Then, and only then, did Spanchetta call the meeting which as its first order of business presumed Scharde's death, announced a vacancy and filled this vacancy from the collateral list. Can you guess who headed the list?"

"Namour!"

"Just so. In effect Spanchetta kicked you out and gave Namour your place. Is it not ironic? Namour professes to care not a fig for the House. Still, he demurred not an instant when the opportunity appeared."

Glawen sighed. "At the moment I don't much care one way or the other."

"Your father would not want you to be passive."

"True. I will look into the situation."

"Until your affairs are in order, you shall be my guest here at Wook House. Kirdy will be unhappy and Ticia may well pretend not to see you, but pay her no heed; it is her way of calling attention to herself. Otherwise, you will find us congenial."

In the morning Glawen took breakfast alone in the rooms Bodwyn
Wook had put at his disposal, then set off down Wansey Way, under
a sky full of small scudding clouds: fugitives from a tremendous storm,
now five hundred miles out to sea, but advancing inexorably toward
the coast. At Beach Road, Glawen returned north and proceeded to
the airport, where he found Chilke sitting in his office drinking tea.
Chilke looked up in surprise. "I thought you were dead! That was the
rumor that came to my ears."

"I'm alive. It's my father who seems to be dead."

"That is the general assumption. I don't know any more than you
already know." Chilke brought out a map. "He flew on a standard
patrol: northeast over Pandora Plain, past the Mahadions, around
Lake Garnet, north to the ocean, then along the Marmion Foreshore
and back down the coast: at least, that was the course that went into
his autopilot."

Glawen asked further questions, but Chilke had nothing to add
except speculations and suspicions. "Under almost any circumstances
we should have heard the distress signal, if only a single yelp. We
heard nothing, and nothing registered on the monitor. We found no
wreckage. That's all I know for sure. What about you? What has
happened to cause such pessimistic rumors? You look pale but strong."

"I've been exercising in a cave." Glawen told Chilke of his adventures, then brought out the photograph he had taken from Zaa's desk.
"What do you make of this?"

Chilke studied the photograph with care. "Those are stern-looking
ladies. Unless my eyes deceive me, I see my old friend Madame
Zigonie, who still owes me money."

"Which is she?"

"This one, third from the left. When I knew her she wore her hair
longer, or it might have been a wig. Who are these ladies?"

"Members of a philosophical cult. They call themselves Monomantics. This one here is Sibil, who was in charge out at Thurben Island.
This one is the Ordene Zaa, who fell in love with me—I guess you
would call it that. I escaped by climbing down a rope of torn bed
sheets, and I'm truly glad to be home: such as it is."

"Why do you say that?"

"Namour is now a Clattuc and I'm a collateral. You have more
status than I do."

"It makes one wonder," said Chilke.

Glawen returned to Wook House. He went to the library and spent the rest of the morning cogitating and making notes. Bodwyn Wook came past. He patted Glawen's shoulder. "I am happy to see you taking some rest. You have been through a great deal and now you need time to readjust! Doze on! No one will disturb you until lunchtime."

Glawen looked up indignantly. "I am awake; in fact, I am thinking."

Bodwyn Wook laughed indulgently. "Surely, in Zab Zonk's tomb you must have thought your fill, to the point of repletion!"

"These are different thoughts, and rather more interesting. But I have something to show you." Glawen produced the photograph.

Bodwyn Wook's eyes suddenly became sharp as skewers. "Where did you get this?"

"At Pogan's Point, from the Ordene's desk." Glawen pointed to a face. "This is Zaa. And this is Sibil."

"Why did you not show me this before?"

"I wanted to see if Chilke could identify his 'Madame Zigonie.' Then I would have something to show you."

"And could he? But let me guess. It was this lady here."

"Right! How did you know?"

"At one time she was known as Smonny—which is to say, Simonetta, Spanchetta's little sister."

Glawen studied the faces with new interest. "Now that you mention it, I can see a resemblance."

"If you will allow me, I will take charge of this photograph," said Bodwyn Wook. "Let us say nothing about it to anyone. I will instruct Chilke along these lines. It is most intriguing information."

"Namour must know."

Bodwyn Wook settled into a chair beside Glawen. "One day we will catch Namour out in one of his peccadillos, and then all his precious secrets will be revealed in full dimension, in glowing color, fresh and vivid!"

"Namour will be careful to give you no such opportunity."

"That has been true so far. Incidentally, I had a few words with Drusilla this morning, and she confirms Floreste's guilt with eager protestations of virtue." Bodwyn Wook squinted down at the papers in front of Glawen. "What are all these notes and lists?"

"They represent points still obscure to me: mysteries, if you like."

Bodwyn Wook peered down at the notes. "So many? I thought that we had wiped the slate clean of mysteries."

"For one thing, I am puzzled by Floreste's easy connection with the Monomantics. I want to put some questions to him."

"Hmm. If you wish to question Floreste, why not? It will be good practice for you, if nothing else. I spoke with him this morning, but learned nothing. He is master of a tantalizing opacity, which at last becomes unendurable. You will fare no better."

"Unless he takes me lightly and becomes careless."

"Possible. Be prepared to deal with a saintly martyr, whose only crime is artistic expression. I pointed out the virulence of his deeds, but he only laughed gently, as if he knew better than I. The folk of Araminta Station had never truly appreciated his great genius, so he assured me. He considers himself a 'citizen of the universe.' Araminta Station is a turgid little backwater, with a stupid and incestuous social system, which rewards its fools and blunderers and forces its talented folk to fulfill themselves elsewhere. These are his words, not mine, and of course they contain a leavening of half-truths.

"In any event—and for an instant we catch a glimpse of the naked and unadorned Floreste—what has Araminta Station done for him? Where are his official honors and high rank, his wealth and private mansion! How is his great genius rewarded? In a patter of applause for his marvelous productions and the patronage of the Fine Arts Committee. I pointed out that he was basically no more than a skillful public entertainer, and it was not our way to sanctify or ennoble such folk. He said no more, but clearly he has no love for either the Conservancy or the Charter or Araminta Station."

"I wonder why he should want to build his new Orpheum here?"

"Where else? The situation is ideal. Why not put the question to Floreste? From sheer perversity he will evade a direct answer. He is impervious."

Glawen leaned back in his chair. "As I sat here thinking—dozing, as you put it—I realized that Floreste must have accumulated a large sum of money. Do you know where this money is kept?"

"As a matter of fact, I do. It is on deposit at the Bank of Mircea in Soumjiana."

"I have decided to bring a civil suit against Floreste. My chances of a large settlement seem to be good—especially if the case is tried in the High Court here at the Station, which would have the jurisdiction."

"Hah!" cried Bodwyn Wook. "You have mastered that dastardly Clattuc art of attacking your enemy in his most sensitive parts! Even in the very shadow of doom, Floreste will suffer agonies if his money is threatened."

"This was my own thinking. How would I institute such a suit?"

"Wilfred Offaw will draw up the papers this very day, and Floreste's money will be impounded as if it were encased in durastrang and guarded by a hundred Gray Helmets."

"Floreste should be disconcerted, at the very least."

"Beyond a doubt. When do you wish to question him? Anytime is suitable; Floreste has no engagements elsewhere."

"This afternoon will do well enough."

"I will mention to Marcus that you are to be assisted in every way."

Immediately after lunch Glawen wrapped himself in a cloak and walked leaning against the blustering wind to the ponderous old jail across the river from the Orpheum. In the front office he was searched by Marcus Diffin, the jailer. "I will not apologize, since I pass no one without a search, including Bodwyn Wook himself, and it was he who gave the orders. And what, may I ask, is this parcel?"

"It is what it seems to be. If I need it, I'll give you a signal."

Glawen entered the chamber, and stood for a moment with his back to the door. Floreste sat in a wooden armchair at a rough plank table, his attention fixed upon a small white flower in a slender blue vase. The intensity of his gaze suggested mystical inversion, or perhaps he merely hoped that Glawen might notice his preoccupation and tiptoe abashed from the cell. Anything was possible, thought Glawen. After a moment he said gently: "Let me know as soon as I may conveniently break into your meditation."

Without so much as shifting his gaze, Floreste made a gesture of weary resignation. "Speak! I have no choice but to listen. My only hope is hope itself. I look everywhere, but I find it only as a symbol expressed by this little flower, so brave and winsome!"

"It is indeed a nice flower," said Glawen. He pulled up a chair and seated himself across the table from Floreste. "I want to ask you a few questions, which I hope that you will answer."

"I am not in an expansive mood. I doubt if you will be gratified by my answers."

"From sheer curiosity: how long have you known Zaa? I refer, of course, to the Ordene at Pogan's Point."

"Names mean nothing to me," said Floreste. "I have known thousands of folk, of every ilk and description. Some I might recall, for their style of being, or a certain flair which sets them apart from all other Gaeans. Others are like footprints in last year's sand: dismal creatures best forgotten."

"In which category do you place the Ordene Zaa?"

"These finicky little classifications are both pointless and tiresome."

"Perhaps you will tell me this: how and why did Zaa, a woman of intelligence, become involved in Monomantics?"

Floreste gave a cool chuckle. "A fact is a fact, is it not? Things are as they are, and that is enough for the man of deeds."

"As a dramatist, are you not concerned for motivations?"

"Only as a dramatist. Empathies, sympathies—by such means the insecure try to rationalize their murky and frightening universes."

"That is an interesting point of view."

"So it is. I have now said all I care to say and you may leave."

Glawen pretended not to hear the suggestion. "The day is probably not too young for a glass of wine; I suppose that you feel as I do on the subject, since we are both men of cultivated taste."

Floreste darted Glawen a haughty glance. "Do you think to gain my favor with such footling tactics? I want none of your wine, early or late."

"I expected that you would take this position," said Glawen. "I brought no wine."

"Bah," muttered Floreste. "Your prattle is both inane and insipid. Did you hear me correctly? I gave you permission to leave."

"Just as you like. But I have not told you the news!"

"I am not interested in news. I only wish to live out my days in peace."

"Even when the news concerns you?"

Floreste looked down at the white flower. He shook his head and sighed. "Grace and gentility: goodbye: no doubt forever. I am embroiled in vulgarity against my will." He looked Glawen up and down as if seeing him for the first time. "Well—why not? The wise man, as he travels through life, enjoys the scenery to either side, since he knows he will not come this way again. The road ahead winds back and forth, over the hills and far away, and who knows where it leads?"

"Sometimes it is easy to guess," said Glawen. "As, for instance, in your own case."

Floreste, jumping to his feet, marched back and forth across the room, arms clasped behind his back. Glawen watched in silence. Floreste returned to his chair. "These are dismal times. I will drink wine."

"It's all the same with me," said Glawen. "I came prepared for either contingency." He went to the door and rapped on the panel.

Marcus Diffin opened the shutter to the peephole. "What do you want?"

"My parcel."

"I must pour it into a synthan container and supply synthan cups. Criminals are not allowed the use of glass."

"Don't call me a criminal!" roared Floreste. "I am a dramatic artist! There is a notable difference!"

"If you say so, sir. Here is the wine. Drink with joy."

"What an idiot!" stormed Floreste. "Still—what does it matter? The wise man rejoices in each fleeting instant! Pour the wine with a loose hand!"

"It is a sad affair," said Glawen. "Your termination will bring tears to many an eye."

"Including my own. It is shameful to treat me so."

"What of your grotesque crimes? You deserve much worse."

"Nonsense! Those so-called crimes were a means to an end: small coins spent to buy a great prize! They are finished and forgotten. But now—think of it, if you will! I am obliged to dance a part, all unwilling, in this macabre ballet you call justice—and to what end? Who benefits? Certainly not I. Far better to put all this foolishness aside and start afresh, like the urbane gentlemen we are!"

"I must ask my father's views on the subject—if ever I see him again. He has disappeared; were you aware of this?"

"I heard talk to this effect."

"What has happened to him? Do you know?"

Floreste drained the cup at a gulp. "Why should I tell you, even if I knew? It is by your act that I am here, counting off the minutes of my life."

"It might be considered a generous act."

"Generosity, is it?" Floreste filled his cup from the synthan flask. "All my life I have been generous! Have I been ennobled, or in any way rewarded? I am still listed as a far collateral. Meanwhile I have given of my genius with both hands! I am giving my personal fortune to the new Orpheum, even though I will never see the splendid reality. But I will still give! It shall be my memorial, and folk down the ages will speak my name with awe!"

Glawen gave his head a skeptical shake. "This may not be possible, which is the news I came to bring you. Not happy news, I fear."

"What are you saying?"

"It is simple enough. I have suffered great damages by reason of your wanton, cruel and purposeful acts. Therefore I have placed an action at law against you, your property and all your fortune in money. I have been assured of a very large award. Your plans for an Orpheum must be postponed."

Floreste stared at Glawen in consternation. "You cannot be serious! It would be the act of a maniac!"

"Not at all. You arranged a terrible fate for me, and I suffered greatly. As I think back it seems a true nightmare! Why should you not recompense me? My case is legitimate."

"In theory only! You want my money, the treasure I have pieced

453

together sol by sol, always with the grand dream in mind! And now, with the dream at last attainable, you would shatter my universe!"

"You were not concerned with my plight at Pogan's Point. I am not concerned with yours."

With sagging features Floreste sat staring at the white flower. On sudden thought he hitched himself up in the chair. "You are belaboring the wrong person. It was Kirdy, not I, who insisted on the call to Pogan's Point. I acceded, true, but without emotion; your fate meant nothing to me. It was Kirdy who contrived the deed and enjoyed it enormously. Take his money if you must; leave mine alone."

"I can't really believe this," said Glawen. "Kirdy had nothing in his mind but confusion."

"My dear fellow, how can you be so dense? Kirdy's hatred for you might have caused his confusion, but it was not the other way around! He has detested you since you were children!"

Glawen looked off across the room and down through the years. Floreste, in this case, was telling him the brutal truth. "It's a feeling I've had at the back of my mind—but I always kept it repressed, down and out of sight. Kirdy was considered a fine upright fellow; it was wrong to think such things of Kirdy—even when they could hardly be disguised. But—I can't understand why. He had no reason to hate me."

Floreste sat looking at his flower. "After he called Pogan's Point it spilled out of him like vomit. He held nothing back. It seems that all his life, you took everything he wanted: without effort or strain. He was mad for Sessily Veder; he craved her so badly it made him sick to look at her. She avoided him as if he were deformed, but she went gladly to you. You won school honors and Bureau B rank, and all without apparent effort. At Yipton he tried his best to implicate you but the Oomps wouldn't listen and placed him under arrest. He told me that thereafter he hated you so much that whenever he saw you his knees went weak."

"It makes me a bit sick to hear of it."

"It is sickening stuff. At last you left him alone at Fexelburg, and with great gladness Kirdy knew that the time had come. The telephone call to Pogan's Point was his moment to even the score. In all candor, I was appalled by so much ferocity."

Glawen sighed. "All this is interesting, in a horrid way, but not what I wanted to know."

"And what was that?"

"Where is my father?"

"Now? I am not sure that I know."

"But he is alive?"

Floreste blinked, irritated that he had revealed even a glimmer of information. "If my suppositions are correct: it is possible."

"Tell me what you know."

"What do you offer in return? My life and freedom?"

"I can't do that. I have power only over your money."

Floreste, wincing, poured himself wine. "That is an idea not to be contemplated."

"Tell me what you know. If I am able to find my father, your money will be safe from me."

"Obviously, I cannot trust you."

"Of course you can trust me! I would give all your money and my money and everything else to bring my father home! Why should you not trust me? It is your only chance!"

"I will consider the matter. When is my trial?"

"You have refused defending counsel, so there is no reason for delay. The trial will take place two days from now. When will you have an answer for me?"

"See me after the trial," said Floreste, pouring out the last of the wine.

4

The Court of High Justice sat in the Moot Hall of the Old Agency: a wide circular chamber under a high dome of green and blue glass, with rosewood panels and a floor laid in a checker of gray marble streaked with green and dense white quartz. To one side the court conducted its business; to the other, a semicircular three-tiered gallery allowed the entire population of Araminta Station, if it so chose, to observe proceedings.

At the stroke of noon the three High Judges entered the hall and took their places: Dame Melba Veder, Rowan Clattuc and Conservator Egon Tamm, who presided at the trial. The judges seated themselves and the Nunciator called out: "Attention, all! The court is now in session! Let the gentleman under accusation be brought to his place of judgment!"

Stumbling and looking angrily over his shoulder as if to discover who had pushed him forward, Floreste entered the chamber.

"The accused may take his place in the dock," called the Nunciator. "Bailiff, be good enough to escort Sir Floreste to his place."

"This way, sir."

"Don't hurry me!" snapped Floreste. "Nothing will start until I arrive; you may be sure of that."

"Yes, sir. This is your place."

Floreste at last was properly seated. The Nunciator uttered a sonorous command: "Sir, you are here to answer grave charges! Raise your right hand on high and state your name, so that all present shall know who sits in the dock."

Floreste showed the Nunciator a sneer of pure contempt. "Are you serious? I am well-known! Call out your own name and let us inquire into your crimes. It will suit me just as well, and it may prove amusing."

Egon Tamm spoke gravely: "The formalities seem to impede our work, and we shall forgo them, if Sir Floreste will agree."

"I agree to anything which will expedite this farce. I have already been adjudged guilty and condemned. I accept this, and I will deny nothing; it would only mean confusion and aggravation for everyone. As for my forthcoming death, what of that? I have long suffered that incurable disease known as life. So now I meet my end with neither regrets nor shame. Yes! I acknowledge my mistakes, but if I explained them I would seem to make excuses, so I will keep a dignified tongue in my head. But I will say this much: my motives were those of grandeur! I rode like a god on dreams of glory! And now these visions will dwindle and wither and lapse into dust. My going is a great tragedy for all of us. Look upon me well, you folk of Araminta! You shall not see my like again!" Floreste turned to the judges. "So far as I am concerned, the trial is over. Make your dreary utterance, and also I would suggest a sentence of six months at hard labor for the Nunciator, on sheer suspicion, since everything about him suggests venality."

"Three days hence, at sundown, you shall be terminated," said Egon Tamm. "As for the Nunciator, this time he shall escape with a warning."

Floreste rose to his feet and started to leave the dock. The Conservator called him back: "One moment, sir! We must deal with peripheral matters, where your testimony may be needed."

With poor grace Floreste resumed his seat. The Nunciator called: "Namour Clattuc! Approach the bench!"

Namour came slowly forward, showing a face of smiling bewilderment. "Did I hear correctly? You called me?"

Egon Tamm said: "Quite right, sir. We have a few questions to ask of you. You are well-acquainted with both Floreste and Titus Pompo. Did you know of the Thurben Island excursions?"

Namour considered carefully before speaking. Then he said: "I had only an inkling that something was going on. I asked no questions, for fear that I might learn more than I wanted to know. To set the record straight: I am not well-acquainted with Titus Pompo."

Egon Tamm asked Floreste: "Does this accord with your own recollection?"

"Closely enough."

"That will be all, Namour. You may step down."

Namour returned to his seat, still smiling his soft vague smile.

The Nunciator called out: "Drusilla co-Laverty Clattuc! Please step forward!"

Drusilla, sitting between Arles and Spanchetta, rose uncertainly to her feet. "Do you mean me?"

"Was your name called?"

"Oh, yes! That was my name."

"Then why should I not mean you?"

"I'm sure I don't know."

"Come forward, if you please."

Drusilla twitched her rather unsuitable black and persimmon-pink gown to its best advantage, then sauntered across the chamber to the chair reserved for witnesses.

"Please be seated," said the bailiff. "You understand that you must answer all questions truthfully and in full detail?"

"Of course!" Drusilla, seating herself, gave Floreste a gay fluttering little wave of the fingers. Floreste, watching somberly, made no response. "I'm sure I don't know what I can tell you," said Drusilla. "I know nothing of this affair."

Egon Tamm asked: "You were not aware of the Thurben Island excursions?"

"I knew something was going on, and I suspected that it might be just a bit naughty—but naturally I had nothing to do with it."

"You were the representative of Ogmo Enterprises, were you not?"

Drusilla made a flippant gesture. "Oh, that! I just carried around advertising material and dropped it off here and there."

The judge Dame Melba Veder asked sharply: "You did not actively solicit custom for the enterprise?"

Drusilla blinked. "I'm not sure that I understand what you mean."

Floreste spoke in a dreary voice: "Don't badger the poor creature. She knew nothing."

Dame Melba paid him no heed. "You were on terms of intimate friendship with Namour. Did you not discuss Ogmo Enterprises and the excursions with him?"

"Not really. He looked at a brochure once or twice, and just laughed and threw it aside, and that was all there was to it."

"What of your husband, Arles?"

"About the same."

"That is all."

Egon Tamm said: "You may step down."

With patent relief and a cheerful smile for Floreste, Drusilla rejoined Arles and Spanchetta. Bodwyn Wook now approached the bench and spoke in a low voice to Egon Tamm, who in turn conferred with his colleagues. Bodwyn Wook went to the side and waited.

Egon Tamm addressed the chamber: "The Superintendent of Bureau B has brought another matter to our attention, which might as well be dealt with now. Sir Floreste, the affair does not concern you, and you may retire."

Floreste rose to his feet and looking neither right nor left, marched from the chamber. Egon Tamm said: "I now ask that Bodwyn Wook acquaint us with the details of the case he has brought to our attention."

Bodwyn Wook came forward. "This matter concerns a particularly nasty little fraud, perpetrated, apparently, from motives of sheer malice. I refer to the Agency status of Captain Glawen Clattuc. Several months ago, and well before his critical birthday, his index was 22. Then Artwain Clattuc retired and Erl Clattuc was killed in a landslide at Cape Journal. Glawen's index became 20.

"Shortly afterward, Glawen's father, Scharde Clattuc, flew out on a routine patrol and never returned. We searched carefully but at last were forced to give Scharde up for lost.

"Now, then: what happens next? Curious events! Two weeks before Glawen's birthday a ship comes down from space, bringing Arles, Drusilla and their son, Gorton! A great surprise indeed, and bad news for Glawen! He is superseded by Gorton and his index rises to 21.

"At any time the Clattuc House Election Committee—chaired, incidentally, by Spanchetta—could meet and declare a presumption of death for Scharde. If this happens before Glawen's birthday, as would seem reasonable and proper, Glawen's index becomes 20, and in effect he assumes his father's place in Clattuc House. Spanchetta, despite angry protests from others of the committee, delays until two weeks after Glawen's birthday, when Glawen has become a collateral. Scharde is pronounced dead, leaving a vacant slot, and who is nominated to become the new Clattuc? Namour! Is it not superb?"

Spanchetta could contain herself no longer. She jumped to her feet. "I protest these vile slanders with all the vehemence at my command! I am totally amazed that the High Judges allow this mad little baboon to strut up and down their court, making a mockery of all dignity and vilifying decent folk! I demand an explanation!"

Egon Tamm said soberly: "Superintendent, you have heard Dame Spanchetta's request. Can you amplify your case?"

"I want no amplification!" cried Spanchetta. "I want a full apology and a retraction of all these infamous charges."

"I have not yet brought charges," said Bodwyn Wook. "As for apologies, the record of your conduct speaks for itself. Do you want me to apologize for citing your record?"

"I have done nothing illegal! The Election Board meets whenever I deem that circumstances warrant. You can prove neither illegality nor malice. As for Gorton, he rightfully superseded Glawen; again, that is the process of the law."

"Aha!" said Bodwyn Wook. "There we differ. Over the last few days we have looked very carefully into the case of Gorton. In the first place we find that he was born barely six months after the formal wedding of Arles and Drusilla."

"That is sheer taradiddle! Arles and Drusilla were informally married somewhat earlier at Soumjiana. And even if they were not married: what of that? Arles acknowledges the child as his own."

"All very well, but the law expressly denies status to adopted children."

"What are you saying? Gorton was not adopted by Arles, or anyone else!"

"Just so," said Bodwyn Wook. "As I say, we have gone into the case very thoroughly. First, by one means or another, we obtained material which afforded us the genetic patterns of Arles, Drusilla and Gorton respectively. This particular research was performed by eminent experts, who can give evidence if such evidence is needed."

"This is all bluster and puff," declared Spanchetta, her voice rich and scornful. "Deal with facts, if you please!"

"The evidence proved that Gorton was the son of Drusilla; there is no doubt as to this. Regarding the other half of the parentage, there is no such clarity, although typical Clattuc gene clusters are found."

"Your test tubes are telling you what I have already made clear! Is it not enough? Now will you leave us in peace?"

"Patience, Spanchetta! Listen intently, and you will hear more! We go back in time several years, to when, with truly reckless audacity, Arles attempted rape upon the person of Wayness Tamm, the Conservator's daughter. He was unsuccessful, and captured. I will let the High Judge describe the punishment meted out to Arles."

"Arles wore a mask and hood, which concealed his identity," said

Egon Tamm. "For this reason we presumed that he intended rape only, and not rape with murder, and so we spared him his life.

"However, to ensure that Arles might never again attempt a similar deed, he was subjected to a surgical process which rendered him sterile and almost totally incapable of tumescence. The procedure was permanent and irreversible. Gorton is not the child of Arles."

Spanchetta emitted a strange wailing cry of outrage. "Not true, not true, not true!"

"It is true," said Egon Tamm.

Bodwyn Wook pointed to Drusilla. "Stand up."

Drusilla reluctantly rose to her feet.

Bodwyn Wook asked: "Who is Gorton's father?"

Drusilla hesitated, looked right and left, licked her lips, then said in a sulky voice: "Namour."

"Arles knew this?"

"Of course! How could he not know?"

"Did Spanchetta understand any of this?"

"I don't know and I don't care. Ask her yourself."

"You may sit down." Bodwyn Wook looked at Arles. "Well, then: what do you have to say for yourself?"

"At the moment, nothing."

"Did your mother know that Gorton was not your child?"

Arles glanced sidewise toward Spanchetta, who sat slumped, her great pile of brown curls askew. "I guess not," he growled.

Glawen, sitting to the side beside Bodwyn Wook, rose to his feet. "If the Court pleases, I have a question I want to put to Arles."

"Ask your question."

Glawen turned to Arles. "What have you done with my mail?"

"We did what was proper and right!" declared Arles in a blustering voice. "You weren't on hand, and neither was Scharde, and no one knew where you were, so we sent it back to where it came from, marked 'Address unknown.'"

Glawen turned away. He told Egon Tamm: "That is all, sir."

Egon Tamm nodded, a faint grim smile on his hard features. He conferred with his colleagues, then spoke: "Our judgment is as follows: Glawen Clattuc is awarded his rightful status. The Court regrets that he was subjected to what Superintendent Wook has accurately called a malicious fraud. Arles and Drusilla are stripped of all status, and may not even consider themselves collaterals. They must instantly depart from Clattuc House, this very day. The chambers must be restored as quickly as possible to their exact previous condition, to the total satisfaction of Captain Clattuc. 'As quickly as possible' means just that: work must begin at once and proceed night and day, regardless of cost. If Arles and Drusilla lack the necessary funds, Dame Spanchetta must bear the expense, and make whatever arrangements for repayment she deems suitable with Arles.

"Further, Arles and Drusilla are sentenced to eighty-five days of hard labor at the Cape Journal Labor Camp. The Court hopes that the experience will prove salutary. It is a minimal sentence, and they should consider themselves lucky."

From Drusilla came a wail of pure dismay. Arles stared silently at the floor.

Egon Tamm continued. "The Court cannot escape the suspicion that Dame Spanchetta knew considerably more of the matter than the evidence indicates. This is only common sense. Still, we cannot act on suspicion alone, and Dame Spanchetta will not, on this occasion, join Arles and Drusilla at Cape Journal. We have no jurisdiction over the internal government of Clattuc House, but we suggest that Dame Spanchetta is an unsuitable chairman for the Election Board, or for any other committee of importance. We recommend that the Clattuc House Elders take executive action along these lines.

"If there is no more business for the Court, we will stand adjourned."

5

During the afternoon of the following day Glawen visited the jail once again. Entering the cell, he found Floreste sitting at the table, hunched over a book bound in elegant pink leather. Floreste turned Glawen a look of displeasure. "What do you want now?"

"What I wanted before."

"I'm afraid I can't help you. I have little time to waste and I must make my arrangements." Floreste returned to his book and appeared to dismiss Glawen from his mind. Glawen crossed the room and seated himself on the chair across the table from Floreste.

A moment passed. Floreste looked up with a frown. "Are you still here?"

"I just arrived."

"It has been long enough. As you see, I am busy with this book."

"You must make a definite decision, one way or the other."

Floreste gave a sour laugh. "All the most urgent decisions have definitely been made."

"And your new Orpheum?"

"The Fine Arts Committee will carry on the work. The chairman

461

is Lady Skellane Laverty; I have known her many years and she is devoted to the cause. She has brought me this book, long one of my favorites. Is it known to you?"

"You have not shown me its title."

"*The Lyrics of Mad Navarth.* His songs hang in the mind forever."

"I am familiar with some of them."

"Hmm! I am surprised! You seem a—well, I will not call you a dull dog—let us say, a rather somber fellow."

"I don't think that of myself. The fact is that I am worried about my father."

"Let us talk about Navarth instead. Here is a particularly delicious segment. He glimpses a face for a single instant, but before he can look around it is gone. Navarth is haunted for days, and at last he pours his imaginings into a dozen wonderful quatrains, wild and fateful, surging with rhythm, and each tagged with the refrain:

"'So shall she live and so shall she die
And so shall the winds of the world blow by.'"

"Very nice," said Glawen. "Do you intend only to recite poetry to me?"

Floreste haughtily raised his eyebrows. "You are privileged!"

"I want to know what has happened to my father. It seems that you know. I can't understand why you won't tell me."

"Do not try to understand me," said Floreste. "I myself make no effort in those directions. I use the plural form advisedly."

"Tell me at least if, for a fact, you know what has happened. Which is it: yes or no?"

Floreste rubbed his chin. "Knowledge is a complex commodity," he said at last. "It must not be flung here and there like a farmer scattering manure. Knowledge is power! That is an aphorism worth committing to memory."

"You still have given me no answer. Do you intend to tell me anything whatever?"

Floreste spoke weightedly: "I will say this, and you should listen closely. Clearly our universe is subtle and, one might say, palpitant. Nothing moves without jostling something else. Change is immanent to the structure of the cosmos; not even Cadwal of the Charter can evade change. Ah, beautiful Cadwal, with its fine lands and noble provinces! The meadows are verdant in the sunlight; they invite the general habitancy wherein all creatures may take their special pleasures. Animals may browse and birds may fly, while men sing their songs and dance their dances, in peace and harmony. So it should be, with each consuming his share and each performing the work he finds needful. This is the vision of many noble folk, both here and elsewhere."

"So it may be. But what of my father?"

Floreste scowled and made an impatient gesture. "Are you so dense? Must everything be shouted into your ear? Do you subscribe to those ideals I have just cited?"

"No."

"What of Bodwyn Wook?"

"Not Bodwyn Wook, either."

"What of your father?"

"Nor my father. In fact, almost no one at Araminta Station."

"Others elsewhere have more advanced views. But I have said enough and now you must go."

"Certainly," said Glawen. "Just as you wish."

Glawen departed the jail and went off about his affairs, which kept him busy the rest of the day and the following morning as well. At noon, Bodwyn Wook found him taking his lunch in the Old Arbor.

"Where have you been hiding?" demanded Bodwyn Wook. "We have searched everywhere for you!"

"You did not search in the Archives, or you would have found me. What is so urgent?"

"Floreste is beside himself with excitement. He insists upon conferring with you at the earliest possible moment."

Glawen rose to his feet. "I'll look in on him now."

Glawen crossed the river and proceeded to the jail. Marcus Diffin said: "Here you are at last."

"I'm surprised to find myself so popular. The last time I was here he couldn't get rid of me fast enough."

"Be warned: he's had a bad day and it's put him out of sorts."

"How so?"

"First it was Namour, and the two had a rousing quarrel. I was about to interfere when Namour left, his face like a thundercloud. Next, Dame Skellane. She upset Floreste all over again, and he began shouting for you."

"I think I know what's troubling him," said Glawen. "Perhaps I can calm him down a bit."

Marcus Diffin opened the door and called into the chamber: "Glawen Clattuc is here."

"None too soon! Send him in!"

Glawen found Floreste standing by the table, glowering in angry accusation. "Your conduct is brazen beyond belief! How dare you interfere with my arrangements?"

"You refer to my conversation with Dame Skellane Laverty?"

"I do indeed! My money is impounded and she learns that you will be made some absolutely grotesque settlement! Our plans will be smashed!"

"I explained this, but you chose not to listen."

"Naturally I ignored such poppycock."

"I will explain again. In exchange for information, I will not prosecute. Quite simple, don't you agree?"

"I do not agree and it is not simple! You put me in an abominable dilemma! Haven't I made that clear?"

"Not in terms that I understand."

"No need for you to understand. You must accept my assurances."

"I'd rather take a million sols of your money."

Floreste sagged back against the table. "You are vandalizing my last few hours!"

"You need only give me the information I want."

Floreste struck his fists together. "Could I trust you?"

"I must trust you, to tell me all you know. You must trust me."

Floreste gave a weary sigh. "I have no other choice, and for a fact I believe you to be honest, though vicious."

"So what is it: yes or no?"

Floreste asked craftily: "Exactly what must I tell you?"

"If I knew, why should I ask? In the main, I want to know everything there is to know about my father: how he disappeared, why, and who is responsible, where he is now. There may be other questions which I will also want answered."

"How should I know all these things?" grumbled Floreste. He walked back and forth across the room. "So I must choose. Give me time to think. Come back in a day or so."

"It will then be too late, and if you think that I will relent after you are dead, think again. Your Orpheum means nothing to me. I will take all your money and buy the space yacht I have long coveted."

Floreste seated himself in the wooden armchair and glared across the table at Glawen. "You force me to break one faith in order to honor another."

"That is a side issue, so far as I am concerned."

"So be it. I will do your bidding. I will write out certain information which I hope will satisfy you. But you may read it only after I am dead."

"Why not just tell me now what I want to know?"

"I have certain arrangements which might be compromised if I told you now."

"That is not entirely satisfactory. You might choose to withhold some critical fact."

"By the same token you might consider it wise to accept a large settlement from my estate. Trust must be a bond between us, disparate creatures as we are."

"In that case"—Glawen brought out the photograph he had taken from Zaa's desk—"look at this picture and name off these ladies."

Floreste studied the faces with care. He peered sidewise at Glawen. "Why do you show this to me?"

"You spoke of trust. If there is no truth, there can be no trust. And if I cannot trust you, then you cannot trust me. Am I clear?"

"Unnecessarily clear." Again Floreste studied the photograph. "I must forgo all reserve. This is Zaa, as you know. Her name originally, as I recall, was Zadine Babbs. This is Sibil Devella. And this"—here Floreste hesitated—"this is Simonetta Clattuc."

"By what other name do you know her?"

Floreste reacted to the question with remarkable vehemence. He jerked up his head and stared at Glawen, then blurted: "Who told you this other name?"

"It's enough that I know. I want to hear what you have to say."

"It is incredible!" muttered Floreste. "Did Namour tell you? No, of course not; he would never dare. Who, then? Zaa? Yes! It must have been Zaa! Why should she do such a thing?"

"She intended to kill me—at your suggestion, of course. She talked for hours."

"Perverse demented woman! Now all cohesion is gone!"

"I don't understand what you are saying."

"No matter. I do not intend that you understand. Come back tomorrow at noon. Your papers will be ready."

Glawen returned to Archives in the recesses of the Old Agency. Halfway through the afternoon he came upon what he had hoped, though not with any assurance, that he might find. He immediately telephoned Bodwyn Wook. "I have something to show you. Can you come to Archives?"

"Now?"

"If possible."

"You sound morose."

"I've just stirred up a swarm of old emotions. I thought they had lost their force, but I was wrong."

"I will be there at once."

Bodwyn Wook arrived, and Glawen took him to the viewing room. "Something Floreste said gave me an idea. I went to look—well, you shall see for yourself."

The two went into the viewing room. Two hours later they emerged, Glawen wan and silent, Bodwyn Wook grim and taut to the strain of his own emotions.

Out in Wansey Way they found that evening had come to Araminta Station. Bodwyn Wook halted, and for a moment stood pondering. "I would like to clear this matter up now, at this very instant—but the time is late, and tomorrow will do as well. Tomorrow at noon it shall be. I will issue the necessary instructions after we take our supper."

The two dined alone in Bodwyn Wook's chambers. Glawen told of his interview with Floreste. "I left him, as usual, with my head spinning. I asked him in regard to Simonetta's other name, thinking of Madame Zigonie on Rosalia. Floreste was extremely perturbed: who would dare tell me such secret information. He must know her by another name. Who could it be, that would cause him such excitement?

"Then again: he will write what he knows about my father, but I may not read the material until after he is dead. I tried to learn his reasons; he would not tell me. I am confused! Where is the difference?"

"It is not all that confusing," said Bodwyn Wook. "There is the notable difference of an entire day, during which much can happen."

"That must be the reason," said Glawen. "I am ashamed to be so dense. And since a day makes no difference to Floreste, the time must be important to someone else. Who?"

"We will watch events with great care and be ready for anything."

6

Halfway through the following morning Glawen went to the jail, to find Floreste closeted with Dame Skellane Laverty. Neither seemed pleased when he entered the cell.

Floreste waved toward the door. "As you see I am conferring with Dame Skellane."

Glawen asked: "What of the information you were to prepare for me?"

"It is not ready. Come back later!"

"There is not much 'later' left. Time is getting short."

"I need no reminders! I think often of this fact."

Glawen addressed Dame Skellane. "Please don't distract him. If he doesn't do his work you will see none of his money. I will cruise the Reach in my space yacht, and you will whistle for the new Orpheum."

"Truly, that is crass language!" cried Dame Skellane in a passion. "I am shocked!" She turned to Floreste. "It seems that we must abbreviate our little chat, which I had hoped might comfort you."

"My fate is upon me, dear lady! I must obey this saturnine young Clattuc, and reveal all my secrets. Glawen, come back later! I am not yet ready for you. Dame Skellane, you must excuse me."

Dame Skellane turned angrily upon Glawen. "You should not hector poor Floreste during the last hours of his life! You should soothe and console him."

"In Floreste's case the only remedy is time," said Glawen. "In thirty years his crimes will be forgotten and everyone will think him a saintly old martyr. What a fine joke! He would cut your throat on this instant if he thought he could gain his liberty or save himself a hundred sols."

Dame Skellane turned to Floreste. "How can you tolerate this abuse so placidly?"

"Because, my dear, it is true. The first and most noble function of life is art! My own art, in particular. I am a mighty vehicle which careens across the cosmos bearing a precious if frangible cargo. Should anything impede my progress, or my existence, or my convenience, or my account at the Bank of Mircea, it must yield or be overridden by my trundling wheels! 'Ars gratia artis': that was a favorite dictum of the poet Navarth. And there you have it!"

"Oh, Floreste, I will never believe such things."

Glawen went to the door. "Come, Dame Skellane, we must go."

Dame Skellane had a final word for Floreste: "At least I have restored you to your normal high spirits!"

"Quite so, dear lady! Thanks to you, I will die happy."

7

At noon Bodwyn Wook entered his office. Looking neither right nor left, he marched to his black tall-backed chair and seated himself. Finally he allowed himself to survey the occupants of the room. "Is everyone present? I see Kirdy, Drusilla and Arles. I see Glawen, Ysel Laverty, Rune Offaw, and yonder sits Lieutenant Larke Diffin of the militia. Who is missing? Namour? Rune, where is Namour?"

"Namour has been somewhat fractious," said Rune Offaw. "He declares himself too busy to attend the meeting. I sent a pair of sergeants in full uniform to bring him here, and if I am not mistaken, I hear them now."

The door opened and Namour came into the chamber.

"Ah, Namour!" said Bodwyn Wook. "I am pleased that you are able to appear after all! It is just possible that we will need you to confirm or elaborate upon some element of our inquiry."

"Into what are you inquiring?" demanded Namour, with no show of cordiality. "In all probability I know nothing of the matter, in which case I would wish to excuse myself, since today I am pressed for time."

"Come, come, Namour! You are too modest! It is widely believed that you know everything!"

"Not so! I am interested only in my own concerns."

Bodwyn Wook gave his hand a casual flourish. "Today they must be subordinated to the work of Bureau B, which, as an organ of the Charter, naturally commands the full cooperation of everyone."

Namour smiled a cool sardonic smile. "I have been brought willy-nilly to your inquiry; please do not expect me to kowtow as well. As soon as my help is no longer necessary, I hope that you will allow me to leave."

"Of course!" said Bodwyn Wook heartily. He reflected a moment, then signaled to Rune Offaw and Ysel Laverty. They came forward and the three conferred a few moments in soft voices. Then the "Boar" and the "Stoat" returned to their places.

Bodwyn Wook cleared his throat. "Today we revert to a most unpleasant subject which many of us have relegated to the back of our minds. We do so only for good reasons, which will satisfy even Namour when he hears them. I refer to the atrocious murder of Sessily Veder, at the Parilia of several years ago.

"The files have never been closed, but only the persistence of Captain Glawen Clattuc has allowed us to resolve the case. Glawen, I will ask you to present the findings, since you are more familiar with the details than I."

"Just as you like. I will try not to be discursive. To start with, we had the clues discovered during the original investigation: mainly fibers found in the winery truck. They might have come from either Namour's satyr legs or two 'primordial' costumes in the Mummers' wardrobe. All the Bold Lion costumes were cut from different stuff.

"Namour was able to account for his movements during the critical time. Arles and Kirdy were supposed to be marching patrol at the Yip compound. Their signatures and countersignatures seemed to exculpate them both.

"However! Ysel Laverty discovered in the photographic record a

468

figure sitting in the Old Arbor. It turned out to be Arles, wearing a primordial costume. It seemed certain that we had discovered the murderer. Arles admitted falsifying the record. Kirdy admitted that he had tolerated the falsification, on the grounds that he and Arles were both Bold Lions and so could do no wrong. Arles admitted going to the Mummers' wardrobe, which is in a warehouse close by the compound. He dressed in his primordial costume, then hurried to the Old Arbor to keep his appointment with Drusilla. Kirdy was left to walk the patrol alone.

"Drusilla corroborated Arles' statement, more or less, though without any firm conviction; in fact, she was drunk. Still, they apparently watched the Phantasmagoria together, and it seems unlikely that Arles would have rushed from Drusilla's fascinating company to perform a set of outrages upon Sessily.

"As I checked the photographic record again, I saw Namour in his satyr costume stop outside the Arbor, look in through one of the arches and talk a few moments with someone sitting just inside. Namour, do you remember this episode?"

"No. I can't say that I do. It's a long time ago, and I had been drinking wine."

"I remember very well," said Arles with feeling. "He laughed at my headpiece, which was not proper Bold Lion equipment. He told me I looked like a toad in a fright wig. I explained that it was the best I could do at the moment, but he wouldn't listen; he was too busy cajoling Drusilla."

Namour chuckled. "True. It all comes back to me. I remember well; it went just as Arles describes it."

"The time of this episode is shortly after the Phantasmagoria. Arles, like Namour, is removed from the list of suspects.

"So: what do we have? Bold Lions are here and there. Kirdy bravely marches his solitary patrol along the fence. Namour, after leaving the arbor, dances the pavane with Spanchetta. Arles sits sulking in the Old Arbor. And there the situation has rested for years, while sweet innocent Sessily drifts away into memory.

"But in two minds, at least, the recollection stays fresh. The murderer thinks of her often—and so do I. For two months I sat in Zab Zonk's tomb, and I thought of many things. One special idea seemed interesting and surprising. We had searched the camera record carefully. When we found Arles we looked no further. At the time it seemed enough.

"That was the first crack in the case, because—to make a long story short—I looked further ahead in time. I discovered another skulking shape, and this one is the guilty skulking shape, beyond all doubt. He comes hurrying from behind the Orpheum a few minutes before midnight, and goes off half running down Wansey Way. He must be back on patrol before the next shift arrives.

"Floreste also jogged my memory, while he reminisced about the Mummers. He mentioned that Kirdy yearned greatly for Sessily, but in vain. Sessily would have nothing to do with either him or Arles. What of the patrol? Another idea clicked into place. Kirdy once told me that he never obeyed orders which he thought foolish or useless. Kirdy had a grandiose vision of himself: he was unique, and set apart from ordinary rules and regulations. The order to patrol outside the Yip compound in Kirdy's mind was pointless and foolish. As soon as Arles left, Kirdy decided to go too. He followed Arles to the Mummers' wardrobe, dressed in the other primordial costume, and now he was free! He could do as he liked, unhampered by inhibition. And most of all he wanted to impinge himself upon Sessily—to acquaint her with his mighty lust and to punish her severely for what she had done!

"This seemed a good idea and he acted upon it. It was the most glorious moment of his life."

Glawen paused. Everyone looked askance at Kirdy, who sat like a stone.

Namour said abruptly: "All very well, and it's none of my affair, but where is your evidence?"

"He appears in the camera record," said Glawen. "He is in a hurry to get back to the patrol and he is careless. So there we see him lumbering down Wansey Way in his primordial costume, and there is no mistaking him."

"It is all a lie," said Kirdy. "Every word is false."

"You admit nothing, then?" asked Bodwyn Wook.

"I cannot admit to a lie."

"And you performed the full stint of your patrol?"

"Certainly. Glawen has always been jealous of me, because I am who I am—a Wook of pedigree—while he is a born mongrel."

Bodwyn Wook spoke without intonation: "Larke Diffin, step forward if you please."

Namour spoke in a long-suffering voice: "If you are finished with me, I will now excuse myself."

Bodwyn Wook looked at Glawen: "Have you any further questions to put to Namour?"

"At this particular moment, no."

"You may go."

Without a word Namour departed the chamber. Ysel Laverty waited a brief period, then followed. Meanwhile Larke Diffin had come from the corner of the room where he had been sitting: a blond young man of good address, tall and a few comfortable pounds overweight, with bristling mustaches and an air of confident affability.

Bodwyn Wook spoke to the chamber at large: "Everyone here, surely, is acquainted with Larke Diffin, who is a lieutenant of the militia. Larke came on duty at the Yip compound immediately after the shift which should have been kept by Kirdy and Arles. Lieutenant, repeat what you have already told me."

Larke Diffin pulled at his mustache and cast a troubled gaze toward Kirdy. "I will report facts because they are as they are, and my telling will not alter them. On the occasion in question, the last night of Parilia, I came on duty ten minutes early, to make sure that I would not be late. I found neither Kirdy nor Arles at the patrol station; however, to my surprise, I found that all the patrols had been signed and countersigned, which of course is strictly against regulations. The signatures certify that the patrols have been performed and clearly the last patrol had not yet been completed.

"A few minutes later Kirdy appeared, out of breath and seriously out of uniform; in fact he wore what I now know to be a primordial costume. He was taken aback to find me early, and embarrassed by my evident disapproval. He said that he had just stepped over to the Mummers' wardrobe for the costume, in order to save time. Arles, he said, had done the same.

"I found it impossible to be harsh during those last few hours of Parilia. I pointed out, as sternly as I could, that both he and Arles had falsified patrol certifications, which was most irregular. I remarked that I should properly report the occurrence, but since all was peaceful and no harm had been done, I would overlook the offense. That is where the matter stood, and I never thought of it again until Glawen questioned me. As I think back, Kirdy came in not from the direction of the warehouse, but from Wansey Way."

Glawen looked at Kirdy. "Well, what of that, Kirdy? More lies?"

"I will say no more. I must go my way alone. It has always been me against the world."

Bodwyn Wook said abruptly: "That is all for today. This is not a formal hearing and you have not been arraigned. Still, do not attempt to leave the station. I will consult my associates and we will decide upon our procedures. I suggest that you find counsel to help you represent yourself."

Glawen lunched alone at the Old Arbor, then, with nothing better to do, sat quietly drinking what remained in the decanter of the wine, while Syrene moved across the sky.

The time became middle afternoon. Glawen could wait no longer. He took himself to the jail, where, without comment, Marcus Diffin admitted him to the cell.

Floreste sat at the table writing across sheets of orange paper, using black ink. He looked up and gave Glawen a curt nod. "I am just finishing." He inserted the papers into a heavy envelope, upon which he wrote: "Not to be examined until sunset!"

He sealed the envelope and tossed it to Glawen. "I have done your bidding. You must heed the instruction."

"I don't understand it but I'll do as you ask." Glawen thoughtfully tucked the envelope into his pocket.

Floreste turned him a quick wolfish grin. "Tomorrow, or even sooner, my motives may become clear. Our transaction is now complete, and you must abandon your litigation."

"It depends on what is in this envelope. If it is nothing but breast-beating and claptrap I will take every dinket you own. So think well, Floreste, and make your changes now, if any are needed."

Floreste shook his head ruefully. "I would not dare thwart you! I know something of your mettle. You are merciless!"

"Not so. But I will do what I can to help my father."

"I cannot fault you for your loyalty," said Floreste. "I wish I could feel the same emotion in those I am trusting to guard my interests." He jumped to his feet and paced up and down the chamber. "In all candor, I am troubled. I wonder if my associates are as truly dedicated to my goals as they claim." He halted beside the table. "I must be logical. Can I truly trust Namour? Will he subordinate his own interests to my goals through loyalty?"

"The answer would seem to be no," said Glawen.

"I tend to agree," said Floreste. "As for Smonny, she also claims to share my ideals, but there is small evidence in this direction at Yipton. When she thinks 'Araminta' she thinks 'vengeance,' not glorious new honors. Again let us be brutally realistic: if she had access to my money, would she work toward the new Orpheum or would she invest in flyers and weapons? What is your opinion?"

With great effort Glawen managed to conceal his stupefaction. Could Floreste be saying what he seemed to be saying? Glawen managed to say: "My opinion is the same as yours."

Floreste, pacing back and forth, paid Glawen no heed. "Perhaps I have been too trusting. My account at the Bank of Mircea includes not just my personal moneys, but also funds listed to Ogmo Enterprises. This is an account used by Smonny for her convenience, and includes some very large recent deposits. Your litigation of course froze these funds and denied them to Smonny, causing her great anxiety. Namour prevailed upon me to write out a will, bequeathing all properties to Smonny, who would then turn over my personal fortune to the Fine Arts Committee, and this is where my doubts arise. Would she in fact do so?"

"At a guess," said Glawen, "I would think not."

"I incline in this same direction. My new Orpheum will be realized only in the context of present conditions. I wonder—" Floreste stared thoughtfully down at the table. "Perhaps it is not too late to make a few small changes."

"Why not? Call in Namour and retrieve your will."

Floreste gave a bark of sour laughter. "Is it not clear? But no matter. I am only concerned with consequences and now I see a way to assure my goals. Just as a matter of curiosity, how did you learn so much about Smonny? It was supposedly a great secret. Zaa told you, of course, but I wonder why."

In this case falsehood was easier and cleaner than the truth. "Zaa planned to kill me, after I had serviced enough of her females. She took a perverse pleasure in telling me anything I wanted to know."

"Aha! 'Perverse' is the proper word for Zaa. I could tell a hundred strange tales in this connection. It was Zaa who conceived the Thurben Island events, that she might teach her torpid Zubenites to breed. At least that was the pretext. Sibil contrived the tactics, and since she had what was called a love-hate kink in her nature for pretty young girls, she did her part with zeal. Smonny provided the girls, indifferent to their fate. And I? I ignored the affair, and turned my back on details, so long as I was paid the money, and there was little enough remaining after Smonny took her share. Though now, is it not ironic? All the money is in my account, and Smonny has never even collected her expenses."

"It is a good joke on Smonny," said Glawen.

"So it is! Though she has absolutely no sense of the absurd."

"How did she arrive at her present position? Zaa told me nothing of this."

"Smonny married a rich rancher, a certain Titus Zigonie, on the world Rosalia. The two visited Yipton to contract for Yip labor. Old Calyactus was then the Oomphaw. By some means they inveigled

Calyactus into visiting them on Rosalia. Poor old Calyactus was never heard from again.

"Smonny and Titus returned to Yipton. Titus began calling himself Titus Pompo. But he had no taste for authority and the real Oomphaw was Smonny—a position which brought her untold pleasure.

"Namour somehow became involved in the situation—perhaps as Smonny's lover? Who knows? Namour is a man of iron discipline and no scruples whatever—a dangerous combination. That is all I know."

For a period he paced up and down. Glawen said: "Our transaction is complete, and now—"

Floreste made an imperious gesture. "Not yet! Grant me still a few moments."

"Certainly; just as you like."

Floreste strode back and forth. "For years I have been a man of far vision; my gaze has ranged the horizons and meanwhile I ignored the ground at my feet. Now, in these final hours, I must make changes." He went to the table, and seated himself; taking up pen and paper he indited a short document with great care. He raised his head and listened. "Who is out in the front office?"

"Marcus Diffin, or so I suppose."

"Someone else is with him. Ask both persons to step in here."

Glawen rapped on the door. Marcus Diffin looked through the peephole. "What do you want?"

"Who is out there?"

"It is Bodwyn Wook."

"Floreste wants the two of you to step in for a moment."

The door opened; Marcus Diffin and Bodwyn Wook entered the chamber.

Floreste rose to his feet. "I have come to an important decision. It may seem strange to everyone here, but I consider it right and proper, and at last I find myself at peace." He indicated the document he had just composed. "This is my will. It is dated and the exact hour of the day is specified. I will read it:

"To whom it may concern:
    "This is my last and final will, inscribed during the afternoon previous to my death. I am of sound mind and calm in disposition, as the witnesses will attest. This will supersedes all others, specifically and particularly that will wherein I bequeathed my belongings to Simonetta co-Clattuc Zigonie: which will is here and now declared canceled and invalid in each and all of its provisions. Now, of my free will and upon careful judgment, I bequeath everything of which I die possessed, including all monies, bank accounts, items on deposit in the vaults at

the Bank of Mircea in Soumjiana, all precious articles, gems and works of art, all lands, properties, estates, personal effects and all other possessions, to Captain Glawen Clattuc, in the hope and expectation that he will put these funds and derived income to the uses which he knows to be dear to my heart: namely, the construction of a so-called New Orpheum at Araminta Station. I sign this will in the presence of the undersigned witnesses."

Floreste took up the pen and appended his name to the document, then handed the pen to Marcus Diffin. "Sign."

Marcus Diffin signed.

Floreste gave the pen to Bodwyn Wook. "Sign."

Bodwyn Wook signed as instructed.

Floreste folded the will and handed it to Bodwyn Wook. "I entrust this into your keeping. Execute it quickly and make sure of the property! There will be great complaint since in my account are funds which Smonny reckons to be her own. Namour is on his way to Soumjiana to execute my previous will and withdraw those funds."

"So this is the reason for Namour's anxiety at the meeting. Is there a ship leaving today?"

"There is indeed," said Floreste. "The *Karessimuss*. Namour will be aboard."

Bodwyn Wook ran from the room, to avail himself of the telephone in Marcus Diffin's office.

"That is all," Floreste told Glawen. "You may go, and I will sit here reflecting upon the strange lands I shall be wandering through tomorrow."

"Would you like a bottle of wine to enliven your thoughts?"

Floreste asked suspiciously: "What kind of wine? The last you brought was proper gut-wrench."

"Marcus will bring in some good Green Zoquel."

"That will do."

"I will make sure your money is used as you would wish."

"I have no worries on that score. I am at peace."

Glawen departed the chamber. He told Marcus: "I promised Floreste a bottle of Green Zoquel. Will you see to it?"

"I will do so at once."

Bodwyn Wook came slowly away from the telephone. "The *Karessimuss* departed over an hour ago. Namour was aboard. Somehow he gave my men the slip. Ysel Laverty is out looking for them now."

"When Namour arrives at Soumjiana—what of Floreste's money?"

"It is safe. First of all, it is still bound tight by your litigation, which has not yet been lifted. Secondly, such affairs go with deliberation. The will must be validated, and the records searched; and Floreste must be proved dead. The process might take anywhere from a month to three months. In the meantime the latest will can be probated here, and much more quickly. Floreste's property is safe."

"Now we also know why Floreste insisted on writing his information."

"How so?"

"Are you ready for a shock?"

"As ready as I'll ever be."

"Why do you think Titus Pompo is so careful to remain unseen and unknown?"

"I have often wondered."

Glawen provided the explanation.

At last Bodwyn Wook found his tongue. "This may be the principal reason for Namour's hurry to leave. He is now demonstrated to be at least a passive co-conspirator in Ogmo Enterprises and the Thurben Island affair, and he would not escape stringent punishment: at least twenty years at Cape Journal. Perhaps worse. We will not see him at Araminta Station again. Now, if you will excuse me, I have a few melancholy details to arrange."

"At least Floreste will be drinking good wine when the gas enters his cell."

"There are worse ways of dying. Do you have your information?"

"I am not allowed to look at it until sunset."

"It makes no difference now. Namour has flown the coop."

"Still, I'll honor Floreste's last wishes. I'd feel strange otherwise."

"Glawen, you are either overly sentimental or extremely superstitious, or both . . . Upon reflection, perhaps here is the essential definition of 'honor.'"

"As to that, I can't say." Glawen turned away and departed the jail.

9

Glawen walked slowly down Wansey Way. Sunlight slanted through the trees along the riverbank, striking long pink blurs upon the road. Glawen looked over his shoulder. Syrene still hung its own diameter above the western hills; sunset was an hour away.

Glawen stopped to look into the Old Arbor. Late afternoon activity filled the air with the sound of lighthearted voices and muted laughter, somewhat at discord with Glawen's mood. In a far corner sat Kirdy, morose and alone, staring into nothingness.

Glawen had no present inclination for the Old Arbor. He continued down Wansey Way past the avenue leading up to Wook House, then a second similar avenue to Veder House, and a third to Clattuc House. Glawen paused and surveyed the familiar façade. Tomorrow he would look in to make sure that the work was going properly, without improvisations, shortcuts and that general scamping of the job which Spanchetta would be sure to attempt.

His thoughts turned to Spanchetta. How intimately was she involved in Simonetta's machinations? How much, in fact, did she know? Certainly, with pious indignation, she would deny all knowledge. At the moment Glawen refused to so much as speculate. He looked toward Syrene, still a pink-orange globe not yet in contact with the hills. He tucked the envelope securely into the inside pocket of his jacket and continued down Wansey Way. He passed the lyceum, now still and quiet but reverberating with a multitude of memories. He looked across the river to the site of Floreste's projected new Orpheum. Floreste's account at the Bank of Mircea included Ogmo Enterprise funds, and Glawen laughed aloud. The news of Floreste's final arrangements would bring consternation to Yipton.

Wansey Way joined Beach Road Highway. Glawen crossed the road and went down upon the beach. The surf was running high; a series of storms out at sea had generated massive swells; one after the other they rolled against the shore, to tumble and crash into foam.

Glawen went to stand where the sheets of hissing bubbles almost wet his feet. The envelope weighed in his pocket; he took it out and examined it on both sides, and read the inscription. The envelope was of excellent quality, fabricated of stiff glossy parchment, mottled tan and gray, of the sort used to enclose legal documents. Had Floreste intended to emphasize the significance of the message within? Hardly necessary, thought Glawen. Perhaps Floreste was merely indulging himself in a final dramatic flourish. Or perhaps this was the only envelope he had on hand.

It made no great difference one way or the other, he thought, so long as the message within was explicit. Glawen forced his mind away from speculation and tucked the envelope back into the inner pocket of his jacket, and buttoned down the flap. He looked back at Syrene, now almost brushing the hills. At the edge of the road a man stood watching him. Glawen squinted against the sunlight, and his heart sank. The brooding posture was unmistakable. It was Kirdy, who apparently had followed him from the Old Arbor.

With careful steps Kirdy descended the slope from the road and picked his way across the sand, never taking his gaze from Glawen. Today he wore black garments: black breeches, low black boots, a black long-sleeved shirt and a broad-brimmed black hat. His pink face was set; his china-blue eyes were as empty as the eyes of a great dead fish.

Glawen looked right and left, up and down the beach. No other person was in sight. He and Kirdy were alone.

Glawen calculated his choices. The prudent course was to walk away, or, if necessary: run. He had nothing to gain and everything to lose from a confrontation with Kirdy.

Glawen sidled off along the beach. Kirdy altered his own course, angling to cut off Glawen's line of retreat, thus defining his intentions. They were sinister.

Kirdy moved closer on stealthy feet, as if by this tactic he hoped not to startle or alarm Glawen.

But Glawen's apprehensions were not so easily allayed and he continued to move away at a slant, down upon the wet sand where the footing was better, in the event that he chose to run—still a feasible if somewhat embarrassing option. Glawen moved more briskly, but Kirdy sprang to cut him off. Kirdy seemed to be grinning; the tips of his big white teeth were visible between his drawn-back lips.

Glawen halted. At his back a ponderous mass of water tumbled over with a thundering crash; foam surged up the shore. Glawen had often played among the breakers and felt no fear of the surf. Kirdy, however, was a weak swimmer who hated and feared the sea; he must shortly tire of the game and depart, with whatever satisfaction he could find from having chased Glawen into the surf.

In fascination Glawen watched the twitching muscles in Kirdy's cheeks. Surely Kirdy would turn and march away rather than approach the dreadful deep water any more closely.

Kirdy indeed paused and gazed out over the sea. His jaw sagged and the grin abruptly left his face. The foam advanced, wetting Glawen's feet. Kirdy drew fastidiously back. The foam receded, leaving an expanse of clear wet sand which Kirdy found irresistible. He cast caution to the wind and charged in a lumbering rush, arms raised to grapple Glawen and bear him down to where he could be properly controlled and dealt with.

Glawen jumped back through the incoming surf and stopped to watch as the foam washed up over Kirdy's heavy shins. Kirdy frowned in vast distaste, but nevertheless splashed forward in graceless splay-footed jumps, convinced that finally Glawen was trapped where he dared retreat no farther. Glawen must now start to reason with him, or even to plead for moderation. That would be rich entertainment for a fact!

But Glawen was not yet ready to beg for mercy, and stood just beyond Kirdy's reach. Kirdy lunged, but again Glawen backed away, step by step, with the foam now swirling and bubbling around his legs. Kirdy splashed recklessly in pursuit. Glawen remained maddeningly a few yards beyond his reach. Would he never stop and take what was coming to him? Close at his back was the dim deep water where one sank forever and at last, still living, became putrid gray slime!

Glawen seemed oblivious to the danger. But now he could go no farther! Kirdy moved grimly forward to catch him.

The new surge raced shoreward past Kirdy, wetting him to the belly. He stopped short. Glawen, now less than three yards to seaward, scooped water into Kirdy's face. Kirdy blinked and gave his head a furious shake.

The foam receded, sucking and pulling; Glawen and Kirdy were tugged a few steps down the beach. The water ebbed; Glawen stood close at hand, and Kirdy, maddened, made a spraddle-legged dive but came up short; Glawen had moved smartly away. Kirdy gained his footing, but now he had lost his hat.

A great swell toppled and crashed; Kirdy was distracted and awed. The foam thrust at Glawen; he braced his feet and held his position; Kirdy was thrust a few yards up the beach. The surge returned and with it came Kirdy, half running, and at last he found himself at grips with Glawen. Uttering a glad snort he threw Glawen into the water and tried to kneel on his neck. Glawen swallowed a mouthful of brine and sand. Kirdy's weight pressed on him, but without great effect. He brought up his legs, planted a foot in Kirdy's stomach and heaved. Kirdy toppled over backward, and was carried away on the departing surge, out and under an enormous tumbling breaker. Glawen, rising to his feet, was propelled up the beach. Kirdy, caught in the undertow, had been carried out past the first line of breakers.

Glawen felt for his envelope. It was secure. He unbuttoned the flap, pulled it out and examined it. The heavy parchment had suffered not at all from its momentary contact with the salt water; its message, whether for good or ill, was secure.

Glawen began to shiver from chill and fatigue. He looked out over the water. Where was Kirdy? The incoming breakers hid the offshore water from view. Somewhere out there was Kirdy, floundering about and wondering why he was suddenly lost out on the ocean, when only an hour before he had been sitting in the Old Arbor.

Glawen trudged up the beach. He felt no emotion: certainly neither triumph nor gratification. He mused briefly upon his own conduct, then told himself: "What difference does it make, one way or the other? I am glad that he is gone."

Glawen climbed to the road, and turned to look out over the ocean, and for an instant thought to see in the melancholy light of sunset a flailing black-clad arm and the flash of a pink face. When he looked again, he saw only heaving water.

Shivering from the chill of wet clothes, Glawen studied the western sky. Syrene could still be seen, with half of its substance showing vermilion-pink above the hills.

Where Wansey Way joined the beach highway, a bench had been arranged for the convenience of pedestrians. Arriving at this bench, Glawen again studied the western sky. Trees obscured the hills, but the light had started to fade and he decided that at last Syrene was gone. Sunset was now in progress.

Glawen seated himself on the bench. With his teeth chattering, he brought out the envelope, and with some difficulty broke into the stiff parchment. He withdrew the enclosed orange papers and began to read. Rapidly he skimmed through the three pages, then returned to the first paragraph, which was short and succinct, but which told him what he wanted to know.

For the information of Glawen Clattuc:
  Scharde Clattuc, so I am told and so I believe, is now held captive in a most unusual and difficult place. Why has he been treated so cruelly? I can only guess.

The wind blew in Glawen's wet clothes, and set his teeth to chattering anew. He folded the pages, tucked them into the envelope, which he returned to his pocket. He looked once more out over the ocean, already indistinct in the afterglow. He saw nothing. He turned and at best speed trotted up Wansey Way.